# James A. Michener

# THE
## FIRES
### OF
#### SPRING

FAWCETT CREST • NEW YORK

# To C. S. and S. C.

*THE FIRES OF SPRING*

THIS BOOK CONTAINS THE COMPLETE TEXT OF THE
ORIGINAL HARDCOVER EDITION.

Published by Fawcett Crest Books, a unit of CBS Publications,
the Consumer Publishing Division of CBS Inc., by
arrangement with Random House, Inc.

Copyright © 1949 by James A. Michener.

ISBN: 0-449-23860-1

Printed in the United States of America

25  24  23  22  21  20  19

# PART 1

# The Poorhouse

DAVID HARPER could scarcely sit still. It was Friday afternoon, and Miss Clapp was reading from the blue book. For three weeks now she had been reading about Hector and Achilles. This afternoon Hector would go forth to battle. David, who had been a Trojan for almost a month, shivered with excitement. He knew that when Achilles met a real fighter things would be different.

Then Miss Clapp closed the book!

"What happened next?" David cried.

Miss Clapp smiled primly. "We'll find out next week."

"Oh!" David gasped. He was eleven that year, and next Friday was as far away as next year.

Miss Clapp gave a self-contented smile. With her left hand she deftly tapped the pile of brown report cards. "I suppose you know why I had to stop early today," she said unctuously. Like all teachers, she savored the little climaxes that were permitted her.

"Report cards!" the children in Grade Five chimed.

Miss Clapp smiled warmly, as if her students had mastered the multiplication table. As she called the happy litany of names, each child went forward to receive the decisive card. Returning to their seats, the children stole furtive glances at their grades. Those who were pleased smiled.

"David Harper."

David rose, sandy-haired, freckled, grinning. Miss Clapp handed him his card. Holding it against his badly worn shirt, he sneaked a quick glance at the grades: "Doylestown Public Schools. Grade Five. English 71. Spelling 82. Geography 74. Arithmetic . . ." He gasped. There it was again. That horrible mark! "Arithmetic 99."

"What's the matter, David?" Miss Clapp inquired.

"Arithmetic!" he blurted out, thrusting his face back toward the teacher.

"What's the matter with arithmetic?" Miss Clapp asked in astonishment.

"It's 99 again. I didn't miss a single question all month."

"No, he didn't!" the boys of Grade Five cried, egging their classmate on.

Carefully Miss Clapp placed the remaining cards on her desk. She stood very tall and folded her hands. Then, instead of growling, she smiled softly at David and said quietly, "Of course you didn't miss any questions, David. But nobody is good enough for 100. Never."

"But I didn't miss any!" the little boy argued stubbornly.

"Of course you didn't," Miss Clapp reasoned patiently. "But 100, David! That means the very best that anyone could ever do. Ninety-nine means good, but you could do better."

The incentive was lost on David. He pointed his stumpy nose at the desk and argued, "How could I get more right than all of them? How could I?"

Miss Clapp ignored the boy's anger. Softly she reasoned, "Were your papers as neat as they could have been? Were your 5's made with one line? Was your pencil always sharpened?"

The nose dropped to half mast. "Oh," David grunted. "That's what you mean?"

"Yes. That's what 100 means."

David released a huge grin. "Good! Next month I'll do all those things, too."

"And if you do," Miss Clapp said quietly, "your mark will still be 99."

David gritted his teeth and stared at his teacher. He was mad, fighting mad. He wished he knew a thousand swear words. Abruptly he went to his seat and shook his head at Harry Moomaugh. "Teachers are crazy!" he whispered. "Especially Miss Clapp."

The teacher heard this but ignored it. "Gracey Kelley," she called.

A thin, scrawny girl with red spots on her face rose from the back of the room. She lived in Worthington's Alley and was almost always dirty. But when she passed David on this day he saw that she was wearing a pretty red dress. She swung her way up the aisle and received her card. Clutching it in her hand, she smiled bravely at the rest of the children. Her marks were poor, but she didn't care. She had on a good dress.

But from the second row another little girl said in a loud whisper, "That used to be Mary Gray's dress!"

Right away David remembered. Of course it was Mary's old dress! But the whisper was so loud that Gracey Kelley heard it, too. The bitter words struck her in the face and in the heart. Dropping her report card, she threw her long arms over her face and broke into impulsive sobbing.

Miss Clapp, unaware of what had happened, left her desk and tried to comfort Gracey. "Don't cry," she pleaded. "You'll get better marks next month."

Gracey Kelley turned away. "It's my dress," she wept. One of the boys laughed nervously and she swung on the class, her eyes deep with hate. "I hate you all!" she screamed. Then she slapped Miss Clapp's hands away and rushed into the cloakroom. David could hear her sobbing there and kicking at the wall. Miss Clapp hurried after her, and when the teacher came back to the room, she was crying, too. Seeing this, the little girl whose cruel whisper had launched the trouble also began to cry.

David leaned over and whispered to his friend, Harry Moomaugh, "I told you Miss Clapp was nuts."

"Women are funny," Harry agreed.

"What's the matter with Gracey Kelley?" David demanded. "All that fuss about a dress! Everybody knows I wear your second-hand clothes. So what?" The two good friends shrugged their shoulders, but David was disturbed, for from the cloakroom came the inconsolable sobbing of a heartbroken girl.

The poorhouse lay three miles south of Doylestown among the wonderful rolling hills of Bucks County. Hunched up in back of the poorhouse truck, David watched the familiar sights as he sped homeward. Down the long hill, out of town, past the fine, winding bridge at Edison, then up a hill, through some woods, and there before him were the two long, gray buildings of the poorhouse.

To David these bleak stone buildings were not the last stop of the world's defeated. Not at all! For nearly a month they had been the walls of Troy, and would be for three more searching weeks. Then, although David did not yet know it, the poorhouse walls would become the home of Lancelot. Later, Oliver Twist would live there. Indeed, it was more fun living in a poorhouse than almost any kind of place you could imagine.

But right now David was worried. Because if the poorhouse was truly his castle, he now had the unpleasant job of visiting the witch that lived in the dungeon. As long as he could remember he had lived at the poorhouse with his Aunt Reba. She was in charge of the women's building, and long ago she had brought David to the two forbidding buildings. His parents were dead—"No better than they should have been," his aunt said—and he had come to live with the ugly, unloving witch.

Gingerly, he edged his way into the women's building. The air was hot, smelly with the strong juice they used for keeping bedbugs under control. A very old woman in blue and white denim winked at David and shrugged her shoulder toward Aunt Reba's door. "She's in there," the old woman said with pleased and obvious loathing.

David took a deep breath. "Oh, well," he sighed, knocking lightly on the door.

From within came a harsh, sharp cry, "Komm in." Reluctantly David pushed open the door. Before him stood a thin woman of forty. Her hair was stringy and her face was sallow. She didn't come out in front, the way Miss Clapp did. She never smiled. Her eyes were a watery blue, and never since David had lived with her had her thin lips kissed him. Whatever she did, she did grudgingly as if she wanted to save something of each act for herself. "You're late" she said, reaching for the pen.

Without looking at the card—for she hated schools—she scratched her obligatory signature on the cover. "You're late," she repeated.

"I missed the bus," David explained reluctantly.

"So!" she mimicked in Pennsylvania Dutch. "I missed the *bus*, yet." She spoke in an angry sing-song, accenting the first word of each sentence, singing the last. "It's *wery* nice. *Spend*ing money, I suppose we were. *Yes?*"

"I was talking with Harry Moomaugh," David confessed.

"*Talking*, was it?" she hissed. "*Wery* nice, talking when you should be *verking*, yet." Angrily she reached out and smashed her hand against David's ear. He stumbled sideways against a chair.

"Get aht!" his aunt commanded. He recovered his balance and went to the door. In the hallway he was embarrassed by a half dozen old poorhouse women who had been eavesdropping. One of them patted him on the shoulder, but he merely grinned at her.

"She can't hurt me," he said.

When David was ten he had moved from the women's building into a room of his own on the long hall where the most interesting men in the world lived. There had been many bad moments in the poorhouse during the first ten years when he lived with Aunt Reba, but the past fifteen months had been like a wonderful dream. Now, as he climbed the stairs to his own hall, a glow of fine joy engulfed him. One more step, and he would turn to the right, and there would be the long hall with the many doors and the many, many friends. As always, he paused on the top step and closed his eyes. Then he turned and slowly opened them. And there at the far end of the hall, sitting on his bench, was Old Daniel.

"Hello, Daniel!" David cried.

"Hello, David!" the thin old man chirped back.

Happily, the young boy moved down the hall. From every door old men called greetings and some fell in behind him as he moved like a young god to the bench where Old Daniel waited.

"How was school?" Daniel asked. He was more than seventy, a drying-up old man with a full set of false teeth that clicked when he talked. He had gossamer hair, and flint-sparked blue eyes, and a terrible pain in his stomach that never quite went away. "Isn't this the day for your report card?"

A crazy Dutchman moved in close to David. He was a madman, but not mad enough to be placed in the mad cells. He was harmless, a kind of wonderfully vacant house that had known much fine living. The people had moved away, but the house, like a memory, was left to stand. "Yes!" this eager madman cried. "It's report time." He clamped a tremendous hand on David's shoulder, and when David's bones began to hurt the boy pulled away and smiled up at the big, mad Dutchman.

"Let's see your card," Old Daniel said, reaching out a hand that was mostly bone and delicate fingers. The frail old man tenderly removed the card from its folder and studied the grades.

"Read 'em," cried a tall, gaunt man with no teeth.

"English 71," Old Daniel intoned.

"English is wery hard," the mad Dutchman said.

"Spelling 82."

"Spelling," said the madman, "is wery difficult."

No one made a fool of the Dutchman. They all knew he had never been to school. He couldn't even sign his name. But when he boasted about his grades in school or about the cigar factory he owned, no one shamed him. That was one of the nicest things about the poorhouse. A man could lie his heart out, could tell in fantastic fables all the things he had dreamed of and never accomplished. No one contradicted him, for all the men in the poorhouse lived their last years with ancient lies, and if you pointed out that Luther Detwiler, the mad Dutchman, couldn't possibly have owned a cigar factory, somebody might remember that your wife hadn't really been pretty at all. There was gentle tolerance, and David loved to hear the fabulous stories that this tolerance engendered.

"You always get 99 in arithmetic," Old Daniel said approvingly.

"Yes!" the toothless man agreed. "Why don't you try to get a 100?"

"Well," David explained patiently, "you could never get a 100! That would be perfect."

"And nobody's perfect," the mad Dutchman agreed. "That stands to reason."

"But this English mark," Old Daniel said gravely. "That's a pretty bad mark, David."

"English is wery hard," the Dutchman said consolingly.

"It's sissy stuff," David explained.

"What do you mean?" the frail old man on the bench asked. The great pain swept over him, and his small body shivered for a moment. At such times it was agreed that the others would look away.

So David stared up at the tall, toothless man and said, "It's sissy stuff. Like 'You and I went to the store.'" He spoke in exaggerated accents, like Miss Clapp. The men laughed. "Not, 'You and me went fishin'.' "

Now the pain retreated and Old Daniel resumed command of his body. "What's funny about learning to speak correctly?" He spoke with a trace of acid in his voice, and the men stopped laughing.

"It's girls' stuff," David argued weakly.

"Oh, no!" the frail old man argued. He leaned forward from his bench and said in a quietly passionate voice, "You were meant to read all the books, David. To study wonderful things. You will wander about the world and see kings and maybe even talk with presidents. You'll ride on ships and airplanes. You'll see the deserts and mountains and trees so tall you cannot reach the top. If you study hard, David, all these things will come to pass." The old man sat with his hands in his lap and stared directly at the boy.

"You'll go where we neffer got to see," the mad Dutchman droned.

David grinned at his friends. This was the kind of talk he loved. Lately he had entertained a premonition that he might be called upon to accomplish certain unusual things, and now Daniel spoke of them as if he somehow knew the boy's secret. "When you grow up, what do you intend doing?" the old man inquired. "You once said you might like to write a book. Or become a lawyer. Or maybe a minister. Do you think you can do those things without good English?" Again the sparkling eyes stared out from the sunken face, and David was somewhat ashamed.

"It's sissy stuff, I think," he repeated stolidly, for want of a better argument.

Old Daniel laughed. "Of course it is!" he agreed. "Almost everything worthwhile is sissy stuff. But if you want to be a good man, David, you've got to be master of the sissy stuff. It's all right for Toothless Tom to say, 'Him and me ain't here,' and nobody's ashamed of Tom because he talks that way." The tall, toothless man laughed nervously. "But if you want to do the things you say, David, English isn't sissy stuff. It's very hard and very important." He returned the card to David, and just before the lights went out on the long hall he cried, "Oh, the world you have before you!"

In some embarrassment, David went down the hall to his room. He could not know with what encompassing love the old men watched him disappear. He was a young, sandy-haired kid, resolute and kind, and yet as he walked away from the old men it seemed as if a transubstantiation took place. He was the man! He was the man who would accomplish what they had not accomplished. He was the man who would avoid the terrible errors that had brought them to the poorhouse. And they were the children, looking forward to the distant day that would never dawn for them.

There was a moment of breathless silence in the poorhouse as David went to his room. Old Daniel, the mad Dutchman, Toothless Tom, and all the old men watched the boy. Then the lights went out.

Door 8 was David's door. Inside the air smelled thick with bug juice. The tiny closet held only eight pieces of clothing, counting socks and underwear and everything. Not one piece had been bought for him. His washstand had a dirty thin towel and no soap. In the darkness David could feel the stub of pencil three inches long and the half tablet of writing paper sneaked home from school. There was no rug on the floor, no paper on the walls, no picture, no mirror, no shade on the window. He had no slippers, no bathrobe, no raincoat, no rubbers. His toothbrush was three years old. He had no watch, of course, no books, no maps, no album of stamps, no baseball glove, no winter overcoat, no collection of bird eggs.

But when David entered the darkness of Door 8, the room seemed all aglow. His heart and his mind were simply bursting with emotion. To see the world! To talk with a president! To read all the good books! Oh, the illimitable world that lay ahead! The glory and the wonder of it, the variegated charm, the endless invitation to far thoughts, deep wells of beauty, and strange sounds! How could a poorhouse or a prison or handed-down clothes or barren rooms contain such a boy?

He went to the gaunt window of his room and looked out across the snowy fields and up to the crystal heavens. There were the stars that Old Daniel had traced out for him: "Since the world began they've been there. When you and I have been dead a thousand years they'll still be there. That's Andromeda you're looking at." A room might be swamped in bug juice, but the fathomless universe came crashing in nevertheless. "It's pretty nice out there," David mused. Then he thought of Old Daniel. "It's pretty nice in here, too."

Then came a knocking at his door! That would be Toothless Tom with some food. Eagerly David ran to the door. "Here's the waiter!" the toothless old man joked. "A little something from the kitchen."

Like David, Toothless Tom was always hungry. He was a lean fellow from Solebury. Once he had owned a farm. Now his nephew owned it. Something had gone wrong, somehow, and Tom's nephew owned the farm. Tom was in the poorhouse, and he was always hungry, but he would never eat alone. Not when a growing boy was about!

Tonight Toothless had an apple, fresh and cold from the apple barrels of some farm. He had begged it that afternoon from a trucker. "You done pretty well this month," he said in the darkness. "Studyin' is a fine thing for a boy, David. Never forget that. If I had of done a little studyin' . . ."

Toothless never finished sentences beginning with *if*. In the poorhouse such clauses were constant currency. They filled the long hall like dead leaves clogging an alley in autumn, and whenever the old men talked to David, the sentences with *if* broke forth in profusion. The men would see his frank freckles, his eyes popping with delight at the prospect of extra food, or his eagerness to understand the ways of life, and they would cry, "If I had told Crouthamel '*No*' when he suggested a mortgage . . ." "If I had only of finished high school . . ." "If I had had the operation when the doctor said . . ." "If . . . If . . . If . . ."

Toothless alone refused to finish those sentences which ride the lonely winds of a poorhouse. He alone had the honesty to realize that even if he had studied, his particular nature was one which ends its day in a poorhouse. Defeat and poverty were the destiny of the kind of man he was. His nephew was much smarter than he, a better farmer, too. Were the old days miraculously restored, were Tom to have his teeth and his farm once more, he knew in his heart that sooner or later his nephew—or some clever man like his nephew—would somehow or other get that farm.

"Gee!" David confessed, "I ate almost all the apple, Tom."

"You're a growin' boy, ain't you?"

"Tom! You're very kind. I swear on a Bible, next time you get more'n half." Positively, absolutely, next time Tom must get his share. David spit on his finger and crossed his heart. Of course, he had made this solemn promise at least sixty times before, but this was the first time he had ever spit on his finger, too.

The toothless old man gummed the last of the core and raised David's window to throw it away. "Say!" he whis-

pered in a farmer's speculative voice. "Spring's comin'." He
sniffed the air. 'Sure'n shootin', spring's comin'.'"

David stepped beside him and like a little farmer sniffed at
the air. It was very cold, and he could perceive no spring in
it. But he felt good, standing there with Tom. He took a
deep breath. "Say!" he said. "Seems to me you can feel it.
Spring's comin'."

When Tom left, David lay straight and quiet for a long
time. There were so many wonderful things to think about.
Hector in Troy. The rotten Greeks. Why you could never
get a 100. The strange sobbing of Gracey Kelley. How could
a boy's brain ever stop hammering and let him get some sleep?

There was a gentle knocking at his door. Shivering in the
cold night air, he jumped out of bed and admitted Old
Daniel. The little old man didn't have his teeth in. He was
in a long nightshirt, and he carried a candle.

"I brought you something, David," he whispered. He
closed the door and cautiously lit the candle. "Sometimes
you may want to read," he said.

"I don't have any books," David explained.

"I brought you one," said the shadowy old man. He handed
a well-worn book to David and then stood away from the
bed.

David opened the front cover of *Oliver Twist,* and there
were the magic words: THIS BOOK BELONGS TO DAVID HARPER.

"Oh, Daniel!" he cried, running his fingers along the careful printing. The old man fixed the candle above David's head
and started to leave. "Is the candle mine, too?" the boy asked.

"Of course." Daniel laughed. "How else could you read
in bed?"

David wanted to laugh, too, but tears filled his eyes. There
were many things he did not understand about the poorhouse.
Twice he had found old men hanging by their necks in the
barn, but he had not understood the passionate tragedy that
put them there. He had watched an old woman go crazy, one
spring, when she thought that the fields of the poorhouse farm
were her garden in Doylestown. She had tried to till them all.
There were other things, too, that he did not understand, but
he did know the meaning of a candle that cost a penny.

In his eleven years he had spent—of his very own money—
some twenty-eight pennies. They had not come from his aunt,
of course, but from the old men on the hall, and every one
of the twenty-eight had represented a real and terrible
proportion of the wealth of the man who had given it. Pres-

ents in a poorhouse were not like presents at Christmas, when the kind people of Doylestown brought good things for everybody, and never seemed to miss them in the giving. No! When a poorhouse man gave even so much as a candle that cost a penny, he gave part of his decency, part of the miserable hoard that kept him from being a complete and utter pauper.

The candle flickered and Old Daniel's white silken hair cast strange shadows on the wall. David rubbed his eyes and began to read, but as he did so the frail old man cried, "It's so wonderful!"

"What is?" David asked.

"Reading your first book."

"Why?" David asked, pulling the smelly bedclothes about him.

"It's so wonderful to begin reading! And so terrible. Do you know what you're doing? Learning leads only to unhappiness, David. When you start to learn and think and feel . . . Well, you step blindly into a fight you can never win."

"I don't want to fight," David said.

"Your report card," the old man said as he opened the door. "You must make it better next month."

But David scarcely heard him. He was already lying on his stomach, starting that magic journey from which no boy returns the same. He was reading, for the first time in his life, a book which was his own.

It was not because of blindness or insensitivity that David loved his life in the poorhouse. During three seasons of the year, life in the long gray buildings was delightful. The men, no longer having money or position to protect, were kind and friendly.

And there was surprisingly little recrimination—that is, during three seasons of the year. Of course, men who had lost their farms were inclined to blame Mr. Crouthamel, but such gossip against rich men was inevitable. It was the other kind of recrimination that was not heard: the blind railing against fate as such.

Uncle Daniel, for example, found no one to blame. The wispy little old man had been a brilliant scholar in his youth. But the evil thing had happened. One day along the canal he had watched a loaded barge drifting down to Bristol, and like a magnet the barge had dragged him away, to Bristol, to Philadelphia, and on to Rome and Cyprus, and strange cities and to the Pyramids themselves. He had seen the world, even the Southern Cross. And now he was in the poorhouse.

Toothless Tom accepted his lot without complaint. He was at peace with the world and did not even blame his nephew for stealing the farm. "He's a better farmer than I am," the toothless fellow admitted.

Even crazy Luther Detwiler gave no one any trouble. He, like the rest, conjured up a fable that he was in the poorhouse because Mr. Crouthamel had stolen a cigar factory from him, but the mad Dutchman wouldn't have known Mr. Crouthamel from a butcher boy.

Very occasionally some strange man, shadowy and terrible, would be forced into the poorhouse for a few days. Having lost position and wealth suddenly, he would be unprepared for poverty, and he would skulk along the corridor, stare into his food, and shiver. Young as he was, David learned that such men always followed the same pattern. Either relatives came to rescue these men, or the men sat apart in the poorhouse and shook as if the cold winds of death were upon them. Within a few days they hung themselves.

The two suicides that David found hanging in the barn were such men, and Old Daniel was much afraid of the effect their violent deaths might have upon the boy. "They were so miserable," Daniel explained, "that they preferred death. That leaves the hall to the rest of us who are happy." This explanation seemed so simple and correct that David never realized the truth. He did not see that the unhappiness of one lonely old man might bespeak the vast unhappiness of a village, or a city, or a world.

So, insulated by men who loved him, he grew up happy and untouched. He especially liked summer at the poorhouse. Corn grew in the lovely fields of Bucks County, and lima beans climbed on poles. Horses smelled strong and sweaty. Wagons creaked in the early morning and groaned their protests at night. Birds sang, and at every meal green things were served. In summer David went swimming at Edison. There were woods to explore, animals to track, and ripeness riot through all the land.

Autumn was golden and exciting. Then wagons worked overtime bringing in corn and pumpkins. After the first frost, apples were picked. Pears were wrapped in paper and stored in dark bins. Cider was made at the press, and celery was buried beneath the earth. Hundreds of heads of cabbage were sliced up for sauerkraut, and David helped Toothless Tom wire down the lids of the fermenting barrels. After the baling wire was drawn taut Tom would tap the barrels of kraut approvingly and cry, "Now let 'er fizz!"

But winter was best of all! A pleasing warmth settled over the poorhouse. For one thing, there wasn't so much work to do. The stars were brighter, and Orion dominated the frozen skies. Like that vast warrior, David too went out to hunt. Day after day he rose at four and went with Toothless Tom along the creeks to see if their traps had snared any muskrats. Night came earlier, too, and on the long hall there was much good talking.

So for three seasons of the year, life was not at all bad in the poorhouse.

On the last Friday in February, David received a shocking jolt. Miss Clapp opened her blue book and continued the story about Achilles and the Trojans. David sat back and smiled. This time he knew that Achilles was not going to meet the second team. Hector was in the field for the Trojans!

As the great story of battle unfolded, David Harper sat transfixed, his mouth open a little, his tousled head tilted to one side. When the inevitability of Hector's death bore in upon him, his sandy head lowered, not in defeat, but in despair. And when the flaming Trojan was trussed to the victor's chariot and hauled through the dust, David could do nothing but sit and twist Harry Moomaugh's pants, which were now his pants.

He did not protest to Miss Clapp. She was a funny woman, but he trusted her. If she read it that way, that's the way it was. Nor did he blame the book. He had long since learned that books merely tell what happened. No, his despair was greater because it was formless. An evil thing had happened.

When the day ended, he closed his desk, went to the cloakroom in silence, and slipped into his thin coat. Harry Moomaugh punched him in a friendly manner. "You guessed wrong this time," he joked.

David stopped and looked at Harry across a considerable void. Silently, he turned away from his friend and left the school. When he reached the poorhouse truck he climbed in back and did not speak to the driver. Grimly he reviewed what he had heard. Hector, the peer of them all, was dead. He was not only dead; he lay disgraced outside the walls of Troy.

At the poorhouse, meals were served in a long, dismal hall, which the women entered by one door and the men by another. Usually the women chattered and argued about seats, while the men were quieter, staring at the kitchen to get a hint of what the food was to be. But this night even the women were quiet, and David had the strange sensation of feeling that as they somberly entered the long hall they were acting out a lamentation over the body of dead Hector. The scene was so lonely and terrible that he had to leave the table, his food untouched.

That night he could not talk to the men on the long hall. He went directly to Door 8 and slammed it behind him. He fell upon his narrow bed and tried to understand what had happened at Troy. Always before he had been able to guess the ending of a story after the first instalment. But this time the story baffled him.

After lights were out Toothless Tom crept into his room with some cheese. David did not want any. "I'm not hungry, Tom," he said.

"You ain't et!" Tom insisted.

"I don't want any," the boy said dully.

When he found sleep impossible, he crept down the hall to Old Daniel's room. The wizened man was reading in bed with a candle. "What's up?" he asked.

"It's about Hector," David explained.

"Wrap yourself in those pants. It's cold."

"Hector was better than Achilles."

"Of course he was."

"Then why did Achilles win?"

Daniel lay in bed with the covers tightly around his thin neck. His delicate hands lay beneath the blankets, and now, as if he were about to say something of great importance, he stuck his left hand out and pointed to his visitor. "David," he began earnestly. Then he reconsidered and laughed. "Did Miss Clapp finish the story?" he asked.

"Next week," David explained.

The old man looked at the candle for a long time, so long that David thought he had fallen asleep. Finally he asked, "What do you think will happen next week?"

In the shadows the boy's face brightened. "Well," he exploded, "somebody from Troy will kill Achilles and the Greeks will go home."

Old Daniel chuckled at the eager boy huddled in the blue denim pants. The round face was so pleased, so freckled, so pug-nosed and sure of itself. "That's what you think will happen?" Daniel asked.

"Sure!" David added. "Troy is the best side."

Again Daniel started to explain the tragedy that awaited every Hector, and Achilles, and Priam, and each city, whether it be Troy or Carthage or Sparta. But again he stopped. He realized that in every thinking life the moment must come when the bearer of that life must face the inexplicability of things as they are. By and large, the more penetrating the initial blow the better chance a man has of diffusing its meaning over his entire soul and welcoming this savage truth into the heart of his being. Old Daniel saw clearly that within a week this bright, cheery boy would receive his initial blow, for a boy may help to cut down two suicides and miss entirely their meaning, but when a boy grieves abstractly about the death of Hector, and when within a week he must also learn of the perfidy by which Achilles himself died and the foul trick that tumbled the topless towers of Troy, then he is dabbling with the soul's fire and he must surely be burnt.

"It's cold," Daniel said. "Go to bed. Next week tell me how the story ends."

"Sure!" the shivering little boy replied. "I'll find out what happened for you." He hung up Daniel's pants and crept back to his own room. There, upon his pillow, was a chunk of cheese. Hungrily he ate it in the dark.

As Friday afternoon dragged on, David found himself nervous with anticipation. Finally Miss Clapp picked up the blue book. "This afternoon we are going to say good-bye to our friends the Greeks and the Trojans," she said. She coughed, waited a moment for that strained silence which delighted her teacher's heart, and began: "At night the Trojans crept out to get the body of Hector and give it decent burial within the walls." David gasped when Achilles was tricked to death. Even Achilles should have been allowed to fight. Now the March sunlight crept across the blackboard like the hand of a clock rushing to end the tale. A wooden horse was built, and David chuckled to himself. The Trojans wouldn't be that dumb!

The sunlight was clear across the board, filling the room like music, and Miss Clapp read on, her voice fraught with suspense. Now the walls of the city were knocked down to admit the horse. The treacherous beast was hauled into the heart of Troy. Stop them! It's a trick! Night came on and much feasting. Oh, put a guard there! Trojans, Trojans! To the walls! But the city ignored all of David's warnings, and from the bowels of the horse came forth a fearful burden. Kill them now! Now! But the city caroused, and in a moment it was aflame, and the proud towers of Troy were gone forever.

This time David could not keep silent. With sunlight flooding the room like the flames of Troy, he rose and asked, "Is that what it says in the book?"

Miss Clapp, who had been working for a crushing finale, was exasperated. "Of course that's what it says!"

"I don't believe it!" David blurted out.

"Oh!" Miss Clapp gasped. "You sit down!"

To his own great surprise, David glared at his teacher and cried, "No! It's a crazy story!" And he dashed into the cloakroom exactly as Gracey Kelley had done. But instead of sobbing or kicking the wall, he grabbed his coat and ran out into the street. He ignored the poorhouse truck and wandered down the hill, down into the fields leading to Edison.

The ground under his feet was still frozen, but he could sense spring fighting for possession of the earth. In places a mild thaw had set in. Here the earth was moist and David's feet sloshed up and down in rich mud. A path through the woods led him to a sunny spot where jack-in-the-pulpits were growing. Beside him the soft earth was pierced by the glorious leaves of the dogtooth violet.

David's shoes were now a mess, but his turbulent heart was quieter. When he reached the stream he was fully decided as to what he must do. Miss Clapp could have the story her way. He would have it his way. His fingers were truly burning to get hold of a pencil! "I'll write a book," he mumbled defiantly, "that'll take care of the Greeks!"

There are many reasons why men write books: vanity, a longing for old days, the need of money, a bursting desire to expostulate or to share experience. But in David Harper's first aching desire to write he struck upon one of the finest and most difficult-to-control of all motivations: he was burning angry, fiery mad, and come gods or schoolteachers or friends or thrashings from his aunt or hunger or poorhouses or the despair of his own heart he would do something about it!

Night fell before he reached the poorhouse. Deep in the west his old friend Orion waved a last farewell. The air was colder now, and the fields were no longer soft beneath his feet. He climbed the last hill and there below him gleamed the lights of the poorhouse.

His heart dancing with energy, he hurried across the remaining fields. He hid in shadows as the old women returned from supper to their own building. He saw one of them stop, sniff at the air and try the ground with her finger. He watched another kick at the earth of the sleeping flower beds. Then Aunt Reba, thin and angry, appeared and hurried the old women to their hall.

The sight of Aunt Reba made him shiver, and he realized that he was both hungry and cold. He would slip in the back way, and Aunt Reba need never know. But there was no such luck. Miss Clapp had already reported him by telephone. The truck was running up and down the road looking for David Harper. In Doylestown the policemen were doing the same. "Here he is!" cried an old woman.

"Catch him!" Aunt Reba yelled. She dashed across the open space between the buildings and grabbed her nephew. "*So*, ve got to run avay from *school*, yet! *Look* at them shoes. Them pants, yet. *Look* at Mr. Smarty!"

Mumbling with rage, she dragged David into the pantry and grabbed a small board from the top of a flour barrel. Stretching the boy across her lap, she did not whip; she beat him. With a fury born of desperation she beat David until, indifferent as he was, he had to scream for mercy.

"*Vell!*" the frantic woman cried above his noise. "*So* it's trouble in *school*, yet!" And she beat him still harder. On the long hall the men, hearing David's screams, were ashamed and did not look at one another.

Finally David could bear the pain no longer. He wrenched himself free, and in doing so he stumbled. Like a swift cat, his frenzied aunt was upon him, thrashing him wherever she could land a blow. The board caught him on the head, across his cheek, in the back, on the legs. He scrambled to his feet and dodged the frantic blows until he made his way out of the pantry and up the dark stairs.

"Komm *back* here, you!" his enraged aunt bellowed. But he was safe. He stopped on the dark steps and listened to his aunt puffing. He saw her peer into the stairway, her face flushed and furious. Then she threw the board down and left.

For a long moment David stood in the darkness. He was

ashamed to enter the hall where the men might speak to him. He touched the blood on his cheek and felt sick. Then he hoisted up his pants. Mortified, he entered the hall, and to his great joy there was no one there to watch him. Daniel had herded them to their rooms. They listened as he plodded down to Door 8. They heard him stand for a moment by the threshold of his room and cry defiantly to no one at all: "She can't hurt me!" The door slammed violently, and the hall was empty.

Inside his barren room David kicked off his muddy clothes and grimly arranged them along the floor. Then he picked up his stubby pencil and sat at the washstand, his tablet of stolen paper before him. He sucked his pencil for a long time and then began to write. A great, inconsolable rage welled up within him. But Aunt Reba had nothing to do with it.

When Toothless brought him a sandwich, he refused to let the old man in. Someone else knocked, probably Daniel, but he too was ignored. When lights went out he lit his candle. All day Saturday he worked, and Sunday, too.

On Wednesday night he finished writing. With a grandiloquent flourish he signed his name and walked to the end of the hall, where Old Daniel and the men were waiting. "You been workin' a long time," the mad Dutchman said.

"I've been writing," the little boy said.

"What?" Luther demanded contentiously.

"A poem!" David snapped.

The mad Dutchman nodded. "Writin' pomes is wery hard," he said.

Old Daniel took charge. "If it's a poem," he said, "it should be read. Would you like me to read it?"

"I'll read it," David said. A place was made for him on the bench, and about him stood a circle of wondering old men. The boy's eyes flashed as he started his new version of the *Iliad*. At lights out he was only half finished, and his audience crept into the light of Daniel's candle.

David had now reached the part about the death of Achilles, and for a moment he had to pause, for the candle in Daniel's hand wavered, wavered in the night. The great pain was upon the old man, the pain that tore at one's stomach as if the vultures of Prometheus were come back, and once the candle almost went out. Then Tom took it, and David killed the matchless Achilles, and Ajax, and Agamemnon. Hector

" . . . lit a fire beneath the horse
And burned up every Greek."

His voice was quivering with joy at wrong righted, David finished his poem. Not seeking admiration—for he had modestly established his own—he looked up at the old faces in the candlelight. Toothless was rapt in admiration. "We ought to send that right in to *The Intelligencer*," he said.

When the men were gone Old Daniel asked, "Why did you write it that way?"

"It was wrong the other way," David explained.

"But you can't change things like that," Daniel argued.

"If it's wrong you can."

"We better go to bed," Daniel said, but before David left he confided, "Some things happen the way the teacher read."

"You mean killing people by tricks?"

"Tricks? Yes. That's why some of these men are in the poorhouse, David."

"Well, then they oughtn't to be!" the boy cried impulsively.

"But the good people don't always win, David."

The little boy stuck out his chin. "When I write a story, they win," he said defiantly.

Spring in a country poorhouse is a time of pain. Then hearts break and overflow into the somber faces of the defeated. The men, gaunt from their long surrender, look at the stirring earth and compare their present lot with what they had hoped for. In the evenings they stand along the walls and watch the fresh-plowed hilltops. It is different from summer, this watching at dusk, for the men do not await refreshing breezes. They await the haunting memories of their youth.

When David was eleven, even Old Daniel, suspecting that this was his last spring, grew reminiscent. "When I was a boy," he mused, "there were sometimes as many as forty barges a day, passing up and down the canal. Bells on the mules tinkled merrily along the towpath, and bargekeepers blew their winding horns to warn the lockmen of their approach. David, you could hear the horns for more than a mile!"

"What were the barges like?" David asked.

"They were like ships at sea. They were truly glorious, when I was a boy." As he recalled the happy days, pain attacked, and he shifted his body into various positions until he found one that was comfortable. His silence gave the mad Dutchman a chance to speak.

"They had fancy barges for picnics," Luther explained. "When I bought my cigar factory we hired a barge. To Erwinna we went. Oh, the pretty girls that day! Then we took a hayride home. Wery nice, the barges!"

"Did you ever ride the barges?" David asked Old Daniel.

"Did I ever!" the frail old man glowed. "The bargemen knew me well."

"Warious people lived right on the barges," Luther explained.

"There was one family," Daniel mused. "They were gypsies, we claimed. I rode up and down the canal with them all one summer. I wanted to marry their daughter."

"I never got married," Toothless Tom said.

An old man interrupted. "On a farm women are good. In a city, no."

"I got married," Luther Detwiler said. He scratched his mad head. "My wife . . ." He looked beseechingly at David. "Where . . ." Then he grinned. "My wife's in Delaware."

A sudden breeze swept up from the grove of oak trees. This was spring! Spring, as only it can be, a quiet, searching, overwhelming thing, sweet with lilies-of-the-valley and dogwood.

"That smells like lily-of-the-valley," Luther said. The men stopped talking as the perfume of spring, like that of a delicate woman, passed them by, and every man thought of what paradise, great or small, he had lost.

David never forgot that moment. Luther was the first to speak and he droned on about his cigar factory: "I lost my factory. I lost my house. I lost my wife. I never should of signed them papers Mr. Crouthamel give me."

Nor did David ever forget that when poorhouse men speak of the worlds they lost, they speak always of those distant worlds as they were in spring. It was the barges of spring that Daniel recalled. Other men remembered their homes surrounded by spring flowers, or that memorable spring when ice stayed in the Delaware through April. They thought of the plowing, not the harvesting, the thawing of earth, not its freezing. They remembered the branches of their trees twisting in the agony of blossom-birth: they did not boast of the many apples they had picked.

David also noticed that old men who came to the poorhouse in spring were inconsolable. A man might enter in

January and praise the warmth of the long hall, but the men who came in spring could praise nothing. Then the poorhouse was a prison terrible to the spirit. Spring men often ran away, and the two men whose dangling bodies David had found in the barn, they were spring men.

There was little surprise, therefore, when an old man from Bensalem reached the poorhouse one Saturday in late March and disappeared the following Monday. For two nights he had lived in Door 10. Endlessly he had walked up and down, an old man of seventy-three walking up and down.

David went in to see him on Sunday and said, "Would you like to come to church with me this afternoon? It's the Baptists this week. They sing fine."

"Get out of here!" the old man snapped. "Leave me alone."

In a way, it was good for David that the old man did run away. For the next occupant of Door 10 was an interesting man. He was younger than most of the occupants, less stoop-shouldered, and possessed of his own teeth. On the second night, that was Wednesday, he gave David a chocolate bar. On Thursday he gave the boy two apples. Late that night, after Toothless had visited with some cheese, the stranger tapped lightly on Door 8.

"May I come in?" he asked.

"Yes," David cried eagerly. "Thanks for the apples."

"Did you like them?" the man asked. His face was clean and bright in the candlelight.

"They were good," David beamed.

"Well, I know little boys like apples," the friendly man laughed, sitting on the edge of the bed. "They tell me you're pretty good in the games at school."

"I like to play basketball," David admitted. "But I'm too short right now."

"You'll grow!" the man assured him. He leaned forward and felt the muscles in David's arm. The boy's small arm had goose pimples from the chill air. "You'd better cover up," the man said very quietly. He snapped the meager poorhouse covers over the boy in such a way as to extinguish the candle. "I'm sorry," he said. "I have no matches."

"There's some over there," David said eagerly.

"Never mind," the man reassured him. Gently he forced David back onto the pillow. "You must be sleepy." He stroked David's forehead, and then his cheek.

"I guess I am," David said. He felt funny. The man's

hands smelled funny, like that soap they used at Paradise Park, where the band played.

"You go to sleep, David," the stranger said, "and when you grow up those arms will be fine for basketball. Your legs, too." Gently, he tested David's muscles through the thin sheets. "Get some sleep now," the soft voice repeated. "You'll be all right."

There was a sharp sound at the door. David heard the stranger hiss air between his teeth. The door wrenched open. In the candlelight the old men of the hall looked into David's room. Old Daniel cried, "Why, you . . ."

Toothless Tom was first to reach the stranger. He lunged awkwardly forward, missed him, and plunged across the bed. David saw the stranger's face in the shadows. It was ugly and distorted.

Now Luther grabbed the stranger. In a brutal Dutch grip he hauled the man from the corner and out into the hall. David, not wanting to miss anything, pushed Toothless from on top of him and scrambled out of bed to see what was happening.

"Boy!" Toothless roared, his mouth slobbering because he had no teeth. "Close that door!"

David did so, but as he stood shivering in his skimpy nightshirt, standing with his hand in Tom's, he could hear the old men of the poorhouse beating up the stranger. He could hear that soft voice whining, pleading, screaming, and cursing while the poorhouse men, silent, breathed hard.

Door 10 slammed shut. David could hear the bed creak heavily. Then there was silence. His own door opened. It was Old Daniel, oh, how thin and tired. Toothless rose to leave. "You stay!" Daniel ordered.

"I never been married," Toothless protested.

"Sit down!" Daniel commanded. The two old men put David, who felt fine, tenderly to bed. In the candlelight they stood over him, Toothless shifting from foot to foot, Daniel talking.

The astonishing things David heard that night would probably have perplexed him for a long time except that early the next morning the wardens found the runaway man from Bensalem. They found him floating face downward in the big tank on top of the women's building. And this was the tank from which all the drinking water came.

Before breakfast three doctors from Doylestown rushed down to the poorhouse and inspected the tank where the man's bloated body had contaminated the water. The poorhouse people were called into the mess hall, wardens and everybody. A new man stumbled and knocked over a bucket of water. As the clear liquid ran onto the floor, a woman got very sick. She rushed out and David could hear her vomiting in the flower beds. Aunt Reba followed her out, commanding the woman to stop.

"We don't think there's anything wrong," the overseer said reassuringly.

"We'll give everybody two pills," a fat doctor said. "For safety!" he joked.

"We tested the water and it's all right," the overseer cajoled. But another woman started to vomit and rushed out.

"So everybody line up!" the fat doctor laughed. "Here!" he said to the overseer. "You're first."

The overseer grinned broadly and picked up his two pills. Then the doctor handed him a glass of water. Instinctively the overseer shuddered, and the poorhouse people laughed nervously. "This water's from the Barish farm!" the overseer explained. With exaggerated gestures he swallowed the pills and stared happily at the doctors. "I took 'em!" he cried proudly. "That wasn't bad!" But another woman had to leave, all the same.

When David took his pills he tasted the water carefully to see if he could detect any difference between it and the contaminated poorhouse water. Later, on the playground, he announced judiciously to Grade Five that he couldn't taste the dead man. A little girl got very sick.

At that moment David saw a housewife walking down Court Street with a basket of spring vegetables, scallions and lettuce. And suddenly for the first time in his life David saw a woman as a woman. She was clean, wore good clothes, walked straight. She was not old and faded like the poorhouse women, not stiff and proper like Miss Clapp. She was just a woman, and David thought that women were very funny people. They got sick and had to vomit over a little thing like water. But they never hung themselves in the barn. They did not die of broken hearts merely because they were in the poorhouse, nor did they beat their brains out because they had lost a farm. No, the women went right on living, fighting, being mean, elbowing for the best seats at supper. It was the men who quit and died.

In mid-April Mrs. Moomaugh sent David a large bundle

of clothes. Its arrival was a great event, and Old Daniel said that something must be done to fix up the boy's closet, now that he had some clothes.

So accordingly three men worked all one day building shelves and hammering nails into convenient spots. "I'm going to check this closet every day," Daniel said. "A boy has to learn to be neat."

It was good to have fresh clothes, especially Harry Moomaugh's, for they fitted fine, and on Sunday morning David dressed in the choice items and reported to his aunt for inspection "*Vhere'*d you get them *clothes?*" she demanded.

"Mrs. Moomaugh," David explained.

"She should *ought* to 've brought 'em to me," his aunt protested.

"She brought them to Daniel. Because he asked her for them." The implied censure angered Aunt Reba and she gouged her finger into David's ears.

"They clean?" she whined.

"Yes," David replied. She turned him around.

"*Don't* get messed before church, yet," she commanded. Then she dismissed him, thinking grimly to herself: "Chust vait! He be fourteen *soon. Then* we see!"

Church in the poorhouse was held in the afternoon so that David had time on his hands. The day was brilliant and warm, and gradually he wandered over to the woods that fringed the poorhouse fields. As he walked he saw birds flying and the nests of field mice. At the stream a lazy carp drifted with the current. Active sunnies darted among reeds, and a few cattails were beginning to show brown stalks. Milkweed was growing, too, and he noted his three spring favorites: jack-in-the-pulpits, skunk cabbage in fascinating colors, and the superb dogtooth violet.

"Lots of stuff out today," he mused. Upstream bullfrogs leaped from the bank. David never tired of watching the lithe young frogs arching into the sunlight, trailing their legs behind as they flashed noiselessly into the pools. One fellow in particular watched him as he approached and then leaped gracefully into the stream. "That's nice!" David cried approvingly.

The cool splash of the frog excited him. Looking about, he decided that he was alone, and before he knew what he was about he was naked by the bank. He dipped his toe into the water. It was very cold, but not too cold, he thought. It wouldn't be so bad if he could leap in all at once, but Toothless had warned about ever doing that in a strange pool. So he drove the frogs before him and edged into the water. "Whew!" he whistled. "This is mighty cold!"

He thought: I'll get out now. It'll be almost the same as if I had ducked." So he retired to the bank, but immediately felt ashamed of himself, so he splashed back into the water and submerged. Chattering, he regained the bank and shivered in the sunlight. He felt tingly. A venturesome bullfrog, thinking no one was about, garrumphed onto a log, saw the boy, and dove far into the pool. "That's nice!" David laughed.

At lunch he whispered to Tom, "Went swimming this morning!"

Tom asked, "Footsie or all the way under?"

"All the way!" David said belligerently. He could tell when each man at table got the news, for each one stopped eating and stared at him, shivering their shoulders as if they were cold. David shook his head and said, without making sounds, "It wasn't so cold."

After the noonday meal he and crazy Luther Detwiler went down to the highway to mark off the cars. David would read the license plates as they whizzed by. When a state like Montana or Nevada appeared, the men would talk about it for weeks. It didn't matter to Luther what the licenses were, because for some inexplicable reason he thought that all cars came from Delaware. David said, "That one was from Ohio."

"That's in Delaware," Luther replied.

"The dogtooth violets are out," David gossiped.

"Wery nice, dogtooth wiolets," Luther agreed. "Yellow."

At two-thirty Luther jumped up and down and pointed to three cars turning into the drive. "The Quakers is coming!" he shouted. "Got to get our hats!" Long ago he had been told that Quakers did not mind if a man wore his hat to church, and now he tore up the lane so that he would be ready for worship.

Each Sunday some religious group came to the poorhouse to conduct services. On this Sunday in April the Quakers from Solebury Meeting had come. The Quakers, David had noticed, always came a little early. They talked with the poorhouse people, not bending down a little as others did, but straight up. Women would look right at Toothless and say, "Tom, thy old farm looks very good," and Tom would say, "How's the winter wheat?" and nobody looked away in embarrassment because that farm was no longer Tom's. The

Presbyterians and Baptists were more fun than the Quakers, because they sang, but the Quakers came earlier and looked right at you.

When church started David and Luther wandered in as if it were to be any Sunday in the world, but this day was to be different. In the first place, Luther forgot to put his hat on until fifteen minutes of silence had passed. Then he glared defiantly at the tall Quaker on the facing bench and slapped his torn hat on his head. This Sunday was different, too, because David had a penny for collection. Toothless Tom had given it to him. And finally, there was a girl at services this day, a young Quaker girl about David's age. She sat with her father on the facing bench and looked very solemn.

Marcia Paxson was taller than David, even then, more sure of herself, darker, quicker when she turned her head than he. Through the long service David sat in rich silence, clutching his penny and staring at the girl. Across the poorhouse church she stared back. Twice her father nudged her not to be so rude, but her flashing eyes came again and again to rest upon the snub-nosed face.

David would never forget that quiet Sunday. Sometimes the Quakers spoke at meeting, sometimes not. On this day no one spoke, and a fly, drowsily awakened from winter, droned more noisily than all the Quakers. A mad woman who spent some days in the mad row and some days semi-free was free this day. She rocked back and forth, and suddenly began to hum a whispery, airy chant. The fly flew past and she was diverted. The ghostly singing stopped.

Now sunlight from the glowing spring day moved across the hall as it had when Troy burned. The Quakers from Solebury pondered in their hearts the will of God and found no reason to speak aloud, so the pregnant silence continued, and David stared at the strange girl. Finally, after an hour, the girl's father leaned over and shook hands with a white-haired woman. The meeting was over and men began to talk. Luther said, "Hmmm! No singin'. No sermon. Hmmm!" He tried to drag David out with him, but the boy lagged behind.

He had no clear reason as to why he stayed that day, but he was very glad that he did, for the girl's father and mother came up to him and said, "Thee is David Harper. Miss Clapp told us about thee." They reached down and shook hands with him as if he were a man. The man said, "I'm Richard Paxson. This is my daughter, Marcia."

The four of them walked out into the brilliant sunlight and stood between the two gray buildings. Mrs. Paxson said, "Some day thee must come to visit us," and David felt that a very important thing was happening to him. He was assured of this when Mrs. Paxson went to their car and produced four books: *Buccaneers and Pirates of Our Coast* was one of them. He held the books in his hands, but Luther Detwiler, who had been watching, rushed up and took the books.

"Did he say thank you?" the mad Dutchman demanded.

"No," Mrs. Paxson replied truthfully. Luther kicked his little friend.

"Thank you," David said. "I like books."

Then Marcia spoke. "I want thee to visit us, too." She held out her hand. It was longer than David's, and stronger.

But when their car rolled down the lane, Luther threw the books on the ground and started cuffing David about the head. "Daniel tells you! I tell you! When you get somethin', you say thank you!" David recovered the books and took them tenderly to his room.

The Krusens were different. They were like no other couple that ever came to the poorhouse. They arrived one evening about five. It was not the manner of their coming that was unusual. A truck drove up to the women's building, and two bundles of meager belongings were tossed onto the porch. The driver—like all such drivers—was most careful to explain that *he* wasn't related to the Krusens. "Not me! They ain't my kin! I drove 'em up here for a friend." The driver shivered as he saw the poorhouse doors open, and then he was gone with a memory that would plague him whenever he spent a dollar.

Mr. Krusen was a tall man, very bent in the shoulders, rheumy-eyed and unhappy. He was put in Door 11, across the hall from David. At first the boy noticed nothing peculiar, but at dinner on the second night David saw that Mr. Krusen was different. The boy had grown accustomed to watching married men when their wives first came through the women's door. There was a terrible wrench that even David could understand. Here was the woman this man had sworn to protect, and because of his faulty judgment she would die in the poorhouse. It seemed to David that married women took the poorhouse in their stride, but to their husbands it was agony.

Mr. Krusen wasn't that way. When Mrs. Krusen entered the barren hall she put her hands on her hips, surveyed the room, and said, "It could do with some flowers." Mr. Krusen looked across the hall at her as if she were no concern of his, and then he never looked at her again. He kept his eyes on his plate and as soon as the meal was over he hurried back to Door 11, where he locked himself in and spoke to no one.

Three days later Mr. Krusen got a letter. David took it up to him. It was from Lancaster, and the old man eagerly ripped away one corner, then hurried into his room. Even in the half hour when men and women could visit he remained locked in his room.

Mrs. Krusen was in the visiting area, however. She was apparently waiting for her husband. When he did not appear, she sat on a bench with two old women. David walked near them, and they called him over. He was reluctant to go, for he did not like old women. Mrs. Krusen smiled at him and asked, "Have you seen Mr. Krusen?"

"He's up in his room," David said.

"Will you please be a dear little boy and ask him to come down?"

"He knows you're here," David said loudly. "He was looking at you a minute ago."

Mrs. Krusen's head snapped back as if he had struck her. The other old women were ashamed and looked away. Finally Mrs. Krusen licked her lips and asked, "What is he doing?"

"He's reading a letter," David replied. "I took it up to him."

Mrs. Krusen gave a sharp cry and put her hands to her face. Now her two friends turned back to her and said, "There, there."

"Was it from . . . Lancaster?"

"Yes," David said, and Mrs. Krusen began to cry. At first David thought she was crying for herself, but apparently she wasn't, for she said many times, "Jonas, Jonas!"

That night Mr. Krusen refused to look at his wife. She stared at him throughout the long meal, but he would not look up. When he was through eating, he wiped his mouth furtively and sneaked back to Door 11.

Next morning Mrs. Krusen waited by the messhall door so that her husband must pass her on the way to breakfast. "What's the matter, Jonas?" she whispered.

"Nothin'," the man grunted, pulling himself away from her. "They wrote to you, Jonas. I know." He rudely thrust his way past her and David heard her cry. "I'm not sorry for me, Jonas. It's for you! They'll kill you, Jonas."

Angrily the big man hurried from the messhall without waiting for breakfast, and that night it was clear to see that Mrs. Krusen had been crying. But her husband would not look at her.

On Saturday there were two visitors to the poorhouse, and they affected David deeply. The first was Mr. Paxson, from Solebury, with his daughter Marcia. They drove into the circle and asked for David. He was in the barn helping Tom, and when he appeared he was well dusted with the fine, smelly dust of hayseed.

"Hello, farmer!" the tall Quaker said. "Thee's been hard at it, eh?"

"I help out on Saturdays," David explained.

"Is thy aunt about?" Mr. Paxson inquired.

"She's in there," David pointed. "I'll get her." He ran for his aunt, and that lonely, antagonistic woman came out into the spring sunlight. Mr. Paxson introduced himself and his daughter and said, "I've come to ask thy permission to take thy nephew to Quaker Meeting in Solebury some Sunday."

"Hmmm!" Aunt Reba snorted. She quickly saw that this was some kind of trap.

"His father, you know, was a Quaker." The words fell heavily upon David, for he had not known this about his father. He looked quizzically at his aunt and she took his gaze to be condemnatory.

"I don't *want* Daywid traipsing about the *coun*try, yet," she said stolidly, and the vast difference between her penuriousness of spirit and the calm dignity of Mr. Paxson was so great that David blurted out, "I'd like to go."

But Mr. Paxson was not to be so trapped. Bowing gently he asked Aunt Reba, "Then I don't have thy permission?"

Now Aunt Reba was cornered and she scowled at David. "All right," she said and stomped back to her quarters.

"I'll call for thee some Sunday," Mr. Paxson said, and shook hands with David, as if the boy were a man, but even as he spoke David stared into the car at the dark, confident girl who stared speculatively back.

When the car left, Aunt Reba darted out in the areaway and shouted for her nephew. Reluctantly David went to her and she dragged him into her room. "*Look* here, young fellow," she snorted. "You leave them Paxsons *alone!* Don't go gettin' *ideas.*"

"I didn't know my father was a Quaker," David protested.

"There's lots you don't know," she snorted. "Less you know about your father the better."

David was inclined to fight with his aunt. Seeing her beside calm Mr. Paxson had shown him how much he hated her, but his attention was diverted by a black car that came into the areaway. He dashed away from his ugly aunt to see what was happening.

"They've come for the Krusens!" Toothless reported joyfully. The men on the long hall, all of them, were glad when one of their members escaped. Quickly David bounded up the stairs and into the hall. He banged noisily into his own room and then tiptoed back to Door 11 to eavesdrop.

"You told me that before," Mr. Krusen whined.

The visitor replied, in an unpleasant, nasal voice, "I told you. Erma told you. That woman would bring you nothin' but disgrace." He spoke with a complaining Dutch accent: *tawld* and *nawthin'.* "But oh, no! You wouldn't listen yet. Now see where you land."

"All right," Mr. Krusen snapped. "You knew best."

"If you had only listened to me 'n' Erma when we was up to Sellersville . . ." The monitory voice droned on while Mr. Krusen stuffed his clothes into a bag.

David had long before noticed a peculiarity about people who came to take other people away from the poorhouse. Young men who came could always explain exactly what mistakes their old relatives had made. Young men knew how to keep out of the poorhouse. But when old men came to take their friends away, there was no preaching.

When Mr. Krusen and the unpleasant young man came out into the hall, David was lounging by Door 8. "What's he doin' here?" the young man snapped. "He ought to be in some decent home." And the way he said those words, "decent home," made David hope that he never got forced into such a place.

In the driveway below, the black car waited. Mr. Krusen hurried to it and quickly sneaked into the back seat, where he hid himself in a corner. Erma sat grimly in front, staring straight ahead. Her jaw stuck out and she was dressed in black. The engine started and David realized to his horror that Mrs. Krusen was being left behind.

At this moment the old woman banged open the screen

door of the women's building and rushed over to the black car. "Jonas!" she cried. "You mustn't go away like this."

Her husband hid lower in the back. The driver leaned out and snarled, "Watch aht, there!" He jammed the car into reverse and continued to shout, "Watch aht!"

"Jonas!" Mrs. Krusen implored. "Don't let them do this!"

"I'm comin' for'erd!" the driver warned.

"They don't love you," Mrs. Krusen wailed. "You'll die with them. They'll kill you, Jonas."

"Stahnd clear!" the driver bellowed. Three old men came forward and took Mrs. Krusen by the arms. The car gained speed and started toward the road. Erma looked straight ahead.

In wild energy, Mrs. Krusen burst free of her reluctant captors and dashed into the roadway. Her old skirts flashed in the dust, and she seemed to fall ever forward toward the retreating car. "Jonas, Jonas!" she pleaded.

As the car made its last turn before it was free of the wailing woman, Erma leaned out, her neck swathed in black, and hissed justification of herself: "She ain't one of us. Dirty old whore."

David had not heard this word before, but the manner in which it struck across the faces of the poorhouse people lived with him for many days. But to Mrs. Krusen not even the word mattered. She made a last effort to reach the car and stumbled finally to the roadway, covered in dust.

Luther Detwiler picked her up. David saw that even in the Dutchman's strong arms the woman struggled and wept. Luther carried her over to the women's porch, where Aunt Reba was waiting. "Lay her dahn!" Reba commanded with bitter contempt. Luther did so, and three old women gathered about their stricken friend, but Aunt Reba was relentless. "Let her be!" she warned. "She wasn't married to him."

That night it became apparent to the men on the long hall that Old Daniel was dying. The pains that racked him had become so frequent that no man of seventy could long resist them. David, having yet had no real experience of death, could not interpret the signs, but he noticed that from the day Mrs. Krusen was left behind, Old Daniel lived and spoke with a sense of great urgency.

When David asked, "Why was Aunt Reba so mad at Mrs. Krusen?" he replied. "Your aunt's not a bad woman, David. It's just that she wants to be good. And she doesn't know how."

"But why does her wanting to be good make her mad at Mrs. Krusen?"

The old man became quite eager in his explanation, and he explained the anomaly this way: "You must talk to Mrs. Krusen some time. Tell you what, David! You get up real early tomorrow morning and pick the biggest bunch of flowers you can find. Then you take them up to Mrs. Krusen's room."

"Aunt Reba would beat me," David protested.

"So what does that matter?" the frail old man asked. "David, it's important to you and to Mrs. Krusen both."

"How could it be important to me?" the boy asked, and then something in the thin face staring at him warned David that he must ask no more questions.

Early in the morning he rose and sneaked out of the long hall. In the damp woods he collected a large bouquet of spring flowers. Joe-pye weed and violets and lilies-of-the-valley filled his arms when he crept back to Daniel's room. The old man had found an empty jar that could almost have been a vase, and he got Toothless to arrange the flowers so that they looked large and important. Then mad Luther Detwiler was sent to ask Aunt Reba a question while David slipped into the women's building through the back.

"Where's Mrs. Krusen's room?" he asked in a whisper. The old women, pleased with any conspiracy against Aunt Reba, led him to the right door. He knocked softly and a low voice said, "Come in."

David stepped into the room, and he was unprepared for what he saw. Mrs. Krusen had lived there only a few days, but already it was a fine, clean room, different from any he had previously seen. There was no smell of bedbug juice. Instead, some kind of sweet smell dominated. About the windows were small strips of colored cloth, tied back in bowknots. Over the bed there was cloth of another color, and on it rested a pillow with a knitted cover. The bed was very neat, and above it on the wall were four colored pictures from the *Ladies' Home Journal*.

"I brought you some flowers," David said.

The little old woman rose and curtseyed. "Thank you," she said. With three or four touches of her fingers she made the flowers look different, more spread out, perhaps.

"I'm sorry about yesterday," the boy added. "I'm sorry for you, left behind."

The little woman smiled. "Oh," she protested. "Don't be

sorry for me. It's poor Jonas. He's going to a house with no love. He'll die. He'll die." Tears effaced her smile, and David had to look away.

On the wall he saw a picture of a mill on a hillside with handsome trees about. "That's a pretty picture," he said.

"It's from a magazine," Mrs. Krusen explained. Then she patted David on the head, although she wasn't a great deal taller than he. "They tell me you do well in school," she said approvingly. David grinned, for the little old woman made him feel at ease. "So the boys who do well deserve presents!" And she jumped up on the neat bed and pulled down the picture David had admired. "This is for you," she said happily, "and here's the tack, too!"

"I didn't mean I wanted it," David protested. Mrs. Krusen rolled the picture into a trim tube and placed the tack inside.

"Now you have a picture, too," she said. David nodded and started for the door. "Aren't you going to say, 'Thank you'?" Mrs. Krusen asked.

"I forgot," David admitted. "Thank you for the picture." He stepped out into the hall and a very old woman hobbled up to him.

"Miss Reba coming!" the old woman whispered.

"Day*wid*!" came the searching whine.

"Oh, my gosh!" David cried.

"Hide in here," the very old woman suggested, shoving the boy into her room.

"Don't bend that picture!" David cautioned.

"Iss *Day*wid up *here*, yet?" Aunt Reba probed.

"No," the very old woman lied.

Reba stormed past and into Mrs. Krusen's room. "*Some*body chust *said* my *boy* wass up *here*," she whined.

"Now!" the very old woman cried to David. He slipped from her room and hurried downstairs. He could hear his aunt threatening Mrs. Krusen. Carefully he crept behind the milkhouse and through the woods behind the barn.

"Day*wid*!" his aunt bellowed.

Old Daniel's window snapped up. "He's up here, Miss Reba," the thin voice cried. Breathlessly David dashed down the hall to his friend's room. Sticking his head out the window at the last moment he cried casually, "You want me?"

"*Where* you been *at?*" his aunt shouted.

"Talking with Daniel," the boy lied.

And when the threat was over he showed Daniel the picture. "That's by Rembrandt," the old man explained.

"I'm going to put it over my bed," the boy replied. Then he shared his bewilderment with Daniel. "I don't think Mrs. Krusen was sorry for herself yesterday. She was sorry for Mr. Krusen."

"I was sorry for him, too, David. To turn his back upon an old friend, that's most evil. Could you deny Toothless or me or mad Luther? No! You're too much of a man to deny your friends. And did you see the young fool Mr. Krusen went away with? How would you like to live with that one?"

"He said I oughtn't to be in the poorhouse," David said, shivering from memory of the ugly, self-satisfied man. "He said I ought to be in a decent home."

"Like his, I guess!" Daniel snorted. "Did you see his wife? How would you like to live with them, David?"

The boy did not even answer but asked, "Did you ever see the rooms in the women's building? They aren't like these. Mrs. Krusen's was really pretty. And that other old woman who walks with a cane. Even her room was pretty and smelled nice."

"That's what women are for, David," the wasted old man explained. "Over here things are clean, but they're ugly. I remember when I traveled up and down the canal. Nothing can be dirtier than a barge. And the gypsy barge was dirtiest of all. But the girl had one corner of a room on deck, all to herself. And it was beautiful all summer long."

"Aunt Reba's room is never like that," David said.

"No, I imagine it isn't," Daniel agreed. "That's why I wanted you to take the flowers to Mrs. Krusen. You have a lot to learn."

As he spoke the pain became too great for him to bear, and he fell to the floor in a faint. David was terribly frightened and called for Tom. The poorhouse men crowded into the room and lifted the small man to his bed.

"It's his cancer," Luther Detwiler said. The other men gasped and rushed David from the room. In his own quarters he trembled for a moment and then sneaked across the hall to talk with Toothless.

"Is he going to die?" the boy implored.

"Not yet," Toothless said patiently. Then he added, "We're all old men, David. Pretty soon we'll all die."

Quietly, and with a heavy burden, David returned to his room. It was Sunday, and he had nothing to do. He was confused, and then at his feet he saw the Rembrandt. Gently he pressed it flat and, with his shoe, tacked it to the wall over his bed. The sunlight illuminated the ancient mill and made it seem alive.

David did not want to think of Old Daniel, lying faint in bed, so he thought of Mrs. Krusen instead: "A nice woman like her. You wait. Some day Mr. Krusen will come back for her."

But he never did.

Late in the afternoon they carried Old Daniel out of his room and into the sick quarters. Four men came for him with a stretcher, but when they lifted it with Daniel, even David could see the surprise on their faces. And no wonder, for the little old man weighed less than ninety pounds, and of those pounds the cancer weighed one in four.

At every door an old man stood to say good-bye to his stricken friend. And when the stretcher reached the end of the long hall, the bearers paused a moment so that the old man could look one last time at the bench and the afternoon sunlight and the faces of his friends. There was no make-believe on anyone's part that Daniel would ever return. When old men left the long hall on stretchers they never came back.

In the sick room they placed the little old man near a window. David thought: "You can't really see outdoors from here. But you can see that tree."

The dying man looked up and saw his familiar friend. There was the boy's freckled face, the turned-up nose, the smudge of dirt above the left eye. He was, thought Old Daniel, the inheritor of the earth; and suddenly the frail man burned with energy to tell this boy all the things he knew.

"David!" he cried imperatively. "Listen!" And that was the beginning of the long talks he engaged in as he lay dying. He would brook no interruptions, and often he skipped madly from topic to topic, merely gleaning large generalizations from his rich memory. At times he would stop and beat his hand against the sheets to impress an idea into the boy's mind. In a final surge of desire to project his spirit into some kind of life after the body's death, the old man spent his accumulated philosophy upon the boy.

That first afternoon he said: "David, the world is not an evil place. Never believe that. You will see wars and famines and betrayals. But the world itself cannot be evil. It's just that evil people, having nothing kind within themselves to feed upon, are driven like mad animals to accomplishment.

So you'll always find that one evil person makes more noise than four good men.

"I never found a way to tell a good man from an evil one except by what he did. It's popular now to say all men are good and evil both. But I don't believe that. Men are on one side or the other. Of course, sometimes a good man will do an evil thing. But he regrets it. And so will you, whenever you do wrong. And if you do wrong too often, regrets come so easily that you forget what wrong is. Then you've become an evil man, and you're all tied up inside, and you work and fight against others. And do you know why? Because you have no peace in your heart to satisfy you when you are alone.

"I tried to be a good man, David, and I think I was. When you grow up you'll ask yourself, 'But why did he wind up in the poorhouse?' Let me tell you that America is a wonderful country. I've seen all the countries in the world, I guess, and there is none to compare with ours. But it's quite possible for a man in America to lead a good life and die in the poorhouse. It's pretty hard for an evil man to do that." Then the frail hands beat unmercifully upon the bed, and the old man cried, "But you must never forget that evil men don't get into this poorhouse of ours because they live forever in a miserable poorhouse of their own spirit. All their lives!

"So when you're thirty years old or forty and you remember your friends on the long hall, don't jump at wrong answers as to why we were here. The world wasn't all wrong. America was not an evil place. We were not bad men. It's . . ." He looked up at the fragmentary tree. "It's like the burning of Troy. There is no explanation."

A terrible paroxysm gripped him. His face became bluish. He clutched at the covers and writhed upon his bed. The sunlight beamed across his forehead and showed sweat standing in tiny balls, like a crown of jewels. But beneath the sheets his knees hammered together until David could hear them.

"Ugh . . . ugh . . ." he gasped.

"Daniel!" David pleaded softly. He thought: "If he were dead like the old men in the barn, his pain would stop. But look at his eyes. He doesn't want to be dead."

"Oh, David!" the nurse cried, rushing up. "Get out of here!" She grabbed the boy tenderly and led him to the door. But David kept looking back at Daniel, who did not want to die. The boy saw this thing and remembered it.

Daniel did not die that day. David had many more visits with him. As the old man grew weaker, so that even his face contracted, he talked with greater speed. He jumped more in his speech, too, cutting at the topic sentences of his mortal essay: "Lots of people start things in January, with the beginning of the year. But that's ruling your life by a calendar. Always start things in the spring. Work at them through the summer. Finish them in the winter. Most great men are started in spring. Women carry them through the summer and autumn. That's why we celebrate so many birthdays in February. People are like the earth.

"You can look at any great man and say, 'He's no better than a hog. He eats and sweats and goes to the toilet and some day he dies.' But you can also say, of the meanest man you ever saw, 'He is more than an eagle.'

"You can't save enough money to make sure that everything will turn out all right. Lots of times when you do have money you can't use it, so what good does it do? But it's fine to have. I've heard fifty ministers try to explain why a rich man cannot enter into the kingdom of heaven, and I've never heard an explanation yet. But as surely as I've lived, there are other things worth more than money. Again, America is not a bad place. But it's very hard in America for you to have money and the important things, too. You must decide on four or five things that are of most importance to you. Look at me! They will be more important than money, David, and if you turn your back on those things, your heart will wither and die.

"David, I don't want to turn you against your Aunt Reba. She's not evil. She's stupid. She has lots of money, and she could buy you clothes and books and pencils. But she won't do it. She thinks she can save that money and spend it on something better than a human being. What, I ask you? What's better? I sent four boys to college, and if they knew I was here now I think their hearts would break. But I've never told them. They weren't even my sons. Look! If they spent money on me now it would soon be buried with me. But if they do something good for a boy just growing up, it'll go on forever."

When the great pain came, Daniel fought with all his frail strength. He turned and threw his skinny shoulders into the chest of the pain, kicked at it, clutched its gray outlines with his bare hands.

"Oh, David!" the nurse cried again. "Please call me when it

starts!" Her voice broke and she sniffled. "Why doesn't your goddamned aunt take you out of here? That old bitch!" As if she were angry with David she thrust him violently from the room.

On Sunday Daniel said: "Reading and travel are the two best things besides people. Travel is best, but some books are very great. You should read all the books you can get before you're twenty. If you don't need glasses by the time you're thirty, you can consider your life wasted. Maybe books are best, because you don't have to . have money to read. And there's this difference, too. A man can travel all over the world and come back the same kind of fool he was when he started. You can't do that with books.

"But you needn't spend a great deal on travel, either. Nor do you have to go very far. Just set out for yourself some day and walk to the canal. I've been all over the world, and the canal north of New Hope is the best place of all, because there the land is just the way God made it. But in spring, of course, any place is beautiful, because in spring fires leap from your heart, and you can see things that aren't there.

"And wherever you go on the face of the earth have the humility to think that a thousand years ago someone pretty much like you stood there and a thousand years from now a boy like you will be there. And in two thousand years boys and places and people will have been pretty much the same.

"A lot of nonsense is spoken about work. Some of the finest men I've known were the laziest. Never work because it's expected of you. Find out how much work you must do to live and be happy. Don't do any more.

"But thinking is something different, altogether! Think always as if the hot hand of hell were grabbing for you. Think to the limit of your mind. Imagine, dream, hope, want things, drive yourself to goodness. Whatever you do, David, do it to the absolute best of your ability. Never take the easy way where thinking is concerned.

"As for churches, they do much more good than harm, but churches where women are in command are often evil places, for no minister can speak honestly there."

In these days of monologue David sometimes interrupted with strange questions. He was living in a world of ferment. Outside his window a horse-chestnut tree had broken into handsome pyramids of flowers. All day and through the evening bees gossiped among the stately blossoms until the tree seemed like a village store on Saturday night. There was a glorious ache, a marvelous energy in the world. One night a peach tree would appear frail and green. Next noon it was bedecked with flowers, like a young girl painting her cheeks with abandon in her first attempt.

"Were you ever married?" David asked on the last day.

"Me?" the old man asked, his knees shaking with pain. "Sure I was married."

"The gypsy girl?"

"No!" the wasted fellow laughed. "No, I married a big woman in Detroit. We had three children. One was a fine boy, like you."

"Where are they now?"

"I . . . Well . . . It's this way, David. There are many things that can't be explained. But remember this thing that you can understand. It's better to marry any woman at all than never to marry. This is what I mean. It would be much better for your withered-up aunt to marry Toothless Tom than to live the way she does. If you tell her that, she'll fizz up and bust. But it's true."

Now sovereign pain gripped at the old man with final fury, for this time there also came the ally death. Daniel must have seen the terrible pair, for he jerked his head back and raised his hands as if to fight once more against them. But now the visitors would not be denied. Shaken in their icy grip, the old man writhed in mortal torment.

David clearly perceived what was happening. He knew that this pain was different from the others. This was all-possessing pain.

"Sam! Sam!" the old man shouted, and the boy wondered: "Who is Sam?"

"Sam! Goddamn you, Sam!" the dying man roared.

Back in some distant passion Old Daniel died. He forgot David, and his pain, and the poorhouse, and all the wonderful things he had seen and read. "Sam!" he pleaded. Then he whispered the word again: "Sam!" Getting no response, he summoned his final energy, raised his gaunt neck and bellowed mightily: "Sam!"

This cry brought the nurse, and David said, "He's dead."

"Poor old man," she said, and methodically she covered up the ancient face.

But the picture of the man was not erased from David's mind. For a long time he could see his old friend, beset by more than human pain, alone, his children gone from him, lost in a country poorhouse, fighting death to the last wild cry. David did not clearly reason out what he instinctively knew to be true: Daniel had known something in life that was sweet beyond words; he had never quite described it for the boy, but he had proved its presence in the world.

On the day of Daniel's burial Mr. Paxson said that he would come by for David on Sunday and take him to Quaker Meeting. When David told the men on the long hall about his good fortune, they were strangely silent. He repeated his message and finally one of them asked bluntly, "What are you going to wear?"

"I'll wash up, and Tom can mend my shirt."

"But you can't go to the Paxsons' that way!" a man from Solebury said. "Why, the Paxsons . . ."

David interrupted. "I don't think Mr. Paxson would mind."

"But look at you!" the man protested. The men of the poorhouse studied the boy. Old shoes, scuffed beyond repair. Harry Moomaugh's pants torn on a stone fence. A bedraggled shirt, and a mop of untrimmed hair.

"I'll tell you what!" Tom said brightly. "Old Daniel gimme somethin' before he died. Said to spend it on you when you needed it. Looks like now's the time." He went to his room and returned with a Bull Durham tobacco pouch. Toothless emptied the pouch into his hand. It contained more than two dollars!

"Won't be enough for shoes, too," an old man said.

Tom scratched his chin. "Tell you what, David. You go beg some money from your Aunt Reba."

"Not me!"

An old man said, "You go, Tom. I'll cut the boy's hair." So Tom left while the men made a stool for David to sit on while experimenting barbers trimmed his long hair. At Aunt Reba's door Tom said, " 'Scuse me for buttin' in, but your boy needs shoes."

"*He's* got *shoes!*" Reba snapped.

"He's got old shoes, Miss Reba. All wore out."

"I seen 'em the other *day*. Nothin' wrong with 'em."

"But Miss Reba!" Tom pleaded. "They ain't good enough for him to go to church in. And maybe the Paxsons'll take him to they home atterwards."

"The *Pax*sons! Them against *Sole*bury?" She flung her thin arms into the air and rushed at Tom. "*You* done *this!* I know it! *Fillin'* that boy's *head* with big *ideas. Makin'* a poorhouse boy so high and *mighty*."

Doggedly Tom insisted, "The boy's just got to have shoes, Miss Reba."

"No!" she screamed. "And *if* he leave*s this* place *Sunday* I'll beat him till he can't sit *down*. Nor lay down, *neither!*"

Tom reported Reba's decision to the long hall. "We'll figure some other way," he said, and next morning he and Luther sneaked David and Daniel's tobacco pouch into Doylestown. They went to Ely's and said, "We want a pair of pants for this boy."

"What size?"

"You kin see 'im! That size."

The clerk studied David and said, "He's big enough for a suit."

"We only want pants," Tom replied.

"Here, sonny. Try these on." The clerk handed David a trim pair of boy's pants, stiff and clean. David started to take his own off. "Not here!" the man said. He opened a cubicle, and when he saw David's underwear he gasped.

"I told him to wear clean ones!" Tom protested, but David blandly reached for the new pants. He could never understand why people worried about underwear. He had two pairs and this pair had been worn for much less than two months. There were walnut stains, ink stains, green stains from leaves, and other odd marks on the cloth. But they weren't torn.

"Thank heavens the pants fit!" the clerk said to himself. Aloud he waxed enthusiastic. "Perfect. Turn round in a circle, my little man." David complied and decided that the view he caught in the mirrors showed a well-dressed chap. The brown pants made his hair look darker, the way he liked it.

"And how much would some shoes be?" Tom asked.

"$1.30," the clerk replied. Tom and Luther retired to count their money.

"Could I speak to you, please?" Tom asked the clerk.

The two men went to the back of the store, and pretty soon the clerk blew his nose. Then he wiped his glasses and went to the phone. "Wilmer?" he called. "That you, Wilmer? Is there any more money left in that fund?" There was a long silence and then the clerk whispered something. "OK, Wilmer." He blew his nose again and said, "First! Some underwear."

"What shall I do with the ones I have on?" David asked.

"Throw them in the corner!" the clerk directed. "No! Don't! Put them in this bag." Shoes, stockings, two shirts, a coat to match his pants, four sets of underwear! That's what Old Daniel's pouch of dimes and quarters and one bill purchased.

"A pretty neat little man!" the clerk beamed. When the trio left the store the clerk joked, "Now when you grow up, remember where you bought your first suit!" He winked at David and shook hands with him. When David opened his fist there was a bright dime in it.

"What can we get for ten cents?" he asked his cronies. Luther, being a Dutchman, was all for saving the dime. Toothless felt that a celebration was in order, so David led the way to a candy store.

"I like suckers," Luther said.

"I like marshmallows," Toothless reported. But there were some jelly beans left over from Easter and the storekeeper gave David two pounds for ten cents. Luther popped a handful in his mouth and started chewing violently, but Tom said he didn't care for any. David was about to eat a black one, but he looked up at Tom with childish horror. He had forgotten that Tom had no teeth.

"I'll trade 'em back for some marshmallows," he insisted.

"I'll suck one," Tom said. But to David the candy was sour, and mad Luther ate the whole two pounds.

On Sunday morning they stationed Luther at the roadside to flag down the Paxson car, lest Aunt Reba see it. Then Tom and the other men dressed David in his new clothes and combed his hair. "Remember!" they said. "If you eat dinner at the Paxsons', say thank you!"

The drive to Solebury that Sunday morning was magnificent. David had never before ridden in the rear seat of a good car. Nor had he ever ridden with a primped and pretty girl. The fields of Bucks County were superb, as if they too were in their Sunday best, and birds sang from every tree.

At the Meeting House the wealthy Quakers of the county stood solemnly on the porch to greet their neighbors. The Paxsons led David and Marcia to a bench and then assumed their own positions as heads of the meeting. Now the spirit of God descended on the place, and there was silence.

After many minutes a woman rose, a housewife from New Hope, and she spoke words David could not understand.

But there was a calm and handsome beauty about her face. When she sat down, no one else spoke.

As the old men had predicted, the Paxsons invited David to Sunday dinner. Mr. Paxson said, "We have some other guests, too. This man's a famous painter."

"I have a painting on my wall," David said. "It's by Rembrandt."

"Joe's no Rembrandt," Mrs. Paxson laughed.

"Tell me, son," the painter said. "How do you like the Rembrandt?"

"It's pretty dark," David said thoughtfully. "Lots of it he didn't paint, but where he did, the light shines." Mr. Paxson and the painter nodded.

Then the painter asked, "How do you like my picture? That one by the fireplace?"

"Why, that's the canal!" David cried.

"Do you know the canal?" the painter asked.

"I've never seen it, but a friend of mine used to work there. He said it was just like that picture!"

"David!" Marcia cried. "Look out here!"

The boy turned abruptly and ran into the yard. There was a swing, a pool for fish, a total world for children to play in. At dinner all the men, and David, had two dishes of ice cream.

On the way home, riding once more in the comfortable car, David tried to recall each joyous moment of the day. Men and women—not old poorhouse people, but men with jobs—had talked with him. There had been a room filled with books. There had been music, and a pond for fish. As the car neared the poorhouse David leaned forward and said, "It was a very nice day. Thank you."

"Thee sees, Margaret," Mr. Paxson whispered to his wife. "The boy's all right. He doesn't even know he's living in a poorhouse."

But this time Mr. Paxson was dead wrong. For when David leaned back after his thank-you's, Marcia Paxson, black haired and deep eyed, had put her hand in David's and whispered, "Thee can come to lots of parties now. Harry Moomaugh said thee had no good suit. But thee does."

Crushed, David did not sneak behind the hedges to escape his aunt. With a great burden of discovery he walked stolidly up the lane where everyone could see him. "A good suit!" he muttered. "Because I didn't have a good suit I couldn't go to the parties. Now I have one and I can go!" He thought with overwhelming bitterness of the music and the good food and the fun he had missed.

"Day*wid*!" came a strident voice. "Komm *here*!" He shuffled disconsolately on, ignoring his aunt.

"Day*wid*!" came a new command. "I said, 'Komm *here*!' " The boy looked up as if he had never before seen his aunt and with studied care walked right through the bed of tulips.

"Och!" his aunt cried. She leaped from her chair and dashed across the lawn, catching her nephew by the hair. "*When* I say stop, you *stop*!" She gave him a stiff blow across the face. He stumbled back into the tulips. This infuriated her.

"*Church,* is it? *Party,* is it?" she cried with an angry, hopeless ache in her voice. "And who gave you new *shoes,* yet?" She struck at him again, for she saw in the brightly dressed boy a symbol of those plans which she feared could never come to fulfillment.

"A new *suit,* too?" she bellowed, and reaching out with her bony hands, she ripped the coat down the front. She tore at the shirt. Still unappeased, she slapped David violently, and his nose began to bleed.

Crazy Luther, seeing this, could stand the scene no longer and grabbed Miss Reba by the waist. "He's *crazy*!" Aunt Reba screamed in fright, but mad Luther gripped her furiously.

"Luther!" David shouted. "Put her down!" Impersonally, Luther dropped the frantic woman and went to David.

"Look what she done to that suit!" the mad Dutchman mumbled.

"I don't want it," David cried, and even though Luther tried to stop him, the boy ripped away the remainder of his coat and threw it among the crushed flowers. When he was gone, Luther salvaged the garment and sneaked it over to Mrs. Krusen.

"Don't let the old witch see it!" Luther cautioned.

"If she says a word," Mrs. Krusen threatened, "I'll stab her eyes out with a needle."

In three days the coat was back, almost as good as new. David never asked how it got there, for he had no desire to wear it. It was a bloody thing, bought with Old Daniel's pennies, and David despised it. In his old poorhouse clothes he had walked with kings, fought at Troy, wandered across Arabia, lived in a mill with Rembrandt, and made a dozen friends. It was the new coat that put him in a poorhouse.

David was convinced that he would have to fight Harry Moomaugh. Harry had said things about him, and that was that. But next day, when he looked at Harry in school, his ardor was considerably diminished. Harry was a big boy. He was two inches taller than David and at least fifteen pounds heavier.

Nevertheless, David was determined to avenge his honor, and all week he picked on Harry, but Moomaugh, never having lost a fight, had no inner compulsion to hit anyone, so he laughed at David's arrogance.

On Sunday David was in a surly mood. Even the minister's words made him angry: "As I look at you people I have come to call my friends, I see that the finest of you all has gone. I knew Daniel Brisbane as well as one man can know another. He was noble, good in all ways, kind to everyone, jealous of no one, a true servant of the Lord. He was a great comfort to me when I started preaching in Doylestown. When my faith grew weary, I refreshed it at the soul and smile of Daniel Brisbane. He never complained. He spent his worldly goods helping others and refused to call upon them for repayment. He taught the teachers and he ministered to the ministers. He lived with the Lord, and when he died he returned to the Lord. He called on no man for aid. His call was upon God, and God replied by giving him that sweetness of life which is denied so many."

At first David wanted to cry as he remembered Old Daniel, but instead he took refuge by laughing at the minister. "A lot he knows!" the boy grunted to himself. "Called upon the Lord, did he? Well, I was there when he died. And he called on Sam Somebody. And when he died he cursed something awful." David dropped his head and glared at the minister.

But late that night he considered what the man had said. Had he, this minister, come to the poorhouse for help? That was incredible. To David it had always been the other way around. Mrs. Moomaugh brought things to the poorhouse. So did the other women, at Christmas and Thanksgiving. When the inmates became sick, the nurse phoned their names in to town, and people brought them flowers and baked custard. Suddenly he hated charity: the smirk on women's faces when they brought things, the smell of another boy's clothes, and Marcia Paxson. Caught in the bursting realizations of life, he became the impotent slave of his resentment. "I'll smash Harry Moomaugh in the nose!" he groaned.

Like every trouble-seeker, David got his chance. He was playing Hold-the-Fort on the school cinder pile, and he gave Harry a tremendous shove, so that the boy spread-eagled across the cinders and cut himself. "You pushed me!" Harry cried.

"What are you gonna do about it?" David demanded.

Like a doctor about to perform an operation, Harry took off his jacket and rubbed his hands. David wasn't quite sure what happened next. There was a flailing of arms, a smashing of fists, and he went down. He sucked in his breath and thought: "He can hit harder than Aunt Reba." Then he struggled to his feet and tried to land a blow on his swift adversary. But again the windmill arms mowed him down.

He would have been badly beaten had not those students who enjoy a brawl started screaming, "Fight, fight!" The provocative words reached the principal's office and he rushed onto the playground and stopped the struggle in time to save David.

It was the custom in Doylestown for the principal to administer frequent thrashings when his young charges got out of hand. This seemed an appropriate occasion, and he took the two boys into Grade Five and made them bend publicly over the waiting chair. Before he started he asked Harry, "What was this fight about?" Harry, not knowing, remained silent. When David's turn came the principal said, "You look bad enough already. What was the fight about?" If Harry could keep his mouth shut, so could David. He mustered up enough strength for a schoolboy snarl, and the principal hammered him twenty times.

When David got back to his seat, he had had enough. He sat very quietly, and when school was over he was glad to hurry home. But Harry Moomaugh stopped him. "What was the fight about, Dave?" Harry asked.

"You said things about me," David replied.

"Like what?"

"Like you told Marcia Paxson I had to wear your old clothes."

Harry looked away and bit his lip. That isn't what he had said, not at all, but he knew there was no use to argue. "Dave," he said, "on Saturday I'm giving a party. I want you to come." Proudly, David shook his head no. Then Harry cut all the ground away from his stubbornness. He said, "We're going over to the canal."

David swallowed and thought: "The canal!" In surrender

he said, "Sure," but then he added defiantly. "I'm gonna wear my old clothes!"

Harry grinned at his friend. "I don't care what you wear, Dave. If you want to, you can come naked."

When Harry's party was over, David lay in bed and thought: "I'll bet that's the best day I ever lived." It had started inauspiciously when he dressed in his very best clothes and tried to sneak out to the highway. Aunt Reba caught him.

"*Where* are you going *to*?" she demanded.

"To a party."

"*Over* to Solebury *again*?" she whined.

"To Harry Moomaugh's."

His aunt paused a moment in sullen despair at seeing her nephew slipping out of her grasp. If he went on this way he would be no use to her when he did reach fourteen. "*Where* did you get the money for the *suit*?" she whined.

There was a very tense moment. David had learned that if he started things, he must bear the consequences, and yet he felt a surge of power within himself. He said with great precision, "Daniel gave me the money. He said you had lots of money but wouldn't give me any."

"*Day*wid!" his aunt bellowed in hurt rage. She grabbed him by the arm and dragged him into her barren room. Standing high above him, she slapped him across the face. David gasped. He had been beaten too much that week. He pulled away and would have left the room, but his aunt was determined to have a final understanding. She struck the boy again and he cried, "Aunt Reba! Don't you hit me!"

"*Talk*ing back it *is*!" she stormed.

Now David was committed to a showdown. He stuck his small face up at her and taunted: "Not only that, but Daniel said you were a dried-up old witch. And you are!"

His aunt, with rage long repressed for a scene like this, struck her nephew forcefully in the face with her fist. Immediately David could feel his eye begin to swell shut. "And Daniel said why don't you marry somebody? It would do you good!"

His withered aunt could stand no more. Swiftly she clapped her hand over David's mouth and dragged him to a corner. With her body pressed close to his she bent her face forward until her breath was against his face. "*When* there was no one in the *world*," she wailed, "I took *care* of you. Eight *years* I been *here* in the *poor*hass, taking *care* of you. Your mother was no *good*. Your father was *worse*. You think I *like* it here in the *poor*hass? No! Every *penny* I got for eight *years* I saved to get us aht of *here*. *Look!*" her voice was hollow from some epic despair. Rummaging through her papers, she produced a thin book, which she thrust into David's face.

"For eight *years*, Daywid!" she pleaded, "every *penny*! For me no *dresses*. For you no *clothes*. These *other* ones like the poor*hass*, but not me. Look *here!*" she cried hoarsely. Opening the book, she showed him the figures: "Reba Stücke has paid to Crouthamel and Company $2,763.28." The effort of that scrimping overcame her in retrospect and she sat down. Her voice was agitated and eager like a young girl's.

"Pretty soon *you* get a chob, *too*. We'll *save* every penny, *Daywid*. When *you're* fourteen you don't have to go to *school* no more . . ."

"I'm going to high school," David said.

"No!" his aunt screamed. "*Chust* like your *father*. Books! What did it get *him*? Don't go to *Sole*bury no *more*! When you'll be four*teen* you'll get a nice, steady *chob* in Sellerswille pants *fact*ory . . ."

"Daniel said I should go to college," David persisted in his first great battle.

"*Col*lege is it *now?*" his aunt screamed. Beside herself with the disappointment she had feared, she threw her scrawny fury at him. But when she jumped at him, David saw a ruler on the table. He dodged his aunt and dove for the weapon.

"*Oh*, so it's the *rul*er?" his aunt screamed. She tried to forestall him, but too late. David clutched the heavy ruler and ran around the other side of the table.

"Don't come over here," he threatened.

"*Day*wid!" his aunt shouted, rushing at him.

He swung the ruler with all his might. It caught his aunt a glancing blow on the shoulder and bounced off against her head. Breathing hoarsely, she made another lunge at the boy. Once more the ruler struck her. She winced and doubled up. David, seeing that she could not hurt him now, threw the ruler onto the floor beside the book with her penurious accounts. When he opened the door, he found that all the poorhouse women had been listening.

"Run away!" Mrs. Krusen urged, wiping his blackened eye with spit.

"He *hit* me!" Aunt Reba cried. "Oh, he *hit* me!"

Mrs. Krusen blocked the door and said consolingly, "He's a bad boy, Miss Reba."

"Call the guard!" Reba demanded.

"I don't see how you stand him," Mrs. Krusen lamented, holding the beaten woman firmly by the shoulders.

The second momentous event happened at Harry Moomaugh's party. Of course, everyone teased David about his eye. Harry said, "What's the other fellow look like?" David recalled his aunt doubled up with pain and replied, "Not so good."

Marcia Paxson stood apart and studied David's eye. "It looks awful," she said. "Did thy aunt do it?"

David thought: "Like a Quaker. She asks whatever's in her mind." David knew that all the kids in Grade Five understood about the thrashings he got from his aunt, but what they didn't understand was that he was never going to take another one. Never. Suddenly he felt like sharing his secret with Marcia. "Yes," he admitted. "She did it. But she'll never do it again."

"Can I feel it?" Marcia asked. He stood very still while she probed it with her finger. "We'll put some beefsteak on it," she said.

"Why?" David asked.

"It takes away the blackness. My aunt does that for her husband. He drinks a lot."

So, with his chunk of beefsteak, David climbed into the truck and set off to see, for the first time in his life, the canal and the barges. He could sense, by the feel of the air, when they had come close to the placid Delaware. At the top of the hill in New Hope, Harry's uncle stopped the truck to have his little joke. Like most Pennsylvania villages, New Hope had a Civil War cannon, but the iron balls that actually fitted the cannon were unimpressive, so someone had donated a pyramid of immense ammunition. "Now you tell me how they got those balls into that cannon!" David listened to the foolish answers and wondered: "Why don't he drive on down the hill?"

And then, below him, stretched the canal. It was clean and grassy along the banks. People had built fine homes there, and there were more flowers than David could see with his good left eye. The canal itself was brown with rippling water, and the towpath was sandy invitation to wander among the trees that shaded it. There was a red bridge and beneath it the canal crept in silent beauty.

"Look!" Marcia cried. "The barge."

Around the bend came a canal boat, its mules plodding northward, its driver swinging a birch switch. There was a tiny house on deck, and from the doorway of that house an old man looked across the canal at David Harper. Instinctively, David waved, and the old bargeman waved back.

Now the mules dragged their burden around a corner, and the barge was lost among the trees. But back to David floated a long-drawn, mournful blast of the bargeman's horn. The mules were approaching a lock, and the keeper must be warned.

"I always love that sound," Marcia said, and the word "always" struck David with peculiar force. He thought: "You mean she comes here all the time?" Then a strange thing happened. As if Marcia had guessed David's thoughts, she said, "Yes. I come down here often. Uncle Clarence lives down here. He's the one that gets eyes like yours!"

When Harry's uncle stopped the truck beside the canal, David assumed that food would be served, but the baskets were kept covered. Although he was disappointed, David forgot his appetite, for a second barge had hove into view, and on its prow stood a young boy. Immediately David felt a complete identification with that boy. He was awestruck, therefore, when the barge reached an iron bridge. Deftly the boy leaped up and grasped one of the girders. Suspended there, he allowed the barge to pass beneath him. At the last permissible moment he dropped back onto the barge, his home.

"Whew!" David whistled.

His excitement grew more intense when the barge nosed its ugly snout into the bank. "Surprise! Surprise!" Harry's uncle cried. "We'll eat on board!"

There was a mad scramble, and David threw away his piece of raw meat. Aboard the scow, he felt that he was back home. He knew where each thing was, so often had he talked with Old Daniel. Now the baskets were unpacked, and with a gentle motion the barge tore itself loose from the bank and headed downstream.

It was Marcia who proposed that they offer the barge family some of their food. The boy ate ravenously, and for the rest of the dreamlike journey David and Marcia sat with him and talked. The questions that David wanted to ask, Marcia asked, and when the hallowed trip ended at a bridge far downstream David said, "Why don't we write to each other?" He gave the barge boy his name, but no letter ever came.

It was twilight when the barge drifted away to the next lock. Its mournful cry made David's entire body leap. For the first time in his life he wanted to imprison a moment, to see indelibly the particular quality of that barge and that boy and that beautiful day. He was pleased beyond words when Marcia came to stand beside him on the bank. Of all the people on the picnic he guessed that she was the only one who might know what he was thinking. But not even she could sense the passionate wildness of his thoughts as he recalled Old Daniel and the gypsy girl, and the barges drifting down year after year through all the old man's life, the call and echo of the horns, the creaking gates, the dank lock walls, and the far vistas of the Delaware. Half-formed, the words came to his mind: "I'll put it in a book some day."

"Thee'll never forget this, will thee?" Marcia asked.

"I saw it before," David said.

"But thee said this was the first time."

"Yes." David stammered. "But . . ." Then he found a way out. "That picture in your house."

"Oh, sure," Marcia laughed. But she wasn't fooled. Not a bit, and she looked at David in a certain knowing way to let him know she wasn't fooled. David blushed.

He blushed even more at what happened at the close of this remarkable day. At Harry Moomaugh's Denis Bigelow cried, "Let's play *Heavy Heavy*!" The girls squealed and Marcia said, "No!" but Denis insisted, so everyone gave Eleanor Morris a pencil or a piece of hair-ribbon or a button or something, and she mixed them all up together. The first thing she pulled out of the hat was the pencil David had given her.

"Heavy Heavy! What hangs over?"

"Fine or superfine?"

Eleanor grinned at David, who admitted the pencil was his. "Fine!" she announced, meaning that the pencil belonged to a boy. Then she whispered so that Denis could hear, "It's David's."

In a deep voice Denis said, "Fine will go out into the hall, and he will kiss Marcia Paxson."

Again the girls squealed and Marcia said, "I will not!"

"Coward! Coward!" the other girls squealed. So blushingly Marcia stomped from the room.

David was perplexed and asked, "What do I do?" The

children yelled with joy and the boys pushed him out into the hall. "You kiss her!" they shouted. Denis Bigelow became very excited and jumped up and down. When the door closed, he stood guard and listened.

In the hallway Marcia waited for David. Her black hair was pulled tight behind her ears. Her dark eyes were bright, and she was nervous; her hands were twisting and untwisting. "It's a silly game," she said.

"Marcia," David said in gulps. "If you don't want to . . ."

"It's only a game," she repeated.

David stepped close to her, and since she was taller than he, she bent her lips slightly toward his. He tried to kiss her, but merely brushed her lips. So he placed his hands on her shoulders and kissed her again. He discovered that kissing was cool, and that Marcia's lips were strange. He did not think too much of kissing, but when this kind, understanding girl trembled, he felt an overwhelming compassion for her. Quickly he grasped her hand and stood close to her.

"You're always the most fun," he said.

She made no effort to move either toward David or away. "What were you thinking when the barge disappeared?" she asked.

In the dark hallway David whispered, "I was remembering."

"What?"

"How it looked. How it sounded."

"Why?"

"Some day . . ."

"Hey!" Denis Bigelow shouted. "That's some kiss!" He flung open the door. Marcia and David stood in the darkness, hand in hand.

Back in the circle, David blushed for some time. He hoped and hoped that his pencil would not be drawn again. Kissing was pretty disturbing, after all. You said things you had not intended to say.

As if his cup were meant to run over, the Paxsons invited David to go on a picnic with them to Paradise Park. On the appointed day David rose at five. He was scrubbed and polished by six. His new suit had been pressed under the mattress, the way the old men had showed him.

He could not sit still long enough to eat breakfast, but later on he did stand very straight while the old men inspected him. "He looks good," Luther grunted. "Wery clean."

"Now, remember," said an old man with a hump, "whenever you take a girl out, you got to buy her somethin'. You got any money?"

David had four pennies. He dug them from his pocket for the old men to see. An angry hush fell upon the hall. Then Tom snorted, "Why, four cents . . ."

"You can't buy much with four cents," Luther grunted.

"You be still," the humped man commanded. He looked with a kind of desperation at the boy. "Sonny," he said, "if you're taking a girl on your first date . . ." Slowly, as if a portion of his blood were being drained away, he hauled a nickel from his watch pocket. "Here," he said.

Another man produced three cents he had been saving for tobacco, and a third rummaged for more pennies. Then the men stared at Luther, who was suspected of hoarding, but the Dutchman stared back and said nothing. He knew the difference that poorhouse pennies made. With a few coins one could swagger into a Doylestown store and say, "I'll take some of that!" Pennies held a man's head up.

"Now how do you buy a treat for a young lady?" the humped man reviewed.

"Like you said," David explained. "After we eat in the grove, we're walking past the rootbeer stand. I say, 'Wouldn't you folks like a rootbeer?' and Marcia says, 'Don't mind if I do,' and Mr. Paxson says, 'I'll get the tickets,' but I hold up my hand and say, 'Nope, these are on me,' and I get four tickets, and they're twenty cents, and then I hand Marcia her rootbeer like this."

"Whoa!" the humped man interrupted.

"Of course," David blushed, "Mrs. Paxson gets hers first."

Then came a voice of doom. A sour-faced newcomer said, "Rootbeer is ten cents."

The poorhouse men looked at him as if he were a Judas. "That's ridiculous!"

"It's ten cents," the killjoy insisted. "I was there last year."

"That's too much!" David protested. "What shall I do?"

"Well!" Tom proposed brightly. "You could get two bags of popcorn!"

"That's silly!" Luther snapped. "With a girl you get her somethin' for herself. You get two rootbeers, David, one for you, one for her. Let that old Quaker Paxson get his own." Suddenly the madman became furious at Mr. Paxson. "Why don't he take his hat off and sing like other people, that's what?"

"You be still!" the humped man commanded. "Two root-

beers! You want the boy to look cheap?" The word had a
horrible sound in the long hall, for these men had never been
cheap. They had not scrimped nor saved the cores of life,
but with splendid largesse they had spent themselves and their
substance; and they would die in the poorhouse while the
mean and ugly prospered. Angrily, the humped man stared at
his companions. "This boy needs twenty cents!" he said in
threatening tones.

The old misers looked away. There was a terrible pull
upon the secret places in which they hid their pennies. Hands
started reluctantly toward the petty hoards, but there was
no need of this, for Luther Detwiler, violating every principle of Dutch thrift his mother had taught him sixty years
ago, sat down on the poorhouse floor. Slowly he took off his
right shoe. His sock was worn into funny shreds that clung between his toes. Tugging at the fragments, he disclosed two
dimes that had been wedged away for seven months. Without rising, he handed them to David, but when he saw the
boy actually place the precious coins in his pocket, the old
Dutchman hobbled to his feet and clutched the boy by the
arm. "If rootbeers is only a nickel," he begged, "you'll give
me back the money, yes?"

Paradise Park was a magnificent place with rides and crazy
houses and all sorts of jovial scenes, but there was one
aspect of it for which David was totally unprepared. After
lunch Mr. Paxson led the way to the lake where a motor
launch took passengers for a short spin, and David expected
to get aboard for a ride; but the Paxsons went right past the
lake and into a pavilion, on the stage of which sat more than
fifty men in uniform. They were a band, the first that
David had seen with so many members. When the instruments tuned, David felt a shiver playing upon him and he
whispered to himself: "That sounds nice!" Then silence fell,
and suddenly the audience began to clap and cheer.

A man with white hair, in a blue uniform, walked onto
the stage. He moved stiffly, nodded stiffly, and stiffly started
to wave his baton. "That's John Philip Sousa," Marcia said,
and before her words were out, the pavilion broke into wonderful sound.

Mr. Sousa played three pieces of music, and each piece
was better and louder than the one before. But the last selection so far exceeded David's expectation of what music
could be that he never forgot that day at Paradise. Mr.

Sousa started the music by waving his baton back and forth, not doing much, but the first swelling sound was glorious. And then it got better! When David thought it had ended, it started all over again, but this time four flutes and four piccolos moved down and stood at the front edge of the stage. They played furiously, up and down, until the audience gasped with delight. Then eight saxophones joined the flutes. Finally, eight trombones and eight cornets moved forward until the stage was jammed. Mr. Sousa didn't even look at them. He just waved his baton back and forth in choppy strokes, but each player blew as if his cheeks must burst, and at the end there was so much noise and glory that David could not hear it all. It came over him like a flood. Then Mr. Sousa gave two short chops, and the music ended.

"Whew!" David cried as the audience cheered.

Mr. Sousa nodded several times, stiff little nods, and Marcia whispered, "That was *Stars and Stripes Forever.*"

"What was?" David asked.

"That music," Marcia explained.

The boy was still in a happy stupor when they passed the rootbeer stand. The Paxsons were well past it when David realized where he was. "Hey!" he shouted ahead. "How would you folks like some rootbeer?"

Mr. and Mrs. Paxson stopped and looked at each other. "I'd like . . ." Mrs. Paxson began, but Marcia cried, "That would be swell!"

"The stand's back here," David explained. He jammed his hands into his pockets. Luther's two dimes were in his left pocket. The pennies were in his right. He had a feeling that rootbeer would be five cents. He had a strong feeling that's what it would be.

He walked up to the man and said in a clear voice, "Four rootbeers."

"Where's ya tickets?" the man asked.

David plopped the pennies on the counter. "Four tickets," he said.

The quick little sodajerk laughed and said, "Ya get 'em over there."

In some embarrassment David scooped up the pennies and went to the cashier's box, looking for the dreaded sign, 10¢. When he saw no sign he reasoned: "If it was 10¢, they'd say so. Else how would people know it wasn't 5¢?" Confidently he banged his fist on the cashier's board. "Four rootbeers," he said.

" 'At's forty cents," the cashier said. "Can't you read the sign?" Far above David's head was the smallest sign he had ever seen: "Rootbeer 10¢." Grimly, from way down in his left pocket, he dragged up Luther's dimes. Deftly, the cashier swept the dimes into a pile and shoved the boy four tickets.

"Four rootbeers!" David ordered, placing his tickets before the sodajerk.

"We ain't got any rootbeer," the little man said. "We got loganberry."

David looked protestingly at Mr. Paxson and then at the man. "The sign says 'Rootbeer,' " he insisted quietly.

"Rootbeer we ain't go. Loganberry's nice."

"Why didn't you tell me before?" David pleaded. The quick little man turned away to serve another customer while David tried to fathom a place where they sold rootbeer tickets with a tiny 10¢ sign and then didn't have any rootbeer. He felt wretched and tears would have come to his eyes except that he happened to look at Mr. Paxson. The man didn't exactly wink at David. The corners of his mouth pulled up, that was all.

"I'll take four loganberries," David said firmly.

Rapidly the man served four tall glasses of deep red juice. David handed Mrs. Paxson hers, the way the men had said. Then he gave Marcia hers. She smiled and looked very pleased. Mr. Paxson reached for his own. David sighed and took his.

Then he got a real shock. The loganberry was astonishingly good! It was sour, yet sweet, and tasted of berries picked in spring. It had a tingle, too, different from anything he had tasted before. "Say," he cried, his upper lip covered with pale red foam, "that's good."

The sodajerk laughed. "You never try nothin', you never learn."

"That *is* good," Mrs. Paxson said.

Slowly, David drained his ebbing glass of loganberry. Marcia and her father put their glasses down. "That was awfully good," Marcia said. Mr. Paxson raised his glass again to drain the last drop. David watched him through the rim of his own glass. The boy had a wonderful feeling inside, and it was not from loganberry.

"How'd you like that, sonny?" the little clerk asked.

"That's some drink!" David said.

"I'll tell ya what I'm a gonna do," the man said quickly,

snatching up the four glasses. "We're innerducin' loganberry in the East. For you and the young lady, who I guess is your sweetheart, since you're buyin' her drinks, I'm gonna give you each a free drink. But the grown-ups is gotta buy their own." He winked at Mr. Paxson, and before Marcia's father could speak the little man placed four glasses of loganberry on the counter.

With all his heart, more than anything else he had ever wanted before in the world, David wanted to swagger over to the window and say, "Two more tickets." But his pockets were empty. Mr. Paxson bought the tickets.

This time David drank his loganberry more slowly. It was, if possible, better than before. Once at Christmas he had eaten dinner at a home in Doylestown and the lady had served mashed cranberries. They were fine that way, about the best thing David could remember eating. Well, cold loganberry juice was twice as good.

"Thank thee, David, for showing us something very nice," Mrs. Paxson said.

"That's lots better than rootbeer," Marcia said, squeezing the boy's hand.

It was late at night before David got back to the poorhouse. From Neshaminy on Marcia had slept, resting on David's shoulder. He thought: "It's the first time today she's missed anything." In the driveway she bade him a muffled good night, and he laughed, for he was aware that she did not know who he was.

"Thee'll have to excuse her," Mrs. Paxson said softly. "She's had a wonderful day."

On the long hall more than a dozen night-shirted figures waited for the boy. They found a candle and huddled together in Old Daniel's room, and the first thought that David had before he spoke was that it would have been good if Daniel could have been there.

"Paradise Park must be the best on earth," he exploded, and words tumbled furiously from him, striking sparks of light in old eyes. "You never heard a band like Captain Sousa's!" he confided. "Everybody up front, blowing his head off! I just . . ." And the words stopped.

Then, from down the hall, a door creaked, and mad Luther Detwiler, in a nightshirt too long for him, came suspiciously into the circle. "How was the drinks?" he asked probingly.

"It was loganberry," David replied.

"What's loganberry?" Luther asked suspiciously.

"It was expensive," David said, and Luther uttered a sharp cry.

The humped man interrupted. "But was it good?" he asked.

"Loganberry," David said judiciously, "is about the best drink there could be."

"Then what are you complainin' about?" the humped man asked. "What's money for but to spend?"

David looked at the crippled man's face in the candle-light, and although it was not a handsome face, there was beauty in it. Suddenly the boy felt the tremendous quality of life, the sweep of it, the grandeur, the twisting, contrary nature of living that made every day a thing of wonder. He sensed the passion with which old people cling to the hopes of young people and he saw for the first time the tremendous dignity of these old men huddled in their nightshirts. His heart was so full of emotion that he wanted to say something to that humped old man, to say some special word about Captain Sousa or the small boats on the lake. But he hesitated, and the chance was gone forever. Luther Detwiler had heard enough.

"The drinks?" Luther demanded. "Was they a nickel?"

"They were ten cents," David replied.

The crazy Dutchman gave a cry of wounded rage and dashed off toward his room. But as he ran an old warning of his mother's came back to him. "You wait and see!" he shouted back. "Spendin' money on girls like it was water. You keep that up and you'll end in the poorhouse!"

Door 5 slammed with a great echo and soon the men could hear mad Luther smashing his furniture. In a paroxysm of rage he stormed and cursed at David for his prodigality. Tom grabbed David and said, "If he smashes all his stuff they'll lock him up."

"Stop him!" David pleaded as the breakage increased.

"Not me!" Tom declined, remembering the gorilla-like strength of the crazy man.

The poorhouse men withdrew from Door 5, and David was left there alone. "Luther!" he called.

"Go away!" the destructive Dutchman bellowed.

"Hey, Luther," David pleaded at the door, and finally the crashing ceased. There was a long moment of silence and David called, "The loganberry juice you bought me . . ."

The door opened slowly and revealed a heart-broken crazy man. Luther held in his right hand a chair leg and for a moment it appeared as if he might strike David with it. Instead, the crazy man stared at the boy with profound reproach. "You spent my two dimes," he half sobbed. "You little pig! You little glutton! Go to bed!" He slammed the door. Then the violence resumed.

"Luther, Luther!" pleaded the little boy.

The news reached the poorhouse one Thursday afternoon. Like wildfire it swept the dismal halls and evoked passions that had seemingly long since died.

As if the news were indeed a crackling fire of despair, David could hear it pass from room to room. "Oh, my God!" a woman screamed. "I told John!"

"It ain't true!" a woman from Bensalem cried, and immediately she began wailing across the flower beds to the men's building, "Henry! Henry! You hear?"

"What's going *on*?" Aunt Reba shouted at the women. When they explained, she threw her hand to her mouth and uttered a terrible, animal scream. "He wouldn't do that!" she protested. Then she stumbled back and fell into a sitting position on the women's porch.

"Get some water!" Mrs. Krusen called.

"It ain't true!" Aunt Reba sobbed.

But it was true. Shamefully, it was true that from hidden nooks and crannies of Bucks County the respected citizen Crouthamel had stolen more than $200,000. How he had accomplished this mammoth theft, no one would know, for the financier had fled.

Reba Stücke, a warden in the poorhouse, contributed $2,763.28 intended for a home in Sellersville. An old couple in Buckingham gave $4,816.95, savings upon which they had expected to bury themselves after their long lives ended. From New Hope, from Quakertown, Erwinna, Chalfont and Doylestown the vast kitty for this indecent poker game had come. Mortgages had been collected but never paid off. Rent money had been sequestered. Rights-of-way had been purchased but never acquired. The horrible pattern of rural theft, which has scarred one American community after another, was now squeezed down upon the foolish people of Bucks County.

On Monday the dispossessed started arriving at the poorhouse. The first couple came from a farm near Lahaska. For three years they had believed the farm was theirs. Now they knew the truth. The old woman went into the ground-floor room next to Aunt Reba's. For the first time in her life Reba Stücke became interested in a woman inmate. Endlessly she sat with the woman and went step by step through the filthy processes whereby Mr. Crouthamel had bedazzled his victims.

"He always dressed so *nice*, yet!" Aunt Reba recalled.

"He give us papers, too. Signed with red wax," the woman sighed.

By the end of the week Aunt Reba had grown to like this woman from Lahaska. She even suggested to Mrs. Krusen that they get together and try to make the woman forget her misery. Mrs. Krusen said that was a good idea, and she and the warden bought some chintz to brighten up the newcomer's room.

Two other couples and an old man also reported that week. Their frugal lives, spent lately in a long battle against this very poorhouse, were now ending in the wreckage they had fought to avoid. There was a terrible, spring sadness about these old people, and for the first time David began to understand how miserable the poorhouse must seem—from the outside.

Then his mind was distracted from these sad-faced old men and women, for into the poorhouse came a strange and violent couple. The man was moved into Door 10, and David never forgot that first night. The stranger was well over six feet tall, very thin and with a large Adam's apple. When the door closed behind him, David, through the thin walls, could hear the tall man fighting with himself: "I'll kill him. I'll break out of here and twist his throat to pieces. I won't stay in a poorhouse!" The man stormed back and forth across his room, crying the great, profane oaths that free men use. At supper time David knocked on the man's door and cried, "Time for chow!" and the violent man slammed open the door and stared in frenzy at the boy. Catching him under the arms, he swung David into the air. "What are you doing here?" he roared. He peered deeply into the boy's eyes, and David saw there was no madness in this man's face, only anger of the kind David had never before known.

Violently, the man tossed David back into the hall and slammed his door shut. He would not eat, and during dinner there was much commotion on the grounds, for the guards caught the tall old fellow and his wife half-running, half-walking across the fields to escape the poorhouse.

On Tuesday the two old people ran away again. That

was when David first saw the tall man's wife. She, too, was thin. Her hair was almost white, but she seemed scarcely half so tall as her husband. David noticed her particularly, because most poorhouse wives sniffled, but this woman leaped out and hit the guard when he shoved her husband. "It ain't his fault!" she said with a forceful, low voice. "Don't you touch him!"

But the guard simply had to push the old man along, whereupon the woman flew upon the guard and slapped his face. "You shan't touch him!" she said even more quietly. "He's a good man. This ain't his fault, and we won't stay."

A big lump came into David's throat when he saw what Aunt Reba did. The mean, thin warden came out wiping her hands on her apron. She and Mrs. Krusen had been making some little cakes. "Come along," Aunt Reba said to the little woman. "He stole from me, too."

But the little woman marched along beside the guard, as if daring him to touch her husband again.

The tall man stayed alone in his room that night and swore himself to sleep. That is, David thought he had gone to sleep, but toward morning the guards found him climbing down the waterspout. This time the man was locked into a barred room, but for the rest of that night he and his wife kept shouting back and forth across the garden space between the two buildings. The man swore terrible oaths, and the woman encouraged him.

About ten o'clock the next morning Mr. Paxson, from Solebury, drove up to the poorhouse. He talked quietly with the overseer and with the man's wife. The little old woman bobbed up and down like a sparrow, trying to persuade Mr. Paxson about something. Soon the tall man was released. Mr. Paxson met him on the long hall, and the tall man stared with bitter hatred at that avenue of cells. "I need men like you," Mr. Paxson said quietly, looking right at the tall man.

When they left the building, the man's wife hurried up and grabbed her husband's hand in a strong, almost manly gesture. David, watching nearby, thought: "I've never seen men and women like that." Their minds and their bodies seemed to clash in midair, violently, as if a mighty gong should have sounded when they looked at each other. David watched them as they went to the car, and to his surprise he saw that Marcia Paxson was watching them, too.

The escaping couple looked straight ahead, grim people,

clothed in purple fury, shining in the morning air like Venus in the dawn. Other people came to the poorhouse because of Mr. Crouthamel. They wept a little, sighed for their lost hopes, and soon fitted into the routine. For a few days the women cried over their husbands, who were undone through an alien agent; or the men felt disgraced that their wives finally fell into the poorhouse. But adjust they did. They did fit in. Within two weeks David could not tell the Crouthamel inmates from the regulars. Only the violent couple had fought against their fate, and they escaped.

In fact, Mr. Crouthamel's vast theft would certainly have been forgotten had not a trivial incident thrown it boldly into the poorhouse like a ghostly shadow outlining an evil deed done at a distance. In checking Mr. Crouthamel's papers it was found that a feeble-minded Dutchman from Quakertown, one Luther Detwiler, had paid $2.50 a week for eleven years in the belief that he was buying a cigar factory, which was, in fact, owned by a rich German in Reading. The enormity of this deception so preyed upon the public conscience that a Philadelphia newspaperman wrote the obscene story and flashed it across the country.

The next afternoon a photographer from Trenton came to see the crazy Dutchman and took his picture. Luther was pleased with the attention and explained where his factory was. He was careful to say that he happened to be in the poorhouse right now only because his wife was visiting in Delaware.

But that night after dinner the Dutchman began to brood about this factory which somehow or other he didn't have, and the wife who was gone, and a feral melancholy possessed him. Somberly he rose and looked at the old men about him. He tried twice to explain to these men about his factory. Then he bowed his head and walked quietly to Door 5.

"He's got a right to be sad," a newcomer said. "What they did to him!"

"He ain't sad," an old-timer said. "He's nuts."

With no warning a chair crashed against Door 5. Toothless Tom blanched and said, "Somebody better get the guards." As he spoke a teacup smashed through Luther's window and clattered, with broken glass, to the areaway below.

Toothless Tom and David went down to Door 5. "You get away from here!" Luther screamed at Tom. Then, with an icy grip, he hauled David into the room and banged the door shut.

David saw that the room was a shambles. In the corner lay the broken chair. Glass was scattered about, and the bedclothes had been ripped into ragged strips.

The crazy Dutchman clasped David to him and moaned, "Oh, David! I did have that factory. I made lots of cigars. Good cigars!" His tortured brain collapsed and he bellowed, "I MADE CIGARS!" His hands twisted madly in the cigar-maker's pattern. With a jagged chunk of wood from the chair he sliced away imaginary ends of Havana wrapper. His eyes were wild with fury, old confusion, old anguish.

He now roared about his factory senselessly, standing between David and the door. The boy stood very still. He had seen many mad people in the poorhouse, over on crazy row. He knew what he must do. He smiled at Luther, who became calm.

"David!" the man began to weep. "I don't know. I done everything right. They only had to tell me once. 'Don't use spit,' the man said. 'Use water from that pitcher.'" He looked about the broken room wildly for the missing pitcher.

In an excess of violence he thrust David away from him. "You got my pitcher! Paul! Where you hide my pitcher?" David stood very still. In a wild rage the crazy Dutchman heaved his chunk of broken wood through the broken window. Then he leaped at David, shouting, "I'll kill you, Paul!"

But David managed to evade the frenzied dive, and Luther sprawled into the broken glass. With a cry of pain he brushed away the slivers of glass that tore at his hands and leaped once more at the boy. This time he caught David by the belt. With a tremendous jerk he ripped the boy backwards and lifted him high in the air. For a long moment he stood with the boy, ready to throw him through the broken window. And then some glimmer of light found its way into his addled mind. The Dutchman grinned at David and tossed the trembling boy onto the bed.

The door burst open and two guards leaped at the crazy man. Feeling their hands upon his body, Luther made a last violent gesture and threw the men against the wall. Then he leaped for the open door, but one of the guards tripped him, and he fell forward, so that his face smashed sickeningly into the sharp corner of the door jamb. Mad Luther, his face smashed in, his hands stabbed with glass, and his knees bleeding, fell backwards into the room.

The scene had been so macabre that for a moment the old men forgot David, and while the guards hauled Luther over to crazy row, the boy slipped into his own room to wash away the flecks of blood that Luther's frenzied hands had left. Suddenly Toothless Tom cried, "Where's the boy?"

From the door of his own room David answered, "I'm all right."

"Did he hurt you?" the excited men demanded, and David, remembering that single flash of recognition on the madman's face, replied, "He wouldn't hurt anybody."

Lights went out, and the old men, nervous from having seen something of themselves in mad Luther, went silently to their lonely rooms. After a time Toothless rapped on Door 8. "Come in!" David whispered eagerly, for he too was lonely, but from a different cause.

"I don't think Luther would hurt you," Tom reasoned.

"I don't think so, either," David agreed. He knew that what had happened between him and Luther had been a kind of game, a passionate, wild affair in which one of the players was mad, but not so mad as to forget who the sandy-haired boy was.

But it was more than a game, and David asked, "Did lots of these people come to the poorhouse because of things other people did to them?"

"I wouldn't say so," the toothless old man replied. "Luther did, but he ain't bright enough to run loose, anyway. I don't know about Old Daniel. Some men just ain't intended to make a livin'. As for me?" Tom paused. "I tell you what, David. You seen that long skinny man come in here a while ago? Iron bars couldn't keep him in. Nor his wife, neither. If I been like him, I'd sure be outta here by now. Don't that stand to reason?" He paused again, for a very long time, and in the darkness David could almost hear him thinking. Finally he said, "You mark my words. For the next fifteen years ain't nobody comin' on this hall but what he claims Mr. Crouthamel done it to him. Whadda you think? You think one man done it all?"

For a moment Toothless Tom's argument convinced the boy, but then on the crazy row Luther Detwiler recovered consciousness. He moved his aching body on the smelly bed. His mind wandered in past days, and he tried vainly to figure where he was and why. All he could remember was that he had been a faithful workman and a frugal man, so he surrendered to mad confusion with a piercing cry that echoed through the poorhouse and filled David's room: "I MADE CIGARS."

In Bucks County spring ended on the day when the girls went swimming. Not dipping a toe in, either, but the warm fine day when with giggles and delight they plunged to the sandy bottom of the pool.

In David's eleventh year summer began in late May. A series of warm days heated the earth, and on Friday morning David asked the poorhouse driver to wait a minute at the bridge. The boy got out, felt the water, swished his arm among the reeds, and grinned. At school he reported, "Felt good today!"

The little girls asked, "Warm . . . enough, that is?" He nodded.

So on Saturday a crowd gathered at the swimming hole behind the hill. The little girls, laughing merrily, ducked into a wooded cave, where traditionally they changed into their suits. David was swinging high on a limb above the water when they arrived, and he thought their giggling especially silly on that fine day.

"How's the water?" Harry shouted up to him.

"It's peachy!" David replied.

"How would you know?" Harry teased.

"Look! My suit's already wet. I went in from up here a while ago!"

"Do it now!" Harry challenged. David swung back and forth, but suddenly he became frightened and began to laugh nervously.

"I'll wait," he said sheepishly. Some older boys along the bank began to tease him when suddenly their attention was diverted from the sandy-haired boy in the tree. From the girls' cave had come a big, well-rounded girl named Betty.

"Hello!" she cried in a bright, edgy voice. The boys began to cluster about her. "Watch out! Them wet suits!" she squealed. This encouraged the boys, and they grabbed at her, eagerly. She struggled happily with them for a while and then screamed murderously as they mauled her into the chilly water. "My God A'mighty!" she squealed. "You're killin' me!" From the bank a boy dashed madly into the air and plunged right beside the struggling group. A spray of cold water deluged the big girl. "Watch out, will ya?" she demanded. Two of the boys began to brush the water off her suit, especially around her chest. She protested mildly, and then uttered a playful scream as another boy grabbed her by the legs and pulled her under the water.

But as she submerged David heard another scream, and this one came not in play. It was a girl's voice, and she was screaming in the cave. Instantly, David plunged from his high perch, but he was beaten to shore by the strong swimmers who had been grabbing at the girl's legs. David had to wait till they scrambled out, and then he followed them breathlessly to the cave. Four little girls from Grade Five, two almost undressed, were pointing to the woods.

"A man!" they cried, and they were trembling.

"Just somebody tryin' to get a peek," a know-it-all boy said.

"No!" a little girl screamed. "He took his pants down."

Silently, the big boys looked at the girl. She clutched a petticoat over her body and nodded. "Yes, he did," she said. In disgust her three companions agreed.

The boys dashed into the woods. One of them—who had himself many times hidden near the caves—cried knowingly, "He'd go this way!" The mob followed him, and soon David heard great shouts.

"Knock him down!"

"Grab his legs!"

"Club his brains out."

There was a sullen crashing in the woods, and David hurried up just as two stones struck the intruder in the head. He fell to the earth, and two boys jumped on him. His pants were not yet buttoned. "That's him!" a little girl cried, hurrying up to stare. Four boys slugged at the fallen man. Finally the leader made them stop and roll the trespasser over on his back. It was Toothless Tom.

David felt sick. A little girl from Grade Five took his hand and whispered, "That's the man, Dave." But the words came to the boy from far away, filled with strange and horrible loathing.

"Get the cops!" an older boy directed. "You!" he said, pointing to David. "Go out and stop a car."

Mechanically David started to do so, but he took only three steps. Then he stopped. "Whatsa matter?" the leader asked, standing with a heavy club over Tom's head.

"Why don't we let him go?" David asked. A shout of derision howled him down.

"We oughta beat his brains out. Now you scram!" The leader left Tom and shoved David along the path, but the boy would not move. He stuck his jaw out, not much, but some.

"Let's let him go," David said quietly. "We already done enough to him." He pointed at old Tom's face where a stone had hit below he eye.

"He took his pants down, didn't he?" the leader demanded, pushing David again.

"We hurt him enough," David repeated.

He might have won his argument but the big girl now bustled up and stared with disgust at the fallen intruder. "You filthy bum!" she shouted, spitting at him. "Guys like you oughta be shot!"

"Yeah!" the boys agreed, and they began to kick the old man.

"Stop it!" David insisted. His voice rose to a high squeak. The older boys laughed.

"You oughta beat him up some more!" the big girl said, kicking at Tom's chest.

David leaped at her. "You stay out of this!" he cried. "This is for boys!" The big girl laughed at him and pushed him backwards.

Then she snapped her fingers and cried, "I know you, you little runt. You're the poorhouse kid! And this old sonofabitch is a poorhouse crum, ain't he?" The words inflamed the boys and they began to thump Tom again.

"Is he a poorhouse crum?" the leader demanded.

"No!" David said. There was a moment's pause, but the big girl was beside herself with excitement.

"They oughta operate on a guy like him!" she snarled, kicking at Tom again. The boys would have joined in but David, with tears welling into his eyes, said, "He's an old man." In spite of his determination not to cry, tears bubbled onto his red cheeks. He kept his face turned up to the bigger boys, and the unwelcome tears stood like little pools beside his nose. "He's an old man," the boy insisted.

There was a moment of long thought. Then Harry Moomaugh, who was bigger than David and therefore more to be respected, said, "Let's let him go."

So the bigger boys pulled Toothless Tom to his feet. The old man's knees actually refused to lock. Pathetically, he slumped forward into the arms of his attackers. Blood from his bruised face stained the naked shoulder of the leader, who

snapped back in unhidden horror. David took the scared
boy's place and held Tom up.

"If you ever come back here," the big girl cried, "we'll
kill you."

Stumbling and staggering into trees, Toothless Tom left
the swimming hole. The little girls finished dressing and
came down to swim. The leader of the boys washed blood
from his shoulder, and for a while it seemed as if the
swimming hole had returned to normal; but David noticed
one big difference. Now the big girl was left alone. Boys did
not run their hands beneath her swimming suit to squeeze
her legs.

As David dressed, on this first day of summer, Harry
Moomaugh whispered to him, "He was a poorhouse crum,
wasn't he?"

"No!" David insisted.

"But I saw him down there!" Harry recalled.

"I never saw him before," David said.

And that evening, walking home across the hills, David
tried to comprehend what he had seen. That Toothless Tom
had done something very wrong was obvious. But why did
the big girl want Tom killed? Why did the boys beat him
so hard? And why did the little girls shiver and scream in
the cave? And the big girl, too! One minute all the boys
were eager to grab at her and wrestle with her. The next,
and she was left alone as if they were ashamed.

David paused and in the sweet evening of soft sounds
tried to remember what Old Daniel had told him about
men and women, that dark night behind Door 8. Apparently Daniel hadn't told him everything, but there was one
incident of that night which David now recalled. It had
happened when Daniel had started to speak. Toothless had
tried to scuttle from the room. "I never been married!" he
had pleaded, and while Daniel had talked, it had been Tom,
tall and almost seventy, who had blushed and fidgeted. "I
guess it's because he didn't get married," David reasoned.
But immediately he saw that he had come to a conclusion
which explained nothing. "Maybe," he argued stubbornly,
"it was because of things like today that he didn't get married." The boy was torn with confusion, and he wondered
much about men and women.

But on one point there was no confusion. When he reached
the poorhouse he would walk right into his room and toss
his swimming suit in a corner. Then, as if nothing had happened, he would yell for Tom. When he found the man he

would look right at him, like the Quakers, and ask, "What happened to your face?" And that night—he knew—Tom would be ashamed to tap on Door 8, so he, David, would tap on Tom's door.

With this idea in mind, David slipped into the pantry and begged for two pieces of cheese and some bread. Stuffing the repast into his pocket, he climbed the steps to the long hall. "You can't run away from a friend," David muttered. "Not even if he gets into trouble with little girls."

David did not comprehend the heartbreak and tragedy of a country poorhouse because he had taken his residence upon an island. When he retreated doggedly to that fortress, nothing could touch him, not death nor humiliation nor the visible decay of defeated old men. He was king of his island, its sole inhabitant, the watcher of its hills and the guardian of its sunsets. The moat of his island was the protecting wonder of his vagabond mind that saw tragedy as an invitation to experience. The castle was David's unfailing belief in himself; and the ultimate sanctuary of the castle was the boy's quiet love for other people. He lived in a kind of dream world where Hector always won.

It took a shocking experience to blow aside, even for a brief moment, the veil of unseeing from his boyish eyes; and it was this episode that forced him to perceive a vision that was in later years to save him from the folly of his dreaming.

On a hot day in early summer mad Luther Detwiler began to scream for David, and before supper Aunt Reba sought out the boy and commanded him to stay away from the Dutchman. Aunt Reba now had another account book, and she was already well started in accumulating a small fund for a house in Sellersville; and with the slow growth of this money the bitter woman's hatred of David and the women in her building returned. Naked, she had sought affection; clothed in a few pennies, she could afford to hate once more.

But David ignored her command and went to see mad Luther. He had often been on crazy row and had grown to like some of the fey creatures there: the woman who saw sheep crowding her room, the man who believed himself to be a preacher, the daft man who nodded his head back and forth some thousands of times a day, the mumblers, the slobberers, and those who could not go to the toilet by themselves. Some of them recognized the bright-faced little boy and stopped their nothingness to smile at him.

At Luther's room the guards were washing the crazy Dutchman and asked David to wait in the hall. Idling there, he stared through the bars at an old mad woman. She sat still and intent. Suddenly her right arm shot out quicker than David's eye could follow. She had caught a fly. Methodically she ripped off its wings and placed the flightless creature upon her barren table. Then, with a finger of spit, she drew a wide circle about the dismembered fly. Composed, calm, like an Aztec god, she watched the fly as it stumbled about the table top. As long as the fly stayed within its circle, which was ample, the mad woman followed it patiently, with her great eyes rolling this way or that. But when the fly once touched the forbidden line, the old woman's face clouded like an angry Jehovah. Then she raised her right hand, and with a brutal spatulate finger, crushed the fly.

Then, like a spider, she waited until another fly came into her ken. Flashingly she would snatch it from the air. Wingless, the fly would wander across the surface of his restricted world. It was free until it transgressed the line. Then the horrible forefinger ended all feeble wanderings.

When the old woman had five flies piled one upon the other, she ate them.

Sweating with fright, David stared transfixed through the madhouse bars. For the first time in his life he knew terror, the stark wild terror that invades every room in every house in every town.

"All right, sonny!" the guard said. When he saw how David trembled, he added, "Now you don't need to be afraid. Luther won't hurt nobody."

David shook himself and tried to halt his shivering. Mechanically he moved toward Luther's cell. He blinked his eyes to bring himself back to a world he understood.

The crazy Dutchman embraced him. "Oh, David," he sobbed, shedding lucid tears, "you don't need to be afraid of me. You know I wouldn't hurt you."

The frightened boy placed his small hand in Luther's hairy fist. "I know," he mumbled. Then he saw, impersonally as if from another world, that his friend's face was bandaged, his right hand badly bruised, and the sleeve upon the right elbow torn as if from some epic struggle.

All of this happened one spring in the poorhouse near Doylestown. David saw these things, and much more, but he did not understand what he saw. That was to come later.

# PART 2

# Paradise

WHEN DAVID HARPER was fourteen years old his Aunt Reba Stücke got one of the major surprises of her life. She discovered that the laws of Pennsylvania prevented her from taking David out of school and putting him to work at the pants factory in Sellersville.

All of Reba Stücke's friends had gone to work when they were fourteen, or much sooner. To her frugal German mind it was indecent for her nephew—who was now a big boy—to delay getting about the deadly serious business of earning a living, both for himself and for her. In Reba's orderly world aunts raised nephews until they were old enough to work, and then the nephews "took care of the old ones." She could not believe that child-labor laws applied to "sensible people like me and the Schultzes."

She was somewhat mollified, however, when she discovered that with permission from parents and school a boy of fourteen could work summers. She readily gave her permission and prevailed upon the Doylestown authorities to do the same. David would be sent to Sellersville to learn the rudiments of the pants industry. Then, when he was sixteen, he could start work in earnest "and no more of this education nonsense."

With the sure insight of a little animal smelling out a

baited trap, David sensed that once he put his foot in the Sellersville factory he would never again be free. His aunt would find every reason for him to go on making pants. And where then would be Old Daniel's vision of learning and travel?

So, with an intuition based upon a flashing memory of rumor heard years before at the swimming hole ("Joe got a good job just by askin' Judge Harmon"), David went in to Doylestown and sought out the old judge. It was June. Summer was upon the town as David walked out Court Street past the school whose very stones seemed warm and friendly to him. Hot summer lay over Bucks County, and the sweet smell of warm earth was everywhere. A milkman's horse had urinated in the gutter, and the keen, penetrating odor tingled in the air a moment and was swept aside. In the junkman's yard, cherry and peach blossoms had long since faded. Tiny fruit, green but with the promise of rare delights, expanded in the sun. It was summer. School was out, and David was applying for his first job.

Judge Harmon sat on the porch watching the mutes at the deaf home clean their lawn. His vast stomach slumped between his knees as he wheezily told David to sit down. "What d'y' want, son?" he asked, mopping his forehead. "Hot today."

"I want to get a job," David said.

"Y're Reba Stücke's boy? Yes, I heard about you. George Paxson said you were a good boy. They tell me you're a good worker." The fat judge shifted his stomach and turned to look at the boy. David beamed at him, acknowledging that so far as he knew he was a fine worker.

"I've been pretty good at school," he said.

"What kind of job d'y' want, son?" the judge asked.

"I don't know, sir," David replied. "I heard some fellows say that you got Joe Axenfield a job."

"Joe Axenfield!" the judge said. He scowled and shifted his mammoth body around toward his visitor. "Y're a young lad," the judge said, "Are y' strong?"

"Oh, yes!" David said eagerly. "I play basketball. Against the first team, even."

"I mean have y' courage?"

"I don't know," David said earnestly. "I been in some fights, but I never do too well. I don't run away, though." His frank brown eyes looked directly at the perspiring judge.

"Y' don't know what I mean, boy," the judge said, wheezing heavily. He leaned far over his stomach and pointed a finger at David's chin. "Are y' honest? Can y' stand temptation? Y're not a weaklin', are y'?"

"I never been in trouble, Judge Harmon," David replied. "I think I'm all right."

"Well, son. The only job I got for y' needs a strong man. Not a weak boy." The judge leaned still farther toward his guest. "The boys were right, son. I got Joe Axenfield a job. And a year later Joe got eight months in jail. Now are you another Joe or are y' a clean, strong young man? Because if y' get this job, y'aren't a boy any longer. Y're a man."

David heard these rich words with a strong feeling of adventure about his heart. He knew then what he was: a young man, strong and honest. He told the judge so.

"All right, son. Y' asked for it. There's a job waitin' for y' down at Paradise Park. Bella! Bring me some paper." The German maid appeared with the judge's portfolio. He breathed heavily as he wrote a few lines. He folded the letter and was about to place it in an envelope. Changing his mind, he opened the letter again and thrust it at David.

> "Dear Lewis:
>     I am sending you a fine young man of whom I have had excellent reports. Give him some kind of work. He is an honest and deserving youth.
>                         Matthew Harmon"

Solemnly the judge placed his recommendation in the envelope. "Son," he said. "Don't y' ever dare to make me regret those words. This is y'r first job. Remember this. What y' do on this job will haunt y' as long as y' live. Y're a man now." The judge extended his wet hand and puffed noisily as David grasped both it and the letter.

"Thank you, Judge!" he said in great excitement.

"I hope y'll want to thank me ten years from now," the judge said. At the deaf home across the beautiful street two mutes were arguing about a lawnmower. In fury, one pushed the other. They struggled for a moment, and in the hot summer air David and the judge could hear the weird, ghostlike mouthings of the mutes. David looked at the judge and shivered. The fat judge swallowed hard. In eighteen years of listening to that strange penetrating sound of mutes quarreling he had never grown accustomed to it. He wiped his face and signified by his scowl that David was to be gone.

David hitch-hiked to his first job. A big Packard pulled up and a man with a cigar invited him to jump in. "Where y' off to, son?" the man asked with real interest.

"I'm getting a job," David replied as nonchalantly as he could.

The man tilted his cigar into an imperative angle and studied his passenger. "Well! What's a little twerp like you good for?" When David grinned, the business man asked seriously, "Do ya smoke?"

"No."

"Do ya gamble? Spend a lot of money? Get drunk?"

"No," David reported proudly.

"How about women? Do ya chase after every skirt ya see?"

"Oh, no!"

"Well!" the man shouted, banging the steering wheel and roaring with laughter. "Ya may be goin' to a job, but ya could never work for me!"

"Why not?" David asked somewhat crestfallen.

"I'll tell ya why! I run a real tough business. Competition! Terrific! I got to have men who are in trouble, men with two or three women their wife don't know about. Heavy drinkers, gamblers. Especially men who play the horses. Because a man in trouble has damned well gotta work."

"How can you trust men like that?" David asked.

"Ya can't!" The big fellow chuckled. "But ya' watch 'em like hawks so they don't steal ya blind, and ya just work 'em till they collapse. Because when they make money, you make money!" He looked suspiciously at David and concluded, "So maybe what the Sunday-school teachers has been tellin' ya is a lotta bunk! Be a bum and be rich! That's the new rule!"

When the Packard stopped at Paradise the talkative business man grabbed David's arm. "Son," he whispered, "I just give you ten thousand dollars' worth of advice. Now I'm gonna give ya some more. Likewise free. Son, you're goin' in to ask for your first job. Here's a buck. Get yourself a haircut. A shoe shine. Smile. Look neat. Make folks think you're prosperous. When ya smoke, smoke cigars. Because everybody loves the poor but honest farm boy. But nobody hires him. And right now, son, you look like a farm boy." The big car whirred away, and before the dust had settled, David was in search of a barber shop.

"You like me to fix your hair up real nice?" the barber asked.

"Yes," David replied. When the job was done—shine, facial, singe, shampoo—the barber said. "That'll be a dollar and ten cents."

"Whew!" David whistled.

"You got that much, ain't you?" the barber asked suspiciously.

"I got it."

The barber breathed more easily and said, "And I may say that you got in return just about the finest all-in-one special we ever turned out. Look at him, Oscar!"

In an aura of sweet smells and high hopes David entered Paradise Park and sought out the manager. He remained in a kind of twitching daze until he heard the wonderful words, "Well, Mr. Harper! You're hired!"

A guide was dispatched to take him to his job. No sooner had they left the office building than the guide whispered, "Boy, are you lucky!"

"I know," David replied, for he knew how lucky he was to have a man's job at fourteen.

"What I mean is," the sharp-eyed guide explained, "you're gettin' the one job where you can steal as much as you want."

"Steal?" David repeated.

"Ssssh!" the wiry guide cautioned. "See that big skinny bastard? He's a stoolpigeon. Watch out for that one!"

"What do you mean, steal?" David pursued.

"Here we are!" the guide announced, leading his charge into a grove of pleasant trees. "You're a lucky dog!"

A ruggedly built man in overalls stepped out from a little building that looked like a railway station and reached for David's hand. "Glad to see ya, kid. You ever run one of these things?"

The *thing* was a miniature train for children, the Pennsylvania and Reading Rail Road. It consisted of an electric locomotive, a coal car, six gondola passenger cars, and a caboose. There was much gilt, a powerful headlight and a whistle. "It runs by electricity," the man in overalls explained. "It's a lot of fun. You oughta pay for this job. Now this handle works exactly like a motorman's control on a trolley. Four speeds ahead. Two back. No brakes, so you got to judge things carefully. Because every time you jump the track we fine you one buck. Let's take a spin."

By this time nine passengers were seated in the train, and the locomotive started slowly on its beautiful trail through the grove of tall trees. It passed among shadows and out into the brilliant light along the lake. Then it darted among the thrilling jungle of props and spars which held up the Hurricane. High aloft a carload of screaming girls sped over the violent dips of the great ride. The railroad left the tortuous trestles and crept back among the delicate shadows, around a bend, up a tiny hill and home to the station. The passengers left and others climbed aboard.

"Now you take her around!" the man said.

"Not yet!" David protested.

"Well, you're goin' to!" the man said. "Wait'll I get the fares." He grabbed an alligator bag and cried, "All fares on the Pennsylvania and Reading Rail Road. Everybody pay up, or out you go. There's no foolin' on this line." He treated the grown-ups like children and the children like grown-ups. Then he shouted "All aboard!" raising his voice on the *board* the way real conductors did. "Take 'er out!" he commanded imperiously.

David pulled the whistle cord and his train went "Whoo! Whoooooooo!" He threw the pointer into the first notch. Thrillingly, the wheels whirred. Then they caught, and the P and R was off on its first trip under new management.

"Now this bend is a bad one," the man warned. "Some day we'll rebuild this. You need speed for the next hill, so just about here . . . Let her have it!" David wrenched the pointer hard right, and his train whizzed around the bend and in among the trestles of the Hurricane. Above him a tandem of cars roared past. The Hurricane passengers screamed, and in the railroad the children squealed with vicarious pleasure. The man said, "That's good timing. Always try to have the train under here when the Hurricane goes by. Kids love it."

Exhilarated and confident, David led his train back toward the wooden station. At his ear the engineer gave instructions: "Lots of speed here . . . watch . . . now . . . toss her hard into reverse!" The engine groaned and came to a protesting halt. "That's it!" the man said approvingly.

On the next trip he showed David how to jump the track. After the locomotive had ripped up the grass he called, "Everybody out! But keep away from the third rail!" An old man picking up paper came over to help.

"Worst wreck in forty years!" he said in a high voice to the children. Some onlookers helped and the locomotive was shoved back into place. "Everybody push 'er up the hill!" the old man cackled, and as people strained, the wheels slowly took hold. "All a*board!*" the engineer shouted, and children scrambled into their seats. "That's all there is to that," the man said.

"Doesn't anybody ever get hurt?" David asked.

"Nah!" the man said deprecatingly. "Up there!" he said, pointing to the cars roaring past on the Hurricane. "That's where they get hurt. Forever!"

"You mean those cars jump the track, too?" David asked in awe.

"You bet they do!" the engineer replied. "You'll see one of 'em rip over the edge some day. People fly through the air like crazy birds. See that lilac tree? All its branches torn off. A full train landed there last year."

"What happened to the people?" David asked dully.

"What the hell do you suppose happened to them?" the man countered. "One thing you can be sure. They ain't smellin' lilacs. They got a snootful of lilacs that day." He laughed at his grisly joke.

"It wasn't in the papers," David observed.

"It's never in the papers," the man said reassuringly. "That would be bad for business." David looked up at the towering structure while the man droned on, "It's really pretty safe. Two men walk over every inch of it every day. Then somebody takes an empty car around just as fast as he can. Sometimes he goes too fast, and he gets killed. The last guy went too fast. Now I have the job." David gaped at his instructor with astonishment.

"You took the empty car around today?" he asked.

"Every day."

"What are you doing on this little ride?" David inquired.

"Fillin' in," the man explained. "The boy that had this job got arrested yesterday. Stole too much money."

"Stole?" David repeated.

The engineer nudged David's hand to indicate that more speed was necessary for the last hill. "It's like this," he explained. "When you sell a ticket, you get a dime. Each ticket is numbered, so in the morning the Company takes down the number on your first ticket. At night all they have to do is subtract the number on your last ticket, multiply by ten cents, and that's how much you owe."

"How could a fellow steal against such a system?" David asked.

"He can't, usually," the engineer agreed. "Because on all other rides one guy sells and another collects. But here we don't do enough business to hire two men. You sell and you also collect, so what's to prevent you from sellin' the same cardboards over and over? Huh?"

David's attention was diverted by a peculiar circumstance, and he began, "That woman . . ." but the engineer gripped his wrist in an icy grasp. When the woman had seated herself in the train, David whispered, "She gave you a two-dollar bill!" Again the engineer squeezed David's wrist and dragged him along to the locomotive. They made the trip in silence, and when the woman led her children away, the man took a big, deep breath and handed David fifty cents.

"That's yours," he said.

David left the coin in his open hand. "Are you going to keep that dollar?" he asked.

"Sure!" the engineer explained, folding David's fingers over the money. "That's the rule. You mustn't steal from the Company. But if somebody leaves her change, that's yours. When you've been here a while, you'll learn how to get rich on other people's mistakes."

"What do you mean?" David asked.

"You'll find out!" the engineer replied with a big wink. "This is my last trip." He hurried down the long line of passengers and sold each one a ticket, but David noticed that he was reselling old ones and pocketing the money. The boy said nothing about this, but when the Pennsylvania and Reading was under the trestles the man whispered, "About them tickets. The Company expects you to steal a little dough each day. Hell, they pay you only $2.14 for a fifteen-hour day. Hardly covers carfare and meals. So if you steal a couple of bucks daily, nobody'll howl. But don't try to steal more'n that, or I'll catch you sure."

"You?" David gasped.

"Sure," the man said, wiping his nose. "I'm your boss. I run this railroad."

Paradise Park paid its cashiers $2.14 a day. Grown men with fine winter jobs gave up those jobs to work at the Park. Men with families and automobiles drove thirty miles to work for $15 a week. In his first ten days David found out why.

At nine o'clock one night a woman with three children—two of her own and one of her sister's in Manyunk—came to the train, obviously harried by the sticky, noisy children. David gave her four tickets and stuffed the bill she handed him into his alligator bag. Not until this woman was well on her way home to Torresdale did he discover that she had given him a five-dollar bill.

Two nights later a party of adult drunks boarded the train for a noisy spree. Two different men paid for the tickets and one gave David a two-dollar bill, which was forgotten in the clamor. David made eight extra dollars that week. Then, slowly, he began practicing ways to make people forget their money. He did not admit to himself that this was dishonest, for he was not stealing from the Company, and then one day he cashiered for Max Volo, and that night he had to admit to himself that he was becoming a crook.

The rheostat on the locomotive broke, and David was ordered to sell tickets at the loganberry stand. He remembered the cool drinks he had bought Marcia Paxson and her parents, and he approached the stand with pleasant memories, but he was even more pleased when he saw behind the counter the same excited, flash-smiled little man. "My name's Dave Harper!" the boy reported. "I remember you from when I was just a kid. First forty cents I ever spent at one time. I was standing right here, and you made my girl's father buy two extra drinks!"

"I know! I know!" the quick little man said, wiping the metal bar with great speed. "We were innerducin' the stuff. You'll like it here."

"Hey! You!" a guard yelled. "Don't you know cashiers is not supposed to talk to ticket-takers! Get in your box." An elderly man appeared and showed David his badge. "No selling tickets over on my beat. You get in that box and stay there."

David climbed into his narrow booth and grinned back at Max Volo. The little manager of the loganberry stand was about five-feet-three. He even wore his white apron with a flair, and his black hair was always combed. He had big teeth, which he showed liberally when he smiled. His quick eyes seemed to miss nothing, and he moved his head jerkily as if vainly trying to keep up with his inquisitive stares. Less than twenty minutes after the guard had warned David, Max started swearing at his pimply-faced clean-up boy: "I told you a dozen times to clean out that box!" He dragged his helper over to David's booth and tore open the door. "Look at that dirt!" he cried, belting the boy across the head. Then, quick as a viper on hot sand, he thrust a wad of old tickets into David's hand and slammed the door. "We'll get this cleaned up," he said.

Under the change board David fumbled with the second-hand tickets but would not take them from their tight rubber bands. At the end of an hour Max Volo, standing behind the loganberry dispenser, glared at David. In a flash that no one else could have seen he held up an untorn ticket, whisked it under the counter and indicated by cutting his left forefinger in half with his right that he and David would split all stolen money fifty-fifty.

As the day wore on, David tried slipping one or two of the old tickets into his left hand and palming them so they looked as if he were tearing them off the regular roll. He had disposed of perhaps a hundred in this manner when a thin man approached the booth. David watched him coming, but out of the corner of his eye he also saw Max Volo suddenly freeze into an attitude which fairly telegraphed terror. David had only a few seconds in which to interpret this unsent signal, but he guessed that the approaching man was one of the Company spotters, the stoolpigeons that spied on everyone in a vain effort to prevent theft. With exaggerated gestures of honesty, David clearly tore off a fresh, new ticket and handed it to the spotter. Almost imperceptibly the stoolpigeon studied the ticket and its number. Then he handed it to Max Volo who ostentatiously tore it cleanly in half and tossed it into the chopper.

For a long time David was afraid to pass any old tickets, but as night fell and crowds continued to buy drinks, he disposed of his last seventy-five. When he added up his accounts, he had $29.80 too much. He stuffed the money into his shoe and walked slowly down to the cashier's office, where he delivered his unused tickets and the Company's money.

A middle-aged man in a black alpaca coat sat at a table with four armed guards. Each cashier walked up, dropped his alligator bag on the table and stood at attention. The head cashier droned: "Tickets morning, 31857. Tickets night 35085. Tickets sold, 3228. Receipts, $322.80. Plus morning change, $50.00. Money deposited, $372.80." The man in alpaca checked the numbers and tossed the money to a guard to count. If there was any money extra, the Company kept it. If there was a shortage, it was deducted from the weekly pay of $15.00.

From the cashiers' office to the trolley that would take

David home to the poorhouse was a distance of about a mile, and it was along this dark pathway that thieving ticket men lay in wait for their cashiers and their share of the day's stolen profits. As David walked the lonely mile, watching the stars, he wondered at what point Max Volo would appear to demand his cut, for the money was bulky in his shoe. Suddenly a dark form melted from a tree trunk, grabbed David by the wrist, and hauled him back into the bushes.

"You were swell, kid!" Max chortled. "I figure you owe me $13.20. And I was real proud of you when you got my signal about the stoolpigeon. I'd like to knife that creep."

"This is too risky for me," David admitted.

"Easy goes!" Max whispered, pressing his quick, hard hand over David's lips. "You and me could tear this Park wide open. You're smart! You're my type. But look, I have to pay a rake-off to my helper, who knows all about this. So I think you oughta give me an extra, say, four bucks." His voice was cold, demanding. David gave him two two-dollar bills. Max lit a match to check the bills and handed them back in horror. "Me take a two! Christ, kid, don't jinx me!" He wouldn't touch the unlucky bills, and when David handed him a five he said, "Why don't we make it five even, hmm?" Then he grabbed David by the elbow and whispered, "Now for fifty dollars I can get you transferred to the loganberry stand permanent. We could steal the brass rails, you and me!"

"Not me," David said with complete finality.

"Think it over," Max said and magically disappeared among the shadows. David looked carefully about him and stepped unobtrusively back into the road.

But he was not undetected. A slim figure in a straw hat and neat gray suit stepped quietly beside him and grabbed him by the arm. David's heart actually stopped for a moment. This was the arrest! Then he saw that his captor was Mr. Stone, the silent, efficient man who cashiered at the greatest amusement of all, the Hurricane. He always wore gray suits and straw hats, and he stayed far away from the messy business of selling tickets twice. "Well!" he said icily. "Doing business with Max Volo, eh?"

"No, sir!" David lied impulsively.

"Don't lie about it," Mr. Stone said quietly. "Everybody does business with Max. For a while. Then they wind up in jail, and Max stays free."

"I don't know what you mean," David whispered, for his arm hurt.

Fiercely, quietly, Mr. Stone slapped David's face four times and twisted his wrist until the skin ached. "You're a good boy," Mr. Stone said angrily. "In the office they think you're one of the few honest cashiers, so don't get mixed up with Max Volo. He'll ruin you, just as he's ruining the business for the rest of us. Soon the Company'll bring in more detectives, and even short-changing will be outlawed. Be smart, kid. Play the game honestly. You don't have to steal. All you have to do is learn to make change fast. Practice. Practice."

"Max made me take the tickets," David said quietly.

Mr. Stone slapped him another stinging blow. "Did he make you sell them?" he asked. "Max gives everybody tickets, but only fools sell them. I like you, kid. You're real. I know who you are and where you came from. Stay away from Max Volo." The slim gray man disappeared into the darkness.

But Max Volo was not an easy man to stay away from. David found that out the afternoon of the wreck. He was driving his train downgrade toward the trestles of the Hurricane when a string of cars high above him plunged through a railing and screamed madly to earth. The brakeman rode the deathly cars into the ground and was killed. The four occupants—two girls and two sailors from the Navy Yard— were thrown clear of the cars. They floated majestically to earth. One of the girls hit a tree. Her body seemed to come apart. The two sailors were horribly mangled. But the fourth girl, screaming like a meteor in flight through weird space, plunged into a lilac tree near David. She was not killed. An eye was ripped out by a branch, but she was not killed.

The Pennsylvania and Reading was approaching the curve when this accident took place. David, in grim fixation, watched the four figures flying in the sunlight. He forgot to decelerate his train, and it jumped the track. But everyone was concerned with the greater accident, and he was not fined. He got some boys to heave the cars back onto the track. When he finally got the train into the station—his passengers stayed behind to watch the ambulance come for the bodies—Max Volo was waiting for him.

"They'll be closing you up pretty quick, kid," Max said.

"Why?" David asked, confused.

"Oh, they always do!" Max said. "Every time a car goes

off the edge, they close the Hurricane. And this place, too. Don't want nobody pokin' around. In fifteen minutes you'll be my cashier!"

"I don't want to . . ." David began.

"Skip it, kid!" Max interrupted. "In a year you'll be one of the best crooks in the business." He winked and hurried off.

A messenger from the cashiers' office checked David's money and tickets. "Report to Max at the loganberry stand," he directed. "Take over there for the rest of the day."

When David reached the cashier's booth he looked for Max Volo, but the little man was nowhere to be seen. So David opened the door, squeezed himself into the booth, and climbed upon the high chair. His right leg struck something soft. Below him, huddled in a corner, was Max Volo. His quick, beady eyes smiled up at David. "Now we can talk!" he whispered. "Cross your legs if that tall spotter comes along. Here's a fistful of old tickets. We'll split fifty-fifty."

"I don't want this job!" David protested. But he did not then or ever protest sufficiently to have Max arrested. No one ever did that, for Max made it perfectly clear to everyone who worked with him that if even so much as a word leaked out to the Park police, he, Max Volo, would . . .

For more than an hour and a half Max huddled in the corner of the booth and explained to David the possibilities the boy would have from either stealing money from the Pennsylvania and Reading, or, better still, moving into the loganberry stand as Max's permanent cashier. "At the railroad it's easier money, sure. Alone you could probably knock off ten bucks a day and nobody ever know about it. But that's tops. You can't go any higher than that, see? Now here we do a big business," he droned on in a persuasive whisper.

"The spotter's coming!" David warned. The tall man purchased a ticket, looked slyly at the number, watched to see if the ticket was torn up by the clerk, ducked behind a tree to write down the number, and passed on. Max Volo knew the thin man was a spotter. He bribed a clerk in the cashiers' office to find out.

"He's gone!" David said.

"But here!" Max resumed. "Here we do a big business. On a good day $450.00. On such a day we can knock down 10 per cent, easy. That's twenty-two fifty for you. Of course, you give me two-fifty for the fix. That's only fair."

Half accepting the idea, half rejecting it, David asked, "Won't they find out?"

"It's all fixed!" Max explained. He shifted position and worked his face closer to David's. "About the tickets, I know the nights they check to see if any old tickets are mixed in. So, watch! We never sell yesterday's tickets that day. Only the tickets that I can palm during the first couple hours. I got a million ways to slip 'em to you. So when they check, they find only that day's tickets! On the other days, I slip you a big bundle of old ones. Keep feedin' them tickets out, kid. You get rid of that bunch, I can get you lots more."

"But don't they count the loganberry?" David said.

"I got it all fixed!" Max replied. "We water it. Then I slip in some extra citric acid. I can get it wholesale. For the carbonation I get the truck driver to leave four extra cylinders a week. He steals 'em from his company. Nobody knows a thing about it. I pay him for 'em, slip him five bucks a week, and who knows?"

"I'll take a loganberry!" a customer said. David looked up in astonishment. It was Mr. Stone.

"They put me here!" David muttered, handing Mr. Stone a new ticket. The cashier tilted his straw hat back, reached through the window and grasped David's left hand. Forcing it open he saw the fifty-odd old tickets the boy had been palming. He closed David's hand over the old tickets. "That's a good way to the penitentiary, kid!" he said. He kicked the booth a violent blow. "I suppose that's Max down there. His regular game." Mr. Stone stared at David. "You get A in arithmetic, they tell me. But you can't see this is the penitentiary for you!" He tore up his ticket and threw it back into the booth.

That night Max Volo received $16.40 plus $4.00 for David's share of the various fixes. David took home $12.40 plus another $2.85 for short-changing. He now had $57.50 hidden in the poorhouse. After he had cashed his day's take he sat for a long time in his room behind closely locked Door 8. He stayed awake until almost four o'clock writing a poem. David called this poem "People in the Air." Five people were floating in the air. But nothing bad happened to them. For they were floating idly above the earth, above the lilac bushes. They just floated off and never came back.

After David had worked on the railroad about six weeks the spotter turned in his report: "Harper seems to be more honest than any boy we have had on this job. As you are well aware, only a boy's honesty prevents him from stealing what he will. I judge that Harper has never taken much more than forty of fifty cents a day. Even on days when the total reported receipts were above fifty dollars, his returns checked very closely with my estimates. Recommended: That he be given the job at the loganberry stand." The spotter received fifteen dollars from Max Volo for that last line. The preceding portion of the report was unbiased fact. David Harper, when not working with Max Volo, was a reasonably honest cashier. That made him a phenomenon at the Park.

David had no wish to work for Volo, but he accepted the job. He had been in the booth half an hour when a pimply-faced boy bought a ticket and gave him a copy of *Passionate Love*. From the feel of the cheap magazine David guessed that it contained two bundles of old tickets. He nonchalantly read the cover page. "Beasts in the Night!" A pale, frantic girl wept in terror while a hairy hand ripped away her dress. The men working in the Park loved such magazines. He slipped the tickets into his lap. Then he looked up in horror. The tall spotter was watching him!

"What you got there, son?" the man asked.

"A magazine!" David said weakly. This was it! This was the way they arrested cashiers. No fuss. He had seen the young fellow at the popcorn stand get it. They just walked him away.

"Let me see it a minute," the spotter said quietly.

Sweating profusely, David lifted the magazine up to the money board and slipped it through the opening. He kept the tickets in his lap, squeezed between his legs. He tried not to show any emotion. The tall man studied the magazine a moment. "Just as I thought!" he said. "This magazine's mine!" He showed David the name written painstakingly across the top: "Michael McDermott." He rolled the magazine up. "Sorry, kid! But somebody swiped that magazine when I was eating lunch. I'll give it to you when I'm finished." He smiled slowly at David. The boy tried to smile back, but couldn't. He saw that the man hadn't been studying his name on the cover at all. He had been looking into the folds of the magazine where Max Volo had secreted the tickets. The man knew David had old tickets for sale. And David knew he knew. The spotter smiled a long, agonizing, slow smile. "I'll be back!" he said.

David could hardly see, he was so excited and frightened.

There was nothing he could do with the tickets. There they were, in his lap. And the spotter was coming back! Suddenly the boy had an idea. He started coughing, violently. A guard hurried up. "What's the matter, kid?" the guard asked.

"A cracker!" David replied weakly.

"I'll get you a drink!" the guard said.

Feigning not to have understood, David left his booth, a forbidden thing to do, and rushed over to the loganberry stand. "Hey, son! Back in your box!" the guard cried. But before he could reach David, the boy had slipped Max Volo the two wads of tickets. In massive relief he drank a glass of cold water. It tasted wonderful.

But in less than half an hour the same pimply-faced boy was back with another magazine, *Great Crimes*. In it David could feel the two wads of tickets. He permitted them to slip into his lap. In terrible confusion he tried to hide the tickets but found that Max had enclosed a note: "Don't be a sucker! That spotter's fixed!" David looked across the gravel roadway to the loganberry stand. Max was grinning at him.

David was growing up. He was almost fifteen now, strong in the shoulders, long in reach. There was a slight growth of hair on his chin. At night, on the trolley, he often had a great urge to reach out and wrestle with some boy. Occasionally he fought on the trolley, and the conductor laughed until the punches became too rough. "That's enough!" the conductor would cry, and then David and the other boy would swap one or two real blows, as hard as they could swing, furious, deadly socks. They felt good, even when they hurt. Then the boys would sink back in their seats and each would think: "I could lick that guy . . . if I had to." David ate good meals now, with his stolen money, but he was always hungry. Walking up the poorhouse lane late at night, after the trolley had hurried over the hill to Doylestown, he would sometimes dart quickly from shadow to shadow as if he were an Indian scout. He would stop sharply, whirl about to meet an unknown assailant, double up, lash out at the darkness, and then step calmly back into the road. He knew exactly what he would do if attacked. Thinking of this, he would come upon the women's building, long and gray in the night, and he would smile. He would think of how Aunt Reba had beaten him, and he would smile.

At Paradise he began to watch the girls. They came to the

Park in summer dresses and stood quietly by the loganberry stand while their escorts bought tickets. There would be thin lines of dew upon their lips, and David wondered what it would be like to kiss such lips. Then he became awkwardly ashamed of his thoughts and contented himself with reading *Passionate Love* and staring at the illustrations. Sometimes he would look up suddenly and see the wind tugging at some girl's dress, and the form of her living body was a million times more exciting than the stories in *Passionate Love*. And once a girl from Philly had arranged to meet a young man at the loganberry stand. He was late, and she stood nervously away from the crowd so that finally David spoke to her. She blushed angrily, against her will, and she looked so lovely that David said, "How'd you like a drink?" and she agreed, and they joked with one another, and David said, "I'll bet he's not coming at all," and she blushed again and said, "I'll tell you what! If he don't come, you and me'll make a night of it!" David's knees grew weak, and through the bars of his cage he held her hand, but the young man came and glared at David, and the night was empty, so that on the trolley going home David really slugged another boy and drew blood.

Max Volo, who was a very clever man, noticed these things about the growing boy and whispered one day. "You oughta come down to the Coal Mine for a while. That'd fix you up!" David, thinking Max referred only to the immense, dark ride, agreed. Max's eyes grew bright as he whispered instructions: "Then you duck right in under the waterfall!"

The Coal Mine was famous for its two fearful drops through gloomy darkness and for the imitation waterfall which carried a constant burden of green and brackish water across imitation rocks. David walked there slowly and studied the waterfall. Magically, from behind it, Max Volo whistled to him. David looked sharply and saw that a door led through the papier-mâché rocks. "This way!" Max called.

David entered the narrow doorway and about him saw the gaunt outlines of scaffolding which sustained the flimsy structure. Water dripped from old and rotting beams, and mossy slime clung to every board. Far above him, a car bearing a few hardy celebrants roared along the lofty tracks and then plunged into the darkness. The occupants screamed, and David could hear the car roar past on a lower level.

The scaffolding trembled, and moisture was shaken loose. Then the Coal Mine was silent again, and very black.

"Hssst!" Max whistled. "This way!" He led David along a path of planking and suddenly opened a door through the scaffolding. A bright line shone into the darkness and illuminated the slimy water at David's feet. "Well!" Max announced proudly. "Here we are!" but before David could enter the room Max whispered harshly. "It's three bucks, please."

When he had been paid, he led David into a fairly large room. Originally intended as a storehouse for extra cars used only on Sundays, it had been rebuilt by Max into a crudely sumptuous entertainment room. Three girls, one of them wearing almost nothing, were seated in heavy chairs. A brakeman from the Coal Mine was sitting in the lap of the girl with almost no clothes on. The two other girls rose to greet Max, and to his astonishment David saw that the prettier of the two was that same big Betty who, at the swimming hole, had insisted that the boys stone and arrest old Toothless Tom.

"Do you know Betty?" Max asked.

"He's the poorhouse kid!" Betty laughed. "Hear you're in fast time, kid? How you like it?"

David smiled. Max answered for him. "He's doin' fine, Betty. And how are you doin'? Miss me today?" She came over to him and threw her arms about his neck. He placed both hands in the small of her back and drew her warmly to him. Then he moved his quick hands to her breasts. Betty twisted away. "She's good for me!" Max told David.

The brakeman raised his head from kissing the girl in the big chair. "Janet says hello, kid!" The girl waved a bare arm and grinned at David. She was a handsome girl, big, broad-shouldered. Her legs were bare to where they lost themselves beneath the brakeman. They were very white.

"It's a nice place we got here," Max said to David as Betty and the third girl started to make some sandwiches. "I make more money here than I do anywhere else." He nodded to the smaller of the girls making sandwiches. "That's Nora. She's a nice little thing."

When the sandwiches were served, the brakeman and his girl each took one. "Hey, cover up!" the brakeman yelled, pulling the girl's clothes about her shoulders.

"What you see never hurts you!" the girl laughed, winking at David. "Ain't that right, sonny?" She ostentatiously adjusted her brassiere. "You know, kid! In about four more years there ain't no woman goin' to be able to say no to you!"

"When did you ever say no to anybody?" the brakeman asked. He buried his head in her neck. Then he rose from her lap and pulled her into an alcove. Overhead another lonely car roared through the Coal Mine, echoing and making the scaffolds sway.

"Betty says you live in the poorhouse!" Max said.

"Yes," David replied. He felt strange in this hidden room. He knew that Nora was watching him. He wanted to look at her, too, but he was afraid.

"Well," Max continued, "a few more summers like this and you won't have to live in a poorhouse. I'm tellin' you that!"

Betty kissed Max heavily on the ear. She was bigger than Max. "Hey!" she said huskily. "Nora! The kid's your date. Get workin'."

Nora went to David's chair and sat on the arm. Her bare legs rested beside David's. "Don't mind them others!" she said. Max and Betty disappeared into another alcove. "Max has a nice place down here, don't you think?"

David looked about him. He could see the brakeman's feet sticking out beyond the alcove. There were pictures on the wall. Undressed women, all looking very serious. There were the big chairs and a place to make sandwiches. The floor was made of old packing boxes and was damp.

"How old are you?" Nora asked.

"Almost fifteen," David said. He smiled at the girl. She was not pretty, like the other two, but she had nicer teeth than they. She wore her hair long.

"How old do you think I am?" she asked, tilting her head. Her chin was firm.

"I think you're twenty-one," David replied.

"Nah!" she cried. "I'm nineteen!" She slipped down onto David's lap. "Do you like girls?" she asked. Then, before David could reply, she asked, "Have you ever kissed a girl?"

"Don't ask so many questions!" Betty cried from the dark corner where she and Max were lying.

"Yes," David nodded.

"Like this?" Nora asked. She brushed David's lips with hers, delicately. She wore perfume. David's heart leaped with surging pleasure. Nora squeezed his shoulders. "You're only a kid," she said. "You come back in four years! Oooo-la-la!" She raised her eyebrows and kissed him lightly.

He threw his arms about her and held her next to him. She pressed her face against his.

"You don't shave, do you?" she asked. "Ah, you're a sweet kid!" She hugged him again and lay back in the big chair. Her right hand gripped his knee. "You've got the world before you, kid," she said dreamily. "What you goin' to be when you grow up?"

"I don't know," David said.

"You go to school? Oh, sure you do! You get good marks?"

"Pretty good!" David said eagerly.

"I'll bet you're the best kid in the class, aren't you?" she teased.

"Sometimes I am," David replied. Nora hugged him.

"How did a sweet kid like you get mixed up with Volo?" she asked.

"Are they making love?" David asked, pointing to the alcoves.

"What do you think?" she asked, looking at him sideways. David grinned and said nothing. "Don't you worry about that stuff, kid. You got plenty of time to worry about that. Take my word for it. You're gonna be a fine fellow when you grow up. You can have any girl you want. You ever slept with a girl, kid?"

"Nope," David said. "Not yet."

"Well, don't say it that way!" Nora cried. "Let me tell you something. Bend your ear way over." She bit it and then whispered: "Don't rush things, kid. You got plenty of time. But when you want to make love to a girl, always be nice to her. Understand? Give her little presents. Write her nice letters. Take her out. Tell her she's the most beautiful girl in all the world. And listen, kid. Whenever you're out with a girl don't look at any other girl. See? Always your girl is the best. Not like these lunks!" She jerked her thumb at Volo and the brakeman.

"Do you have a fellow?" David asked. The smell of her sweet perfume was lovelier than anything he had previously known. He hoped that she didn't have a fellow.

"We got lots of fellows," she said. "Didn't Volo tell you?"

"No," David said.

"We work for Volo." She turned her pretty eyes right at David. She swished her hair back with her left hand. "Betty lives here. Me and Janet come here most of the time. Max makes a lot of money, don't he?"

"You mean you work here?" David asked, trying to get things clear in his mind. "Like Janet?"

Nora looked at him and smiled. "Now don't get to worryin' about things, kid. We like Volo. He's a good fellow. And you're sweet!" She swished her hair back again. "How soon do you have to get back to work?"

"It's a rainy day," David said. "I've been out pretty long already."

"Look at this floor!" Nora said. "I'll say it's rainy! Tell me the truth, kid. Did you ever kiss a girl?"

"Mmm-hmm!" David said firmly.

"What was it like?" Nora insisted.

"Sort of funny."

"Sort of funny!" she repeated, laughing. "Hey, Betty! He says kissing is sort of funny!"

"Give him one of your specials!" Betty cried harshly.

"Look, kid!" Nora laughed. "This'll be your first kiss." She wrapped David in her arms and kissed him feverishly. She placed his hand at the open buttons of her dress and pressed him to her. The boy, feeling as he did when fighting imaginary shadows on the road home, caught hold of the warm, fragrant girl and returned the kiss. She, feeling the surge of manhood in the awkward boy, relaxed for a moment. Then slowly she pushed him away and fixed her dress. "You've been kissed, kid. You kissed a girl," she whispered. "That wasn't funny, was it?" She stood up.

David had lost all sense of co-ordination. He seemed to be nothing but elbows and knees. He sat very still and watched the girl. She fixed her dress and her hair. She tilted her chin and grabbed her left hand with her right. Then she smiled down at him, extending her hand to help him up. As he rose, she pulled him to her. "You're a sweet kid." She laughed nervously. "We could have a good time together. You come back to see me next year." David looked at her. She was his own height. He put his arms about her.

"I think you're a fine girl," he said huskily.

"How about buyin' me a hot dog and some rootbeer?" she asked.

"Let's!" he said eagerly. "How about them?"

"They're good for hours!" she said, casting a contemptuous look at the brakeman's feet.

David and Nora left the hidden room. Back among the dark scaffolding they picked their way along the narrow boards leading to the secret doorway beneath the waterfall.

Overhead the mysterious dark hid the walls of the Coal Mine. Near the door the soft splashing of the waterfall on imitation rock made lovely music. Nora paused, and David caught up to her. His face was against hers and with an instinct born of the most fragmentary experience he fumbled with her dress until his hand and lips found soft sanctuary. "Oh, kid!" she sighed in the darkness. "Damn it all! Cut it out!" She pushed him away. He slipped on the slippery boards. One foot went into slimy water. "I'm sorry, kid!" she whispered, pulling him toward the door. Outside, the Park was its same magnificent, lonely, rainy self. The carrousel played softly in the distance. A wandering car shot echoing through the Coal Mine. And everywhere was the smell of burnt caramel from the popcorn stands.

David bought Nora two hot dogs and two glasses of rootbeer. She was soft and lovely, standing in the mist which blew down from the imitation waterfall. David suddenly had tears in his eyes. He wanted to imprison in his mind the vision of this girl, but while he watched he saw the vision fade, a pattern lost, a flashing beauty in the mind's night that glimmered and was seen no more.

Nora walked with him to the loganberry stand. Before she got out of sight a short, thin man hurried up to her and took her possessively by the arm. An immense stab of pain captured David, and tears filled his eyes. He called for the stupid assistant who helped Max Volo. "Take the booth!" he said.

"You know I can't do that!" the boy grunted.

But he had to, nevertheless, for David was hurrying down the gravel walk to the cashiers' office. "I don't want to work for Max Volo any more," he announced.

"Why not?" the suspicious head cashier demanded. David stared back at the man. The head cashier started to ask a question, but thought better of it. Man to man, in the cold, mist-filled office he looked at the boy. He saw David's determined chin, the broad, quick eyes that bespoke a certain moral stability. And David, in his turn, saw the man who tried to do his best, tried to keep stealing at a minimum, worked as decently as he could in a dirty, despicable job. Man to man they looked at each other. "All right," the cashier said.

And that was how David came to be Mr. Stone's assistant. Max Volo got a new cashier next morning. On the third day an uncontaminated spotter caught the unfortunate youth selling old tickets. The boy was sent to jail, but he never betrayed the man who gave him the tickets.

"So you finally got some sense!" Mr. Stone observed when his new assistant reported. "Max Volo's loss is my gain." He shook David's hand with great formality and said, "When you work for me, you wear a clean shirt. And keep your fingernails scraped."

He appointed David to the second-fare platform and fixed to his belt a register with a loud, tinkling bell. "When the cars unload," he said, "you hurry along the train and ask the passengers if they'd like a second ride. If they do, collect the money and ring this register. Spotters will check you all the time, so don't try to short-change the Company. If you do, I'll know about it, and I'll send you to jail. If you need money, ask me and I'll give you some. Understand?"

David nodded at the austere man and adjusted the register. Mr. Stone studied him approvingly and said, "You're in big business now. Some days you'll do $500. So the smart trick is to learn the game right. Learn to make change. Work. Work. Work."

He placed his arm about David and said, "I'm proud of the way you've behaved, so I'll give you a few hints. When the train comes in, always stand up here at the front and work to the back. See why?"

"No," David said.

"Because that way people lose sight of you as soon as you've short-changed them. If you stay in sight, they'll remember their money. So make change very fast and get out of sight. Another thing. As soon as a train comes in, take a quick look for guys that have been having a hot time with their girls. Especially if a guy has been up a girl's pants, he's an easy touch, because his mind is on only one thing. Rush up, suggest another ride, slap the change into the hand he's been working with, and he'll pop it right into his pocket."

Mr. Stone taught David much more about how to work the second-fare platform. Never stealing from the Company, David learned all the tricks. If he managed to swindle a man of five dollars he gave scrupulously correct change to everyone else in that car, so as to prevent arguments which might remind the robbed man of his money. He also learned to hand customers coins with each hand so as to make them think they were getting a lot of money.

The job never bored him. He was free of the awful pressure

that working with Max Volo entailed. There was no ride in Pennsylvania like the Hurricane. The wild drops and twists frightened even the most durable spirits. Sometimes children would leave the ride in hysterics. Women would throw up and middle-aged men would be wild-eyed. But most of them reveled in the sheer agony of the ride, even though every year saw its fatal accident. High in the air, something would go wrong, and a car would shoot far into the sky and crash among the trees. Other cars would be whizzing around the Hurricane while the death car still sped to earth, and these later riders would see people flying through the air. David dreaded such moments, for it meant that when the others cars pulled into his platform people would faint and scream with fear. And yet he saw clearly that those who were thus saved always looked back toward the broken railing with grim satisfaction. They had got through! The deaths of others merely heightened their own miraculous salvation.

David further saw that after an accident the men of the Hurricane took a keener interest in their work. Their senses were sharpened, and their feeling of comradeship intensified. And finally, David discovered to his great surprise that even though the Hurricane killed at least one person every year, business never dropped off. Next day after an accident there would be more riders than before. Thrill seekers, young men and their girls, mauled one another as before and felt themselves to be extra brave for daring the high ride; and even those who had fainted returned to the scene of their horror. They fainted on Tuesday, but they came back on Wednesday.

"People are cattle!" Mr. Stone snorted contemptuously. "If you closed everything in this Park where a guy can gorge himself or get a good feel, we'd all go broke in a week. Study the swine carefully, kid. Notice everything they do to make fools of themselves. Then help them do it, and you can short-change them blind."

There was one horrible aspect to the tragedies, however. Young girls were almost always involved. If they lived, they were disfigured for life. If they died, you saw them on the grass, their dresses over their heads, their white legs sprawled apart. Some man always hurried up, fixed their dresses and covered them with a coat.

One of these mangled girls had ridden around twice with a sailor. They were fine kids, breathless and in love. David saw the girl lying on the grass near the tracks of his old railroad, the Pennsylvania and Reading. "I feel sick," he said to Mr. Stone.

"Don't you worry, kid," the cashier said. "It's brutal, but it's true. There's more pretty girls in the world than can ever be used up. When you're my age you see them all around you. Dried-up old maids. Not worth a penny to themselves or to anyone else. Never worry about what happens to young girls, kid. It's what don't happen to them that should really worry you."

Max Volo took David's escape from the loganberry stand philosophically. He apparently bore no grudge, for early in David's tenure at the second-fare platform Max appeared clothed in mysteriousness. "It's sensational!" he whispered.

"What is?" David asked suspiciously.

"The bell!" Max replied cryptically.

"What bell?"

"It's like this," Max explained enthusiastically. "You wear this bell under your shirt, and it ain't no ordinary bell. A man who works for the company that makes your fare bell slips me this special one on the side."

"What's this all about?" David demanded.

"Like I said!" Max wheezed. "Under your shirt is this bell. You ring it with your elbow and pocket the fare. Nobody can tell the difference." The little man beamed at David.

"I don't want your bell," David said.

"Look!" Max explained. He flicked his elbow imperceptibly and a sound exactly like David's fare bell sounded. "I pay the guy fifty bucks to give me this. I let you have it for seventy-five. In a month you could knock off five hundred dollars!"

"No!" David exploded.

"OK," Max agreed promptly. "You think that's too risky. I got another angle. I know the spotter who works your beat. For twenty bucks a week I tip you off. Why, you could palm fares so fast nobody could see you."

David was disgusted. "Get the hell out of here, Max!" he exploded.

"Sure!" the little man said. "But I think you'd like this!" He whisked before David's startled eyes a glossy photograph of Nora, completely undressed and smiling at the camera. Max moved the picture just slowly enough for David to see clearly and indelibly what the picture was. "Costs only two bucks," Max whispered.

Three thoughts flashed through David's mind in that fragmentary moment. "I could beat this guy up," he thought at first. Then as the exquisite thrill of the picture took effect he thought: "I'd like to have that." And instantly he thought: "Nora! She's a good kid." He shared none of his thoughts with Volo, who stared at the boy, sighed heavily, and walked away.

David saw Nora several times after that, but not at the Coal Mine. He saw her sidling through the Park, walking aimlessly until some young man picked her up. Then she insisted upon riding the Hurricane. Thin, tense, her lips white with fear, she swept through the heights and dizzy depths of the wild ride. When the car stopped at David's platform she stepped out, dazed. Then, clenching her fists, she would take a deep breath and smile at David before she disappeared with her young man toward the Coal Mine.

Occasionally she would ride alone, sitting by herself in a corner of the car, trembling violently when the mad dash was over. "What do you ride for if you're so scared?" David asked her one day.

"You gotta do something," she joked.

"Want another one?" he asked.

"With you? Sure!" He tossed his register to a brakeman and jumped in beside the shivering girl. Then, far above Paradise, he and Nora clung to each other and surveyed the tawdry land below them, the crooks, the whorehouse beneath the Coal Mine, the spotters, and the thieves. The car dipped wildly, and Nora shrieked. David did not try to kiss her or clutch at her dress, and as the car reached the long, slow dip before the platform, Nora gripped his hand and whispered, "You're the best kid in the Park!"

She returned often to the Hurricane and told David that if he ever wanted to revisit the room beneath the waterfall he could. "You're a big boy now. You know what goes on down there, but I guess you don't wanta be mixed up in it, do you? Well, you're smart, but if you ever want to come down, we can have a good time. Just kissing and stuff like that. Not like Max and Betty." David usually took her to dinner on such days, and they ate hog dogs with sauerkraut.

"Max showed me your picture," David said one evening as they ate.

"You mean?" She flicked her fingers down the front of her dress.

"Yes," David replied, his voice choked with excitement.

"I'm skinny, ain't I?" she teased.

"You're a sweet girl!" he avowed passionately.

"Sure I am," she said softly, piling more sauerkraut on her hot dog. "Only I got some bad breaks. But I got some good ones, too. Right now a gentleman wants to marry me. Only he's a Polack. Achh!" She spit into the gravel. "You'd never catch me marryin' a Polack. They beat their women somethin' awful." She looked at David with deep, flashing eyes. "I'd never marry a guy who beat his wife. I'd kill him, that's what."

One night Mr. Stone saw David talking with Nora and after the little prostitute had gone, the gray cashier said, "I suppose you know who she is."

"Yes," David said, not certain that he did know.

"I suppose you know that she's one of the girls Max Volo keeps in the Coal Mine? He rents them out. To anybody who wants them. Have you been fooling around there?" David did not reply, and the older man asked sharply, "How much do you know, kid?"

"Oh, I know!" David said bravely.

"Well, do you know this?" Mr. Stone asked forcefully. In ten minutes he told David more than Old Daniel had been able to explain in an hour and a half. They stood beneath a carrousel shed, where the waltz from *Faust* played on and on, mixed with the unfeeling words of Mr. Stone as he described what David's future would be if he caught certain diseases.

David was shocked and bewildered. He had guessed much of what Mr. Stone was saying, but he had not known, for sure. When the icy lecture ended he was badly confused. He wanted to believe that sex was the solemn, grandiose thing Old Daniel had said. But he also knew from what he had seen beneath the Coal Mine—especially from things Nora started to say but couldn't—that sex was also the brutal, retributive thing that Mr. Stone claimed. David never entirely reconciled these two views of life, in which respect he was exactly like most men who live, including Old Daniel and Mr. Stone.

As a reward for the boy's honesty, Mr. Stone taught him the master tricks of short-changing. "Some men like talcum powder best, but I prefer pumice," the precise, gray cashier explained. "Run your hand over my board. Smooth as glass, eh? Now watch!" With his left middle finger Mr. Stone deftly slid a dime across the polished change board. The coin came to rest exactly where a customer could not see it. "That's what pumice does!"

"Wouldn't talcum do as well?" David inquired.

"Better, sometimes, but you'll notice that we're close to the lake. The humidity makes talcum gum up. Always stick to pumice." He produced a cotton bag filled with dust and patiently polished his board. Then he flipped a few nickels and dimes across it, laying them where they could not be seen.

"There's one idea to master," he continued. "A customer is a hand, and a voice, and an eye. He lays his money down. That's the hand. He says, 'Two,' and that's the voice. But it's his eye that you have to work on. So here's how to do it. As soon as he speaks, have the tickets out there for him. Put them so he'll have to move forward to get them, and that carries him past his change."

Mr. Stone stopped and looked at David. "How tough are you, kid?" he asked.

"I'm pretty tough," David replied.

"Short-changing is a test of whether you're tougher than the customer. Because you've got to judge the next second. Is the yokel going to leave? If you make a single move, he'll remember his change. So you watch his coat sleeve like a hawk, and that's when you've got to be tough. Outlast him. Out-brazen him. But you've got to do it in the flash of a second, because the minute he hesitates, you shove part of his change at him, in the direction he's moving. The part you want to keep you shove way back over here."

With beautiful gestures Mr. Stone showed David exactly how to work: "Tickets way over here. The pause. Then a quarter and some dimes right beside the tickets. A quarter and a nickel way back here." David could not detect a single variation in the cashier's movements.

"You certainly do it smoothly," David said admiringly.

"Some cashiers don't like that left-hand trick of mine," Mr. Stone explained.

"I see why," David agreed. "Your left hand slides the money you want to keep right into the face of the next person in line. Then it's the next guy who messes up the deal by shouting, 'Mister! You forgot your change.' That's what happened to me at the loganberry stand."

"There's a way to beat that," Mr. Stone explained. "See that sign?" David left the booth and studied the traditional Park sign that ran across the front of the bars: COUNT YOUR

CHANGE. In front of the word COUNT Mr. Stone had erected an immense sign with the single word PLEASE. He had placed it so precisely that people waiting to buy tickets could not see the spot on his change board where the errant coins lay hidden.

"It cuts off people's faces," David said. "How can you see them?"

"Ah!" Mr. Stone cried, "that's the beauty of it. If you really go into this business, you never look at people's faces. Remember what I said: a hand, a voice, an eye. That's all. You short-change everybody. You don't try to guess who you can ream and who you can't. You ream them all. Then you're in the big time."

"How about women?" David asked.

"They're people, aren't they?" Mr. Stone countered.

The day finally came when David was permitted to sit in Mr. Stone's chair and try his skill; but he was most maladroit, and soon he had a line of customers arguing about their change, and in his confusion he slid out more coins than he should have. Mr. Stone watched in amusement for some time and then took over. "You can't expect to be a champion in one day. Tell you what! You come to work early and practice on my board. But remember! Never look at a sucker's face. You felt sorry for those yokels and lost your shirt."

Frequently thereafter Mr. Stone allowed David to try his hand. In time the boy became fairly skilled at the dirty business, and to his great surprise he was informed one morning that he would henceforth be cashier at the third largest concession in the Park, the Coal Mine! He erected his sign, PLEASE COUNT YOUR CHANGE, and polished his board with pumice. He spent hours each day flipping coins idly, speedily, purposefully across his shimmering board and discovered one evening that he had become psychologically tough enough to outbrazen the yokels. He tried to cheat every customer, never looked at their faces, was icily undisturbed when they insisted on their right change, and made at least $50.00 a week.

"You've learned a lot this summer," Mr. Stone said admiringly on the last night. "But the biggest thing you learned was to play the game honestly. Don't ever fool around with men like Max Volo." Side by side, in warm friendship, David and Mr. Stone left the Park. It was a cold night in September, and the lights went out for the last time that year. The wind was midnight chill, and there was a grand loneliness in the air.

"You were very kind to me," David said impulsively as they reached the trolley line.

"See you next summer, kid!" Mr. Stone said impassively. "You're all right, kid. You got a good head on your shoulders." He waved goodbye and disappeared. Funny, but David did not know where Mr. Stone lived. Somewhere near Philadelphia. He didn't work in the winter but went down to Florida for a rest.

David stood thinking of Mr. Stone when he felt a soft push in the middle of his back. "Guess who?" a thin voice teased. It was Nora!

"I was wondering about you," he said.

"Don't you worry about me," she replied.

"What are you going to do now?" he asked.

"There's a man wants to take me down to Florida," she replied.

"Are you getting married?" David asked, his voice betraying his disappointment.

"Oh, no!" the thin girl explained. "This guy's in his fifties. He came to arrange it with Max."

"Are you going?" David asked.

"I guess so," she said. She pulled a very thin coat about her shoulders, and David was perplexed as to what he should say next. He was glad she wasn't getting married, and at the same time he was unhappy about her going to Florida with a man of fifty. Yet he liked the idea of her going south for the winter.

"I don't know what to say!" he admitted. Nora smiled at him and clasped his hand. His blood began to circulate furiously.

"Don't you say anything," she whispered. "I know what you're thinking."

But he did say something. He said a very foolish thing. "That's the only coat you have, isn't it?" he asked.

"Yes," she said.

"Well, here!" Impulsively he handed her fifty dollars which that night would have been hidden in the poorhouse barn. She pushed the money back at him.

"If I go to Florida my man'll buy me all the clothes I want," she explained.

"All right," David said. "Then you take this for yourself."

He thrust the money into the ragged pocket of her thin coat, and as he did so she clutched him by the arm and they stepped back among the shadows that now possessed the Park. She held her warm lips up to his and placed his hands upon her body.

"Oh, kid!" she whispered. "Let's just stand here for a minute." She pressed herself against him and moved her body slowly. "Does that feel good?" she whispered hoarsely. David could only mumble and she gripped him by the shoulders, pushing him away. She spoke very quickly: "First time we met you told me you had a girl. You go home and be very nice to her. You kiss her and do all sorts of things with her." She hurried David back onto the graveled walk, but when the time came to say good night she stood very straight before him, her breasts projecting toward him, and she said with great force, "Next year you'll be old enough, Dave. The time we'll have!"

Nora kissed him one last long time and then disappeared toward the Philadelphia trolleys. He watched the strange manner in which darkness folds about the body of a retreating woman, and long after she had gone that darkness seemed still to contain her. She was the first of the nameless people he was to know. She had no family, and no one cared where she went or when she lay down to sleep. A succession of cheap rooms formed her home, and she had a mind that no one had ever cared to cultivate. Sometimes in the winter when she was sick, she lay for days in dirty sheets until the fever wore itself out, and in the warmer summers she slept with many men. She was nobody, and she had no nationality. She was not French nor Polish nor Italian . . . some indiscriminate race that retained long names which people in America could not pronounce. David did not know her name, nor where she lived, nor could he write to her; yet this strange, nameless thing was David's first girl, and her departing promise of a great time next summer haunted him for seven months.

In that first summer at Paradise Park David had every opportunity to become a cheap thief, a hanger-on, a whoremonger, or a bum; but at every deciding point an inner voice of conscience kept him clear of the vilest entanglements.

This voice was a very real thing! It actually spoke to him, and he could hear its stern command: "Come on, Harper! Get going!" It was not the voice of his aunt, nor of Old

Daniel, nor of any minister, nor of his own inner light. It was the very solid voice of Bobby Creighton crying, "Come on Harper!" and it was by all odds the most imperative voice David would ever hear.

Bobby Creighton had come to Doylestown some years before. He was a dumpy, round, quick-eyed man and looked completely unlike any other teacher David had known. He was the basketball coach and while David was still in grammar school Bobby Creighton had spotted him. "You got a fine natural shot," the coach had said. David could remember the precise inflection of Bobby's voice. There was hope in it, for the coach saw that with quick, rangy kids like David coming along, Doylestown would have more championship teams. He had smiled at David and added, "How would you like to scrimmage against the varsity some afternoon?" David had swallowed hard and said he'd like it. That night he lay in bed and held his breath for two-minute spells so as to get his lungs in training. He could not sleep and imagined himself slipping under Fred Baker's arms for shot after shot.

Three days later Bobby had stopped by the grammar school and asked, in an off-hand way, "Why don't you drop down tonight?" and David had twisted his shoulders indifferently and replied, "OK, I may do that." He stayed in after school and cleaned the blackboards. He did tomorrow's arithmetic, dusted the desks and finally could think of nothing else to waste time. Slowly he sauntered down to the gym.

"You fellows know Dave Harper," Bobby said, standing with his pudgy arm on David's shoulder. "He's small, like the Hatboro forwards. I asked him to drop down." David nodded at the big men on Doylestown's championship team and loafed into the dressing room. When he returned in uniform Bobby studied his strong legs and long arms. "How's about stepping in at forward?" he asked.

"Now?" David inquired.

"Sure!" Bobby said, but suddenly David was attacked with the athlete's urge. He felt that his kidneys must burst —that very minute—if he didn't run to the urinal. He got red in the face.

"Excuse me?" he asked. "Just for a second?" The big men laughed and waited. He was furious and muttered to himself, "You wait! You wait!"

The scrimmage started, and it was very rough. The big

men passed far too swiftly for him to handle, and he looked bad. Bobby took him out. "You're pretty nervous, kid."

"I'll be all right."

"Sure you will!" Bobby said. He threw his arm about David's shoulder and whispered, "Now watch how Gulick leaves that spot open. Hang there and then cut like mad. Think you can do it?"

"Sure," David replied, and Bobby had sent him back in. He hung back toward the open spot and suddenly caught the ball winging toward him. With two fast dribbles he swivel-hipped his way into the goal and laid the ball up mechanically, his left elbow jabbing a guard in the face, his right leg pushing high in the air.

"Come on, Harper!" Bobby Creighton yelled, and that afternoon David hung up three more goals.

"You're all right!" Gulick and the big men said in the dressing room, but it was Bobby Creighton's comment that David would never forget. "Practice, practice, practice!" Bobby said. "I'll be waitin' for you."

More than religion or school or all that his friends had taught him, basketball kept David hard and clean. The game was sheer magic. Many words are wasted about high-school athletics: *body-building, character formation, sportsmanship*. Rarely do sports achieve those flowery ends; but what they do achieve is something even finer. They help boys find a place in society, especially boys who might otherwise live on the fringes of the world. In games, such boys can be momentary heroes and win the wild approval of their community. Young fellows who wear ill-fitting clothes, whose fathers lie drunk in the town gutters, or whose mothers rouse whispers on street corners, boys whose entire future is nothingness can have their day of glory; and some of them like the taste of that glory and determine that the town gutters are not for them.

Fortunately for David, Doylestown was basketball crazy. There was a tradition that its teams, playing against those of much larger schools, should win most of the championships. As early as David could remember he had known that he would be on the championship teams. Toothless Tom had built him a basket in the poorhouse barn. The truck driver had found him an old basketball. He learned to dribble with either hand, pivot, pass from the chest, and fake break. But most of all he learned to shoot baskets. Some Saturday mornings he would practice a single shot four or five hundred times. He became a master of english and a precisionist from any spot within the foul circle.

But most of all he liked to hang around with Bobby Creighton. The fat coach seemed to know what boys were interested in. More than a hundred times David listened to Bobby as the pudgy man stood with his right leg on a bench and told some new gang of kids about the Dedham-Swarthmore game. "It was the big game of the season! Swarthmore won about eighteen games that year. We were the underdogs. Coach said before the game, 'Bobby? Are you hot tonight?' I said, 'Yes, Coach, I am.' 'Well,' Coach said, 'Bobby, we're goin' to start you at guard. We'll let Lemons run wild. If he can score, let him. Don't worry about him. You, Bobby, keep down the floor and shoot.' That's what Coach said. So at half time I had six baskets, we were only two points behind, and the crowd was crazy wild. Second half, Swarthmore kept two points ahead. All the way. It was truly heart-breakin'. Right down to the last minute, two points ahead. On a jump we got the ball. They passed back court to me. I was goin' to dribble and shoot when I saw the pistol go up in the air. So I just twisted to one side and let 'er ride."

At such moments there would be a solemn hush among the listening boys. "How did you shoot it, Bobby?" someone would always ask.

"Well," Bobby would reply, "I figured I was too far away to make the basket, so I leaned way down and shot it from between my legs, underhand. Just in chance it might get that far." At this point some boy would toss Bobby a basketball. Bouncing it once or twice the chunky fellow would blush and apologize.

"Of course, I'm out of practice," he would say. Then he would pat his belly and add, "And now I got a spare tire, too." Holding the ball low, he would shoot it underhand. Once in ten the ball would spin through the air and pass accurately through the hoop, the way it had done that night long ago in the Dedham-Swarthmore game.

"So the score was tied! 41-41," Bobby would say, his eyes aglow. "You know, they had to get the police to clear the floor so we could play an extra period. Swarthmore got the lead. They held it till right at the end, then I busted loose with another long shot. This time everybody really did go wild. So the police came out again and we waited till the ropes were stretched tight. In the second extra period it was murder. I made three baskets. Swarthmore none!"

It was part of the mythology of Doylestown, that Dedham-Swarthmore game. Moerman's barbershop had a framed clipping from the Philadelphia *North American* and a picture from the *Press:* "Dedham Miracle Man Topples Swarthmore." Bobby got his hair cut at Moerman's, and once or twice a month he would tell the older men of the town about that fabulous game. The story never grew tedious, for when fat, unpretentious Bobby started to talk, old men and young enjoyed his eager words, as if they were part of a beautiful world far, far away in space.

It was in the fall after David's first year at Paradise that Bobby announced in the barbershop that whether the kids were young or not he was starting David Harper and Harry Moomaugh at forward that year! "This kid Harper's got an absolute lust for the basket!" Bobby explained. "And Moomaugh's a big, tough guy. Good in a roughhouse. Confidentially," Bobby said in a whisper which the barber relayed to David, also confidentially, "if those two kids can stand up, we've got another championship!"

The word sped about Doylestown that Bobby Creighton thought his team was in. And then David experienced the sweet subtle thrill of athletics! Men watched him as he walked to school. Important men like the policeman and the head of the National Guard would stop him and chat idly with him, slipping in hints here and there: "Hoagey always shoots from the right corner. Watch Smoot! He's got a fake start. Moyer's good, but keep jabbing your elbow in his belly." And the young fellows—in the fifth and sixth grades—who imagined themselves as stars one day began to mimic the way David walked with his right arm crooked as if waiting for a fast cut to the basket. So in a town where education and religion and every other possible aspect of society had failed to make David Harper feel that he was important—that he belonged—basketball succeeded; and it was this sense of belonging that David defended when he turned his back on Max Volo. Going to jail as a crook would be evil. David could see that in the terror the cashiers showed when they were finally caught; but to bring disgrace upon the shaded streets of Doylestown, to humiliate a team of one's own friends—that would be terrible indeed!

Bobby Creighton understood David very well. If the opposing team could be demoralized, everyone passed to

David. The slim wiry boy could easily score four or five baskets in the first half, and the rout would be on. But when the opponents were big and tough—the favorites—Harry Moomaugh got most of the passes. He was rugged and fearless and never wilted under fire; so after he had mauled the guards for three quarters and been ejected on fouls, the team would pass to David, still fresh and springy, and David would shoot from any position and ring up three or four goals in a hurry.

David understood this strategy. He sensed that much as Bobby Creighton liked him, the coach knew that there was only one dependable, utterly fearless competitor on the team, and that one was Harry Moomaugh. The young fighter understood, too, and a warm friendship grew between the two stars. They always rode together when the team played away from home, and when in the distance the enemy city appeared they would share a moment of intense excitement. Each boy would mutter to himself: "They'll be laying for us tonight. Because we're the champs!"

At the gymnasium David and Harry would grab their bags and step into the cold air. "That's them!" the hangers-on would cry. "The big one's roughneck Moomaugh. Nnnyaaah!" But David was the special butt of jeers, for his habit of staying out of the roughhouses until he got a good pass infuriated the spectators. "There he is! Harper the Sleeper! Nnnyaaah!"

That was the glorious moment! To feel yourself among the hostile crowd, to hear them shouting at you, and to know that later that night when you dropped a couple in from the middle of the floor they would be cheering—that was exciting. At such moments he liked to be near Harry Moomaugh, for he knew that under his breath Harry was swearing: "Wait, you muggs! Wait till the whistle blows!"

But even more cherishable were the games at home when he could hear the last wild shout of obvious pride the people of Doylestown took in their team. At times the cheering became so intoxicating that David began to make impossible shots, as if he were not responsible for them, and the roar would increase; but always underlying it, like the firm beat of the sea beneath spurious waves, came the quiet voice of Bobby Creighton: "Come on, Harper!" It was the strongest voice David had ever known. It was his conscience and his will.

David's second summer at Paradise was more exciting

than the first. He became known as an important cashier. He began to shave, too, and stood very straight, for word had circulated that he was a star athlete.

After diligent application, he regained his nimbleness in making false change. Once or twice the conscience that had begun to develop in basketball troubled him, and he spoke to Mr. Stone. "Forget it," the lean gray man advised. "You got to accept the customs of any job. The Company don't call it stealing, if you concentrate on the customers. You and I are expected to make our salary off the peasants."

David became known as an incorruptible. He carried himself like a man and discovered with pleasure that he was now taller than Mr. Stone. He went several times to the secret room in the Coal Mine, but Nora had not yet returned from Florida. "She's a thin little number," big Betty joked, "but I'll bet she's giving that old man the ride of his life." Then a happy thought came to her. "There's a new girl here, Dave. You'd like her. Name's Louise."

"I was looking for Nora," David explained.

"I saw you in the Perkasie game," Betty added. "You were red hot."

"Thanks," David replied, retreating through the murky scaffolding.

Paradise was excellent that summer, for that was the year he became friends with Capt. John Philip Sousa, then an old man. For many years Sousa had conducted summer concerts at Paradise, where he was revered and loved. At his table in the big Casino celebrities gathered daily to pay him homage. The March King was modest, quiet, friendly to the young, and courteous to everyone. Mr. Stone said, "This is a young admirer of yours," and Capt. Sousa nodded gravely. He looked across the white and silvery Casino to where a man stood with a very beautiful woman. David noticed that the man was dark and that he moved with a delicate grace. But he forgot the man when he saw the young woman who that summer was singing for Capt. Sousa. Mary Meigs was then about twenty, slim, blue-eyed, blonde, and lovely in a breath-taking way. David never lost that first image of her, nor did he ever forget his first involuntary thought: "The man's embarrassed, but she likes to stand there. Look! She's turning her head so that more people can see her."

"Klementi!" Capt. Sousa cried. The tall man, blushing at the sound of his name, saluted the great bandmaster by clicking his heels and bowing stiffly from the waist. Sousa raised his right forefinger and dropped it, quite in the manner he used to start his concerts. The tall visitor led his partner to the table, and she walked with a grace that seemed to be unreal, keeping her head forward in a bored sort of way, but twisting it ever so slightly so that her exquisite profile showed to advantage.

"Miss Mary Meigs," Capt. Sousa began. "My friend Mr. Stone, and his friend, Master Harper." David winced at the appellation. "And this is Klementi Kol, a very fine musician of the Philadelphia Orchestra. Klementi is going to conduct his own orchestra during my vacation. My friends, be seated." He dropped his hands at them as if they were so many clarinetists. "How's your orchestra, Klim?" he inquired.

"I can't get all the men I want," Kol replied. "You can imagine how it is. Playing with Kincaid and Tabuteau all winter spoils you for the summer." The tall musician spoke with lovely grace.

"It's been pleasant up here," Sousa replied. "I do miss Victor Herbert, though." He chuckled. "People used to come to me and whisper, 'I like you ever so much better than Victor Herbert.' I'm sure they told him the same."

"What are you singing tonight, Miss Meigs?" Mr. Stone inquired.

"*Ah, Sweet Mystery of Life* and *Just a Kiss*," the lovely singer replied. David was delighted with the quality of her voice. He thought: "I've never seen such fine people. I'll bet she's in love with Mr. Kol." He hoped his surmise was correct.

As the dinner progressed—David's first in a fine restaurant—Sousa insisted that his guests occupy his private box at the concerts. David was so pleased by such an unexpected pleasure that he actually closed his eyes and bit his lips. Sousa noted this and asked, "Do you like music?" David did not reply and Mr. Stone nudged him.

"Me?" he blurted. "Oh, yes!"

"Then I'll play the encore for you," Sousa said graciously. "What would you like?"

David could think of nothing. He knew no music by name, but then he recalled his picnic with Mr. Paxson. "*Stars and Stripes!*" he shouted.

Capt. Sousa laughed and said, "We have to save that for

the last concert." He became interested in David and bent toward him. "What's your second choice?" he asked.

There was a wretched moment of silence and Mr. Stone guessed what was the matter. "How about *Semper Fidelis*?" he suggested.

"That's it!" David fairly shouted. Then, ashamed of himself and determined to retrieve his position, he took a blind stab. "Isn't that the one that goes . . ." He hummed very softly. Capt. Sousa smiled and patted him on the hand.

"That's exactly the way it goes," he said. "Only louder." David blushed. He wanted to throw his arms wide and embrace these exciting people. He said to himself: "Mr Stone was right! Suppose I had got mixed up with Max Volo? What if that spotter had caught me? I'd be in jail now." As on the basketball floor, the thought was horrible. He felt that everyone must be watching him squirm. Only Miss Meigs was. She smiled at him.

"What kind of music do you like best?" she asked.

"All kinds!" he replied expansively.

"Do you like *Carmen*?" she continued. "That's my favorite." David gulped. Again he had trapped himself. His mind started to work furiously. "What do I know about *Carmen*? I've heard that name before." Then he saw Old Daniel's book. There was the woodcut of the passionate gypsy.

"Yes," he exploded. "About the Spanish gypsy." Miss Meigs studied the boy's eager face and liked the frank look of joy it wore. She was about to speak when Capt. Sousa rose.

"In the second concert you'll hear excerpts from *Carmen*," he announced.

"*Carmen*! With a full band!" Klementi cried. "Excellent!" He shook Capt. Sousa's hand with pleasure. In the excitement of leaving the Casino and going to the concert David was forgotten by everyone except Miss Meigs. She continued to watch him and laughed to herself as she saw him studying Klementi Kol so as to know how to behave and how to say the right things, for less than three years ago Klementi had taught her the same things.

Between the first and second concerts Mr. Stone took his friends about the Park. He was careful to explain everything to Miss Meigs, and David clearly saw that Mr. Stone was proud to be seen with the handsome girl. Cool, fixing her hair with her left hand, tilting her chin when she was being watched, she glided along with her three escorts; and David discovered that he, too, was very proud when he heard visitors whispering, "That's Sousa's new singer!"

They rode on the gentler rides and laughed together on the gondola that took them through the dark Canals of Venice. The evening was spoiled, however, shortly after they left Venice, for David's name was called by a bright, brassy voice. It was Nora. She was dressed in a tight-fitting dress that accentuated her slimness and her full bosom. Her hair was in curls and she had on a good deal of make-up.

"Hello, kid!" she cried, and then, seeing the well-dressed people with David, she put her hand to her bright mouth and said, "I didn't know you were with a party."

David was embarrassed and wished that Nora had not seen him. Then he thought: "Well, she's my friend," and awkwardly he introduced her. Then he asked, "Whyn't you join us?" He hoped she would say no.

"Could I?" she asked eagerly. There was a long pause, during which David twisted his toes waiting for Mr. Stone to speak, but the gray cashier stared angrily at the lake. Finally David took Nora by the hand and said, "Sure, come along. It's not fair for Miss Meigs to have three men. Heh, heh." But nobody laughed.

On the rides Nora sat with David and put her arm about him, for even short dips frightened her, but she sensed that this embarrassed the boy and she whispered, "I feel rotten with these people. I don't belong." David looked at her and winked, even though he knew that the enraged Mr. Stone was watching him. In added perversity he insisted that Nora join them in Capt. Sousa's box, but this made Mr. Stone so furious that the concert was a chilly failure. That is, it was a failure until the very end of *Stars and Stripes*, when Nora gripped David and cried, "God! The way those flutes tear up and down! It makes you shiver!" and that was precisely how David always felt, but of all the people he would ever know in the world, only Nora would ever react to the music as he did.

He became glad that he had invited her, and in front of everyone he kissed her good night. This was too much for Mr. Stone, and when the others had left, he hauled David down to the lakeside. "You stupid fool!" he exclaimed. He would have struck David, but crowds had gathered for the fountain display. Instead he twisted the boy's arm until the skin ached. "I introduce you to my friends! Great musicians! And you dig up a cheap, perfumed little whore." He grew pale in the face and said harshly, "You're a poorhouse kid and you don't know anything. It's time you learned. There's two worlds, you stupid ass, and they don't mix. If you want to throw away your life in Max Volo's Coal Mine, all right. But you can't drag that filth into my parties! A cheap South Philadelphia whore!"

That night, when the rest of the poorhouse slept, David tried to write a poem. Sousa, Mr. Stone, Klementi Kol, and Nora were all mixed up in it, and it was terrible. He took a fresh sheet and wrote, almost without effort, a poem of clear and sensitive focus. It began: "*By the dark moss a dog-tooth violet . . .*" It was his first love poem, but in it no girl appeared. When he finished, dawn had come from the east, and he found that his poem expressed exactly what was in his heart. It was a love poem to the confused wonder of the world, the throbbing, simple things that had been about him since that first cold, silent night when his mother had carried him into the yard to listen for the wild geese flying north.

The day finally came when Capt. Sousa started his vacation, and then Klementi Kol took charge of the music. With a group of musicians from the Philadelphia Orchestra he formed the Kol Symphony. When the first concert was given, David listened attentively and decided firmly that a symphony orchestra was a pretty poor substitute for a band. There wasn't much noise and the pieces they played were not easy to whistle. He wondered contemptuously what Klementi Kol and his swaying fiddlers could do with a piece like *Field Artillery*! "What would they use for bass drums? Who would fire the pistol?"

At the second concert, however, Klementi started with that good music which David had learned from Capt. Sousa, *William Tell Overture*. Reluctantly David had to admit that this was pretty thrilling stuff, even with a symphony. Then Kol rapped for attention, and the audience leaned forward as if some great thing were to happen. The baton fell with startling suddenness, and from the orchestra came a whisper of strings, then a cascading melody, then flight and retreat, and epic marching. When the drums rumbled softly they seemed to be more like violins than tympani. The flutes and horns did strange, unpredictable things, and always the strings rustled on and danced and cried out. The music was unbearably majestic, and in that moment David swore: "I'll hear all the music in the world if it's like that!"

Others in the audience must have felt the same way, for they cheered and stamped and made Klementi take many bows. "What was that music?" David asked. A man in a high stiff collar and black suit smiled.

"You don't know that, sonny? Well, you just heard the music from *Tannhäuser*."

"What's that?" David inquired.

"It's an opera," the man beamed.

"I thought people sang in an opera," David said.

"Oh!" the man quickly explained. "A real opera is twice as good as this. Tonight was just the music."

"Twice as good?" David queried. When the man nodded enthusiastically, David stuck his eager nose into the night air and stared back. "Hmm," he said.

After the concert David felt that he must speak with Klementi Kol, so he dawdled by the bandstand until the musicians filed out.

Finally the tall conductor appeared, accompanied by Mary Meigs, fair and beautiful. David hurried up to them and mumbled, "Excuse me. I met you with Capt. Sousa."

"Of course you did!" the tall man replied, bowing graciously.

"I thought the music was wonderful," David said quietly.

"Thank you," Kol replied. "Do you work here in the Park?"

"Yes. I listen to the music whenever I can."

"Then why don't you come by some Tuesday or Thursday and help us practice?"

David did not know what to say or do. Obviously he should not shake hands, so he bowed from the waist, very low.

"How sweet!" Mary Meigs said. She smiled at the boy.

On Tuesday David was waiting at the bandstand at nine in the morning. He was still there, alone, at ten and at eleven. At eleven-thirty musicians started to appear, clean, interesting-looking men. Toward twelve Kol himself came onstage and seeing David cried, "Oh, no! You sit up here with me!" He placed David on a chair beside him and the rehearsal started. It was the first movement of Beethoven's *Seventh Symphony,* and from that noble start David launched into the full, wonderful world of symphonic music. He felt an immediate sympathy between himself and the music and within a week he sensed the perfect structure of the finest symphonies.

Kol insisted that David have lunch with him, and occasionally Mary Meigs joined them. She called David, "Our young Toscanini," and from that chance remark David built his knowledge of the leading conductors.

And the things they talked about! One day Klementi said, "I wasn't much older than you are now, David, when the new century began, and we celebrated wildly. I had just fallen in love with a model who lived near the Seine, and we were in a café when news came: 'Wilde is dead!' We knew this great poet, and now he was dead. Persecuted and outcast, he died in Paris. So the model and I went to his funeral and wept for that fine artist."

"Was he an artist or a poet?" David inquired.

"A poet. A very great one. Do you know his poems?"

"I never heard of him or his poems," David admitted.

"*Diable!* What do they teach you in school?"

"Sir Walter Scott."

"Ach, no!" Furiously Klementi left the lunch table and dragged David back to the bandstand, muttering as he went, "Scott! No Keats, I suppose. No Shelley? And of course no Spitteler or Baudelaire! Ah, the corruption of youth!" He rummaged among his personal luggage and produced a dog-eared volume of poems. "Read this!" he commanded.

One of the poems David could not understand. He called it *The Ballad of Reading Gaol*. The title was confusing and finally he asked Klementi about it. "It's simple," Kol said. "That's where they put him, in Reading gaol." David looked at the title again and blushed. "So while he was in gaol," Klementi continued, "he studied this man who had killed his sweetheart. Now do you understand?"

"Yes." David said weakly.

Kol brought David many books that summer. He said that if you did not read when you were young, you might never catch the disease and then what would be the use of living? The books were strange and not easy to understand. There was, for example, that twisted thing called *Renée Mauperin*, written by two brothers. Almost nothing happened in it, but you remembered the scenes for a long time. The same was true of that astonishing tale of a madman in Russia who painted his house blue "just because he wanted to." A sillier story had never been written, but for more than a year David looked at certain persons with a kindlier eye, saying to himself: "Let him alone. He's painting his house blue."

The conductor said, "Now's the time to store up ideas.

Then when you're a man and something happens! Behold! You have a treasure house with which to compare it. Why do you like *Field Artillery* so much? I'll tell you. Because you know the drummer is going to fire a pistol. Well, my young friend—and don't breathe a word of this to Capt. Sousa, bless him—that's a poor way to win an effect. Now in *Whistler and His Dog* you look for the bark. That's one degree better. But in *Tannhäuser*, what? Only the divine music. You catch what I mean. You can teach a horse to recognize a pistol shot. A bark is important to another dog, but not to a man. For it takes a mind to remember the rise and fall of music." He whirled about the empty stage and hummed a few passages from Wagner. At their now-familiar sound David's eyes brightened, and Klementi cried, "See! The glow of recognition!"

He sat down and spoke very earnestly with David. "When you are at home with Immanuel Kant and Beethoven and Rubens and Thomas Jefferson . . . Then you're living." He paused and studied the placid lake where lovers were rowing, and he said, "You haven't much time, David. You don't know Mozart or Tschaikowsky. I'll wager you haven't read Turgenev or Goethe. I suppose you don't even know Balzac?"

"He's a writer, isn't he?" David asked.

"He's no one thing, Balzac. He's an architect and a musician and a poet. Let's call him a novelist. He and Thomas Hardy . . ." Suddenly the musician slapped his forehead. "I'll bet you don't even know Hardy, do you?" He brought David a copy of *Jude the Obscure,* and if David had once imagined himself to be Hector, he now actually was Jude. With breathless anxiety he read the book and shuddered. He learned the meaning of the terrible jest the new fat man played at the poorhouse. This fat man sat in the long hall as the men came up from dinner, and he said in a sepulchral voice as each inmate walked past, "There but for the grace of God, go I." Then he bellowed and slapped his leg and roared at his own humor. When David finished reading *Jude,* he thought the fat man's joke obscene.

He said to Klementi, "The book gives me an awful feeling inside, as if Jude were I."

"He is you," Kol replied. "Only by a miracle have you been saved. Don't you understand? If you were a poorhouse boy in Poland, or Russia, or even France . . . God, your life would be desolate, now and forever. In America, things are . . . well . . . different."

"Are you an American?" David asked.

Kol looked away and after a long time said, "Artists are citizens of everywhere."

In August the red-bound novels of Balzac began to appear as Klementi Kol promised they would. The first one was a curious thing, ill suited for a boy to read: *Memoirs of Two Young Married Women.* For a brief moment David thought it was merely another cheap love story bound in hard covers. He found to his intense delight that Balzac was never *merely* anything, not merely a love story nor merely an adventure story nor merely an analysis. Balzac was a complete interpretation of life, and the great novelist's tortured style was much to David's liking. From the very first chapter the boy sensed that here was a writer whose words could be lived.

The second Balzac novel Klementi sent him was in most ways the finest book David read as a boy: *The Quest of the Absolute.* It told about a half-demented Dutchman trying to make the philosopher's stone. Clays was his name and he lived in Douai. Into his fruitless search he poured all of his resources, and found nothing. As David read the story he was transfixed with the reality of it. He wondered: "How could Balzac write this if he did not know my poorhouse?" Yet there it was, in the simple grandeur of that story: all that David had felt about the meaning of life up to that time. Clays was so much like Old Daniel that David sometimes had a wonderful feeling of the old man's continued existence.

One aspect of the story David could not understand. Clays was attached to certain paintings by Dutch masters. It was as if the paintings had living personalities. He spoke to Klementi about this one day. "Why was the selling of those paintings such a tragedy?" he asked.

"Haven't you ever seen paintings?" the musician asked.

"I have a Rembrandt in my room," David replied.

"But the real thing?" Klementi asked. "No? Then we must go!" He made David hire a substitute for one day. That morning he met the boy at Paradise and took him into Philadelphia on a Route 55 trolley. At the end of the line the musician and his guest walked up to Broad Street and down that ample thoroughfare. "This is where I play music in the wintertime," Klementi said. David looked at the red Academy of Music. On a poster he saw Stokowski's picture. He thought the face looked interesting. Another poster showed Klementi Kol himself, thin and fiery, about to play his violin. Farther down Broad Street Klementi stopped at a dirty, ordinary-looking graystone house. "This is it!" he said with some excitement.

"What's here?" David inquired.

"This is the Johnson Collection!" Klementi said in the manner of a priest indicating a fragment of the true cross.

They climbed a short flight of stone steps and went into a dark hall. A very old man in a blue suit hurried up, nodded to Klementi, and clapped his hands. Slowly another old man pulled some cords and turned on the lights. About him, in rich, crowded display, hung the gems of the Johnson Collection.

The first original picture that David ever saw was a small, brightly lighted scene of a drunken man on a donkey which was being urged on by three fauns with men's bodies and horses' hoofs. They were by a seashore. A funny little boat stood behind the men, and on the opposite shore appeared a tiny town of towers.

"Oh!" David cried. "That's just like the town Daniel told me about. That's in Italy, isn't it?" He hurried up to the picture. Klementi smiled and thought: "That lovely Cima, golden and happy through the centuries, spelling its charm again."

"How do you say that name?" David asked.

"Cheemah dah Konayleeahno," Klementi replied. In the dark museum, cluttered with the glories of Europe, the musician gave David his first lesson in Italian, showed him the Rembrandts and the Rubenses, the Botticelli, the Breughel, and the superb Flemish primitives.

"Which one do you like best?" David asked.

"Well, most people say that very small Van Eyck is the gem of the collection. I don't like it much."

"I don't either. It's too small."

Klementi smiled. "I think I prefer the one you saw first. It's such a happy thing! Before concerts I come down here to look at it and I feel deep and happy all over!"

"You mean the one I liked? That's yours, too?"

"Not exactly," Klementi said. "I waver. Really, I guess it's the Crivelli." He led David upstairs to a dark room. The old attendant followed them and turned on the lights. "This one," Klementi said.

David stood before a beautifully decorated picture in which two grief-stricken baby angels mourned for the dead Christ they held between them. The agony of the scene was so apparent and the crucifixion of Christ so terribly visible in that gaunt body that David could say nothing. He and the musician looked at the masterpiece. The boy needed not one word of art instruction, none of the jargon or the cant of painting. This was a superb picture, a terrifying yet glorious thing, satisfying to the point of overflowing.

"Can anybody come in here?" David asked. "They knew you."

"Certainly anyone can come in!" Klementi said. "It's a gift to all the people of Philadelphia."

David looked around the room. There was the dark and speckled Guardi, the lusty Wouwermans, the Signorelli, and the calm beauty of Cuyp. "Oh!" he cried. "Those are the painters that Clays had, aren't they? Cuyp was one of them!"

For almost two months Mr. Stone did not speak to David. The austere short-change artist was still outraged that David should have brought a prostitute into the middle of his party, and he would not even nod aloofly to David as he did to the other cashiers. Finally David said to himself. "I've been a damned fool. I'll go apologize."

But Mr. Stone saw him first and said, "Hello, kid. I'm sorry about that night. How's a poorhouse kid supposed to know?" He explained that for thousands of years men have known two kinds of women—and have treasured each— "but a wise man never mixes them."

"I don't bother with Nora any more," David said.

"You're wise," Mr. Stone replied, and then so suddenly that David guessed how much the lonely man had missed him, the cashier said, "I'll tell you what, kid. I've never told anyone the real tricks of short-changing bills. How'd you like to work with me for a day or two?" It was arranged in the head office, and David sat with the icy, gentleman ticket-seller.

"The government makes bills so that smart men like you and me can grow rich," Mr. Stone explained. "Everytime a boob lays down a big bill, make believe it's a one and keep the change for yourself."

"I try to," David replied.

"Ah, but you have no system. Work out an iron-clad routine. If a man places any kind of a bill larger than a one before you, give him the correct small change at once and try to shoo him on."

"I can do that," David said with determination.

"That's what I mean, kid," the gray-haired man said with

the only enthusiasm he ever showed, a slight tightening of his eyelids. "I almost came over to see you last month . . . To tell you that if you hadn't of had guts enough to pick up that whore when you saw we didn't want you to, I'd of had no respect for you. I could of bashed your brains in, but I admired you, at the same time."

"I sort of felt she was my friend," David explained.

Mr. Stone ignored him and said, "You're a good, steely-nerved kid." He then briefed David on ways to defraud the boobs. "Confidentially," he whispered, "I make about two hundred dollars a week on bills."

David applied himself to Mr. Stone's theories. Like all other cashiers he found the two-dollar bills to be the short-changer's delight. Even customers who habitually tore off the corners of such bills nevertheless forgot they had them. David got a glint in his eye whenever he saw one of the lucky twos.

He concentrated so upon his evil artistry that he was able to forget Nora. Sometimes he saw her straggling through the Park. Once she stopped by his booth and asked, "Your high-class friends tell you to stay away? I'm sorry, kid. I wouldn't hurt you for the world." David treated her as if she were a customer complaining about short change.

"That's all right, Nora," he said, but when she was gone he was appalled at himself for having spoken so abruptly.

He forgot her next morning when it was announced that henceforth the Company would install change-making machines for each cashier. Coins rolled from the machines into a metallic tray with enough clatter to remind even the most forgetful customer of his money. Mr. Stone met David at lunch and reasoned, "It should help with the bills." He moved his machine far to the left so that customers would have to reach in the direction of their own motion. His theory was correct. Grabbing for their noisy nickels and dimes did divert attention from the bills. Mr. Stone said he was making more money with the machine than without it.

Max Volo studied the new system for two days and then slipped into David's booth with a completely different angle. "It's sensational!" he exploded. "To you I'm giving it free for a workout." Deftly he filed away two spots in the coin chute. Into these spots he rested a quarter and a dime. Then he was ready.

"Watch this woman!" he cried. He short-changed her a dime and a quarter.

"That's not the right change!" she whined.

PARADISE 123

"It's stuck again!" Max said patiently. "Knock the chute right there." The woman did so and the dime rolled down. Happily, she picked it up and smiled at Volo. When she was gone, Max flipped a quarter into his pocket.

"If she still squawks about the quarter, why you let her knock the other side of the chute!" It was uncanny, the way Max had the machine rigged. The special dime and quarter never rolled loose, and only one could be dislodged at a time. David worked the system all one day, and he was astonished at how often a man who had been short-changed thirty-five cents would be as pleased as a child when he was permitted to recover the dime all by himself.

Max Volo sold the idea to forty-three cashiers for $10 apiece. Mr. Stone didn't buy. He had figured it out for himself the second day.

Preoccupied with art and music and reading and short-changing, David would have kept his promise not to see Nora if it had not been for the Sheik. At the Canals of Venice the cashier was caught selling old tickets, and David was promoted to the second-best job in Paradise. He moved his PLEASE sign to the new box and lamented to Mr. Stone, "I notice whenever a guy sells tickets twice he lets his board go to pieces." Mr. Stone laughed and said that so far as he was concerned the easiest way to anything was always the poorest.

The Sheik was a low-grade moron who hauled gondolas from the low level of the Canal up to the high level where the passengers climbed aboard. The Sheik was powerful, with heavy eyebrows and a guttural moan in which few words could be distinguished. The men at Venice had to watch the Sheik, for the moron delighted to help young girls out of the gondolas, but he grabbed their arms too tightly and had to be kept below on the lift, where he had worked for eighteen years.

David first spoke to him at a taffy machine, where the Sheik stood watching the mechanical arms twisting the sweet burden of mint and honey. "My God, 'at smells good!" the monster drooled. He sniffed the air like a dog.

"Would you like me to get you some?" David asked.

"Fanks," the Sheik slobbered. "I jus' like to smell. Hurts ma toof," he explained, disclosing a jagged molar.

"Then we'll have a drink," David suggested. They had two

loganberries, and the hulking man clapped his hand on David's shoulder.

"I like you," he grunted. "How 'bout you get me job up front. I like to he'p the priiy gi'ls."

But the Sheik was kept below. Occasionally David rode with him through the dark papier-mâché scenes of Venice. The ride was distinguished because the gondolas drifted noiselessly past animated scenes in which mechanical peasants kissed dairymaids who kicked one leg high in the air. There was a palace, too, labeled in big letters THE DOGES PALACE. David often wondered where the apostrophe should be put, but most customers saw only the mechanical princess who blew kisses to each gondola. She was the one the Sheik got into trouble with.

One day, when there were few people in Paradise, David and some handlers rode the canals to check on leakage. As their gondola swung around a corner leading to the palace, the inspecting party looked up in disgust. In a bestial, indecent manner the Sheik was making love to the mechanical princess.

He was not fired. He was half-crazy, true, but he was also very strong and it would take two men to replace him. He was made to buy a new dress for the princess, and he was teased a great deal. One of the men brought him a little doll to play with. He grinned and kept hauling the heavy gondolas onto the lift.

It was now late August, and David sat idly in his booth watching the moron's great sweating arms muscle the gondolas about. The heat was intense and the Sheik seemed like an animal, panting at his work. Then suddenly the massive form stopped and stared past David. The Sheik's dull eyes brightened, and he began to lick his lips. In surprise David looked in the direction of the moron's stare and saw that Nora, in a new dress, was standing by the booth.

"Hello," she said.

"Hello, Nora," he replied.

"It's hot today, isn't it?" she asked.

"The Park doesn't like girls to hang around cashiers," David said.

"The Park knows me," Nora replied. "Now if you don't want me to hang around . . ."

"Don't go!" David blurted. There was a long silence.

"I haven't seen you much this year," Nora finally said. "How do you like my new dress?"

"It's very pretty," David said. His relief came and David left the box. "How'd you like to ride the Hurricane?" he asked.

"Say, I'd like that!" Nora said. "It scares me, but I like it." When they approached the ride, David avoided the main booth and slipped into the second-fare platform. As they rode up the steep incline Nora huddled close to David and said, "I get it. Mr. Stone don't want you to be seen with me." David did not reply and suddenly their car shot into its wild decline. Nora clung to him and cried, "God, this is worse than before," yet even more than before she thrilled to the violence of the Hurricane.

After the ride David asked, "Why do you like it so much if you're so afraid?" and the thin girl looked at him and said, "A short life and a merry!"

"What do you mean, short life?" He was annoyed at this sentiment and led the excited girl to a bench by the lake. He was looking at her and speaking to her as if she were a man.

"Nobody lives forever," Nora said. Her good teeth and still-clear eyes belied this, and David laughed.

"You talk like a ghost," he said.

"Sometimes I feel like one," she said. "This sun feels good, don't it? Mostly I'm cold."

"How did you like Florida?" David asked, still talking with her on a man-to-man basis.

The thin girl, who grew prettier as she grew older, laughed merrily. "What a trip!" she said. "His wife went along. She said a man deserved one last fling when he was past fifty. Well, I gave him a good one. One day his wife saw me in a bathing suit and said, 'You're skinny!' Her! She must of weighed a ton. Her husband laughed at her and said, right to her face, 'My wife is the best woman on this earth, and one of the biggest.' We had a fine time, I can tell you."

And as she talked she became a woman. Later on David could remember exactly when this occurred. She was telling about Florida, laughing at the man's jovial wife, when she moved her position and her dress caught above her left knee. David saw that this knee was rounded. It bore no protruding bones as his did, and it looked quite unlike the knees of basketball players when they scrimmaged. The dress fluttered and the knee was gone, but David wanted Nora very much.

She sensed this, perhaps from his breathing, and said, "Remember what we said on closing night last year? Summer's almost gone, David."

Wildly he told his secret. "I followed you to the Coal Mine

one night, Nora. I wanted to talk with you and even make love with you. But I looked through a crack and you had a man. And the new girl wasn't wearing anything . . ."

"You were afraid," Nora said softly.

"Yes! And I swore I'd never go there again. And I never shall."

Nora drew back and looked at the young cashier. He was freckled and snub-nosed, throbbing with fire and vast dreams; and in her own lung there was a persistent cough. Not even Florida had warmed that away. "David," she said quietly. "When you looked at the new girl undressed and saw her breasts . . ." she paused. "I'm twice that pretty," she said.

"I swore I'd never go back there," David repeated, burning to touch this frail girl.

"We don't have to go there," she said quietly. He swallowed very hard and nervously cried out to a passing man.

"What's the time, mister?"

"It's six-twenty," the man said.

"Gee, thanks! Time to go!" He rose and hurried back to Venice. Nora trailed a few steps behind him, so he waited for her, and then she walked with tiny steps, smiling at him, and beneath her new dress he could sense her knees. "Maybe we'll find a place," he muttered huskily.

And that very night the Sheik came to thank David for being a friend. "You the bes' frien' I ever got," the lowering hulk blubbered. His eyes were not close-set like those of idiots but wide and expressive. "Because you my frien' I like to show you somethin'." He insisted that David follow him along the canal paths and into the caverns of Venice. There he showed David the interior of the palace from which the mechanical princess threw kisses. It was a small room walled in by canvas. A single light showed so as to reflect upon the clicking princess. Outside the canal ran, and even as David stood in the strange palace he could hear a gondola drift by with boys making jokes about the princess. Voices echoed along the canal and then deep silence followed until the next gondola drifted by.

"You can peek," the Sheik said, ducking low behind the princess and peering into the darkness. A gondola passed with a single couple. Thinking themselves alone, they embraced passionately and David looked away. "Mos' nights I s'eep here," the ape-man drooled. "But if you . . ."

"I don't want it," David snapped. "What made you think . . ."

"I saw 'at priiy gi'l," the moron said. He looked right at David and his lips were slightly parted. "If you an' 'at gi'l . . .'"

"Let me out of here!" David cried. That night he made change very fast, his arms tight to his sides and his full attention on the sliding coins. At midnight he checked in his accounts and hurried directly to the trolley. He breathed easily when he felt the clanging wheels turn on their noisy way to the poorhouse. Safe behind Door 8 he thought of Nora. "She said she was prettier than the other girl," he mused, thinking of the delicate curves of the first breasts he had seen. "How could she be?" Then the flashing memory of Max Volo's post card hung above his bed. Now he did not deceive himself. He said, "I want to be with her. Tomorrow I'll see her and we'll arrange it." With that admission he forced himself to go to sleep.

But in the morning he said, "I won't go to the Park today! Mr. Stone was right. Why, Nora . . ." Reassuring himself that he did not want to see the girl, he fooled around the poorhouse until the last possible trolley had gone. "Well," he breathed easily, "that's that!" Then he dashed down to the highway and flagged a truck which took him to Paradise.

The head cashier said, "You were eight dollars over last night." The other cashiers laughed and the head continued, "What were you dreaming about?"

At work David avoided the Sheik. When the hulking man came to his booth David ordered him back to work. Then, although the day was still cool, he began to perspire. He wiped his face and muttered, "I know just what'll happen! Mr. Stone'll come along and say, 'How about dinner with Capt. Sousa?' and we'll have a fine time!" He chuckled and felt good, reasoning, "I'll talk with Sousa and tell him what to play! Won't that be something!" But his pleasure was short lived, for he stopped daydreaming and saw a man who looked like the Baptist minister when he preached at the poorhouse: "Sin is upon you, and only the blood of the Lord can wash it away, not the waters of the Neshaminy nor of the Mississippi nor even of Jordan. For sin is upon you!"

He felt sick, for now he knew what sin was. In the poorhouse it had been stealing cheese, and Toothless Tom had always done that, but he had helped eat it. That was sinful. But now sin was Nora and the Sheik's room, and he knew that was really sinful. "I feel awful!" he said to the assistant

manager. "I'm going home." He hurried from the booth and
ran toward the main office, but as he did so, he heard a voice
calling to him.

"Where's the fire, Dave?" Nora cried. He stopped and
looked toward the rootbeer stand. In a simple gingham dress,
peasant style, buttoning in back and drawn tight against her
bosom, the thin girl stood with a glass of loganberry in her
hand. "Taste it!" she said. "It's cool." Her hair cascaded
down in the sunlight.

"I couldn't sleep last night," David said, sipping her drink,
and the fizzing water tasted brackish, for he knew that his
resolves—and the pleading voice of the Baptist minister—
were lost. He added, "When I was in bed, I could see you in
my room."

"I would like to be in bed with you," she said simply. And
then she slipped her arm through his, and they walked back
to the Canals of Venice.

The assistant manager saw them and joked, "You feelin' a
lot better, I see."

"Were you sick?" Nora asked, her breath catching.

"I didn't feel so good," David explained, and then she
understood. She gripped his arm and whispered. "It's all
right to be afraid, the first time. Everybody is! You should
be a girl! I can tell you! But you'll remember today as
long . . ." She jumped back and cried, "God Almighty!
What's that thing?"

David was glad of a chance to laugh. "That's the Sheik,"
he said.

"What a monster!" Nora cried.

"He's lending us his place," David explained. As if the
monstrous thing had touched her, Nora shivered.

"It's all right?" she asked, and that afternoon, during his
relief, David led her into the Venetian castle. The room had
nothing but a wooden bed with a rope spring and a single
unshaded bulb that lighted the princess. "Can we turn that
out?" Nora asked.

"No," David said. "That's part of the scenery." Nora
clasped her arms across her waist.

"I don't mind if you don't mind," she said.

"I'm sorry it's such a place," David said, kissing her awkwardly and fumbling at her tight buttons.

Nora sat upon the bed and smiled up at her agitated lover.
"Dave," she said softly, "when you love a girl be very
gentle. Take it easy. Say nice things and don't rush. Don't

be like those lunks at Max Volo's." She indicated that he was to sit by her and when he had done so she ran her fingers through his hair. "It's criminal," she said, "that men have to lose their hair."

David continued to work upon the tight buttons and Nora teased him again. Then quickly she exhausted her lungs and the buttons slipped easily through the cloth. "Why couldn't you sleep last night?" she whispered.

Her dress had now worked loose and the silver cascade of her body tumbled forth. David stared for a moment at the miracle he had accomplished and then buried his lips against her bosom. She clasped his head and after a long moment asked again why he had not slept. "Because you haunted me," he said, "and because I was saying a poem over and over to myself."

"A poem?" Nora asked nervously.

"Yes!" he replied, and for a moment the urgency left him. "That first night you joined our party I wrote a poem. I didn't think then that you were mixed up in it. It was all about dog-tooth violets . . ."

"What are they?" Nora asked.

"Haven't you ever seen one?" he asked, and quickly he told her of the imperial flower of spring and of how from his earliest days . . .

"What was the poem?" she asked.

He recited the verses: "*By the dark moss a dog-tooth violet . . .*" and as he said the words he realized that this poem like all poems was dedicated to his love, not his mystic love of the vast world, but his slim, pretty, warm Nora. "I was thinking of you when I wrote it," he said, and his hands went to her soft, rounded knees.

The effect of this poem upon Nora was even greater than upon David. She had not learned in school that men have traditionally, when young and foolish or when old and very wise, dedicated their finest thoughts to the full love of some woman, so she was unprepared for the idea; but even without instruction she sensed that it was sweet and proper for David to have thought of her. "Imagine!" she whimpered. "Before, I never even got so much as a letter. Not from no one." She buried her head upon his shoulder and rested thus while David pulled away her clothes. Then she pressed his face to hers and kissed him a hundred times. "I knew this was right," she whispered. "You got nothing to fear, Dave. You'll never forget this night. I'll make your old poem look sick."

On the other side of the canvas wall soft waters of the canal kept drifting past in metal troughs. In the darkness the Sheik stood guard, sacrificing his evening hour to the young lovers. In drifting gondolas boys and girls and pregnant women and old men swept by. They stared at the mechanical Venetian princess, and the Sheik, who peered at them with one eye through a slit he had made years ago in the palace wall, sneered at the travelers, wondering what they would think if they could see the real princess behind the canvas: for he could see her! He had cut a peephole into the room, and he swore in his dumb way that no girl had ever been so beautiful.

Like a summer storm exploding through long prepared grasslands, David's desire for Nora rapidly exceeded the bounds of both reason and propriety. At first he fooled himself with resolutions like: "Well, that's that! Never again. Mr. Stone was right." Then he tried the usual manly chatter: "Well, there's got to be a first time for everything. A guy's got to grow up. If you never try, you'll never know." But there was always a residue of experience not covered by any phrases. Nora was a powerful girl, adept in the ways of love and hovering upon the brink of intensity. She had a rare gift of sharing, and she wrapped David very closely to her, as much by the tentacles of her mind as by her hungry arms and legs.

On three successive afternoons David led her to the Venetian palace, and they were days of explosive sharing. The Sheik, unknown to the lovers, stood guard and panted heavily as he watched Nora. He was prepared, therefore, when David approached him and said, "If I pay your room rent, will you sleep in town?"

"I be glad to," the giant replied.

David told Nora, "I don't want you ever to go back to the Coal Mine," he said.

"I can't live here," she said simply.

"Why can't you get a room somewhere?" David insisted.

"With what?" she asked, holding up her empty hands.

"With this," David replied, handing her a roll of bills.

"I can't take your money, Dave," she said. "You and me's different."

He flushed and said quickly, "Yes! We are different! That's why I don't want you to go back to Max's." She was about to explain to him that winter was coming and that she had to depend on Max, but caution told her not to speak.

"All right," she said. "We'll stay here tonight. It'll be fun." Then, while David returned to his booth, she slipped out and talked with Max. "He's a good clean kid, you know that, Max. I'm dropping out of the Coal Mine, but I'll see you in Philly."

So Max was the first to know—after the Sheik—and before the Park closed the quick little man stopped by Venice and said, "Somebody tells me you're stealing one of my girls." David colored and grew furious, but Max ignored this. "It's a good idea, kid, but I got a better one. Why leave her when winter comes? Why don't you move into Philly and work in the theatre I'm buyin' into? What a time we could have!"

Not realizing the extreme inappropriateness of his reply, David said, "I can't quit school. I'm only fifteen."

Max leaned against the booth and laughed outright. "You're too young to quit school but you're runnin' off with one of my girls. This is gettin' to be a screwy world. What's Mr. Stone goin' to say?"

"It's none of his business," David replied bravely. "Now why don't you beat it. You see that gorilla over there?" He pointed to the dripping Sheik. "First thing you know, I'll sic him on you." He was surprised at his words and quickly laughed at his own joke.

"This whole thing is costing me money," Max said, not joking.

"Beat it!" David replied, and he was no longer joking, either.

That night, when Paradise closed, he hurried along the canals and found Nora waiting in the palace. "We can turn off the light now," he said. Outside, the Sheik frowned and then grew happy as Nora said, "Let's leave it on, at least till I pile my clothes in the corner. I don't want to look like a ragamuffin in the morning." David was glad she said this, for he had never seen a girl undress, and the soft ripple of her clothes was a delight. He watched her fold each piece neatly and then turn to face him as she had faced the camera for Max Volo.

"You're like a cat we had in the barn," he said.

"If there's one thing I'm not, it's a cat," she objected. Then, reaching high above her head so that she looked more than ever like a stretching cat, she turned out the light. The Sheik hung about the palace for some hours until all talking died, and then he crept away and went to the bed David had arranged for him in the village.

David found that actually sleeping with a girl was much different from being with her for a passionate hour. "It's like being married," Nora said snugly, making herself into a capital C inside the curve of his body. But to David it was more than being married. He had never before, in his memory, slept with another human being. The sudden warmth of this body next to his, the smell of hair, and the noise of breathing were strange to him. Nor could he decide what to do with his arms. "Nora!" he finally had to cry, "roll over. My arm's about to drop off."

"It's asleep," she said drowsily. "Shake it."

Only fitfully could David doze that night. He tried to stay awake to savor the feel of that rare warmth. Impulsively at times he drew the sleeping body closer to him, as if to make her compensate for all the nights he had slept in his cold poorhouse bed. When she rolled over, her sharp hipbones dug into him and he laughed with pleasure. He felt them and compared them to his own. Nora's were like needles. Then he felt her knees and could not understand why they were so rounded. He was much annoyed that sleeping face to face was impossible, and so he made himself a curve inside Nora's curve, and she sleepily threw her arms about his chest and strands of her hair crept across his face, and her knees jabbed into the V in back of his legs, and she was like a warm blanket to his back, and in that position he fell asleep.

If Nora had meant to David only the newness of sex, her fascination for him would soon have worn away; but she became also the symbol of human warmth, something he had not known before, so that when Mr. Stone and his friends lectured him about Nora they always met a wall of stubbornness, for they did not see Nora as David saw her. "She's a wretched thing," Mr. Stone said on his last visit to David's booth. "The whole Park is talking about this and you're going to ruin yourself."

"It's nobody's business!" David insisted.

"It's everybody's business when a good kid makes a damn fool of himself," Mr. Stone argued. "Remember when you started taking second fares? I told you how you should always watch which way a man was headed and then ease him along. Well, right now, kid, you're headed for the junk heap." The gray man looked at David with open disgust and asked for the last time, "You won't change your mind?"

"Nora is all right," David countered.

"Of course she is!" Mr. Stone snapped. "She's a clean, sweet Sunday-school girl. You know that and I know. But does the Park know? Kid, did you ever hear about the dog and the railroad tracks? This dog was hopping across the tracks when a locomotive snipped off the end of its tail. The dog yelped and turned around to see what had happened. Another train came along, whoosh! And cut off the dog's head. And the moral of this story is: Never lose your head for a little piece of tail!" He stamped away from the booth, and that afternoon the relief cashier said, "I hear you're all mixed up with Max Volo's girls. That's bad, kid."

David's only support came from an unexpected source. During the second week of his shameless attachment to Nora, Klementi Kol stopped by to see him. "Mr. Stone asked me to talk with you," the tall conductor said. "He thinks you're ruining your life."

David polished his change board vigorously and said, "Mr. Stone is wrong."

"Of course he is!" Kol agreed. "He's never been in love. But a boy who isn't interested in girls isn't much of a boy. It's no good saying, 'Wait till you're thirty and some nice girl comes along.' There's no good to that, is there?"

David looked up at the tall Pole and said, "Are you kidding me, Mr. Kol?"

The musician looked away and asked quietly, "How would I dare?"

"Then wait a minute!" David cried eagerly. He called the assistant manager and told him to watch the booth. "I don't care if you sell a thousand old tickets," he said. Then he crawled out to join Mr. Kol. "I need to talk to you," he said.

They went to a bench by the lake and the conductor said, "In Warsaw I used to watch families weep when their sons fell in love with prostitutes or actresses. But it never signified. A young boy who has not fallen desperately in love has missed getting started in the world of feeling. At any age love is wrong only if it means nothing."

"I don't understand," David said.

"You!" the musician said slowly. "You must be the criterion of any love."

"What's a criterion?" David asked.

The conductor grew impatient. "There's only one test, David. Does the love you feel make you a bigger and a stronger person? Do you spend your mind and heart and goodness on this little prostitute, or only your body? Always ask yourself that about any love, for by this test thousands of proper marriages in Philadelphia, or Warsaw, are filthy, terrible things. But if any love makes you stronger and more determined to share, then it's much finer than most people ever attain."

David and his mentor stared at the lake. Boats with white sails drifted back and forth, toyed with by vagrant winds that could not make up their minds. The carrousels played *Faust*, and dust, like jewels, hung in the air. David said simply, "I had more than three hundred dollars saved. I don't know for what. I made Nora take it, because she ought to have things." His lip began to tremble and the musician looked away. After a long silence David said, "A man came to our poorhouse once . . . Mr. Kol, I saw a lot of old men die. But this man had a cough and I thought the rest of us would go crazy listening to him. He couldn't clear his lungs, and finally he died. Nora has that kind of cough . . ." He lost control of his voice, and his eyes filled to the brimming point. He wanted to rub them but was ashamed to do so.

Klementi Kol waited for a moment and then observed, "If a relationship is spiritually sound, a minor question still remains. Can it hurt you in some other way? Will it cost you your job? Will it prevent you from getting ahead? Might it alienate your friends? *Alienate* means to *make angry*, like Mr. Stone. There's nothing more difficult in life than answering those questions about a sexual relationship that is spiritually very right." The tall man looked steadfastly at the lake and said, "You'll see more men kill themselves spiritually that way than any other. They love a girl but feel she won't help them to get ahead, whatever that phrase means. And so they make the terrible compromise, and when they're fifty, they're ahead . . . and they are desolate."

No person in recent years had made so much sense as Klementi Kol, and David wanted to ask him many questions, but he still had not gained control of his voice, and after a moment Kol continued. "I am sure old men forget what it was to be young and to be wholly in love. Not even I can remember those breathless moments. That's why they give old men important jobs and big salaries and orchestras to lead. To pay us back for the terrible loss we have sustained."

The musician stared at the lake, and David felt that it was

he, Kol, who needed comfort. In a low voice the boy asked, "Then you don't think I'm being a fool?"

"Of course you are!" Kol laughed. "But I can't give you Balzac one week and then deny life the next." Great laughter was in his eyes and he held David's hands. "You'll love this little girl, and she'll die, and you'll break your heart and wish that you had never lived, and some day you'll be a man. For hearts are like springs. They snap back."

It was then that David knew how deeply he loved Nora. He said, "I've talked her into going out to Denver, Mr. Kol. It's very high there, you know, and she can get a job. A waitress, maybe. Next summer, when school's out, I'll go to Denver myself . . ."

"You've taken a lot of responsibility, haven't you?" Kol asked.

"Maybe we'll stay in Colorado," David said eagerly. "Maybe she'll get well."

"That's possible," Kol said quietly. "But promise me one thing, David. Before you do anything big like going to Denver, promise you'll talk to me or Mr. Stone."

"I thought you were disgusted with Mr. Stone."

"In some ways he's a very intelligent man. Neither of us wants you to get into trouble, David."

"I'll behave myself!" David promised. "And I'll sure keep out of trouble."

As the season drew to a close, David worked diligently at short-changing. He must save enough money to start Nora in the West. He added two hundred dollars to the fund he had already provided, and she said, "I don't need so much dough! I'll go by bus and have a job in no time." But he continued to cadge dimes and quarters from the customers, and he continued also to use the Sheik's palace.

"It's very damp in here for you," he pointed out to Nora.

"It was worse at Max's," she reasoned. "That was dirty damp. Here the water keeps movin'."

"You'll find it good and dry in Denver," he assured her. Like a schoolboy he rattled off a table of facts about humidity. He was surprised at how methodically he and Nora now talked.

"It's like I said," she laughed. "We're as good as married!" They came to know each other casually, often to sleep without awareness of sex, and always to think of the other's well being. In fact, David began to think that his love for the frail girl had worn down, and he began to wonder what courses he should take in high school that year. Then one afternoon the Sheik coughed.

The sound was lonely and gruesome, echoing along the canals. David jumped up from the barren iron bed and cried, "Who's out there?" He jerked on his pants and leaped for the door, where he met the immense Sheik. "What are you doing here?" David cried.

"I jus' standin' here," the badly frightened moron replied.

"Well, get out!" David ordered, and then he saw the peephole through which the Sheik had observed the iron bed. Instinctively he swung about and clouted the monster above the ear. The big man moved back along the runway and pleaded, "I di'n do no wrong!" The ape-man would have stumbled off except that Nora, frightened by the noise, came to the door and thus stopped his retreat. The sight of the hulking brute terrorized her, and she struck at him, clawing his face. Then she fled through the superstructure.

The Sheik was stunned by her behavior and gritted his teeth, moving ape-like toward David. "You tol' 'at priiy gi'l!" he bellowed.

There was no way for David to escape, and he cried, "Sheik! Go back!" But the big man, his face smarting more from Nora's scratches than from David's solid blow, lunged on. He clutched at David and pulled him into the now-empty palace room. With a crunching sound he tried to crush the boy in his massive arms, but David doubled up his knees and dealt him a vile blow in the pit of the stomach. There was a thud, and the big man slipped backwards. From the floor he leered up at David and mumbled, "I gonna kill you!" He struggled to his feet and dived brutally at the boy, so that they crashed together into the palace wall and ripped it.

A gondola came round the corner and smart-aleck boys started to joke about the mechanical princess, but the girls started to scream. "Look at the fight!" Slowly, inevitably, the gondola drifted right beneath David's head. With a violent effort, he pushed his left hand against the prow and regained the castle room. The gondola banged against the walls, and the boys riding it began to shout.

Now there was silence, and the gasping moron spread his fingers very wide to grab at David. He caught one arm and ripped David off his feet. "You tol' the priiy gi'l!" the great brute mourned, as if he were sorry that he must destroy David. But the young athlete summoned fresh strength and beat the Sheik heavily about the face. Blood trickled from the monster's eyes and nose, but he continued to wail, "You tol' 'a priiy gi'l."

With a tremendous effort David drove his fist in the Sheik's windpipe, so that the man's monstrous tongue protruded and he had to drop the boy. "Acchhh," he groaned, trying to get air, and when he did so, he lunged bear-like at his enemy, crying, "I smash you plenty!" His foot slipped, and his right leg tore away a large portion of canvas. Seeing this, David leaped for the door, but the strong man reached out and grabbed his ankle. David collapsed into a painful heap and the brute leaped upon him. Grunting and sweating, the big moron began to hammer David about the face and shoulders. The boy's energy was almost gone, but in the distance he heard shouts of men dashing through the runways of the canal. They were yelling instructions at one another, and someone fired off a revolver.

"I've got to stop him!" David grunted. "Sheik! Sheik!" he pleaded. "If they see you . . ." A monstrous fist hammered into his mouth, and things grew dark. With a last effort, David doubled his knees once more and tried to kick the ape-man loose. He could not, and the fist fell again. There was another pistol shot, and the voices were near. With almost superhuman effort, the boy shot his knees out and the tired moron spun across the floor and through the torn canvas into the canal.

A gondola came by and the occupants screamed at the sight of the Sheik's bleeding face peering at them from the dark waters. Their cries were doubled when he made weird, gurgling sounds at them. Then the workmen from the Canals rushed up and cried, "There he is! Shoot him in the legs!" Like a monster from Greek mythology the Sheik rose from the waters with green slime about him. A workman had a heavy club which he shied across the canal and at the moron's head. "Accchhh!" the wounded man grunted, and for a moment it seemed that he had been killed. But soon he rose farther downstream, and a young boy began clubbing him in the face. Like a wounded otter, the great hulk beat his way to safety.

"Come over here!" the Canal manager shouted. Obediently the moron pawed his way to shore, like a dog. "What were you doing?" the manager asked.

"I 'sn't doin' nothin'," the exhausted fool replied.

"He had too much whiskey," David said quickly. The

manager looked suspiciously at David and then at the panting Sheik, who mouthed a confession of being drunk.

"You'll have to pay ten dollars for that damage," the manager said, and the Sheik mumbled a series of inchoate vowels. The workmen led their giant charge back to his heavy job of hauling gondolas. David watched them go and wondered both at them and at himself. They knew what the Sheik had been doing, and they recognized how dangerous he was; but they also knew that if he were fired they would have to do his ugly work. It seemed that every job David knew of was like this one: certain men took it easy and stole from others, while way down in the caverns monsters and fools and the dispossessed labored in bitter sweat.

And then he thought of another person he had known in the cavern, frail Nora who had worked for Max Volo, and he dashed out into the sunlight of Paradise to look for her. He found her by a rootbeer stand. "Cripes!" she whimpered. "Your face looks awful."

"Nothing broken," David assured her.

"You shouldn't of hit him," the thin girl said, wiping David's lips.

"To think of him spying there!" David blustered.

"You're one to talk!" Nora chided. "Didn't you spy into Max's room? Huh?"

David gave the best excuse in the world for anything: "That was different. I had reasons." He wanted to tell her that the idea of anyone's looking at her or touching her infuriated him, but even then he did not comprehend how love can transform any man into an automatic creature. It took the Hurricane to teach him that.

Shortly before Nora was to leave for Denver, Klementi Kol arranged a dinner for the young lovers. Miss Meigs was there, but not Mr. Stone. That austere man had primly refused to share a meal with a "rotten little baggage."

The dinner was excellent, and Nora acquitted herself decently. David had coached her on what he had learned of table manners, and she sat very straight and kept her elbows on her lap. When Kol asked David what he would like to hear as an encore, David replied, "The Grand March from Aïda." Then Kol asked Nora, and she grinned happily, saying, "What's good enough for Dave is good enough for me!"

At the concert she sat in the front row and between numbers kept up a merry chatter which David found better than the music. She thought that Miss Meigs was quite a singer. "She sure makes eyes at Mr. Kol! Her dress must cost a fortune. Do you suppose she's in love with Mr. Kol? That guy who blows the big thing is sure giving her the eye!" She clutched David's arm warmly and whispered, "Who'd ever thought such people would ask me to dinner?"

When the last cymbals crashed, the young lovers went backstage to thank Mr. Kol and to congratulate Miss Meigs. "It was a swell concert," David admitted. "About the best. Now you'll have to excuse me, since I've got to get back to work." He led Nora off past the lake, and when she saw the Hurricane she said, "Say, how's about a ride? One quick one?"

"I can't do it," David protested. "My relief'll raise the devil as is." He refused to go, but when Nora pouted he gave her the money, and she smiled so winsomely that he wanted to kiss her then, but people were watching. She was very proper and lovely as she walked to the booth. From a distance David saw her slide past Mr. Stone without his ever looking up. "I'm glad of that!" he sighed.

He watched her board a car and start the long climb up the incline. He shot a kiss at her and then started to run back to Venice. But he had taken only a few steps when he heard wild screams. There was a crashing sound as the topmost railing ripped loose, and then came the long night wail of another car riding to death.

He stopped rigidly and prayed: "Oh, God! Don't let it be Nora!" But it was Nora! He knew it, and he started to run toward the lilac trees. Ahead of him others ran, and by the time he got to the crashed cars, men were already throwing coats upon the dead bodies.

"Was there a single girl?" he shouted.

"All sorts of people," a man replied.

"Where?" David screamed, running from body to body. As always, most of the victims were young. He looked in horror at five of them. Nora was not there, but other bodies had been thrown beyond the lilacs. He scrambled across a ditch and searched among the ruins. A boy held the head of another boy.

"Get a doctor, mister!" the first boy cried. "He ain't dead."

"Was there a single girl?" he shouted.

"Me? I wouldn't know. Catch me in one of them death traps?" the boy asked. "I work here!"

David looked at the remaining bodies. Still there was no Nora, and for a moment he believed that his prayer had been answered. Then he saw still a third group of people, and he became pale. Even his hands blanched and he climbed back across the ditch. He was reaching down to pull away a coat when he saw Nora standing at the edge of the crowd.

"David!" she cried. He leaped across the body and grasped her hands. "Was I ever scared?" she asked. "I was in the next car."

Trembling, he led her from the crowds. When they were alone she confided, "I could see them all the way down to earth. The cars were running too close. They make more money that way. It went off not twenty feet from us. David! We just scraped by." Above them the lights went out. No more that year would the Hurricane roar.

"Nora," David finally said, "I thought my heart would never beat again. It isn't only because . . . I mean, in the palace . . ." He could find no words. He held her closely and smelled the heavy perfume in her hair. "But if I thought we'd never . . ." Again the right words could not come and he took refuge in the simplest idea he could command: "I was so lonely until this summer."

They walked a long time, and he took no thought of his job, nor of the people about him, nor of anything. By the lake he met Klementi Kol and the singer. He rushed up to them crying: "I thought she was on the Hurricane, but she wasn't. She was, of course, but she wasn't on that car. She's all right!"

All the way home on the trolley he thought of the strange passion that had possessed him when he believed Nora to be dead. It was like nothing he knew, not even like the fragile moments when he lay deep upon her. It was wrenching and terrible, that passion. He had to acknowledge that one day Nora would be dead. He even suspected that sending her to Denver was not much good; yet he could still reason that the day of death was in the future. But tonight! That had been now! This day! This moment of time, and after it was gone he would never see her again nor feel her soft body nor hear her whisper: "Now you get some sleep, Dave."

He wondered how men could live till they were seventy if they endured such passions as he had known that fifteenth summer, and although he knew many things, and although he tossed on his poorhouse bed all night, he did not even guess that men are able to live because slowly, one by one, they snuff out the fires of spring until only embers burn in white dignity, in loneliness, and often in cold despair.

Paradise closed and Nora went to Denver. Almost as if his own good common sense had dictated it, David plunged into the boy's world of high-school politics and basketball. This was his sixteenth winter, and he was becoming a wiry fellow. Away from the Park he was a boy again, and he alternately rode the crests of fortune when his team won, or wallowed in the troughs of dismay when they lost. Especially in games away from home he was prone to go wild with excitement and want to fight the entire crowd. He played at his best then and on the way home Bobby Creighton would sit beside him and say, "All right now, Dave. Cool down. You've got to learn to master yourself if you want to be a star." Bobby spoke to him as if he were a fledgling boy and David looked forward to being with the coach.

Sometimes after practice Bobby would hold Dave and Harry Moomaugh back. "You're my two sleeping tablets," he'd joke, but they knew what he meant. Doylestown forged ahead in the race and maintained a substantial lead. "Dave," he argued one night, holding David's shoulder as if he were still a kid in grammar school, "tomorrow night I want you to drive for the basket like you never did before. Because if you can ring up three baskets in the first quarter . . ."

The stratagems of basketball quite took David's mind off the murky summer and he became a healthy young animal replenishing itself at the springs of strength. For every evil trick Max Volo had taught him, Bobby Creighton taught him one of the American virtues. "No matter if they knee your crotch loose, my team don't play dirty!" Bobby shouted at his center when the big man kneed an opponent. For every snide approach to life that Mr. Stone inculcated in the boy, Bobby Creighton taught him the fundamental optimism that governs most American thinking. "Unless your arm is cut off above the elbow, I want to see you keep fightin'. I want it said everywhere in Pennsylvania: A Doylestown team don't quit." And to the murky Coal Mine, or the forbidden palaces of Venice, Bobby opposed an attitude toward girls that was almost sacrosanct. "A man who will defile the name of a girl," he said with deep seriousness, "well, he'd quit or do anything." It was an open-and-shut world that Bobby preached, a world in which goodness reigned, strong men were clean, and Doylestown won more than half its games.

David had almost forgotten Nora when her postcard arrived from Denver. It showed a picture of the mountains and bore only three words: "Some place Nora."

The message reached him after an exhilarating victory over Souderton and he was about to crush the card into his pocket when he looked at it again, and he forgot the game and began to wonder where the thin girl was. He read the message at least fifty times, but he could not even determine whether Nora's reaction to Denver was delight or disgust. "Some place!" Poignantly, he wished he were with Nora. He thought of Max's suggestion: "Take a job in my theatre. You could have a nest somewheres with the girl." The vision of such a place came to him. Nora waited for him and when they went to bed she curled up inside his arms and legs. He closed his eyes and thought of her warm body, and like fire in a country barn he flamed into wanting her. But the next day Bobby Creighton had a bright idea about stopping Perkasie, and he said, "Dave? Do you think you're man enough to count three before you shoot your long ones?"

David said he thought he could, but in the game he trembled like a child, and tossed the ball quickly toward the basket as he had always done. At intermission Bobby looked at him with disgust and said, "You make a lot of promises, kid."

"I get excited," David explained.

"Sure you do!" Bobby stormed. "Everyone does. But a real ball player learns. Now are you a man or just a kid?"

In the second half David proved he was fifty-fifty. He couldn't count to three, but he did get up to two. Creighton said, "That's better!" and David said, "Those guards look so damned big . . ." Bobby stopped him short. "Who gave you permission to say *damn*?" he asked. "Apologize!" David blushed and said he was sorry. "You better be!" Bobby said. "If you're so eager to grow up, do it on the floor. Stick your face right in the guard's and outwait him. But don't try to be a man by sayin' tough words. It don't fit you!"

There was another aspect of basketball that made David feel he was still a boy. After the games, and the drinks at the soda fountain, and the recounted glories, David drove back to the poorhouse in some car. The young drivers loved to whirl around the circle and deposit him before the men's building. Then gears would grind and the car would spurt off through the night. A window would rise, Toothless Tom's, and David would look up to his ultimate audience. If his team

had won, he would raise his thumb, and he would hear
Tom cry along the hall: "We win! We win!" But if Doylestown had lost, David would wave his hand low above the
earth, like an umpire signaling safe. Then Tom would glumly
report: "We lose. Tonight we lose."

And then, no matter what the hour, when he got to Door
8 the old men of the poorhouse would troop by in the
darkness to congratulate or console him. "I hear we win,
Dave!" they would say. They were proud of their player, but
not even their congratulations could quite equal the dumb
warmth of Luther Detwiler's comment on defeat. He always
said the same thing: "You can't win 'em all!" Then he would
chuckle as if he had made a very clever remark.

Only a healthy young boy could have lived in David's
multiple schizophrenic worlds; an adult would have been destroyed mentally by the process of jumping back and forth.
In winters David was a clean athlete, a diligent student, an
official in school government. In summers he was a professional short-change artist, a music student, the lover of a
young prostitute, and an art fancier. He thought none of
these things mutually contradictory, and at the beginning
of his third year at Paradise he bought a vellum edition of
Shakespeare's sonnets and memorized some thirty of them, for
they came close to representing what he believed to be beautiful and good. Like a book of many sonnets, his life was cut
up into neat octets and sestets with terminal couplets at the
end of each experience. He gloried in each passing day and
was like a grub delving in carrion, certain that one time in
the future he would be a soaring, winged creature. In other
words, he was young.

He was not disturbed, therefore, when the Park, in desperation, did away with tickets and installed foolproof turnstiles. A customer paid his money, went through a narrow
space, and an impersonal cogwheel registered a number. At
night the cashier paid ten cents for each click, and there
would be no more stealing!

It took Mr. Stone one day to figure out a way to beat the
stile honestly. "Suppose," he whispered to David, "a woman
with a lot of kids comes up. They always do. You hold the
stile back and the woman gets mad. They always do. She
pushes the kids, thinks it's their fault. So the kids squeeze in,
two or three to a stile. It's going to be easy!" The Park

caught on quickly and changed the spaces so that children couldn't double up.

Max Volo solved that dilemma promptly. He appeared with a loud clicking device, so that when a woman appeared with children the cashier could make a click and say patiently, "I'm sorry, madam, but your son turned the stile. That'll be ten cents extra." When the woman exploded the cashier said, "If you don't want to pay, you'll have to lift the child over."

The Park caught on to this, too, and made it an offense to lift children over any stile for any reason. Then Max produced his masterpiece. "This is truly terrific!" he whispered to David one hot afternoon.

"Beat it!" David said.

"You'll be very sorry," Max said sorrowfully. "This makes everything else prehistoric."

A few days later the Canals of Venice sprang its yearly leak, and David was sent to another ride. Before he left he saw the Sheik hauling great chunks of lumber from a distant pile, working like an animal under the direction of men who stood about in the shade. David was in his new booth only a few minutes when a sandy-haired boy hurried up with a letter and said, "Tommy gave me this for you. For his sake don't do nothin'."

Tommy was the regular cashier and his note read, "Whoever relieves me. I'm sick. You can have all the dough but for God's sake, protect me." David could make nothing of the message until time for evening meal. When he made his routine check of money he found he had $66 more than the stile called for! He refused to leave for food and had a sandwich sent in. At nine he checked again, and now he had over a hundred dollars. He wiped his face.

Suddenly, from the crowd, Max Volo darted into his booth and lay upon the floor. "That's the trouble with this new racket. You got to cover up for people." He began to take the turnstile apart.

"What are you doing?" David demanded.

"You keep on makin' change, kid," Max ordered. With a pair of pliers he noiselessly disassembled the lower part of the stile. From his pocket he produced the legitimate cog that had turned the tally numbers. It contained four spurs. From the defrauded stile he withdrew a spurious cog with only three spurs. "Wonderful, ain't it?" he beamed. "With this we make twenty-five per cent each and every day!"

"How many machines are you working?" David asked, quite dry in the mouth.

"Some here, some there," the little man evaded. "Now about that money, kid. You keep it."

"Max," David said firmly, "I don't want it and you don't get it. As soon as you leave, I'm going to call the office and report a screwy stile. Let them figure it out."

"Hey, kid!" Max cried, grabbing him by the leg. "You can't do that!"

"Watch me."

"I'm tellin' you, Dave. Don't do it."

"You don't scare me, Max," David replied. "You run along, because they'll catch you sooner or later if you keep up this racket."

"You're makin' a big mistake!" Max warned, but David's mind was made up. Later, when Max was a bigshot Philadelphia crook, David could say, "Once I took a hundred bucks from Volo, and he didn't do a thing about it!"

The Company officials were in a turmoil when the extra hundred dollars was reported. They deduced what must have happened, so they put special locks on all the stiles. This stopped Volo for more than a month. Then one day he appeared all smiles and winked at David. "Thanks for helping me go straight!" he joked. "Because now I got something that nobody can stop!"

He had found a crooked engineer in the company that made the turnstiles and together the two men had devised a magnet that would cause the ten's digit to jump backward. Every time this was accomplished the cashier made an even dollar. Max paid the crooked engineer two hundred dollars for the magnets and installed six of them in the biggest rides. Now cashiers who had been stealing seventy dollars a week on tickets started to carry black lunch boxes like railroad laborers, for they were making so much money they had to have a way to smuggle it out.

Ultimately the officials found a way to make their cogwheels magnetic proof, but before they did a clever cashier had whittled out for himself a piece of wood which could be substituted opposite the turnstile so that thin people could slip through without clicking the stile.

In this way the never-ending fight went on. Precautionary measures which the Park introduced one week were circumvented the next. There was no job too high, none too low to attract the racketeers. Even the boy who unloaded mustard stole it in gallon lots, and the spotters had spotters who spotted on them, and Max Volo paid everyone he could contaminate a few dollars for special information.

"Don't worry about it!" Mr. Stone said. "Every business is run this way. You should see politics in Philadelphia!"

"But why doesn't the Park arrest Max Volo?" David insisted.

"Because they know what kind of crook he is," Mr. Stone replied. "They know his limits, you might say, so in self-protection they keep him on the payroll. There are good crooks and bad ones. We're all lucky that Max is a good one."

"I don't understand," David confessed.

"Why does Philadelphia have such rotten politics?" Mr. Stone countered. "Because the citizens can trust that particular bunch of thieves. Why don't you read about the accidents here at Paradise? Because people don't want to know anything that's bad for business. It's like the famous case up your way," Mr. Stone continued. "What was his name? Crouthamel? Took over $200,000. Got away clean. Don't tell me people didn't know what was going on! But it's easier to let things slide than to start a mess. Why, if you had whispered that this fellow Crouthamel was a crook . . . I'll bet even the churches would have been on your neck. Bad for business, so you always hold onto crooks you know rather than flee to those you know not of."

"I don't think Doylestown is like that," David said. "On our basketball team . . ."

Mr. Stone interrupted. "All people are suckers," he said. "In crowds they're even bigger suckers. Take this turnstile! They put it here to keep us honest cashiers honester. But it helps my business fifteen per cent."

"What do you mean?" David asked.

"Well, it's a trade secret, but I work my stile this way. When a fellow and a girl come up for a ride, I see to it that the girl gets in first. Then I make a false start with the stile. Like this. The girl moves forward and I stop her with a bang. The yokel slams into her bottom, and it feels real nice. The girl is maybe a little bit pleased herself and turns back to smile. Then I release twice, real fast, and the boob is so hot to chase his girl he don't know if he gave me one dollar or fifty."

"Does it work very often?" David inquired professionally.

"Like I said," Mr. Stone reasoned. "You got to study

people till you find what their weakness is. Then you give them a tiny shove in that direction. Every business is run that way. So I wouldn't be surprised if maybe you couldn't even give the President of the United States a nudge now and then." He adjusted the hung coins in his change machine. "That is, if you knew how Mr. Harding was leaning."

In July Nora came back. David had no warning of her return, and he was shocked when he saw her walking along a gravel path toward the Coal Mine. "Nora!" he called, and the thin girl stopped in great embarrassment. She seemed taller, but then David noticed she was wearing high-heeled shoes. She was thinner and her eyes were much brighter. She moved with increased nervousness, but her slim body was more desirable than before, for it was set off by clothes that better fitted her enticing bosom and hips.

"Hello, Dave," she said dryly. David noticed that she was wearing more lipstick than before.

"Aren't you glad to see me?" he asked.

"Sure I am," she said without much enthusiasm. He took her by the arm, and she pulled away slightly. He drew her to him, and after another attempt to pull her arm loose, she pressed it against his body.

"How was Denver?" he asked.

"That's some place," she said without betraying her feelings.

"That must be some place!" David repeated. "Anyway, it made you look lots better," he lied. She walked with her shoulders more bent in toward her chest.

"Denver's all right," she said.

"I've been saving a lot of money for you," David confided. He reached into his pocket for a roll of bills he had kept for this moment.

"I don't want it Dave!" she protested quickly. "I did all right in Denver."

"This is for you," he insisted, thrusting the bills into her hand.

"I don't want it!" she cried, shoving them back. "I had a good job."

"You get many tips, waiting?" he asked, holding the bills until he could find a chance to make Nora take them.

"So-so," she replied.

"You come back by bus?" he continued. There would never be enough time to talk with her about the winter. "We lost the championship this year," he said. "Perkasie was too big."

"Were they?" Nora asked dully. Then quickly she gripped David by the arm and asked, "Did you fall in love with some nice girl? Does that Marcia . . . Is she your girl?"

"She doesn't go to my school," he said. "She goes to New Hope," he explained patiently. "Of course, lots of kids from New Hope sometimes come to Doylestown . . ."

Nora held his arm warmly against her body. "Let's sit by the lake," she suggested. "I'm sorry your team lost this year."

David laughed nervously. "We have a Dutchman who always says, 'Well, you can't win 'em all.' " He repeated the sentence and grinned at Nora.

"Did you get my card?" she asked.

"Yes! I guess I read it till the ink came off." He had to fight his hands to keep them from clasping the knees that were pressed against his. "Nora, Nora!" he whispered. "I've thought about you. I've just been waiting until we could go somewhere. I . . ."

"Ssssh!" she protested, pressing her warm hand upon his lips. She looked away and started twice to speak, but her own words were too confused to share. Finally she said lamely, "Don't talk that way, kid."

"But Nora!" he confessed, words welling up within him as if they were a penny a dozen, "I could see you in the palace. I could feel you sleeping against me. I wished I were in Denver so that I could buy you things you might need. But I didn't have any money and I didn't know your address. Let's go right over to the palace?"

The thin girl shivered, as if a wind had blown upon her that hot July day. "I can't go to the palace," she said abruptly. "I'm staying with Betty at the Coal Mine."

It took some moments for the import of these words to strike David and then he said, "But Betty isn't your friend, Nora. I am. Why didn't you ask me for help?"

"I don't need help!" the confused girl protested. "And I don't need you! Now get the hell away from me!" She rose and started to hurry along the gravel paths. David ran after her, unashamed of the scene he made, a long-legged boy running after a very thin girl in high heels and a dress that was just a bit too tight.

"Nora!" he cried, grabbing her by the arm. "If you're in trouble, don't go to Max Volo. Take this!" He jammed the bills into her dress pocket so forcefully as to tear the pocket.

"Oh, look!" she mumbled. She stopped running and looked

at her torn dress as if a terrible thing had happened. "Oh, David!" she repeated several times, her thin hand pressed to her lips and tears splashing upon her cheeks.

Tenderly David led the bewildered girl away from the Coal Mine and back toward Venice. "No!" she objected, pulling away from him so violently that he was afraid she would begin to run again. He allowed her to choose the way and finally they paused beneath the lilac bushes under the Hurricane. Overhead the cars whizzed by, but they were not so dizzy with the dusk as David.

Nora stood very still against David but would not sit upon the grass. He drew her deeper among the lilacs and she stood upon the withered flowers that had fallen that spring. "I've wanted you so much!" David whispered, and for the first time she kissed him warmly and replied, "So have I, kid." Impassioned, he parted her dress and found the soft breasts that had slept beside him and the burning thighs that had cooled his own desires. She stood with her eyes closed and pressed herself close to him.

"Dave! Dave!" she muttered and then as if activated by the spring of a child's toy, she thrust him away and buttoned her dress. "I've got to go!" she cried, and this time she ran all the way to the Coal Mine. At the obscure door under the waterfall she darted in among the trestles, and David stood in the gravel, more bewildered than at any previous time in his life.

His confusion lasted for a week. Nora would not talk with him, but twice he saw her on the arm of a red-haired man who leered down at her as if she were a very small child. A third time he saw her standing by a drink stand. He left his booth unattended and dashed over to talk with her, but before he could reach her a different man spoke to her, and she walked away with him.

Against his sworn promise to himself, he finally plunged into the swampy shadows of the Coal Mine. Betty was there alone and she said, "You better knock off, kid. Take my advice. Nora is too old for you. She don't care to have anything more to do with you."

"Does she need money?" David asked.

"Everybody needs money," Betty replied.

"Will you give her this?" He handed Betty his takings for the week. Then he pleaded, "What's wrong, Betty? You can tell me. We used to live in Doylestown together."

"Nothing's wrong!" Betty insisted. She was matter-of-fact

and cold. "Now why don't you beat it before she gets back with some fellow? Only make a scene."

He left the dripping trestles and went to see Max Volo at the loganberry stand. "Max," he said, "I'm worried. What's the matter with Nora? Why won't she talk with me?"

"Girls is girls," Max said philosophically. "I hired about sixty in my day, here and in Philly, and I could write a book. The guy that can explain girls is gonna make a million dollars."

"But what about Nora? Is she working for you now?"

"Yep. She came back the last of June, I guess. I didn't see her all winter. Now if you're hot for her, come down some night."

"I don't mean that!" David snapped. "Max, I love Nora . . . and she won't even speak to me."

"Whores," said Max, drawing upon his long experience, "are damned queer people. They cry their eyes out over some nice clean guy. They're gonna marry him. Settle down in Kentucky. I bet I listened to more stories about nice clean guys than God ever had time to make. Last year, when Nora left the Coal Mine, she gave me the old song and dance. Well, now it's this year and the song is different."

The days dragged on and David lived in a world of misery. He would catch glimpses of Nora, and she would tantalize his mind, even when he tried to sleep at night. As he worked, he could see the loftiest peaks of the timbered mountains that rose above the Coal Mine, and they mocked him with their secrets of what Nora was doing with some strange man far beneath their summits. Klementi Kol came to relieve Sousa and one day David frankly poured his problem on the big musician, who listened gravely and said about what Max Volo had reported: "Nobody has ever understood a woman." But he also added, "Not even another woman." He told David to forget the girl. "I know it's impossible, David, and I know you'll never forget her. But you've got to divert your mind. The girl doesn't want you, that's clear. Now, have you been reading?" He brought David *Eugénie Grandet*, but David could not follow the story because tears came to his eyes at every indignity the heroine suffered, for it was clear that Eugénie was meant to be Nora.

Finally he went to see aloof Mr. Stone. They talked of Park politics for half an hour, David standing with his left foot on the booth foundations. When the stupid men who ran Paradise had been sufficiently vilified David stood silent for several minutes and Mr. Stone asked gruffly, "Well, what's eating you?"

"That girl you don't like," David began. "She won't . . ."

"You don't have to tell me," Mr. Stone said. "You thought she was in Denver. I met her in Florida. She was with the biggest, noisiest, drunkenest bastard I ever saw in Palm Beach."

David gasped. "I don't see how . . ."

"It's pretty simple," Mr. Stone said. "She got to Denver and found she had to work for a change. Some guy in a check suit came along and said, 'You oughtn't a be workin' yourself to death, baby.' 'What better can I do?' she asked, and he said, 'Like to go to Florida?' She'd been there the year before, so she went."

David hated to hear words which he himself would probably have framed later. "She's not a strong girl, Mr. Stone," he argued. "Maybe the work was too hard for her."

"Girls like her," Mr. Stone pontificated as he rolled nickels into dollar lots, "any work is too much for them. Except one kind, that is."

"You can't say that!" David flared up.

"For God's sake!" Mr. Stone snapped. "Don't you know any clean, pretty girls?"

David left the Hurricane, but the tornado of his spirit stayed with him. He could not then—or ever—reconcile the way Mr. Stone looked at life with the way Klementi Kol did. Kol had said: "If you see a picture you like, stand before it until your head swims. You can never see enough beauty. Play music that you love a thousand times. Take all experience into your heart. That's why, with Nora, you have a right to love her as long as she brings meaning to you. Because even if love is unsatisfactory, or ridiculous, it's still the best thing we know." Opposed to this was Mr. Stone's cruel imperative: "Cut her out of your mind, kid. She'll poison you."

David drifted about the Park until he simply had to return to work. Then immediately he hired a substitute and ran down to the Coal Mine and under the waterfall. He found Nora and she said, "You don't take 'No' for an answer, do you?"

"Nora!" he blurted out. "Why did you go back to Florida?"

"How did you know?" she demanded.

"Mr. Stone saw you," he explained.

"Oh, that devil!" she cried. She became very angry, not with herself, but with Mr. Stone. "He's a nosy, David. So high and mighty. You'd do well to stay away from that devil. I'll bet he's never kissed a girl. Would warm him up a bit if he did."

"But why did you . . . Why didn't you write to me? I'd've gotten you money. Anything, Nora."

She said, "Let's get out of here. Betty's coming back pretty soon and she may have a guy with her." They walked down by the trolley tracks, where no one would see them. "It was hard work in Denver," she said. "I'm not strong any more. Three or four hours and I feel, honest to God, I got to lay down. A man used to come into the restaurant, and he was taking a long vacation. All those nice, warm places." She stopped and then said, "I went along."

For some time David could not look at her. He was too ashamed and too unwilling to believe that Mr. Stone should have guessed so clearly. He felt as if a part of his world had changed forever. The dream of fair women was gone. Standing by the trolley tracks he thought of the finest girls he knew. Miss Meigs and Marcia, probably. He wondered what they were like, and suddenly he realized, for the first time, that everything Klementi Kol had said about love could be explained if Miss Meigs were a lot like Nora, only better dressed. But Marcia Paxson wasn't like that, and then he saw that she was like Mr. Stone: hard and tough and never in love with anyone. Finally he said, "Nora, you're kinder and sweeter than any person I've ever known. I don't care if you did go to Florida." Tenderly he caught her by the shoulders and kissed her without passion. The thin wanderer stayed close to him until the kiss was spent and then stepped away.

"Go away!" she pleaded. "Get a decent job somewheres else. The Park's no good for you, and I'm no good, either. I'm rotten bad for you, kid." He stopped the flow of her words by pressing his hand across her mouth, and she kissed the palm of his hand, proving to his satisfaction that her words were false.

He began to cry and she looked away until he gained control of his quivering lip. Then she said, "I'm going back to the Coal Mine now." He could not stop her, nor could he follow her. Forlorn, he stayed beside the weed-grown tracks and listened to the distant carrousels.

"Nora! Nora!" he lamented. She was the first member he

had met of the world's willfully defeated, and the tragedy he saw in her was more than he could bear.

Klementi Kol guessed at what was happening and he came several days to have dinner with Capt. Sousa. During each visit he stopped by David's booth to talk with him. One day David bluntly asked, "Are you in love with Miss Meigs?"

"Of course I am," the conductor replied.

"I just wondered," David added.

"I'm sure I know what you're wondering, too. But I won't answer, David. When my concerts begin you'll hear a new piece. By me. It won't say so on the program, but it's a love song to Miss Meigs."

David was about to ask, "Then why don't you get married?" but the disclosures of the past week imposed caution. There were things everywhere that could not easily be explained. Instead of probing further, he took down his own love songs, the poems he had written to Nora. The musician looked at them with increasing interest.

"These are good," he said. "This one? What's it mean?" He returned a scrap of paper with a short elegy beginning:

#### THE IMPROVIDENT HUSBANDMAN

This is the field that was not plowed,
The tree that bore no fruit.
And in the dropping time this was the barren sow . . .

"I wrote it last night on the trolley," David said. "I was looking at the wasted fields."

"You have a talent!" Kol said. He repeated the word to Sousa and to Miss Meigs. "This boy has a talent!" The word was like a magic key. Sousa and his singer looked at David quite differently. He perceived that for these people all the world was divided into those who had a talent and those who did not. Up to now he had been merely an amusing youngster in what the Europeans properly call a *lustgarten.* But if he had a talent . . .

Capt. Sousa said, "Perhaps you'll write a book one day." Miss Meigs laughed and said, "He already has!" David felt very pleased, but Capt. Sousa nodded in his old man's way and said, "It's never music until it's played. It's never a book until it's printed."

The difference in their reception of him at dinner was carried over into all fields. Even when Capt. Sousa was host, he now asked David what he would like to order, more as if David had a mind of his own. It was quite unlike the great musician's former condescension. And Klementi discussed concerts with David as if he actually wanted to know what David thought of Tschaikowsky. For almost a month Kol succeeded in driving David's attention from his self-flagel-lation, and then Kol destroyed all of his therapy by playing his love song to Miss Meigs.

He called it simply *Fugue,* and it was less like a love song than anything David had yet heard. Two groups of violins argued with each other, and the contention grew vigorous, so that other instruments took up the quarrel, and a mighty, swelling pressure resulted. David listened as if his mind were growing out of his skull, and when the surging music stopped his hands dropped limp into his lap. He stared at the conductor and wondered how he could have com-pressed so much feeling into so short a piece of music. Then he saw Kol leave the stage, and Miss Meigs was so eager to congratulate him that her white hands showed for a moment from the wings.

For the rest of that day David could think only of Nora. He was lost and hopeless in his desire to see her. Knowing that men willfully destroy themselves, he nevertheless determined to be with her again. During his evening relief he walked to the waterfall three different times, and left each time without going through the hidden door. He was about to return when he noticed with relief that his time was up and he hurried back to work.

On the trolley he heard her name with every clacking of the wheels, and in the stars above the poorhouse he saw her face, her thin and ever-present form.

The next day was hot, a grim, sticky, hot Pennsylvania day. Crowds from Philadelphia streamed out to Paradise, but by midafternoon the Park was boiling in the August sun.

Venice did a big business that day. Steaming couples flowed through the stiles, hot, arguing with each other. Even the music from the carrousels seemed sticky with heat as it came, moist and dull, across the hot gravel.

David was busy from the moment he opened his booth, but as the day wore on not even his preoccupation with dimes and quarters sufficed to keep Nora from his mind. Once he saw her idling by a candy stand and he summoned the Sheik. "Quick!" he ordered. "Run over there and tell her I want to see her!"

The big moron ambled over to the thin girl and mumbled something. She looked at David's booth and shook her head. The Sheik walked dejectedly back, kicking pebbles. "She 'on't come," he reported sadly.

The day wore on and David kept watching the paths. Betty came by and David shouted at her. She didn't hear him calling, so again he dispatched the Sheik. This time the ape-man came back grinning, leading Betty by the hand as if she were a child. "I go' this one!" he announced proudly.

"Some day!" Betty said, wiping her face.

"It's about the record," David said.

"Nice and cool in there!" Betty joked, pointing toward the Venetian palace. "You should know."

"Most of the rides are cool," David continued cautiously.

"I don't like 'em on a day like today," Betty said professionally. "Too big of a crowd. You got to stand in line, and you don't get a seat to yourself. Somebody piling in on top of you, making passes on the curves. I like Mondays best. You get a car all to yourself."

There was a pause and David said, "Must be a lot of business today."

"There is!" Betty agreed. "That fat brakeman. The one that fell off the Hurricane and lived. He come down a little while ago for a quickie . . ." Betty put her hand to her mouth and blushed. "We don't see you much any more."

"You know why," David said directly.

"Yes!" Betty said primly. "And I think Nora is being pretty foolish." She took out her compact and fixed her lips. "Everything gets sticky on a day like this," she said. Then she folded her compact with extreme precision and said, "Why don't you and me go down and talk to Nora?"

"Would you?" David begged.

"It's only proper," Betty said. "After all, you and me's from the same town."

"I can get off in about twenty minutes," David said, so eagerly that his hands shook.

"Fine!" Betty said. She reached inside the cage and took a dollar. "I'll get us some hotdogs." She soon returned and stood by the booth as David waited for his relief. "Nora told me a lot about you, Dave," she said. "I think you treated her very fair." Then she added quickly, "Max treats me all right, too. There's many a man that doesn't." Then she became confidential. "You can always tell how a man was brought up by the way he treats a girl. He don't have to spend a fortune on her." She tapped her foot as the minutes passed and said, "Your relief must of stopped down for a quickie, too." David felt disgusted that he had to utilize this brazen girl as an intermediary with Nora.

But the relief finally came, and David and Betty ducked under the waterfall and into the cool, damp shadows of the Cave. Only the new girl was in the room. She wore a skimpy brassiere and black lace panties. "Boy, is this day ever a scorcher?" she asked, fanning her armpits.

"Nora'll be back soon," Betty assured David. "This is about the only cool spot in the Park and Nora ain't dumb. You like a beer or a Whistle?" Suddenly she snapped her fingers and started whispering to the new girl, who quickly popped into a robe and left the room. David guessed that she would be stationed among the trestles to forewarn Nora if a man came, too.

"Now, Dave!" Betty said. "You be firm with Nora. Ain't no reason why you and she shouldn't have a good time this summer." She fussed around with some sandwiches and peered out the door. "You want me to scram when she comes?" she asked.

"Would you?" David asked eagerly. Then he added, "Not that I . . ."

"That's what they all say!" Betty laughed.

Footsteps sounded along the damp walk and David's heart began to beat quite rapidly. The door pushed open and Nora looked into the room. "I thought she was kidding," she said.

"I'm going out for a hotdog!" Betty announced sententiously. She slatterned past Nora and slapped her on the bottom. "Good huntin', kids!" she laughed.

The young lovers stood apart and studied each other. Nora was paler and her shoulders dipped. Her hair was more beautiful than David had remembered, but her eyes were the same, intense and dark. Her thin face was handsome and her long fingers nervously twined and untwined, as if she were a young girl meeting a boy after church. "You shouldn't have come," she said.

"I've almost gone mad," David said slowly.

"Oh, David!" she replied. She avoided him and hung her cheap beaded bag on a nail. "You like beer or a Whistle?" she asked.

"I decided that . . ."

She went to the door. "Hey! Don't stay out there!" she cried. The new girl came in slowly and shrugged her shoulders at David.

"Do you mind?" she asked, taking off her robe and hanging it beside Nora's bag. She fell heavily into a chair and read desultorily from *Passionate Love*. "Some of the things that go on in the world!" she said, thumbing the pages idly.

Nora brought David a bottle of Whistle, and the bright orange drink tasted cool. "Well," she said, "it was good seein' you." She led him to the door, but as she was about to close it upon him she grabbed his hand and whispered, "I'll walk you out. You might slip."

They walked beneath the trestles for a moment, David in front, and when he stopped she hurried to him and kissed him on the face and over his eyes in his ears. "It was rotten of me today," she said. "Not coming to see you." She laughed. "The Sheik almost started to cry."

They found a damp post, and she leaned against it. He slipped her dress away from her shoulders and loosened her clothing. "Oh, Nora," he cried, "we've wasted a year." She said nothing, not even when her dress trailed in the dank water nor when David started to press himself against her body. She hardly breathed, but slowly the warmth and the desire of this boy captured her and she placed her hands upon his hips. She held them there for a moment and then thrust him away.

"Listen, kid!" she said quickly. "I want to, too. But let's do it right. Tonight, when it's cooler . . . Say when the Park closes. We'll go wherever you want. You're such a sweet kid! I love you so much."

She pulled her dress about her shoulders and winced as the cold water trickled down her back. David felt the mossy water and said, "We ruined your dress."

"What do I care?" she cried happily. "Think what we'll do tonight! Dave! Dave! I'm going in and take a nap. Won't we have a time!"

Back in his booth David could scarcely make change. He could think only of Nora and of how they would spend that night. "We'll go to the palace!" he decided. "Hey, Sheik!" The big man stalked over to the booth. "Can I have the palace room tonight?" The moron grinned broadly. "Yeah . . ." he said in six syllables. "I s'eep in town." David gave him two dollars. "I 'on't look 'is time," the immense creature promised. David watched him go and was appalled by what others before him had learned: sin enlists the most wretched accomplices.

Betty reminded him of this when she stopped by the booth. "I heard!" she said with great pleasure. "And I don't blame you a bit for likin' that girl. She's wonderful, Dave. She's neat, too. She washes her clothes all the time." She leaned upon the booth and said very confidentially, "Now when you make up with a girl, like you 'n' Nora's doing tonight. Always take her a present. A pair of silk stockings, maybe. Girls like fellas that do nice things for them."

"How could I get stockings?" David asked.

"I never thought of that!" Betty said. Again she reached into his cash pile. "Tell you what!" she said. "I'll go buy a box of real nice candy. Candy's almost as good as stockings. And Nora likes candy!" She sighed. "Y'know?" she mused. "If I et like Nora does, I'd be a perfect pig." She walked sedately off through the stifled evening crowds and returned shortly with a florid heart-shaped box wrapped in red ribbons and lettered in satin: "To My Sweetheart." "It was eighty-five cents!" she protested. "Robbery! But it is sort of nice."

At nine o'clock that very hot night a man outside David's booth remarked to his wife, "It looks like a volcano." A Venice guard looked where the man was pointing and screamed, "Christ! The Coal Mine's on fire!" The was when David looked up and saw the topmost peak of the mountains burst into flame. Before he could leave his booth the entire fantastic structure blazed in the night.

He rushed toward the fire and saw a last train of cars roar with maddening speed to safety. The passengers were singed and hysterical, and even as they fled from the platform, the central portion of the mountain caved in with a giant hiss.

David leaped at the door beneath the waterfall, but a solid body of flame engulfed that portion of the Mine, and he dashed to the workmen's entrance. It, too, was burning, but a man might get through. He hesitated a moment and then heard Betty's agonized voice screaming above the flames, "The girls! The girls are in there!"

David threw his arms above his face and started to run to the door. A burst of flame forced him back. Again Betty screamed, and this time he said, "I'll get there or else," but a swift blow from a hard fist struck his chin. His knees crumpled and he lost consciousness. Max Volo had knocked him out.

No one in Philadelphia—or Doylestown, either—ever read about the two girls who burned to death in the great fire at Paradise. There were stories about the flames being visible for miles and about how fire engines had reported from fifteen different towns. On one engine a volunteer fireman who had not missed a fire for thirty-one years fell off but got to the immense blaze by hitch-hiking in a car with two women. There was much publicity about that incident. Editors said it showed how strong habit is and how much devotion to duty some volunteer firemen have.

David never discovered whether Park officials and the police knew about the two girls. If they did, nothing was said. It would have been difficult to identify those girls. Who were they? They were wanderers. They had neither criminal records nor homes. David guessed that Max Volo had bribed the police to let him search the ruins and destroy any evidence.

But the evidence in David's mind was never disposed of. When the guards, finding his booth empty, swept up his money for protection, they also saved a box of candy. "We don't know what to say," the officials complained. "Running off and leaving your booth like that! But we were proud of you, the way you tried to see if anyone was trapped in the Coal Mine. All our workmen got out, thank God!" They wiped their faces and told him to take a few days off.

He wandered about the gravel paths as if he were a ghost in a banqueting hall where fine feasts had filled the night. "Oh, Nora!" he cried when some memory of that thin girl appeared before him. There were the towers of the Hurricane to which she had come when he was second fare. In the opposite direction he could always see the gaunt and broken timbers of the Mine, standing jagged like a fractured tooth in a smile that once was beautiful. The cable, snapped by the heat, twisted madly in the air, and David's mind was twisted, too.

With that flood of sentiment which adolescent boys must have if they are ever to be good men, he began to see Nora, not as she was but as death had made her: the glowing, passionate, unattained girl, half dressed among the shadows. He said: "She was different from the other girls! Don't tell me she was a . . ." He would not say the word, not even to himself. Immolated within the Mine whose death sparks had been seen for miles, Nora became far more than she had been.

Capt. Sousa met him the second afternoon, standing by the lake. "That was a bad fire," the bandmaster said. "They tell me you were quite a hero."

"It was . . ." David bit his lip and looked at the old musician.

"Won't you have dinner with me tonight?" Sousa asked. With courtly grace he ordered for the boy, sensing that David was suffering from shock. "Would you sit in my box tonight?" he asked. But when Mary Meigs came out to sing love songs, tears filled David's eyes and the concert was ruined. "Nora!" he mumbled to himself. "I didn't even know her last name." After the concert Miss Meigs spoke with him.

"Capt. Sousa tells me you were a hero!" she said. She leaned over and kissed him. It was a strange kiss, one that he scarcely felt. For his lips were burning from a kiss of much different quality.

On the third day Mr. Stone met him wandering about the lake. "What really happened at the fire?" he inquired. David reported formally, but Mr. Stone said, "No! I mean . . . Why were you trying to get into that door? Your little baggage trapped in there?"

"Nora was inside," David said.

"I thought so," Mr. Stone said. He was inspired to console the boy, but David stood aloof.

"You never understood her, Mr. Stone," David insisted. "She wasn't like the rest."

"They never are," Mr. Stone said sadly. "Now look, David. You've got to be sensible. You've got to admit to yourself the way things actually were. She never slept with you when she came back from Florida. And you know why. She was rotten sick, kid! She picked up a dose in Florida. All the fellows around the Park knew it. If she had let you fool with her just once . . ." He snapped his fingers. "There goes your fine young life. It's bitter, but it's true. That fire was a godsend. Straight from the hand of Providence."

Mr. Stone kneeled down and picked up a handful of pebbles. One by one he tossed them into the lake. They splashed crisply, and lone, clean circles started for the shore. "You knew what I'm telling you, didn't you?" the cashier asked.

"Maybe I did," David confessed. Tears came to his eyes,

but he fought them back. Somehow, it would be improper to have Mr. Stone see him cry. After a moment he asked, "Mr. Stone, why can't we ever tell ourselves the way-down-deep truth?"

"Lots of people do!" the gray cashier insisted. "I do."

"You do?" David repeated.

"As nearly as anyone can," the self-contained short-change artist replied. He tossed another stone into the lake. "But I can see that you don't. I've watched you for two days drifting about this Park. Dreaming about that girl. Well, I'll bet you can't even spell her last name."

David looked at the lake and Mr. Stone pitched a pebble at that very spot. David became badly confused. "When I was a kid," he said, "a friend of mine was caught doing something bad. I could have kept my mouth shut, but I didn't. I even lied to help him. I was ready to fight boys bigger than I was. The other night it was the same way, but now you tell me that every man should go his own way. Never fool himself about anything."

"I'm right," the cool gray cashier insisted. "When you interfere in things like that you're always a fool. There's good an' bad in the world. You've seen that. You can see it right here every day. Well, it's no one man's job to fight all the bad there is. Keep your own nose clean. Certain people, David, are going to wind up in the garbage heap no matter what you or I or they or God Himself does. They're not your problem, kid."

He pitched two pebbles into the lake, and their wavering circles soon became tangled like David's thoughts. "Suppose," Mr. Stone reasoned, "that you had reached the door. You'd surely have been burned alive. There wasn't a thing you could have accomplished, and you'd have spread the whole dirty story over the country. This way, everything's worked out all right."

"But what about Nora?" David doggedly insisted.

"How long did she have to live, David? You know she was dying, and she was doing more harm in the world than good. Max knew that when he knocked you down. His girl Betty was setting up a howl, too, so he belted her in the mouth. Knocked a front tooth out. Well, Max can pay to fix that tooth. But if Betty had kept shooting her mouth off, who could have fixed that?"

The icy man in the gray suit stared at his confused friend.

David was breathing deeply. "I don't like things that way," the boy said.

"But that's the way they are," Mr. Stone concluded. "Believe me, everything has been worked out to an easy balance. Leave things alone. Tell yourself the truth, the rock-bottom, absolute truth. Because if you do, you'll be miles ahead of the boobs who feed on dreams."

The bitter, Old-Testament moralist pitched his remaining pebbles into the water. He wanted to put his arm about David and console him, but instead he coughed and said, "Get back to work. Work solves everything. And forget this nonsense."

By the lake now filled with dusk David slumped down upon a bench and surveyed the world he had inherited: a moral jungle, a thief's paradise, a world of loneliness and death and spiritual hunger. It was his world and he did not like it. As the stars came out he thought of that other world he had known in the poorhouse, where a report card or a glimpse of Orion or Old Daniel's fine talk could set the heart pounding. Where had it gone? That world of beauty and sharing, that infinity of wild surmise, where had it fled?

It was Miss Chaloner who led David back to clarity and decency. Even more than Bobby Creighton she showed him the dignity of life. She was perplexing, though, for in her brawl with Bobby Creighton David sided with Bobby and was almost instrumental in getting her fired; but in her quiet way she revolutionized the lives of her students.

"She don't look like much!" Harry Moomaugh observed after the first class in geometry.

"She's got a nose like a baseball," David agreed.

At the poolroom the snooker men said, "That one won't last long. She buys her things in Philly." The barbershop men noticed this too and explained why it could not be tolerated. "We pay taxes and taxes pay her, and she spends the money in Philly. She oughta be fired."

The church people, who also paid taxes, said you couldn't expect anything else from an atheist. And the businessmen, who paid the heaviest taxes of all, said that Miss Chaloner was a Russian, which explained everything. So many protests were made that the school board had to consider firing her, one-third because she was a Russian, one-third because she was an atheist, and one-third because she bought her clothes in Philadelphia. But when the question came actually to a vote, no one could seriously consider firing her, for she was obviously the finest teacher the school had had in twenty years.

She taught as if every student before her had an immortal soul thirsting for knowledge and guidance. Those who were good in mathematics might be geniuses, she thought. Those who were hopelessly poor in math might still be great mothers or fine coalyard men, or politicians or school-board members. They happened not to have a knack for math, and that was no evil. It was an unfortunate fact.

During the third week of geometry Harry said, "Old Baseball Nose can explain stuff, can't she?" But not even then did he and David know that this undistinguished woman whose dresses were too long—as if to hide three-year-old shoes—would change their lives forever. But in the fourth week they understood.

It was Friday, the loveliest of all days in school, and Miss Chaloner brought into class a big map of the United States. "You study geometry," she said, "only to understand the laws of proportion and beauty. What you might call the properness of life. You should learn to see the beautiful simplicity of geometry wherever you look. Now this map of your own country. How beautiful it is! How much it tells you!

"See what a perfect proportion it is! How pleasing to the eye! The longest distance from east to west. A rectangle. When you have seen a thousand great pictures you will know that the rectangle is the easiest mathematical form for achieving beauty. Your country is like the outlines of the finest pictures ever painted. A rectangle, in perfect proportions.

"But see how the variations creep in. The beautiful sweep of the western shoreline. The jagged, handsome sweep of the Atlantic coast. That long, beautiful Canadian border. And the fine breaking shore around the lakes. See how majestic the lines of the Mississippi are. If you were a great artist, you would place the Mississippi just about where it is. Slightly to the right of center. Yet leaning to the west. And you'd have all those other rivers running into it. Just the way they do. You wouldn't change it by a hair's breadth.

"And see how the map speaks of the people who live on it. In the east the chopped up, tight little states, crooked lines, powerful concentrations of things and people. Then look west. How the lines straighten out! Those slashing lines right across rivers and mountains and deserts and everything else. How beautiful they are! How they balance the tight little lines of the east! There are even three states whose boundaries are nothing but straight lines on the map.

"And do you see how the Rocky Mountains balance everything else? They follow the curve of the Pacific, but they give the land character. They're in beautiful proportion. That's what you should see in everything you study. Try to see the proportions, the way things link together. Mathematics can help you do that, because mathematics sets the rules."

The students were astonished by this lesson. They talked about it for a long time. Even the dullest student could comprehend what Miss Chaloner was talking about. For when she spoke there was a quiet compulsion. She never had to discipline a student. Not one. For she spoke directly to each mind, and more than that, to each consciousness and each heart. She seemed to say to each student: "Watch what great thought I will give you today." But she never moralized. Students who led the class were not held up for approbation. Boys who got into trouble, the two girls who were found undressed in the coal shed, suffered no indignities in Miss Chaloner's class.

One day she had David and Harry hold up the American flag. "Only a mathematician could have figured this out," she said. "He didn't have to know mathematics, of course. But he had to have that feeling for mathematics that I told you about. How could you divide space more perfectly than this flag does? See? The blue takes up its right proportion. Exactly. The red and white have added effect because some lines stop here and others run straight across. The jagged points of the stars add variety, but they're kept in line. How beautifully it is constructed. Do you see how everything falls into place?" She stood back to survey the perfection. David and Harry twisted their heads to see the flag. It was so simple, the way she explained it.

"If we have any more states for stars, it'll all be spoiled, won't it?" a student asked.

"Oh, no!" Miss Chaloner said. "That's the beauty of mathematics. It's so adaptable to new ideas. If you know the laws, you can fit them into any situation. See? With forty-nine states? What a beautiful flag you would have! And with fifty, spaced out so?"

"What about fifty-one?" a boy asked.

Miss Chaloner smiled at him. "I haven't worked that out yet," she said, laughing.

Another day she brought in a vase, made in Trenton.

She explained the proportions of the curves and why the vase was a fine example of mathematical thought. "Of course," she said, "maybe the person who made the vase didn't even know how to add two and two. I doubt it, but it might be so. The important thing is that he had a feeling for the rules. Or maybe it was a woman!" She laughed.

When David turned in his first notebook, with twenty original propositions worked out to the final Q.E.D., he expected to get an A. Instead Miss Chaloner called him and Harry and two other students to her desk after school. "Why did you turn in notebooks like this? Only twenty propositions each? Do you think that's reasonable for people who learn as easily as you do? And the lines? I see you spending money every week. All of you. Can't you spend ten cents for a bottle of red ink? And a good compass? You spend money for soft drinks and candy. And what have you? Nothing. But you spend that same money for some red ink and a good compass and you may acquire habits that will serve you a lifetime. Use sharp points on your pencils. Do your construction lines in different ink. And when you finish the twenty in half the time these other students do theirs, go on and do twenty more. Of the really hard ones." The students were astounded at such a view of learning! They reached for their unmarked notebooks. Miss Chaloner continued: "You! Harry Moomaugh. You want to grow up to be an engineer! When are you going to start? I don't know what you want to do, David. But why should a boy like you turn in a paper that isn't typewritten? Boys! There's always a best way to do things."

Because of geometry David had to work for the first time in his school career. Really work! Slave over smeared drawings. Try to show construction lines. Because of geometry he learned to type, to draw with a fine pen, to outline his work, to learn how to find word-derivations in the dictionary, to write in complete sentences, and to turn in a final twenty propositions that were as beautiful on the page as Miss Chaloner had known they could be. David got A in geometry, and he felt that he had earned it. From then on he never looked at the plane surfaces of the world without seeing their proportions. They were organized according to plan. "And the plan," Miss Chaloner said over and over, "is in your own mind. All the rules of the world can be found there, and if you worked forever, you'd not exhaust the wonders of your mind."

Marcia Paxson also helped David forget Paradise. She transferred to Doylestown High School because the classical education there was the best in Bucks County, and her impact upon the school was terrific. Like many Quaker women, she was determined to improve any society of which she was part, and her intransigent character soon made her the logical choice for class president. "She's an outsider!" some argued, but David and Harry served as her campaign managers. They reasoned, "Maybe she is an outsider. Maybe we need some new ideas," but the protesting students retorted, "You got that idea from Miss Chaloner, and it's common knowledge she's going to be fired."

Marcia was elected and she ran a ruthless, benevolent administration. She organized gift baskets for needy families, and she proposed a system whereby seniors took examinations on the honor system. "If you don't learn how to be honest in school," she pleaded, "where will you?" She appointed David chief student proctor. From this and other hints he guessed that she liked him. She liked Harry Moomaugh, too, but she never indicated that she wanted to be either David's or Harry's girl—at least not in the Bucks County sense.

In the Dutch region of Pennsylvania young courtship was an astonishing thing. At fifteen or sixteen boys and girls paired off and were acknowledged lovers. Each evening the boy visited the girl's home. He would talk to her parents until nine, and promptly at that hour the elders would cough and go to bed.

For a half hour or more the young couple would keep the lights on, or until they had finished their home work. Then, darkening the house, they would lie on the davenport. Some of them undressed and threw a blanket over themselves. At midnight, the father's bedside alarm would explode and he would cry: "Hey, Chonnie! Time to go yet!" Lingeringly at the door, Johnnie would say good night.

On the davenport a delicious variety of things might happen. A few couples became actual lovers and lay with each other night after night, the girls avoiding pregnancy by some miracle or becoming pregnant, engaged, and married within the same month. Others loosened their clothing and went to sleep, wrapped tightly in each other's arms. Two or three times a year they might make fumbling, passionate love, leading to nothing but deeper affection and worse confusion. Still others lay in darkness, kissed hesitatingly, talked, argued about school, laughed nervously and slipped tenderly into odd liberties and were ashamed of themselves next morning. And there were many who slept night after night on the davenports, satisfied with kissing and the tenderness of promised love. Boys were expected five or six nights a week, and if they did not appear the girl's father would say, "Where's young Eddie at tonight, Bertha?" "He's got play rehearsal," Bertha would reply. "He'll be out around midnight." The parents would shrug their shoulders and go to bed. Toward midnight Eddie would appear and slip into the darkened parlor. Bertha might be asleep on the davenport. Softly he would slide down beside her and take her in his arms. On such nights, and always on Saturday, the boy would be permitted to stay until two or three or four o'clock, as the morality of the girl's parents determined.

This was a fine system of courtship, and in a Dutch world where pregnant women were rarely deserted, it worked. By gradual stages men slipped from sleeping on the davenport to sleeping in a real bed; and Dutch marriages were fruitful, happy and secure, for the husband and wife both knew what they were getting.

But the Paxsons would tolerate no such courtship for Marcia. In the strange ways that girls have, she knew which of her friends were conducting their courtships in which degree. She was interested, but not envious. She knew that when she wanted a "fella" she could have one. Practically anyone she wanted.

Nor did David become involved in the country courtships. At first he was too interested in basketball—Bobby Creighton defended girls to the death, but he implied that boys who went with them too much were a bit silly—and later on he was so numbed by his experience with Nora that he became almost afraid of the strong clean girls of his school.

Yet he noticed that whereas before he had never been able to hear any voice but Bobby's howling at him during a game, he now became aware of another voice. It was a girl's clear, low cry: "Come on! Dave! Shoot!" It was Marcia's and it came to have great meaning for David, giving him the extra courage he needed when the going was tough.

After the game, of course, there was an awkward moment. Most of the players—even those on the second team—would have girls waiting for them. Bobby Creighton absolutely forbade his players to ride to games with girls, but he could not prevent them from going home that way. So, through the cold nights, sweethearts hurried home to davenports, spread out in fine exhaustion, and fell asleep, their relaxed, tired hands beneath the dresses of the girls who loved them.

With David and Harry it was different. They had no girls. Or rather, they had the same girl. When Marcia was seventeen, her parents let her have a car, and after the games she would drive the boys home. They were proud of the dark Quaker girl, and she showed no favoritism, analyzing each game fairly and apportioning the praise or blame justly. Some giddy girls were fooled by the fact that David did most of the scoring. But Marcia knew that it was because Harry passed so well. The boys liked her for her good sense.

David liked her because she seemed so much a part of the world he had missed at Paradise, and even though he was not in love with her, he was glad when Harry Moomaugh, feeling the urge of life, started going with a prematurely developed girl from New Britain. The davenport creaked six or seven times a month, and the girl's parents lay awake and pondered what might happen. "Harry's a fine boy!" the mother reasoned. "A wery good catch!" Her husband wondered how much his daughter really knew. Apparently she knew enough, for she got neither a baby nor Harry. She was a handsome Dutch girl, pink and white and soft. It was not long after Harry left for college that she shared the davenport with an older man. He knew a good catch when he slept with one, and they married promptly and had twins, two girls almost exactly like their mother.

So on the night after the Allentown game, while Harry hurried to a new davenport, Marcia drove David to the poorhouse and said, "You played better than ever before."

"I heard you calling my name," he explained.

"You fight so hard for what you want," she said.

"In a game I do," he said thoughtfully. "Other times . . ."

"You'll find out what you want to do," she said with great assurance. By some sign she signified that she would not be unhappy if David kissed her. Blushing and ill at ease, he climbed back in the car and tried to do so. She twisted to meet him, but the kiss was a maladroit, unsatisfying thing. "Good night, David!" she called as she shifted gears. "I was proud of you tonight."

He watched her disappear among the trees. She left the poorhouse lane and turned onto the Doylestown road. It was almost spring. Soon the last game of the year—and of all years so far as David's play at Doylestown was concerned—

would be over. The maples would begin to sprout and in the woods the dog-tooth violets . . .

David stood between the two buildings for a long time and then slowly started walking toward the road. Three cars whizzed by and the fourth stopped. "Hey?" the man asked. "Aren't you Dave Harper? That was some game you played tonight! Where you goin'?" The man drove him to Doylestown, where he walked about the streets for a long time.

He thought mostly about Nora, dead in the fire, and the smell of an early lilac tree reminded him of the time he had stood with Nora beneath the Hurricane. That was it! He'd go see Betty and talk with her about Nora.

He walked out Oakland Avenue trying to recall where the big girl lived. "She won't be at the Park yet," he reasoned. A drunk came reeling down the street. "You know where a girl named Betty lives?" David inquired. "Whosh Betty?" the drunk demanded, staggering on. "A big girl with a gold tooth in front," David explained. The drunk ignored him and went into a house, where his wife was waiting. "Oh, God! Have mercy on me!" she screamed as the man tottered into the door and fell upon the stairs. "Elsie! Elsie! Come look at your father!" She slammed the door and drove away all thoughts of big Betty with the gold tooth.

By this time David had reached the Catholic Church, so he walked on toward open country. A car picked him up. "You're Dave Harper!" the man exclaimed. "What a night you had! Where you goin'?" Then David knew.

"To Solebury," he said.

He reached the Paxson farm about one-thirty. The grass was already showing green and a few trees were in bud. The Lion was high in the heavens, its stars gloriously bright in the cool yet springlike air. And there was Marcia's window, by the coping. He threw a pebble at it. Quickly Marcia appeared. "David!" she whispered and then hurried to a side door. With no pretense she flung herself cleanly into his arms. "I couldn't sleep, either," she said. "How did you get here?"

"Hops most of the way, and a little walking," he said. She pressed him closely to her and allowed him to kiss her full upon the lips. David thought: "They're cool. Not like Nora's." His hands felt for her breasts, and they were different, too. Hard and firm, like the girl herself.

"Oh, David!" she said softly. "I'm sorry you came. You've got to go."

But they stood together looking at the agitated night, and

the air seemed to grow softer as if it knew spring were about to burst upon Bucks County. "You don't have to go right away," Marcia said, clinging to his arm and stopping his hungry hands.

They stood in the doorway for more than an hour, talking of school and what they would be when they grew up. Marcia would go to college and be a lawyer, or a social worker, or perhaps a writer, or a college teacher. David started to lead her to a large chair, but she protested in fright. She would not trust them together in a chair, for this meeting was not high-school fooling. They were looking at each other with ultimate penetration, asking: "Is this the one I am to marry?"

Three times David started to pour out his strange feelings for this quiet Quaker girl, but he could not speak, and after an hour of standing with her, talking of inconsequential things, he realized with dismay that he was afraid of Marcia. Her aloofness and the sharp quality of her mind differentiated her from all the other girls he had known, and he was afraid. Finally he stood with his hands at his side, staring at her, and she knew what troubled him. She leaned forward so that her nightgown hung in magnificent folds like angel garments in the museum, and she kissed him.

Suddenly his tongue was loosened and he babbled, "Marcia! That day at the poorhouse when your father came to get the man and his wife. I saw you watching them."

"Yes," Marcia said softly. "I knew what you were thinking when they rushed away together."

"I was thinking that everyone else in the poorhouse was old and worn out. But they weren't. You're like . . ."

"Hush!" she said, stopping him with a warm hand. "But if we ever do love each other, David, it'll be like that." Then she sent him away.

And when he had walked back to the hills that looked down on Doylestown, dawn overtook him, and the fabulous castles of Doylestown shimmered in the golden light of morning. He had never spoken of those castles—built by a wild and powerful man who thought houses dull—to a person in the world, for they were strangely his, and this morning he watched them for a long time, thinking: "It's not fun to kiss Marcia. But the world . . . It seems to be bigger. And brighter, like the castles this morning."

Miss Chaloner felt that she could not, in the restricted

periods allowed her, teach all the math her students would later need. She therefore obtained permission to hold additional senior classes after school. Through September and October the extra sessions were a keen pleasure, but in November the serious business of education began so that David and Harry had to drop math for basketball.

Miss Chaloner asked them twice if they thought this was wise. "Why don't you cut practice one day a week?" she asked. The thought was abhorrent to the young athletes, and Miss Chaloner said no more; but she arranged for Marcia to teach the boys on Saturday morning those principles which she, Miss Chaloner, had explained in the special sessions. Everything would have been fine except that trigonometry intervened and spoiled the system.

When Miss Chaloner first explained the theory of logarithms David said to Harry, "That's marvelous! A genius must have dreamed that up!" Daily he fell deeper under the spell of logarithms and refused to believe that one man could have devised such a magnificent system. When special after-school classes resumed he was much disturbed. On Tuesday he hung around school, fingering his five-place tables and edging toward the math room, but finally, with a show of courage, he tossed the book back into his desk and rushed off to practice.

There was violent excitement in Doylestown that year, for Hazleton and Allentown each had fine teams. A delirium had settled over both town and school, and Bobby Creighton walked with his face staring at pavement cracks. Gossip flashed through the town like fire: "Moomaugh's got a blister!" "Harper had indigestion, and the Reading game's tomorrow!"

Yet in math class Miss Chaloner continued to expound the impartial orderliness of the universe, and across David's impeccable notebook marched the magnificent logarithmic processes like trained soldiers of the mind. He derived real, physical pleasure in ordering his columns of figures until each triangle added up to the required $180°$ $0'$ $0''$.

The break came during the Reading game. Harry's blister broke, and for three quarters David was lost and ineffectual. In the final minutes Harry limped back into the game, roughed up the guards, and permitted David to slip through for three easy goals. Hours later there was still a dull roar in his ears, and he said to Moomaugh, "Tomorrow I'm signing up for the special math class."

"Me, too," Moomaugh replied.

Then the barbershops and poolhalls exploded! "Why the Allentown game is coming up!" the citizens wailed. "Those kids forget the honor of this town is at stake!" They went in small delegations to see the school board and argued: "A tight race like this is good for business. A championship gives a town color. You know Dave and Harry are bright boys. They know all they need to know right now! Stands to reason, Tom, you and I did mighty well without trigonometry. That Miss Chaloner's nothing but a troublemaker, and I said so before."

A board meeting was called, and the boys attended. Bobby Creighton, worried and sweating, stood by the door. Near the president of the board sat Miss Chaloner, unperturbed. "Now what is the need of extra classes?" the president asked sympathetically.

"Schools must take care of their brightest pupils," Miss Chaloner said primly, as if explaining a knotty algebraic formula. David could see she was making a poor impression. "These boys need to know all they can learn," she said like a frigid schoolmarm.

"But Miss Chaloner," a member argued, "surely these boys do well enough in their studies."

"One never learns enough," Miss Chaloner responded.

"You can carry things to extremes!" the member insisted.

"Learning should be carried to extremes!" the teacher snapped. For her sake, David wished she would not speak so much. The president rapped.

"Bobby?" he asked the coach. "How do you see this?"

Bobby Creighton coughed deferentially and blushed. With fidgets and solecisms he won the sympathy of the entire board, whose members recognized in him a fine, clean, average, honest, unpretentious fellow like themselves. "Miss Chaloner," he began, "is about the best teacher we've ever had in this town. She's a wonderful influence on these two boys. They'll tell you that. And I can see it in practice, too. . . that is, when they show up. But my idea is this. We play Bethlehem, Perkasie and Hazleton, in that order. Our school is smaller than any of them, and by rights we ought to be licked each game. But if we had the undivided help of Harry and Dave—and I think they ought to go right back to math classes after the race is over—well, if they'd pitch in and fight the way they used to, if I could only count on Harry and Dave . . ." Bobby's voice broke and he sniffed a couple of times, concluding. "Why, with Harry and Dave in there fighting I'd take on any team." His voice broke again, and Harry Moomaugh had to blow his nose. David felt simply rotten.

The kindly president leaned way back in his chair and asked in a most fatherly voice, "Well, young men? Sort of looks as if we ought to get back to practice, doesn't it?"

There was a moment of silence and then David turned his back on Miss Chaloner. "I guess we ought to," he sniffed.

The president smiled very warmly at Miss Chaloner and said, "We'll just suspend the extra classes, for a while." Then he chuckled. "That is, until Bobby's won the championship for us again. And by the way, Miss Chaloner, we've heard the most excellent things about your work."

The brilliant math teacher was a good loser. She smiled placidly at the board members and nodded to the two boys. In leaving the room she had to pass by Bobby Creighton, who eyed her nervously. Delicately she patted him on the arm. "If anyone can show the boys how to win, Bobby, you can," she said. "Good luck."

In class she taught with added intensity. To David and Harry going to Trig became something like going to church; they were uneasy but they were impressed. They understood their quiet teacher when she said, "You see how beautiful logarithms are. They are the essence of real numbers. As in chemistry, you boil away the useless water and retain a distillate. Now if you are truly smart you'll always approach every problem you meet in that manner. Boil away the needless water. Get right to the essence of your problem. If you can do that, you can never be defeated."

After the Bethlehem game she said, "Dave and Harry gave a good example last night of what I mean by going to the heart of the problem." The boys were astonished. They had never seen Miss Chaloner at a game of any kind. "The other team was bigger, so by saving their energy for spots where it would be most useful they won."

She lay down her chalk and smiled at the two heroes, but they weren't fooled a bit. They knew that she was castigating them and they were not surprised when she announced that she would not teach next year in Doylestown. They went to her after class and she said simply, "Most American schools despise learning. I thought this one might be different. It isn't."

When the championship was won, she resumed her special class, and it was jammed, for now students and parents alike recognized that in Miss Chaloner they had found that rarity beyond a price: a teacher who could inflame young minds. At her first session she said, "There is no reason why anyone should learn to use a slide rule, but it is so magnificent an instrument that I think you will enjoy knowing about it for its own sake." She distributed eight cheap K and E rules she had purchased with her own money. "These will give you a rough idea," she explained. "If any one of you is going on to higher learning, I strongly advise you to buy a good rule of your own." She passed among the students her own excellent rule. "Using this," she explained, "is like having a complete set of logarithmic tables in your brain." She demonstrated each of the processes, hammering away relentlessly at underlying principles. "Now, Marcia, explain again how you can tell by simple inspection $\sqrt[3]{x^2}$ and $\sqrt{x^3}$ ." She never bothered to ask why anyone would want to know the cube root of $x$ squared. She assumed that young people of growing intelligence would want to know hundreds of things for exactly the same reasons that boys hanging about a garage liked to know what a carburetor was, even though they drove perfectly well without knowing.

If every teacher in Doylestown had been as able as Miss Chaloner, David could never have digested the wonders paraded before him, for this undistinguished-looking math teacher demonstrated what was to David a revolutionary world: a universe of order and beauty. After the tangled morass of Paradise he was eager for such a vision, and as he slowly mastered the slide rule he often recalled that dismal meeting with the school board. "I turned my back on the only good teacher I ever had," he confessed to himself. Then he studied like mad.

He was surprised when the Philadelphia papers announced that Miss Chaloner was going to marry a Dr. Rossley, who taught at Yale. "See!" the people of the town whispered. "He's probably a Russian, too." But Harry and David were disturbed, and they went to see their teacher.

"We're ashamed of what we said at the school board," they said.

"Don't be!" she pleaded. "People have to acknowledge many loyalties. Sometimes they conflict."

"Then you're not mad at us?"

"Two fine boys like you!" she said in real surprise. "How could I be?"

The boys went among their fellow students and said, "If

she's getting married, let's buy her one hell of a fine wedding present!" David insisted upon handling the money so that he could slip into the fund ten dollars from his hoard hidden in the poorhouse barn. Then Marcia showed them what pieces of silver Miss Chaloner might like to have. Later the entire special class went into Philadelphia to meet Dr. Rossley. He was tall and thin, much older than Miss Chaloner. He talked gravely with the visitors and was both surprised and pleased at the real affection these children had for his intended wife. When the time came to say good-bye he left the room. Each of the girls kissed Miss Chaloner, who smiled and shook their hands. The boys were flustered, but when only Harry and David remained Harry bent forward and kissed his teacher on the cheek. "Lots of luck!" he said.

It was David's turn, Miss Chaloner gripped his hand and he was very nervous. "You must work hard to make something of yourself," she began. Then Harry pushed him, and he kissed her. She was the first grown woman he had ever kissed, and he blushed in great confusion.

"Oh, boys!" Miss Chaloner cried impulsively. "Don't be ashamed of saying thank you! Suppose you had never told me! I might have thought . . ." She pressed her large nose and said, "Sometimes thank you is better than a big salary." She laughed nervously, and the boys left.

At graduation David was dismayed. He heard the principal say: ". . . the prize each year to the best student. This year it is our great honor to award it to Marcia Paxson." Flashing, dark, self-confident, Marcia rose, bowed gracefully, and accepted the prize. Not for a moment could David believe that she had fairly won it. Only in Latin did she excel him.

Then, to his dismay, he heard the prize for the best all-round boy awarded to Harry Moomaugh. Tall, rangy and tough, Harry rose, smiled at the principal, and stepped smartly back with the prize.

"A special prize," the principal announced. "Only rarely does such an honor come to this school. Or to any school. By special arrangements which I am not at liberty to divulge, a special four-year scholarship covering tuition and all expenses to the college of his choice, to David Harper."

The boy could not rise. Out of the despair of his indecision, from the depths of his moral confusion a new miracle had been wrought. He could not believe it. This noise in his ears was not like the cheering at the basketball game. That was a game. But this was life! This was his future, his illimitable hopes and yearnings. The principal motioned to David to come forward. One sharp look at the boy showed the man it was hopeless to expect a word of acknowledgment. He handed David a small piece of paper. He smiled at the assembly and raised his hands as David stumbled back to his chair.

Dragging his mental and moral feet, David went back to Paradise for one last summer. He was astonished at how ugly Max Volo seemed when the little fellow whispered, eagerly, "It's positively sensational . . ."

"You get the hell out of here!" David commanded, but that night Max met him along the path leading to the trolley.

"Pssst!" Volo whispered. "Kid, give me a minute. I've got the rum-running concession for all the area north of Philly. Look! I got a fast car for you and a promise that there's to be no gun play."

"Max, you know I'm not in your league. Let me alone."

He walked to the trolley and slumped nervously into a seat, but outside he could hear loud voices. A woman of perhaps thirty-five, very plain, held two children by the hand. They were weeping.

"I had the money right in my pocketbook," the woman wailed.

"What money?" the conductor asked.

"A two-dollar bill," the woman insisted. She appealed to the boy. "I did have it, didn't I?"

"I saw it," the boy wept.

"What did you do with it?" the conductor asked. "Say!" he cried. "I'll bet you mistook it for a one!"

"Oh, God, no!" the woman cried. "I need it." She began to recount the places she had been: "Popcorn. Two hotdogs— I didn't buy one for myself—three rides . . ."

"It's no good," the conductor said. "Them Park cashiers, once they get hold of a two-dollar bill!" The woman sat on the step of the car and buried her face in her hands.

"What will I do?" she wailed.

"Don't you have any money?" the conductor asked.

"Where would I have it?" she screamed.

David intervened. "Here," he said. "Take this." He gave her two dollars.

"Oh, thank you!" the woman cried.

When the trolley dropped David at the poorhouse he thought: "That woman! You mean to say I've been stealing from women like that?" Then he understood why the cashiers of Paradise never looked at their victims. "Hell!" he cried to the night. "I'm no better than Mr. Crouthamel."

In stark, indecent colors he saw himself as he was, a petty thief preying upon women and children and lovers. He was a minor Max Volo, and in shame he walked to his poorhouse room. "Thank God Daniel's dead!" he muttered when he reached the long hall. "I'd be ashamed for him to see me tonight." And early next morning he quit his job at Paradise.

Mr. Stone's reaction surprised David. The gray cashier looked very glum and said, "You're the only person I ever shared a secret with," and David sensed that the grim, controlled man was lonely. Mr. Stone was a rugged, moral man who saw the world in only one light, and David could not brazenly say to him: "Your tricks for robbing people aren't much better than Max Volo's." He couldn't say: "This Park is a filthy place," because with Capt. Sousa and Klementi Kol and Mr. Stone it wasn't altogether filthy. "I'm going to work on a farm," David lied. "Training for college football."

Mr. Stone shrugged his shoulders and said, "Well, if that's what you want."

"I'll tell you what I do want!" David cried. "I want to have dinner with you and Sousa." Mr. Stone arranged it, and in the interval of waiting David wandered along the gravel paths of Paradise. He would never forget this Park: the tinkling carrousels that played *Faust*, the smell of popcorn, the distant thunder of the Hurricane . . . His throat choked up, for a new Coal Mine was being built, with peaks higher than before. "Nora, Nora!" he mumbled to himself.

The lilacs were in bloom and he asked the young conductor of the Philadelphia and Reading if he might whisk the little train beneath the trestles one more time. "No indeed!" the boy said firmly, protecting his alligator bag of tickets. So David walked among the lilacs and thought: "Look how these bushes grow up every year. You can't seem to kill them." As he walked through these familiar scenes for the last time he tasted the death that clings to the coattails of life. He had outgrown this turbulent and wonderful Park, but each garish spot was burned into his heart, and rejecting Paradise was like dying.

At dinner he remembered what Miss Chaloner had said

about thanking people and he shook Capt. Sousa's hand. "I'll never forget how kind you've been. You didn't have to bother with me, Capt. Sousa."

The elderly musician nodded gravely and said, "Tonight we'll fire the pistols just for you!"

And the pistols fired and Capt. Sousa himself nodded from the bandstand, and when the concert ended David went backstage and said the same thing to Miss Meigs: "You've taught me to like music. You didn't have to bother with me, and I appreciate it."

The singer smiled at the grave young man and asked, "Doesn't the fountain play pretty soon?" When David nodded she asked, teasingly, "Will you be my escort?"

At the lakeside David said, "I like the way you sing, Mary."

"Mary," she repeated slowly, holding on to each syllable. "Mary Meigs?" She touched David's arm and asked, "Do you like that name? Does it sound right to you?"

"It's a fine name!" David cried enthusiastically as the lights came on.

"But I mean . . . Is it a name you'd remember?"

"I could never forget it," David affirmed as if taking an oath.

"I don't mean you," she argued. "I mean just anybody. How would Maris Meigs be?"

"Too many s's," David objected.

"How about Mona Meigs?"

"Not bad. Sounds sort of Persian. But what's the matter with Mary?"

"It's sort of common and I want a name that people will remember." The lights came surging up through the leaping fountain and the tense singer cried, "Like that! When my name is in lights, nobody must ever forget it."

David stood close to her and felt the determination that consumed her. Colored shadows played across her face as she continued. "These new movies they're talking about. Do you honestly think they can make people sing? Because if they can . . ." The lights died away and in the distance the Hurricane roared.

Then Mary Meigs burst into wild speech. "You watch! Some day you'll see my name everywhere. Because I can sing, Dave! I can sing like mad!" The vibrancy of her passion enthralled David, for he had often heard girls in Doylestown say they wanted to become nurses or teachers. But this was different. Mary Meigs saw the entire world as her enemy and she had the courage to cry, "Why, some day I'll spit on this lousy Park. And I'll be up there when I do it." She pointed at the stars.

"You will, too!" David said reassuringly, and although Mary was five years older than he, he kissed her. He did so in an awkward manner and she whispered, "Watch out! You'll muss my hair!" Then she saw how agitated this simple kiss had made the boy and she patted his hand. "I'll sing the next song only to you."

And when the music started she kept her promise. She smiled only at David and began to sing, *"Just a kiss in the dark . . ."* But before she had finished five measures she felt the breathing audience in front of her and she poured forth her soaring notes to every man sitting there, and every man as he listened could honestly say: "She was singing right at me." Some remarked to their wives, "That girl can really warble. She'll go places."

That was when David knew what he wanted to do. He wanted to write words the way Mary Meigs could sing them. He wanted to fling angry phrases at the world's teeth, and to hell with it! But even as he sat with his arms clasped about his knees he knew that he was somehow different from Mary and that he would never say to hell with the world. He lacked her all-consuming vanity. Even now he could remember her tenseness and preoccupation with herself as she whispered, "You'll muss my hair!"

# PART 3

# Fair Dedham

LIKE A WISE ANIMAL retreating caveward to repair his wounds, David lost himself in the willing anonymity of freshman year in college. After the violent excitement of Paradise, he was glad for the refuge of books.

The fraternities were content to let him hide. Their scouts reported: "He's got no money. Not a cent. How could he pay dues, let alone dance fees?" Men who had seen him play basketball said: "In his jerk-water league he was all-county for three years. But you know the small-town athletes. They bloom in the bushes but they bust in college." Most damning of all, one of the scouts discovered his marks: "Another brain trust. Probably wind up as a radical. Hands off! We've got our share of headaches as is."

In spite of David's satisfaction with the sanctuary of college, he experienced the bitter moment of knowing that the fraternities did not want him. The realization was heavy upon him, as if he were a small boy. "Well," he mumbled when the others opened their envelopes and there was none for him, "I didn't want much to join anyway."

He could not delude himself, however, when football started. He was not heavy enough to make the team and for the first time sat in the bleachers while men his own age played a thrilling game. Again he consoled himself: "I don't care much for football anyway. Basketball's my dish." But as the Dedham-Swarthmore football game approached he became unbearably excited. He even found himself whispering at night: "I hope we win this year." And on the day of the game he shouted with wild joy at the Dedham victory.

He had chosen Dedham principally because of Bobby Creighton. Fellows in Doylestown could laugh about Bobby and the long-ago basketball game, but most of them knew that if they ever went to college they would select Dedham. It was a quiet, somnolent place, some fifteen miles west of Philadelphia, and was dedicated to the Republican party, the glories of English literature, the perfection of Philadelphia society as opposed to New York's hurly-burly, and the eventual triumph of everything that was good and beautiful and true. Dedham was a Quaker college, and although the tenets of Quakerism did not intrude, the quiet simplicity of that religion dominated college life, so that even when the dead average of Philadelphia living was being held up as the world's ideal, Dedham always had room for a minority report from an abiding genius like Dr. Tschilczynski. For David, the towering Russian became a symbol of the difference between Dedham and Doylestown; for in his home town many citizens had argued whether Miss Chaloner were an atheist or a Russian or something equally awful, whereas at Dedham everyone was proud to explain that their Immanuel Tschilczynski was both. At least six students whispered to David: "You know he's a genius, don't you?" No one liked to take the Russian's classes, for his English was not adequate to explain mathematical processes, but all the students were pleased that among the dead wood of their faculty there was one genius.

There were other excellent aspects of Dedham that David savored in the early days of his anonymity. It had the first real library he had seen, a wonderful place of old stacks and corners filled with books that must some day be catalogued. He was allowed to rummage through these musty corners and thus developed the first criterion of a scholar: that any book of any size or color or date or language or complexion be considered an avenue to some great adventure. In the dark enclaves of the library David punished his eyes and rebuilt his enthusiasm for all the facets of human knowledge; and never would he be able to forget the average autumn day when he made so unaverage a discovery: he stumbled upon

*The Greek Anthology;* it was done into verse by some eighteenth-century scholar so that dead men seemed to be standing all around David with their tombstones and he was reminded of those fields of Troy upon which he had set out to redress each of the world's wrongs.

As he tasted the deep pleasures of college life David began to feel that he had at last discovered a spiritual haven where the ugly life of Paradise could never intrude. Of course, that was before the Coronation of the May Queen or the shocking Case of the Assy Nude. But in his freshman ignorance he withdrew into a shell of quiet learning, and he would have stayed there, recapturing the innocent adolescence he had missed because of Paradise, had it not been for Professor Tschilczynski and Joe Vaux. Quietly at first, and then with a rush, they dragged him back into the main stream of life, whereby he saw that all living in the world is of a piece and there is no retreat.

It was autumn, in 1925, and the air was crisp and fine. In gutters old leaves burned and filled the town with Hallowe'en incense. The rich smell of it lingered for days. The earth was dusty green and then a dying brown, for all green things were dying.

That was the wonder of autumn in a college town! As the earth died, people grew into beings. The professors who had been rusticating on their farms sprang back into life and began to teach as if this were their last class before the final dismissal bell. Young men and women burst into flowering thought and started to write sonnet sequences or swore to themselves that this year they would master chemistry. The promises that were made! The old hopes that were taken out and dusted off! Why, it was spring itself in the human mind, and all the while the earth lay dying.

David's close association with the seasons at the poorhouse had made him unusually aware of their sequence, and autumn had always been a lonely, confusing time. He had never believed that a given year ended in December. That was the glorious time of birth and violent happiness and the deep friendship of cold winter nights. No, it was obvious that the old year died and the new one began some time in late October or November when irresponsible gusts of wind ripped the last leaves loose and sent them howling into the long nights.

He felt, therefore, that this autumn he was being born

anew. Sometimes he shuddered when he thought of Paradise and swore to himself: "I'll never get mixed up in anything like that again!" In his clean new life he noticed the people about him and for the first time met young men and women his own age who could think more quickly than he. There was the girl, thin and wasted-looking, whose poems had been published in the *Atlantic*. A chemistry student had perfected a process for making hard-grained soap, and a large company was paying him royalty on it. Another man with an expressive face played weekly at the Hedgerow Players and had been asked to take a role on Broadway. It was exciting to be among such people.

But more exciting than anyone else was Joe Vaux. He was from Boston and went to Mass. "My mother's name was Feeney!" he announced. "Do you want to make something of it?" He was a wiry, gnarled fellow and bore the scars of many street brawls. "I came here because I got a scholarship," he said pugnaciously. "You might say I was a wizard in history."

Vaux quickly settled upon David as his principal friend. "You look smart," he said. "Tell me! What's the lowdown on this Tschilczynski? Who is he? Is he a White Russian? If he's as good as everybody says, why isn't he in Russia?" The wiry Bostonian jerked his head from side to side like a ferret on a strange path. He seemed to probe at David with his nose. Dropping his voice to a whisper he asked, "Do you suppose he's a Trotskyite? Hmmmm?"

David had never before heard of Trotsky. "Who's Trotsky?" he asked.

Vaux jumped back as if he had been struck. "Who's Lenin?" he countered.

"He had the Czar shot," David explained.

"Oh, my God!" Vaux shouted. He dashed off to his room and hurried back with a dirty, worn book. "Read this!" he commanded. It was *Ten Days That Shook the World*. "By the way," he asked, "what do you think about the Revolution?"

"Which revolution?" David asked.

With great contempt Vaux snorted, "The Russian."

"Well," David said, quoting the Doylestown paper, "they refused to pay their debts, didn't they?"

This time Vaux showed no anger. He cocked his head on one side and studied David. Then he thrust his thin nose forward and asked, "How old are you, Dave?"

"I'm eighteen," David replied.

Vaux leaned back and smiled. "You sure don't act it," he said. Then he added with acute intensity, "Look! In your lifetime! The greatest event of modern history has taken place. And you don't know anything about it!" He stamped about the room and suddenly extended his chin like a professor, crying, "What have you been doing?"

David learned that if he wanted to talk with Joe Vaux he would have to learn a great deal about Russia. He read many books and never quite understood what it was that had happened. But for some strange reason he would not tell Vaux what he knew about Tschilczynski. He had learned, for example, that the great mathematician had taught in St. Petersburg and that he had fled to Paris during the Revolution. A Quaker had met him there and brought him back to Dedham, where other Quakers had taught him the rudiments of English and had paid his salary at the college.

Then one day Joe Vaux burst into David's room and cried, "I knew! I knew if I stuck on his neck long enough I'd find out!" He closed the door with soft caution and confided to David, "Tschilczynski's a counter-revolutionist! He's meeting with a group of White Russians in Philadelphia."

David refused to comment. Instead, he asked, "Why are you so worried about the Revolution?"

Vaux dropped his hands and stared at his friend. "I'm worried about everything!" he said. "I'm worried about Mexico and Yugoslavia and Germany. Aren't you?"

"No," David admitted.

The slim, gnarled Bostonian was about to explode but he controlled himself and grinned at David. "You'll wake up some day! Guys from . . . Where is it? Cow Center? You just need more sleep than the rest of us."

And that first autumn at Dedham there were other stirrings and brooding thoughts that must be part of any good college. A droning professor would say somthing that suddenly illuminated the known world like a vast light. Or at night the student body would burst into an unpredictable display of emotion over a football game. Bonfires would flame toward the sky and florid speeches such as Scipio might have delivered erupted from student leaders. The meager college band would play, mostly off key, and a hundred night voices would softly intone the opening words of the song that would forever haunt David's mind with a sense of autumn: "Fair Dedham, in that distant day . . ."

Immanuel Tschilczynski was a mammoth man. He was well over six feet tall and towered above the rostrum from which he tried to explain the principles of mathematics. He wore a shaggy moustache that spilled over his lip like a muddy waterfall, and a dull scar led from the right corner of his mouth. Students were of two opinions about that scar. Some said Tschilczynski got it when his wife gashed him—in Lwow, of all places—with a razor. Others maintained that it was a relic of the professor's student days in Germany.

If David had kept his mouth shut he would not have become involved with Professor Tschilczynski, but he had a habit of solving algebraic equations instantaneously, under his breath. He had worked so diligently with Miss Chaloner that college algebra was quite a bore, for when the Russian wrote an equation like $x^2 + 45x = -164$, David would see at once that the answer must be $(x+41)$ and $(x+4)$.

One day Dr. Tschilczynski saw David's lips moving and guessed what was happening. He asked his student to solve four quadratics in rapid succession. "How are you doink it?" the Russian demanded.

"I think of them as compensating reciprocals on a slide rule."

"You knowink the rule, yes?"

"Yes, sir. I imagine the reciprocal index to C. Then I guess what the factors are."

The professor dropped his chalk and said, "You mean . . . you gan wisualize a rule? Set? In your head?"

"Yes," David replied.

Tschilczynski wrote three complicated quadratics on the board. Then, where David could not see, he wrote the correct answers for the class to watch. "Now, you like to tryink this one?" he asked. David rattled off the answers and grinned as the students applauded. "Now this one," Tschilczynski directed. Again the answer was relatively simple. "And now!" the Russian said. "We tryink maybe this one, too!"

"I don't seem to get that one," David said. "Must be some decimal places. If I had to guess I'd say 3.6 and something like 43.7."

Professor Tschilczynski opened a drawer and produced a beautiful twenty-inch rule. "Try this," he said. David fumbled with it for a moment and then found two scales he knew.

"Well," he laughed nervously. "I was off on that one!"

"The gorrect answers?" Tschilczynski asked. David read them rapidly and the class applauded again. The towering

Russian nodded gravely, as if the accolade were for him. "How were you disgoverink this?" he asked David.

"I had a very good teacher," David replied.

The professor's face broke into a massive grin. He raised his big, stubby hands in the air and said, "You had one egzellent teacher! Tomorrow you report to galgulus. Algebra you know already too much."

But calculus was too difficult for David. He studied hard to catch up, but whenever he faced the difficult formulae his mind came to a jolting stop. After several such experiences his stomach muscles began to tighten up and he underwent sweaty frustration.

"I can get this!" he swore to himself. "If those other lunks can get it, I can." But he did not catch on. Much of his difficulty was caused by Professor Tschilczynski, whose explanations of the calculus merely confused him. The great Russian would stand at the board and his eyes would light up with pleasure at the beautiful process he was about to unravel. But after a few bumbling phrases he would start to write equations with either his left or right hand—or with both—and when the board was in hopeless chaos he would start to erase terms with the heel of his hand until only a simple equation remained. Then he would smile like a child and cry, "So you seeink! It's obwious!" He was known among his students as Old Obwious, but David did not learn the calculus.

For a week he ignored his other classes and started painstakingly at the beginning of his book, pondering each step. Still he did not learn and became irritated. He remained after class and said, "I don't think I can keep up with this class."

The big Russian grinned with real pleasure. "Is wery diffgult, galgulus? Good! Pretty soon it all gomes glear, like daylight. Then you seeink how beautiful it is!"

So David went back to his midnight desk and his calculus book. "I'll learn this damned thing," he muttered over and over. He cut classes for two days and stayed pinned to the slim volume of principles that eluded him. At night he could not sleep because of the writhing formulae that twisted through his mind, and then on the third day, about eleven o'clock in the morning, the vast design took shape. It was wonderful and pleasing. He closed his hot eyes and admitted, "I'd like to be a math professor. This is what I've been looking for." He did not confide to himself that what he sought was a world of neat categories organized into known patterns.

At Paradise he had tried submerging himself in the fiery, intemperate world of poetry and love. The experience had been too vital for him to hammer into neat shapes. "I want to be a mathematician," he said that morning. "I like the cleanness of it."

When he informed Tschilczynski of this the big Russian clapped him on the shoulder. "Fine! Today you begome my assistant. Then we plan your future! University of Tchicago. Maybe Leipsic! Gambridge!"

But when David submitted his first batch of corrected exam papers for the Russian's review he received a shock. "What you runnink?" Tschilczynski cried. "Yet a kindergarten?" He pointed to a red 15 that David had added onto an otherwise dull paper. "What's this?" he demanded.

"We always got 15 for neatness and setting up the paper right," he explained.

In a rage Tschilczynski tore up the papers and grabbed a fresh pile. "Like this we gorrect!" he stormed. With a red pencil he flashed through the papers. "In one million years this one don't gatch the idea!" he bellowed. "Zero!" He stamped it furiously upon the offending paper. "Is too much, already, zero!" he shouted at the next. He whisked through the yellow sheets, looking always for those papers which displayed correct processes of analysis. When he had them segregated, he marked each with a violent 100. He started to give the others zero, but David interrupted.

"Some of those are not so bad!" he insisted.

The brooding Russian hesitated. "Which ones you think-ink?" he asked.

David shuffled the papers for more than four minutes, with Tschilczynski staring over his shoulder. "These," he said. "You can't give them zero."

"By me is OK," Tschilczynski cried. "Them we give 60." He splashed the mark across each paper and David thought: "I'll change them later." Then the Russian asked, "What's this neatness you talk about?"

David explained Miss Chaloner's theory of mathematics as training in precision and beauty. At this Tschilczynski exploded. "Neatness, margins, straight lines!" he bellowed. "In mathematigs is only one thing! That understanding, way down deep. Is he got that? OK, he's yet a mathematician."

The big Russian continued, stamping up and down his narrow office. "Nice lines! Bah! For twelf dollars a week you are gettink draftsmen to do that. Nice lines anybody can draw. InAmeriga you got already one million men gan draw nice lines. But to wisualize a problem! To see all sides at once. That don't come from no nice lines! I'm tellink you, David, the best way to be a rotten man is to bother with nice lines!"

Suddenly Tschilczynski stopped ranting and grabbed a pencil. He scribbled equations until they spilled over onto a second sheet. "Look!" he cried joyously. "I knew it! All day long I been tryink to solve that equation. How beautiful it is!" He stood back and studied the problem that had preyed upon his mind since breakfast. Even when quarreling with David he had been pondering that complex thought. He dropped the sheet and said quietly, "I tell you what, David. You takink them papers home. You give some of them higher marks. Maybe I was too egzited."

But if Tschilczynski thought a fugitive equation could get him excited, he had much to learn. Joe Vaux started auditing second-semester calculus. He sat in profound contemplation of Tschilczynski's more than customarily turgid explanations. He leaned far forward in his chair and nodded sagely whenever the Russian said, "From there, it's obvious . . ." Tschilczynski derived comfort from the fact that at last a student could keep up with him. He was a bit surprised, therefore, when Vaux rose to his feet upon the invitation: "Any qvestions?"

"Yes, professor," the wiry young man said. "Do you think that the free spirit of science can flourish in a capitalist society?"

Tschilczynski wiped his forehead. "What kind of a qvestion is that?" he asked. "We go on with the lesson."

That night the story about Joe Vaux's question skipped about the campus. The sager students took it as further proof that Joe was a trouble maker. On Thursday some of the senior men discussed the problem of what to do with this difficult freshman, and on Friday Dr. Tschilczynski's class was crowded.

When his first demonstration ended in customary obscurity, Tschilczynski asked if there were any questions. Vaux rose and asked, "Do you agree that in the field of abstract science as well as in the field of applied science Soviet specialists are far ahead of those in capitalist countries?"

"I must ask you . . ." the professor began.

"Throw him out!" an engineer cried, and before Tschilczynski could intercede, four husky football players grabbed lean Joe Vaux and dragged him from the room.

This caused consternation on the campus. A faculty investigation followed which uncovered embarrassing situations. For example, Dr. Tschilczynski had no idea who was in his classes. Furthermore, Joe Vaux was attending nine different classes and flunking three for which he was duly registered.

It was agreed that Joe would have to be dismissed, and news of this was welcomed on the campus; but before the sentence could be put into effect Dr. Tschilczynski reported to the president and argued with him for more than an hour. That night the Russian said to David, "A uniwersity is got no right to set itself up as a geeper of little rules and regulations. Let Mr. Waux take fifty glasses, if he can get an eduGation that way. A uniwersity is . . ."

"This is only a college," David interrupted. The Russian stopped and looked at him.

"True," the professor said. "A collitch is yet a small uniwersity. But it must not be small in the big things. Things like gettink an eduGation."

The upshot was that Mr. and Mrs. Vaux were called down to Dedham. They were remarkable people, not at all like the substantial parents from Philadelphia who preened themselves on the fact that their daughters had been invited to the Phi Kappi Psi dance or that their sons played football. The Vauxes were tight, belligerent Irish people who had worked bitterly hard all their lives. They were bewildered by Dedham and mortified that their son should be in trouble. They made him promise to behave. "No more roisterin'," Mr. Vaux warned him. "A boy like you gets a chance like this once in a million years."

They liked David and cautiously asked him if he would keep an eye on their son. "Watch after him," Mrs. Vaux pleaded; but the entire visit was torn into a wrenching experience when it came time for the bewildered couple to go back to Boston. Joe and David took them to the station, where Joe promised them again that he would behave. Then, as the train came around the bend, Joe suddenly caught his parents' hands and held them, gnarled and knotted, in David's face.

"These are the badges of their honor!" Vaux said, as if he were about to cry. "Look at them!"

The train puffed to a stop and Joe kissed his parents good-bye. "What did you mean by doing that?" David asked.

Vaux turned on him furiously as the train chugged away. "What have you ever done to justify yourself on this earth?" he demanded. All the way back to the dormitory he railed at David as if he hated him, and before David could reply four big upper-classmen came to take Vaux away.

"We want to talk with you!" the big men said.

Next day the story broke all over the campus. The student leaders had taken Joe to a room and messed him up a bit "to knock some sense into his head." But Joe had broken loose and had grabbed a chair. He had also kicked one of the seniors in the crotch, so that a true roughhouse had developed. "He's a regular alley fighter!" the senior men reported.

The faculty heard about this and considered firing Joe for good, but when they saw the respect that Joe and the seniors now had for one another they dropped proceedings. Dr. Tschilczynski explained this to David: "Sometimes is even Qvakers got to see that a little physical wiolence is necessary. It glears up the air, sort of."

If David had avoided going to Dr. Tschilczynski's room, he might still have escaped involvement with the big Russian; but one day the professor said, "You like to gorrect your papers with me, yes?" and he led David to his quarters.

His room was a gloomy, forbidding place, in the home of a Greek restaurant-keeper's widow. She was a blowsy Southern European who took no pains to keep the professor's room clean. At first she had tried to do so, but he had complained that she mussed his papers. Now she left the big, sloppy man alone.

There was a samovar in the middle of the room and beneath it a battered tin of solidified alcohol. His clothes closet was merely a section of the room partitioned off by beaver board and green draperies that did not close. There were two unmatched stuffed chairs, and it was easy to detect which was the professor's, for it was smeared with butter. There was a sink in the corner filled with saucers and glasses.

But more than the dirt David noticed the books and papers. Tschilczynski had hundreds of books piled about the floor in toppling stacks. His two tables were hidden by jumbled papers, on top of which rested the plates from which he had eaten his lunch. With a generous brush of his hand the Russian indicated his American quarters and said, "I abologize for the appearance. I'm yet a wery dirty man." He cleared a space for David at one of the tables and dragged up the battered chair. "I let you use my chair," he said.

Soon David was immersed in his work, oblivious of the confusion about him. Then he looked up and saw that the restaurant-keeper's widow was cleaning the room and Tschilczynski was gone. David smiled at her and she blushed like a peasant. "You ought to clean this place up," he said to her. "No matter what Professor Tschilczynski says!"

The widow giggled, grabbed a trayful of dishes and said in parting, "Men! Men!"

Outside, in the yard, the Russian called lustily for David to come to the window. "A robin!" he cried. "Loog at him chumping!" The big man studied the friendly bird for some minutes and banged his way back into the room. "Gomes sprink," he said like a poet, "I got to be movink. Listen to me, David. Never make good resolutions in the winter. Always in the sprink. That's when life starts to roll, I tell you."

That night he walked David back to the dormitories and in the quadrangle he had a happy idea. "Tomorrow we both gut glasses and go into Philadelphia! We go to Leary's!"

They went into Philadelphia on an early train and wandered down Market Street to the famous old bookstore that had served generations of scholars. "Now we see somethink!" he cried like a boy on his first trip to Paradise. He pulled from the long shelves book after book on a bewildering variety of subjects.

"What do we want all these for?" David asked.

"These are for you!" the Russian replied in much surprise. "My assistant with no library! Ah, no!" He picked out one book in particular, a treatise by Karl Pearson. "And this one special! This Karl Pearson! He is the father of all modern knowledge. In biology, medicine, egonomics, edugation, chemistry . . . At the foundation of any positive science is always Karl Pearson." He would not let Leary's wrap that book. "He takes it with him!" he announced to the manager. "It's for him the beginnink of a new life."

The two mathematicians—David with his new bible—walked up Market Street and felt the quiet breath of spring upon the city. "It's nice!" Tschilczynski said. "Even in a city is nice, sprink." At the Earle Theatre the Russian noticed that vaudeville was showing. "Well!" he cried exuberantly. "In the theatre best of all is waudewille!" He bought two tickets and led David into the darkened theatre. A cheap movie was three-quarters finished. In a loud whisper the

Russian announced, "But with waudewille the worst part is the movies."

"Sssssh!" the other customers warned in irritation.

"We mustn't talk!" the Russian whispered hoarsely.

"Please sit down!" a woman begged. With a massive hand Tschilczynski pushed David into a seat.

The movie ended and a brassy orchestra started to play extremely rapidly. The professor clapped his hands like a child and whispered, "Good, eh?" The curtains opened and a chorus of ten pretty girls danced out in ballet costumes. "Wery nice!" Tschilczynski beamed.

An hour later the show reached a noisy climax with all performers onstage. They bowed flashily and the orchestra ripped into a vigorous march. "We go now," the professor said, dragging David after him. But as David struggled through the aisle he suddenly stopped so that Tschilczynski was caught between two women. They muttered at the clumsy man and the Russian pulled David's arm again; but David was staring at the screen, where brilliant letters proclaimed: "NEXT WEEK. TELL YOUR FRIENDS. AMERICA'S FAVORITE SONG-STRESS. MARY MEIGS." David gasped and would not move while the beautiful pink and white slide remained on the screen, showing Mary Meigs in a daring evening gown. Her hair was more blonde than ever, and she wore a string of pearls about her white neck. In the picture her eyes were an exaggerated blue, and she had her head raised in that insolent, attractive way she had practiced so long at Paradise. "TELL YOUR FRIENDS!" a new slide commanded, and Professor Tschilczynski finally dragged David loose.

So on the trip back to Dedham the professor and his student were each in a state of mild exhilaration. Tschilczynski hummed snatches of old songs he had learned in the music halls of St. Petersburg. "When I was a student," he began, but interrupted himself to sing *Gaudeamus Igitur*. Then he told David of the manner in which he had practiced duplicity in order to visit the theatre, which his parents could not approve. He grew increasingly agitated, and when the train reached Dedham he insisted that David have dinner with him that night. The blowsy landlady produced a tableful of smelly and delicious food. "Like an angel she makes food, that one!" Tschilczynski said approvingly as the heavy woman disappeared.

When dinner ended the big Russian still wanted to talk. He clasped his huge hands about his knees and laughed.

"Everybody wants to know who I am. I tellink you." He was the son of a wealthy Russian merchant. He left home for some reason and became a student. He had been to the Universities of St. Petersburg, Utrecht, Uppsala and Berlin. On his return to Russia he taught at the University in Moscow. His father, seeing him at last respectable, gave him a great deal of money. He married the daughter of a minor government official who was also wealthy. In the Revolution this woman became one of the most violent supporters of Lenin. He himself had no interest in the Revolution. Not understanding what it was about, he slipped out of the country, to Paris.

"But what about your wife?" David asked.

"I don't know. I guess she's dead."

David looked at his professor. He was the first great man David had known, greater even than Sousa, and as he talked David learned that neither a man's greatness nor his goodness can be measured by the happiness he has attained. This disturbed David, and he felt drawn toward the towering Russian. He remembered his own surging bitterness in the poorhouse when Hector was debased, and in the intervening years he had come to think that there ought to be a true correlation between happiness and goodness; but now he saw his professor, as kind as a man could be, and he was not happy. He was an outcast from home, a wanderer, a man who did not even know if his wife lived or was dead.

In the dark and messy room David brooded silently upon this unwelcome discovery. Evil men prosper, and good men die in the poorhouse. Other evil men are caught and executed. There was no mathematical certainty in life. Right now Max Volo was one of the richest men in Philadelphia with all kinds of corruption under his control. His name appeared in the papers: "Max Volo says it's time for a change in City Hall!" "Max Volo returns from Florida." Even though the warmth of spring was already in the air, David shivered.

He was not prepared for what happened next. Immanuel Tschilczynski, trembling like a boy, was over him blurting out, "I got to tell somebody." Then, expansively, he kicked open the door into the kitchen. "You gome in now!" he ordered. Bashfully, the giggling widow joined the two men. Tschilczynski held out his big hand and she stood awkwardly beside him. "Three days ago we were married, yet," the professor announced, like a child confessing a petty guilt.

David did not want to share this secret. He did not want

to be dragged back into the vast messiness of life, and he hated thinking of his great, brilliant professor married to a clumsy peasant. Awkwardly, and in shame, he congratulated the two middle-aged people and hurried to his own rooms.

"Why would he do that?" he muttered. "A man like him! Why, he could marry the best . . ." He stopped short. "Suppose his other wife is alive!" And the whole turgid tumult of living swarmed back upon him. He lay down on his bed and felt weak. Then he began to chuckle at something Tschilczynski had said: "She gan gook like an angel, that one." He wondered if that's what men wanted, the buxom warmth of a good cook.

Each day that week David bought copies of the *Inquirer*, *Bulletin*, *Ledger* and *Record*. As Saturday approached, both the advertisements and stories about the new vaudeville at the Earle made more mention of Mary Meigs. She was, it seemed, a brilliant singer whom Philadelphia would take to its heart. On Friday a group of pictures and a long story appeared, and it was with difficulty that he restrained himself from running to all the rooms on his hall shouting, "I know this girl!" It was warm and good to know a person who was successful.

At the same time David was deeply worried about Professor Tschilczynski. What would the college authorities say if they knew that he had married his peasant housekeeper? And what would they do—or the law, for that matter—if it was discovered that his Russian wife were actually living? Suddenly Tschilczynski seemed like Nora; they were the wanderers. They had no homes, no families, nothing to tie them into one place. And David felt agitated and sorrowful for them.

Yet he continued to be angry with Tschilczynski. He felt that his huge professor should not have placed on him the burden of the secret wedding; and he adopted the trick of mentioning the Russian's name at frequent intervals, to see if the story had yet become common knowledge. He avoided Tschilczynski's office for fear the towering man might want to indulge in further confidences.

Then his vague excitement about Mary Meigs and his irritation with Tschilczynski were each knocked out of him. Through Joe Vaux's intervention he was drawn forcibly into the very vortex of college life, and the days of his isolation were ended. They were beaten out of him with clubs.

The strange events began on Friday afternoon, just after he finished reading about Mary Meigs' gala opening next day at the Earle. Joe burst into the room, his pointed, hungry face livid with rage. "God Almighty!" he shouted. "Did you hear who's going to be May Queen?"

"No," David replied, shivering with an uncontrolled fear that was not really a part of him. "Did they pick me?"

"No!" Vaux shouted, and again against his will David relaxed. "It's worse! If you thought all night you couldn't pick a worse Queen."

"Who is it?" David asked, needled with excitement.

"Dave?" Joe asked in deep seriousness. "Are you willing to risk your neck?"

"It depends," David replied. "I don't want to get mixed up . . ."

"But this isn't getting mixed up, Dave. This is where you either stand for a decent college or you don't." Vaux paused and looked at his friend. "They're going to choose Porterfield for Queen." David gasped. "And it's Askleton for Prince!"

David felt sick and ashamed. "They wouldn't dare to do that," he protested.

"They're doing it," Vaux yelled.

"What do you think we ought to do?" David asked.

"I have a letter here," the Bostonian said. "I want you to sign it with me. I'll take the worst end. But I want someone like you with me."

David picked up the typed page and read the flaming words. *"Stupid and Disgusting Committee of Self-appointed Gods, Clowns and Damned Fools:"* He took a deep breath. "That's some beginning," he said.

"Wait till you get farther down," Vaux replied.

David read the words he was expected to sign: "The practice of electing from among the freshmen men a May Queen and a Prince of Wails to be hauled through the streets of Dedham and held up to ridicule is a barbarous custom which only utter jackasses like you would dare to perpetuate. But for you to select Porterfield and Askleton is indecent and inhuman. The undersigned therefore volunteer to be Queen and Prince respectively and furthermore offer to fight your whole, lousy, rotten committee one by one."

"I don't like the fighting part," David said.

"No!" Vaux protested. "In a thing like this you either go whole-hog or not at all." With a great flourish he signed his name. It looked as big as John Hancock's. Then he thrust the pen at David, who signed in smaller letters.

Joe grabbed the paper and marched across the quadrangle to the room where the big men of the freshman class were meeting to make official the choice of Porterfield and Askleton. Vaux burst into the conclave, looked at each of the self-appointed senators, and threw his epistle at the captain of the freshman basketball team. "There! You lousy bastards!" he cried and left the room.

But the big men of the freshman class did not accept Joe and David for the golden chariot. No, as in all previous years, they selected two of the most inoffensive men on the campus. Porterfield had glandular trouble. This made him very fat, prevented a beard, and caused him to speak in a high voice. Secretly he wanted to play football, but his glands made him different and therefore a thing to be despised. His fellow students called him Poet Porterfield, and he was Queen. Askleton was a quiet boy from a small town in Delaware. He got A in every class and had a furious complexion that burst into eruption at regular intervals each month. The girls of Dedham used to say: "I'm so lonesome for a date I'd even go out with Askleton." He was different, so he was the Prince.

At dusk the golden chariot was hauled into the quadrangle and decked with old vegetables and toilet paper. Ridiculous and funny signs were posted on it. Upon the seats of honor were placed the poet and the pimply one. Before they had time even to hide their faces, tomatoes and eggs struck them.

The leading men of the freshman class directed others to haul the chariot and its agonized cargo about the town. As dusk fell the grotesque fat boy sat bitterly erect and refused to duck any longer when old fruit was thrown at him. Askleton, on the other hand, was so terrified at the raging roar about him that he could not keep from crying, and his tears mixed with the rotten vegetables and the sour eggs.

The lights of the town came on, and the weird procession started to chant, "On to Belle Forest!" A sense of keen excitement gripped the crowd. New men stepped forward to haul the golden chariot to the exclusive girls' school on the edge of town. "On to Belle Forest!" rose the ever more exciting cry. "The proposal! The proposal!"

At the entrance to the girls' school the chariot almost upset. Eager hands from the freshman football team reached out to hold it up. The fat Queen, thrown off balance, slipped from the seat and slid to the floor. Again eager men helped the Queen back to the throne. The men who helped in this way stopped to wipe their hands on the spring grass, and as they did so, they made ugly faces, for the sticky mess on their fingers was repugnant.

At Belle Forest the girls were waiting. Each year they looked forward to this serenade. Now all the lights in the fashionable school were extinguished. In nightgowns and pyjamas girls huddled in the windows. There was a strange hush upon the crowd. A man's voice, deep and clear, began to sing the beautiful songs of college. The hidden girls sighed. Finally the singer began the rich, sweet song: "Fair Dedham, in that distant day . . . !" It rang out magnificently through the still spring night; but the flashlights that played upon the Queen showed that his fat lips were not moving.

The serenade ended, and from the girls' windows began the cry: "Now the proposal!" In the courtyard the men roared back: "Yes! The proposal!"

All lights focused upon the Queen, who looked straight ahead. The last few eggs and fruit were thrown. The girls shrieked with delight when an egg actually struck the pimply Prince on the forehead. He looked funny and ridiculous.

"Silence!" the president of the freshman class commanded. "Queen! You look at the Prince! Prince! You propose!"

"The proposal!" cried the excited girls in their high voices.

But at that moment from a lower window came a girl's piercing scream. "Oh God!" she cried. "How terrible!"

And it was this unknown girl's cry that finally broke the spell of horror that had enveloped Joe Vaux and David Harper. That solitary voice was their conscience, returning to their bodies. All that pale and sorry evening the two freshmen had been thinking: "Well, we offered to be up there. I'm glad they didn't take us." But that girl's wild cry drove thoughts of self-safety from their minds..

With a vigorous leap Joe sprang forward and knocked an especially offensive man who carried the special eggs for the coronation. He grabbed the bag and started throwing eggs wildly at the darkened windows. Horrified screams told the crowd that some of the eggs had hit the mark.

"Why, that dirty swine!" the big freshmen shouted. "That's that Joe Vaux! Get that guy!"

But Joe and David were already streaking across the fields back to the dormitories. They arrived there breathless, and in a dumb rage they took the remaining eggs and broke them in the bureau drawers of the president of the student body. Then they ranged through the upper-class dormitories pulling furniture down, mixing hair tonic and shaving cream in piles of fresh shirts, smearing shoe polish across clean laundry.

They were caught before they had wrecked more than a half dozen rooms. From an upper window two chairs were tossed into the quadrangle, and across them Joe and David were stretched and beaten until David thought he must either faint or scream for mercy. But he was like the fat Queen. He would not open his lips.

Vaux, on the other hand, cursed and reviled his tormentors. In his pain he dug up old scurrilities from Boston gutters and flung them at the men with the paddles. Since he was thinner than David, the wicked wood cut deeper toward his bones. He understood the frenzy in which the ashamed men of Dedham were caught, and he tormented them with words which hurt more than the paddle strokes.

Finally the head of the YMCA threatened to hit the paddlers with a chair if they didn't stop. The YMCA man wanted to take Dave and Joe to the infirmary, but now that the beating was over David was crying and he said, "You go to hell!" And Vaux was about to say something much viler when he saw, limping across the quadrangle, the fat Queen sneaking home to his college room. "Attaboy, Porterfield!" Joe shouted. "Keep your chin up, Porterfield! You're my man!"

A cheer went up. And then another. The quadrangle filled with students. Vaux kept on shouting, "You're a real man, Porterfield!" Then a senior man grabbed the fat boy by the hand. Another cheer filled the darkness.

It had been Porterfield's intention to look at no one and to go straight to bed as if nothing had happened. But the sudden cheering was too much for him. He turned and waved to the men of Dedham. He had eggs and fruit all over him and a certain proud nobility which David had helped put there.

But no one ever saw Askleton again. He did not even come back to college for his clothes.

Early the next morning there was a meeting of student government. The hall was crowded when the grim-faced chairman took his seat. The gavel hit once before Joe Vaux leaped to his feet. "Want to make a motion . . ."

Before he could say more the president of the senior class cried, "Second the motion!"

"Moved and seconded," began the chairman, but before he finished there was a shout of "Aye!"

The chairman banged his gavel. "Motion carried." He banged the table again. "Meeting adjourned." And there was never another May Queen at Dedham.

In his room Joe said, "Think of it, Dave! They've been doing that for years. And see how easy it was to stop it."

But David was thinking: "Joe and I stood there and watched until that girl couldn't stand it any longer. We took it, all right. But she wouldn't." Then the thought of this girl made him jump to his feet, and the pain in his legs was great.

"Where you going?" Vaux asked.

"I almost forgot a vaudeville show!" David replied.

It was four o'clock before David reached the theatre. He had to stand in line, and his bruised legs hurt. When he finally got to his seat he fidgeted to find a comfortable way to sit. When the orchestra struck up an abbreviated *Tannhäuser Overture* he felt an indescribable excitement. He waited nervously for the curtains to part, and then fidgeted through four interminable acts.

But finally the orchestra burst into a lively potpourri of Victor Herbert's melodies. The lights turned from pale blue to rich gold. Only the violins played, and onto the stage stepped Mary Meigs. She was twenty-four years old, tall and thin with up-swept blonde hair that made her seem extremely fragile. David leaned back into a little ball, his elbows against his ribs, his chin on his fists. "Boy!" he muttered. "Look at that!"

He saw once more the thin line of her jawbone lending a sense of brittleness. He noticed that she started singing with her hands pressed close against her sides, raising them to her bosom as she climbed effortlessly to higher and higher notes. But most of all he marked the manner in which she sang directly to him, and to every other man in the audience. "She's breathtaking!" he said happily. "That's what she is. And can she sing!"

When her songs were ended he saw how reluctantly she left the stage. He beat his hands together. She came onstage again and sang her first great success, the song Sousa had taught her: "Love Sends a Little Gift of Roses." Chills ran across David's body like catfeet upon a carelessly outstretched hand.

As soon as the singer left the stage for good—unwillingly

and with a chin-high glance at the balcony—David left the theatre and hurried around to the stage door. The tough young man stationed there laughed at him. "Then at least give her a note," David pleaded. "For how much?" the tough doorkeeper inquired. "For . . . a quarter," David blurted. He grabbed a piece of paper and wrote: "David Harper from Paradise Park would like to pay his respects. Friend of Conductor Kol's."

The doorkeeper disappeared, and in a moment Mary Meigs herself, wrapped in a flimsy gown, hurried to the door. "Why, it's Dave!" she cried. "It's wonderful to see you. Were you out there?"

She led him through a maze of people and ropes and scenery. At her dressing-room door she stopped and laughed. "No star!" she mock-pouted. "No name in gold!" She kicked open the colorless door and laughed, "No maid, either." But the room was already rich with Mary Meigs. She had two dresses hung on wire hooks. Her make-up was scattered about in various places. She was messy, David saw, but from the mess she created a picture of cool lyric loveliness for the stage. Now she was merely going out on the street, so she took no pains. With a slap-dash she pulled off her wispy robe, and before she ducked into a thin dress David saw the white flash of her body. "You're supposed to look the other way," she chided. Then she caught a hat from another hook and pulled a heavy coat about her shoulders. David tried to hold it for her but she laughed and said, "Only yokels put their arms in the sleeves."

On Market Street she looked into the spring dusk over Billy Penn's statue and said, "We'll go see Klementi! How would you like that?" She hailed a cab and gave directions, paying the fare when they reached the apartment.

"Klim!" she cried as she burst into a large and handsome room. "Guess who this is!" But before David saw the conductor, he saw one of Mary's dresses lying on the bed in the next room. Kol shoved the door shut and hurried to greet his young friend.

"David!" he cried warmly. "It's so good to see you."

"I saw her name in lights," David laughed. "Just like she said. She sings better than anybody I ever heard. She's some singer, Mr. Kol."

Mary moved deftly about the apartment in a familiar manner, getting drinks. "What have you been doing?" Kol asked.

"I'm in college," David explained. "Dedham." Then his eye was caught by a picture of Mary above the fireplace. "That's a neat picture," he said admiringly.

"You recognize it?" Kol asked. "When I first met her. Very good, too."

"Oh, Klim!" Mary cried petulantly. "You didn't send a telegram?" She pointed a crumpled paper at the musician.

Kol leaped to his feet. "Indeed I did!" he stormed. "I was so furious!"

"You shouldn't have done it!" Mary insisted, handing David a drink in a tall glass. "You know that with a critic you can never win."

"But to say a thing like that!" the musician cried. He stamped about the room and David guessed that Kol wanted to talk.

"What happened?" he asked. Behind Klementi's back Mary shook her head vigorously "No! No!" but the angry musician had already grabbed a newspaper and thrust it at David. It contained a disparaging review of Kol's conducting at a Boston concert. The harsh sentences looked forbidding in cold print: "No feeling for the master's work and no attempt to attain any . . ."

Klementi repeated the last words. "That's the rotten part!" he cried. "That strips honor from a man. No attempt to do the thing right! Why, if I try and fail, that's all right. Then I must stick to my fiddle playing in Philadelphia and not presume to be a conductor. I could take that. But if I don't even try! Then I'm neither a musician nor a man. No honor, no dignity, no sincerity."

"Sit down!" Mary laughed. "Klim, at your age you must learn to take digs like that in stride."

"You don't understand," Klim explained patiently. "I learn from bad reviews, if they're just." He thrust a book of clippings into David's hand. The latter leafed through them: Cleveland, Chicago, Buenos Aires. Whenever adverse comments appeared, Kol had underlined them in red. "This one!" he said. *"Insufficient practice.* How true! I should never have attempted that piece." He shook his head and then added softly, "But to say a man did not try to do the great thing! That strips honor from a man."

David noticed that as Kol spoke of the musician's honor, Mary sat watching, her chin resting low on her interlaced fingers. Finally she said, "Take it easy, Klim. Concert tonight." Kol snapped back to his urbane self and grinned at David.

"I wish I could join you two for dinner," he said, "but I don't eat much before a concert." He laughed and added, "Mary's always hungry." He showed them to the door and kissed Mary lightly on the hair.

In the cab the singer asked David if he would like to see the vaudeville again. When he showed his delight, even in the darkened cab, she told the driver to stop a minute, and she purchased a bagful of sandwiches and two malted milks. At the theatre she took David to her dressing room and said, "Forget what Klim said. He has a pick-up concert tonight and he's excited. All winter he plays fiddle for Stokowski. The rest of the time he conducts wherever he can. He takes it very seriously."

When the vaudeville started David offered to go out front, but Mary insisted that he stay in the wings. He turned his head when she dressed, yet as he did so Mary asked suddenly, "Dave! What do you honestly think of Uncle Klim?" He turned quickly to answer and saw the slim and delicate singer pulling on a sheer silk stocking. "I told you!" she warned him laughingly. "You're supposed to look the other way." But he stared at her, and she slowly continued her dressing.

"You're beautiful!" he said huskily. Mary hooked her stocking in place and ruffed out her slip.

"You might as well button me up," she said. "I can make believe I have a maid." She lifted a dress from its hook and popped it over her head, wriggling her arms until it slipped softly into place. David watched entranced as the inanimate dress came alive with handsome curves and deep, delicious dips. He made no move to fix the buttons, and Mary laughed quietly at him. "Didn't you ever button up the little girl's dress at Paradise?" she teased. David blushed deeply and shook his head no. "Well," Mary began. Then she stopped and listened to the music. "This week I'm billed fourth. Later on I guess I'll be fifth. You know, of course, that closing isn't really the best spot. Fifth is the choice one."

She leaned against the door, listening to the music, while David finished the buttons on her golden dress. She felt his hands poised in the air about her bare shoulders, lingering there, warm and confused. She could sense the look that must be in his excited eyes and the tousled look of his college-cut hair. And then softly the orchestra violins began to play the music of Victor Herbert. She dropped her right hand and allowed it to brush against the boy's leg. Quickly his hand fell to grasp hers.

"Mary!" he whispered. "You're so very beautiful!"

"Ssssh!" she teased. "I've got to sing! Don't get me upset." She gave his trembling hand a slight squeeze and seemed to float off toward the stage.

"Some girl, that!" a stagehand said as she began to sing "Kiss in the Dark." "You know her?"

"What?" David mumbled. "Who?"

The stagehand moved away and allowed David to watch the fragile singer. She had now raised her clasped hands to her bosom and was singing the gently rising song from *No, No, Nanette*. All during her performance David watched her, studied the way in which she built her voice to climaxes, the tricks she used to turn her delicate profile to the audience, and the way she pulled her whole body backwards in her bows of acknowledgment. "Even her shoes act!" he thought.

After the first evening performance she said, "Why don't we go out to see Klim again?" and David was about to say, "Klim's got a concert!" but instead he mumbled, "Yeah. Why don't we?"

At the apartment Mary rang several times, then took a key from her purse and let herself in. "I guess he's still at the concert," she said with airy surprise. She went immediately to the bathroom and washed her face with cold water. She reappeared wiping herself vigorously with a heavy towel. "I live here," she said simply.

"Are you and Klim married?" David asked.

Mary's face was covered with the towel at the moment and she rubbed herself briskly, seeking time to arrange her reply. Then she tossed the towel backwards into the bathroom and smiled at David as she started to mix a drink. "Surely," she said over her shoulder, "you must have guessed."

"Guessed what?" David asked.

She looked away and tinkled some bottles. "Do you like vermouth?" she asked.

David went to the sideboard and awkwardly pulled Mary away from the glasses. "What should I have guessed?" he asked.

The actress looked at him frankly and said, "That Klim's never going to marry me."

A surge of possessiveness came over David and he cried

like a wronged Bucks County farmer, "He ought to be horse-whipped!"

Then Mary started to laugh and pushed him back into a chair. "David!" she pleaded with a half chuckle. "It's so hard to explain things to a college man." She bit her lip and stood above him for more than a minute. Finally she said quietly, "Don't you understand, Dave? Klim's no good for a girl. And he's too fine to waste my life by marrying me."

The ideas were far too complex for David. He blushed, as if he should be ashamed for someone. A long silence followed during which he tried to fathom the meaning of the words, and then like any man he started to bluster. "Well, why . . ."

"To us!" Mary interrupted. She spun quickly and produced the two drinks. Dancing gaily, with her left shoulder dipping toward the floor, she handed David his and cried, "To my clean-faced stagedoor Johnny!"

David struggled to his feet and countered awkwardly, "To the most beautiful girl in the theatre!" The words gave him courage, and he felt very much a man, smiling across his glass at a real actress. "Skoal!" he shouted and took a deep drink.

They sat on the davenport and Mary said in a kind of sing-song voice: "Klim was very good to me. When I was starting, that is. He took me to see Sousa. As long as I live I'll owe Klim a real debt." Her arms were stretched along the top of the davenport and she seemed completely relaxed. She closed her eyes and said, "It's terrible to hurt people you love."

There was a long silence and David asked, "What do you mean?" Mary rolled her delicate head toward him and smiled. The upstretched tension of her arms made her firm breasts show clearly even beneath the loose knockabout dress she wore outside the theatre. She did not answer his question and then he did a very foolish thing. "Mary!" he gulped. "Could I kiss you?"

"Of course not!" she snapped, and her eyes chastised him so that he blushed even more furiously than before and mumbled, "I'm sorry. I apologize."

She continued to lie back against the davenport and mused again upon an old theme: "Would you think me silly if I changed my name to Mona Meigs?"

"Nothing you could do would be silly," he said huskily. She clenched her hands with great determination.

"From now on I am Mona Meigs! I'll be a great singer. I'm going into the movies and everyone will know that name!"

She rose and started to walk about the room, holding her elbows back as actresses did to accentuate their breasts. She talked wildly and took long, swinging steps. "Dave! You'll remember that name as long as you live. You'll see it everywhere! You'll tell people you knew me when I sang with a band and the goddamned saxophones drowned me out every lousy, rotten night. You can say you heard me sing with a second-rate orchestra when the fiddles were always too slow. And in the Earle Theatre. You can say you stood in the wings . . . "

David had never before seen a person totally dedicated to success. He had never watched the deep and burning longings explode in shameless frenzy and deep hunger for the accolades. He was shocked, as if a naked woman were walking before him, and he could not see the fragile line of Mary's face, for it was hard, hard with hope.

The young singer stopped abruptly before him and stood with her hands contentiously on her hips. "Now you know!" she said, and David rushed at her as if he were an animal and clasped her thin face to his and kissed her until his lips hurt. His hands fought for her provocative bosom, and finally he was thrust backwards onto the davenport.

"Dave!" the newly christened singer cried. "Be careful! Klim might come in!" But she looked at the sprawling college student with happy pleasure in her eyes. "Anyway," she said. "The first kiss Mona Meigs got was a good one. You ought to go out for football."

David had intended dropping into his classmates' rooms and asking in an offhand manner, "Any you guys see the show this week at the Earle? Well, that singer . . . " Instead, he was confused and said nothing to anyone about Mary.

The words she had used, and her actions, too, haunted him, and for the first four days of the week he pondered many times each inflection she had used: "What did she mean, 'Klim is no good for girls'? Come to think of it, she meant for me to kiss her all along. But why did she fight that way? There are some things I just don't understand. And why should she want to change her name? There at the end, too, when she was racing up and down that room, telling me what she was going to do! That was pretty silly. Most girls would give a leg to sing at the Earle . . . " Then his words would be driven away by memory of that magnificent white leg, and his hand would burn for the feel of her unforgettable breast.

"I better forget about her," he commanded himself, but as luck would have it, that very week he was given charge of the night hours at the observatory, and there, seeing for the first time through a large telescope the ancient stars and the massive formations beyond the sun and the moon, all the imperishable vastness of the universe was intermingled with his feelings for Mary Meigs.

On Thursday night he was so bewildered that when his hours at the observatory were ended he could not sleep. At first he thought he would visit Tschilczynski, who had got him the job, but sharing the Russian's secret made it impossible for David now to thrust his own secret—he considered the kiss a secret—upon his professor. Instead he went to see Joe Vaux. The Irishman was curled up in a chair reading Veblen, spitting contempt at passages he did not like.

"Joe?" David began. "If a girl were to say . . . Now just for instance, you understand. If she were to say that such-and-such a man was no good for girls, what would that mean?"

"Well, it would mean that he wasn't any good for girls," Joe explained.

"That much I know!" David said uneasily. "But what would it signify?"

"Well, it might mean he was a fairy."

"Oh, no!" David protested promptly. "Not this guy! He's a good, clean guy, and I've seen some fairies in my day! I can assure you, this guy isn't a fairy! He simply isn't."

Joe laughed and said, "I thought you said this was a f'rinstance?"

David gaped and thought of six or seven explanations, but none was any good. "What do you think the phrase might mean?"

"I'll tell you what we'll do!" Joe said. "We'll ask Eddy. He's pre-med." The future doctor was called into consultation, along with a half dozen vagrant minds. In considerable ignorance they discussed David's problem and launched off into others of their own. They knew astronomy, these young men, and Chaucer and German verbs and geology and even the advanced formulae of Karl Pearson, but no one had ever told them about the human body. Their groping session lasted until dawn, and when it was over David still did not understand what Mary Meigs meant when she said that Klementi Kol was no good for girls. In his embarrassment he began to laugh in short, hysterical chuckles. "Damnedest thing I ever heard of!" he cried to no one in particular. "In our town there was this guy. Let me tell you, he was some guy! A red head and very awkward! You'd of died to see him. Well, he got a crush on the prettiest girl in town and one night she let him walk her home. Well, at her door this yokel actually says, 'Could I kiss you good night?' He asks her, mind you. So she slams the door in his face!"

The freshmen laughed uproariously at this and started telling their own hilarious stories, and bells for the eight o'clock classes rang. David went to bed and that afternoon he said to Joe, "What do you say we go into Philly and see a movie?"

"Why not?" Joe agreed. "We've messed up the day anyway!" So they caught a train into the city, but during the trip they began to argue. Joe wanted to see the show at the Stanton and David preferred the Earle. "All right!" Joe finally cried. "We'll match for it!"

David said a brief prayer and tossed his coin. He won, and they went to the Earle. They got there during the second act of the vaudeville, and before long Mary Meigs appeared. David slumped way down in his seat and watched the beautiful singer. Joe fidgeted and said in a loud voice, "This is what killed vaudeville." David winced and stared at the stage. When the picture came on, it was terrible and Joe heckled his friend. "You sure pick 'em!" he chided. "Say? Does your tail still hurt from that May Queen stuff?"

"I'll say!" David replied. He could guess what was going to happen next.

"Then let's blow. Let's get an Italian dinner somewheres."

"Joe!" David said. "Let's see the first part of the vaudeville."

"I don't like seals," the Bostonian replied. He started to leave, but an imperative tug at his arm prevented him. He said nothing but sat back quietly and watched David. He saw the tense excitement that flooded his friend when the orchestra began to play, and the manner in which David bent forward to watch the seals perform. And then he saw Mary Meigs come onstage for the second time. He felt David relax and tie himself together with his arms about his knees and drink in the motions and the singing and the beauty of that slim, fragile girl.

Later, while they ate spaghetti on Thirteenth Street, Joe

commanded the waiter to bring the wine list. "I don't like wine," David objected.

"But tonight! Special!" Joe laughed. He raised his glass and said, "To Mary Meigs." David gasped and was ashamed to look at his friend. "To a damned pretty girl!" Joe added. They drank the toast and then David said, "I knew her at Paradise."

"You talk like Dante!" Joe quipped.

"It was a park," David explained. "She sang for Sousa."

As they crossed through the City Hall, as they climbed the stairs of the dirty station, and as they rode homeward David told Joe of each item he could remember about Mary. With guesswork and perception the Bostonian asked leading questions: "So this Klim is the guy who's no good for girls! And so you, like a country bumpkin asked her for a kiss!" He laughed in commiserating fun at David. "You're deep and complex!" he said sagely. "Like a saucer of skim milk."

"So that's that," David said as they reached the quadrangle.

Joe stopped dead and grabbed him by the hand. "What do you mean, that's that! You're certainly going back to sleep with her, aren't you?"

The words were very sharp, the words that David had been refusing to admit into his reveries. "I've got to take some pictures at the observatory," he said hurriedly.

"Good!" Vaux cried. "I've always wanted to see that place." He accompanied his friend to the silent and rounded room where the telescope and cameras were kept and where the stars alone gave light.

"Your eyes get accustomed to it," David explained. He went about the business of setting up the camera.

"I know how you feel about this singer," Joe said. "Same thing happened to me in Boston. There was a damned good-looking young girl wanted to get married. The three of us on our block who might have—even though she was an Italian, she was Catholic, you see—all wanted to go away to school or sea or something. So she married the worst bum on the block. And during Christmas vacation I was lounging in the candy store . . . Dave, if you stood in that candy store a week and just watched, you could write a book. So she came in wearing a thin coat and I could cut my tongue out but I said, 'What's the matter, Becky? Louis can't buy you a real coat?' And she stuck her face into mine and said, 'No.' And she looked at me a long time and it was perfectly clear she wanted me to take her home, and it was clear to everybody else in the store, and we went home right in broad daylight, because no one on our block is scared of Louis, and we weren't inside the room three minutes before we were in bed, and only last summer she slapped my face for kissing her."

David worked at the camera and set the huge gears in motion so that the telescope would follow the motion of the earth and remain fixed upon a single star, as his mind followed Mary Meigs and focused upon her tender beauty. He could think of nothing to say to Joe.

So the tough Irishman continued his monologue and said: "All you got to do is stand in that candy store and you can see that the world is a poorhouse . . . "

"Have you ever seen a poorhouse?" David asked.

"I see one all about me!" the fiery student replied. "A poorhouse of the spirit!"

"Joe! Listen!" David began. "You were very smart guessing about Mary Meigs. But sometimes you shoot off at the mouth too much. What would you say if I told you I lived in a poorhouse?"

The shadowy Irishman stopped making huge gestures with his hands and asked, "You what?"

"I lived in a poorhouse. From the time I was a kid. It's not so bad. As a matter of fact, I had a pretty good time there."

"You actually lived in a poorhouse!" Vaux repeated mechanically. "What was it like?" For hours the inquisitive Irishman cross-examined David on everything that had happened in the poorhouse. The stars came and went, and in the east the moon rose, a thin crescent motioning its two fingers for the dawn to follow. When David spoke about certain things—the old men hanging themselves in the springtime and Mr. Crouthamel—Vaux stormed up and down in the growing light.

"But that was only a small part!" David protested. "Those things were incidents. The important part was the happiness and the love I saw there."

Joe stopped walking and glared at his friend. "You blind fool!" he cried. "You didn't see the terror because you live in a dream world you crept into when you were a baby. You don't see social injustice because you're lost in it yourself."

"Don't talk like that!" David objected. "I was immersed in poverty. Up to my heart, if you like. But it wasn't the way you say. What harm did it do me? Poverty never hurts anyone unless it breaks his spirit. I got to college all right. And I'll get through college."

"Stop it!" Joe shouted. "You! They buy you off! They give you a cheap scholarship and you never see what's happening to you."

"There's no point in shouting," David said, piling the photographic plates into rows. "You see it one way. I see it another."

But Vaux was obsessed with the poorhouse and he would not let David go to bed. "This old fellow who drowned himself in the water tank. You say you didn't know him very well. Tell me, how did it feel at night, after a basketball game, when you went back to the poorhouse?"

"I felt I was going home."

"Home!" Joe exploded.

"Yes. The old men were always waiting to hear the score. It was very exciting."

"Now this Crouthamel. How did he make his money in the first place? How many families did he actually force into the poorhouse?"

"Look, Joe!" David interrupted. "You have it all wrong. Of the families that came, only one couple really down deep insisted on getting out. They weren't in the poorhouse a week."

"Dave!" Vaux shouted. "Don't say that again. It's irrelevant and horrible. Of course, only one couple was strong enough to fight what the capitalist system had done to them. But haven't you ever conceived of society as a system in which the useless ones are protected and sustained as a sort of public trust? You and I know that four-fifths of the people on this earth don't mean a damn to man or God. They're miserable, useless things. Suppose you were a crook! Why, you could steal from those damned fools day after day and they'd never know it. But they're society! They are the blood of my heart."

He flung his arms about in wild gestures. Immense morning shadows spun through the observatory, a kind of visual prediction of the person Joe Vaux would one day become. "And you live in the body of the poorhouse and you don't see it!" he cried. "Dave! I want you to tell me one thing. You've talked about this man Crouthamel four times tonight. And you've told me about how your aunt got sick and wanted to die because her money was all gone. Yet you've never once altered your voice to show that you give a damn for her misery. Why?"

"It's time for breakfast," David said nervously.

"No!" Vaux insisted. "Let's have this out, Dave. Why?"

David, nineteen years old and uncertain of himself, stood with his right foot on the observatory ladder. He wanted deeply to tell Joe all the things he felt, but he was aware that he could never do that, not to Joe nor to anyone else. He once thought that Nora might have understood, but now he was convinced that there were certain things he would never discuss . . . not with anybody.

"I'll tell you this much, Joe," he said slowly. "The first thing I can remember in my life was a very cold night in Sellersville. I was with my mother then. She was so poor she used to tie the bread up in a bag and hide it under her pillow so that neither she nor I would eat any. She rented a house from Mr. Crouthamel, the worst house in the whole town, except one. She missed a rent payment and Mr. Crouthamel told her she would have to move into that other house. I remember going down to see it in the snow. There was a plum tree in the back yard, but all Mom could see were the bedbugs. They were crawling from the boards, even without beds being there. Mom brought me back to the house we were living in and left me alone while she went to visit her sister Reba. But Reba wouldn't lend her any money. So Mom came home and we went to bed. I was so terribly hungry I couldn't sleep, and I remember pulling out the bag of bread from under Mom's pillow and trying to untie the knot. I couldn't, and I wakened Mom. She was furious. She beat me and started to cry. But just then we heard a noise, and Mom bundled us both up and we went out into the frosty night. We waited a long time, and then the noise came again. It was wild geese flying north. Soon there was enough light for us to see the V in the sky, heading north.

"The sight made Mom feel wonderful. She caught me up and cried: 'It's no sin to be poor!' She carried me to a neighbor's house where a German family was just getting up for breakfast. She burst into the door and cried: 'I can go without, but not this boy!' She made them give me breakfast. I remember everything very clearly. A big German breakfast. Meat and fried potatoes and pie. Mom wouldn't eat any, so I asked for a second piece of pie and she said: 'Don't be a pig!' But two ministers heard about us and paid for moving us into the other house. They gave us some food and some clothes. Joe, the bugs were terrible. Mom wouldn't go to sleep. She sat up all night killing them. She died in that house. So I went to live at the poorhouse, where Aunt Reba got a job. And if I sat here in this room and watched her right hand burn off, I wouldn't feel a bit of pain."

Joe sat looking at the floor for some time and then said in a very low voice, "If you carry a thing like that around with you long enough it'll eat away your mind. You must get it out of your system. Talking's good, but discharging the poison is better."

"What do you mean?" David asked.

"It's all explained in books. You ought to read Jung and Adler. Haven't you figured it out? Crouthamel treated your mother rotten. Your aunt treated you rotten. So you take delight from the fact that Crouthamel got even with your aunt. And you say: 'To hell with the poor people! I was poor, once.' That's evil, Dave."

David knew that Joe's quiet words were true. He shoved his foot back and forth along the ladder and asked, "What do you think I should do?"

"I'm no doctor," Vaux replied. "But you should take into your heart the problems of everyone who is hungry or lonely. You should work against the poorhouses of the world." The wiry Bostonian laughed at the pompousness of his words and said, "I'm going to bed."

David remained in the empty observatory. It was incomprehensible that this tough alley fighter from Boston should be able to thrust so neatly into the heart of things, probing at the seat of sickness. But David thought: "I'm not like him. In math or any kind of studying I can go right to the center of the problem. But with people . . . Even myself . . . People are surrounded by a glowing fog I can't penetrate. I see them as characters in a book or magnificent figures in a painting. I don't see them as naked people. Or going to the toilet. I guess I've loved ninety-nine people out of every hundred I've met. But I'm not interested in them the way Joe is. I don't care if a man loses his job or starves. Because I know that if I were with him I would do anything for him or even starve with him, and find him the best friend I ever had. Joe talks about abstract things, but I don't care about them. It's real people I like. I can't think of a person on earth I don't like . . . " He closed the book in which he kept his records, then added, "That is, except Aunt Reba."

Joe Vaux was completely convinced that some day the revolutionists would break into all homes and ask to see the calluses upon the hands of the workers. "And it's a fair bet," he argued, "that those who have done no physical labor will be liquidated." This reasoning confused David, because in Joe's mind it was always someone else who was to revolt. It was *they,* the downtrodden, the masses. Joe and David would be hauled before *their* tribunals to be judged by *them.*

"But who are *they?*" David inquired.

"The hungry masses," Joe replied.

"Look!" David argued. "This country is getting richer and richer every year. There are no downtrodden masses, Joe."

Vaux looked sorrowfully at David and sighed. "You still refuse to see? You think we'll go on, year after year, making more money?"

"I don't see why not," David replied. "Joe! I know the downtrodden masses. They're just like you and me, only with less courage."

Vaux became angry and cried, "You know the old ones. You ought to spend this summer catching up on yourself, Dave." He dumped in David's room his studies of the French and Russian revolutions. "Old men from poorhouses didn't lead those babies," he joked.

"I want to know what laboring ten hours a day means," he said as the college term ended. Then he left for a summer of work with a construction gang in Fall River.

David stayed at the observatory all that fine, hot summer of 1926. He had been engaged to make a systematic mapping of the Milky Way in an effort to track down the variable stars. At intervals he would photograph a small portion of the sky. The developed plates would show a thousand mottled stars, and David would place two of them side by side in an oscillograph box with rapidly flashing lights. Almost magically, one variable star—among the thousands visible—would begin to dance in the darkness, so that even the most untrained eye could see that there was the star that was different.

David liked his work. He slept most of the day, read Joe Vaux's books, and thought about Mary Meigs. He could still recall every incident of his meeting with her. He was increasingly confused over the fact that a girl could have a thin, delicate body and a perfect face and still swear and betray angry passions. He decided that it was because Mary was older than the girls he knew in college, and it never occurred to him that in their dormitories college girls were the same way.

He was ashamed of his thoughts about Mary—about wanting to be with her again on Klementi's davenport—because he could not dissociate her from Klementi; and whether Klim was good for girls or not was irrelevant, for David was indebted to him. "I'll never see her again," he swore to himself in schoolboy fashion.

Then Kol himself played David a mean trick. He called the college one day and left a curt message: "Tell Mr. Harper Klementi Kol wants to talk with him." David studied the message and called Philadelphia. "Yes," Kol said brusquely. "I want to ask you about something. You'd better come up here."

David was sweating when he hung up the receiver. What had Kol discovered? Did he want to talk about Mary Meigs? David felt a resentment against the musician and against the world. "I don't want to get mixed up in things!" he cried to himself as he hurried to the station. "Damn it all! I want to read this summer."

At Kol's apartment there was a note. "D.H. Come to the Academy. We're recording." So David hopped aboard a trolley and reported to the famous music hall. He slipped quietly into a back seat and listened as Stokowski prepared his men in Schubert's Seventh, that bright and brassy thing of a hundred themes. And as he listened he stared nervously at the violins, where Klementi Kol sat very straight.

"How did you like it?" Kol asked when the recording was completed.

"He uses so many melodies!" David replied cautiously. "Any one of them could be made into a symphony."

"The word is *prodigal*," Kol explained. "Why don't we go down to the gallery?"

"I'd like that," David agreed. They walked the few steps down to the Johnson Collection, where in the quiet, cool rooms a few art lovers studied the gems which the rich and parsimonious lawyer had surreptitiously purchased over many years. Already David thought of these pictures as his friends: the laughing Cima, the cool Cuyps, the sleepy Hobbemas, and the wrenched and bleeding primitives.

But this day Klementi asked the guard to move two chairs into the small room where the Rembrandt studies were. There he sat with David and pointed to the earthy picture of the massive beeves, hung on hooks, half-butchered, with their suet gleaming in the light. *"Prodigal* is the word," Kol repeated.

"What do you mean?" David hazarded. He was looking at Kol, not at the Rembrandt.

"Lots of men," Kol explained, "have so much talent they can waste ideas. Like the Schubert symphony. But there are others who have one talent, and they husband it very carefully. And often they're better than the prodigal geniuses like Schubert. I'm thinking of Brahms, for example. And Watteau." There was a long pause and David guessed that next Kol would speak of Mary Meigs. But instead the tall musician turned in his chair and looked at David, saying, "I met Immanuel Tschilczynski at a chamber-music session the other night. Could it be true what he said? That you plan to become a mathematician?"

David felt relieved, as if the attendants had come into that little room and lifted one of Rembrandt's beeves from his chest. He laughed and said, "Yes. That's right."

He was unprepared for what happened next. Kol jumped up into the air like a strong, tribal dancer and cried, "But you have the talent! When I knew you at Paradise you could write! You had the vision, too, and I thought that maybe you would spend your life on something worthy. But to be a mathematician! What's that, David?" He flailed his arms about and a wretched thought assailed the young student.

"Sometimes he is just like a girl!" David said under his breath.

Then the musician sat down and put his hands on David's and said very quietly, "Leschetizky once told me that several of his finest students were like you. They knew they were going to be great pianists. But they fought against it. They struggled and cried out against their own destiny. Leschetizky told me that's why they were wonderful when they finally surrendered. There was the fire of hell in them."

Kol drew back and dropped his hands so that they almost dragged along the museum floor. "Anyone can be a mathematician," he said. "But look at the Rembrandt! See with what wonderful invention he twists his paint to make it appear like suet. If you can possibly get even a foothold in art, you should never be a mathematician." Then he lifted his right hand to point at the Rembrandt, and the hand was powerful, like a blacksmith's, and David thought: "There's nothing wrong with him! Why, he could play tackle with those mitts."

Kol knew he had said enough, so now he clapped his

hands and said, "After the lecture, good news! Mary is arriving on the afternoon train from Cleveland! And we're going to have dinner tonight!"

"I've got to get back to college," David protested. "The observatory."

"That can wait!" Kol insisted, and he led David to the dirty station where Mary was to arrive. The train was late, of course, and Kol said, "I'm glad. I forgot to tell you something, David. Mary has changed her name. For professional reasons." He pressed the side of his nose and tried not to smile. "Now you should learn that whenever a girl changes her hat, or her hairdo, or her name, it's very important. Won't you please remember to call her Mona?"

"Mona!" David repeated. "That's an interesting name."

The train puffed in and David's heart pounded like the thundering wheels. Finally Mona appeared, a rich coat thrown over her shoulders and a porter carrying five or six boxes. "Klim!" she cried, rushing up to the tall musician and kissing him. Across Kol's shoulder she saw David and slowly drew her lips away from Klim's cheek.

"Hello!" she said, extending her hand.

"Hello, Mona," David replied. A slight twinkle flashed in her eyes and she pressed his hand. "See!" she cried to Kol. "He knows my name already!"

They ate, very formally, at a German restaurant and then went by taxi to Kol's apartment. David was tremendously excited. Mona was much prettier than even his accurate mind remembered. He noticed that she was not wearing much make-up and that her pale cheeks were not rouged. At the apartment a message was waiting and Klim said, "Stokowski called. He's furious about the recording. The brasses, rumbling like beer wagons! I'll run along now. I won't be long. You wait here."

But he was gone a long time, and as the minutes passed David could do nothing but stare at the actress, and she sat still and tired in a large chair. Finally she asked, "What are you thinking, Dave?" And he replied, "I was comparing you with that portrait. You seem to get younger." And she said, "I'm one of the lucky ones, Dave. I don't put on weight. I've got good teeth. I'll be young for a long time." Then David sucked in his breath and said, "You talk of yourself the way farmers talk about horses." And she laughed and said, "Most people are like horses, but they don't admit it. I'm one of the lucky ones. I keep my looks a long time."

They lapsed into silence and David finally said, "Klim's gone a long time." And Mona replied, "When he and Stokey get together they talk forever." She dropped her head as she said this so that she looked at David out of only part of her eyes, and he had to restrain himself from leaping at her again. He said, "I'm ashamed of how I acted last time, Mona." And she held out her hands and said, "Don't be silly! Never be ashamed of anything! If you've made a fool of yourself, just don't do it again. But being ashamed is only being a fool twice for the same reason." He rose slowly, almost indifferently, and thought: "How do you start to kiss a girl who's sitting in a chair?" He walked stiffly to the chair and bent awkwardly down. As he did so he realized he couldn't possibly kiss the actress unless he knelt on the floor, but quietly she raised her lips, and he did not feel awkward any longer. "Let's sit over here," he said, pulling her gently to the davenport.

Together they looked at the door, thinking that Klim might appear at any moment. "Wouldn't it be better . . . " David began. "Why don't you lock the door?" Mona asked. David jumped to the task and laughed nervously as he returned to the davenport. Again he wondered: "What am I supposed to do now?" Tentatively, he sat close to her and kissed her on the cheek, then on the lips. Mona closed her eyes and leaned back against the cushions.

"It was a long trip from Cleveland," she said. "What a smelly theatre!"

Even more tentatively David began to loosen the buttons at the throat of her dress. Instinctively, as if she were again a girl of fifteen on her first date, she pressed her hand against his to stop him. Then, as if she remembered who she was and what she needed, she rose calmly and undressed.

With his mouth open, David watched the expensive traveling clothes slip away from her perfect body. When she at last stood free and naked before him, he was breathless in wonder, but his mind—that impartial machine that must work and compare to live—said: "She's so much whiter than Nora! Her breasts are smaller and harder, too. But it's strange how much alike girls look when they're undressed." Then he himself, David, rushed back to his mind and cried, "What if Klim should come in?"

Angrily Mona clenched her fists and muttered, "Klim's no part of this. If he comes back, that's our risk. And his." With a quick jump she landed on the davenport beside David and allowed him to clutch her lips to his. But instinctively she knew that he was afraid of Klim, and his fear gave her added courage. Deftly she slipped away from him and danced from light to light, snapping switches and kicking her small pink-and-gray heels as she did so. She circled the room like the goddess of night, leaving behind a trail of lovers' darkness. Then she crept beside David and whispered, "Don't you understand? Whenever a grown man rants about his honor it means he's no good in bed."

She was a wild and violent woman, a human, twisting spring, tortured and yet deeply alive. Her breasts were firm like muscles and her neck was never relaxed. There was a passion in her love-making and a gurgling, triumphant conclusion. For a moment, she was set free of her tireless ambition and was merely an exhausted, breathless woman.

But it was only for a moment. Suddenly she cried, "Now for God's sake get dressed, Dave. Turn on the lights and unlock the door. Oh, my God! If Klim had come home!" She fluffed up the pillows and made David turn around in a circle to be sure he looked all right. Then she said, "I know! Why don't you leave right now? I'll say you couldn't wait. Had to get back to take your pictures." She rushed him from the apartment and into the warm night air.

Hours later he sleepily set two photographs into the oscillograph and even his exhausted eyes could catch the fluttering star, the star among all the others that rose and fell in brilliance, throbbing millions of miles away, exploding in fiery wonder like a woman in love.

The light in which David saw himself next morning was not pleasant. He had betrayed a friend. In Klim's own house he had seduced the musician's mistress. But he knew the word *seduce* was meaningless when applied to Mona. She had merely used him as her automatic fool, and that fact, added to David's memory of kind, friendly Klim, produced a vague nausea.

David said to himself: "No more of that!" Then he added a current college tag line: "That's how guys get shot." He immersed himself in his studies and for several days succeeded in expelling Mona from his thoughts.

But her banishment was soon revoked, for whether he willed it or not, he was forced to submit to his vision of her. She was completely unlike anyone he had previously imagined, for she was one of those women whom a few fortunate men meet: she filled the hazy confines of the dream of love and made imaginings real. Let her once be glimpsed, running naked to extinguish the lights, and she was perpetually in the mind. Five days after David had denounced himself for having betrayed Klim, he was subconsciously plotting how he might again get into bed with her.

His connivings were subconscious because openly he reassured himself: "Like I said! No more of that dame. Not for me!" Then he added: "I'll study like mad." He began by reading a life of Castiglione, which led naturally to a consideration of Titian, which made a trip to the Johnson Collection—which had no Titian—a likely idea, and before two hours had elapsed he was standing before Cima's laughing, lovely panel of the satyrs.

"Look at those rascals!" he laughed, not admitting that he envied their conscienceless revels. He cocked his head and studied the delicate brown shading of the picture, and one of the rubaiyat of Omar came to his mind from those rainy days at Paradise when he had memorized the indolent poem.

> Come, fill the Cup, and in the fire of Spring
> Your Winter-garment of Repentance fling:
>     The Bird of Time has but a little way
> To flutter—and the Bird is on the Wing.

Goaded by the words, he prevailed upon the caretaker to let him use the phone. When he called Klim's number, Mona answered and David asked breathlessly, "Is Klim there?"

"No," she cautiously replied.

"I'll be right up," he whispered.

"Take a cab," Mona said in a noncommittal voice.

Twelve minutes later he burst into Klim's apartment and cried, "I've been dying to see you."

"Hey!" she protested. "Take it easy!" She pushed him into a chair and started laughing. He joined in and for some minutes they made fun of each other, laughing ever more boisterously. Finally Mona cried, "You came busting in here like Tarzan."

"That's how I felt," David admitted, and then they chuckled over David's ever becoming an uncontrolled apeman.

"Don't you think it's fun when people aren't too serious?" Mona teased.

David grabbed at her and said, "You can't talk me out of being serious over you. Don't try!" He pulled her onto the couch beside him, and she pressed her clean, cool face against his.

"Klim's always so dull," she whispered, and that was when David learned how utterly delightful can be the revels of love, how winged and how joyous.

The experience affected him deeply. Instinctively he knew —because of his Bucks County upbringing—that it was reprehensible to enjoy with abandon any act of life; but to enjoy sleeping with a woman must be inescapably sinful, and it was irrelevant that an old Persian had advised tossing the ashcloths of repentance into the fires of spring. That might be all right for a Persian, but it simply didn't apply to a Pennsylvania Quaker.

So, as most young men would have done, David stayed away from Mona for more than a week. Then suddenly he dropped all pretense and hurried shamelessly to the actress. "I'll bet you've been having a great argument with yourself," she teased.

David stood back to study this remarkable girl. She had not bothered to finish high school, but she knew more about how people behaved than David would ever know. "How do you happen to guess right so often?" he asked.

"Books bore me," she explained. "When you want to be an actress, you study how people do things. Want to see yourself?" With affectionate yet acid burlesques of David she portrayed an indecisive college student hastening to and hiding from a fatal charmer.

"I don't look as silly as that!" David objected.

"Sure you do! You're my silly Stage-door Johnny!" she teased, peering nervously around the edge of an imaginary door. Then she stopped teasing and allowed David to kiss her. "And like they say in plays," she whispered, "you're my lover. If you hadn't of come today I'd've died."

David wanted to ask, "What about Klim?" but he had reached the point at which Klim could be exorcized at will. In fact, on this day David himself went methodically from window to window, lowering the shades, but when he reached the darkened davenport, method ceased, and Mona crushed him to her. "You are my lover!" she said over and over, repeating the phrase even when they lay back exhausted; but David had the strange feeling that she was saying this only because she had heard it in some play. He didn't believe for a moment that she meant the words. He even doubted that she understood what they were intended to convey.

In the late 1920's most American colleges were little more than outposts of England, and as long as David lived he would bear a peculiar love for that tight little island. This was because his teachers had really loved only one thing: English culture. They extolled the grandeur of English common law and the sovereign accomplishment of English writers. Since Dedham was a Quaker college which considered art and music probably immoral, David did not discover until late how barren England was in those twin fields which illuminate so much of life.

For students of David's generation the excellence of the world lay distilled in England, and those few of his professors who had chanced to study in that fortunate realm comprised the Dedham hierarchy. The accepted Dedham pronunciation was a bastard British; the style of clothes and the look of life were English; and the Nirvana to which even the lowliest student might properly aspire was "a summer in the Lake District."

The result of this shameless sycophancy was snobbery on the one hand and ridicule of American culture on the other. Only three American writers were deemed worthy of study: Emerson, Howells, Henry James, and they were dealt with condescendingly. Most students graduated without ever having had a course in American history, and as for the concept of a rough and sometimes brutal American freedom, the idea would have been lashed from the halls of Dedham as vulgar and offensive. What civil freedoms America had attained were thought of as stolen from early English settlers.

In fact, anything American was slyly laughed at as unfortunate, or grotesque, or immature, or downright uncouth. And as David slowly built his moral and cultural judgments, he accepted blindly this evaluation of his own land. He was taught to be ashamed of it, for it was so deficient in quality. In the normal course of events he would have graduated with honors in German mathematics and English affectation. Then he would do graduate work in Chicago and Leipsic, after which he would find himself to be a pallid imitation of a pallid interpretation of an essentially pallid mock-European culture. Then he would be enshrined as a professor, and he would seduce other young Americans into the same folly. He would laugh snidely as he referred to "American Corin-

thian, the Bible Belt, Longfellow, and the great unwashed."
He would, in short, have become an American intellectual.
Fortunately, a moonfaced Texan changed all that.

Doc Chisholm was a professor of English in one of the
Texas colleges. He was built like a barrel, had very long
apelike arms and a florid complexion. He massacred pronunciation and drawled in a voice that was sometimes so
low as to be inaudible. He was becoming bald. And he had
a gittar.

How a man like that ever got to Dedham, David never
knew, but the roly-poly man appeared one Friday night and
it was announced that he would teach three special classes.
Purely because of a schedule mix-up, David took Doc
Chisholm in the novel. And as long as he lived the results
of that accident would haunt him.

For Doc Chisholm was a free man. He was the first completely free man David had ever known. Even cold Mr. Stone
was tied to his glossy change board, but fat Doc Chisholm
was free. His mind was a thing of placid, rare excellence, as
beautiful as a lake in summer when the slightest feather
from a passing bird establishes a ripple that ultimately finds
shore.

In his third lecture—in which he reported on the first
batch of papers: "My Three Favorite Novels"—Doc Chisholm
spoke in a very low and soft voice. "Ah won't tear up yore
papers," he said softly, "for Ah gotta admit that anithin'
once written has value to the guy that did the writin'. But
these papers!" He waved them contemptuously. "Yawl tryin'
to impress me? Yew men are the hope of this nation. Yew
mean to admit that the books yew tellin' me about are what
yore greatness feeds upon! Or yew jes' tryin' to impress me
wid the fact yew read all the best books? Hmmmm?" He
brushed back the fringe of hair about his red face and peered
at the students.

Then his voice mounted in slowly rising scorn as he read
off the novelists mentioned: "Thomas Hardy. John Gals-
worthy. R. D. Blackmore. Richardson. Defoe. Walpole!" He
crumpled the list he had made and tossed it in the air. Then,
like a strong halfback, he punted it out the window.

"Lissen, students!" he begged. "Yew and I got to get down
to fundamentals. And quick. Ah not gonna be here long."
He dropped words from sentences when he felt them needless.
"But this nation is a meltin' pot. Yew people before me, yew
come f'um all corners of the known world. Ah see Jews here,

and Poles and Russians and Slovaks and Dutch and Nor-
wegians! Yet yew tryin' to tell me that all yew ever read
was the watered thought of a few Englishmen! Yew tryin'
to get good marks f'um me 'cause Ah'm an English teacher?
Well, doan' do it, 'cause Ah'm a Scotsman. Mah pappy came
to Texiss years ago to drink in the air of freedom. And yew
believe this! The air of freedom is not composed from the
wind of jes' one nation. It's a magnificent and complex pro-
duction from all the known quarters of the world." He stood
fat and mouselike by his desk and said in organ tones, "Yew
are the inheritors of all the world. Yew're a new brand of
people. Yew're Americans." His voice was strange, as if he
were singing, and it was that very night that Doc Chisholm
first appeared in the dormitory with his gittar.

He arrived about eight and dropped into a room down the
hall from David's. He carried with him a battered guitar,
sweat-stained on the hand side. He introduced himself and
asked, "Yawl do much singin' 'round here?" The room's
occupants were so baffled they didn't know what to say, so
Chisholm pulled up a chair and started to plunk his gittar.
"Yawl know *Red River Valley?*"

From his room David heard the strange music and cried
brashly, "Can the racket!" but the racket continued and he
stamped down the hall to see what was happening. He saw
fat Doc Chisholm plunking on a gittar and singing faraway
notes through his nose. The professor nodded quietly at
David and when the song was ended asked, " 'M I disturbin'
yew?"

"I couldn't guess what it was!" David laughed.

"Siddown!" the Texan said. Soon the room was filled and
Doc Chisholm kept plunking his gittar, not strumming it but
hitting soft notes here and there. "Yawl know *Camptown
Races?*" he asked. When singing, he had a strong, nasal
twang that David had never heard before. "It's cowboy
singin', mostly," the florid man explained. "Jes' some cow-
hands singin' to theyselves at night. Ah picked up most of
these songs goin' here, goin' there."

They sang from eight until eleven that first night, the
unaffected songs of Foster and the nameless troubadours of
the West. Finally the professor laughed and said, "Ah got
to be goin'. Ah'm pourin' it on mah students in the mornin'.
Ah'll knock some sense in their heads elsen Ah'll die a-tryin'."

And the next morning he made a frontal assault on David
in particular. "Mr. Harper," he said slowly, "Ah've looked

into your record. It's a distinguished one, so Ah have no hesitancy in sayin' what Ah've got, in all sincerity, to say. Yore paper in particular is a disappointment. It says nothin' and it says it well. But when yew write a paper like this yew should always begin with a holy vow to yorese'f, somethin' like this." He closed his eyes, and looked up at the ceiling. "'Once there was an immortal mind, against which a thousand arrows were loosed. The multitude fell short or overshot their mark. A slim few reached that mind but all of them were glanced aside by its prejudices. Yet of the thousand, one sped true and shot into the very core of that mind and turned it into all confusion, whereupon the man who owned the mind had to set hisself down and make a new pattern of convolutions.' Whenever yew start to write, think of that, and then doan' waste yore time wid enny of the arrows that fell short." Suddenly his voice rose to a shout. "What books have blasted yore mind loose, Mr. Harper?"

David was so surprised he could not reply. "That's right!" the professor said very quietly. "Take yore time! All of yew. Go back to yore rooms and write me some new papers. Doan' impress me wid what yew had last year in Freshman Lit. But tell me in simple words what arrows blasted yore shallow stupidities and forced yew to rebuild yore world on a more secure footin'. If it was *Black Beauty*, say so! For me I guess it was a handwritten book of some cowboy ballads. But once I read those words I could never be the same again. Now this time tell me the truth." He looked at the clock. "No more class today," he said. "When a man's got to do some hard thinkin', he needs lots of spare time."

Doc stayed out of the dormitory that night, and the next night, too, but on Sunday he appeared with his gittar and started to sing the real cowboy songs of the West, songs no one in Dedham had ever heard before. And as the fat man sang the whining songs of loneliness and love's complaint, David began to sense the vastness of the land from which this strange man had come. New words crept through the songs: *sage, dogies, corral, arroyo.* More than words, however, was the spacious, quiet flow of life as it was lived in a land of immense distances and hard-hewn culture.

Doc was not an impressive figure when he sang. He allowed a cigar to hang in the left corner of his mouth and even when he was not playing the gittar his right hand continued a series of nervous plucking motions. His round face began to sweat and his hair soon became rumpled, for whenever he changed the position of his cigar he passed his hand on up and across his head. But when he sang, everyone listened.

They listened, too, on Monday morning when he said in quiet disgust, "Today I see real livin' people. But Ah see also a poverty of mind that is appallin'. Yawl think life is goin' to wait for yew? For yew alone? Yawl think yew can grow to full manhood" (He never admitted that girls existed.) "feedin' yoreselves on the wretched stuff yew been readin'?" He threw the new essays on his desk.

"Yore national genius! Has it never been reborn in yore own precious minds? Melville? Nobody mentioned him. Frank Norris? No one! Upton Sinclair? Nobody. Dreiser? Three people! Out of forty! Willa Cather? Edith Wharton? Mark Twain?

"All right! Yew turn yore back upon yore own country. What about the great geniuses of the world? How do they fare in yore hands? Students!" he bellowed. "Yew are already in yore twenties! And yew have not met the Russians, or the Scandinavians? Reymont? Who has heard of him? Couperus? No one knows his name! and Balzac! Now there's a name to sigh upon! How many of yew . . . No, doan' raise yore hands. But how many of yew joined this class because some day yew hope to be writers. Fine! Ah'm proud you had the energy! But in twenty years yew had not the sense to find Balzac for yorese'f, and he is the supreme teacher! Only one of yew mentioned him. What are yew doin' with yore lives?"

Following this class the run on the library was sensational. Dostoevsky, Tolstoy, Turgenev and Frank Norris were gone in a moment. There was no Upton Sinclair, of course, and Dreiser was kept locked up. Nor had the librarians ever heard of Couperus, Reymont, or Nexo.

Doc Chisholm was not at all perturbed when his students reported the deficiency of the library. "Colleges are not for education," he observed. "Colleges merely tell yew what to do if yew honest-to-God want an education. Yawl got some money! Ah see you spendin' it on the most ridiculous things. Take it an' buy books!" He broke into an expansive smile. "Yew are students!" he cried joyously. "That word is sacred. It gives yew the right to do strange and wonderful things. Like spendin' all yore money for a book they never heard of in yore proper little library. And if yew want to underline the spicy passages and send the book from hand to hand . . . Why, students have always done that, too."

On that night Doc Chisholm first sang *Foggy Foggy Dew*, and the men liked the song so much that he had to sing it many times, teaching them the fine musical words. The song had a powerful effect upon David. It spoke to him of a life not bound in by the narrow conventions of his Aunt Reba's poorhouse maxims nor by the niceties of Dedham's proper and British-yearning education. It was as if Old Daniel were singing the song, and it was a promise of prairies and starlight. For several days David read Willa Cather and hummed, "He reminds me of the winter time, part of the summer, too . . ." He was lost in a dream world, but Doc Chisholm blasted him out of it with his lecture on Nexo.

"How many yawl plannin' to go into business or gov'mint? Or maybe into the labor movement? Why yawl think yew have a right to enter those professions if yew haven't read *Pelle, the Conqueror?* 'Course, yew won't find it in the library. I 'spose yew never even heard of the author, Martin Andersen Nexo. It's a long book, four volumes, but for a young man, it's the key to. . . ."

He sent David and Joe Vaux into Philadelphia to buy some copies, if they could be found, and as the train jogged along David thought: "It's strange. Doc Chisholm is a free man. He doesn't have to act up about anything. He doesn't pose about having been to Europe, because he lived there, and I guess he's read most of the novels in the world. He's the only teacher I've had who is willing to tell the whole truth. Even Miss Chaloner made the world a little better than it is."

"What's eating you?" Vaux asked.

"Doc Chisholm," David said. "I was thinking that he's a citizen of the entire world. Somehow or other he became a free man."

"That's right," Joe agreed. "He doesn't pose much, does he?"

"Unless," David added suspiciously, "it's all a pose." The two students looked at each other as must have looked the students of Socrates, or Abelard, or William James, and none of them ever knew whether their great teachers were merely simple men of truth or the most consummate poseurs.

"I don't know," Vaux mused. "Sometimes I think that guitar of his an act, but the other night that song of the Negro labor camp. Jesus! That hit me over the heart!"

But *Pelle, the Conqueror* hit them much harder. They were able to find only one second-hand copy of the first two volumes, bound together in red and with the penciled notation: "Laura Estervelt, London. May 6, 1924. See the Rubens' landscape."

It was a terrible thing Doc Chisholm did, sending David to that book. For six days the young student could think of nothing but Pelle, the little Danish boy living in the Ark, pushing his way ahead in the world and bearing in his heart the grief of an entire people. A dozen times David slammed the book shut in real confusion of spirit and vowed he would read no more. Then he would be lured back to the relentless steps by which Nexo explained the working-class movement. David could sense every climax the young workman went through. He felt as if Pelle were dragging him, willy-nilly, along the same path. But David refused to go. The brilliant and terrifying story was Pelle's, not his. He had been able to imagine himself Hector slain in dust, or Père Goriot betrayed and alone, or Old Clays, or even an impossible prince in a fairy tale. But he could not imagine himself Pelle, the fighter and the conqueror. He was not Pelle, and he would never be. He was not a man sprung from the people, fighting for a dim social justice that would make all men decent.

He closed the first two volumes in tremendous spiritual agitation. He was glad the rest of the novel was missing, for he never wanted to finish the book. He knew that it was a merciless indictment of David Harper, who had seen most of what Pelle had seen, but who felt no burning sympathy for the writhing masses for the simple reason that he had long since closed his eyes and told himself over and over again: "It isn't like that! People don't sicken and die from lack of food! In America it isn't like that! It isn't! It isn't!" David felt wretched and vastly disturbed.

He was not surprised, however, when Joe Vaux picked up the agitating book and thumbed through it. "This book as good as Moon Face said it was?" he asked.

"It's . . ." David stopped. How could he describe it?

"I'll give it a fling," Vaux replied. He pulled his knees up and forthwith launched into the novel. For two days he stayed in David's room entranced. On the third afternoon he rubbed his tired eyes and cried, "My God! Dave! We've got to find the last two parts."

He called his father in Boston and asked him to have someone search the bookshops. "Go to all the old stores," he begged. He cut class for two days and reread the first two parts. "This is some book!" he said.

Most of the students in Doc Chisholm's class were goaded

into reading some one book which had upon their minds an effect equal in purpose if not in intensity to the effect of *Pelle* upon Joe and David. The books which Doc Chisholm recommended were what he called "the mordant novels." He said, "Mordant novels are those which cut away all pretense, not within their own character, mind yew, but in the inner being of the person who reads. Mordant novels are often ugly novels. There is sand and gristle in them, and Ah can't name four that are well written." He directed his students to *Vanity Fair, Moby Dick, Casuals of the Sea,* and *Oblomov.* He especially recommended *The Old Wives' Tale.* "There isn't much Ah'd like to gamble on," he said, "but Ah would gamble that a thousand years from now this book is goin' to be held up as the model of its age. Ah commend it to yew wid great warmth!" Three students read it and said they didn't catch the greatness. He was pleased with their honesty, for he made it clear that he thought it one of the great books.

"Ah doan' expect yew to see in a book what Ah see in it," he said. "But Ah think our nation is goin' to be the battleground for the mighty struggle between the cities and the countryside. It's a mighty admission for me to say that. Ah was brought up on ranches where the eye could look beyond the horizon itse'f. Then in Europe Ah saw the mean cities, and right yere in America, too, and Ah was thoroughly repelled by them. But Ah got to admit that the future lies wid the cities." He paused and looked out the window.

"Yew may ask why it is, then, that Ah've dedicated my intellectual life, as it were, to range songs. Well, a man doan' have to dedicate his life to what he knows is true. Ah know the world rides wid the cities, but Ah choose to ignore that fact. Ah choose to say to hell wid the cities, and Ah cast my lot wid the open land." He grinned at his students and added, "A fool says in his heart, 'If Ah want to do a thing, then that's the right thing to do,' and a truly great man says, 'No matter what Ah want to do, Ah'm goin' to do what Ah know to be right.' But most of us, yew and me alike, is neither fools nor great men, and so we say, 'Ah know what is right, and Ah praise those who follow that, but in my weakness Ah must pursue another course.' "

From that day on the night songs of Doc Chisholm had an effect on David—and on many of his friends—more powerful than the music of Beethoven. They became the deep, penetrating songs of a free man, imprisoned within his own longings and follies, a man of conflict and emotional disturbance. When Chisholm sang, David could hear the hammer of men across a prairie, or the whimpering of a coyote when night had fallen. The round-faced Texan became a symbol of the splendid confusion in which all men live, the good and the bad alike. They knew where the future of the world lay, but they lusted after another road.

When the time came to write a term paper David launched into a sententious essay on "Social Conflicts in Five Modern Novelists." But he could not deceive himself as to the emptiness of his writing. One night in the observatory he found courage to tear up the pompous paper and to start again. He thought of Doc Chisholm singing and vowed: "I have an immortal mind! It was operating before I got it and it'll go on after I'm dead. I'll tell that damned Texan exactly what I think!"

For some reason he was furious at Doc Chisholm, and he worked for five days on a carefully worded essay. "The Earth," he called it. In glowing terms he spoke of the novels which had come close to expressing and explaining the earth as he had loved it in Bucks County. He wrote of Hardy, Rolvaag, Reymont, Mrs. Gaskell, Turgenev, Chaucer, and Balzac. He culled, sometimes from memory, illuminating passages which came close to the thoughts of a boy upon a farm, the smells, the sound of animals at dawn, the richness of milk pouring from a clean can. He built a solid structure of impassioned reasoning to prove that no matter what happened in the cities, men would always be forced back to the earth for spiritual as well as physical sustenance.

David wrote with fervor, but when he studied his work he found it much too florid. Again he threw away most of it and sat quietly in the dark observatory trying to imagine what he really did think. It was the first time in his life he ever cut away all the sham of words and acquired education and pretty moral phrases. What, in the presence of his naked self, did he believe?

And as he sat there he thought of Eustacia Vye watching on the moors, and he could see her and the Reddleman more clearly than he could see the dim distant wall of the observatory, and it came to him that what he was more interested in than any other thing were the passions of men upon earth. He started to write again and quoted a long passage from *Oblomov*, and this time—at last—he wrote freely, saying almost exactly what was in his mind.

He had to write in longhand, for Joe Vaux was banging

away on the typewriter. Joe called his paper "Foreshadows of the Great Decline." He based it mostly upon *Pelle,* but he did not refer very often to the novel. If Doc Chisholm wanted the picture of a mind torn apart by a book, Joe Vaux would give him just that! The second volume of *Pelle* had arrived from Boston, and as soon as he had finished it, Joe handed it breathlessly to David. "Don't write your paper till you've read it!" he implored, but David would not take the book.

"It's too long," he said. Joe smiled at him knowingly and never again mentioned the great novel. He understood that it cut much too close to David's inner thoughts.

Instead, David read *Oblomov* again. He found the brooding Russian novel much to his liking. He had it with him when he went to type his paper at Dr. Tschilczynski's. When the mathematician saw the book he grabbed it unceremoniously and started to read stray passages. Tears came into his eyes. "My Ongle Peter!" he chuckled. "Goncharov he could have sued. Oblomov is my ongle!" He burst into a florid account of his worthless uncle, who sat by the fire and read English novels. Uncle Peter was very fond of Walpole—that is, the elder Walpole of Strawberry Hill. Warm tears of memory trickled down Tschilczynski's scarred cheeks. "Ongle Peter and my father and especially my sister Elizabeth's husband. They were no good! But they were lovely people. My father destroyed a business . . . How you say it? Sixty thousand dollars a year profit. My father and Ongle Peter ran it down to ten thousand a year, gross. He survived the revolution because everyone knew he wasn't a businessman. He used to write to me in Paris, 'They have ruined me!' " He patted the book affectionately, as if it were indeed his Uncle Peter, and handed it back to David.

When Doc Chisholm reported on the term papers there was an extra silence. He said, in a very low voice, blowing his red nose on a dirty handkerchief, "Yew have made some progress. Ah had sublime faith that yew would. Some of these yere papers are mighty creditable." He returned each with a comment. Vaux's was "stirring." David's was "disorganized and essentially disappointing." David gritted his teeth and refused to listen to the rest of the comments, but when he got his paper he saw scratched on it an untidy A —.

At the end of class the fat Texan asked David to remain for a moment. "Yew doin' anithin'?" he asked. David winced and thought of Science II. It was a dismal class.

"I'm free," he said, glad of any excuse to cut the dreadful monotony of science as taught at Dedham.

"Ah've got a bottle of beer in my ice chest," the professor said. "Why don't we discuss that bottle and yore paper at the same time?" He led David to the bootleg beer and mused, "Yore fund of knowledge is both refreshin' and superior. But yew seem to have no standards of judgment. And yew have no idea at all about paragraphin'."

The Texan guzzled his beer and wiped his red face. "Yew seem unwillin' to come right out and say somethin' is either good or bad. Like an enormous sponge, suckin' things up. Yew got no character to yore thought." He insulted David for some minutes and then asked, "Doan' yew ever fight back?"

"I'm trying to get a lot of things straightened out all at once," David replied.

"Good!" Chisholm cried. "That's fine! But, son, yew been followin' the wrong track. Ah truly think yore country and mine is headin' for leadership of the known world! There is no glory on earth that is beyond us. But we got to have a knowledge worthy of that leadership. We got to rely upon strong young men like yew to know somethin'."

"I study," David contested.

"But yew know nothin' about the spirit of man! Yore papers sound as if books were only paper and some ink and some words. But books are the spirit of man! I grant yew, sometimes, they're purty, like yew said in yore paper, but . . ." He fumbled for words and put his beer bottle down. "David," he said, "the spirit of man jes' plain ain't purty. Yew can call it magnificent or bewilderin' or powerful to the point of despair. But it ain't college-English purty. And yew ought to stop writin' as if it was."

When Chisholm left Dedham several other students besides David felt a regretful longing. The roly-poly, bald, red-faced Texan was remembered as a new kind of man. He had a mind that played honestly upon the broad experience of the world. He saw things pretty much as they were, and his vast learning in many fields never seduced him into an Oxford accent nor lured him to the apostasy of alien values. He spoke in a low voice, and many of his songs were vulgar. He spoke through his nose, and he wore sloppy clothes; but he was a free man.

Not even the unpleasant facts uncovered by the head of science after Doc Chisholm had left changed David's opinion of the Texan. On the very afternoon when the scandal broke David tossed a book through the observatory window and muttered, "To hell with them all! I'd like to be Doc Chisholm." That was when he decided not to be a mathematician. "I'll study people!" he pledged. "People, just as they are." And that was the beginning of his education.

Yet at the very moment when David was most sincerely dedicating himself to the understanding of what was best in American life, he was involving himself more deeply with Mona Meigs. They had reached the point at which she called him at the college to tell him when Klementi would be out of town. Then David would hurry into the city.

For sentimental reasons they met in mid-town and went to the vaudeville at the Earle. Mona carried on a kind of machine-gun comment on the acts: "Look at her legs! She'll get nowhere. You watch Milton Berle, the way he sort of comes in on the up-beat when you're already beginning to chuckle. That's timing, Dave."

Then, at the apartment, she would revel in the security of locked doors and Klim's absence. She would skip about the room and cry, "It's wonderful to have a place all to yourself."

On the day Doc Chisholm left Dedham David watched Mona dance about the room, her arms high above her head. Overcome with desire for her, he caught her and carried her into Klim's bedroom. She laughed and kicked vigorously as he tried to take off her stockings. "Nothing to worry about tonight!" she cried. "Make as much noise as you want!" She beat him with pillows, laughed and squealed like a little girl. Again David was impressed by the fact that for Mona sex was nothing but a violent, super-urgent release. She was like the young animals he had seen on the poorhouse farm. When the great urge was upon them neither fences nor barns could restrain them, and when the act was completed they stood in shadows, lowing softly. There was something wild and glorious in those animals, and much of that primitive grandeur Mona exhibited that night when she returned from the shower and sat with a towel about her shoulders, fixing her hair. She took infinite pains with each wastrel lock at the back of her neck.

"Does it look right, Dave?" she asked, turning her head this way and that.

"It looks heavenly," David replied drowsily.

Mona laughed merrily. "Hair's very important for a girl."

"I'm sure it is," David grunted.

She continued combing her hair and said, "I'm trying out a couple of new styles. Did you notice? I'll bet you'd never guess why. When I was in Chicago two men flew there to see me. Guess from where? From Hollywood! They took pictures of me until the lipstick melted. I must have kissed one of the fellows in our troupe a hundred times. I knew when they were going to take the profiles, so I asked to be excused and got my other brassiere. You know, the one I told you about. Well, I put that one on, Dave, and when I came back one of the men laughed and said, 'You're not so dumb, baby!' But I made out I didn't understand. I saw the shots, Dave. I don't want to boast . . . My God, I've got my fingers crossed until they hurt. But honestly, the shots did look wonderful. Really they did, Dave. One of the men said, 'You take shots like a professional,' and I said I'd been planning them for eleven years. Then he said, 'I'm not president of the company, but I think you're in!' That's just what he said, Dave. I don't want to gloat, because maybe I'm to be the heartbroken one, but I think I'm going to get a contract. Even if it's only a small part! What if it is, Dave? All a real actress needs is one chance." She did not look at the bed on which David lay, but speaking very softly she said, "I'm no fool, Dave. I've always known I needed someone like you. With Klim I was all tied up inside. I loved him and I was grateful to him, but that's not enough. I knew it during the tests. Dave, I was like a queen. So sure of myself! I wasn't afraid of anything, because I knew my body was no longer important. I could make it move about as I commanded. And you helped. If it had still been Klim I would have been uncertain and afraid. Please, Dave! Don't think of me as conceited. I'm not. But I've wanted this for so long." She began to cry, softly, and pulled the towel about her naked body. Then slowly she discovered that David was asleep, that he had heard nothing of what she had said; but she would not fully acknowledge this, and so, still not looking at the bed, she continued whispering: "You understand, Dave, that in a test they have real movie cameras. And the make-up is lots heavier than on the stage. I looked in the mirror when I was finally ready, and I was like a queen. Maybe the part won't be much, but all a girl really needs . . . If she's got talent, that is . . . All she needs is to get her foot in the door . . ."

The next morning when David left Klementi's apartment he walked down Walnut Street, and at Forty-ninth he was aware that a long, black Packard had drawn up to the curb beside him. "Psssst, kid!" a quick, eager voice called. David looked into the sleek car and saw Max Volo.

"Hello, Max," he said.

"Some car, eh?" the little fellow asked. In front rode a driver and a guard. Two extra guards rode in back. Max sat in the middle, well dressed and with his hair pasted down. He wore an extravagant diamond on his left hand. "Well," he said expansively, waving the diamond, "I should be doing all right. I'm paying protection like you never dreamed." Then he smiled self-consciously and added, "You no doubt read about it in the papers."

"I see the headlines," David replied.

"You!" Max commanded one of his guards. "Fix that seat for the kid."

The big guard pulled down a folding seat, and somewhat reluctantly David eased himself into the expensive car. The guard asked, "This the kid from the Park?"

"You bet he is!" Volo cried warmly. "See, kid? I tell everybody about you. About how you was a great star in basketball and all that stuff. He goes to college, too."

"Where you go, kid?" the guard asked.

"Dedham."

"Hmmmm. My brother he goes to Temple."

"Keep your mouth shut!" Volo commanded roughly. "This kid don't have to cheat to pass his exams. Do you, kid? But what I never forget about you, never so long as I live, was when them girls was caught in the fire. You woulda gone right in, wouldn't you? That's what I call bravery. I never forget that!" The little man spoke approvingly of that far-off day. It was apparently much more vivid in his mind than in David's.

"That's why I was glad to see you just now," Volo continued. "Kid, you need any money?"

"No," David replied.

"You need any books or stuff like that? You studyin' to be a doctor?"

"I don't need anything, Max."

"Well, if you ever do . . . Say, listen. How about a girl? You got a steady girl?"

"Well . . ."

"Just what I thought!" Max cried. "You quiet guys don't

know nothin'. You remember Betty? The one with the gold tooth in front? Well, I never forget a friend. Betty has a very swell house on Race Street. Any time you find you need a girl drop around and see Betty. She often speaks of you. Say . . . Even better! How you like to come up to the hills with me some week-end? I can get you a girl, you'll think she's a movie star!" Quickly he flashed from his inner coat pocket photographs of four girls. They were posed as before, but they were much more beautiful than Nora. "This one," Max said approvingly. "She'd go for you. She's crazy about college men. Went to school herself, somewhere."

Max insisted that David take the girl's picture, but David grinned and handed it back. "OK!" Max said. "You can drink milk if you like. Because I know that when the chips was down . . ." He winked happily at his former cashier. "Boy! Did we rape Paradise Park! Kid, do you ever think back on them days?"

Made sentimental by his memories of the old days, Volo impulsively pulled out a roll of bills. He ripped off a hundred-dollar note and stuffed it in David's pocket. "Remember!" he said. "Any time you want something from me, it's OK."

The big car hummed sedately down Walnut Street, as if it were carrying a banker to work, and David felt the hundred dollars in his pocket. Quickly he turned and ran back to the apartment. Mona was in shorts, exercising to keep her hips slim. Awkwardly David thrust Max Volo's bill into her hand. "You may need this," he said.

Mona looked at the money and a lovely, relaxed smile possessed her face. "I don't need money from you, Dave," she said softly. "I know college kids need dough. You keep it. But when you're a big name I may come around for help. Let's wait till then."

"But didn't you say something last night about going to have a screen test? Won't you need lots of clothes and things for that?" He smiled at the actress in great embarrassment. "I could never be happier, Mary," he said. "I mean, Mona, than if you become a great person!" He looked away from her and said rapidly, "I dream of your success, Mona. You're bound to be wonderful. So won't you please let me help you . . . Even a little bit, on your first test?"

"I've already . . ." Mona began. Then she stopped and took the hundred-dollar bill. "All right," she said. "For luck." She kissed him on the nose and said he was a dear and that one of these days he'd grow up and wouldn't be a dear any longer. Then she shoved him out the door and back to college.

As it is for most able boys, college was an intellectual disappointment to David. With Doc Chisholm gone, only Tschilczynski imbued him with any fire, yet David had already decided not to be a mathematician. The other courses were dreadful. Freshman English had been hopelessly dull. History was pedantic and French sodden. But for the abominable science there was no excuse. Botany and zoology were art courses. No attempt was made to explain the coldly passionate development of life. No great principles were established, nor was the mystery of mutation expounded. No! In morning classes all living cells were classified and in afternoon laboratory periods the same cells were drawn in neat circles and well-spaced dots. David passed his science courses because in geometry he had learned to draw. His precise art work was copied by at least twenty students, each of whom also passed. In an age when science was about to assume command of human destiny the students of Dedham were taught to despise the subject. Along with future Congressmen, editors, business men, and voting housewives, David generated intense disgust for science. It seemed—and was— a trivial, wasteful, unimaginative study, fit only for drones.

Nor was David able to lose himself in basketball, as he had done in high school. The college game was too fast for him, and with many tall, aggressive players available the coach would have been foolish to waste his time with a dead-eye forward who hogged the ball and held back when the game got rough. David was eleventh man on the freshman team, but did not even make the squad in his sophomore year. He therefore felt a twinge of deep disappointment when he read about Harry Moomaugh at Swarthmore. Harry was now six feet tall and a rugged man. He was a star guard, and in the Dedham-Swarthmore game scored eleven points. David did not bother to go to the game.

College would therefore have been a failure for David had not, throughout America, a group of thoughtful men been pondering the future of American education. They saw that most colleges failed to educate the gifted student who did not fit exactly into patterns. At Dedham, Doc Chisholm spurred the introspection by saying to the open faculty: "This yere college is takin' money under false pretenses! Yore students simply cannot think! Even bright lads like yore

Mr. Harper. He's picked up a fair stock of stray knowledge, but he's got no critical faculties. What's a college for?"

The head of science rebelled at such iconoclasm. "Dedham turns out solid young men," he snorted. "My graduates do top work at Harvard and M.I.T. And who's this Chisholm, anyway?" he demanded. "I looked him up! Why, he doesn't even have a Ph.D. They call him Doc because he used to medicine horses on a ranch! The man's a fraud!"

There was embarrassed laughter over Dedham's having accepted a gittar-playing horse doctor. Wretched teachers like the head of science—who year after year methodically killed intelligence—took solace in the fact that they had Ph.D.'s whereas Doc Chisholm didn't. By giggling at the disruptive Texan they avoided reviewing their own incompetence.

"We don't need prescriptions from a horse doctor!" they chuckled. "A good, average education. That's what our students need." And that's what American college students got.

But a few determined scholars at Dedham fought the mediocrities and finally established a system of Readings. David was elected to join the experiment and the toothy dean talked with him for more than an hour. "Both Tschilczynski and Chisholm nominated you," he explained. "You're not forced to accept, because what we propose is frankly a risk. For two years you'll have no classes and no examinations. You'll read and argue with professors and write papers. At the end of two years we'll invite eminent scholars from other colleges and universities to test you. Good luck!"

David was surprised at the difference Readings made. Twice a week he visited his professor and argued for several hours. He came away rededicated and worked long hours over many books, culling information for essays which he wrote on diverse subjects. He was becoming a scholar.

And what a change that was! Now his Dedham professors had to explain things, for they knew that when he was examined they would be examined, too. Now there was no posing, for the professors were eager to share all they knew; and for the first time David began to appreciate the fine and polished minds his small college contained.

He was somewhat ashamed when he had to designate the fields in which he would read. He knew that Dr. Tschilczynski would be hurt, but he nevertheless thought of Klementi Kol's arguments before the Rembrandt, and he put down: "English and History." He fell particularly under the spell of the tumultuous Tudor period. He spent months exploring the fascinating fabric of that rich age: Francis, Carlos Quinto, Maximilian, Suleiman the Magnificent, Walsingham, and the Fuggers; but always as he read of the cruel devices by which England became a national state, he thought: "That's the way America is now. We're only just beginning, too!"

Finally David had to face Dr. Tschilczynski, and to his surprise the giant Russian did not berate him. "You likink very much Chaucer?" the mathematician inquired.

"Very much," David replied with embarrassment.

"You givink up the idea, mathematigs, yes?"

David looked up at the big man who had been so good a friend. "I guess so," he said.

"You lookink like you're all mixed up wid people, yes?" Tschilczynski continued.

"Yes," David replied. He wanted to blurt out that Doc Chisholm and Klementi Kol had seduced him from the rigid path of mathematics. He wanted to say proudly: "I'm dedicating myself to the study of great books and the passions that are imprisoned within them," but the words sounded phony, and he could not say them.

But the Russian could speak. He tapped his head vigorously. "All day I workink on nuclear physics. I got one good headache!" David noticed that Tschilczynski's moustache was longer now and drooped a bit. The scar was more pallid and he was becoming noticeably round shouldered. Finally he banged his head twice and said, "Is wery good bright young men start to study human beinks. Soon we rewolutionize the world of science. We profit greatly from a rewolution in human relationships."

Four days later he showed David a telegram from Chicago. With considerable embarrassment to himself, Tschilczynski had arranged for the graduate scholarship in math to be changed into one for English. David felt extremely humble when he saw the telegram and tried to express his appreciation, but the Russian would have none of it. "Is nothink!" he insisted. "What is any sugzessful scholar? A monument to the love some older scholar had for him. What I have arranged for you! The dean says is OK you keep up a minor in mathematics. I teach you on the side."

And that was the meaning of Readings! The hard work, the long papers, the arguments, the conflict with adult minds, the symphony tickets, the art galleries, the laboratories, but most of all that sense that had pervaded every decent university since the days of Athens: the fellowship of able and high-thinking spirits.

The more that people did to help David—like Tschilczynski and the graduate scholarship—the more disturbed he became about his own treatment of Klementi Kol. Now, when he was with Mona, they took Uncle Klim for granted: a kindly musician who fortunately had to take long trips. But when David was alone in the observatory he could not keep his mind from Kol. It was all very well for Mona to laugh at Klim's remarks on honor, but in his Readings David found repeatedly that it has been the strong men of the world and not the weaklings who have stood—at last—upon the grounds of honor. And he, at twenty, had surrendered that strange and precious commodity. Then the shocking Case of the Assy Nude reminded David of what honor was.

If the Case had never occurred, David would certainly have retained a most sentimental picture of Dedham as a cultural haven far removed from the ugly strains of Philadelphia. But the Assy Nude showed him that all places and all people are pretty much alike and that the time comes in each personal or institutional history when honor is the ultimate guide to action.

Young Mr. Thorpe was a Harvard man, almost a fop, trained at the Fogg Museum. When Dedham hired him as the college's first art instructor, he was considered quite a catch, for he came of an excellent Boston family and had been a Rhodes Scholar, as well. It was felt that if anyone could safely teach art in a Quaker school, Mr. Thorpe was the man.

But the honeymoon ended when he started his classes. He was an avowed and utter modernist. That was the year Philadelphia was fighting to keep the Johnson Collection in the city, and Mr. Thorpe was quoted in the papers as having said that "the collection was little more than a bunch of junk in the first place, and that the money Philadelphia proposed spending to house it could much better be spent on a couple of good Van Goghs."

One of the Philadelphia papers carried a reproduction of two pictures: an old saint and a bunch of messy sunflowers by Van Gogh, whom no one had heard of. The caption was straight to the point: Anyone with good sense could see that the saint was great art and the other . . . Well, you name it! The Dedham faculty was embarrassed, especially the head of science. "It's undignified!" he insisted. "Why does that damned fool have to stir up trouble?" The Board of Managers requested that Mr. Thorpe attend to teaching his classes. One gentle lady said that everyone knew the Johnson pictures were great art. "They look old and nice, just like Raphaels."

Probably the whole affair would have ended there had not another newspaper got hold of one of Mr. Thorpe's examinations. When the questions were printed, they created quite a stir. David remembered them well. They were the first simple-answer questions he had seen, and he was much impressed by them. *"You are at a swanky dinner. Your hostess says, 'This morning the art gallery delivered my Picasso.' You reply airily: (1) I adore his chiaroscuro; (2) No man gets distance behind cattle better than he; (3) I'm mad about his blue period; (4) It's a pity we haven't any really fine frescoes in America."*

The questions were held up to ridicule, whereupon Mr. Thorpe interviewed the press. He said: "Ninety per cent of art appreciation is social gush, indulged in to impress one's friends. If that's the case, the best thing I can do is to make sure the gush is accurate. Don't you honestly admit that Philadelphia wants the Johnson Collection only because the paintings are old? Obviously there are twenty artists in the city right now who can paint better than most of those dead old fuddies."

The interview aroused a storm. It was held to violate the gag rule imposed by the Board. Mr. Thorpe was reprimanded and ordered not to mention the Johnson Collection again. And he was to stop giving preposterous examinations. From then on his questions had a proper academic quality: "Compare Perugino's use of space with Claude Lorrain's."

Yet not even the gag rule quenched his ebullient nature, and David formed the habit of dropping in to hear his lectures. He could remember many things Mr. Thorpe said: "No student in this college can possibly see his world unless he has studied Cezanne and Manet." "Some time when you are older and have forgotten poetry you will see a Vermeer, and your tight little hearts will explode." "Rembrandt is like a wintry storm, stirring up the universe, but Frans Hals is sunshine bursting into a fish market."

Under Mr. Thorpe's guidance David went to New York to see the Bache and Frick collections. For the first time he saw the magisterial masterpieces of painting, and he was quietly ashamed that he had ever thought the Johnson Collection superb. Then Mr. Thorpe took him to the Barnes gallery, and the glory of French modernism exploded about him! At his first sight of Matisse and Renoir and Van Gogh and Gauguin he knew that here was a world he was meant to inhabit. The colors were his, and the frenzied shapes, and he said, "If I could paint, I'd paint that way." He wrote a letter to the papers, defending Mr. Thorpe's attack on the Johnson Collection. "Essentially second rate," he said. But when he next stopped by the old house and saw the many trivial paintings—valued because they were ancient—he had to admit with peculiar shock that the three he had come to love were not trivial, and they were not second rate: the Cima and the Van Eyck and the Rembrandt beeves. He looked at them and thought how sad it was that learning consisted of acquiring new understandings with which to kill old pleasures. He had loved the soft sentiment of Thomas Hardy, but Doc Chisholm had killed that. He had liked the old paintings of the Johnson Collection, but Cezanne destroyed such nonsense. As he learned Mahler, Schubert died; and Emily Dickinson made Omar Khayyam seem wordy. "Why can't a man learn just one set of things . . ." he mused. But then a nun entered the museum with a horde of noisy children. They stormed the place and made reverie impossible. David was about to leave when he saw a young boy standing on one foot, daring the Cima to please him. "That's a fine picture," David said. The boy looked up and then stared again at the little picture. David could see that the drunken satyrs and the fairy quality of the picture were beginning to win the boy. "It's a wonderful picture," he said. "It's a masterpiece!" But the little barbarian was not going to surrender that day. Before David could finish extolling the Cima, the boy moved on.

So even though Mr. Thorpe destroyed something much to be cherished, David continued to visit the art class, for he sensed that destruction and the brushing away of false loyalties is the only true education. He was in class the day hell broke loose. The prissy young instructor was showing slides of modern pictures. "What do you make of this?" he asked. "It's a late Picasso, and frankly I don't make much of it either. Now this one. Oh, yes! This has an amusing story."

He permitted the Modigliani to rest on the screen for some minutes. It showed a large nude clutching a towel. Some students began to snicker, for the girl displayed a perfectly immense bottom. "It was the title of this pictured that misled me," Mr. Thorpe said in quiet, clipped tones. "Unfortunately, I knew no French at the time and when I saw the title, *Nu Assis,* I naturally thought it meant the nude with the imposing *derrière.*"

There was a moment of silence. Mr. Thorpe coughed. Some French students began to chuckle and David whispered, "What? What?"

"Don't you get it?" a girl majoring in French explained. "The Assy Nude." A boy in back started to laugh outright and soon the room was rollicking with pleasure; and all the while the statuesque Modigliani, with the pinched eyes and vast rump, stared from the screen.

By noon the campus buzzed with Mr. Thorpe's latest quip. By evening the faculty had heard of the young instructor's continued insolence, and by noon next day Mr. Thorpe was called to an executive meeting. David never knew what occurred at that acrimonious debate or what kind of ultimatum was delivered; but when the meeting ended Mr. Thorpe was fired. Then, in the strange manner that colleges adopt to protect academic freedom, the condemned man was given a hearty breakfast: he was permitted to meet his classes for the last time.

The hall was crowded and he spoke simply, as if he had much to say. "Art appreciation is silly rot," he insisted. "Art has meaning not when it is appreciated but when it is sucked into the heart of your living. Fifteen years from now you'll all have your own homes. Then you'll find that the noisome trash in the Johnson Collection has no meaning for you. You'll decorate with bright, live pictures. Cezannes, Renoirs, Van Goghs. You watch! Or a really good Rembrandt or Vermeer. But I think you'll find it's the moderns who speak to you. You study novels so that you can understand human principles. You study poetry so you won't be ashamed of yourself when you're alone. And you study art so that you can see the world. Without it you can see nothing.

After Mr. Thorpe had left Dedham, David often remembered that last phrase, and it was true. Until he studied Cezanne he had never seen a tree. With profound shock he realized that of himself he was nothing. It was only when he studied with Miss Chaloner that he perceived how the world could be organized. Until Klim taught him to read Balzac he had no conception of the manner in which people subtly or brutally interact upon one another. By his friends he had been taught to understand music and art and logic and sportsmanship and even the rudiments of honesty. He had been a formless thing until the affectionate interest of others had made him into a sentient being. Mr. Thorpe had taught him to see.

David was therefore disgusted almost to the point of nausea when he discovered that this brilliant teacher had been fired principally because the head of science had insisted that "Thorpe's a bad influence on the college. Brings it into disrepute." David railed about this to Joe Vaux, who was now deep in economic theory, and the wiry Bostonian laughed. "You certainly aren't defending a Harvard man, are you? Don't you see that the faculty is just like the students? Porterfield and that pimply-faced kid were different, so the students threw eggs at them. I knew Thorpe wouldn't last a year at Dedham the minute I saw he wore his handkerchief up his coat sleeve. The faculty couldn't tolerate that." He paused and grinned sardonically at David, adding, "But seriously, the big point was that Thorpe was willing to stand on principles."

The word *honor* was never used in the Thorpe case; but as David remembered Thorpe, *that* was the significant word, and the young instructor's closing message rung about the Dedham campus for a long time: "If I had been willing to shut up and stifle my beliefs, turn my back on what the world knows, I could have been your teacher for a long time to come. You can be sure that the old men in politics or religion or art or even education will always hate to the death young men with new ideas. That's why, if you're young, you've got to fight so desperately for what you know to be true, because it won't be long before you're one of the old ones. Then all you can do is hate."

It was during the Christmas season of David's senior year that Klementi Kol finally came home and caught the lovers. Actually, the incident was trivial. Klim was supposed to be in Cleveland arranging for a spring festival, but the local backers withdrew and he returned to Philadelphia. When he reached his apartment, Mona was dressing for a dance and David was sitting in a chair, looking at her portrait.

When she saw Klementi, she instinctively slammed the bedroom door closed. The sound alarmed David and he sprang from his chair and cried, "Mona!" Then he saw the tall conductor. Klementi had a fawn topcoat which he carefully placed on the arm of the lounge. Mona's handkerchief

was there. Klementi looked at it and then at David. There
was a long pause during which David tried to speak but
could say nothing.

Shortly Mona appeared in a silvery gown which Klim
had bought her. "Hello!" she cried merrily. "David's taking
me to a dance at his college. Pretty?" She spun in a tight
circle and the stiff dress twirled out from her slim legs. Kol
sat down in a chair.

Mona shoved David from the apartment and whispered,
"You wait downstairs." Before he had left the hallway, David
heard Mona talking very rapidly to the musician. In a few
moments she joined David. "Klim's a dear," she said. "He
understands."

"What did you tell him?" David asked.

"You never have to tell men like Klim much. They understand." She would say no more, but grabbed David's arm
and whispered, "Mmmmm. Prom night!"

She was the sensation of the evening. There could be no
doubt of that. The young men of Dedham clustered about
her, and David was visibly proud of the way the stags cut
into her dances. She was overcome by the pleasure of such
a night. "I've never been to college before," she confided,
and she held her head back like a spirited young animal so
that everyone could see the joy she was experiencing. "Boys
in college look so clean!" she laughed. "Why do people have
to grow old?"

At intermission David led her to a corner of the solarium
overlooking the eighteenth green. Outside the snow lay deep.
A few couples, bundled in fur, made galosh-tracks through
the drifts, the tracks converging now and then into trampled
circles where the young lovers had kissed. Mona clasped
David's hand and whispered, "It's come! Like I said!"

"What?" David asked.

"I have a part in a movie. Yes!"

The news seemed so appropriate to the fairy-tale quality
of a formal dance with golden slippers and silver dresses that
David caught her in his arms and kissed her. Some men who
had been staring at Mona started to cheer and David heard
those taunts which make a young man's heart happy at a
college dance: "Who is she? Spill it, Harper. A movie queen?"
And David grinned, thinking: "Oh, boy! If you only knew!"

But when the eager dancers whisked Mona away, David
discovered that some of the bloom of that tantalizing night
had been brushed away by a newcomer. It was Marcia Pax-

son, who appeared after intermission with a tall young Quaker boy. She was straight and strong in a blue silk dress that did not cling to her body as Mona's did above the waist. She stood by the door with one shoulder raised higher than the other, watching the minor sensation Mona was creating. When she saw David she peremptorily left her escort and greeted her friend.

"Isn't that Sousa's singer?" she asked.

"Yes," David said with an unsuccessful attempt to hide his pleasure.

"She's the best dancer here," Marcia said, getting David off balance. "In a flashy way, that is." She heard David draw in his breath and then she added, "Do you suppose her hair is natural? It couldn't be." Then she patted David on the arm as might a condescending aunt. "I must run along now," she said, and when she left the evening was somehow changed, as she had meant it to be.

And on the train back to Philadelphia David caught himself looking at Mona's hair. Then he thought of Klim and asked, "Did Klim guess about us, Mona?"

"Don't you worry about Uncle Klim," she assured him, but when they hailed a taxi at West Philly she said nervously, "You'd better not come up tonight."

At the apartment house a crowd had gathered and when Mona saw the gawking people she cried, "Oh, my God!" Then quickly she spoke to the driver. "Right on past, please."

The cab squealed to a halt on Walnut Street and Mona jumped out into the snow. As David paid the driver he could hear the voices: "A shot! From up there! The police knocked the door down! But what do you expect? He was a Rooshian." The voices continued and all that they said added up to one fact: *He* was dead.

Mona took David firmly by the arm. "Let's walk for a minute," she said. Underneath a street lamp they stopped and Mona stood for some time tapping her high left heel against the packed snow. "He shot himself," she said over and over. Then she looked pathetically at David and asked, "What can I do now?"

"What do you mean?" he asked numbly.

"Mean?" she cried. "My clothes! They're all up there."

"What can we do?" David asked.

"Do?" Mona screamed in great anger. "Goddamnit! Don't stand there like a college boy. Think of something!"

She walked up and down the dark street and started pounding her right fist into her left palm. "I could brazen it out and say I didn't know him. But that's no good. Think of something! You're supposed to be so bright."

David's mind was working as eagerly as Mona's and he, too, banged his hands together. Suddenly he stopped and cried, "I've got it! Klim's notebook. I was looking at it tonight. You remember that critic up in Boston? Klim's been fighting with him again. He had the clippings underlined in heavy red. . . ."

Mona grabbed him furiously. "You're positive?"

"I saw them."

Mona began to sob. "Dave! Dave! Do you think I'd have the nerve to sell them that story? Frustrated genius?"

David took her by both hands. "If anybody can, Mona, you can."

In a flash Mona saw the possibilities. "You let me talk, Dave," she insisted. And when she explained to the police, and showed them the clippings, and when they tracked down Klim's bitter letter protesting about the artist's honor, it was obvious that another demented genius had committed suicide.

Mona escaped lightly. In fact, if there was a villain it was the Boston critic. His picture appeared in several Sunday supplements: DID HIS BITTER PEN KILL GREAT MUSICIAN?

The consciousness of guilt rested heavily upon David. Even though the critical two-year examinations loomed ahead, he could not study, for no matter what the book he held, across it moved the shadowy figure of Klementi Kol, silent but accusing.

Mona summoned him into the city one evening. She had a suite at the Bellevue. She seemed more slim and silvery than ever. She began to reassure David. "You've seen how the papers handled it," she said. "They gave me a good play all over the East, and not too sexy. Frankly, I think . . ."

David stared suddenly at Mona and said, "We did a terrible thing to Klim."

"Don't make a fool of yourself, Dave!" the determined actress commanded. "Let me tell you something, David. To do her best work a girl has got to be in love. And not pretty-pretty book love like Klim's. But honest-to-God all-or-nothing love. And don't ever let anyone tell you different."

"Would you mind very much, Mona, if I went on back to college?"

"You goddamned men!" she cried with sudden ferocity.

"You make me sick! You never know what you want! I never knew a single man who would look at life as it is."

Mona was twenty-seven then, and she felt greatly inspired to tell David that in spite of her love for Klim, the musician's death had been a boon to her, for it had forced her to stop depending upon an enervating support; but she took one look at David and thought: "How could I say that to a dumb kid like him?" So she dropped her arms about his quivering shoulders and said, "You've got to forget this, Dave. Klim was good to an endless number of people. Once he sent a young French girl to music school, but she ran off with a meat wholesaler and gave up music. That was when he met me. He said: 'We all hurt other people, especially those we love.' He said that civilized people were the ones who had learned to hurt according to rules. Dave, would it rest your mind if I told you he knew about you for a long time? He did."

David pressed his face against Mona's shoulder and then asked, "Then why did he kill himself?"

"It was coming in like that, and both of us so guilty for ourselves. Even though he knew about us, that was like rubbing his face in it." She dug her nails into David's back, right through his coat and shirt, the tips of her polished nails biting at him. "I loved Klim as I'll never love anyone. I loved him. But I thought that if I ever saw him again, standing by the bed at night, looking at me as if he wanted me more than anything in life, and yet absolutely power-less . . ." She trembled for a moment, and then David be-came increasingly aware of the fingernails, and like a different man—not David Harper at all—he pulled himself free and lifted Mona in his arms, carrying her to the gaudy bed.

But when he returned to Dedham late the next afternoon he found that her reassurances had disrupted him even more completely than his own recriminations. Now he wondered not only about Klim, but about himself: "How could I have slept with her again?" he demanded, abusing himself for such an action. I don't want anything to do with her. All the way in on the train I tell myself that. I tell her that Klim haunts me . . . and then we go to bed!"

Even this deep disgust had to give way to a greater, for as he recalled events of that night he remembered one of Mona's explanations: "Klim was good to a lot of people. He sent a French girl to school." He stopped motionless above the observatory cameras and thought, far away in his mind: "Klim sent me to school, too. Oh, God! What have I done?"

The enormity of his crime ate at him, and for a while he considered leaving Dedham. He even packed the half dozen books he thought he would like to keep, but the prospect of slinking off without sure knowledge oppressed him and he rushed one afternoon into the dean's office.

"Could you tell me," he blurted out, "who gave me my scholarship?"

The dean smiled in the reassuring way that deans and undertakers acquire. "It's an unannounced grant, isn't it?" he asked.

"Yes."

"Then how could I possibly announce it?" he asked, turning his palms up.

"It's very important, sir!" David begged, but the dean shook his head. Then David asked suddenly, "If he were dead? You could tell me then, couldn't you?"

The dean made no promise but went to a locked file and carefully procured a folder. He shuffled through the papers. "Harper. Harper," he muttered. Then he looked up at David and grinned reassuringly. "He's alive, Harper." He returned the folder and locked the file. Then he put his arm on David's shoulder and said, "From what I hear of your work he must be very proud of you. We are, David. Do you mind being told that all the faculty hopes you will do wonderfully well in your exams? Good luck, and don't let anything trouble you for the next weeks. Not anything."

David was astonished at how reassuring the dean was, but as soon as he left the office he saw through the stratagem: "That damned liar!" he muttered. "Why, of course it was Klim! That damned liar wouldn't tell me because he wants me to do well in his lousy rotten exams. Well, to hell with them! And to hell with him, too!"

In fury at the trickery David spent two weeks doing nothing. He could not bear to see Mona and books were an abomination. Then one day in the Philadelphia *Ledger* he saw the name *Doylestown* in a date line. He didn't even read the story, for he was humbled with shame. "I've got to pass those exams!" he said. "I could never go home if I were a failure." He did not think of the poorhouse as home, nor of his Aunt Reba as part of his home; his home was a town with towers, and he could never return to it a failure.

Then he knew what he wanted. He dashed out onto the

highway leading past Dedham and flagged down a car. "Could you take me into Swarthmore?" he asked, and when he reached that college town he asked where he might find Marcia Paxson. He was directed to a quadrangle built like an English monastery, and in a few minutes he met Marcia.

"David!" she cried. "It took you four years to get here!"

"Could I talk with you, Marcia?" he asked. She seemed very strong and clean as she stood in the doorway of the monastery, and she knew that David had come to talk with her because she was like that.

"Is it about the singer and Mr. Kol?" she asked. "Were you involved?"

"Well, not exactly," David began with great reassurance. Then he saw her quiet Quaker face and said, "Yes."

"Why don't we walk?" she asked. She led him to a winding path along a small stream, and for a moment he could imagine himself back in the springtime woods of Bucks County. She waited for him to speak, but she was hardly prepared for what he said.

"You and I were pretty lucky," he finally began. "We grew up in the only town I ever heard of around here that has a real castle. And our town had two of them. I guess it was foolish to waste money building castles, but did you ever see them, Marcia? I guess I saw them in every light and every way there is. When I came to school in the morning I used to look at the red one where the museum is. But the other one was even more . . . Well, it was particularly mine. I've never told another person in the world this, but whenever we had a tough game or an important examination I used to walk out and take a look at that . . . Well," he coughed and they were silent for some time.

Then he said, "The night I walked out to see you I got back to Doylestown just about dawn, and I thought I'd seen that castle in about every possible way, but that morning was like nothing I've ever seen before. Believe me, that was something to see!"

They wandered for a long time through the woods and finally the time came when they had to turn back. "Wouldn't you like to take dinner here?" she asked. "With me?"

"I'd like to!" David said. "But wouldn't Harry . . ."

In the subtle way that Quaker girls have of conveying ideas, Marcia swung her body provocatively sideways and implied without speaking that Harry Moomaugh was no problem. Then she said, "And after dinner I could drive thee back to college."

It was the word *thee* that David had wanted to hear, that and his own memories of the castles he had watched as a boy. "It's good to see you, Marcia," he said.

"There's no reason why this has to be your only visit," she said. "That is, after you've passed your exams."

David actually jumped away. He had come twenty-three miles so that Marcia might goad him back to work, and yet when she did just that he was angry and afraid of her. But as soon as he recovered from his instinctive action he took her hand in his and said, "Marcia, you're more than a castle to me. I haven't studied for a month."

"I guessed that," she said. Then she added, "But you've got to! How could you bear to go home if you did less than you could?"

David stopped and kicked at the spring earth. It was rich with the promise of flowers and it was powerfully sweet. Quietly he pulled Marcia to him and kissed her. "I needed someone to say that," he whispered.

But before he could get started studying, Mona summoned him back to Philadelphia. They met in a cheap hotel he had never before heard of, and she got right down to business. "I'm desperate, Dave," she said.

"Are the police . . ."

"Oh, no!" she interrupted impatiently. "But the Hollywood deal has come through."

"That's wonderful!" he cried.

"I know, I know," she half-growled. "But I don't have a cent of money. Look at me! Look at this dump!"

"I could let you have . . ."

"How much?" she asked eagerly. "I've got to have some clothes. I can't go out there like a dime-store girl."

"I could let you have $260."

Mona dropped her hands and laughed with a touch of hysteria. "You're sweet, Dave. No wonder I like you so much. But I got to have about five thousand dollars."

"Five thousand?" David repeated dully.

"Yes!" Mona snapped. "If I go out there looking as if I need money, I'll get pushed around like I was a poor relation. But I'm going to land there in style. This is everything for me! Dave, I'm over twenty . . ." She stopped and added reluctantly, "I'm more than twenty-five, and I've got to land a job out there." Suddenly the fight went out of her. "I'm scared, Dave. I don't have hardly a cent. I don't even have anything to hock."

She sat heavily on the edge of her cheap white-metal bed and began to bite her lip. She would not cry, but she did have tears in her eyes. "What can we do?" she asked.

David stood above her in acute embarrassment. His mind worked rapidly: "Tschilczynski never had $5,000. Maybe his wife has! Oh, but she's a Greek and she'd hold on to it in the face of God himself. Joe Vaux has nothing. I can't ask Marcia. Can't let her know I came back here after the other night. Her father would have $5,000. But Marcia would surely . . . Say!" He banged his fist into his hand and cried, "Mona! I know where you can get it!"

"Where?" the actress cried, bounding at him.

"Do you know Max Volo?"

"The big shot?" she asked, obviously impressed.

"Yes. He'd lend me five thousand."

"Dave!" Mona cried delightedly. "Why, Max Volo is one of the biggest men in Philly!"

"He'd have to know what it was for," David said cautiously. "It would be bad for you to get mixed up with a man like him."

"Ho! Ho!" Mona chortled. "You let me take care of myself!"

"You want me to try him?" David asked carefully.

"I'm not afraid of Max Volo," Mona said evenly. "Not if he has $5,000. I can handle punks like him, just fine." She shoved David from the door.

"It may take some time for me to find him," David warned.

"I'll be here," the actress said.

On the street David considered what he should do. Volo wouldn't be in the phone book, and he had no idea how to find him. Then he thought of Betty, with the gold tooth. Hadn't Max said, "A house on Race Street"?

He walked up Thirteenth Street. Billy Penn's clock said midnight. On Market the all-night movies were grinding on. At Race he turned right and wandered down that bedizened alley. He looked for the night-prowlers who would know where Betty's house was. Drunks, old and young, male and female, lurched along the lurid street. A Chinese laundryman locked his door and tucked the key into his pocket. At Ninth Street David approached a young man lounging under a light. "Where's Betty's house?" he asked.

"That the one Max Volo runs?" the lounger inquired.
"Yes."

The lounging man blew smoke through his nose. "The yellow house," he said.

When David knocked at the door a Negro opened it and said, "We don't want nothin'."

"I'm looking for Betty," David insisted.

"Betty don't live here."

"Max Volo sent me."

"Where you know Max Volo?" the Negro asked suspiciously.

"Paradise."

"Mis' Betty!" the Negro called. A handsome woman appeared and asked imperiously, "Who are you?"

"I'm David Harper."

"Yes!" the handsome woman cried. "I didn't remember you!" She thrust out a big, firm hand. Expansively she led David through a hallway and into a large, carefully furnished room. There were pictures on the wall, mountain scenes mostly, and expensive furniture. Some men in their fifties, quite at ease, sat about the room talking to four attractive girls who wore perfectly laundered summer dresses.

"This is David Harper," Betty gushed expansively. "And this is Helen and Patty and Louise and this lovely little girl is Floramae. Floramae is from Charlottesville, down in Virginia."

Quietly Betty took Floramae by the hand and said, "Max told me that if you ever showed up I was to be very nice to you. Floramae, why don't you show Dave the place?" The little Southern girl placed her hand in David's.

"I've got to see Max," David said.

"Why don't you and Floramae just look around a bit?"

"Thanks, Floramae, but I've got to see Max right away."

Betty sent Floramae back to the other girls. "You in trouble, Dave?" she asked.

"No!" he insisted, reassuringly.

"Then what do you want to see Max for?"

"A friend of mine's in trouble," he explained.

"A girl?"

"Yes."

Betty laughed heartily. Her gold tooth sparkled brilliantly. "A friend in trouble. A girl friend. Dave, we hear that every day. She going to have a baby?"

"Heavens no!" David laughed. Somehow he never thought of Mona having a baby.

"I don't get what you're driving at, Dave, but Max has never forgotten how you behaved at the fire. He said you could see him any time. I'll send you over with Hampton."

The Negro shrugged his shoulders and left to get a car. Soon David was riding up Race Street toward the center of town. Hampton parked the car and led David to Volo's expensive suite of rooms. Max was there.

"What's up, kid?" the little man asked brusquely.

"A very beautiful girl I know has a chance to bust into pictures. She needs a five-thousand-dollar stake."

"Five grand! Just like that!"

"She's a good risk. She has talent."

"You been sleepin' with her? Guys sleepin' with dames always think they have talent."

"No, Max. I met her up at Paradise. You know her. The girl who sang with Klementi Kol."

"I don't know Kol," Max snapped in an extremely business-like manner.

"The orchestra leader."

"Dance band?"

"No, Max!" David explained. "The good musician who took Sousa's place each summer."

"Oh! That Kol! The guy who croaked himself. *That* dame! Hell, kid! That girl's got all kinds of class!"

"She needs five thousand."

"What for?" Volo asked suspiciously.

"It may sound funny," David said slowly. "She has an offer from Hollywood. But she has no money. She says that if she goes out there broke, they'll treat her like nobody. She wants to make a splash so she'll be too big to be pushed around."

Volo snapped his fingers loudly. "That girl's smart. Where is she?"

There was a long pause during which David thought: "I shouldn't let Max meet her." But the hour was late and Max Volo was in a hurry; so against his better judgment David led Max to Mona's dingy hotel. When he knocked on her door, Mona threw a thin robe about her shoulders and allowed her nightgown to twist awry as if she had just risen from sleep. She pulled at it until her bosom partially showed. Slowly she opened the door.

"Oh, Dave!" she cried. "You shouldn't have come here!"

Quickly she pressed her nightgown against her throat. Then slowly she brought her other arm across her bosom and stood with her wrists crossed. She was tenderly exquisite and blushed in embarrassment. "This awful room!" she said.

Max closed the door and proceeded to business. David was astonished at how quickly Max and Mona understood each other. "Miss Meigs," Max said graciously after the loan had been arranged, "I got friends in Hollywood. Important people, I can assure you. When you get there I arrange flowers, cars, and even should you want it a band."

"That's sweet of you, Mr. Volo," Mona said. "I'm scared, and I'm going to need all the luck I can scrape together." She smiled brilliantly at Max, showing her iridescent teeth.

Then Volo did a very silly thing. He bent low and kissed Mona's hand. David was already in the hallway and did not hear what happened next, but Mona permitted her hand to linger in the little man's and said softly, "But all you get out of this is the five thousand paid back. That's all, Mr. Volo."

"I'm willing to gamble on that," Max replied. He was smiling happily when he overtook David. "Any time you want favors like tonight, look me up! It's a pleasure!"

When the list of visiting examiners was posted David received a jolt. In American legal development, Thurman Arnold. In English history, Mr. David Dalling, of Oxford. David looked at the list and whistled. "I'm to be examined by such men!" He became panicky and hurried off to study in all directions. "Boy!" he grunted when his long absence from books started to tell. "I waited too long!"

But Joe Vaux helped him to get organized. Joe reviewed the books that Dalling had written and pronounced the man to be archconservative, anti-Macaulay, pro-Walpole, anti-Earl Grey, and pro-Sir Thomas More. Following this analysis he tracked down a dozen books and joined with David in a systematic summary of the great writers: Ostrogorski, Dicey and the rest. But at night Joe snarled at the men on his hall: "It's a damned disgrace to bring a man like Dalling to America. Reactionary, Troy, anti-labor. And an Englishman! Well, here's one Boston Irishman that don't give a damn if he graduates or not. Wait till you see what I do to Mr. David Dalling!"

The written exams came first, ten days of them with three-hour papers each morning and afternoon. On the first day David felt chilly and truly afraid, but then he saw Mr.

Dalling's exam. It was one question: "What events in British constitutional history might be studied in an effort to understand Andrew Jackson and Abraham Lincoln in their defense of union?" David grinned at the question and a sweet sense of power came upon him. "I could write for days on that one!" he muttered.

He did well for eight days, and when students compared notes, word flashed across the campus: "Dave is knocking them dead." He was not sure, but he did know that few questions were asked which he and Joe had not studied. At the beginning of each exam they nodded gravely to each other; and then on the eighth afternoon David was handed a telegram as he left the examination room: "Must see you tonight. Dinner. The Bellevue. Mona."

"No!" he cried, immersed in the problems of the next exam. Then, as he stood with the crumpled paper in his hand, he sensed the terrible right of intrusion that people retain if they have slept with each other. "Mona!" he mumbled to himself. "I'd like to see you tonight, but I just can't leave!"

He destroyed the telegram and said nothing to Joe, but Mona forced her way into his book and he rubbed his eyes. "No!" he cried again. "Damn it all, no!"

Outside his window there was a honking and students began to shout, "Harper! Harper! It's the longest car east of Hollywood!" He went to the window and recognized Max Volo's special limousine. Two plug-uglies were in front. "Hiya, kid," they called. "Max is giving a farewell for the blonde. You're to come along." For a moment David was determined to slam the window and get back to work. Then he thought of Mona and her last night in Philly.

"Vaux!" he shouted. "Leave me your outlines of Chaucer. I'll be back late."

The farewell dinner was a gala affair and all during it David pushed away the glasses and bottles of Max's bootleg. But when Mona toasted "The first man to tell me I'd make good! Dave Harper!" he felt a lump in his throat and drank a full glass to her success. He had two more following Max's speech and two more after a tearful tribute to Klementi Kol. Then he waved his empty glass and said, "To the best of them all, John Philip Sousa!"

At eleven two limousines drove the party to West Philadelphia, where Mona boarded the train for Chicago. She had a suite, and Max had ordered it filled with flowers. David lugged her baggage in, and then he and Max stood in the doorway. "Thank you!" she cried in thick tones. "Thank you both!" But it was David she kissed.

The conductor cried, "Everybody off that's getting off!" and Max disappeared; but the announcement of actual departure frightened David, and he had a sense that he might never again see Mona. Swaying gently, he watched her shaking her lovely head to clear away the mists, and in this last moment of their time he blurted out: "Mona? What was wrong with Uncle Klim?"

"What do you mean?" she snapped, trying to focus her champagned eyes on David. "Who said there was anything wrong with good old Klim?"

"Was he injured when he was a boy? Or in the war?" David was fighting for one last understanding of the man he had wronged. "I mean, why couldn't he make love to you?"

"Why, you dirty . . ." Mona began. "You get out of here with your filthy mind!" She shoved him toward the door and then recognized who he was. She stood swaying before him, and the conductor blew his whistle. "Dave," she explained hurriedly. "Sometimes a man can be the best man in the world. He can be kind to people and love a girl until his heart breaks. But things don't work out for him, so he shoots himself." Her lips moved vacantly and then, as if she knew that one day she might herself be subjected to the whim of an implacable injustice, she flung her unsteady arms about David and begged, "Wish me luck, kid. Wish me luck!"

When the train chugged away Max asked, "Were you sweet on that dame?"

"Sure!" David replied defiantly. "Who wasn't?" Then he saw a clock and cried, "My God, Max! I got to get back to college!"

"They lock you in at night?" Max asked.

"Exams."

"You're smart enough already," Max objected roughly, shoving David toward the cars. "We'll celebrate."

"Max!" David protested weakly, and even when he staggered up the steps to Betty's house on Race Street he was still talking about Chaucer.

"Meet Mr. Chaucer!" Max cried in taut accents. The girls were delighted and laughed at the unsteady college student.

"Sing us a college song!" they demanded. Their voices were shrill and exciting and David said, "I'll sing you the daddy of 'em all!" And he began to intone "Fair Dedham, in that distant day . . ." The words reminded him of college. "Hey!" he roared. "I got to get to college!"

The night wore on. Betty and the girls sang. An expensive radio picked up stations ever westward as the eastern ones closed down. Max sat regally in a red chair and studied the clowns about him as might Caesar have studied Egyptian dancing girls and Grecian fools. At three he said, "OK. Let's get going." He and Betty piled into the limousine and ordered three men to lift David in after them. The big car roared back to West Philly, and Max boarded a Pullman. The train disappeared into the night and David asked, "Where's he going?" And big Betty replied, "He's going out to Hollywood. He catches up with Mona's train in Chicago."

There was a buzzing in David's head and he never knew how he got back to Dedham or how the two men dragged him up to Joe Vaux's room. The first thing he remembered was looking up at Joe from a bed. "You look just fine!" Joe declared.

"God! My head!" David moaned. He belched and added, "My stomach, too."

"Get into the shower!" Carefully Joe herded him under the cold water and then gave him a brisk rubdown. "Drink this," he said.

"I don't wanna drink anything!" David protested."

Joe smacked him in the face. "Dave!" he said pleadingly. "This is where they separate the men from the boys!" He propped him up and started reading the notes on Chaucer, but before he had reached the second page David was asleep. Joe allowed him to lie in his stupor until ten minutes to nine. Then he thrashed the half-drunken student into shape and dragged him off to the examination room.

"My head!" David repeated. When he sat down, the room remained standing and he could not get it to obey him. Then he saw the white paper staring up at him and three thoughts flashed through his throbbing mind. First he thought: "I'm going to be sick, like the women in the poorhouse." Next he tensed his stomach muscles and thought: "This is where they separate the men from the boys." Finally he saw that name on the examination paper: Chaucer! And he began to grin. If there was in all the history of the world one man upon whom to write after a night of drunken foolery and kissing fair women good-bye and singing to the stars and being young and turbulent and in love and confused and wildly happy, that man was Geoffrey Chaucer. And David thought: "Especially in the spring."

In the public interrogation David did very well and experienced a new sense of affection for Dedham and its intellectual fellowship. At each question the Dedham faculty leaned forward, visibly hoping that their prize student would answer with distinction. But it was the interrogation of Joe Vaux that filled the hall! For three weeks Joe had publicly been threatening to humiliate the crisp English visitor. "If you want to hear something good," Joe had said grimly, "listen to me tear into that pompous ass." He launched his assault on Mr. Dalling's first question: "In your opinion, Mr. Vaux, how do you account for Pitt the Younger's intransigent resistance to Napoleon?"

Joe thrust his Irish chin toward the Englishman and said, "I imagine, sir, that he was held up by two outmoded beliefs. *One*, an ingrained love of imperialism, his brand. *Two*, like all members of the ruling classes everywhere, Pitt was constitutionally afraid of any progress, French or English."

From that blast the interrogation continued. Mr. Dalling never betrayed the least irritation with Joe's astonishing replies. Nor did this disturb Joe, who called upon all of his learning to antagonize the cool Englishman. The Dedham faculty was both embarrassed and surprised at the depth of Joe's knowledge. They were humiliated by his behavior.

At the end of an hour Mr. Dalling rose and smiled at the audience. "I understand that I must submit my reports in private, but in view of the interest in this interrogation I shall submit this report publicly." He bowed crisply to the Dedham faculty as if to say: "What can you do about it?"

"I must award Mr. Vaux two marks instead of one. For his grasp of British history. Very, very superior. But when I was a small lad in a school where unruly boys were whipped, I was often whipped and given a rating that disturbed my mother very much. I now pass that on to Mr. Vaux. Deportment, Failing." Then he grinned and reached across the platform to shake Joe's hand.

At seven that night the student body gathered to hear the final marks read. On a small platform the visiting scholars sat informally. The dean raised his typed sheet and read with impressive pauses. Joe Vaux, Magna Cum Laude. A few students applauded. Then, in conclusion, he said, "The examiners were especially pleased to award David Harper Summa

Cum Laude in two fields: English and history." The Dedham faculty started to applaud politely but was interrupted by a twilight voice that sang: "Fair Dedham, in that distant day . . ." and David was so filled with emotion that he dared not look up, for in those days Dedham was the only American college where the student body could get as excited about distinguished scholarships as it did about football.

That summer Joe Vaux worked in a steel factory. He tried to make David join him. "Don't you see?" he pleaded. "Chisholm was right. The future of the world is in the cities. What happens there is what's important."

But Marcia Paxson had other plans. She drove to Dedham on graduation day and said, "Daddy'd like to hire you for the farm this summer." She spoke firmly and with no embarrassment, yet she and David each knew that what she was suggesting was as truly a proposal of marriage as if she had said: "Let's spend the summer studying each other. I don't really like Harry Moomaugh, and if you and I find that we are in love, there's no reason we shouldn't marry and go to Chicago together."

"I'd enjoy such a summer," David replied, but inwardly he was afraid that he was signing his life away. Marcia drove him to Solebury and when they passed the poorhouse he laughed and said, "If I had any spunk I'd go in there and spit in Aunt Reba's eye. She'll blow a gasket when she hears I'm not going to work in the pants factory."

"Was she so awful?"

"She's a perfect example of old people hating young people," David replied.

"Where did you ever hear such a silly idea?" Marcia demanded.

David explained about Mr. Thorpe; and all through the June days when he plowed the rich fields of Solebury, he thought again and again of something the art teacher had said: "You study poetry so you won't be ashamed of yourself when you're alone."

So as he worked the fields and watched the swallows and the barn owls and the mice, he started to recall the snatches of poetry he had learned, odd bits and fragments of felicitous summary: "Music when soft voices die vibrates in the memory." "Blow, blow, thou winter wind, thou art not so unkind as man's ingratitude." Sometimes he could not recall much of a poem, only a phrase that hung in memory as if some ancient hand had arranged the words and put a spell upon them so they could never be changed: "Bare ruined choirs where late the sweet birds sang." "Huge cloudy symbols of a high romance." "Nor the prophetic soul of the wide world dreaming on things to come."

As such words clung about him David felt that he was indeed the inheritor of the world's accumulated beauty. He could do no single thing that someone before him had not done, and relished and compressed into memorable wisdom. He would look across the fields of Bucks County, and they had been described long, long ago by Wordsworth and by Shelley. Keats was with him, and Thomas Campion, and Shakespeare everywhere. He could find Robbie Burns under any stone, or brooding Goethe or the far-flung glories of Homer.

He marveled constantly at the seductive power of words, the way they possessed him forever: "Thy soul was like a Star, and dwelt apart." "The holy time is quiet as a Nun breathless with adoration." "O where hae ye been, Lord Randal, my son?" "While greasy Joan doth keep the pot . . ."

There were special poems which he found he knew fairly well by heart, Milton on his blindness or the sonnets of Shakespeare. As he plowed, he would sometimes recite a single sonnet a half dozen times, savoring the nuances of expression, and from these special poems certain lines stood out as if intended for him:

> Haply I think on thee, and then my state,
> Like to the lark at break of day arising
> From sullen earth, sings hymns at heaven's gate.

Those lines were particularly disturbing because in David's life they applied to no one person. His heart simply did not leap up when he beheld Marcia. She was a fine friend to him in those early June days. She saw to it that there were towels in his room when he came in from the fields, and in the evenings she was always ready to go where he wished.

On Sundays they went to Solebury Quaker Meeting, and by the third week it was acknowledged in the community that David and Marcia would marry, even before he went to Chicago to become a professor of English. But in the long weekdays under the warm sun, working again with the earth he knew, David became increasingly opposed to his easy destiny. A phrase from Shakespeare possessed his mind:

"When to the sessions of sweet silent thought I summon up remembrance of things past . . ." It recurred endlessly, in time to the hammering of the tractor pistons, and as he drove across the fields, back and forth toward the canal that had lured him so strongly when he was a boy, he felt offended with himself that he should drift into a marriage that contained no passion and into a profession that dealt not with the fires of spring but with the learned ashes of winter.

"No! No!" he muttered to himself as he shepherded his noisy tractor home at night. "The testimony of everything I know tells me this is wrong!" Restlessly he went to his room and saw by chance a map of America. He was vividly called back to Miss Chaloner's math class, and he could hear her speaking of the Rockies. "I've never seen a mountain!" he muttered.

"David!" Marcia called. "Dinner's on."

"All right," he replied grudgingly, and all during the meal he felt resentment against the quiet girl.

"What's the matter?" Marcia asked.

"Did you study much about America in Swarthmore?" he asked.

"No," she replied, reflecting the college tradition of the time, "we didn't study it at all."

"Neither did I," he replied. "This is a pretty big country." Mr. Paxson looked at him and agreed.

For two days he was depressed and would have nothing to do with Marcia. Her father noticed this and waited for his daughter to mention it. When Marcia did, he laughed easily and reassured her that "Dave's pretty much like a new-broken horse. He's testing his shoulders against the harness."

But David's agitation went deeper than that. He did not want to be a college professor. He felt that surely somewhere there must be a more urgent life than that. Nor did he want to marry Marcia. He could not help comparing her with Mona, and the terrible fable of American middle-class life plagued him: Marcia was a nice girl, therefore she would be cold and distant. He shivered at the prospect and stayed by himself among the horses and the cows.

As he worked, new fragments of poetry flashed through his mind, all bearing testimony to the fact that there is in life a fiery passion which alone makes the long years tenable: "About, about, in reel and rout, the death-fires danced at night," he chanted, swinging over to the chopped lines of

Blake: "What immortal hand or eye, dare frame thy fearful symmetry?"

Finally David became so nervous that he could not eat with the Paxsons. He felt like an intruder. He walked about the farm studying the fall of the fields and the trees at dusk. A single line of poetry, remembered from high-school days, but unplaced among the jumbled ends that cluttered his mind, slipped into his consciousness: "Shades of the prison house begin to close upon the growing boy." He began to repeat the words and wondered from their strange beat what poem they were attached to. Then, slowly, the meaning of the words broke upon him, and he felt quite breathless, as if he had been running.

"That's what I'm afraid of," he admitted. "I refused to work in a pants factory. But this is worse, because I'm doing all of this consciously." He leaned against a fence and surveyed himself. By hard experience he had learned what honesty was, had acquired a certain physical courage. Mr. Chisholm had taught him what intellectual integrity consisted of, but the inner integrity whose absence breaks a man had not yet developed. He was twenty-two years old, and he was slipping dreamily from one choice to another.

"No!" he shouted at the sunset. "I won't go to prison!" He would rush in and tell the Paxsons, but he heard Marcia calling him. He was wanted on the telephone.

# PART 4

# Chautauqua

MONA CAME BACK. She reached North Philadelphia at dusk and immediately called David at Dedham. The operator said, "He's gone back to Doylestown." Mona called the poorhouse and after a long interval heard an elderly woman's plaintive voice, "Daywid ain't *here* yet. He won't *be* here. He's *against* the *Pax*sons by Carwers*ville.* I told him to *come* . . ." Mona sensed that the complaining voice would continue, so she hung up. These calls were costing money, but she decided on one more. This time she reached David.

"It's Mona," she said.

"As if I wouldn't know!" an excited voice cried. It made her feel good. She threw her shoulders back. "Good news?" the eager voice inquired.

"No!" she snapped, and her shoulders dropped. "You read *Variety*? Those dirty bastards! Said I went west lit up like a Christmas tree. I didn't get to first base."

There was a long silence and then David said, "Oh."

"But there's one thing you can be sure of," Mona said with much satisfaction. "That dirty little pimp Max Volo didn't get any good out of it. He trailed me all the way to the coast. And he came back, too. Alone."

There was another awkward silence and David asked, "What are you going to do?"

"That's what I called about, kid. How would you like a job? Yes, a real job! With a play company? Sure, you'd act!"

From the scrambled sounds that reached her, Mona judged that David was bursting for such a job. "Are you kidding?" he exploded.

"No!" she assured him. "I have a six-months' tour with Chautauqua. A swell comedy. There's a part for you. And you're to help with a marionette show in the afternoons. How about it?"

"Do I travel with you?" David asked.

"All over the country," she said. "But I've got to warn you . . ."

The telephone whistled, like the escape valve of a long-pent engine. David interrupted her warning. "Mona," he cried, "I'm sorry for your bad luck in Hollywood. I've prayed for you, but I've also had my heart crossed, hoping for some job like this one . . ."

"Look, Dave," Mona cautioned. "There's one thing about the job you may not understand . . ."

"If it's with you, it's all right!" he cried.

She gave him directions and then added, "Now I want to tell you, Dave . . ." but the operator broke in, asking for twenty cents. "All right!" Mona cried. "Here's two dimes, and you know what you can do with them!" But David was gone. She shook her head and muttered, "He'll raise hell when he finds out, but he's got to grow up some time."

She stepped back into the shoving crowd. Two men passed her and turned back. "Why don't you put your arms in the sleeves, baby?" they asked. She ignored them and they teased her, "You're gonna lose that lovely coat wearin' it thataway. Then who'll keep you warm?"

She smiled to herself and whispered, "Men, men."

When Marcia answered the phone and called David from the fields, she sensed that the woman's voice was Mona's. "Long distance," she told David as he hurried into the house. While he talked she brought him a pencil and some paper. He nodded his thanks, but she could see that even his eyes were absorbed in the telephone conversation.

Marcia felt that she must not eavesdrop, but she could not force herself to leave the room. She sensed that this was the climactic moment of her life so far. That afternoon she had quarreled with her parents: "If David isn't ready, I'll simply have to wait for him. No! I've gone with Harry Moomaugh for three and a half years. That's a good trial, and I don't love him." She had thought: "It's funny! I always think of Harry as a man, but I don't love him."

Now David's eager voice was speaking: *Where are you, Mona?* So it was that silly singer. Marcia could remember the day when she and David first heard John Philip Sousa. "I wonder if Mona Meigs was singing then? She could have been. She's as old as Methuselah." The thought gave her pleasure and she leaned against the door, watching David twist the phone cord about his thumb.

It had been a grand spring, so far. On First Days they attended Solebury Meeting. They sat in deep silence, and in the quietness of those stately sessions it was apparent that they were intended to marry, to live among the quiet trees of Solebury, and to have children who would attend First Day School in that very building.

*I don't get a chance to see* Variety *very often.* David had promised her that he would accept the scholarship to Chicago, but she sensed that he was not happy about his decision. Yet, deep within, she knew that in being a college professor there was stability. He would get a job at Haverford or Dedham, and in the summer they would live at Solebury, and the happy years would go on forever.

*Oh, that's rotten luck, Mona!* Marcia pressed her head against the door jamb. Sunset light from the fields fell upon her strong head and along her starched, precise dress. David looked at her with far-away eyes, as if she were part of an ancient Quaker sampler. *That's really tough, Mona!* It was Marcia's intention to accompany David to Chicago. She'd study social work, for she knew that even if she had a dozen children—and she would enjoy a dozen—she would have to continue some meaningful work. For as she studied the married people who filled the various Meetings she perceived clearly that those men were happiest whose wives were best. She knew fifty men who had married fluffy young girls who remained fluffy young wives, forever. She would not believe that those men were happy, for in the strangest ways they betrayed their unhappiness. "So what if David does like this singer! He knows it's all wrong. Like Harry and me."

*Chautauqua? Yes! It used to come to Doylestown when I was a kid.* "He's still a kid," she mused. "Look at him!

He doesn't know what he wants or what he'd like to run away from." She guessed it might be his fear of responsibility, and she berated herself for not having told him that her father had agreed to support the marriage for the first three years. "I'll tell him when he hangs up," she said.

*What's this about marionettes?* She twisted her head and looked across the noble fields of Solebury, the soft green fields. How exciting spring had always been! Year after year! The crackling of ice along the Delaware. Then soft days with pussywillows by the barn. Next lilacs and the full tide of earth bursting into fruitfulness! And this spring was finer than any she had known before. David was with her, and often they kissed, not schoolboy kisses, either. True, he was shy and seemed to pull away, spiritually, but she imagined that most good men—certainly the men she saw in Meeting—had been that way: unwilling to tie themselves to one person, but when tied, faithful and sharing till the last wintry day. A dove flew across the sunset fields and she thought of the haunting line she loved so well: "And peace proclaims olives of endless age." Then David's voice broke the spell.

*I've had my heart crossed. Hoping some job like this would come along.* He wrestled with the cord and could not free his hand. "Marcia!" he cried. "Take down this address." With his elbow he pointed to the pencil. She walked slowly to the phone and wrote as he dictated: "Delaware Chautauqua, Delaware, Pa."

David hung up. He was so excited that he had to move about the room, but as soon as he had left the phone he hurried back to study the paper with Marcia's writing. He waved it in the air. "How do you like that?" he cried.

"What's it mean?" Marcia asked.

"Why, it means I've got a real job!" he replied.

Marcia put her hand to her mouth. Something in the way David accented the adjective *real* conveyed his full meaning. But with a stolid determination to hear the worst she asked, "Isn't a fellowship at the University of Chicago a real job?"

David looked away from his inquisitor and thought of what he was about to surrender: Tschilczynski's Chicago fellowship, the chance of being a college professor, the quiet grandeur of Quaker life in Eastern Pennsylvania, and Marcia, too, and the fields of Bucks County. He realized the folly of his decision, but he saw its substitute and found it glowing: a march across the country with a traveling circus, Mona and the dark nights when her desires and ambitions mingled and overflowed, strange people in strange towns!

"I'm not ready to get married, yet," he said.

"Married!" Marcia cried, with her right hand to her lips. "Who . . ."

"We both know," David replied. "We were to spend the summer here studying each other and then get married in late August. Marcia . . ."

"Are you afraid of getting married?" she interrupted.

"In a way, I am," he said. There was a great agitation in his mind, for this quiet Quaker girl disturbed him deeply. "Oh, don't you see?" he cried angrily, ashamed of his own confusion. "I'm not as old as you are. Spiritually, I mean. If I can get away for a couple of years and see this country . . . I'm not sure of myself, Marcia. You might not want to marry me when you see the kind of man I become. If we could wait . . ."

Marcia studied the freshly plowed fields and saw in them the urgency of life, which, like the growing season, is so very short. "I can't wait," she said simply. "I can't suspend life while you wander about. Why must you beat your head against the world? You know in your heart that in the end you'll love me. Then it'll be too late, because I will not wait. If you go, I'll marry Harry Moomaugh."

David felt that it would be decent for him to protest, but he was tremendously relieved that Marcia had worked out an alternative plan for her life. He shook her hand and said, "I'm sure you'll be very happy." Immediately he was ashamed of himself, disgusted, and he pleaded, "Marcia! Why won't you wait?"

She replied with the great frankness that marks Quaker conduct. "For men life seems endless," she said. "But for girls it isn't. While you loaf around, I'll have had two children. While you dream of this or that, I'll be running a farm." She looked across her father's fields and gripped David's hand. "It's almost as if we were two trains on different schedules. We weren't intended to meet nor to share the same stations." She stamped her foot. "Damn it all!" she cried. "God certainly can louse up his timing!"

For the first time since David had known her, she seemed like an ordinary girl, warm and petulant, and David found her deeply appealing. Almost instinctively he tried to kiss her, but she pushed him violently away. "No!" she commanded harshly. "That's past! Go on up and pack! But when I'm married, you're never to visit. And when you've traveled all summer with your cheap singer and seen that everything is empty, not what you wanted at all, don't come cringing back, David! I'd slam the door in your very face."

The Cyril Hargreaves Troupe of Broadway Players consisted of six actors and a telephone. Hargreaves himself was sixty-six, a splendid, well-preserved cenotaph with an aquiline nose, a handsome face like parchment and the remnants of a grand manner. Emma Clews, aged forty-four, was a flaccid, dumpy veteran of twenty-three summers on Chautauqua. She was terrible. Mona Meigs, twenty-seven and hungry for better things, was leading lady. David Harper, twenty-two and aching for the full experience of life, was the juvenile. The dwarf Vito Bellotti was comedian, and the fabulous Wild Man Jensen, a former football star at Illinois, was general muscle man and bit player.

But in a certain sense the telephone was the hero of the troupe, for this was the year 1929, the last year that the good, brown tents of Chautauqua went through the East, and although there was money to burn that year, Chautauqua was slowly dying. Radio, the movies, and the motor car had killed the venerable institution and David was an attendant at the wake. Everything was conducted parsimoniously, and since the play they gave called for some dozen characters, it was necessary to feature the telephone. Whenever it came time for one of the missing characters to speak, the phone rang and Cyril Hargreaves picked it up. "No!" he would ham. "You don't say! That's delightful! Listen to this," and he would repeat word for word the absent actor's dialogue. He played his own role and those of the six missing subordinates. "We save some thousands of dollars that way," he explained.

The play for that summer was *Skidding*. It dealt with the fortunes of Judge Hardy's family in Pocatello, Idaho, and in the play the dwarf Vito had the role that was later to become world famous. Vito was the rambunctious son, Andy Hardy, and the happy little dwarf clowned his way through the part so delightfully that even when a more famous actor assumed the role in the movies, David always thought of Andy Hardy as little Vito had portrayed him.

In fact, David was in that wonderful and sentient moment of his life when he seemed to have no skin upon him, no lids upon his eyes or veils across his mind. He sensed immediately the tremendous effect of each of the other five members of the troupe upon him; and in many ways this summer of 1929 was the most terrifying and meaningful of David's life. He worked hard and grew thin. He drove the Chautauqua truck long hours and for weeks at a time was so sleepy that life seemed like a shadow hung between day and night; and always about him were the five members of the troupe, pressing upon him in various ways. Once he said to himself: "It's as if I were nothing but exposed nerves," and even though the experience was exhausting he felt at the time that this was the way men of greatness had lived: they felt more, they sensed more, they allowed people about them to impress them more deeply, and their nerves were forever exposed.

For example, Cyril Hargreaves, a man of sixty-six, became David's competitor in love, was successful, had David almost killed, and never once lost his temper. He was a tall, icy man and spoke in acquired British accents. He was originally from Oklahoma, a fact to which he had not alluded in forty-eight years. He was stilted, arrogant, pompous, and extraordinarily selfish, but he was also a full-grown man of passion, and after David contended with him, David too became a man.

Trouble started on the first day, when Cyril quietly let David know who was boss. He said, "Mr. Harper, in a prosperous year I could not possibly have tolerated an amateur like you in my troupe. Whether you appear onstage or not is of no possible consequence to me, but if you once fail to ring the telephone when I'm supposed to give a speech the fine is twenty-five dollars."

Cyril also made it clear that during that summer he would escort Miss Meigs to and from the tent, to and from her meals and to and from her bed. When this became apparent, David tried to protest, but Mona stopped him. "You're a grown man now," she said.

"Then why did you invite me for the summer?" he demanded.

"I tried to explain over the phone, but you were being cute like a college boy. We had to have a cheap actor. The cheapest we could get."

"That's a hell of a reason," David snorted.

"And the second reason," Mona continued, "was that I knew damned well you were rotting out on that farm with

Miss Apple Blossom of 1928. You were mighty happy to have me save you."

"Can't we at least have dinner tonight?" he begged.

"I eat with Cyril."

He looked at her with bewilderment. He had not before realized that two people who had been passionately involved with each other could submerge their one-time desire. In confusion he asked, "Don't you love me any more?"

"Love you?" the actress repeated incredulously. "Who ever said I did?"

"But . . . In Klim's apartment?"

"What's that got to do with love?" she parried, leaving him for her dinner with Cyril.

Emma Clews explained things to David. She was round and dumpy and had a sallow complexion. Each thing about her was indiscriminate and blended softly into its neighbor. She had watery eyes, straggly hair, a chin that rested upon her bosom, which sagged onto a protruding stomach, which hung upon fat legs. Her blouse of soft silk joined haphazardly a woolen skirt which bulged at awkward points, and about her shoulders she wore a knitted scarf, for she was always cold.

She was known as the Gonoph, why, no one ever said. She had big yellow teeth which she exposed when she smiled, and she was one of the worst actresses imaginable, delivering all words with identical emphasis, like a mother who refuses to take sides among her equally ill-favored children.

For some reason that David could not guess, Mona despised the Gonoph and ridiculed her bitterly. "Why don't you borrow a razor blade and cut your throat?" she used to ask.

The Gonoph grinned, baring her horse teeth. "Wouldn't you be sorry if I did?" she chided. "Wouldn't you just?"

"Tell you what!" Mona suggested. "You cut your throat! Then later Cyril can tell you how shocked I was. I don't think!"

The Gonoph grinned and tucked in her blouse, patting her fat stomach. "So now it's Cyril this and Cyril that! I've watched better girls than you try that game!"

"Name one!" Mona challenged.

"Me!" the fat woman said quietly.

"Oh, go to hell! Borrow a razor blade and cut your throat!"

When Mona had stamped off, the Gonoph smiled at David. "All right. She can sleep with Cyril this summer, but it won't get her a job on Broadway next winter. Mark my words!"

David said without thinking, "She wouldn't sleep with Cyril. He's old!"

"Actors never get old," the Gonoph laughed. "That's why ordinary men dislike them so much."

"But not Mona!" David insisted.

"All right!" the Gonoph surrendered. "But why do the hotel stairs creak at night?"

That question was the beginning of David's intense dislike for the pasty, dumpy Gonoph. In time he came to think of her as a sodden mass of unleavened dough, yet it was this inept and abominable actress who taught him how to act. It was also she who taught him the essential quality of love. It could be said that of the entire troupe she was the one who scraped her nails most often across his exposed nerves and that therefore she was the one from whom he learned the most.

From the dwarf Vito he learned how to manipulate marionettes, for in the afternoon he and Vito gave a show for children. Vito was forty-one inches high, in no way misshapen. He had a Falstaffian voice that rumbled in his chest like beer barrels rolling along a gutter, but he could make it birdlike in imitation of giddy girls. He rarely allowed his affliction to sober his wonderful good spirits; but he had never known a girl of his own size and his mind dwelled upon love as if it were something forbidden him. In spite of his immense voice, he always whispered when he asked such questions as: "Are you in love with Miss Meigs, Dave?"

"Yes."

"Don't worry, kid. You'll get to love these puppets as if they were human." David thought of the Sheik and his love for the mechanical princess. He was about to speak when he saw that the dwarf Vito actually did love his stringed dolls.

And finally, there was Wild Man Jensen and his pigeons. But the Wild Man was something very special, and when the summer was over David had merely to recall the man's name and the great sun that warms the earth seemed to be with him.

"Of course," the Gonoph leered, "it could have been the chambermaid."

"At four in the morning?" David demanded.

"Maybe the chambermaid left something in Mona's room

which just had to be taken to Mr. Hargreaves'." She turned her pasty face toward David to see the effect of her words. "Or it could be that it was Lord Cyril himself, crawling back to his own room after a night's work well done."

David clenched his teeth and refused to get angry. "Leave Mona alone," he said. "What she does is her business."

"I'm not one to cast the first stone!" the flaccid woman cried. "I'm just disgusted with Mr. Hargreaves. Every summer it's the same way. He looks over all the women and it's sort of like the finger of God. 'You're the one!' Then all summer he's as nice to that girl as he can be. Teaches her everything. And promises that in the winter he'll get her a job on Broadway. The only charge for this service is very modest! His shoes under her bed."

"I don't want to hear any more about it!" David insisted.

"I'm not spreading gossip!" the flabby woman protested. "I just got a hunch you're sweet on Miss Meigs and I'm tipping you off."

"I don't propose to start a fight," David replied.

"Ho ho!" the Gonoph cackled. "That's not what's worrying me. I like you, Dave." She said his name in three syllables, lingeringly. "I wanted to warn you that if you tried to start anything, Lord Cyril would chop you into little bits. Have you ever seen a monkey back into an electric fan? Whirrrr! They're gone! That's the way it is when anybody mixes up with Cyril when he's hot after some girl."

David disliked being drawn into this conversation but he felt that he must flex his muscles. "I can handle Cyril," he assured his informant.

"Cyril don't fight!" the Gonoph said quietly. "He's too smart for that." She chuckled to herself. "Like the time a two-hundred-pound athalete and him was trying to lure the same girl. She couldn't make up her mind who she was sleeping with that summer. Cyril was smarter but the other guy was better-looking. So the other guy never knew what hit him. The cops arrested him for running likker, and there it was!" She pulled her shawl more tightly about her shoulders. "I can say these things," she mused, "because twenty years ago it was my room Mr. Hargreaves was coming to."

David must have gasped, for the Gonoph looked at him and said, "Yes. Twenty years ago I wasn't so bad-looking, if I do say so myself." She tucked in her blouse and patted her fat stomach complacently.

"And is that how you finally got on Broadway?" David asked, fascinated by the Gonoph's information.

"Oh, no!" she protested heatedly. "I've always been a Broadway star." The words were strange when applied to her.

"You have?" David asked, not masking his incredulity.

"Yes, indeed. You see, my mother was an actress, too!" She paused smugly, tugged at her shawl and added, "My father was, too, but he wasn't a very nice man." David sensed that for the Gonoph everyone was either *nice* or *not very nice*.

"What parts did you play?" he asked.

"Little-girl parts till I grew up. Then big-girl parts. Then when I got my growth, women's parts," she explained.

"Which did you like best?" David asked.

"I guess the little-girl parts," she replied, recalling some amusing incident of the past. "You see, my mother was living then. We had a family skit, *The Red-Haired Orphan*. It was fun but it wasn't fun, too. My father wouldn't follow the script. But I got to admit he did work out some funny business. That was the part that wasn't fun. He hit me in the face with a pie. The audiences roared. We played that skit for two years, all across the country. My mother cried when my father insisted on the pie routine. But after a while I didn't mind very much. You see, I learned the trick of putting lots of grease in my hair so the pie just rubbed out! It was as simple as that!" she said triumphantly.

"Do they use real pies?" David asked.

"No!" she explained eagerly. "They's a special powder. Makes wonderful fluff. That's why all the pies you see onstage are lemon meringue." She dropped her voice. "They never see a lemon!" she confided.

"When you got your growth," David asked, caught by the far-away quality of the Gonoph's talk, "what parts did you play?"

"Oh, mainly any kind," she explained. "Mainly the second sister, I guess."

"What do you mean?" David inquired.

"I was usually the plain one to offset the pretty one," she said. "Like in this play. They don't want the mother too good-looking or Miss Meigs won't seem so pretty." She dropped her voice to a whisper. "She's no spring chicken, you know. She does have a beautiful build, though. As if you didn't know!" She poked a pudgy finger at David's rib.

The Gonoph continued her dismal narrative. Overhead the hot sun ceased beating on the brown canvas and the rich smell of baked grass, grease paint, human sweat and dust pervaded the Chautauqua tent. David sniffed approvingly of the fine country aroma and listened as the Gonoph droned on. "This may very well be my last play," she admitted. "I'm getting too old for the second sister. And it's disgraceful the way they type-cast old women in plays. Got to be pawky old devils like May Robson and Marie Dressler. They're good, of course, but they're hardly my type."

She pulled her shawl about her fat shoulders. There was a sodden look in her heavy face. David found it impossible to believe that this woman could have earned a single week's work in any theatre at any time, except perhaps as a charwoman long after the last patron had left.

"Of course," she droned, "twenty years ago I had a better figure. And a better complexion, too. You see me twenty years ago, when I was touring with John Drew, you wouldn't blame Lord Cyril for crawling up the stairs to my room!" A heavy, musty look came into her eyes and she grinned knowingly at David, poking him again in the ribs.

She made an indelible impression on David, deep and disturbing. He perceived that most of the laborers in any art are like the Gonoph. The third and fourth viola players. The writers whose books never quite come off, and the weaker contraltos whose voices can fill neither a theatre nor a heart. Formless, unachieving, dimly perceptive or totally blind to the principles of their art, they stumble on and fill the interstices left by the Kreislers, the Bernhardts, and the Thomas Manns. If growing up is the process of seeing things as they actually are—perhaps only two or three truths in a lifetime—then the Gonoph meant more to David than anyone else he met that summer. For through her bleary eyes he saw the world of art as it was, the tragic, fumbling, ever-seeking world in which so few achieve so much and so many accomplish nothing.

In spite of what the Gonoph had said about Mona and Cyril Hargreaves, David longed to be with the actress. True, he could kiss her five or six times each night in the play but mere kissing was not what he wanted. He desired much more or infinitely less. He yearned, for example, to hear the slim girl become involved with laughter and disgust as she told him about her experience in Hollywood. He wanted to feel her hand eagerly upon his shoulder when she chuckled and cried: "Oh, Dave! Let me tell you something really delightful!" He wanted to be with her in a thousand small and sharing ways, for he had convinced himself that she had become his other self, his alien eyes that saw so much, his extra senses, and the personification of his hopes.

But Mona's preoccupation with Cyril, and David's own duties with the dwarf Vito kept them apart, so that David, like most men in the world who are unhappy, tried to lose his dismay in work. "Why couldn't I operate a doll of my own?" he asked the dwarf one day.

"You could," Vito replied. "But you'd have a hard job learning."

"I'd like that," David replied. So the dwarf handed him a marionette carved into the form of a roistering sailor.

"This is Bosco," the dwarf explained. "He's got fifteen strings. Just watch the things he can do!" Vito deftly grabbed the controls to which the three-foot strings were attached. First he made the sailor strut, then dance, then roll his eyes, then salute. Finally Bosco grunted and sat heavily upon a painted wharf. He began to play an accordion. Then he stopped and reached for a glass of beer, from which he knocked the foam. He drank the amber liquid, rolled his eyes again, and spit lustily into a corner. Then he resumed playing his accordion, tapping time with his toe.

"You do it all with strings," Vito explained.

"I think I could learn that," David replied, and he plunged into the job with all his energy.

The dwarf had a small, collapsible stage made of aluminum piping and beaver board. Eight lovely backdrops were painted on canvas and could be shifted by the quick motion of a wrist. Matching side drops framed the stage, and a florid red curtain, sequined in purple and gold, ran on runners like a real theatrical curtain.

The marionette stage was small. The actors were small, and even the owner undersized, but whenever David worked with Vito he felt at home. The little Italian so loved his dolls and was so quietly happy with them that his entire show assumed a fairy loveliness, and through it David entered a world of delicate fantasy, but the pleasure he found there was very real.

Vito was an extraordinary puppeteer. His remarkable voice enabled him to portray an endless number of characters. He stood on a ramp and rested his stomach on the bar that held up the painted backdrops. Leaning far over the stage he would dance his little dolls deftly in time to phonograph music. Above his head there was a gridwork of latticed boards from which hung huge wire hooks shaped like capital S's. When a doll finished a dance, Vito would grab a hook, twist it quickly to the right length, and hang upon it the controls of the now motionless doll. Then he would grab a new actor and make it perform contortions. Out front the children would scream with delight to see a red-headed boy fighting with an ice-cream cone that spouted smoke! But often Vito would extend a thumb or finger and flick the strings of the suspended marionette. Then, on the stage below, that doll would throw back its head, or raise a hand, or kick, or do something to signify its joy at watching the immense ice-cream cone belabor the hungry boy. So with hooks, a dozen voices, and a love of dolls that bubbled from his very elbows, the dwarf could keep an entire stage alive.

It was David's job to keep the dolls in order. Soon Vito allowed him to handle one doll in each act, but David never found one he enjoyed so much as Bosco. When he brought Bosco on, swaggering, his sailor suit messy and white cap awry, David could hear the little boys in the audience start to laugh. "Watch out there, mate!" Bosco bellowed, squatting on a bale of cotton.

A bartender came out with a huge stein of beer. The little boys roared with pleasure as Bosco deftly grabbed the beer, obviously drained the glass, and shouted, "Bring on the girls!"

As he sat on the cotton and played his accordion, Vito would bring out two girls in tight waterproof dresses. Adroitly they would dance a tough little dance. At the end of the number Bosco rose and chased them. Then Vito screamed in his highest voice, "We'll run away if you stop playing!" At this Bosco would stamp his foot and leer at the boys in the audience. "How can I have any fun if I got to nurse this squeeze box?" With one hand David would start the phonograph again, the needle would scratch, and Bosco would resume his accordion concerto.

The act ended with the toughest little girl dancing steps that defied the law of gravity. She displayed her red panties and Bosco rolled his eyes. The waiter came back with a stein of beer and caught Bosco kissing the girl. Infuriated, he poured the beer down Bosco's neck. And the audience roared approval.

David was delighted with the complexity of the dolls Vito had carved. There was a beer-hall pianist who smoked. A small bellows was filled with white powder and tucked inside the pianist. Attached to the bellows was a bit of tubing that ran to the cigarette. One tug on a specially marked string made the bellows close slightly. Out came the smoke! A heavy magnet was built into the beer stein and another in Bosco's lip. They snapped together with force, and it was then a simple matter to tilt the stein and have the brown fluid run accurately into the sailor's big mouth.

Vito said, "There's nothing a man can do a doll can't, if you've got enough strings!" But the time always came when the strings got tangled. Not one doll escaped. A control might drop. Then the damage was done! Strings that should have hung straight were twisted and crossed, and the doll was hopelessly crippled. One leg might be caught in the air, or the neck might be skewed to one side.

Then Vito would take the ruined doll and patiently study the tangled skein. At such times he never spoke, but after a while he would deftly trace a single string as it wound its way through a maze of twenty others. It would, of course, have been much simpler merely to cut the strings and start anew; but to the dwarf that would have been sacrilege.

"If a man tangled this doll," he insisted, "a man ought to be able to untangle it."

With an artist's infinite patience he would labor over his wounded doll. Soon the strings would be so tangled that David would look away in despair and start to pack the other dolls. Half an hour later he would return, and there the patient dwarf would be, still unwinding the tangled life into which his doll had fallen. Then, when things looked most confused, the industrious dwarf would pull some strings together and the doll would almost miraculously step free. Each string was perfect, doing the work for which it had been ordained.

At such times David had an oppressive, almost mystic feeling that he was watching not the dwarf Vito playing with dolls, but a deity at work upon some tangled human life. And the feeling grew strong upon him that any life in this world, no matter how tangled or distressed, could be set free if only a friend knew which snarled string to unravel.

"I hope you don't mind my taking so much time on one doll," Vito apologized one night. Then, not waiting for comment and not looking at David, he said very rapidly, "These dolls are pretty important to me. You won't understand this, but when I realized I wasn't going to grow up . . . Well, it was pretty awful. I used to dream of stretching machines, and a special kind of cabbage that would make boys grow, and what I would do if God gave me three wishes. 'I'd only need one!' I said. And I wanted to die. Then I saw a marionette show." Tenderly he wrapped up the doll he had repaired. He tried to hand it to David without looking, but his hand stabbed the air and he turned.

"I guess that marionette show changed my life," he said. "Because look!" His eyes danced with excitement. "I can hide back here! Nobody can tell how big I am or anything else. I can have as many voices as I like and as many characters. I can make them do impossible things." Quickly he unwound the mended doll and sent it flying through the air, looping the loop, and shouting for a ham sandwich. David noticed the Vito's dolls were fun because they were always getting into trouble or eating or making love or dancing or singing or having a wonderful time.

Chautauqua played for seven days in each town. First Day was noisy with the band and a comedian. The Swiss bellringers filled the Second Day with music and fun. Dressed in Alpine costumes and long moustaches, they laboriously spelled out hymns and polkas. A pretty girl of nineteen played the little bells until the comedy number was given, whereupon the comedian would lift her and her bells and swing them together. It was good clean fun. Third Day brought the acrobats and an inspirational talk on the good life. Vaudeville and a gala concert filled the Fourth Day. Then, on Fifth Day, came an accordionist to fill time until, in the evening, the Great Man spoke. In the past the Great Man had been William Jennings Bryan or Russell H. Conwell or Robert La Follette; but in this dying year a worn-out schoolteacher tried vainly to fill the spacious shoes that had graced Chautauqua in the fine years up to 1924. The Sixth Day brought Vito's marionettes and the play. All week long each entertainer had been required to say, "I never laughed so much as I did at the play you're going to see on last night." An intense excitement was generated, so that by the time the curtain finally went up on Cyril Hargreaves' troupe the town was prepared to believe that the great days had returned, and gradually this excitement pervaded David, for he knew that when he kissed Mona in the last scene of the play, there would never again be another Chautauqua in that town.

This sense of doom stayed with him, especially when it

fell the players' turn to provide Sunday worship, for Chautauqua was founded on Christian principles and each act conducted church service if they were in a town on Sunday. That was the Seventh Day, and when David heard the mournful old hymns sung in the tent that would soon be dying upon the grass, his heart welled up in longing for Mona, who held her hymn book as properly as a virgin in a church choir afraid to look upon the organist.

"You have a real soft spot in your heart for Chautauqua, don't you?" the Gonoph asked one evening.

"Yes, I do!" David admitted, grinning at the formless woman.

"I like it, too," she sighed. "Some of the best parts I ever had were in Chautauqua. I like fat parts with long speeches. Stars don't impress me no more, because they hog the show. John Drew, Ethel Barrymore, Minnie Maddern Fiske, I traveled with them all."

"What was John Drew like?" David asked.

"He swore!" the pasty woman said reproachfully. "Once he accused Mrs. Fiske of coming onstage drunk and she told him to go to hell." She clucked her tongue, and that was all David learned about John Drew.

"Did you enjoy touring with Ethel Barrymore?" he pursued.

"She has a very low voice," the Gonoph replied.

"How about Walter Hampden?" he asked.

"He made me sick!" she confided. David tried to discover why, but the pudgy woman kept her secret, shaking her head in disgust.

"Didn't you enjoy touring with the stars?" he pressed.

"Well, yes and no," the woman confided. "It had its good points and it had its bad points."

"What do you mean?" he demanded.

"Well, generally speaking, the bigger the star the poorer the part I got. I was usually a maid. Not a comic, you understand. Just the maid. That's why I like average company best. Just an ordinary company like this one. No stars. That's when I've had some really fat parts." She came and sat with David, tapping him on the knee. "Now I'm not boasting, you understand. But this part of Mrs. Hardy is just about the fattest part in the play." She tapped him again for special emphasis and whispered, "Have you noticed how much I'm onstage! That's how you can tell who has the fat part! Lots of actors say they like a part where they stay offstage and are talked about. Then they rush in, beat their

breast, and storm out. Everybody claps. But they don't fool
me a bit. They only kid themselves when they say that.
They're sore because they're not onstage themselves." She
tucked in her blouse and smiled complacently. "Have you
noticed that I'm onstage more than Miss Meigs? That should
tell you something!"

David was appalled by the Gonoph's incapacity to see
herself as she was. He did an ugly thing and asked, "Why
did Cyril take those two speeches from you and give them
to the telephone?"

Instead of being humiliated by this question the Gonoph
smiled complacently and resumed her whispered confidences,
leaning upon David. "Don't you get it?" she asked. "Miss
Meigs is very jealous of me. She knows I used to be where
she is now. I'm sure it was her idea, David. I can just hear
her pestering Mr. Hargreaves at night, bargaining with him.
I guess in the end he just had to give in. After all, I know
him well enough to understand that he'd do anything to
protect his regular summer loving."

She punched David knowingly in the ribs and gave a
superior, condescending smile. "But don't put me down as
being bitchy!" she protested. "I'm probably the last woman
in the world jealous of Miss Meigs. After all, when I knew
Mr. Hargreaves he had his own teeth!"

Day after day she came to the tent with her murky ra-
tionalizations, and, disgusting as she was, David found her a
source of warm and continued interest. For she spoke, un-
knowingly, of the vast lands that comprise America. Names
fell from her fat lips that were music to David's ear: "We
were playing in Sioux City." "Miss Barrymore said that the
entire city of Denver . . ." "It was on a rainy night in
Great Falls."

"Did you ever play in Texas?" David asked.

"Houston, Dallas, San Antonio, Fort Worth and El Paso,"
the dumpy woman recited.

"What were they like?" he asked.

"Hot," she said.

But the litany went on! Kansas City, Albuquerque, Reno,
Aberdeen, Memphis, Baton Rouge, Columbia. The Gonoph
could characterize any city in the country in a single word.
San Francisco was hilly. New Orleans was Frenchified. And
Omaha was railroads. There were no people in these distant
cities, and no meaning in their lives. But even the names
of the cities were beautiful to David.

"What city . . . Now consider them all!" he said. "What one did you like best?"

"Providence, Rhode Island," she said immediately.

"Why?" he asked.

"I was born there," she replied. "And Father stopped drinking for a while."

David found only one subject on which the Gonoph could discourse intelligently. Love had an endless fascination for her. She would sit on the marionette boxes and talk for hours about friends of hers who had fallen in love under strange circumstances. She called it "finding their hearts' desire," which was a line from a play she had known years ago.

"Well, there was this girl I was telling you about," she said one night. "We were playing together in something." She never remembered the names of plays. "We had a Saturday date in Pueblo, Colorado. Some friends stopped by to drive us down to Albuquerque. The young man who drove this girl's car was real nice. They stopped off in Santa Fe. My car drove right on through. Well, when her car got to Albuquerque she had found her heart's desire."

"They get married?" David asked.

"Sure they got married!" the Gonoph replied angrily. "She had her heart's desire, didn't she? I get Christmas cards from her! She's got three kids!" She tucked in her blouse with violent little stabs. "Of course they got married! What do you think?"

"Didn't you ever find your heart's desire?" David asked quietly.

"No!" she said abruptly. She ruffled the pages of the book she was carrying. "It's like Proust says. Sometimes you never find your heart's desire."

"Proust?" David asked. "Do you read Proust?"

The Gonoph, who was used to startled looks when she mentioned the name of the great French novelist, smiled weakly and replied, "Oh, yes! I like his work very much. He seems to have more depth than most modern writers."

David stopped what he was doing and looked at this amazing woman. He had once tried to plow through Proust's involved sentences and had given up; and now here was this disorganized, frowsy woman reading the man with pleasure.

"What do you suppose the Wild Man does with his pigeons?" she asked, returning to topic number one.

"That's his business," David replied.

"I'd like to know!" the Gonoph mumbled. "I've found it a

safe rule that whenever there's a boy and a girl together, there's apt to be trouble."

"That's the Wild Man's affair," David insisted.

"How about your little dwarf?" the Gonoph persisted. "Do you suppose he could have a baby if he wanted to?"

"Look, Emma!" David cried. "Why don't you ask him?"

"He's your friend!" she argued.

David shrugged his shoulders and refused to talk with her any further. He rose and lifted the marionettes into the truck. Quickly the Gonoph ran to his side and helped him with the boxes. "There's no point in getting sore!" she said.

"Don't try to lift those boxes, Emma!" David said patiently.

The drab woman stood aside and leaned against a stay rope. She watched David's muscles ripple along his arms as he hefted the stage into the truck. Then she spoke in a quiet voice. "Have they said anything to you about it?" she asked.

"About what?" David asked, shoving the stage into place.

"Oh, about you and me."

David could scarcely believe what he had heard. With his back still to the Gonoph he replied, "What do you mean?"

"Oh," she replied indifferently. "Wild Man's been teasing about me being in love with you." David gulped and gave the stage a final push. "Not that I mind a bit of teasing!" she added.

"Emma!" David finally cried, turning to her. "What in God's name are you talking about?"

"Oh," she said in embarrassment, pushing on the rope like a schoolgirl. "People like to guess. They've been talking about the way I come out to the tent every day."

It was a warm evening. The sun still hung among the trees that lined the western edge of the field on which the tent stood. On the other side of the stage a group of boys finished lining up the wooden chairs for the evening performance. This was the last night Chautauqua would ever pitch its tents in that town, and there was the lonely quietness of death about the place.

David studied the misshapen Gonoph and smiled. "If they're talking so much, I don't think you ought to come here any more," he said softly.

"I got to come somewhere!" the Gonoph replied.

The answer stopped David for a moment. It was not what

he expected. Finally he recovered and said, "Well, then you come here," he said. "I like to talk with you."

A slow smile spread over the woman's big face. Her yellow horse teeth showed between fat lips and she sighed. "I'm glad!" she said. "Because you're the nicest man on Chautauqua this year. You're really a very nice man!" She reached across the dead grass and the dust and patted David on the arm. All that night she followed him with her big cow eyes, and onstage she muffed two lines watching him. When the curtain fell the Wild Man laughed at David and said, "I see you got yourself a girl!" David thought of three funny answers but offered none of them.

"Sure looks that way!" he agreed.

They were in a small Pennsylvania town called Jersey Shore when David discovered that the Wild Man was something special. His full name was Wild Man Jensen. He was about twenty-three years old and had played halfback at the University of Illinois. He drove the marionette truck while David and Vito slept on bunks built in the rear. He was in the play, too. He had a small speaking part, a local politician who was badgering Judge Hardy. More important, he ran the telephone when David was onstage, and was property man, as well.

The Wild Man was big, already turning to fat. He had a rough, handsome face and a puppy-like manner. He was usually unkempt, knocking about in a football sweater, but each afternoon about five he would start brushing his hair and polishing his shoes. "Where do you go every day?" David asked him in Jersey Shore.

"Usually," the Wild Man grinned, "I go out to dinner with the best-looking pigeon in town." He turned to stuff the shoe polish into the truck when a freckled boy peered around the edge of the tent and motioned a strikingly beautiful girl of seventeen to follow him.

The girl walked up to David and asked, "Are you Mr. Jensen?"

"Hey! Hey!" the Wild Man protested. "I'm Jensen! He just works here!" The girl laughed and held out her hand. "I'm Lucretia Davis," she said.

In Clearfield, David discovered how the Wild Man arranged such attractive dinner dates. David was inside the truck that day, making up the bunks when he heard the Wild Man hail a young boy who was straightening chairs.

"Sonny!" Jensen began very quietly. "You live here in Clearfield?"

"Sure!" the youngster replied.

"Who's the prettiest girl in Clearfield?"

The little boy thought a moment. "I guess it would be Sue Tucker," he said.

"She really beautiful?" Jensen checked.

"Oh, she's gorgeous!" the boy replied.

"You know her?"

"Sure I know her! She lives on our block."

"All right, son! I believe you," Jensen said quietly. "Now here's fifteen cents. And in this pocket there's ten cents more! All you got to do is go find Sue Tucker and tell her exactly what I say. You go up to her and say, 'Sue! I just been down to Chautauqua. There's a fellow there acts in the play. He ain't so good-lookin' but he played football at Illinois. He asked me where a good restaurant was. He ain't had a meal at home for the last two months.' That's all you say, sonny. Then if Miss Sue Tucker says the right thing, you get the extra dime."

The little boy ran off to find Sue Tucker. When he was gone David poked his head out of the truck and cried, "Fine business!"

The Wild Man looked up from the box on which he was shining his shoes. "A guy's got to have his pigeons!" he drawled.

"You mean, you pull that trick in every town?" David asked.

"Son!" the Wild Man replied. "It's shore a warm day. Let's don't pry into trade secrets? OK?" He stretched out on the box and pulled a handkerchief across his face. He was dozing there when the little boy came round the end of the tent.

"Hey! Mister!" the boy called. "Come here a minute!"

Jensen rose, twisted his rugged body, and smoothed down his hair. He went to where the boy was gesticulating. Shyly, from around the canvas, came a dark girl of seventeen, accompanied by a younger sister. She seemed perfect in the afternoon sun, her brown hair and tanned face matching the canvas.

"This here is Sue Tucker," the little boy said proudly. "Didn't I tell you she was pretty?"

Sue blushed and David wished that it was he talking with her, leaning relaxed against the guy ropes the way Jensen did. "I . . ." she began in a half-childish, half-womanly voice. "That is, my mother . . . we heard you've been eating in restaurants . . ."

Sue fumbled with words, so that her little sister broke in, "Mom says, 'Why don't you eat with us?' " Sue blushed again. The Wild Man leaned harder upon the rope as if deeply displeased. He scowled at the little boy.

"You shouldn't of told her about the restaurants!" he chafed. The boy opened his mouth and stared.

"So if you would like to eat with us," Sue continued. She wore a summer dress and seemed to be striving to fill it as if it were a challenge.

"You go to college?" Jensen asked.

"Next year I'll be a sophomore," she said. "At Penn State."

"Say!" Jensen cried. "That's a mighty good school!" He unwound himself from the rope and said, "I'll tell you, Sue. I've got to be back here at seven-thirty. Hardly be fair to your mother . . ."

"We could eat early!" Sue stammered, falling over words in her eagerness to reassure him.

"Then maybe I could make it," the Wild Man admitted, thoughtfully. He slipped the bewildered boy a dime and took the little sister's hand. "What's your name, little girl?" he asked.

They set forth, the three of them, and toward eight Jensen returned. After the show Sue and her mother came back to see the Wild Man. "You were very good!" Sue observed.

"They don't give me much to say," Wild Man replied. There was a moment of hesitation and then Jensen, greasy and big, pulled Sue to him and gave her a tremendous kiss. David saw the kiss and watched the manner in which Sue closed her eyes and broke away with paint upon her cheeks. The girl's mother was embarrassed and grabbed her daughter. Together they picked their way through the tent and Sue turned back to cry, "Write to me!"

Jensen watched them go and then wiped the grease paint from his face. He rubbed the massive growth of hair on his chest. "Beats eatin' in restaurants!" he observed to no one in particular.

In every town he suborned some boy to find him the prettiest girl. Then one day he had to buy a broom, and David understood him much better. Up to that particular day Jensen had been merely a scatter-brained romantic, meeting young girls as they came shyly to invite him to dinner.

He was kind to them, friendly to their little sisters, and most courteous to their mothers who cooked the meals. He kissed them good night and wrote each one at least two fine letters: "We played Farrell, Pennsylvania, tonight and when the tent came down I imagined that you were here again . . ."

But in Charleroi, where he bought the broom, things were different. The prettiest girl in town was well rouged up, and Jensen reported for the play smelling strongly of whiskey. After the show he said to David and Vito, "I'd like to use the truck for about half an hour." He drove off with it and later that night David and Vito found pins and perfume all through their blankets.

"Stop the truck!" Vito suddenly called in his deepest bass.

"What's up?" Jensen cried back through the sliding window.

"What's this in my bed?" Vito roared.

Jensen turned his head. "It's a garter belt!" he announced.

"What do I want with a garter belt?" Vito bellowed.

"Throw it out the back!" Jensen ordered.

But when they stopped that night for two-o'clock coffee Jensen asked the restaurant keeper if he'd sell that broom in the corner. "Whadda you need a broom for?" the man inquired.

"System!" Jensen explained. Later he explained things to David and the dwarf. "When I go looking for a girl," he said, "all I want is a nice girl. I like 'em fine that way. A good meal. A nice home. Maybe a kiss. I just yearn to be with girls, that's all. But sometimes even nice girls like to do a little explorin'. Now when this broom is hangin' out the end of the truck I don't want any interference. Come up, shift gears when it's time to go, and I'll wind everything up in ten minutes. That's a promise."

So through Ohio and much of Indiana and Illinois the Wild Man blew into one town after another. "Son!" he'd say to some dark-haired boy, "Who's the prettiest pigeon in town?" And if that girl, when she appeared—and she almost always did—was chafing at the edge of life, eager to try her new-fledged body, Jensen was an admirable companion. The broom would hang out the end of the dark truck, and Vito, when he climbed in front to shift gears, would hear subdued giggles coming from his bed.

But if the girl was afraid, not yet sure of herself, the Wild Man treated her as tenderly as if she were his own sister. He would be all gallantry and tell her, when the last garish light swung back and forth on the last tent pole, "I'll write to you. Yep. From the very next town."

After such nights he would ask David to ride up front with him as the dark truck rolled westward to the next distant tent. "Everybody in the world wants to be in love," he said one night. "If I was a million guys I couldn't make love or write to all the girls who would like me to. God! I tell you! I see unhappy women like the Gonoph! My heart breaks, Dave! Honest to God, I have so much fun in life I sometimes almost cry for them that don't."

David asked, "Don't you ever fall in love? Really?"

"Me?" Jensen cried, dropping his hands from the wheel. "I'm in love every day. I get almost breathless waiting to see who's comin' round the edge of the tent. I know she's gonna be beautiful because she thinks she's comin' to see an actor! I go day after day through a long string of towns. I'll never see any of 'em again. Never! But for that short visit I can imagine that I'm really somebody. An actor like Cyril. And I can make any girl think so, too! God! In a job like this all girls are beautiful!"

The rolling truck sped through the dark and silent towns. Canton, Wooster, Mansfield. "Imagine!" Jensen cried. "We could stop in any place along the road. Any town at all. And in the afternoon there'd be some pretty girl who'd want to convince herself that she loved me!" He wrenched the truck back onto its course and pointed ahead to a dull glow in the sky. "What's the next town?" he asked.

"Massillon," David said.

"Massillon!" the Wild Man repeated softly, rolling the syllables upon his tongue. "In Massillon there's a beautiful girl. She's sleepin' now, and I'll never see her. But you're beautiful, you little pigeon! Go on sleepin'."

Never before had David heard quite so frank a song of love. It baffled him, and for a long time—until they had passed through Massillon—he rode in silence. Finally he asked, "Don't you use the broom a lot?"

Jensen laughed and bent over the steering wheel. At last he said, "I'll tell you, Dave. Just about the right percentage. Every three or four nights. But don't ever let anybody kid you, fellow. Sleepin' with a lovely woman! That's the better half of livin'."

There was a small town in Western Ohio that David would never forget. He did not know the name of it. In fact, he never saw the town at all. He simply heard a man named Bert urinating against a truck tire at night, but that town and the cheap music drifting out from the all-night hamburger stand were indelible in his mind.

That afternoon they had played in Piqua, and while the Wild Man waited for his pigeon David talked with him. "Of course," the football player agreed, "love ain't everything in life. Jus' half. The other half, seems to me, is workin'. I've got a mighty pretty deal cooked up."

"Like what?" David asked.

"You ever play the stock market?" Jensen asked.

"No."

"Dave, you ought to look into that! Me! I'm as dumb a guy as ever graduated from Illinois. I come from the real backwoods of Kansas, but I played some mighty good football and a rich alumnus come to me and says, 'Wild Man, you brought glory to the Illini. I'm gonna reward you!' So he gave me a thousand-dollar stake and taught me how to play the market."

"You playing it right now?" David asked.

"Sure! Since I joined up with this outfit I make $980. And if Commonwealth and Southern keeps improvin', I'll make a couple of thousand this summer."

"How do you do it?" David asked.

"I study the papers. Keep my eye on what's goin' up and down. It's really very simple. All you got to know is when to sell."

"When do you sell?" David inquired. He was interested in Wild Man as a stock operator.

"When I get to my pigeon's house, like tonight, I say to the mister, 'Can I use your phone? I'll pay the charges.' Then I call a guy in New York and tell him to buy or sell tomorrow. It creates a fine impression." He laughed pleasantly to himself. "How much dough you think I'm worth right now?" he inquired sharply. David shrugged his shoulders. "Eight thousand smackers! Looks to me like America is a ripe melon jus' waitin' for a guy to cut hisse'f a chunk."

The two actors leaned back and contemplated the endlessly beautiful future. Then the Wild Man added, "If I was a guy mad for money I could of parlayed my roll into fifty, sixty thousand bucks. But that's too much dough. What a guy needs is half work, half women!"

He had more to say, but a blonde girl of eighteen, accompanied by a sister of fifteen, appeared. Jensen went up to them and they talked together for some moments, each of them looking at David in turn. Jensen came back and said, "How'd you like to shove your feet under some home cookin'?"

David inadvertently looked at the attractive sister. He very much wanted to join her, to feel her near him and to smell the perfume he was sure she must be wearing. "I can't," he said.

"Why not?" Jensen demanded.

David was stuck for an answer, and then he saw the Gonoph waddling across the dusty field. Cyril's car had only then arrived from the previous town and the distressing woman had hurried directly to the tent. "I told her I'd wait," David said, pointing to the Gonoph.

The Wild Man did not laugh. He sucked in his cheeks and watched Emma Clews pick her way among the rocks of the field. "All women are beautiful," he said and then made David's apologies to the two pigeons.

The Gonoph was sweating when she reached David. With dainty pats of a very small handkerchief she daubed away the moisture on her face. "Well," she announced. "Lord Cyril was on the prowl again last night."

"Look, Emma!" David cried with sudden force. "Don't come here and tell me those things."

The Gonoph kept the handkerchief at her chin and said, "All right! I just keep tabs on him, that's all." She began to chuckle, her round shoulders heaving beneath the shawl. "Last night I thought of a very funny thing," she said. "I saw a movie once about a girls' school. One little devil tied the teacher's door shut. It was really a scream!" She rocked back and forth. "Don't you get it?" she asked.

"Get what?" David asked.

"Sir Cyril!" the pudgy woman cried. "Some night we could tie him in Mona's room! What a scandal!" She showed her big horse teeth and punched David in the ribs.

To change the subject he asked, "Emma, where's your mother?

"In Medford, Oregon," she said instantly.

"What's she doing way out there?"

"Filling a hole in the ground," she said abruptly.

David gulped and asked, "How'd she get to Oregon?"

"When she was taking Pop to be buried she saw a poster about Oregon and she said, saving the word, 'Goddamn if I stay in the stinking East another day.' She got a job as waitress in Medford, Oregon, and she married a Chinese laundryman and she died. If you ask me, I think the Chinaman poisoned her."

Dusk came on and Emma got her make-up kit. She said, "It's fun out here in the evening." David watched her as she patiently plastered her immense face, and slowly the sensation possessed him that this scene was not taking place in time at all. He was so achingly perceptive to every sight and sound that he had the absolute feeling of being suspended outside the universe. Each sense and nerve in his body rushed messages to his brain and he saw indelibly and forever a circus tent at twilight with a dowdy woman remaking her unhappy face.

"Emma!" he cried impulsively. "Knock 'em dead tonight!"

"And don't think I haven't," she leered. "In my day, that is." Then her insistent mind galloped back to love and she whispered, "What with all this paint on my kisser you probably can't see that in my day I was a stunner!" She chuckled to herself and waddled off to dress. As if David had no control over his eyes, they filled with tears and he was vastly confused.

These were the days, the sweet and memorable days, when David hesitated between being a youth and a man, the mystic days whose memory can be the bittersweet seasoning of a life. He was ready to become a man, but he clung obstinately to the impulsive remnants of youth. Wild, lonely, uncontrolled feeling was such a remnant; yet he knew that he was almost a man. He had a full beard, hard and bristly against his razor. He was almost six feet tall, yet when he stood in the wings, waiting to hurry onstage and kiss Mona, his knees trembled like a boy's. His voice would never again crack in awkward adolescence, but his heart did. He steadied himself against the canvas and mumbled, "Me outside the universe looking on! Hell, I can't even see myself."

He would never know what obsessed him that strange evening. Somehow he stumbled through his lines and felt for a moment that he had regained control of himself; but in the deep night, while he waited for Jensen to leave off kissing in the truck, he heard a thin voice calling in the town's outer darkness: "Hey, Eddie, what say we go fishing tomorrow?" And he peered past the truck and beyond the tent that was dying in the dust. Who was that Eddie? Where were the fishing grounds? And he longed to rush into the darkness, to find that distant voice, and to embrace the night crier.

It was not love of man or woman that he sought that night. He was tormented by the vast uncertainty of youth, the surging time, the violent flowing time of manhood to the heart. He sensed the thoughts as yet untested, the fiery glory of words that rushed to his throat and rattled there unspoken, the vagueness, the urgency, the trembling fears and wild resoluteness of youth! It was all his that night. He would have dared anything, yet he was afraid to walk with Jensen's pretty pigeon. He would have volunteered to go, on the instant, to Java or Samarkand, yet when the Wild Man pulled the truck up to the hamburger stand in Western Ohio, David was completely incapable of entering the noisy, friendly place.

"I'll catch some sleep," he said.

"OK!" Vito cried. "But I'm warning you. I'm eating onions!"

David heard them bang their way into the restaurant. There was a slot machine, and Jensen started to play it for dimes. A waitress kidded him in a brassy voice, and David wished that he were in there, kidding the waitress.

A truck rolled up. The driver got out and shouted, "Hey! Bert! Want me to order for you?" The screendoor slammed and David could hear Bert urinating against a tire.

"Two eggs and some coffee cake!" Bert shouted.

"OK!" the driver called back into the night.

Then Vito's astonishing voice boomed out, "Hiya! Stranger!"

"Hey! Bert!" the driver shouted. "Come in! They's a guy six feet six says he'll knock your block off!"

Bert jumped up and down on the driveway and hurried toward the door. Then there was a wild burst of laughter. "Who'n hell's this?" Bert shouted. "Tom Thumb?"

"None o' yer guff, pardner!" Vito roared.

David could hear the men slapping backs. Even the dwarf Vito fitted in. He was a man. He knew what he wanted.

But David was still a youth. He had an agonizing desire to join the noisy crowd in the restaurant, but he could not move. He pulled the covers about his face so that he might seem asleep when Vito returned. But he could not sleep. He lay face up and thought: "Some time! In a book! I'll write this all just the way it happened. A truck will roll up. There'll be a . . . A squeal? No! 'The wheels crunched to a stop on the pinched gravel.' Two men'll get out, and one'll cry, 'Hey! Bert!' " He mulled the words and whispered them to the roof of the truck, but they tore back at him, savagely, the words of men drinking beer together in an all-night restaurant.

After an hour of singing, Vito and Jensen returned to the truck. The dwarf was drunk and had to be lifted into bed. "Ssssh!" Vito whispered to Jensen. "The kid's asleep." Then he began to cry. "Poor kid! No fun!"

"Don't you worry about the kid!" Jensen muttered. "He'll be OK when he begins to feel his oats."

David's confusion was abated somewhat when Wild Man Jensen set out to find a pigeon forty-one inches high. The unusual quest began one afternoon in Indiana. The Wild Man was leaning upon a guy rope, watching the dwarf Vito wrap marionettes and place them between blankets.

"Vito?" he drawled. "You ever go with women?"

The dwarf blushed furiously, all the way down his neck. "Not much," he said.

Jensen shrugged his shoulders at David and continued, "Where does a guy your size find a pigeon to play with?"

Vito blushed again and wrapped up his dolls. "You ain't answered my question, Vito," the Wild Man insisted. "You meet many girls your size?"

The dwarf turned away, but he had no desire to end the conversation. He was delighted with the amiable way in which Jensen—and to a lesser degree, David—treated his infirmity. To them he was merely a little man. He liked the way they spoke, without embarrassment, of his size.

"As I pointed out, you crummy little dwarf," Jensen pursued. "You ain't answered my question. Where do you find girls, Vito? When you want a little refined lovin'?"

"Oh," Vito said seriously, sitting on the packed box, "every town of any size has at least one little girl. Somewhere. Of course," he added hastily, "she might not be my age. Or she might be taller than I am." He spoke eagerly, bubbling with words. "You understand, I wouldn't care if she was a little bit taller."

Jensen stopped swinging on the rope. "You mean to tell me," he asked slowly, "that maybe we passed some little girls right this very summer?"

"Oh, sure!" Vito said eagerly, pulling his knees up under him. "There was one in West Chester. A blonde. I'd say she was about forty-five inches."

"How high are you, Vito?" David asked.

"Forty-three," he lied. "And there was a girl in Du Bois, too. She was about forty inches. She was a blonde, too."

"How do you know all this?" Jensen asked.

"Well," the dwarf said, "I sort of look." There was a long silence and Jensen snapped the rope. Then Vito continued. "I sort of keep watching," he said.

"What you mean," Jensen cried, "is that you stand on the stage and gawk. So that's why you keep starin' at the audience! I'll be damned!" He snapped the rope again. "Tell me, Vito. How can you spot a little woman, say from jus' a little girl?"

"You can tell," Vito replied.

Jensen bit his lips. "You mean to say that already this summer we passed a couple of little girls? Girls your own size?" He kicked the dust angrily. "Why, Goddamnit to hell and little blazes! Why didn't you tell me? This makes me pretty mad, Vito. You're a pretty stupid guy."

The two men looked at each other for more than a minute and Jensen began to smile. "I could probably have gotten you four or five dates!" he said. "How would you like that, you midget?"

"I'd like it," Vito said.

"Well, by God!" Jensen swore. "It's in the bag! If they's a little girl within a hundred miles of any tent, you got a date with her! That's a bet!" The Wild Man walked up and down in great excitement, as if it were a date for himself that was under discussion. Sudden he slapped his leg and cried, "Dave! Vito! We'll go into town right now!"

He herded his two friends into the truck and they stopped at a mean restaurant where he ordered veal fricassee. It was so bad he sent it back. "Western omelette with lots of onions!" he snapped. Then he put his arm on Vito's shoulder. "How's your beef stew?" he asked.

"Not so good," Vito admitted.

"Douse it with ketchup!" he advised. He grabbed a ketchup bottle and drowned the offensive stew. "That any better?" He dipped his own fork into the mess and came up with a chunk of meat. "My God, Vito!" he stormed. "You can't eat that! Another western!" he bellowed.

"What's the matter with the stew?" the proprietor demanded.

"It's lousy!" Jensen replied.

There was a waitress standing by the water cooler. For some time she had been studying Vito. She felt sorry for the poor little man and tears came into her eyes. "Hey! You!" Jensen cried.

"Me?" the girl asked.

"Yes! You!" Jensen insisted. The girl walked along the boards behind the counter. They creaked.

"What do you want?" she asked, keeping her eyes away from Vito.

"Are there any little girls in this town?" Jensen asked.

The waitress was shocked and bit her lip. "I mean any pretty little dwarf girls?" Jensen pursued. The waitress burst into tears and ran back to the manager. He grabbed one of the western sandwiches and hurried back along the boards.

"What's the idea of insulting my waitress?" he cried belligerently.

"I was jus' askin'," Jensen snarled, "if they might be a little dwarf girl livin' around here anywhere. Some little pigeon about his size!" He slapped Vito affectionately on the shoulder.

The manager licked his dry lips and looked away from Vito. "No," he said hoarsely. "We don't have any dwarfs in this town."

"You sure ain't got any beef stew, either!" Jensen snorted. He caught the plate of stew and ketchup and dumped it on the western sandwich. Then he wrapped his arm about Vito. "Come on," he muttered. "Let's get to hell out of here."

In the street the Wild Man scratched his hairy chest and looked about him. Houses were beginning to show lights. The lawns were summer-green, and here and there a tree had begun to drop its leaves. "Vito!" Jensen cried. "Strike me dead, but I'm findin' you a couple of little pigeons about forty inches high. You watch!"

From town to town as the Chautauqua tents moved westward, the Wild Man inquired if there were any little girls who hadn't grown up. The answer was always no. This infuriated Jensen, for Vito swore that in the early weeks he had seen at least three. Finally, in Western Indiana, the Wild Man met a boy who knew of such a girl. She lived on a farm, eighteen miles out in the country. She was a blonde and used to be the angel in Christmas pageants. She could play the piano, too.

"Vito!" Jensen cried, trembling with excitement. "You stay right here!" He jumped into the truck. No one ever knew what he said at the farm, but an hour and a half later he returned with his own customary date on the front seat. And on the seat near the door sat a little girl.

Jensen got out first. His girl followed him. Then he called in a low voice, "Hey! Vito!" The dwarf came slowly from the dressing room, where he had been waiting. He was nervous and licked his lips.

Then from the truck the Wild Man handed down a nineteen-year-old dwarf, forty-three inches tall. She was dressed in blue and very neat. Unlike Vito, her face was slightly pinched, but she had a bouncing little step and a charming smile. "This is Grace," Jensen said.

That was the first of the terrible moments in which David shared. From town to town Jensen found five such little girls. They came to the tent. They were breathing hard beneath their white dresses or their blue dresses, and Vito was always sweating. They would look at each other, the little people, and it was not like the meeting of ordinary people. No, not at all! For in an entire county—or in a dozen counties— there might be only one man to whom such a dwarf might look for love. And now this stranger had come, this little actor of whom Jensen had told such fabulous stories! Out of all the world, only a handful of men! And here was one of them, here in the dusty tent.

The little pigeons were pleased with Vito. They stayed to see the play. Sometimes they had him to their homes for dinner. They played music or laughed at his jokes. But everything was deadly serious. The night was short. The truck rolled on so soon! Wild Man Jensen might say that every town had a girl whom he could love. But the little people knew better.

Once, after Vito and the Wild Man had visited the home of a little girl, they rode together on the front seat. Vito was excited and had no desire for sleep. David heard them talking seriously in the night.

"Vito?" Jensen asked. "You ever kiss them little pigeons?"

There was an embarrassed silence. Jensen repeated his question and the dwarf admitted that he never did. Jensen snorted. "Why the hell you think I spend my time lookin' 'em up? You mean to swear to me, honest to God, you ain't never had one of 'em undressed?"

Vito gasped. "What do you think I am?" he asked.

"Think? I know! You're a guy jus' like me. Or are you? Say? What's the deal with you? Could you have kids if you wanted to?"

"I guess so," the dwarf replied.

"Then what in the hell are you wastin' your time for?" Jensen demanded. "How many of them little pigeons are you writin' to?"

"I'm not writing to any of them."

David could sense that Jensen had dropped his hands from the steering wheel. Then the truck jerked violently back onto the road. "What in hell, Vito, is wrong with your head?" David could hear Jensen slap his leg. "Why, dammit all, fellow! How many little girls you think I can find for you?" He snorted in dismay. "Why do you suppose any girl ever comes to see any man? To see if he's the guy she wants to marry! I watch these little pigeons when I drive 'em up to the tent. They tremble and like to die. Why? Because they wonder, 'Is this the guy I'm to marry?' And what the hell are you thinkin', waitin' in the tent?"

He paused for Vito to explain. There was no sound, so after a moment he sniffed and said, "Why, a little girl is jus' like a big girl. Maybe more concentrated. You mean to tell me you been wastin' the time of them dwarfs?" He spoke in great contempt. "You make me sick!"

David could sense that Jensen had turned away from Vito and was attending to the truck. Speed picked up and there was a long silence. Then Vito asked, "What do you think I should do?"

"Do?" Jensen shouted, and the truck slowed down. "Jus' be a man!"

"Like what?" the dwarf asked hesitantly.

"That's your business," Jensen replied. Then he quickly added, "But I will say this much. Everybody in the world wants to be loved. Little girls! Big boys! It's all the same." He dropped his voice to a whisper. "See if Dave's asleep."

The dwarf peered back into the bunks. "Sound asleep," he said, and David strained to hear the next words.

"Tell me," Jensen said. "You ever see a sorrier woman than the Gonoph? No! And neither did I, except in a freak show." There was a moment's silence and Jensen said. "Sorry if I offended you, Vito. But in my book you ain't no freak."

"That's all right," the dwarf said.

"But even the Gonoph has got to love somebody," Jensen continued. "So she comes out to the tent, day after day, talkin' with Dave. And here's a funny thing! He talks to her, too. She makes him sick at the stomach, but he's glad to see her when she comes waddlin' in. Because everybody has got to have somebody interested in 'em. Did you ever look at it that way?"

"No," Vito said.

"Well, it's time you did," Jensen snorted. "You're jus' like me. You ain't no ordinary dwarf. Like I said, you're no freak. You're a terrific guy! I seen dwarfs with their faces all pinched up. You're good-lookin'. You knock 'em dead in the play. You got a voice I truly envy. Vito," the Wild Man pleaded in the cooling night, "you should ought to write to every one of them pigeons. It don't matter too much what you say. What does a girl want to hear? 'I miss you. I'll always remember that wonderful night. I kicked myself a hundred times for not kissing you good-bye.' And if it comes into your mind to say it, why, add, 'Don't fool yourself, Clara. I'm comin' back.' That is, if you want to say it."

There was another silence and then Vito asked, "Is that what you say?"

"Oh, that and some other stuff," Jensen replied. Then a happy thought struck him and the truck veered off the road again. "And by the way, you sawed-off Casanova. Any time you want the truck and the broom, it's OK. You don't fool me a bit."

But the talk and the jokes and the friendship could not erase one fact. When the little girls came to see Vito there was a terrible moment, as if the world stood still, and it was a moment that men David's size would never know.

The Gonoph was shameless in her love for David. By talking of him incessantly to Cyril and Mona, she picked up odd bits of information about him and these stray tags of intelligence came to have much meaning for her. She discovered, for example, that he liked jelly beans; and even though Easter was long since past she searched for the cheap confection as eagerly as Jensen searched for little girls forty-one inches high. Finally she found a bagful, held over in a store that had bought unwisely. She brought them triumphantly to the tent.

"Look what I found!" she said.

"They're jelly beans!" David cried with the pleasure of a boy. She watched admiringly as he munched a few and then began nervously to eat them herself as she talked. She ate so many that she got sick and belched onstage. David could see Cyril Hargreaves grow furious at the Gonoph. Between acts he fined her five dollars, and this agitated her so that in the last scene she called David by his real name instead of Wayne.

When the curtain fell Cyril stormed at her and would have fined her another five dollars for such a breach of acting, but David interfered and said, "Let her alone!" whereupon Mr. Hargreaves looked down his patrician nose at David and said, "Are you her champion?" and David shouted suddenly, "Yes! And I don't go sneaking down hotel corridors to get in her room, either!"

Mona gasped at this, and Jensen hurried between the actors. "Take it easy, Dave!" he cautioned.

"I won't take it easy!" David cried. "I'm sick and tired of this pompous bag of wind. Every summer he picks out some girl and gives her the big rush!" Words spurted from his lips, words he had never intended to say.

Mona reached across Jensen's restraining arm and slapped David's face. Then the Wild Man had the good sense to clap his hand over David's mouth and drag him offstage. As they drove westward into Illinois, Jensen made David ride up front with him. "You'll only get into trouble, Dave, acting that way," he cautioned. "If I seen it once, I seen it a hundred times. Never interfere with an old man and his love." He slumped over the steering wheel and laughed. "When my old man was over sixty he got a new housekeeper. She wasn't good-lookin' and she wasn't bad-lookin'. He cottoned up to her something disgraceful, and I decided I'd show him a lesson, so I took the housekeeper out, and when I got back my old man was waitin' for me with an axe handle. He like to killed me. I had to run away from home, and that's how I come to the university. No place else to go."

"He ought to lay off Emma," David replied.

"She's really pretty dreadful," the Wild Man observed.

"Sure she is!" David agreed. "But he could speak to her in private."

"Why are you so interested?" Jensen asked.

"You know why!" David snapped. A few more questions, and he would want to fight Jensen, too. "I heard you explaining it all to Vito the other night."

"Oh!" the Wild Man grunted. "Well, what I said is true." He spoke the words in rude challenge.

"You want to stop the truck and make something of it?" David asked.

There was no reply. Then the Wild Man said, "You better take it easy, Dave. Besides, I could massacre you."

"I'm not so sure!" David grunted, and slumped back in his seat. He was twisted up, and the agitation of life was bending him this way and that. He wanted to be a full man like Jensen, rough and ready, loving and brawling across the countryside. But at the same time he had a poet's ear for the Gonoph's strange chatter. He loved the places she spoke of, the distant, beckoning cities of the Western world: St. Paul, Bismarck, Cheyenne, Tallahassee. And he had grown to like her as a person, exactly as he had grown to like anyone he had ever met, if only he met that person often enough.

He was disturbed that anyone should have the courage to love as openly as she did. The cast ridiculed her, but she did not care. She was twice David's age, but that did not matter. She was fat and plain and graceless and ugly, and no doubt she often wept because of those afflictions, but the important thing that summer was that she loved a sandy-haired young man. Shamelessly, shamelessly, she loved him.

David's temper had by now subsided and he said frankly to the Wild Man, "What do you make of the Gonoph? Actually?"

"This is the last," he said. "Last play she'll ever be in. You're the last guy she'll ever dare to love."

"Is it so terrible?" David asked. "The last of a thing, I mean?"

"It's pretty bad," Jensen insisted. "My old man lost his power for a couple of months at age fifty-five. Christ, you'd a thought he'd gone plain crazy. Stormed about Eastern Kansas shootin' at people and raisin' hell. An old nigra figured what was wrong and give a real smart yaller gal four bucks to fix the old man up. Hell, he came home three days later a-singin' like his heart was gonna bust. He give Mom sixty dollars and told her to buy any damned thing she wanted in the Monkey Ward catalogue."

Because of this explanation, David became most considerate of the Gonoph. He made it a point to talk with her each day about the various tours she had made, cataloguing in his mind her vapid observations. "Cornstarch is fattening," she said of blanc-mange. "Until I was thirty-five I watched my figure. Then I said to hell with it." She thought that Richard Mansfield was worth a dozen Cyril Hargreaves, and she confessed, "When I'm wrong I'm the one to admit it. I was pretty snooty when I told Miss Meigs that sleeping with Sir Cyril got nobody a job on Broadway. Well, he signed her up for a position in his repertory company next winter! You know what I think? He's getting so old he'll do anything to hold onto a girl!" The look of dismay that came into David's face made her truly sorry for him and she asked softly, "Were you, if you'll excuse the word, lovers?"

The warmth with which she asked this question inspired David to confess. "And that's what makes this summer so very rotten," he said.

The graceless woman bit her big underlip and said, "I got a way figured out that you could cut Sir Cyril's throat and have a fine time with Miss Meigs the same night!"

The offer was so appalling to David that he would not reply. He could not comprehend the monstrous things people did in the guise of love. Cyril cooked up some trivial job so that he could hold onto Mona. Little Vito stared at the audiences in hope of seeing one small girl. The Wild Man caroused from town to town, to find what? And he himself refused to go with Jensen's pigeons because he felt somehow attached to the lumbering Gonoph. Who could understand a life force that produced such wanton results? In utter confusion David changed the subject and asked, "Emma, what's New Mexico like?"

"It's empty," she explained.

"This is some country!" he replied, meaning: "Who can understand people?"

"It's real big," she agreed.

America creeps quietly upon the objects of its love. The sense of its grandeur and vastness comes slowly to its citizens, so that no one can say, "This morning I discovered what America is." David, wandering westward, gained an increasing awareness of his land.

That summer he saw the steaming restaurants at four in the morning, the black ribbon of road becoming the gray ribbon of dawn, the churches, the ugly schools, the white fences, the gentle hillsides and the sweeping pastures. These things began to be a part of his thinking. No longer was Indiana merely a word on the map. It was a place of homes and dimensions. In one of the towns there had been a murder the day before Chautauqua arrived. At a filling station Jensen had become involved in an argument over gasoline, and elsewhere the state was green, or black, or reddish, or a woman had given them coffee and doughnuts. As long as David lived, the word Indiana would have meaning.

Slowly David began to fashion a picture of his land. It was a country of opportunity. Take his own case! A poorhouse crum pulled from impossible surroundings and offered the world, if he wanted it. Or look at Jensen! A tough kid from Kansas, fairly good in football, and now he made as much as a thousand dollars a month playing the stock market. In America there was plenty for everyone. All you had to do was reach out and grab your share.

That summer there were moments of unforgettable beauty. David did his driving at dawn. He would scramble out of bed and change places with the Wild Man. The sun would break over his shoulder, creeping down green valleys and prying its way under bridges. The birds of summer would sing and an early farmer would whip his horses through the dewy meadows. It was a magnificent country, this America, grand and lovely to the eye.

There were sights David would never forget: the tragic, lonely square of Greencastle, Indiana, waiting at two in the morning as if for a messenger from the Union armies; the rich flow of the Mississippi, the bridges of Pittsburgh and the steel mills of Youngstown, belching in the night like overfed merchants; the red soil of Southern Illinois; the waters of Lake Erie pounding at weirs. Again David felt as if each nerve of his body lay exposed to the impressions about him and he experienced a perceptiveness that made any ordinary trip of fifty miles a journey into the heart of meaning. "What a land!" he cried to himself as he drove.

But there was one night in which the spirit of America seemed to ride his truck, like an evanescent wonder miraculously perceptible. Jensen was driving from Pittsburgh to Charleroi. He got lost and finally wound up on a side road that ran along the Monongahela River. As he rounded a corner he found standing in the path of his bright lights two girls. One was crying. He stopped the truck and spoke to the girls. Then he called back and wakened David.

"Hey!" he shouted. "Two girls in trouble. Make room for 'em."

David kicked open the door and the girls crawled in. The younger was about fourteen. They were sisters, and before long it was apparent that they had gone to a roadhouse with two men. They had made love for several hours and got drunk, too. Then, in fear and shame, they had run away from their men. They were headed back home to Monongahela City—Mon City, they called it.

The younger girl would not stop crying. She wept as if there were no controlling her tears. Vito rose to comfort her, but when the girls saw that he was a dwarf, each screamed. The crying became worse. Finally David knocked on the panel. "You better come back here, Wild Man. Let me drive."

They changed places and David drove toward Mon City. The road was narrow and mean. Black houses and slaked furnaces crowded each intersection. This was the dismal part of America, the home of the black workers whose skins were white.

The girls cried for some time and then David heard Jensen reasoning with them. "So what if you did?" he argued. "It's maybe a sin, like the priest says, but it ain't no crime. Maybe you didn't like it. Maybe it wasn't any fun. But you can bet a dollar that every human bein' on this earth started that way." The youngest girl was now sniffling. Her sister had stopped altogether.

"It's like this," Jensen reasoned. "Sometimes it's fun. Sometimes it ain't fun." He paused, then added, "Mostly it's fun. You'll find a nice boy some day, and you'll see what I mean. You'll have kids, too. Each of you, maybe three kids apiece, and if they're girls the day'll come they'll all find out what I'm sayin' is true."

Now they were in Mon City. The streets were dark and grubby. "Where do you get out?" David asked.

They directed him to an intersection. A hill rose steeply to the right. When they stood in the roadway saying goodbye Jensen advised, "Now sleep till about noon tomorrow. You'll forget all about it!"

"We work," the eldest said. "In a mill."

"Fourteen? And you work? I thought there was a law?"

"There's ways," the girl said. They started up the hill, but when the younger saw the familiar houses she began to cry again. Her sister hushed her at first and then joined in.

The three men in the truck felt strange and torn about. But the impact fell most heavily on David. Driving southward through the murky night he perceived that America was not merely the green fields and opulence of rural life, nor the magnificence of beautiful cities. It was also the hunger, the yearning, the will to happiness of all the people in all houses. It was the young girls crying, too.

Up to this summer David had lived upon the discoveries

of others. In the poorhouse Uncle Daniel had begun to arrange life for him. At school Miss Clapp had read aloud the fine stories that ignited his imagination. Miss Chaloner had taught him what order was, and he had borrowed freely from the experiences of other friends: Joe Vaux, Mr. Stone, and the fat Texan, Doc Chisholm. But this summer David made three discoveries for himself. The first had come when he found the meaning of America.

The second came with the tornado. Bellehaven lay outside the tornado belt, so that when the big Chautauqua tent started to creak at the ropes in the late afternoon no one bothered much. There was an average, wind-blown audience that night, but Wild Man Jensen sensed that something unusual was about to happen. He was driving twin sisters to the play when an extraordinary gust came whipping past.

"Looks like the beginnin' of a tornado," he said.

"We never have tornadoes up here," the twins explained.

"Could be!" Jensen replied.

The tent captain lashed down certain ropes and loosened others. Through years of experience Chautauqua hands had learned how to "let the wind blow through" without damage. Like a whip in a summer meadow, the dry canvas cracked over the heads of the audience.

In the men's dressing room Mr. Hargreaves sniffed the air. "I've heard tents crack a lot louder than this," he mused. "Just a good blow." In the women's tent the Gonoph was nervous. "There'll be thunder and lightning," she sniffed. "I know there'll be."

In the middle of the second act, when David was quarreling with his stage sweetheart, one of the two main tent poles cracked. It snapped off clean about eight feet from the top. The remaining giant stump tottered for a moment and then fell whipping across the audience. The lights flickered and went out. There were shouts and cries of pain.

An emergency light flashed on from the top of the other pole. It swung back and forth in the night. Wind howled in through the torn canvas and billowed the tent this way and that. The light flashed eerily upon the people pinned beneath the pole.

Jensen leaped immediately into the audience and organized a crew to remove the heavy pole. It had fallen across sixteen people. Beneath it lay one of the twins. She was bleeding at the mouth and crying. Two boys tried to lift the pole, but it rolled back down on the people, and she fainted.

—

Meanwhile David stood at the edge of the stage transfixed by a grim sight. The top fragment of the broken pole, badly jagged, was held aloft by strong ropes. Swept by the wind, it flailed through the air. As the great tent sagged, the lashing, splintered pole dropped closer toward the people struggling below. It was like a pendulum whose next arc must descend and strike.

David jumped from the stage and fought his way through the crowd. He crawled over the fallen pole beneath which the people were trapped. Now he was beneath the lashing fragment. Aloft the canvas ripped, and the pole dropped within reach. With a leap David caught it and hung on. The wind whipped him back and forth. He pushed people away with his knees, so that when the pole crashed into them it merely knocked them down and did not break their heads.

Through the broken tent the wind howled in new fury. Far above the crowd the solitary light swayed mournfully back and forth. People struggled madly to get free of the tent before the remaining pole crashed, and all the while David clung to his thrashing pole, hurtling this way and that, above and through the crowd.

He had glimpses of things he would never forget. Jensen lifting the fallen pole from crippled bodies. The gaping rip in the side of the tent, like the mistaken slash of a housewife's knife cutting through a flour sack. The lonely light, smashing against the pole and tearing loose, whipping through the air and crashing into three men. And the tent! The wounded tent crying, flapping, dying in the storm! David saw it rip apart at many points. It was like a harpooned whale, foundered along the shore. Finally the entire canvas billowed up, taking David high in the air. Then it crashed upon the people. David's pole rushed furiously to earth, and at the last moment David tried to jump free. He fell with the pole and was not hurt, but he could tell from a snapping noise that the man upon whom the pole fell was dead.

At the edge of the crowd a man called vainly for his family. When they did not answer, he nervously lit a cigarette. It and the match were whipped from his fingers. They struck a piece of paper which flamed instantly. The paper flew madly into the foundering canvas, and in a moment one entire side of the tent was ablaze.

In a mighty sigh the rest of the canvas exploded into flame. As the last ropes were burned away, the remaining pole roared down upon people still struggling beneath the fallen tent. Swiftly, along the path of the pole, flames swept over the canvas. Screams were muffled and death was sudden-quick.

When this happened David was holding up a portion of the canvas so that people could break free. He saw the flames start to engulf him on either side, and for a moment he let the canvas fall in fear, trapping the remaining spectators. But he had no sooner done this frightful thing than he stooped under the canvas again and raised it so the struggling people within could see their way to flaming safety.

The fire was now upon him. Inside lay the three men who had been struck down by the falling light shade and the man on whom the pole fragment had dropped. There was a woman, too, a dumpy woman of about fifty. She wore cheap clothes and her glasses were broken. "This way!" David screamed, but she was dazed and unable to comprehend.

She lay nine feet beneath the canvas, and fire was on David's left hand, but he shoved the canvas as high in the air as he could and dashed in to the gibbering woman. He grabbed her by the shoulders, and they were soft and boneless. The canvas fell about him and he felt that he must leave her; but, pulling her by the hair, he dragged her to the spot where he had been standing. With one arm above his eyes, he pushed through the burning canvas and hauled her after him. She lay on the ground, slobbering and terrified; but David was free, and the tornado roared about him.

Then, as the last of the brown tent burned, rain came. In tremendous quantity it came, soaking the charred bodies, but too late. A nauseous mixture of smoke and flesh and old wet ashes filled the air. David and a fat man took command. "Put everyone who's wounded over here!" the fat man cried. He was a doctor.

David and some helpers hauled out the dead. Now the police and other doctors arrived. At the edge of the field an immense gust of wind caught a fire truck and tossed it sideways into a culvert. The fireman left the lights on, to aid the work. David found five bodies, and it was his gruesome duty to drag them onto the wet grass. The shafts of light from the fire truck were lonely, piercing the night, and there were cries of all kinds in the air.

It was then that David became a man. He discovered this as he carried a bewildered man of thirty to a doctor. The man had been caught by the pole, and he was afraid that he would die. "I won't die, will I, Doc?" he blubbered through charred lips.

"I'm not the doctor," David said consolingly. He laid the man down and stayed with him until the doctor came.

"He'll be OK," the doctor said, and the man smiled up at David as if he—and not the doctor—had saved him.

In that fleeting smile David found the alchemy that made him a man. He discovered the companionship of all men, the grand and solemn march that all men make together from the darkness of birth to the outer darkness of dying. They were all prisoners together, David, and the man saved from burning, and the Gonoph, and Old Daniel, and the dwarf Vito. They did frightful things to one another in their fear, and even a man like David might consider fleeing the burning tent to save himself while others perished, but they were all members of the same companionship.

The rain beat on his face, and he reviewed his actions in the tent. Not until the very end had he been afraid of dying. He was afraid neither of the slashing pole nor of the fire. And even when fear finally captured him, he was able to fight it off. He was pleased that he had acted so, pleased that he had thought of others as more important than himself. He wiped his face and saw the world for the first time as a superb flowing organization of people of which he was not the selfish center. Whether he lived or died was of no moment; and that discovery—which many young men never make—was the threshold by which David passed from callow youth to manhood. He was unimportant; therefore he was free.

Even as he watched the piling up of dead bodies he saw grief-maddened relatives start to readjust their lives. A girl of nineteen looked at her dead father and threw herself despairingly into the arms of a young man she had previously repulsed. As impersonally as white blood cells rushing to protect a wound, the neighbors of Bellehaven rushed to protect the living. The young man put his arm about the sobbing girl and kissed her for the first time. She looked up in astonishment and blew her nose. That very night the living made arrangements to compensate for the missing dead. Under no circumstances could David imagine that things would have been much different had he been killed. With a grimace he even pieced together the minor substitutions that Mr. Hargreaves would make: "Mr. Jensen! You will take Mr. Harper's role. We'll use the telephone for the part you used to play." And little Vito would have to pull a few more strings. That was all.

Yet at the moment when David concluded he was nothing, the dwarf Vito became terribly important. What had happened to the little man? "Hey!" he started to shout. "Where's Vito?" He stormed about the field and across the charred canvas. "Anybody see the dwarf?" he cried.

"Dwarf?" newcomers shouted back. "We didn't see no dwarf!"

"Vito! Vito!" David cried, and suddenly he was like everyone else. He rushed from group to group crying: "Have you seen the little guy?" When they said no he became increasingly panicky. His newly won manhood vanished and he screamed, "Vito! Vito!"

An elderly policeman grabbed him. "Look, son! Don't get people stirred up."

"I'm looking for the little guy!" David cried, pushing the cop away.

"Everybody's lookin' for somebody," the policeman reasoned patiently. "Now who is this little guy. Your boy?"

"The midget!" David screamed.

"Oh!" the policeman said. "He's over there."

David rushed to a group where Vito stood among a group of crying children, lost from their parents. He was joking with them. David pushed his way through the children and grabbed the dwarf. "You all right?" he asked.

"Sure," the dwarf said.

David sat down in the rain. He was tired and wanted to sleep. Soon Jensen came up and called to Vito, "Is Dave OK?"

"Yeah!" the dwarf cried. "He's sitting over here."

The Wild Man came and sat down, too, right in the rain. The two men looked at each other. "You got no eyebrows!" Jensen said. David rubbed his forehead and charred hair fell to his nose.

"You all right?" he asked the Wild Man.

"I'm OK," Jensen replied. "But the twin died."

David punched Jensen on the shoulder. "I saw you with the pole," he said. Then he jumped to his feet. "You and Vito meet me at the hotel," he said. "I got something to do."

He crawled into the truck, a man bearing with him the solemn franchise of manhood. He gripped the wheel and lowered his face upon its cool rim. He thought: "There at the end I was scared. But I wasn't afraid." He took a deep breath. The dying wind tore at his truck. "God! I hope that man lives!" he muttered.

He drove the truck through mud and reached the highway. "You can't come this way!" the same policeman shouted.

"Chautauqua!" David cried back.

"OK!" the policeman cried. "You find the midget?"

"I found him," David replied. The policeman stepped aside and the truck rolled into town.

The actors were staying at the Washington Arms, an ugly frame hotel lighted with the blaze of much activity. In the crowded lobby people talked about the fire. Newspapermen were there, and as soon as David appeared the Gonoph ran up. "I saw you!" she cried. "Hey! Hey! This is the man I told you about!" The newspapermen crowded around and the Gonoph shrieked, "No eyebrows!"

Then David saw Mona. She was wearing her second-act dress and looked nervously beautiful. For the first time in his life David felt as old as Mona. "I want to talk to you," he said quietly.

"David's safe!" she cried ostentatiously to Cyril.

"Let's go out on the porch," David said.

"David! Not now!" Mona gripped his arm and whispered, "You behave!" She pulled away and went to Hargreaves.

Swiftly David caught her arm and said, "I want to talk to you."

"Excuse me!" Hargreaves said. He twisted David around. "Watch yourself," he said.

To his own surprise, David swung on the elderly actor. Mona screamed and two men grabbed at David's arms. Roughly he twisted himself loose and caught Mona's hand. "Let's get out of here!" he muttered.

"Where we going?" Mona asked, dragging back. He led her to the truck and drove out of town. "Where we going?" she repeated.

They came to a crossroads. The tornado had subsided and the rain was softer now. David headed the truck down a small road that had once been a cattle path. "Let's get in back," he said.

"Say!" Mona cried. "What is this?"

"You know damned well what it is, Mona," David replied. He caught her by the arm and tried to pull her from the truck. She was warm and exciting.

"Let me go!" she cried. There was a rough struggle. Mona held onto the wheel and could not be dragged loose. She was a little animal, scratching with her free hand. "You silly damned fool!" she grunted.

"You've tried to make me one," David puffed. "But I've had enough!" He caught her by the waist and wrestled with her until her stage dress tore. Furiously, he ripped at it, and then Mona stopped his craziness. She began to laugh.

She laughed at him in a shrill voice. She was amused and contemptuous. She stopped holding onto the wheel or resisting in any way. All she did was laugh. "You having any fun?" she chided.

"Stop it!" David insisted.

He pulled her onto the muddy ground. They slipped and he tore away her dress and slip. Her legs were white in the reflected light from the truck, but she kept on laughing. "You are so damned silly!" she cried, not at all hysterically.

Then David stopped. He found that he was powerless against her ridicule. Furious at her and at himself he allowed her to climb back in the truck. He stood outside and let the dying rain beat on his face. "Don't play Napoleon!" she laughed. "Get in!"

He stamped his feet clean of mud and got in beside her. "We can't go on like this," he pleaded. "This is no summer."

The glacial girl wiped the mud from her dress. "What did you expect?" she asked.

"I didn't expect anything," he lied. "But . . . this may sound silly . . ."

"It does," she interrupted.

"Tonight when I was looking for Vito, I couldn't find him, and I felt how much I needed you."

"You'll have to go right on needing," Mona said. Then she added coldly, "There's nothing so dead as last year's love. You ought to get wise to yourself."

"You're a good one to talk!" he growled, determined to goad her from her laughing indifference. "You went to Paradise on Uncle Klim's money. And to Hollywood on Max Volo's. Now you expect to reach Broadway. What does that make you?"

Mona gasped. She slashed at David's face with her muddy shoe. She struck him again and again until he caught her hand and stopped her. "You cheap stinker!" she rasped. "What does that make me? Why, I've worked more than you! I know more than you! I've loved and I've hated more than you. People will remember me when you're a name on a tombstone. Now get me back to town, you cheap hick ham. Or I'll damned well have the cops on you."

David shifted gears and drove the truck slowly back to town. At the hotel Jensen and the dwarf were waiting. Hargreaves, his face bruised from David's blow, had gone disconsolately to bed. "Your head's cut!" Jensen said. "The flying pole get you?"

"No," David explained. "Mona socked me with her shoe."

"Why don't you lay off that alley cat?" the Wild Man asked. "You're headin' for a lot of trouble, Dave. Cyril was fit to be tied."

David flared up. "I'd keep out of this!" he suggested.

The Wild Man ignored his comment and continued to drawl, "I've seen lots of tough cheap women, Dave, and Mona's head of the class."

David felt that he must fight such words. He clenched his fists and the Wild Man patiently groaned. "OK!" he sighed. "If it's gonna make you feel better! I fall down go boom! See?" With sudden force he fell full length on the floor.

At that moment there was a hissing sound from the stairway. Everyone turned to see the Gonoph. She was dressed in a flowered wrap beneath which her formless body sprawled in uncorseted abandon. "David! Hsssst!" she called.

Jensen jumped up and punched David in the ribs. "Go ahead! To the victor belongs the spoiled."

Hesitantly David crossed the lobby. "You wait out in the truck," the Gonoph stage-whispered to Jensen and the dwarf. She winked at them broadly and tried to hold back a chuckle.

On the first landing the excited woman stopped and turned to look at David. "You're cut!" she said. "Did Miss Meigs do that?"

"Yes," David replied, confused by what was happening.

The Gonoph pried beneath his matted hair and inspected the wound. "Does it hurt?" she asked.

"No," David replied. They continued walking up the flight of stairs and at the top the Gonoph put both her fat hands on David's.

"Is Miss Meigs your heart's desire?" she asked.

David looked at the floor. "Yes," he said.

The pudgy woman gripped his hands and said, "Why don't you sneak in and see her?" Then she began to laugh and pointed at a door down the hall. As boys in school pester an angry teacher, so the Gonoph had tied Cyril Hargreaves into his room. There was no way he could break loose without ripping off his doorknob. "Mona's room is that one," she said.

David started to walk toward it, but the shapeless woman in the wrap-around hurried after him and whispered, "Cyril knocks three times and then two times. He's always used that for his signal." She patted David on the shoulder and went chuckling to the other end of the hall.

At Mona's door David gave the signal. From inside there was an exhausted, "All right." He opened the door slightly and slipped into the dark room. "What a day!" Mona sighed.

"Mmmmm-Hmmmm!" David grunted.

"I should think you'd had enough excitement!" Mona said harshly, twisting in her bed. "That damned fool David Harper ought to have his head examined." She tossed again. "Did he hurt you?"

"Mmmmm-Hmmmm!" David grunted again.

"Where?" she asked.

David slipped across the room and to the bed. He reached for Mona's hand and placed it on his head. There was a long moment of silence while Mona explored the long-familiar head and the unexpected quantity of hair. There was a slight gasp, and she whispered, "Dave!"

He placed his hand softly upon her lips. "Yes," he whispered. Mona shuddered and then lay still. He dropped his hand from her lips and felt for her firm breasts. He caressed the long curves of her body, the protruding hip-bones, and the pointed, exciting knees. She did not speak until he pulled away her gown completely so that she lay once again as she had been, a timeless feast for all the sensations of the body. Then she said in a low voice, "It's good. It's very good, Dave."

While they were lost in embracing there came a banging from down the hall. "What's that?" Mona cried. Then she guessed and pulled David terribly close to her. "Is that Cyril?" she asked. When David nodded his head into her neck she twisted her head upon the pillow as she had done in Klim's apartment when the great passion was upon her. "He'll rush in here!" she moaned.

"He's locked in!" David laughed, violently. "He's all locked up. The Gonoph did it!"

When the two lovers fell back upon the bed, exhausted, the distant knocking continued, and Mona suddenly snapped her fingers. "Of course! She told you what the signal was!" But she did not laugh. No, she buried her pounding head against David's and whispered softly, "She must love you very much."

And that was when David made his third discovery of the summer. He found that love is never to be defined, that it grows and changes with every year of life, that each person knows it as a different miracle. Love can beat and scream at the edge of a tornado and then surrender completely an hour later. It can wander and search over the face of the earth and alight nowhere. It can crawl in gutters or hide in the late afternoon behind crocheted gloves serving tea in a garden. Nothing can shame it. Nothing can make it more splendid than it already is. Shared, wantoned or hidden forever, it can fill a life. There is no understanding love, and there is no defeat so precious as trying. No aspect of life is more complex, and none so simple. A look, a word, and the heart is torn forever; a touch, and it is mended. Love is brave and cowardly. In the same person it is secret and garrulous. But above all, love establishes its own rules and no man can know its complete manifestation in the heart of another. It can even drive a person to stand watch in a long hall while the heart's desire is lusting with another.

In the days that followed, Cyril Hargreaves was coldly correct. He called David "Mr. Harper" and was studiously formal to him both off- and onstage. Once he reprimanded David for mispronouncing a word. He treated Wild Man and the Gonoph in the same austere manner, for he had not yet determined who had been David's accomplice.

The Gonoph was delighted with what had happened after the fire. She told David three times about the scene in the long hall. Cyril had finally torn the rope loose, but in doing so had ripped off the door handle. There was no way for him to get out. "He yelled like he was stuck in the belly," the pudgy woman reported, chuckling as she recalled the incident. "He wakened up the clerk, who let him out with a screwdriver. Then he stormed down the hall to see Mona. 'Go away!' she said. I was hiding in the women's toilet, laughing near to death. 'Who's in there?' he shouted at Mona, and people began to come into the hall. Sir Cyril just didn't care. 'Who's in that room with you?' he kept shouting, so finally she unlocked the door and threw it open and the light was on and there wasn't anybody there. 'Go on to bed!' Miss Meigs said, and all the people in the hall laughed. I stuck my head around the corner and saw him stomping down the hall as if he was in a play. He slammed his door shut and the next morning the clerk had to let him out again with a screwdriver."

Because of some ancient slight the Gonoph took real pleasure in Cyril's discomfort. "Look at him!" she would whisper to David during the play. "Lord Cyril's really got a worm eating him! Look at him!"

She now talked with David in their afternoon sessions as if he were her lover, as if he had crept to her room instead of Mona's. "Didn't we have a good time that night?" she chuckled, delighted that no one had thought of such a trick before. She spoke more kindly of Mona, too. "She's not so bad, really," the fat woman mused. "On Broadway she might get by. Of course, she don't have it for Hollywood. That takes class, and she's getting on. But I got to admit, she can act."

She was extremely proud of David's part in the fire. "I saw you go back in," she said quietly. "I was proud of the way Jensen worked on the pole, but, after all, his girl was caught under the pole. You . . ." She leaned back to survey her young man. She liked his sandy hair and muscled neck. "You didn't have to go." She wrote to the Bellehaven paper for pictures of David and sent six copies to friends who had acted with her in one play or another.

And the more David talked with her the more pathetic she seemed. She came to represent, for him, the tragic contradiction of art. She was empty and forlorn, yet onstage she stood for solid family virtues. Cyril was vain and selfish and arrogant, but in the play he was a wise, kindly judge. Vito was a grown man, caught in midstream and tortured by the doubts of ever finding a girl he could marry, but in the play he was a boy. Mona wrestled each night with her vast ambitions, but onstage she was a young girl burdened with success.

That was the nature of art. Deaf Beethoven wrote the fabulous symphonies. Dying Keats sang of life's subtlest beauties, and Van Gogh, mad as the night owls, showed all the world how to see yellow and blue. David looked at the Gonoph, vacant-minded, and thought of the great artists he had loved: Stendhal, Balzac, Dostoevsky, Melville, Giorgione, Duccio. They were tricksters, all of them. There could never be a judge's wife so stupid as the Gonoph, just as there could never be a boat so blue as the one Van Gogh painted.

This fundamental duplicity of art fascinated David, and he tried to comprehend it through comprehending the Gonoph.

One day he asked her, "Why did you help me to trick Cyril?" and she chuckled, pulling her shawl about her shoulders, "I like to have everyone find his heart's desire." He was caught in a passionate desire to know all he could about this formless woman.

"Why did you decide to go on the stage?" he asked, and she replied, "What else was there for me to do? I guess you might honestly say I was a born actress."

"Have you ever had good reviews? That is, rave notices?" She thought a while and said, "In Tulsa, Oklahoma, I got a very good review for a Swedish maid. I was pretty good in that. Comedy, you know."

He asked her many questions, and when he was through he knew no more about her than when he started, for she always returned to a few simple statements. "You must be careful at night," she warned.

"Why?" David asked.

"Sir Cyril's gunning for you," she said solemnly. "He'll get you."

"Not me," David boasted. But Cyril did even the score. It happened in a small Pennsylvania town called Slaghill.

That day at Slaghill started with a bang, for two detectives appeared at the tent to arrest the young man who took tickets. He had been selling them twice and had bilked Chautauqua of something like ninety dollars. Now he was off to jail.

"Ninety dollars!" David gasped. "I used to make that much in a day!" He began to shiver and felt alarmed when he and Cyril had to go to the prison to represent Chautauqua. They spoke very formally to each other and to the thief, who sat dejectedly in a barren cell.

"Couldn't you keep your hands off other people's money?" Cyril asked severely. The young college man did not reply and the actor continued, "All through the years the theatre has suffered from dishonesty in the box office."

"Let's leave him alone," David suggested. "Is there anything we can do for you?" he asked the frightened young man. The ticket-taker looked back through the steel bars and shook his head. He was twenty-three years old, a sand-lot baseball player, and David could remember him in the mornings, playing baseball with the kids around the tent.

Cyril wiped his brow with a carefully folded handkerchief

and said good-bye. "If there's anything you need, let us know. You were stupid to have stolen money when the tickets were all numbered." He huffed and puffed a bit of everyday morality and left, but David turned at the door and saw the panic-stricken baseball player, and it seemed to David that he saw himself sitting there behind the bars.

"God, that must be awful!" he mumbled to Cyril.

"The man's a common thief," Cyril snapped, and that was all he would say.

When the two actors returned to the tent, a group of small boys surrounded them immediately. "Are you Dave Harper?" they cried. "Well, the biggest car you ever saw wants to see you. It's in back!" David hurried through the tent and was greeted with a tough bellow.

"Hiya, kid! Ya look swell!" He recognized some of Max Volo's bodyguards and spoke to them. "Max is over here," they explained, adding in a whisper, "Do ya kiss the babes on the stage? Babes go for actors, don't they?"

"Hello, kid!" Volo said quietly. He wore a much better suit than when David had last seen him.

"Hello, Max!" David replied. "What you doing up here?"

"On my way to New York," Volo said. "Took a detour to see you. And Mona."

"Mona doesn't show up till seven-thirty," David explained.

"I can wait," Volo replied.

"How was Hollywood?" David asked.

"Oh, so-so," Volo replied. He sent his attendants on into town for supper but stayed himself to talk with David. "How you like this racket?" he asked.

"It's fun," David said.

"They tell me you play with dolls!" He persuaded David to unwrap Bosco and make him drink beer. "Say!" the little crook cried. "You're good! Part of the reason I dropped by was to see if you'd go to work for me when the tour's over. I got me nine movie houses in Philly. I think I move into New York, maybe. I could use you for a manager. Maybe even a field manager. Wonderful dough!"

"I don't think so, Max," David replied.

"You're the boss! Say!" he said sharply. "I hope you ain't in love with Miss Meigs."

"No, I'm not," David assured him.

"Good!" Volo said. He walked up and down and then asked, "She tell you about Hollywood? What a flop she was! And on my five grand! She put on dog like she was a queen.

The whole town was laughin' at her. I did my best to get her fixed up with some important people. But she loused up every deal. I don't mind tellin' you, kid, she treated me like I was dirt. But I got a terrific yen for that twisty blonde."

Volo's gang came back. They brought him a cheese sandwich, melted, and two malted milks. He insisted that David take one. At seven-thirty Mona appeared, followed by Cyril and the Gonoph. Volo sidled up and Mona shook hands with him. "Hello, Max," she said in a flat voice.

"Hello, kid!" he replied, eagerly. "I'd like to talk to you."

"It's almost curtain time," she said, but he pulled her into the outer shadows. He talked with her seriously for some minutes and came back to the dressing area trembling with rage.

"Who's Hargreaves?" he demanded sharply. The elderly actor stepped forward and Max grabbed him by the shirt. "I want to talk to you!" he said. With three of his henchmen helping he dragged Cyril into the shadows. They conversed seriously for several minutes and Volo cried, "I'll be damned if he does!" Whereupon he stormed back to the dressing rooms and cried to his gang, pointing at David, "Get that sonofabitch!"

Two men dragged David past the marionette boxes. A third slugged him from behind, so that his neck seemed about to break. "Wild Man!" he shouted, but it was no use. Jensen was absent in the truck and the tent captain was in jail. Quietly, and with maximum efficiency, Volo's thugs administered a masterful beating.

"No snotnose college kid's goin' to make a sucker out of me!" Volo said through tight lips, standing apart as his men finished their work. A big boxer shot four blows to David's face. The third smash knocked his jaw loose. The fourth knocked it back the other way. Then he was allowed to fall into the dust and hay. The long, expensive car squealed in the night, and Volo's gang resumed its way to New York.

The curtain was delayed half an hour. Jensen was switched to David's part and Cyril, calm and possessed, handled the Wild Man's original lines via the telephone. David lay propped up in the men's dressing room. Whenever she was offstage the Gonoph nursed him. She cried when the Slaghill doctor said it was a miracle the jaw wasn't broken. "It'll be painful for two more days, but you should be able to eat by then," the white-haired man said.

"How soon can I act?" David asked through clenched teeth.

"Soon as the swelling goes down," the doctor said. "Little make-up on that eye and you'll be OK." He had a breezy manner and gave David a sedative. "Two days you'll be fine!" He stayed to see the play and gave the Gonoph additional instructions when she pestered him.

Neither Cyril nor Mona spoke to David about his beating. The tall actor dressed in his corner of the canvas dressing room and said, "You were admirable tonight, Mr. Jensen." Then he went to the areaway and called, "Miss Meigs! Miss Clews! Stop!"

Apparently the Gonoph and Mona had been fighting, for David, his head throbbing, heard the former cry, "You cheap alley cat!" She refused to ride with Cyril and Mona. "I'd rather walk!" she shouted contemptuously with more feeling than she had ever crammed into a stage line.

Puffing heavily, she climbed into the truck with David. "You ride up front with Mr. Jensen," she told Vito. David was drowsy from the sedative given him by the Slaghill doctor and he understood only part of what the Gonoph told him in the darkness of the truck. He got the sentences: "Lord Cyril, the dirty bastard, told that little man you were with Mona all the time. I caught the slimy old devil smiling to himself after they beat you up."

David wished the ugly woman would go away and let him sleep. Drowsily he turned on his hard bed, but the movement made him wince with pain. The Gonoph banged on the window. "Drive slower!" she commanded, and then she sat on David's bed. She took his aching head in her hands, but he drew away, hating this fat woman.

But the gesture made his head ache dreadfully, down where the lower jaw joined the skull. "Ughhhh," he grunted, and this sound of pain was more than the Gonoph could bear. Against David's will she cradled his sore face in her soft arms, pressed his bruised head against her fabulous bosom. "Oh, David! David!" she chanted. "You are my one heart's desire."

The whole experience was sickening to David and again he tried to move away, but the combined action of pain and the sedative was too much for him. He fell back in her arms and moaned, "God! I feel awful."

The Gonoph sat with him until he fell asleep. Jensen drove slowly and Vito dozed on the front seat. Toward morning

Jensen looked back to see how David was, and he saw the Gonoph rocking back and forth, her eyes closed.

"Well!" the Gonoph announced some days later. "Everything's all right again. Grand Duke Cyril himself got into bed with her last night."

"Shut up!" David shouted. "Get the hell away from me!" He pushed her out of the tent and resumed packing the dolls. When she returned she was carrying a bag of jelly beans. He refused to take them and shouted, "Leave me alone!" She went to the women's dressing room and sat on a bench, staring at him as he worked, but he would not let her come near him. "Why don't you go for a walk?" he snapped.

Even though David had acknowledged to himself that sexual love is not the prerogative of youth—as most young people suppose—he was shocked that a graceless woman like the Gonoph should actually be in love in a breathless, panting sort of way. And he was repulsed by the thought of old Mr. Hargreaves presuming to sleep with a girl as beautiful as Mona. Suddenly he thought of his math professor, Tschilczynski. "When he married the Greek widow, I thought it was because he wanted someone to cook for him. Gosh! Imagine those two actually sleeping together in bed. It's repulsive!" But when he recalled the Russian's passionate nature he realized that it had been the sexual part of marriage that had inspired the wedding.

Normally David would have sought counsel from Wild Man Jensen, but he had not spoken to the athlete since the fight with Volo's gang. The cause of his disaffection was ridiculous, and David admitted that fact to himself, but when he had sat with ice about his bruised jaw he had listened to the Wild Man usurp his place on the stage. And the big clown had been much better in the role than David had ever been. He was freer, less affected, and more outgiving. David, sulking with his dislocated jaw, suffered the exquisite pain of overhearing Mona and Mr. Hargreaves saying, "We should have used Jensen in that part in the first place!"

So, following the beating in Slaghill, David found himself alienated from the players of Cyril Hargreaves Broadway Troupe. He loathed the Gonoph. He was jealous of Jensen. Mona looked past him as if he did not exist, and he had fallen into a kind of little-boy correctness in his dealings with Cyril. Only Vito remained as before, and David was so acutely aware of the dwarf's unsatiated longings that he felt self-conscious near the little man. But it was Vito who dragged David back into the center of the Cyril Hargreaves Troupe, because early one morning David found a perfect pigeon, forty inches high.

He discovered her in Punxsutawney, Pa. He saw her standing in front of a bakery and he jammed on the brakes so that he could get a better look. Jensen and Vito were sleeping in the rear and their heads banged. "What gives?" the Wild Man cried.

"Checking the oil," David explained, and he slipped out of the truck and asked a man, "Who's that little girl?"

"That's Ed Fletcher's daughter. Real estate."

"How old is she?"

"Say! You're nosy! She's twenty and she's a dwarf."

"Ed Fletcher. Ed Fletcher," David said, and he drove to the next town.

But when the puppet show was unloaded he slipped off to a telephone and asked the operator to get him Ed Fletcher, a real-estate man, in Punxsutawney. During the wait David heard the operators repeating his request, and he became actually frightened. "What the hell am I doing?" he asked himself in astonishment. He was about to hang up and run away from the phone when he heard a professionally hearty voice say, "Ye—sss! Ed speaking!"

"This is going to sound silly as the devil, Mr. Fletcher," David began. "But I'm Dave Harper. I'm from Dedham, Pennsylvania, and I'm an actor on Chautauqua."

"Ye—sss, Mr. Harper. What can I do for you?"

"I'm in Kittanning . . ." There was a long pause.

"Ye—sss, Mr. Harper."

"This morning I saw your daughter . . ." There was an agonizing pause and then David rushed his words. "The man who runs our puppet show is forty-one inches high. He's the finest man I've ever known, Mr. Fletcher, and I want him to meet your daughter. I'll drive back right away if you say the word, so you can see who I am. This is very important."

Now the pause came from Punxsutawney. David was afraid Mr. Fletcher might hang up, but after an endless moment the voice resumed. "We—lll, Mr. Harper . . ."

"I could drive back right now!" David pleaded.

"Why don't you do that?" the voice said quite solemnly. David rushed back to the tent and found Vito. "When

I got beat up," he began, "you handled the show fine. By yourself. Could you do it once more? This afternoon?"

"Sure," Vito said. "What's up?"

"Do we have any of those folders left about the play?" David countered. He rummaged in the truck and found one. Stuffing it in his pocket, he wheeled the truck about and hastened back to Punxsutawney.

He was sweating badly when he met Mr. Fletcher, and the real-estate man was equally nervous. "I'm David Harper. This is my driver's license." There was a moment of embarrassed introduction and then David produced the folder. "This is Vito Bellotti," he said. "He has a good job and makes a decent living."

Mr. Fletcher took the crumpled paper and looked at it for a long time. "Why don't we drive out to the house?" he suggested. He called his wife and said, "I'm bringing a young man out for a short visit. Can you fix some cakes and milk?" Then he laughed nervously and said, to David, "Of course, you being an actor, you'd probably prefer beer."

"Oh, no!" David laughed uneasily. "Milk's OK for me."

Punxsutawney was a little town, but Mr. Fletcher turned at several corners, and each time David felt sweat break out upon his arms, for he had no idea what he was to say. Finally the car stopped and Mr. Fletcher said, "Well! Here we are!" He led David up a studiously winding flagstone path to where a woman in a white-and-blue apron waited at the door. "This is Mr. David Harper," Mr. Fletcher said. "He's an actor."

They went inside and David peered quickly through each room to look for the little girl, but she was not there. "Some refreshment?" Mrs. Fletcher asked, and David knew from her nervousness that she had been told the purpose of his visit. Then his mouth went completely dry as Mrs. Fletcher listened and said, "That sounds like Betty coming now!"

A door closed and there was an echo of small feet. Then Betty appeared. She was forty inches high and weighed about eighty pounds. She had a pleasant face correctly proportioned for her body, and her eyes were bright and happy. She went directly to David and held out her small hand. "You're David Harper!" she said. "It was good of you to come all the way back here on my account." She smiled graciously and asked him to be seated, so that it was no trouble at all for him to say, "I thought it would be good if you and your parents could be my guests at the play tonight."

On the trip back to Kittanning, she rode in the truck with David, and her parents followed in the Fletcher car. David was at ease with Betty and joked with her, and even when he saw the brown tent and knew that soon he must introduce her to Vito, he was not afraid, for he sensed that all her life Betty's sensible parents had taught her not to be worried about her size. But at the critical moment when the truck actually stopped and his hands fell from the wheel, the back of his knees began to sweat furiously, and he saw that Betty was twisting her handkerchief.

Then Jensen appeared and David bellowed, "Hey! Wild Man! Come over here!"

The rugged football player stopped and turned toward the truck. At first he did not see Betty, but when he realized what kind of girl sat beside David he walked slowly over and opened the door. He studied her as if she were a painting of a grand lady, long dead, and a look of immense approval came over his face. "She's beautiful!" he cried, as if she were not a living girl. Then he let out a roar: "Vito! My God! Come here!"

That night, after the play, the Fletchers insisted that everyone drive back to Punxsutawney for a celebration. Vito rode in the car with little Betty. They made a fine pair, like dolls beside a clock in a Frenchwoman's boudoir. David rode in the truck with Jensen. They were silent for the first few miles and then Jensen, tired of the silly antagonism that had eaten David, said, "Looks like you beat me to the finish. She's some little pigeon!"

"You know what I bet?" David asked. "I bet he marries her!"

"He's a fool if he don't!" the Wild Man replied. "But we got to arrange something!" Jensen added. "Come life or death. Dave, that little Eyetalian midget must not drive down to Johnstown with us tonight. You understand?"

They shook hands, and at the party Jensen started at once to build Vito's reputation as a solid citizen. Jensen offered Mr. Fletcher a cigar, patting him condescendingly on the shoulder. "Looks as if you invested in Commonwealth and Southern!" the Wild Man said.

Mr. Fletcher blushed. "Well, sir, as a matter of fact I do have a few shares."

"I play around with it a little myself," Jensen confided. "A sheet to windward."

Mr. Fletcher looked at him strangely, as if trying to untangle that last phrase, whereupon Jensen added, "Sort of like Mr. Bellotti's father." This time Vito looked up in astonishment. "Yes," Jensen mused expansively, "Mr. Bellotti's father was a wealthy man in Sicily. But he had a great love for democracy. And that's what got him into trouble with the Black Hand." He snarled a bit. "It was in nineteen-and-three. Had to fly the country."

"What was the matter?" Mr. Fletcher asked.

Jensen hesitated to see if Vito wished to carry on the tale, but the dwarf was sitting with his mouth open. "He was the leader of the democratic forces," the Wild Man explained.

"I thought the Black Hand wanted democracy," Mrs. Fletcher said.

"Politics!" Jensen replied, cryptically. Then he changed the subject. "What did you think of Mr. Bellotti's voice?" he asked. "D below B to F above C."

Mrs. Fletcher played the piano. "How's that?" she asked.

Jensen pounded himself on the chest. "Very low voice," he said. And the action reminded him of his greatest parlor trick. David, sensing this, gasped.

"Mr. Fletcher!" the Wild Man asked impulsively, "Have you ever seen a man practically burn himself to death?"

"No! Jensen!" David cried. "Mr. Fletcher! Don't let him do it!"

But before anyone could stop him the Wild Man peeled off his shirt. He stood before the party bare to his waist, displaying an immense chestful of black and tangled hair. "You got a seltzer bottle?" he asked. He handed it to David. "He's my fire department!" he explained.

He struck a match and held it to the hair about his navel. The tangled mat caught fire and burned briskly. Explosively it flamed up his chest, so that he blazed like a torch. He started to sing "Jingle bells! Jingle bells!" and then with a loud, smoky cry demanded the seltzer water. David pressed his thumb and there was a fizzing, a sigh of flames, and the rich smell of burnt calcium. "Some act, eh?" the Wild Man asked.

"That's the damnedest thing I ever saw!" Mr. Fletcher said. He liked these young men. They had spirit. Without anyone but Jensen knowing what had happened the tension of the day was relaxed. "Let's have a drink!" Mr. Fletcher proposed.

"I must not!" Jensen replied sententiously. "We of the theatre, you know!" He practically posed as Cyril Hargreaves. "Anyway, I've got to be off."

"Where to?" Mr. Fletcher demanded.

"Oh! I've got to get the truck down to Johnstown!" Jensen hesitated a long moment. "So that it'll be ready when Mr. Bellotti gets there tomorrow."

Mr. Fletcher rubbed his chin. "Why, we could drive Mr. Bellotti down ourselves. Why not?"

"That would indeed be gracious!" Jensen observed. David had never before heard him talking that way. "And why couldn't Mr. Harper drive down with you?"

"Why not?" Mrs. Fletcher asked. But just before the Wild Man drove away he gripped David by the wrist. "Listen!" he grunted. "You see that Mom and Pop go to bed. Leave Betty and Vito alone!"

When the truck rolled off into the night there was a moment of anticlimax. "That Mr. Jensen is a remarkable man," Mr. Fletcher said.

"Yes," David replied. "I get sleepy just thinking of him driving that truck all night." This had no effect, so he added, "I'd better turn in. These long treks." Still the Fletchers made no move to leave their daughter with Vito, so David said directly, "You see, I was driving on the early morning shift . . . when we came through Punxsutawney."

"I think we'll join you," Mrs. Fletcher said with maximum confusion. They left Betty and Vito sitting on the porch. Hours later, when the tiny couple climbed the stairs, David watched from his door and saw that little people kiss in the same way big ones do.

The Fletchers, with little Betty, followed Chautauqua into Eastern Pennsylvania, and from watching the dwarfs together David derived a subtle pleasure. They seemed to be his special wards and he discovered how good it was to do something important for other people. Once some uncertain —and therefore aggressive—boys looked at the dwarfs with disgust and started to tease them: "Midgets! Midgets!" And David chased the boys until he caught two.

"What's the matter with you?" he argued seriously. "You got to ridicule anything different from the way you are?"

Now the boys were frightened as well as uncertain, so they

said, "Aw nuts!" whereupon David slapped them hard. This brought them to their senses and he made them come back to the tent where he introduced Vito and Betty to them. "Show them your low voice!" he said to Vito.

"Hello, kids!" Vito said, and on all sides the tension was broken. The boys went for their friends—those who had escaped David—and Vito showed them how to make marionettes, and David stood near by with little Betty, as if it were his protective love that held these two dwarfs safe in the world.

He felt better toward Jensen, too. Knowing how much the Wild Man had wanted to find Vito the perfect little pigeon, David felt that he had triumphed over the hairy-chested fellow, thus wiping away the disgrace of having Jensen star in David's role. In fact, David felt very warm toward Jensen and talked with him night after night in the truck. "You like everybody, don't you?" he asked the big driver.

"Even the Gonoph," Jensen replied.

"How did you get that way?" David inquired.

"Because nobody's got nothin' I want," the Wild Man said. "I got only two desires in the world."

"Like what?" David asked.

"I'd like to live to be a hundred, and I'd like to be hung for rape," the Wild Man replied. There was a moment of silence and then David burst into a wild guffaw. The two actors laughed at each other and told some more stories, and it was out of this very feeling of warmth toward everyone that David and Jensen devised the fabulous thing they did to the Gonoph. David was squeezing his eyes shut with delight at one of Jensen's jokes when he suddenly slapped his leg and cried, "I've got it!"

"What?"

"The Gonoph! All summer I've been watching her and wondering what we could do to help her along."

"That's simple!" Jensen snorted. "Go to bed with her." David frowned and the Wild Man coughed. "No. I guess there's a limit to everything," he said.

"But now I've got it!" David repeated, and when he explained what they could do at Willamaxon, Jensen laughed till there were tears in his eyes and he cried, "What a night that'll be!"

But in spite of his kind feelings toward the Gonoph, David was still incapable of talking with her in the late afternoons. Even though his experience with Vito and Betty had shown

him that love rides and dismounts where it will, he found
the hulking woman increasingly obnoxious. He tried to do
little things for her to show his appreciation of her interest.
He brought her sandwiches, for example, or jumped to lift
her box into the truck; but what she wanted most hungrily—
to talk with him and to touch him now and then—that he
could not give. "Here's a sandwich," he would say, and her
fishy eyes would fall upon him, lingeringly, so that he felt
embarrassed and forced to run away. It was this confusion
between affection for the flaccid woman and disgust at her
physical grossness that betrayed David into devising his
wicked plan. "We'll give her one hell of a big night!" the
Wild Man promised.

Mona and Hargreaves were having a succession of big
nights. The latter, feeling that he had beaten off David's
challenge, acted with glowing freedom when on the stage and
with courtly grace when off. He was thinner than ever, gray
and handsome. He was unashamedly pleased to escort Mona
to and from the tent, and David, watching him one night,
thought, "He's like an old bull we had at the poorhouse.
Whenever a young bull came around there'd be a hell of a
fight, and after that you could see from the way the old bull
walked that he was pretty pleased with things."

Mona perplexed David, and he gave up trying to understand her. She had a degree of concentration that was alien
to him, and he perceived that her sleeping with Cyril Hargreaves simply did not affect in any way the hard and bitter
core of her being that no man would ever know. David still
caught his breath when he saw her turn suddenly upon the
stage and smile at him. He felt that one cord of his heart
would always be strung to that sensitive doll, so that when
she moved, he moved, and he took much pleasure from the
fact that if he had always been nothing to Mona, her present
love, Sir Cyril, was nothing too. That was consoling.

In this quiet confusion David came back to Doylestown.
The Chautauqua tent was pitched at the foot of Shewell
Avenue and as they approached it Jensen said, "This is some
burg! This is probably the only place in America I couldn't
find a girl to fall in love with." But half an hour after they
unpacked he was explaining to girls from Hamilton Street that
he ate mostly in dirty restaurants.

When the marionette show ended lots of children milled
around to say hello. There were some older folks in the
crowd, too, and David looked with real excitement at one girl

who could have been Marcia. She wasn't, and in a sense he felt relieved. Then a very satisfying idea struck him. "Jensen!" he cried. "I'm going to use the truck!"

He raced the motor and drove to the edge of town, out toward Solebury. Then he dismissed the idea of visiting the Paxson farm and thought of Paradise Park. "That's the idea!" he cried aloud. "I'll see the gang down there!" He whipped the truck around and hurried south. He laughed to himself, nervously, for he could picture the cashiers nodding to him, and there would be the heartache of seeing the Canals of Venice again.

But as he drove, gray buildings loomed upon the horizon. On their hill stood the poorhouse halls, impersonal in the late afternoon yet beckoning him home. He slowed the truck to less than a walk. The engine coughed and stumbled like his own unwilling spirit; but at the driveway he turned right, for he was home.

No one at the poorhouse noticed him as he parked the truck and climbed out. He took a deep breath and faced the women's building. The flowers of late summer smiled along its cold stones. He went into the hallway and knocked on his aunt's door. There was a whine of protest from within and the door opened.

Aunt Reba was dressed exactly as she had been when David last saw her. She wore a cotton dress with green pinstripes. It lay flat against her. She looked at her nephew a moment and said, "Come in." She showed him a chair as if he were some inmate come to complain. "So you're a *play* actor, *yet!*" she said with some contempt.

"Yes."

"By *play* acting? Is it much *money?*" she asked.

"I get pretty good pay," David replied.

"They *say* in Doylestown"—she called it *Doi-liss-tahn*—"you could have married the young *Paxson* yet. She's taken *now.*"

David swallowed. "Who?" he asked.

"The young *Moomaugh,*" his aunt replied. "Now *there's* a fine fellow *yet.* Already he's got a good *chob.* And a wife with *money.* When the play acting's *over?* You got a *chob?*"

"No," David replied.

His aunt leaned forward as if to propose the pants factory in Sellersville, but when she looked at the strange young man in front of her, she shook her head sadly. "By me it's *saywing, saywing,* every *month. A'ready* I got nine *hunnerd* dollars!" She took out a dirty book in which her accounts were scribbled.

David looked at the horrible tight figures that spoke of happiness deferred. That was about the total sum he had spent on Nora, to save her from consumption, and all the days that had intervened were happier for him because he had spent his money so. But what would his aunt ever spend her money on? He wondered how many women were now upstairs in agonizing loneliness. A single tea party from this nine hundred dollars might warm those women until death, but instead his aunt shared nothing.

"I don't suppose you'd like to see the play?" he asked.

"I don't *hold* with *plays*," she sniffed.

For a moment coming up the lane David had sworn, "I'll go in and kiss her. We'll be friends." But now, in Aunt Reba's presence, he could do nothing. He wanted to leave, and he sensed that she wanted him to leave; but he felt that humanity—the something that was neither he nor she—demanded that he make a gesture. Impulsively he took out his wallet and gave her thirty dollars. Greedily she grabbed it and smiled. So far as she could recall this was the first reasonable thing her nephew had ever done. She did not thank him, for she knew this gift was long overdue.

"Daywid," she whined, lining up the bills in a neat pile, "I had a heavy *burden* raising *you*. Now that you're getting good *money* play *acting* . . . Couldn't you *send* a money order each *week?*"

David backed away from the wheedling voice. "What do you do with your money?" he asked coldly.

"I got my *eye* on a little house in Sellers*ville*," she replied. "When you leave off *play* acting, maybe . . ."

But the word *Sellersville* reminded David of his dead mother and he stared at Aunt Reba without seeing her. Then he left. There were no farewells and no expressions of affection or regret, and as he closed the door David had a strong premonition that he would never see his Aunt Reba again. For a moment he stood in the dark hallway and said, "God! A man can't say good-bye like that!" And he reopened the door, but inside he saw his aunt scratching new figures into her greasy notebook and he closed the door upon her forever.

He went to the men's building, and his heart pounded with anticipation as he neared the stone steps. Before him stood the dining hall, the pantry, the secure smell of bug juice, the scrubbed pine boards, and the sense of a small boy's comfort on wintry nights.

He sniffed at the pantry. A good Pennsylvania smell greeted him. Cheese and apples! Then slowly he climbed the dark stairway, back to his own hall. He was frightened and short of breath when he reached the last familiar step. He paused and inhaled deeply. Four paces and then a turn. He closed his eyes and envisaged the long hall with the bench at the far end. Suddenly he felt very good, like Ulysses home from the wars, and his fingers began to tingle.

There before him lay the somber hall. Doors stood ajar as in years gone by. The same wisp of sunlight entered the far window and fell upon an old man dozing on the bench where Old Daniel had taught David the Latin names for flowers. Then, as a lover postpones looking toward a certain pew in church, David looked at the inconsequential doors first. Toothless Tom lived there. Mad Luther Detwiler in the next. The man who had drowned himself in the water tank lived over there. And that door! In the shadows! That was Door 8! An old man was sitting inside, mending a sock. Sunlight came over his shoulder and illuminated the wall, on which was thumbtacked an unframed picture by Rembrandt.

With dismay David looked at the fly-stained picture. The old man stopped his needlework and asked in a squeaky voice, "You visitin'?" David nodded, and the old man put down his darning. "Come right in!" he said. "This is the only room with a picture," he added proudly.

"What is it?" David asked, remembering the distant night when he had hung it there.

"I don't know," the old man said. "It was here when I came."

David turned away from Door 8. The poverty of imagination that would keep a torn picture on a poorhouse wall for eleven years was too much for him to comprehend. He looked down the long hall and for the first time saw it as it was: the home of lost men, the final refuge of the defeated, the lonely tomb of the forlorn. This was where hope died, this the living tomb of stolen farms, wrecked lives, loneliness, frustration and wandering minds more lost than the wandering bodies.

This had been his heritage! His portion of America! Not the green fields and white-fenced homes near golf links. His America was Old Daniel dying of cancer, the young girls sobbing in Mon City, and this was the America known by most of the people from whom he had stolen at Paradise. This was the hidden world.

David stood against the wall and listened to the supper bell. Three hungry men, their days no longer punctuated by living but rather by the meals they ate, hurried down the hall. They did not look at David. He waited till they were gone and then knocked on Toothless Tom's door. "Come in!" an eager voice cried.

"Tom?" David called.

"No," the voice replied in falling disappointment. "Tom, he's dead."

David left the sad door and against his will tears came to his eyes. He laughed nervously and pressed his knuckles into his offending eyes. Then he saw, where before he had refused to see, the tragedy of this wooden catacomb. He saw the old men coming here to die, the hopeless ones, the sick, the maimed, the lost, the robbed, the unwanted servants of a society that needed younger servants, the Americans who hadn't made good, the men who never hit the jackpot.

The old man in Tom's room shoved his way into the hall and repeated angrily, "You mean Tom from Solebury? Him with not teeth. Well, he's dead. It's my room now." He stared contentiously at David and then banged his way down to supper.

But the way the old man walked was the way Tom had walked, and David saw that there would always be a Tom in that room. For the first time in his life David caught a sense of the endlessness of time, that cruel metronome. He saw how inescapably men must grow old and watch their visions perish. He sensed the brief interval of years one has to spend, the petty coinage of days and hours, and how bare the shelves of the candy store are. He was caught up in the vast, shadowy web of living, and the full terror of his nebulous prison bore in upon him.

"Oh, Daniel!" he cried. "The things I didn't understand!"

He wished then that he might talk with Daniel and Toothless Tom just once again. He would not worry them with unimportant questions. No, he would ask, "What is life in a poorhouse like?" But they were dead, and he had a terrible feeling that years from now he would wish in the same vain way that he had talked with Aunt Reba, and he was torn with memories not yet formulated.

Then he heard a strange voice pleading, "Come on, now! Time to eat!"

"Don't wanna eat!" a vacant voice replied.

"Sauerkraut! Maybe dandelion salad!" the first voice wheedled.

"Get out!" the empty voice commanded.

David recognized the speaker. He ran to the room and cried with deep pleasure, "Luther! Luther Detwiler!" The old cigarmaker was thin and white. He looked much as Old Daniel had looked during the last days, but his eyes barely focused.

"He won't eat," complained a little man with no chin.

"Luther!" David cried. "Don't you remember me? I'm David! Lived in Room 8."

The old cigarmaker looked at the young man in the doorway, then looked away, and David experienced the pain of returning to a much-loved place and finding himself unremembered. "Look! Luther!" he pleaded. "The night we fought in here! You lifted me up and threw me on the bed! That bed!"

But the old Dutchman's mind had come to rest in some compromise between living and dying, sanity and hopeless insanity. He stared at David and cried peremptorily, "Let's eat!" He stamped down the hall like a soldier from the Civil War marching to Monument Square. In the dining hall he said to David, "You sit here," but to his chinless friend he cried, "You! Go away! I'm sick and tired of you!" The little man bit his lip, but David grabbed his hand and pulled him down beside Luther, whereupon the mad cigarmaker drew a line with his finger and said he would cut the man's hand off if he trespassed. "On this side there's no line," he assured David. "You're my friend. Who are you?"

Obsessed by Luther, David did not see the poorhouse women coming in to eat; but when he did look up he saw again the never-ending stream of faded dresses, bent figures, used-up bodies. Only the faces were different. The old women shuffled to their places. There was a momentary quarrel—as there had been on most nights years ago—when two women wanted the same seat. David almost shouted, "Why, in God's name, can't you at least agree upon the chairs?"

And this irritation proved to David how much he had grown since his days in the poorhouse. Then nothing irritated him. He even used to laugh when serious young men came and explained patiently to their uncles the exact points at which the great errors had been made. "That's what put you in the poorhouse!" the serious young men said. Now he was like that! He, David, could arrange the poorhouse seating so there would be no more petty bickering. He could explain why people wrecked their lives and died in poverty, and he was ashamed of himself for having grown into such a damned fool.

"I think I'll go," he said to Luther's little friend. But just then the waiters brought in big bowls of dandelion salad, and the Dutchman's eyes grew big. He grabbed David by the hand.

"This is good!" he beamed. He filled David's plate with wild roots and sour cream all wilted with hot bacon fat. Luther ate with his fingers and when he was done he spotted a piece of bacon on David's plate. "Do you mind?" he asked, deftly popping it into his thin old lips. In doing so he looked at David and a faint glimmer of recognition passed his face. "I know you," he said. Eagerly David leaned forward, but the Dutchman could recall no more.

When supper ended David felt that he must go back to the Chautauqua tent, but the passing lights upon mad Luther's face kept him chained to the poorhouse. There was a chance that this crazy man might remember him, and he dreaded leaving without at least one man's recalling him; so he stayed with Luther and they sat on the bench in the long hall. "Old Daniel, Tom, the man who hit the nurse . . ." One by one David repeated the names of men they had known, but still no flicker of recognition returned, and at last David had to go.

He led the crazy cigarmaker back to his room and was about to close the door when Luther cocked his head on one side and said, "That night. I wouldn't hurt you, David."

The two men looked at each other and David said softly, "You got pretty excited."

"I'll tell you something," the madman confided. "That cigar factory. I never owned it. I just worked there." He began to laugh in an old man's devilish glee, pleased with having fooled his friends for so long. "My wife's in Delaware," he added. "She's comin' home one of these days."

The sorrow was gone out of David, for he had been recognized. It was only a daft Dutchman who knew him, but one aching strand leading from the past to the present had been salvaged. Luther was the only living contact with David's days of wonder in the long hall, and as such he was of immortal value. They stood together in the dusk and David placed his arm about the withering man. "It's good to see you," he said.

Luther laughed. "It's good to have someone you can trust," he replied. "Don't tell that little fellow about my wife comin' back. He's a nosy bastard." He chuckled at his skill in having fooled the little man, and David laughed with him. But then Luther said something which destroyed the nostalgic pleasure of that meeting.

He grabbed David impulsively by the wrist and said earnestly, "I can trust you, can't I?" When David nodded he clung to him and confided, "My wife's not comin' home. She ran away with a man from Delaware. When she left she hit me over the head with a board. She's never comin' home."

He stood abjectly by David's side and rambled on about the faraway incident. No matter how crazy he had been previously, he had always kept this one disgrace from Old Daniel and Toothless. Now death was near and there was no pride. Finally David had to say, "It's time to go, Luther."

"You won't tell anyone out there, will you?" the Dutchman begged.

"No," David promised, and he said good-bye to Luther for the last time; but as he drove back to Doylestown he became very ashamed of himself. He had gone to the poorhouse selfishly seeking some kind of spiritual reassurance, and instead he had found only new problems. He had not been big enough to ignore his aunt's meanness and he had resented mad Luther's imposition of this story about his wife. He had sought solace and had been given fresh agitation.

The miserly nature of his reactions shamed him, and even though it was almost curtain time he hurried to a cigar store and emptied his pockets. "Here's $18," he said. "Send as many cigars as you can down to the men at the poorhouse." Self-conscious, he left the surprised clerk, but then came back. "Change that," he said. "Send $12 worth of cigars. And send the rest in candy to the women's building."

"Where you been?" Jensen demanded, but David would not reply, so Jensen nodded his head sagely and warned, "You'll be sorry!" Still David ignored him, and Jensen added, "Because a very stunning dish was here to see you." This time David tightened a bit as he slapped make-up on his face, and Jensen said, "Name of Marcia Moomaugh."

"Did she leave a message?" David asked quickly.

"Oh!" the Wild Man said. "You come to life! Yes, she said to say hello."

David wanted to ask more, but the curtain rose, and when he first entered he could hear the pleasing ripple of voices saying, "That's him. He's grown!" But no matter how carefully he peeked at the audience when others were speaking, he did not find Marcia.

It was not until the tent came down that he found her. He was talking with the tent captain when he heard his name. He turned and looked across the worn space where the tent had been, and there in the garish light stood Marcia Moomaugh. She was wearing a summer dress, freshly starched, and she was not afraid.

"Hello, Marcia," he said, walking through the dusty stubble. "I hear you're married."

"Harry's at Penn State this summer," she replied. "You were very good in the play."

"Thanks," he said. "I thought you'd be with Harry."

"I am," she said. "But I came home this week."

"Watch out!" the tent captain cried. "Pole's comin' down!" Now the solitary light lay sideways on the ground, so that Marcia's shadow was immense, blotting out whole fields. Above, the stars shone once more, and there was a fine clatter of trucks coming to haul away the chairs.

"I guess this'll be the last Chautauqua," Marcia said. "Mother and Father used to bring me in to see all the plays. Did you see them, too?" David noticed that she was avoiding *thee*. He did not bother to answer her manufactured question, and they stood for an awkward moment looking at each other.

The spell was broken by Wild Man Jensen who roared, "Mind waitin' around for a few minutes? I need the truck."

David looked at the silly girls with Jensen and to his own surprise shouted, "Yes, I do mind! I'd like to drive Marcia home!"

Jensen laughed and said, "OK. But how do I get these pigeons home?"

Instinctively Marcia tossed him the keys to her Buick. "You can use my car," she said.

Jensen studied the keys a moment and then said, "That makes sense." The he called, "Hey, girls! We go home in style." There was loud squealing as two girls climbed into Marcia's car and started working the lights.

Marcia smiled at David in the weird fallen light. Half their bodies were in shadow and they seemed an eerie pair of lovers from an old ballad. He took her hand and led her to the truck. For some unaccountable reason he said, "The Wild Man . . . That's the fellow who took your car. He uses the back of this truck to make love in."

"You talk as if it were a profession," Marcia said as she climbed in front.

"It is, sort of," David replied. Then he quickly added, "With him, that is." He shifted gears, and the truck crept across the dusty field and onto the road. "Jensen says it's as good a way to spend time as any he knows of." Then he added, "He also makes a lot of money playing the stock market. He's made over two thousand dollars this summer. But I don't know why I'm telling you this."

"Jensen sounds like fun," Marcia said.

They were using up the fragile moments before their hands touched. They sat apart, yet close together, and finally David placed his hand on Marcia's. As if this were the permissive signal, Marcia grasped his shoulder and unloosed her longing. "I've done such a terrible thing," she whispered. "I love you. I should've waited. I should've followed you about the country like a puppy dog, yipping at your heels until you got some sense."

"You shouldn't talk that way," David mumbled. Like most men, he was bewildered by what he hoped for most. "What about Harry?" he asked.

"He's so good!" Marcia replied. "And so stupid." She pulled her hand free and moved away from David. "What about the singer?" she inquired.

"She won't even look at me," David confessed. This admission pleased Marcia, and David could hear her give a little gasp of satisfaction.

"It's mean of me to say it," she confided. "But I'm glad."

They had now reached a hill above New Hope, and below them lay the broad valley of the Delaware. The quiet river flowed softly in moonlight, and beside it hung the outmoded canal, like an artist's inspired afterthought, making the night and the river beautiful.

David guided the truck into a meadow and hid it beneath a row of drooping trees. There was a moment of awkward silence as he turned out the night-piercing lights, and then he volunteered to kiss Marcia, but the proud girl drew back and said with some disgust, "We've made enough mess. We didn't come out here to neck like tragic village lovers."

Her words had a strange effect, and largely because he knew she would say no, David pleaded, "Let's get in back. Come on, Marcia."

Rudely, she pushed him from her. "You must be crazy!" she cried.

Almost as if this were a game with set rules David replied, "Didn't you want to come out here with me? Don't you want to get in back?"

"Of course I want to!" Marcia exploded, covering her face with her hands. "I've been married three months and every day I've longed for you." She stopped in shame and then added in deep, harsh tones such as old Quaker women use when they pray in Meeting, "I've committed the worst sin a woman can. When I've been with Harry at night . . . I've closed my eyes and imagined it was thee."

The Quaker speech sounded grotesque, ending such a sentence, and David placed his hand upon Marcia's, and now he was trembling with confusion. "I've missed you in every town we played," he confessed, more to himself than to her. "You saw the dwarf tonight. He used to stare at the audience, hoping against hope that he'd find a little girl his own size. We teased him, but all the time I was staring at girls, too, and there always seemed to be one strong, proud girl . . ." His desire for Marcia burst free, and he wanted to pour out his rich longing for this wonderful grown woman. He laughed nervously and said, "One night they roped Mr. Hargreaves in his room. Now you understand that Mr. Hargreaves is in love with Miss Meigs, and she . . ." He became all twisted in his explanation and finally cried, "Well anyway, Marcia. It's been you I've wanted."

She pulled her hand away and shivered, as if the night were wintry. "I know you want me, David. I've always known it, even before you did. But now it would be so wrong." She beat her fists into her knees. "I did a foul thing in marrying Harry. Sleeping with you would start another wrong thing. I've got to clean this up my own way."

"But Marcia!" David began to explain. Then he thought better of his insulting thoughts and kept still. He could not tell her—in view of what she had said—that he did not want her sexually. When he said, "I want you," he meant that he prized her rich and strong character. When he said, "Let's get in back," it was because he knew that's what she expected him to say. He had never longed physically for this powerful girl. When he lay in bed at night, she did not haunt his desire. He had worshipped her more as a weary sailor imagining the inevitable harbor into which his storm-tossed ship will ride peacefully at the end of many days. Something in his up-bringing prevented him from thinking of the straight, clean girl also as a warm, tremulous girl longing for bed. He was, in brief, like most good American men, which explains why the finest American women either do not marry at all or stumble into the arms of a Harry Moomaugh.

Marcia was an extremely bright girl, but she did not even guess David's ambivalent attitude toward her; so she tried to console him for her absolute inability to make love with him as long as she was married to Harry. "It's not being in bed that matters," she whispered, sitting stiffly to herself. "It's wanting to be with someone who sees things as fast as you do. It's wanting the heart fairly to explode when your man comes home. That's how I would be with you, David . . ."

Her voice trailed off, and then quietly they began to imagine how they would live if they had married. David said most of all he wanted a clean bathroom. "It's almost a fetish with me," he confided seriously. "I've never lived where there was a clean bathroom." Marcia twisted her fists into her eyes to stifle even the smallest tears that may have been starting and said, "I'm frightfully selfish. Not for things. But I've thought that if we were married that perhaps in the evening we could talk. Not your job or my work, but say . . . Thomas Mann."

The night wore on, and in distant New Hope a bell sounded. Impulsively Marcia pressed her longing lips into the short hair that straggled over David's collar. "Let me kiss you just once," she whispered. Then she laughed and said, "If we were married, I'd surely make you get a haircut!"

"Oh, no!" he protested automatically. "When you're an actor it's the very devil to get a haircut. It's got to be long because of the bright lights."

Then Marcia buried her face against his shoulder and cried, "Oh, God! What have we done to each other!" David started the car and backed onto the main road. "David!" the wretched girl commanded, "you must not let tonight haunt you. What's happened to me is my own fault. I saw all of this the afternoon I married Harry, and I was too weak to stop." She pressed her hands against her face and then said quietly, "I've done an evil thing to Harry, but he shan't be the loser."

Trying to sleep in the truck that night, David tossed and thought of the Quaker girl. He punched his pillow and cried, "Just talking with her means more than sleeping with Mona." Then he saw the silliness of that statement and thought: "Why can't I want Marcia the same way? Why does a whole part of life seem to die when I'm with her?" Because he felt no surging sexual passion for her he reassured himself that she was—down deep—unimportant. "Hell!" he lectured himself. "She's married to another guy! She's out of my life forever! Tonight was just a schoolboy incident. We weren't even like grownups." But then he thought of her wish: that they might talk together in the evenings, and he felt like a poorhouse boy again, starting a picnic when the morning was rainy. The first steps were disappointing, or even distasteful; but there was the promise of a sunny afternoon and quiet pleasures beyond the imagination. "Marcia's like that!" he admitted. "God! God!" he muttered in the dark and swaying truck.

When the last Chautauqua tent came down and David began hoboing across the country, he would sometimes awaken in a strange town, and he would be sweating. "How could I have done such a thing?" he would ask himself, pounding his hot pillow. Then he would think of the evil trick he had played on the Gonoph, and he would be ashamed. But at the same moment he would recall her night of triumph and he would begin to laugh joyously, and he never succeeded in getting reactions about that night straightened out.

The trick started innocently. David told Jensen and Vito, "We'll give the Gonoph one night of great acting!" He accomplished this by inviting her to dinner. "Say!" she beamed. "I'd like that!" She was annoyed that Jensen and the dwarf had to tag along, but she forgot her displeasure when the Wild Man started serving her large glasses of lemonade. "That's pretty good lemonade!" she said. When the gin began to take effect, the men served her straight whiskey—violent bootleg stuff—and convinced her that they were matching her, drink for drink.

She began to blink her fat eyes. Then she licked her huge lips and started to pat her hair as if everyone in the restaurant were obsessed with her appearance. The drunker she got, the wider she spread her shapeless legs until she sprawled on her chair, her weight falling upon the table.

"Looks to me she's about right," Jensen said, appraising her as if she were a prize sow.

"She'll do!" Vito agreed.

With David's help they guided her to the truck. She was gracious and bland, nodding expansively to everyone. When she stumbled she grabbed David's arm and laughed with no apologies.

The trip back to the tent sobered her enough for her to

lurch to the dressing tent. When Mona saw her there was a loud cry: "Cyril! My God! Look at what David did!"

Mr. Hargreaves burst into the tent and surveyed the leering woman. "Emma!" he barked. "What have you been doing?" It was the only time that summer he called her Emma.

She wagged her finger unsteadily at him. "Don't you worry about me!" she chuckled. In slam-bang fashion she dressed, and slobbered, "Let the play go on!" Her lips grew thick and there was a saucy tilt to her head. She kept chewing the side of her mouth and tried vainly to focus her eyes.

"What will we do?" Mona asked, walking her back and forth before the men. The Gonoph nodded to each actor like a confident heavyweight about to enter the ring.

Cyril stared at her and snapped, "Mr. Harper. You're fined fifty dollars."

"It was my idea," Jensen volunteered.

"Mine, too!" Vito insisted. With broad grins they gave David their share of the fine. Cyril was infuriated.

"All right! You did it! Now you get her out of this!" He turned his back furiously upon the young men, but then returned immediately to the group. "Here's what we'll do," he said. "We'll let her come onstage. Everybody cover up for her. Take her lines if necessary. Forget all about cues." He glared at David. "Somebody must stand beside her all the time. And under no circumstances pull the curtain." At this the Gonoph belched, and Cyril added with a squeamish look on his face," "That is, unless she gets sick onstage."

It was a remarkable play, that night. With improvised lines written from air, Mona and Cyril let the people of William-axon know that Judge Hardy's wife was daffy but lovable. While they were talking the fat woman lurched onstage, tried to focus her eyes on the expanse of faces, and belched. There was a moment of suspense and then the audience began to laugh. Putting one foot carefully before the other, the Gonoph curtseyed and clapped her hand to her mouth. More laughter. Cyril engineered her into a chair, from which she surveyed the stage like a drunken queen.

She remembered most of her first-act lines. She slobbered them up a bit and laughed with high pleasure whenever David came onstage. But with each of her actions Cyril became more furious, and when the curtain fell at the end of the act and the audience applauded the fat comedienne, he stormed backstage and said, "Pour water on her face! Get her sobered up!"

David stayed with her and massaged her arms. "You're wonderful!" he whispered. "To hell with Lord Cyril!"

"I feel fine!" she drooled, but halfway through the second act Cyril had to take her lines and when David came on the elderly actor muttered, "Hold her up! You take care of her!" David did so, and he could feel her stomach retching.

"Not here, Miss Clews!" he whispered sharply, and he could see her fighting back the heaving torment of her insides. When the retching subsided she stroked David's face and said to the audience, "He's a dear, dear boy!"

Between acts Jensen tickled her tongue to make her throw up, but she refused to do so. "I feel just fine!" she insisted, and when the last-act curtain rose she was fairly well under control. By this time the audience waited impatiently for each of her entrances and applauded whenever she appeared. David, watching her from the wings, whispered to Jensen, "Well, she's giving some performance. Even if she had to be drunk."

The came the scene in which the broken and despairing judge came to his wife for comfort, and suddenly David realized that the Gonoph was no longer drunk. She stopped ogling the audience and spoke to Cyril—her long-ago lover— as if a world of passion and compassion lay hidden within the folds of her gross body, as if all the silliness of the world did not matter if two people were man and wife.

A woman in the audience began to sniff. The Gonoph's voice grew very low as she spoke of the love she and the judge had enjoyed. People began to blow their noses, and Jensen cried, "Look at her. Her face is green! Dave! She's gonna toss her cookies! Quick!"

Without cues they ran onstage and David stood beside the sick woman. He saw her glassy face and heard the premonitory rumblings of her stomach. In sober despair she looked at Cyril and Mona. "Hurry up!" she whispered. She fought back the sour whiskey.

"No!" David whispered. "Miss Clews, hold it! Hold it!"

He had to leave her for a moment while he patched up his romance with Mona, and when they stood before the struggling woman for her blessing she had to keep her teeth clenched and wipe tears from her eyes, so that real mothers in the audience had to wipe tears from their eyes, too. Then she closed her eyes, and David and Mona held her up until the curtain closed.

The applause was more vigorous than any they had so far

heard and some voices called for Mrs. Hardy to take a bow, but she could not do so, for David was holding her over a rope while her evil cargo disgorged itself.

When the lights came on a man in his fifties—the English teacher in Willamaxon High—came backstage to pay his respects. He had a young girl with him. "I've never seen a comedy played with such verve!" he said. "Magnificent. I've been telling Julia, here, to relax when she acts. I wonder if we could speak . . ."

Jensen tried to keep the visitors away from the Gonoph, but at that moment she had a new attack and her heavy shoulders wrenched violently. "Why!" the English teacher cried in disgust. "That woman's drunk!"

He pulled the young girl away in horror and would have spoken again, but Jensen intervened. "Forget you saw her," he said to the girl. "But when you act, let yourself go as if you were drunk, too. Then you'll be good, the way she was." He guided the bewildered teacher back into the noisy crowd.

"What'll we do with her?" Mona asked.

"We'll take her back to the hotel," Cyril directed, but when the men got her to her room it was apparent she could not undress herself. "I'll send Miss Meigs in," Cyril said quietly. Shortly Mona returned from the room and said, "She wants you, Dave."

David hung back, unwilling to talk with the sick woman, but Cyril pushed him toward her room. "You started this," he said grimly.

"Wait a minute!" Jensen laughed. "No matter how she feels now, she gave the performance of her life. Tell the truth, Cyril. Wasn't it worth fifty bucks?"

"Don't call me Cyril!" the elderly actor said, leading Mona to her room.

"Go on!" Jensen urged David. "Jolly her up a bit. We'll wait in the truck."

Reluctantly David entered the dismal hotel room. The Gonoph rolled upon her side and stared at him. Then she hid her face in her fat hands and moaned softly, "Why did you have to help them?"

"I . . ." But there was nothing he could say. Her clothes filled the only chair, so he sat gingerly upon the edge of the bed.

The Gonoph rolled onto her other side so that she would not have to see David and mumbled, "When you were sick in love for Miss Meigs I didn't laugh at you. I helped you.

And I didn't laugh when Mr. Jensen was better in your part than you were. I told you things to do." She relaxed and all the fight went out of her formless body. Automatically her stomach tried to disgorge the last of the foul whiskey that had outraged it. Bile burnt her tongue, and she spit into a towel.

"Can I get you some water?" David asked.

"Please," she said, and when he returned she looked up at him to thank him, but her eyes were filled with tears of humiliation.

"I'm so sorry, Emma," he muttered.

"Why did you have to make fun of me?" she pleaded.

"You were very good tonight!" he insisted stubbornly. "Didn't you hear them cheering?"

"I know I'm a lousy actress," she admitted bitterly. "I've always known it. My father and mother knew it, too. For a while they hoped I would be a great person on the stage. Not hacks, like them. But when it was clear I didn't have the talent, Pop got a lot of fun out of hitting me in the face with those pies." She sobbed quietly in the pillow. After a moment she asked, "Why can't people let other people be good or bad, just as they are?" She looked beseechingly at him.

"You look lots better now," he said reassuringly. He made a motion as if to leave, but he could see that she hoped with all her heart that he would stay; so he sat on the bed and talked with her. Her stomach heaved less often and in about twenty minutes she fell asleep.

David looked down at her and pondered her unanswerable question: "Why do people torment other people?" He would never find a reasonable reply to that query. All he had been required to do that summer was talk with the Gonoph and perhaps let her touch him as she did now, with her sleeping hand against his knee. That was all, but it was more than he could give.

Yet as he sat with her toward two in the morning he did find one thing he could do to help her. She was dozing fitfully when he saw on her chair the novel by Proust. To pass the time until she was well enough for him to leave, he picked up the book and saw his his complete astonishment that it wasn't by Marcel Proust at all! It was by Marcel Prevost, a minor French writer whose novels had enjoyed a certain vogue in translation. Years ago the Gonoph had bought it upon the advice of a friend who had said, "Always try your mind on the best." She had often wondered why Proust was spelled with a v but she knew that the French were a funny race. She had not even been able to finish reading Prevost, but over the years she had derived great satisfaction from the fact that she, too, could understand the leading novelist of her time.

David replaced the much-worn volume and tiptoed from the room. At last he had found something he could do for the Gonoph. He could keep this secret. He would never speak of that book. Never.

Nor did Vito and Jensen ever speak of the Gonoph's masterful performance. They knew it was a night that should not have happened, and David guessed that they were as perplexed by it as he. One reason for their silence was the fact that as Chautauqua moved into the Southern states the jumps between towns became intolerable. Frequently the actors had to ride all night and up to twelve o'clock the next day before they could rest.

The schedule was particularly hard on Jensen, who tried to make love to as many pigeons as ever and who had to work harder than before. As they left Tarleton Jensen finally admitted, "Dave, I'm whupped. I jes' gotta get some sleep. You'll have to drive."

"I'm dead on my feet," David protested.

But the Wild Man insisted. "Jes' an hour, and I'll be all right," he pleaded.

"If you'd lay off the pigeons . . ." David started.

"No lectures, kid," the Wild Man begged. "Do you mind?"

So David took the wheel, and before the truck was in high the Wild Man was asleep. But driving that night was torment. David could not keep his eyes open. His eyelids were like rusty iron, and once he woke barely in time to miss a big truck.

"I've got to keep awake!" he muttered. Another truck with terrible lights sped at him around a bend and roared narrowly past. He started to recite all the poetry he knew but it was too musical and again he dozed. A car honked wildly and whizzed past.

He rubbed his eyes, spit on his finger tips and massaged his face, but in spite of himself his head fell forward. "War must be like this," he thought. "You can't go on any more, but you've go to." He slowed the truck to fifteen miles an hour and still he dozed. He was wakened by a screaming horn and the terror of a touring car flashing by on gravel. Sweat broke upon his forehead and he pulled off the road.

He had scarcely stopped the truck before he was asleep. He was awakened by Jensen tugging at him. "I feel better," the Wild Man said. "Vito's gonna ride up front with me."

Shamefully, David crept into the back of the truck and promptly fell asleep. He was wakened some time later by a piercing scream. Vito was crying, "Jensen! No!" A violent light filled the sleeping compartment and there was a furious crash. David flew into the air, and as he fell back the weird light showed the heavy property box crushing down upon him. Darkness came and a stabbing pain in his back. He fainted.

"Never move a man that's been crushed," he heard the policeman say.

From far off he heard Vito cry. "I tell you, he ain't crushed. My box of dolls broke the fall."

"Take it easy, little fellow!" the police advised, but David could still hear Vito's wailing voice reassuring this man or that. Then Jensen barked huskily, "You're all right, ain't you, kid?"

"I feel pretty good," David replied.

And he was. When the doctor told them to drag away the big box everyone saw that Vito was right. The doctor jabbed at David's spine. "No gritty feeling, is there? How are the legs?"

There was a painful throbbing in his back and he was about to say so when he saw Vito and the Wild Man anxiously watching him. "I feel pretty good," he said.

"We'll tape up your back and give you a day's rest," the doctor said.

"Does he have to go to a hospital?" Jensen asked.

"No," the doctor said. "A hotel room's good enough."

Scared and dizzy, David climbed into the ambulance. Jensen rode along and before they had reached town his fertile mind had a plan. "You don't need a hotel!" he said. "You can stay at Alison's."

"Who's Alison?" David asked.

"Girl I was with tonight. You'd like her. She's got plenty brains." He knocked on the panel. "You know Alison Webster?" he asked the doctor.

"Mark Webster's daughter?"

"They live in a white house," Jensen explained.

"That's Mark."

"Dave can stay there tonight." The ambulance muffled its siren and drove down a side street, stopping before an average

American house. Jensen peered at the hedge. "This is it," he said. There was a light burning, and he whistled at it.

"Who's there?" a crisp voice called.

"Hey! Alison! It's me, Jensen!"

"What do you want?" Another light went on.

"Alison! My buddy. The guy in the play. We had a wreck and he needs a place to sleep."

"Hey, Mom!" the girl called over her shoulder. There was a clatter on the stairs and two women opened the door.

"Goodness me!" the older cried. "He looks half dead! What's the matter, Doctor?"

"Nothing much," the doctor said reassuringly. "He ought to sleep in bed. He'll be all right. Unless I've missed something."

"And look Mrs. Webster!" Jensen wheedled. "Feed him some of that good Maryland cookin'. And why don't you and Alison drive him down to our next stop. How would you like that?" He jollied the woman along and soon had her promising all sorts of things.

"First of all, we'll get him to bed!" she said in a motherly manner. She led David to a large room. "My husband's in Baltimore," she said. "We'll bring you some breakfast in the morning."

David relished the cool sheets. It was his first feel of bed since the tour began, and in a moment he was asleep.

In the morning he was awakened by Alison bringing him a tray of healthy size. "This is Pop's tray," she said. She sat in a chair and watched him eat. She was about eighteen and not a beautiful girl. She was too plump, and her face was round; but she had rich red hair which she tossed from side to side, punctuating her sentences.

"It's providential," she said.

"What is?" David asked.

"Your coming back like this," she replied. He noticed her precise speech.

"What about Wild Man?" he asked.

"Oh, him!" She tossed back her hair and laughed. "He's a clown. He tried to pull that broom trick on me. But he's a sweet fellow. I think Mother's in love with him. At first you'd have thought he had the date with her. Of course, later on he got down to business."

"Then what's providential?" David asked.

The red-haired girl became nervous and kept her hands behind her. "Your name's David, isn't it? Well, Dave, would you mind reading something I wrote? I'm always writing and last night . ... After Jensen left, I couldn't go to sleep." She spoke intensely, like Mona in a play. "All I could see was a group of actors trailing across the country. I wrote about it. Would you hear this? Please?" She thrust some pages into his hand, grabbed the tray, and ran off.

She called her story *Pierrot* and in the first eight sentences characterized Jensen so cleverly that David had to stop and laugh. The story concerned Jensen's pursuit of a young girl in a hick town, and the girl, who was made slightly ridiculous, was obviously Alison. A hilarious situation was developed which could have been resolved only by a complete and workmanlike seduction when suddenly the entire mood of the story changed, for as the boisterous lovers were crawling into the truck, the country girl saw the young man who played the lead. He was standing with the beautiful star of the play, and their love seemed so restrained and so genteel "like in the movies," that the country girl had no desire at all to climb into the truck. She wanted to be like the star, tall, aloof, and very beautiful with a self-contained young man standing worshipfully beside her. The story ended up in the air. A woman like the Gonoph walked in with her wig off, and the country girl didn't want to look like that. Not ever.

Apart from the good writing, the story had two remarkable qualities. Alison had seen this troupe only a few hours, but she had caught exactly the spirit of their movement across America. Her exaggerated description of David was so apt as to be embarrassing. He was made slightly ridiculous, but very much alive. The second noticeable aspect was more unusual than the first. Alison had made herself amusing, ridiculous and warm. "I don't see how I could change a line," David thought.

Mrs. Webster came in. "Oh!" she said, "I see Alison's given you one of her stories. She gets A at Goucher. They say she has a real talent." She straightened the bed. "What do you think?"

"I'd be afraid to tell you if it wasn't good," David laughed.

"Oh, but you should!" Mrs. Webster insisted. "All parents want their children to be able to sing or write. But they don't want them to beat their brains out if they lack talent."

"Alison can write," David said forcefully. Mrs. Webster stopped dusting and stood with her hand on her ample hip.

"Do you honestly think so?" she asked.

"Without question," David said. "I'm no critic, but I read a lot."

"That's what Reverend Shay says," Mrs. Webster confided. She seemed deeply troubled. "God knows how terrible it would be for parents to hold back a child with even a touch of genius." She wiped her face. "But there was a boy in this town thought he could paint." She shook her head sorrowfully. "I'd want no child of mine to drag herself through that misery. Lots of people think they can write," she argued.

"But your daughter could sell this story," David countered.

"Do you honestly think so?" the woman asked in serious tones. David raised his hands like a dubious merchant, and Mrs. Webster laughed. "I'm sure it's a worry to know how to do the right thing. But Alison has a very strong will. I don't thing she'll be a failure." She finished dusting and left the room.

It was some hours before Alison reappeared. "Well?" she asked.

"You know it's good," David replied.

"Sure," the cocky redhead laughed. "But do you?"

"Why don't you mail it right off? Just as it is?"

"Where?" the provocative girl asked.

"Well. . . . *The New Yorker,* maybe."

Alison closed her big eyes and smiled. "You're good luck! That's the one I chose last night." She opened her eyes and shook David's hand warmly. Then she sat on his bed until the doctor came. She told him freely of her plans for writing. "Mom's afraid I can't make a go of it, but I know I can. From the time I was a little girl I always saw things in stories. Not full stories like the one you read, but perfect little incidents. Last night, for example. I was ashamed of myself. The real reason I wouldn't get in the truck with Jensen was too ridiculous. Oh, I liked him well enough. We might have had a good friendly tussle. But all of a sudden I saw this story and he was just a character in it. I thought I would burst if I didn't get to a typewriter."

"What year are you at Goucher?" David asked.

"Next year I'm a senior. After that, New York!" She spoke with frank determination.

"Why don't you stay here and write?" David asked.

There was a long pause as if she was wondering whether to tell David the truth, and then she said, "Because I know th    t limits of my ability. I'm probably the smartest girl you've ever known, because I know what I can do. I'll never be great, but I can work till hell freezes over to get the right polish. And New York pays big for polish."

David was disturbed that anyone so young should have so clear a vision of the future. He browsed through the pages, and the polish was there. He guessed that she might go on and on for years, writing as well or better. Yet he felt that when he wrote, things would be different. The words would not line themselves up with such grace, but there would be more power indicated. His words would be tied more securely to what people wanted. The old women of the poorhouse would underline his writing for him.

The doctor said he was fine and that if Mrs. Webster wanted to she could drive him to the next town in time for the play. When they arrived at the brown tent the Gonoph hurried up and stared at David. "Are you all right?" she asked.

"I'm fine, Emma," he said.

"Oh, I'm so glad," she blurted. "We heard about it this afternoon."

When the shapeless woman left, Alison said, "She's in love with you, isn't she?"

"Are you planning another story?" David asked.

"When you're a writer, everything's a story," she replied, but when the time came to say good-bye she said, "It was very important, meeting you," and she kissed him on the lips.

The strangest event of the summer occurred by accident. Wild Man was driving the truck into Virginia and it was long past midnight when the men saw a woman of perhaps thirty-eight cross the road of a small village and go to her home. "She was real pretty!" Jensen said of the strange woman who was abroad at such an unlikely hour.

"You couldn't even see her!" David protested.

"So what?" Jensen asked. "All women are beautiful."

"You really believe that, don't you?" David mused.

"Sure!" the Wild Man replied. "I hate to get very far away from women. I like to eat with them, play with them, sleep with them." He hunched over the wheel. "And I don't necessarily mean sex, either. I just like girls."

"Why?" David pressed. He had sometimes felt the same way himself.

"Well," the Wild Man replied sagely, "I don't rightly know. Guess I've always been that way. In Kansas. We lived in one hell of a grubby town. I discovered that everyone in that town who really enjoyed life liked the other sex. We had some old women, by God, Dave, you wouldn't throw a bone to 'em. But they had a warmth about 'em, a real lovin' warmth. Why, I'd rather spend an afternoon with them than any man I ever knew. And do you know why those worn-out biddies wove such a spell? Because they had always liked men. Even when they were eighty they didn't change. They looked at me as if to say, 'We know you, young Jensen! We know what you're wantin'. Well, go to it, young feller. You ain't gonna live forever!' That's why I liked 'em."

He allowed the truck to weave back and forth across the highway and little Vito cried, "Hey, can't you drive this thing?"

Jensen called back through the opening, "You should be asleep! What's the matter? Little Betty givin' you hot pants?"

"I can wait," Vito replied.

"When you gettin' married?" Jensen called.

"After we close," the dwarf reported. "When you going to get married?"

"Me?" Jensen replied. "I could get married tomorrow. Or I could wait forever and strangle myself with anticipation. It ain't gettin' married that does it."

"Does what?" Vito asked. He poked his head through the slot.

"Makes you feel good," the Wild Man explained.

"Don't you ever fall in love?" the dwarf asked. He could never hear enough talk on this subject.

"Sure!" Jensen laughed. "I'm always in love. This town we're comin' to! I could stop on any street and fall in love and be happy for the rest of my life."

"How you talk!" Vito chided.

"You don't believe me?" Jensen roared, drunk with the starry night. "By God, son! I'll stop at the first likely house and pay such court as you've never seen! No particular woman matters. It's the idea of women that's important." He pushed his foot on the feed and the old truck roared into Claypool, Virginia.

He hunched forward and studied the silent town. It was now toward four, and in the distance a rooster crowed. Jensen drove down the silent streets until he came to a rattling milkman. He looked at the white-coated figure hurrying from house to house like an old woman with gossip.

Jensen turned away from the milkman and saw a light shining in the side street. "There she is!" he cried. "Waitin' for me!" He twisted the wheel violently and sent the truck after the light. A yellow shaft fell across a lawn and dirtied itself in the gutter. Jensen stopped in the middle of it and listened to a piano playing soft, straining music in the night.

He stepped into the gutter and walked across the lawn. He stood on tiptoe and looked into a white room. A woman, thin and angular, about thirty-eight, was playing Chopin. She approached a series of chords and Jensen said quietly, "Up late, aren't you?"

The tall pianist turned her head sharply and looked into the night. Her hands automatically drifted along to a pair of heavenly chords. "Who are you?" she asked.

Jensen pulled himself into the window. "I'm an actor with Chautauqua," he said. "I heard the music."

"Chautauqua doesn't play here any more," she said, trying to pierce the darkness.

"No," Jensen said, thrusting his big face into the room and smiling at the pianist. "We're headed south. Like the birds. Hey, Vito! Dave!" He shoved his feet through the window and said, "I want you to meet a remarkable little guy." He let himself into the room. "Say, what's your name, piano player?"

The tall, thin woman looked quietly at him and said, "Miss Agnes Welch."

"We'll let them in the door, Mi' Sagness." He opened the door and called Vito again. "Mi' Sagness, this is Vito, the puppet master. He can talk lower than you can play. And this is the hero of our little play, Mr. David Harper." Jensen was courtly in his manner, and Miss Agnes, as if it were the most logical thing in the world, welcomed the three young men into her spotless room. She showed them chairs.

"Wontcha go on playin', Mi' Sagness?" Jensen asked.

The tall woman smiled. "It's rather unusual, a concert at this hour. I give my lessons in the morning."

"It's most unusual playin' at all at this hour," Jensen countered. "What was the music? I don't know one note from another."

"Chopin," the music teacher replied.

"Good!" Jensen cried. "Our music teacher in school loved Chopin. Let's hear some more." He pulled his chair close to the piano and grinned at Miss Agnes. She looked at him a moment and then began to play one of the posthumous mazurkas. Jensen closed his eyes and said, "It's like people dancin' in hay."

The words had a terrible impact upon Miss Agnes, for she stopped playing and pressed her hands to her face. "What are you doing here?" she cried. "I must be mad!"

"It's very simple," Jensen replied, speaking softly and with the pronunciation Cyril used. "I bet each of these actors that I could stop at any house in Claypool and find a beautiful woman. Yours was the house I stopped at," he said quietly.

The piano teacher was confused that a stranger should talk so. She rose and said, "This is silliness!"

"Silliness!" Jensen echoed. "By heaven, Mi' Sagness! Do you want to hear some silliness? Come on, men, one of Vito's songs!" He beat time rapidly and made Vito sing one of the puppet songs. The dwarf's voice came very low, and Jensen joined with a mock soprano. Then David found himself caught in the nonsense and bellowed.

The milkman came stumbling through the near dawn and looked in. "You all right, Miss Agnes?" he asked.

The tall music teacher laughed nervously. "Yes," she said hurriedly. "I'm all right." The milkman shook his head and left.

"D'y' have any beer?" Jensen asked.

"Goodness, no!" she replied, fidgeting with her face.

"Well, can you play *Asleep on the Deep?*"

"Yes," she said.

"You play it," Jensen commanded. "Vito, you sing. I'll go make the sandwiches." He left the room and then hurried back to ask, "Mayonnaise all round?" In about ten minutes he appeared with a plateful of food. "Coffee's comin' up!" he said.

The four people ate their snack and Miss Agnes asked, "Are you really players?"

"Look at the truck!" Jensen said. He led her to the door and showed her the sign: Delaware Chautauqua. Then he snapped his fingers and cried, "Mi' Sagness! Why don't you come with us today. You'll see a play and the puppets! You'll dine with us! You can ride in front with me or sleep in back."

"I have students coming in a few hours," she protested.

"School's out!" the hairy-chested fellow cried. He found a pencil and made a big sign: *"No music classes today. Miss Agnes."* He passed it around for approval and predicted. "The kids'll love you for it!"

He banged about the very neat house and found her a light coat and hat. He helped her into these and pulled her to the door. "I must be insane!" she said. "Please, go away!"

The noise brought an old lady, a very old lady, to the head of the stairs. "What is it, Agnes?" she asked tremulously.

The angular music teacher looked into the street where the first rays of sunlight danced along the treetops. "I'm going to a play, Mother," she called.

"Where?" the old woman pleaded.

"Where?" Miss Agnes whispered. Then she called to her mother, "Henryville. Now you go back to bed. I'll be home tonight."

She rode up front with Jensen all the way. At the tent she helped unwrap the dolls and worked with Vito as he made them dance. After the marionettes the three men took her to a Virginia farm to dinner, where she was both amusing and gracious. During the play she remained backstage and helped David ring the telephone bell. "I used to love Chautauqua," she said. "I'm a music teacher because a very beautiful girl played the piano on Chautauqua one summer."

When the play ended Jensen left all the props just as they lay. The tent captain began to scream that things must be packed up. "That's right!" Jensen agreed. "You pack 'em." He and Dave drove Miss Agnes to the station. They stood on the starlit platform and listened for the slow train chugging around the bend. "I'd kiss you good-bye, Mi' Sagness," the Wild Man said, "but that would make everything look planned and ridiculous."

"Yes," she agreed quietly. "That would make things ridiculous."

"One question, Mi' Sagness. Why were you up at four o'clock? Playing?"

The angular woman watched the reluctant train approaching. "You won't laugh?" she asked.

"After today?" Jensen asked with a certain wildness in his voice, "Who would dare?"

"I was playing because the world is so unhappy. And lonely."

"A woman with your smile don't need to be lonely," Jensen protested.

"Oh, I'm not!" she assured him. "But the world! It's so wrong! It can't go on like this."

"What's the matter with it?" Jensen demanded.

"You travel across the country and you don't see the selfishness?" she cried.

"I don't see much wrong," he answered.

"Jensen!" she cried hungrily, catching at his hand. "One

thing! Get married. Find some good, strong girl. In the years that are coming you'll need a rock to lean upon."

"What do you mean?" Jensen asked quietly.

"You're young! Look at you, going about the country like a young stallion! The hard days of struggle are coming, Jensen, and some day you'll grow older." She stared directly into his face. "You are not strong enough to stand alone."

The train chugged into the station and sighed as if thinking of the eighty miles yet to go. Miss Agnes climbed aboard and waved good-bye to her strange friends. The conductor blinked a lantern like the last firefly of summer and the weary train went on.

Jensen watched it go and then turned furiously upon David, demanding. "Say it! Say I'd of wasted my life if I had gone ahead and married her. I dare you to say it!"

"They'll be raising hell at the tent," David warned.

"Let 'em!" the Wild Man shouted. "Christ! I could fight a tiger!"

In this last summer of his youth David had been like a reed at the edge of a marsh. Upon him played the last storms of September, and he bent with the wind. Soon the rains of autumn would come and he would be adrift in the full current out beyond the placid marsh; but for this one summer he was content to stay along the edges and to feel the thrilling winds of life upon him.

He realized his indecisive nature when he heard Jensen at work in the truck—with the broom flying—and discovered how beautifully simple life can be for some people. He had dozed off in the driver's seat of the truck when he was awakened by voices in the rear. The sliding window was open and he heard a splendid Southern voice joking with Jensen. "Why do you think you want to marry me?" the girl asked. She spoke with a deep drawl and pronounced her words as *yew, thank,* and *merry.*

"Well, for one thing," Jensen teased. He fell in with the Southern speech as if it were his own, saying *wun theng.* "For one thing it looks to me as if you was pretty well situated, financially speakin'. For another thing, a woman named Mi' Sagness told me to get married. And for the biggest reason of all, Ella-Mae, I have a sneaking suspicion . . . Only a suspicion, mind you, that you and me would be pretty torrid in bed."

"The things you say!" Ella-Mae laughed. "How'd you like my Cousin Vaban to find us in this yere truck?"

"I shore admire the way you say *cousin*," Jensen replied. "Good to hear a real Southern gal speakin' again."

"You from the South?"

"Ah'm from Kansas," Jensen explained. "When I'm up wid the Yankees I'm a hard-bitten business man. Down here Ah'm a Southerner."

"You one of them Yankees that's always fightin' the War between the States?"

"Ah truly admire to hear you say that phrase, Ella-Mae!" Jensen drawled. "My pappy beat me wid a club when he heard me call it the Civil War. You see, when you from Kansas"—he said *Kann-ziss*—"you don't hold much wid that North-South nonsense. My gran'daddy, he come here from Sweden, and for some screwball reason settled in Kansas. Well, both armies chased up and down acrost his land. He jined up wid whatever side was doin' the chasin'. Then when the other side started comin' back, he jined up wid them. No, if you come from Kansas the regions don't make much difference. Both sides was bastards."

"Ho ho!" Ella-Mae chuckled. "You better not let Cousin Vaban hear you speak like that."

"Cousin Vaban a pretty mean man?" Jensen asked.

"He thinks it's his biggest job in life to protect me."

"Well," Jensen reasoned, "if he's likely to come this way, we ain't got too much time to lose. Ella-Mae, yore sure gonna rumple that pretty dress of yourn. Why'n't chew pitch it over there onto that hook?" There was a long pause and then David heard Jensen sigh, "There . . . Ain't that more comfortable like?" Then he asked, "Do I smell pretty strong?"

"Like soap," Ella-Mae chuckled.

"Doin' this kind of work, a man ain't got too much chance to keep hisself clean. You perfectly comfortable?"

"I will be," the relaxed girl laughed, "if you keep that big mitt of yours to yourself."

"As you say!" the Wild Man promptly agreed. "There! Is that better?"

There was a sharp smack followed by hearty laughter and Ella-Mae said, "You were pretty concerned over not mussing my dress. Well, don't muss me, either."

"Ah, it's sweet!" Jensen exploded. "Lyin' here wid you. Honest, Ella-Mae, I ain't had a meal like that since I left home. Jesus, that was good!"

There was more silence which ended in a solid blow across Jensen's face. "First thing you know," Ella-Mae cried, "I'm gonna pitch you out of this truck."

"Honest to goodness, Ella-Mae, you remind me of David Harper!" Up front David caught his breath.

"Who's he?" the warm and pleasing girl inquired.

"He plays in our show. He's always perplexed about somethin' that's gonna happen in the future. Why don't you lie back here and relax?"

"How do you define *relax?*" she teased.

"Sort of like this," the Wild Man replied. There was a long and humid silence, broken by a sharp cry from the other side of the tent. A tall man with a gun stormed into the marionette area and started shouting for Ella-Mae.

"It's Vaban!" Ella-Mae whispered behind David's ear.

"Better get some clothes on!" Jensen said calmly. There was a rustle in the truck as Ella-Mae's cousin stormed up to where David sat.

"You see my girl?" he bellowed.

"No," David said.

"They told me she ran off on a date with one of them actors. Where is he?"

"He don't show up till about eight," David said.

"Where'd he likely be?" the angry man demanded.

"You got any speakeasies?" David asked. The man growled and went roaring off.

"Vaban's a mean bastard," Ella-Mae whispered.

When the ruckus had subsided, the rear doors of the truck opened slowly and a happy girl climbed down, followed by Wild Man Jensen. He carried in his left hand a lethal chunk of lead pipe which Vito used for propping up one end of the stage. The Wild Man stood content and relaxed, peering about for signs of Cousin Vaban. David hurried up to him and asked, "What would you have done if her cousin had found you?"

"Done?" Jensen echoed, brandishing his lead pipe. "Why, I'd a knocked his goddamn brains in!"

David was unprepared for a Chautauqua closing night. The professionals knew what to expect, and they were smiling even before the curtain went up. The first act was not five minutes old when the Gonoph let out a little scream. Vito had given her a fried egg. She had to make four speeches with it in her left hand, and the yolk was not fried hard. It trickled from her fingers.

Everyone tried to miscue Cyril and threw him lines from the last act. He bore their joking well although a bit stiffly and astonished Jensen by handing him not the letter which established the plot but a picture of a nude woman and Santa Claus. Indeed, Chautauqua did not die somberly. David seeking to imprison in his mind the look of everyone on this last night, studied Mona as she stood gracefully beside him. She seemed more lovely than ever, more controlled, and his heart went out to her, wishing her good luck; but at the close of their kiss she left a dead catfish in his hand.

He stood with the smelly fish and tried to pass it on to Jensen or Vito, but they saw his predicament and kept far away. He stood there with it until the play closed. They gave three curtain calls and Cyril made a little speech. Then, when they were alone on their own side of the curtain, the Gonoph cried and Mona kissed each of the men. Cyril stood very stiff beside her and David had to admit they were a handsome couple. "Best tour we've ever had," Cyril said. "A certain verve, I think." To the Gonoph he bowed from the waist and said, "You were superb, my dear. Superb!"

Reluctantly David left the wooden stage for the last time. Like Lot's wife he turned back and saw his players standing in odd groups: the Gonoph between Mona and Cyril, Vito scratching his nose, and Jensen telling the tent captain to go to hell. David had an overwhelming desire to fix these people forever in his memory as they were then: the players, the fine and wonderful people with whom he had toured! The tent lights flickered out and in their place shone the one strong, glaring light. Now humans became shadows, as in a Shakespearean play, vague drifting things that tangled in one's heart. "I wonder if any of them feel this way," David mused. The intensity of this final moment tormented him, and he went to the dressing room.

Then he had to admit that part of his life was over. A smell accomplished this, a subtle, mixed-up smell of dry canvas, trampled grass turning into hay, and the penetrating odor of grease paint and cold cream. He was slapping a handful of the latter on his tired face when he realized that never again would he smell that particular combination of odors. He rubbed the cool stuff into his cheeks and eyebrows, and when he opened his eyes part of the smell was gone forever. The tent crew had ripped away the canvas.

Vito came to him with a package. "It's Bosco," the dwarf said. "Thought you might like to keep him."

"Thanks," David said. "Where are you going now?"

"Florida," Vito replied. He pointed across the fallen tent to where the Fletchers stood. "Dave!" the little man said passionately. "I could never . . ."

"Forget it!" David replied brusquely. Jensen came up with two girls. "Well!" he announced. "It's a job on Wall Street for me!"

"I want to thank you, Wild Man," the dwarf said.

"It's nothing, son!" Jensen replied expansively. "All I ask is that you advise your father-in-law to buy his stocks from me." The hairy-chested fellow grabbed his girls. "So long, Dave!" he shouted.

Then Mona and Cyril primly picked their way across the fallen tent. Mona avoided an embarrassing farewell, but in spite of this David wanted to shout good wishes to them; yet when he started to do so he saw Cyril place a protecting arm about the girl, as if she were a little child, and everything seemed false and silly. "To hell with them both!" he muttered, turning his back upon them; but immediately he felt ashamed and cried, "Good luck! Good luck! I'll see your name in lights."

And so, in the most ordinary town they had seen all summer, at eleven-thirty one December night, the last Chautauqua tent came down. David watched the crew box up the stage for the last time, and he sensed that someone was staring at him. He turned and there stood the Gonoph. She was like a dumb ox, her body sagging toward the earth.

"Better watch out, Emma," he warned. "That pole's coming down."

"I'm all right," she said.

He reached for his bag and started into town, but decency would not permit such a departure. He looked back at the sodden woman, and her eyes were still following him. He gulped and said, "Emma, how's about a bite to eat?"

She almost stumbled running to him. "Hey!" she cried. "I don't mind if I do!" He took her bag and they started off toward town. When they had walked a short distance she put her arm in his. "Do you mind?" she asked.

"The suitcase'll bump you," he warned.

"Who cares?" she said happily as they walked like lovers through the little Southern town.

# PART 5

# The Valley

WHERE EIGHTH STREET crosses Fourth Avenue in New York City a new thoroughfare begins. It is called Lafayette Street, and its first wide block is like a business square in London or Brussels. It is snugly closed at the north end, but its open vista shows the towering skyscrapers which rise at the tip of New York's island.

This strange block bespeaks the great city of which it is a part, for along its eastern side runs the squat and massive headquarters of the Hebrew Immigrant Aid Society. To this ugly building with its ancient Hebraic instructions carved in red stone came dispossessed Poles and Russians and all the wandering tribes on their first day in the free land. Even now shawled figures or old men in beards come back to Lafayette Street to gaze once more upon that ugly building where their hopes began.

Across the street, on the western side, cluster several neat buildings which are used as warehouses by uptown stores. And between these trim new buildings lies a meaner establishment, a remnant of the old city. Above its grubby door hangs a small wooden sign: THE CLAY PUBLICATIONS. To this sign in the early winter of 1931 came David Harper with a letter.

He was met inside by a thin, acidulous woman who opened his letter, even though it was marked personal, and said,

"Mr. Clay will see you." She led David like a schoolboy through a roaring pressroom where thousands of magazines were stacked and into an immaculately clean office. She sniffled petulantly and whined, "Mr. Clay, this is David Harper."

A small trim man in a dark suit rose and extended a well-washed hand. "Morning," he said with no enthusiasm. "I'm Tremont Clay." The thin woman left.

Mr. Clay nodded primly toward a chair. "Sit down," he said with a nasal twang. When he read the letter of introduction he wrinkled his nose and then looked at David. "How well do you know Miss Webster?" he demanded sharply, as if words were knives to cut away pretensions.

"I met her one night," David replied.

"Out necking?" the little man asked with distaste.

"I was visiting her mother," David lied. "She remembers me because I suggested that she send her first story to *The New Yorker*."

Mr. Clay tossed Alison's letter of introduction onto his desk and laughed, a miserable whining laugh. "Her first story! She wrote things for us before she was out of college."

"Alison did?" David asked.

He heard Miss Adams cry from the outer office, "Coming in!" Shoving her way past David, she tossed onto Mr. Clay's desk a lurid picture splashed with primary colors. A girl was having her dress torn off by a vile man. One breast was almost bare and most of her thigh. She had a look of complete horror in her eyes, which were quite large.

"No, no!" Mr. Clay said with great patience. "You! Look at this quick and tell me what you see first." He flashed the picture before David's face and demanded, "Whadcha see?"

"I saw . . . well, the eyes."

"Certainly!" Clay said softly. Then he spoke to the woman, "Tell him he's got three weeks to learn to make the eyes smaller. Focus here," he said gently, tapping the breast with his pencil. He waved the woman out of his office. Then he stared at David.

"You ever been an editor?" he snapped.

"No."

"Police reporter? Writer? Rewrite man? What have you done?"

"I've always been good in English," David said forcefully.

Clay snorted. Contemptuously he kicked open a door and waved his arm toward five girls huddled over desks. "Everybody comes in here for a job was good in English. It's the most useless thing in the world to be good in. You ever study law?"

"No," David said.

The little man sneered at him and said, "You wouldn't be much use to me, would you?"

David became angry and snapped, "I've been around a lot. I want a job. I can handle it."

The forcefulness of his reply pleased Clay, who suddenly banged a pile of magazines in front of David. On the cover of each a girl was being raped, one by a gorilla. "All right," the thin little man snarled, "how many of these do you know?"

"I used to read *Great Crimes* and *Real Western*. I worked in a park one summer."

"What's the plot of *Great Crimes?*"

"What do you mean?" David asked.

"The plot! The plot!" Clay demanded nervously. "The way each story unfolds."

Dizzily David tried to recall the bright, greasy books of Paradise. They blurred in his mind. "I can't recall," he said.

Clay leaned back and studied the young man with tousled hair. Finally he asked quietly, "You ever submit any stories to me? Under a nom de plume?"

"No," David had to admit.

"Well," Mr. Clay said abruptly, "that's that. Miss Adams!" he called. "Show the young man out."

But at the door David asked. "Did you say that Alison Webster had written stories for you?"

There was something so quizzical in the young man's manner that Mr. Clay saw an opportunity to befuddle him further, and with ghoulish pleasure he said, "Come here a minute." He laughed, and the sound was dreadful, like a pinched-up snicker. Deftly he pulled out a filing drawer and flicked the cards with his forefinger. "She used seven different names. Very imaginative stories of love and crime."

"You mean she had sold you stories before I met her?" David asked suspiciously.

With malignant pleasure Clay laughed and said, "Sure. Look here, son!" Proudly the little man riffled the cards and let David see one well-known name after another.

"Do they all write for you?" he asked.

"Sure!" the tight little man chuckled. "Not by their real

names, of course. You see, we don't pay much, but we pay very promptly." Mr. Clay slammed the drawer shut.

But David had already reached in to see more of the names, and the heavy drawer banged on his wrist. "Damn it!" he cried, and Clay jerked the drawer open. David withdrew his hand, still holding half dozen cards. "I should keep my mitts out of other people's property," he laughed. "But these names fascinate me."

"You'd really like to work here, wouldn't you?" Clay asked.

"I sure would!" David replied.

Clay jumped to his feet and walked around David, making noises in his throat. Suddenly he snapped, "Miss Adams! Take this young feller up to see Morris Binder." With a violent push he shoved David out into the pressroom where the cover of *Sex Detective* was being printed. That was the magazine Tremont Clay himself edited, and the girl on his cover was almost completely nude.

Scrawny Miss Adams led David up a flight of dark stairs. At the top she said, "Morris Binder's in here," but her words ran together as if she had said, "Ris Biner's nere." Then she added ominously, "If you want this job, put your thinking cap on. Morris Binder's a very great editor."

She kicked open a door with the nervous gesture that seemed part of Tremont Clay's publishing house. "There he is!" she snapped, pointing across an incredibly messy office to an immense roll-top desk across which slumped an even more massive man of fifty. Morris Binder looked up. He had gargantuan, sagging jowls that hung upon his soiled shirt. His forehead was huge, and hair grew down upon it. Both his mouth and his eyes drooped at the ends, and when he moved his massive body he did so with ponderous and gasping difficulty.

"Young man to see you," Miss Adams said briskly. "Boss sent him up."

Slowly, like a prehistoric animal, Morris Binder turned toward David and lowered his head so that he could see above the half-glasses that sagged upon his fat nose. He grunted several times. "Ugggh. Ugggh. Yessss." He studied David and asked, "Major?"

"English."

"Ugggh. Yessss. Wasted years. Who was Henryson?"

David thought he should know that name. His brain began to whir, and he said tentatively, "I'd . . . say . . . he . . .

was . . ." Morris Binder looked at him with immense sad eyes, betraying nothing. "Oh, sure!" David cried. "He was the Scottish poet who wrote about Cressida. He made her a leper, and all the evil of the world fell upon her."

At these words the powerful eyes of the huge man lighted up. David saw this, and he knew that Morris Binder liked him. Wheezingly the immense man looked away so that his eyes were hidden by the strange half-glasses. Then deftly he twirled a long, shining letter opener in the air so that it fell quiveringly into the roll-top desk, its point far imbedded in the oak. "He'll do," he grunted.

He indicated that David was to sit beside him. "You'll be my assistant," he said. He pointed with a ponderous and pudgy finger at a calendar which had six dates circled in red. "That's your Bible. It's your Koran, too, and the Bhagavad-Gita. No other days matter, because those are the deadlines for my magazines. Ugggh. Ugggh." He bent over and rummaged from the mess on his desk four lurid journals: *Great Crimes, Bare Confessions, Real Love* and *Rodeo Yarns*. "It's our job to fill 'em up, rain or shine."

A sudden clicking noise interrupted, and Morris Binder ponderously turned to study a wavering ticker-tape as it punched its way into his fat hand. "Crime news," he explained abruptly. Apparently there was little happening, for he ripped the tape from the machine and threw it into the crumpled mess on his desk.

"Run off to the mail room," he grunted, "and haul back the day's bilge."

David returned with a huge basket of brown envelopes. "Dump it right here," Morris Binder said, smashing a clear space on his cluttered desk. The Manila envelopes formed a small mound, and the immense editor ripped his long steel opener from its quivering position in the oak.

"The imperative thing," the hulking man gasped, "is not to lose any of this swill. I don't care whether you read it or not. But the minute you lose any of this garbage it becomes immortal."

"How do you avoid losing them?" David asked, as he watched the editor rip into the pile and scatter the manuscripts into various piles.

"Memory," Morris Binder replied. "Here's the trick. You learn it!" As rapidly as he could, he snatched one manuscript after another, noted it briefly, announced the title to David, and tossed it face down on the floor. His voice came in short grunts: *My Sin at the Roadhouse,* Carpenter, Oklahoma. *Was Duryea Really Murdered?* Lassiter, Maine. *New Light on the Hall-Mills Case,* Stanley, New Jersey. *My Wicked Stepmother,* Chambers, Wyoming.

He droned on through about forty titles of crime and sex. Then he directed David to lift the manuscripts one by one and to announce their titles. David said, *"Was Duryea Really Murdered?"*

"Lassiter of Maine sent that one in," the big man puffed. "We run a story on it every seven or eight months. Wonderful murder. A nude dancer was accused. We got a lot of pictures of her nearly naked. Makes a fine spread."

*"My Sin at the Roadhouse,"* David said.

"That's by this moron Carpenter in Oklahoma. Good standard product. Four dabs of sexual intercourse and never uses a wrong word."

"What do you mean, wrong word?" David asked.

"Lesson one!" Morris Binder said solemnly, staring at David above his funny glasses. "No word can be used that would offend a girl of sixteen." He rumbled off a list of extremely ugly words, the phrases of clandestine passion and eroticism. "They're all *verboten. Nicht!*"

"I never realized that," David replied. "The covers sort of mislead you."

"That's our great secret!" Morris Binder chuckled, flipping the long steel blade into the resisting oak. "Nowhere in America can you find a cleaner set of filth than what we produce. An ugly word never appears. Lots of people wonder why we don't get into trouble. I've told you why. High-tone companies like Scribner and Harper and Macmillan. They get into trouble all the time. Because they have high-tone writers who insist on using the wrong words. Why, there's never even been a *damn* in one of Clay's filthy rags."

David looked doubtfully at his pachydermatous new boss. He couldn't tell whether Morris Binder was joking or not, nor was he ever to know. The immense man would not disclose his inner attitude toward the dismal magazines he edited. To him they were a set of well-established rules, and he happened to know the rules better than anyone else. All over America people lusted for stories of horrible murder and raw sexual passion. And no magazines supplied these appetites so well as Morris Binder's, for the man had a true genius in using erotic images, gory details and suggestive incidents.

Yet Binder was a graduate with honors from Harvard. He

was expert in music and art, and he was certainly more widely read than anyone David had previously known. His memory was prodigious, and he was a criminal expert often consulted by the New York police. But in spite of these great gifts he worked for Tremont Clay.

On pay day Mr. Clay said to David, "You're lucky. Morris Binder turned down eight men before he took you. He's a genius, but don't you try to work the way he does. Set up a system, the way I do." The little man pulled his trim blue suit into position and pointed to a set of intricate files. "Even so," he said petulantly, "I wish I had a mind like Morris Binder's."

With a fox-like gesture he grabbed a copy of *Bare Confessions*. He flipped the pages until he found *My Night of Sin*. His quick finger sought out a line: "Then we went to bed again, if you know what I mean."

"That's wonderful!" Clay said enviously. *"If you know what I mean!* Morris Binder thought that one up some fifteen years ago. It conveys everything but doesn't say anything. No court could hold Binder responsible for corrupting youth with that phrase. Do you see how clever it is? Even a stupid person can reason that if he doesn't know what is meant, he better find out. The peasants write our stories for us! *If you know what I mean!"* The tight little man laughed maliciously as he thought of the numberless morons of America who could be so easily titillated by auto-eroticism.

Thrusting his hands deep in his pockets the little man lectured David. "Always be on the alert for a phrase like that. We print only the cleanest material, but we must be studious to find words that suggest otherwise. And watch Morris Binder! He's the genius around here."

It was obvious that Tremont Clay loved his work. His magazines were the best of their kind. His covers were the sexiest, his illustrations the most provocative, and his stories the most easily followed. It was a standard, filthy product that Clay dispensed, and he did so with no illusions. As a young man he had set out consciously to debauch as many people for as much money as possible. He had been vastly successful, for now he published twenty-six magazines. On some days four different ones appeared, on pulp paper filled with specks, with pulp stories crawling with the specks of passion and human indignity. Murder, sex, despair and spiritual hunger marched beside illiterate cowmen, weird monstrosities of so-called scientific fiction, and imaginary baseball games in which the right team always won in the last half of the ninth inning. It was incredible that a great democracy could digest each month the slops pumped into it by Tremont Clay.

There was not one magazine of the twenty-six that dealt with human beings. They dealt with symbols, tricky words, and innuendoes that suggested erotic events. Not even the blood that filled the crime stories was real. "People don't want real stories," Clay insisted.

Morris Binder expressed it differently. He said, "Lonely lives have got to be spiced up with something. If there's good money in such work, I might as well get some of it." David heard this and wondered what the great heaving man meant, for it was common knowledge that Binder received only a modest salary. "Why does he work here?" David asked himself.

Now, thanks to Alison Webster, David had both a job and a riotous place to live. At Mom Beckett's, where Alison also roomed, he had a dingy hall bedroom on the fourth floor. An unshaded light swayed from the ceiling. A faded rug curled up along the edges of the room, and a bleak window opened onto a barren expanse of brick wall.

But there was a warmth about this room that made David think of it always with the bright happiness of youth, for this room was on MacDougal Street, just off Washington Square, and it took no great imagination to see in it the gay ghosts of Eugene O'Neill, Theodore Dreiser, John Sloan, and Edna St. Vincent Millay. But the actual warmth of the room came from none of these famous inhabitants of Greenwich Village. It came from Mom Beckett herself.

She was a big woman of fifty-odd. She was from Arizona, and the vast expanses of that sun-drenched state shone in her expressive blue eyes. For many years she had been a nurse, of sorts. She said, "They taught me how to make the bed without disturbing the patient. That paid twenty bucks a week. Then I learned to make the patient without mussing the bed. That paid lots better." Admirers had given her various sums of money. Three elderly men had settled retirement annuities upon her, and she ran a restaurant in the Village until the day when the annuities began. "Hell," she cried in her harsh, desert voice, "if that damn fool Al Smith don't repeal prohibition, I'll be a rich woman in five more years."

She sustained a kind of running fight with all officers of the law. Prohibition agents were no more repulsive to Mom

Beckett than fire inspectors. Tax collectors and health authorities alike felt her scorn, and it was a tribute to the freedom of New York that she was tolerated. "I'll tell you why they let me alone," she said to David. "Nobody at City Hall can be sure which big shots used to be my boy friends."

When David had roomed with her for two weeks he saw her in action for the first time. Hearing a great commotion in MacDougal Street, he rushed down to find Mom Beckett holding a fire inspector by the lapels of his uniform. "I'm sure," she said in soft, wheedling tones, "that down at headquarters you're known as quite a little hero. But on Mac-Dougal Street," and she burst into an Arizona bellow, "you're nothin' but a horse's ass." She thrust him away from her, and the distraught man was engulfed by hilarious ridicule.

"He'll padlock your place!" David cried above the racket.

"A pismire like him!" Mom laughed. "Hell, he wasn't inspectin' my place."

"What was he doing?" David asked.

"He was botherin' the Eyetalian," Mom explained. "I don't like upstart shrimps like him." She paused in her conversation to fling a taunt at the retreating fire inspector. Then she invited the hangers-on into her restaurant for a drink of bootleg.

She was a handsome, well-preserved woman. Her hair showed no gray, and her teeth were big and white. She wore heavy corsets and seemed to be completely laced into a buxom feminine form. David never saw her when she was mussed, not even in the midst of public brawls, in which she loved to engage. Her hair was always plastered down with a thick pomade, and her ample face was perpetually ready for an explosive smile.

Her restaurant served very poor food, because she could never keep her Chinese cooks very long. As a young girl, she had traveled with her father through Western camps and had grown to respect Chinese cooks, but they would not tolerate her peremptory manners. "By God!" she stormed, "in my day they'd a horsewhipped you, Ching Lee."

"Not your day, my day!" the cooks would flare.

"You get the hell out of here!" she would storm.

"You bet I get out!" the cooks would scream, and before they left they would usually wreck the place, and there would be a violent scene, and Mom would end it, standing very neat and laced up, at the door, shouting up MacDougal Street at the back of the fleeing cook, "I dare you to come back here, you yellow bastard!"

Then she would come into the restaurant and slump disconsolately in a chair, staring at a tall bearded man who guarded her cash register. "Damn you, Claude!" she would snarl. "You musta been castrated when you were a baby. Why'd you let that lousy Chink insult me? Why he coulda killed me for all you care!"

Then the gentle bearded man behind the counter would grin at Mom and say, in a low voice, "Now who's going to cook?"

"You'll have to cook," Mom always replied. And that's why the food was so bad. Because Claude was a poet. He never made any money, nor did he ever have any, except what Mom gave him. He was in his late forties, a thin, gentle fellow who had written some excellent verse, which had been published to critical acclaim. Mom had paid the bills for his books, and it was pretty well established that Claude either was then or had been her lover. He was like some strange tropical flower that bloomed at intervals of nine or ten years. His whole output was not over a hundred poems, and he had not produced a volume since 1926.

But he had a delicate touch—in everything except cooking —and it was from him that David learned the soft, fiery, passionate, steely-cold, infuriating, tender and earth-moving quality of words. One night, after a departing Chinese cook had upset forty pounds of rice and a gallon of molasses, Claude stood scratching his beard as he surveyed the mess that he would have to clean up. Behind him, in the restaurant, two writers were arguing. One said, "The Village is like a refuge from the banalities of this city."

"No!" the poet said quietly. "We live in the hidden valley between the breasts of Manhattan."

"Say!" one of the men said. "That's good, Claude. Can I use that?"

But the poet was already at work mopping up the rice and molasses. Yet the felicitous phrase hung in David's mind for days, like a fly caught in a web. Then one day he took a ferry ride to Weehawken and on his return chanced to see the skyline of Manhattan with the uptown and downtown skyscrapers forming metallic breasts. His Village lay in between.

Mom's restaurant was in the basement, and contained two dozen small wooden tables with red-and-white-checked oilcloth covers. In one corner stood a piano at which Claude sometimes strummed. An old bar, now officially closed, remained along one wall, and by gradual degrees Mom had reopened it as a full-fledged bar. Bootleg was delivered openly from trucks that backed up to the blue door of her restaurant. Four or five times a year her place was raided, and she was often heavily fined. But by common agreement, the police never looked into the big room next to the one in which Mom slept. For in spite of her unending feud with the law, the police tolerated her as a necessary evil. Men were going to buy liquor somewhere, and Mom behaved herself, more or less.

She looked upon David as she looked upon all young men who worked at writing or editing. "If you're an honest-to-God man, why ain't you got an honest-to-God job?" she demanded.

"If you despise writers so much," David countered, "why do you make such a fuss over Claude?"

Mom didn't bat an eye. She looked firmly at David and said, "Some unfortunates is got to write. They can't help themselves. But why should a clean young fellow like you consciously mess up his life thataway?"

"Mom," David laughed. "They tell me you pay to have Claude's books published."

"Sure I do!" the big woman replied. Then her rasping Arizona voice continued, "In America they's some kind of men can't make a livin'. Somebody's gotta support 'em, even if it's a woman."

And across time came Old Daniel's voice saying the same words: "Sometimes good men don't prosper," and David felt both frightened for himself and strangely alive; for he felt that he was reliving a part of his life, as if time repeated itself, as if there were only a few things in all the world worth knowing, as if Old Daniel and Professor Immanuel Tschilczynski and Mom Beckett were the same person, hammering away at the same truths.

"Why are you trying to scare me?" he asked the big, handsome woman.

"Kid," she said, "in my time I've fed more'n forty writers here. Give 'em handouts like they was paupers. 'N I suppose you wanta be a writer, too?"

"That's right," David said grimly, as if he were taking a solemn oath.

"Well, you're a horse's ass," Mom said, with deep pity.

When David realized that he was going to room only one floor away from Alison Webster, he inadvertently whistled and thought, "Oh, boy!"

But whatever plans that exclamation implied were abortive, for Alison had neither the time nor the inclination to indulge in fooling. She had fled Baltimore and come to New York to make her fortune in the way young men, centuries ago, had come to Paris, to London or to Rome. When David met her in Mom's restaurant she was thinner and did her red hair in bangs that had become fashionable. Her complexion was improved, and she wore trim, stylish clothes to match it. She seemed much neater than her surroundings. In short, she was a New York girl, and, like all of them, the product of a small town.

"You look like a new person!" David exclaimed. "Would you let me take you out to dinner?"

Alison pursed her lips and then smiled generously so that her superb white teeth flashed in the dingy restaurant. "Let's do!" she said with exaggerated eagerness. She led David to a fashionable Chinese restaurant where she instructed him in the best dishes. But he noticed that she merely toyed with her portion.

"Aren't you going to eat the shrimps?" he asked.

"Dave!" she laughed. "Don't you know? Fat girls don't rate in this city." Apparently his jaw dropped, for she added, "You look hungry, Dave. Here. You finish them."

"Aren't you hungry?" he countered.

"Sure I'm hungry!" she cried, pushing the dish at him. "I'm always hungry! But I won't be a blubbery pig." She patted her lean stomach.

"I must admit," David laughed as he chomped on the delicious shrimp, "that you look twice as pretty." Then he noticed the excited, beautiful cast of her face. "You were fat and freckly when I knew you. Alison, why did you kid me about writing? You'd already sold a lot of stories to Tremont Clay."

"How do you like Clay's emporium?" she countered.

"Well," he said thoughtfully, "it's a way to make a living."

"That's how I feel about *Fashion*," she replied.

"That's a pretty glossy magazine, isn't it? Flashy and frothy?"

"Sure it is!" Alison agreed. At times she could be an eager country girl, but immediately she resumed her New York pose and said, pushing away her dessert, "That's how you learn. When I knew all Tremont Clay could teach me, I stopped writing for the pulps. But if you think the flashy *Fashion* touch is easy . . . Say, David! How'd you like to do a story on Chautauqua? You know, Stylized! Lots of schmalz." She became excited and in a flash sketched with her long hands a complete layout. "We'd have a montage with William Jennings Bryan, that ham, and a clown falling off the page."

"There never were any clowns on Chautauqua," David explained.

"So what! That's what people expect. Give it to them."

"Articles aren't my line," David said. "If I ever wrote about Chautauqua it would be . . . Well, it would be very hard for me to do."

"I know that!" Alison said haughtily. "Genius stuff. But I'm talking about a quickie. Call it 'The Old Brown Tents.' New York highbrows'd love it."

"I can't write that way," David insisted. Alison became furious, but the Chinese waiter appeared with the bill, and David used it as an opportunity to change the subject.

But in the street Alison pursued her attack. "You want to be a writer. Mom told me you said so. Then write! Write anything. Advertisements, pulps, *Fashion* goo, even rhymes on toilet walls. People who dream of the great book but never start . . ." Her flashing eyes searched Washington Square and fell upon an old bum panhandling dimes. "Such people," she said harshly, "are self-deceiving sons-a-bitches."

The next day she returned to heckle David about the Chautauqua article. "I spoke to Mrs. Clint," she said, "and she agreed that a zippy article on the traveling tents would be good. Chance for a lot of nostalgia."

David said simply, "It's not my line."

To his surprise, Alison showed no irritation. "Maybe you'll want to write later. By the way, what's your troupe doing now?"

"Mona Meigs, she was the lead you know. She and Cyril Hargreaves are in the repertory theatre uptown."

"And the dwarf?"

"He married the little girl we found him. He does radio work, bits here and there."

"And my hero? What was his name?"

David began to laugh and feel good. "Jensen! The Wild Man! He has a job on Wall Street." Impulsively David reached out and tried to kiss Alison, but she pushed him away.

"You liked Jensen a lot, didn't you?" she asked.

"Just thinking of that galoot makes me feel good all over." David said expansively. Again he tried to kiss the handsome girl who was studying him, but again she eluded him.

"What became of that awful dumpy woman?" she asked.

"I don't know," David replied.

Seven weeks later Mom started to bellow from the restaurant. "Hey, Dave! Dash on down and see what I see!" David galloped downstairs and there stood Mom with a copy of *Fashion.* On page 37 appeared an article by Alison Webster: "The Good Brown Tents." It was flashily done and contained a brilliant montage of William Jennings Bryan, some Swiss bellringers and a clown falling off the page. Even though Alison had falsified the clown on Chautauqua, the idea was effective. Mom Beckett cried, "Stitch my britches with barbed wire! Look at that clown!"

The big woman went out into the street and called in all her neighbors. "We got two geniuses in this dump now!" she cried. And when Alison got home there was a celebration, and the poet Claude made a wreath of vine leaves for her, out of green paper, and Mom broke open some red wine and champagne, and Alison sat flushed and happy, smiling so that her white teeth were brilliant against her red lips, and David felt very happy.

Morris Binder was an excellent teacher. Secure in his own preeminence, he was prodigal in sharing tricks with David. "Learn the rules," he advised. "Get your girls straight first. In this racket girls are either good or bad. Mostly they're good. Establish this in the first few paragraphs. The girl is good to her mother. She sings in a church choir. She's pretty. She wears a simple white dress and has no breasts. She wears curls. She goes to the movies and has ice cream afterwards. She likes one young man. It's possible for two men to like her, but she can never like more than one. Blue is also a good color for a good girl. Avoid the unusual shades. She can be either blonde or brunette. Never a redhead. She doesn't wear sweaters. Never drinks or smokes. She has clean white teeth and frank eyes. But above all, she has nothing to do with sex. She doesn't even know about it. If sex enters the story it's always forced upon her. By a bad man. She absolutely cannot have a child unless she's married. A girl who does is automatically bad. We have no place for wronged girls. They're either good or bad. But a good man by immediately marrying a good girl who has been wronged by a bad man automatically makes her a good girl again. You got that straight!"

The immense man wheezed a few times and then described the bad girl. "For one thing, she wears sweaters. She can drink or smoke, but if she does she's automatically bad. She can be interested in sex, but only as a weapon to tear down some good man. She can't enjoy it with a bad man. She sometimes has a baby out of wedlock, but she mustn't love the baby. That's reserved for good girls. She isn't good to her parents, doesn't go to church, can visit plushy night clubs. She wears strange colors like chartreuse instead of honest yellow. She sports an expensive hairdo and probably has money. Money is always bad. She has a car of her own, a convertible, which she uses in seducing clean young men. She never kisses. She embraces. And so on."

"It sounds silly to me," David said.

"Maybe it is," the big editor wheezed. "But it's what most Americans think. And when they read one of our stories, Socko! Right in the first line! They know whether the girl is good or bad."

"What about the men?" David asked.

"The important thing is always to have bad men chasing good girls or good men in the toils of bad girls. That's what makes a story."

"How can you spot the good men?" David asked.

"Well," Morris Binder said reflectively, "good men aren't interested in sex. They like games and church and their mothers. They work hard for small salaries. But sometimes the good man is very rich, in which case he doesn't care for the wealthy girls of his set, who are always bad. I think it's better if he doesn't go to college. We haven't quite made up our minds as to whether college men are good or bad. Of course, if he's an athlete—especially an end or a basketball player—he can be good. Backfield men are showoffs and seducers. Tennis players are pansies. Give me a garage man or an honest laborer! Everybody knows they're good."

The huge editor continued for several days, dropping hints here and there about the four types of Americans: good and bad men and women. There were no in-between categories, no shades of behavior. This confused David, for he tried to fit his friends into Morris Binder's four groups. They didn't fit. Marcia Moomaugh, for example, was obviously a good girl. She was strong and clean and fine, yet she was interested in sex and was therefore typed by Tremont Clay's magazines as bad. And what about himself? Clearly, he was bad! He had been involved with girls, had stolen money from Paradise, and had despised his aunt. Yet he did not feel like a bad man. He felt merely like a man of confused purposes, and he guessed that most people he had known were like him in that respect.

Not even Mona Meigs conformed to Morris Binder's clear-cut definitions. If David had ever known a bad girl, it was Mona. Yet the first rule of Clay's magazines was that if a girl—any girl—opposed a bad man, she automatically became good. And Mona had opposed Max Volo from the first. But there was something else that lifted Mona from any classification of bad. David knew that of all the people he had met in the world—Old Daniel, Marcia, Doc Chisholm, Vito—Mona was the only one who had a chance of being an absolutely first-rate person. If only she could establish herself on the stage or in the movies she would show living greatness to the world. For she was great, hard, fiery great. And the petty categories of good and bad seemed, when applied to her, terribly inconsequential.

David spoke of this to his new boss, and Morris Binder laughed. "We live in two worlds," he said. "Ninety-nine per cent of our experience falls in the world of Tremont Clay's magazines. Newspapers, radio, novels, plays divide things into hard and fast symbols. Read the headlines! *Beast Murders Beautiful Singer!* I know probably five thousand murders intimately. Apart from a half dozen insane men, who are always very gentle killers, the so-called beasts are amazingly complex. They love their mothers, are kind to their sisters. They give money to the Red Cross. They also abandon pregnant girls and steal from their employers. They're like you and me, but when they do a notable thing they've got to be labeled. *Beast* is a good, short word that fits into headlines. That's why we use it."

"And the other one per cent?" David asked.

Morris Binder closed his eyes and drummed on the desk with his letter opener. "You ever listen to Beethoven's *Eroica?* How complex that is. An ode to Napoleon, that master murderer. Yet the music is noble to the point of rapture. You know Raskolnikov? What do you think of him? Or that black beast, Othello?" He opened his eyes and leaned far back in his heavy chair. Deftly he spun the steel blade into the air and watched it bite into the oak desk. "What about Rigoletto, Violetta, Quasimodo, McTeague, Eustachia Vye, Marcus

Aurelius, Fra Lippo, Alexander Hamilton? Or yourself? Or me?"

The gargantuan man, slobbering out of his clothes, breathed heavily and studied David carefully. "That's the world that matters. The world where people glitter like diamonds with a million facets. Where people are like pearls, luminous as nacre on the surface but each with a speck that would destroy it if you were looking only for specks."

There was a moment of quietness, and David returned the fat editor's inquisitive stare. Now David was certain that Morris Binder worked his life away on the dirty magazines because of some secret compulsion. But when the Westfield murder erupted across the front pages, he wasn't so sure.

Mom Beckett had a low opinion of writers. She had befriended or lived with some dozen scriveners and they had dedicated their books to her. She had not bothered to read them. "Not a damn one of them," she explained to David, "ever so much as left me a cent. What you want, if you're a woman, is a man in wholesale."

"What do you mean?" David asked. He sat with his elbows propped on the restaurant table, listening to the provocative woman as she talked of the old days.

"I mean like wholesale furniture or wholesale food," she explained. "Wholesale men think big, and they get you things for half price. Two-thirds of the money I got stashed away came from wholesale men. I like men that think big."

"But you also like Claude, don't you?" David probed.

"Him!" Mom laughed, jerking a manicured thumb at the cashier's stand where thin Claude had his beard hidden behind a book. "Why, you couldn't help likin' that helpless guy." She looked at the frail poet with the tenderness of a mother watching an ill-favored child.

"Why don't you marry him, Mom?" David asked.

"Oh, no!" the big woman winked. "When a woman marries, she's lost! Suppose we was married and the Chinese cook quit. I say, 'Claude, cook up some stew,' and he like as not says, 'Darlin', I'd like to but I got a headache,' and where the hell would I be? As it is, I'm boss, and if that filthy Chinese bastard quits on me, I know I got me a cook in reserve, because this way if Claude don't cook he knows he goes out of here on his ass."

And yet David noticed that no one on MacDougal Street was more excited than Mom when some great figure in the

world of letters came sniffing into the restaurant looking for
Claude. David could spot them as soon as they came down
the steps from the street. Incredulously, they would peer into
the dingy restaurant and ask tentatively, "Does the poet
Claude . . ."

"He's in the kitchen," David said.

"The kitchen?"

"Yes, he's whipping up an Irish stew. Hey, Claude!"

Through the swinging door the frail, bearded man would
appear with a towel wrapped about his waist. There would
be halting introductions and then Claude would throw aside
the towel and talk quietly with his visitor. It might be a college professor or a famous editor. Often they would find the
stuffy air of the restaurant confining, and they would go into
Washington Square and sit upon the benches. Then Mom
would bellow, "All right, Dave! Hop out there and finish that
stew." That's why the food was so bad at Mom Beckett's.
Claude was an abominable cook, but the people who took
over for him when he left to talk in Washington Square
were worse.

Once David asked, "Mom, why don't you cook?" and
Mom replied, "Not this one! I long ago learned that the only
work in this world too hard for women was what they call
women's work. You know, cookin' and washin' and scrubbin'
and liftin' pots and pans all day. I like men's work, like
keepin' track of money or sittin' on your fat tail and givin'
orders."

Later, when Claude and his visitor returned from their
abstract discussions, Mom would say graciously, "I'd be hon-
ored in the extreme if you would permit me to take you out
to dinner. The food here is lousy." And they would leave the
dingy restaurant and the bootleg gin and the foul stew and
David would watch them do down MacDougal Street, the
big, proud, happy woman, the cave-chested poet, and the
distinguished visitor.

It was four-thirty on a drowsy July afternoon when Morris
Binder's ticker flashed the news that Oliver Banks Westfield
had been murdered. The immense editor shifted his three
hundred pounds quickly and grabbed a telephone. *"World?"*
he shouted with a burst of energy that David had thought
impossible. "Carey? Give me the dope on Beatrice Westfield.
Yep. I have a theory. If it works out, you get the story. Call
me back."

He struggled from his chair and heaved his massive body toward a file of old magazines. Thumbing through them hurriedly failed to disclose what he sought. He closed his eyes and stood very still for more than a minute. Then he said, "Of course!" and went to a steel file where he searched furiously. As he worked a big grin broke over his face. "Sure, that's it!" he repeated to himself.

Returning to his chair he cried, "Harper! Bring me the other phone." With ponderous arms he brushed aside his manuscripts. "Operator. Get me the police in Miami."

Word sped through Clay Publications that Morris Binder was working on another murder. Miss Adams dashed upstairs, thin and fiery with excitement. "Take care of yourself," she warned the hulking man, and something in the proprietary way she spoke betrayed to David that she had long loved the sweating editor. Then Tremont Clay himself appeared.

"Is that the Oliver Banks Westfield of National Trust?" he asked.

"The same," Binder replied without looking up.

"God! We can run this story for years!" Clay cried in real excitement. "Wall Street! Long Island! Is there an orgy angle?"

"Maybe," Binder puffed as he placed another call to the police in San Francisco.

"Who did it?" Clay asked, licking his lips.

"His wife," Morris Binder grunted.

"Unh-unh!" Miss Adams interrupted. "Ticker says his wife has been in Los Angeles for the last three weeks."

"She did it," Binder replied stolidly. Then Carey at the *World* called. Binder listened attentively for several minutes and observed, "That's the way I remember it, Carey. Well, nothing definite yet. But if I were you I'd get a lot of stories ready on Beatrice Westfield. Sure I know she's in L.A. But she murdered her husband, all the same."

Next came a flurry of telephone calls to other parts of the United States. As the sticky evening wore on two police inspectors came into the office and smoked cigars. Tremont Clay, greatly excited by the poisoning of the great banker, sent out for sandwiches and coffee. He was already drafting headlines for *Sex Detectives: "Did Oliver Banks Westfield Play Once Too Often?"* He laughed at himself and said to one of the detectives, "Everybody who gets murdered should be named Oliver Banks Westfield! What a beautiful name!"

At ten Morris Binder got the phone call he was expecting. It was from a small town in Illinois: "Yes, a ham actor named Chester Gates was registered at the hotel. Arrived Thursday. Practically no money. Wouldn't admit anything, either. But he did have a picture of Beatrice Westfield in his wallet. Sure we'll hold him, but what for? Murder! Cripes a'mighty!"

"There it is," Morris Binder announced as he slumped back in his chair. "Beatrice Westfield had this two-bit Chester Gates poison her hubby. Better have the L.A. cops pick her up."

The chief inspector leaned forward. "Do you think, Mr. Binder, that she'll talk?"

"Of course not!" Binder snapped. "But Chester Gates out in Illinois will. All you got to do is prove she played him for a sucker. Now to do that all you have to show Chester is that the fair Beatrice went west to shack up with Tom Barnley."

"Did she?" the inspector asked.

"Sure she did." Then Carey from the *World* called back. The huge editor snarled at him, as if the day had been too long, "Sure it's safe! You say yourself that Tom Barnley and Chester Gates were in the same show. Sure Beatrice Westfield kidded them both along. Sure Chester'll yap his head off when he finds out he was just the stooge for Barnley."

Morris Binder banged the phone down on the desk and took a deep breath. The inspector started to ask additional questions but the gigantic editor brushed them aside. "Wrap it up," he advised. "Pour the full heat on little Chester. I'd arrest Tom Barnley, too. He's innocent, but it'll get your face in all the papers. Play this case for all it's worth, Inspector, and you'll be chief one of these days."

Slowly the office emptied. The ticker was turned off and Tremont Clay asked, "How do you do these things, Morris?"

The fat man grinned at his employer. "I never forget anything," he said.

Miss Adams whispered to David, "It's about the sixth case I've seen him solve. Sits right in that chair and figures them out!"

"Why does he stay on a two-bit job like this?" David inquired.

Miss Adams became ashen gray. "Don't you know?" she asked.

But before she could speak Morris Binder rose from his chair and indicated that she should go home. "Thank you very much," he said quietly, and David again had the sensation that these ill-matched people were lovers. The immense man smiled down at the sparrowy woman and said, "Good night."

When Miss Adams had left, David began turning out the lights. Behind him he heard his huge boss puffing heavily, as if the day's exertions had been great. "How did you guess about Chester Gates?" David asked.

"Murder's my hobby," Morris Binder replied, wearily slamming down the lid on his chaotic desk. Breathing heavily, he slumped back in his chair for a moment and droned. "There's one rule to go by. If a wife is murdered, work on the assumption that it was her husband. If a man is murdered, always assume it was his wife. That's a safe bet, because no two people can live together for long without having a hundred reasons for murder. And then," he added with a chuckle, "if the wife happens to be in L.A. when the murder is done in New York, don't be a bit worried. Just figure out who she got to do it for her. It's really very simple."

"But how did you hit on Chester Gates?" David persisted.

The last light was turned out, and from the hallway shone the dismal glow of a single small bulb. Tediously, Morris Binder snapped on a desk lamp and protestingly pushed up the top of his desk. His fat hands fumbled for a batch of pictures. The top one showed Mr. and Mrs. Oliver Banks Westfield at a lawn party. They happened to be staring at each other in boredom. Behind them stood several actors from a New York hit. With his fat forefinger Morris Binder pointed at Mr. Westfield. "That's the look of murder," he said. "That bored look."

"But he's the one that got killed!" David argued.

"What does it matter?" Slowly the tired editor closed his desk and turned out the light. Then he coughed a couple of times. "Ugggh. Ugggh. I want you to believe, Harper, that two years ago I saw that picture in the paper and thought, 'There's a shot I can use some day in *Great Crimes.*' But I couldn't have told you which one was going to be done in." He closed the door of the office and mused, "I hope to heaven one of those men in the background turns out to be Chester Gates. I have a hunch it will."

On the narrow stairs David was inspired to say, "You ought to be on the police force, Mr. Binder."

The huge man chuckled. "Yes, I should. I suppose they've told you why I'm not."

David was about to ask why, but at the foot of the stairs he saw thin Miss Adams, waiting in the shadows. She looked particularly drab in a gray tweed jacket, but there was a great light in her eyes as she almost pleaded. "Come, Mr. Binder. We'd better hurry."

The city of New York captivated David, as it should any young man with imagination. Mom Beckett's was only nine blocks from where he worked, so each morning he walked along Third Street and watched Italian families haggling over business details. He grew to enjoy the fat women shouting at their little men, and for the first time in his life he realized that he was a fairly big man.

At Lafayette Street there was always a bustle of cargo and men moving it. At Tremont Clay's, huge trucks delivered round cores of cheap pulp paper for the insatiable presses and took away the same paper fouled up with stories of crime and passion. Idle policemen watched the traffic, and old men with beards gathered at the Hebrew Immigrant Aid Society. There was vigorous life on all the streets.

But David had eyes for only one thing when he reached Lafayette Street in the morning. He would turn and look south to the skyscrapers. They were beautiful in the morning, like an etching by Piranesi. Pinnacles leaped into the air, superbly high and secure, forming mysterious shapes. And whenever David saw this congregation of leaping beauty he thought: "They're talking over my day for me." At such moments he fancied himself to be Balzac watching the roofs of Paris, for those skyscrapers, whispering together, were the gossips of the city, relishing the scandals of the previous night.

At night David walked back to Mom Beckett's by way of Fourth Street. It was not so interesting as Third, but it invariably yielded one moment of sheer physical joy, for it broadened out into Washington Square, and David never grew satiated with that beautiful enclave within the great city. The Square was well proportioned and seemed always to be filled with people: students from the university, bums sitting along the fountains, boys playing ball, poets dozing on benches, pretty girls, scrawny maids with other women's children, vendors of this and that, young girls and old prostitutes engaged in the same business of waiting, bored policemen, Fifth Avenue bus drivers arguing the politics of their harried company, worried professors, and elderly women living upon niggardly incomes. The Square was the city, and no matter how tired he was at night, the sight of this tree-filled open space with its trivial humanity made him feel good. The Square was of deep significance to him: he could never fool himself that the petty business of Lafayette Street or the frigid skyscrapers of Wall Street were the end of man; they were mechanical and nothing; but the sprawling people at rest and dreaming and arguing and loving in the Square, they were the end of life, the meaning of the universe.

So there was always a moment of joy for David as he burst, like a lover, into the Square. Like a million other visitors to the city, he felt that the Square was in some peculiar way his own; but immediately he came upon it at night he experienced also a pang of hunger, for just off the Square, at Mom Beckett's, Alison Webster would be waiting.

She would have little to do with him. She was working, she always said. She put in long hours at *Fashion* and was becoming one of the "women to be watched" in that organization. At night she stayed in her room and wrote: stories, articles, novelettes, anything. And she became steadily slimmer and more desirable. A friend at *Fashion* had shown her a new hair-wash which brought out the golden flashes of her red hair. Another friend had sought out heavy brocaded cummerbunds with embroidered designs which accentuated Alison's attractive figure. She no longer put her arms through her coat sleeves, and she spent much of her salary on expensive woolen dresses that had both a tailored and a casual air.

Like an affectionate pup, David insisted on tagging after Alison. In spite of rebuffs, he asked her to dinner. "You can't afford it," she usually replied, but once in a great while she would assent. "Now don't take me to some ritzy place," she commanded, but David was so pleased to know a handsome girl in New York, so happy to be with her, that he spent most of his meager salary on their dinners together. This both flattered and dismayed Alison. Finally, in fairness to David she said bluntly, "Dave, I don't want to go out with you any more. You're spending your money and . . . well . . . frankly, you're not going to get anything for it."

"Being along with you is plenty," David persisted. Then he added a foolish explanation of his behavior: "Besides, I don't know anyone else in New York."

"That's what I mean," Alison laughed. "If you continue to waste your money on me, you'll never meet any girls. Dave, it's no fun for a girl to say this, but I'm never going to fall in love with you. I'm not even going to let you kiss me. Not because I'm mean. I like you, but we're going in two different ways. Rather, I'm going up. I'm going to be a great writer. I don't know where you're going."

"Oh . . . I . . ."

"If you had any guts, Dave, you'd quit Tremont Clay's. They've taught you all you need to know. I can get you a job uptown. Maybe if we worked together, if we had the same ambitions . . . Look, Dave! I'm sure that Miss Clint will commission you to do a series of smart stories on your hoboing around the United States." Again the girl's bright vision conjured up whole lay-outs for stories. "You could do one on Santa Fe, with Indians and pueblos. San Francisco with the funny little cable cars and a smashing view of the bridge they're putting up."

David leaned back in the expensive restaurant chair and waited while the busboy placed fresh pats of butter on the silver plates. "None for me," Alison said. When the man left, David watched the retreating white coat, cut in a flashy way so as to resemble a footman at the court of Louis XIV.

He said, firmly, "I don't want to write like that, Alison."

She dropped the subject completely and said, "Dave, you ought to pay more for your suits. You're in New York now. I'll bet this skirt I'm wearing cost more than your whole suit."

"Alison!" David protested. "That's a shocking thing to say! If you want to know, I paid $22.50. Down on Delancey Street."

"It looks it."

The coldness of her observation bewildered David. "Why do you say things like that?" he pleaded, more in protection of her than of himself. "Why do you boast about the way you made a fool of Miss Clint at the office? Why do you make yourself more important than you are?"

She pursed her lips and studied David, wondering how far she could goad him. "I wouldn't say I gloated over success, because I haven't had any yet. Not compared with what's ahead. But I do mourn over your failure."

"My failure!" David cried. "I'm only twenty-four!"

"Joe Wismer's twenty-four and he's sold stories already."

"From what I've heard you say about Joe Wismer I don't want to be like him."

"He's doing what you say you want to do."

"Alison! I'd never measure myself against Joe Wismer. When I write, it won't be like him."

"What you mean is that Joe and I write tripe."

"I didn't say that!" David protested. The waiter brought

rolls to the table and David nervously began to pick at one. As soon as the waiter disappeared Alison snapped, "But you mean it's tripe, don't you?"

"Alison!" David pleaded. "We have nothing to fight about! Your writing is very clever."

"You say *clever* very distastefully."

"I didn't mean to," David apologized. "I wish I could write as well."

"You're a moody snob," Alison replied, ignoring the apology. "All you do is sit and dream. You loaf in the restaurant and talk with that damned fool Claude. And all the time you're doing that I'm upstairs working. When I've written a best seller, you'll be sitting in some place like this you can't afford, pontificating to some girl who thinks you're wonderful because you want to write. You'll lean back and say, 'Alison's story really isn't much good. You know, she just bats them out. Now Dostoevsky . . .'" She tossed her red hair provokingly. "Isn't that what you'll be saying, David?"

David's face hardened into a hurt mask. "Why don't you go home?" he asked harshly. "You want to fight with me to build yourself up. Get out!"

Slowly Alison rose from the table and with a beautiful, flashing smile looked down upon the bewildered young man. "I've told you a dozen times, Dave, there's no point in your taking me to dinner. Now do you believe me?" She turned abruptly and left the restaurant.

At this moment the footman-waiter appeared with two plates of soup. David looked up at him beseechingly and half-laughed. "She walked out!" he said.

The waiter carefully placed the soup on the table. "You'd be surprised how often that happens in a joint like this," he whispered.

David felt less a fool. "Really?" he asked.

"Sure!" the waiter confided. "Prices are so high here people are under a strain. I saw one young fellow pour a cup of cold consomme on a girl's head."

"What shall I do?" David asked. "I'm not hungry."

The waiter took a furtive glance about the gilded room and whispered, "To hell with the management! Walk out! I'll say you canceled the order."

"Could I do that?" David asked, imploringly.

"Well, not rightfully, but the management here is bloodsuckers. Screw the management!" The tense waiter busied himself with brushing away crumbs so the head waiter would not suspect him of sabotage. Nonchalantly David rose, but the footman tugged at his sleeve. "It would be proper to leave a small tip. After all, I do lose my table this way."

David fumbled with his coins. "Would thirty cents be all right?"

The footman smiled and said, "Thirty cents would be very decent." Then he dropped his voice to a confidential murmur and whispered, "Never lose heart! The revolution is coming!" At the door the head waiter surveyed David suspiciously and began to ask what . . . But David bolted out the door and down the street.

He was bewildered. It was apparent that Alison had set out to cure him of his infatuation, and yet he could not understand her harshness. He walked home and arrived at his room in great agitation. He tried to read a book Doc Chisholm had sent him from Texas, *The House with the Green Shutters,* a minor Scottish novel which was rumored to have been the victim of plagiarism. It was heavy and plodding, but it merited that precious word of Doc Chisholm's: it was mordant. Yet its very quality of passionate life made David restless. Slowly he felt himself being caught up in the spell of his own words and ideas.

Reluctantly, like a bride moving toward an unknown chamber, he went to his typewriter. He sat for a long time, staring at the paper. "Of all the things I've seen," he mused, "what . . ." Across the white paper came a vision of Old Daniel, Morris Binder solving a murder, his Aunt Reba, the wonderful Quaker girl Marcia Paxson who was now hurtingly Marcia Moomaugh. He recalled the unshared things that had happened to him while he hoboed around America after Chautauqua. But when he actually started to peck out words they came not as a flood but one at a time, painfully, and they related to no one of the magnificent things he had experienced: not the days with Sousa, nor his moment of courage in the burning tent, nor the grandeur of Colorado mountains in deep winter. He was picking words from far back in his memory to describe a smell, the most evocative smell he could recall. Toothless Tom was visiting him at night with four slices of new-baked bread and a great chunk of store cheese.

He became lost in his writing, and toward three in the morning Mom Beckett banged on his door. "You're keepin' folks awake," she said. She came into his room and sat on his bed. "You burnin' up the pages with immortality?" she joked. When she saw David gather his sheets protectingly to him she laughed, "Don't worry! I never read any of that crap. Books is for people that can't see MacDougal Street with their own eyes."

David leaned over his typewriter and studied the neat, corseted woman with the perfect hair and the rasping voice. "You don't fool me," he laughed. "Some day you'll write a book yourself. But it'll be so vulgar nobody'll publish it."

"I don't write 'em. I live 'em!" she replied. Then her voice took on a serious note. "I see you and Alison go out to dinner. I see her come back alone and start to write like mad. Then I see you come back and do the same. Fight?"

"Oh, I wouldn't . . ."

"Dave? Tell me one thing. Honestly. You gettin' any good out of datin' that mean, tense, little bitch?"

"No."

Mom Beckett had a wisecrack for every situation, but this time she kept her mouth shut. She was very sorry for all the people in the world who love and love and who get nothing out of it. Like Alison, earlier in the evening, she turned abruptly from David and left him. Ten minutes later the poet Claude climbed up with a tray of food.

"Mom said for you to eat this," the thin bearded man reported.

"Claude, what do you think a novel is?"

"It's a book," the poet said.

"But I mean, in form? Does it have to have a set story?"

As if the room had suddenly changed, Claude put aside the tray of food and stared for a moment at the dark night outside the solitary window. "A novel," he said, "is a golden kettle into which you pour all of experience." His slim hands began to wave in the darkness. "You can toss in great chunks of meat and fragrant bones and stock left over from the meals before. You can add fragments of character or the whole man. You can have scenes that fill a quarter of the book and others that flash by in a fleeting glance. In a novel there's nothing you can't do, if you do it with passion."

All his life David had heard talk about books, but this was the first that made complete sense. Eagerly he made a place for Claude and when the poet was seated he asked, "If you feel that way, why don't you write novels?"

Claude laughed and tugged at his beard. "A poet tries to say it all in a few lines. If everyone who writes could write supremely well, they would all write poetry. But most people don't understand words, or feelings either. So they cover up their deficiencies by writing long books."

"You mean that poems are distillations of books?"

"Good poems are. That's why poor novelists always title their books with jagged bits of poetry. The whole novel has already been said in the poem. But fools have to write it out so that other fools can understand."

David was truly burning to prolong this conversation, but Claude had said enough for one night. With a twinkle in his eye he picked up the tray and started downstairs. Instinctively, David grabbed for the food, but the poet shied away and said, "Mom told me you had been knocked out by love, so she wanted you to eat something. But I see it wasn't love. It was the desire to write. And a man with that desire upon him is crazy if he stuffs himself with a lot of food." He kicked the door shut after him, and in the morning David found in the hallway Mom's tray of food. It made an excellent breakfast.

In the succeeding days David forgot his first attempt at writing, for Morris Binder promoted him to the editorship of *Passionate Love*. "Your pay's $24 a week," the hulking man announced, "and I want the sexiest magazine in New York."

The new job entailed reading some forty manuscripts a week. They were dreadful affairs, laden with musky passion that took place in the back of bars, in the back of automobiles, or in the sullen back places of the mind. More than a third of the manuscripts were so illiterate that they had either to be discarded on sight or completely rewritten. It was then that David discovered the value of an editor's paste pot. He would sit at his typewriter and bang out copy as fast as he could type. With long scissors he would cut apart his own work and paste it over the worst sections of the story. Finally he would have a mangled hodge-podge, but that was the only way to get a good story, one filled with suggestive movement and sexy passion.

Well-written manuscripts usually lacked the force of reality. They were not brutal enough. Morris Binder said, "Tell all your love stories with an eye to using the same characters a couple of years later in a murder magazine." He was not pleased with David's first issue. "You don't have enough of the murderous passion," he said judiciously.

"What do you mean?" David asked.

"Love. Haven't you ever known a girl you loved and yet you'd like to break her neck. Actually?"

"Yes," David said.

"That's the way love is," the big man puffed. "Get it into you stories."

Yet when true stories of the murderous passion arrived, David found they were too gross to be used. They came in dirty envelopes bearing brutal stories told in the unsophisticated words of the outhouse. The came mostly from women, and phrases from them lingered in David's mind for weeks: "He beat me until his arm must of ached." "If you was here I could show you my bruises." "No matter what happened after that, I always remember that one heavenly night. Who could forget?"

In real embarrassment David bundled up such stories and returned them. In time he learned to rely upon a few trusted authors—Alison Webster had once been one—who knew how to hit a high standard of pornography and to maintain it. These writers were usually from small towns in the South or West. They wrote a standard product that played in morbid fascination upon the multiple forms of rape. Their characters, too, were standard brands, engaged in the involved game of suggesting everything and saying nothing.

So without David's ever acknowledging it, he became immersed in the filthy business of polite pornography. He slipped into his evil responsibilities as easily as he had slipped into the thieving tricks of Paradise Park. Yet there was this difference: at Paradise he had been attacking property, and he realized that if he persisted in stealing he would land in jail; whereas at Tremont Clay's he was attacking only men's minds, and it was obvious that no one cared about that.

To his surprise David found that his most valuable mentor was not brilliant Morris Binder but drab, acid Miss Adams. She supervised his work with care, helped him to avoid errors, taught him the systems used within the publishing house. She steered him to the most salacious illustrators and showed him how to fake letters to the editor which would be sure to call forth a flood of angry responses, which in turn permitted him to take a righteous editorial stand: "Yes, indeed, we think girls under seventeen should be home and in bed by ten o'clock!"

The more he worked with Miss Adams the more impressed he became with the subtle way in which she ran Tremont Clay's business. She was his introduction to that marvel of

American industrial life: the pompous front man supported by the obscure, deft woman behind him. And as he moved from one New York office to another—say, the paper plants or the engravers'—he found there too some quiet woman standing behind the blustering boss, and it was to these women he went for crucial decisions; so that when he rode in subways and saw thousands of these prim withdrawing women, he was not fooled. He knew that they were running much of the business of the great city.

When David had made a success of *Passionate Love,* he was given the editorship of *Secret Detective* as well. His salary was raised to $26. The new magazine was different from the first. Now he had to comb the annals of repulsive crime, especially those that had been well photographed. He used ten a month and rigorously fitted them into the established pattern: Describe the crime in two dripping pages. Use the words *lurid, ghastly, thigh, sawed-off shotgun, decaying, breast.* Indicate the complete bewilderment of the law. Establish a definite suspect, but use a fictitious name. Then have superior police work clear the doomed man. Enter the crime on the list of those that will never be solved. Then have an ordinary detective—show him in at least three poses—solve the crime. End with somebody being hanged.

The formula was so well established that David wondered how he could ever find enough cases, but with Miss Adams' help he managed to fill his magazine month after gory month. Once more he found that he had to rely upon three or four dependable writers. He learned to ignore ruthlessly articles which began, "This here is a true story. You can read about it in the *Detroit Free Press.*"

But surprisingly soon he fell into line with Tremont Clay and Morris Binder. If a particularly bloody murder came along, Clay used it first. Then Binder. Then David. Morris Binder laughed and said, "Sure we print the same stuff year after year. But if you uncover a really good murder, make a note of it. Use it two or three times a year. But always call it 'New Light on the Chandler Case.' I have about six gory jobs I use all the time. If a witness moves, or a policeman who worked on the case dies, I brush off the type and run in a new lead: 'Last week a central witness in the Chandler Case went to meet his Maker. When Louis Denman stands face to face with God, what will he confess?' Then you run the same old guff."

Miss Adams, as usual, provided a substantial system. "We

keep a file. If we get a really good murder with sex angles we use it up to four times a year in the different murder magazines. But we like to avoid needless repetition, so when we see that any one magazine has used up all the standard stuff, we change its name and start all over again."

After three months of exhuming loathsome deeds, David was given his third magazine and a salary of $28. The additional rag was *Real Western*. Of it Morris Binder said, "It's a clean family magazine. Your villain must always be a half-breed, a Mexican, or a banker. Good girls get into the stories because their fathers are in trouble. Bad girls are always dance-hall girls, and let it go at that. No description. For comedy use Chinamen, Easterners, or very fat men. It's best to have the chase center on actual property: cows, horses, a written deed, some gold, or a map. If the chase centers on something abstract, like honor, our readers lose interest. And use a heavy sprinkling of words like *corral, dogie, sage* . . ."

"A college professor taught me those words," David laughed.

"Then use 'em!" the big editor commanded. He pointed out that simple though the Western story might seem, it was by far the most complex of the pulp yarns. "For example," he puffed, "you have the villain, a no-good, half-breed killer who uses a knife. He's got to die! But you also have the bad man, who uses a decent revolver and kills men face to face. The bad man doesn't have to die! He can be regenerated, especially by a good woman, and he can become sheriff and shoot down a dozen villains. I guess I make about fifty per cent of my bad men sheriffs. The rest I kill off."

Like most editors, David quickly tired of the Westerns, and he did not understand why until one day he recalled what Wild Man Jensen had said of Kansas: "The best people I knew were the women." That was it! The Westerns were frightfully dull because women were omitted, and David realized with dismay that Western magazines were so popular because all over America men in lonely rooming houses were sick to death of women and wanted to read about brave men and horses. "We leave out the best half of life!" David protested to Morris Binder.

"A lot of men want it that way," the editor observed.

"Even the stupid women who read *Passionate Love* are better off," David reasoned, "because at least they're reading about men."

"If you're going to accept substitutes for real living," Binder grunted, "horses are just as good as paper men."

"I don't know," David reasoned. "This use of symbols for real things perplexes me. For example, I stink up every edition with sage, and I have no idea what it smells like."

"Neither do I!" the fat editor admitted. He stamped on the floor and Miss Adams appeared. "What does sage smell like?" he demanded.

"I'll bring some tomorrow," she said primly, but when she held a pinch for David to smell he was overcome and said nothing, for that was the way the poorhouse turkeys had smelled on the two great feast days each autumn. He turned away from Miss Adams and Morris Binder and considered how much a prisoner of memory men are. They spend their lives accumulating sensory impressions: sights, smells, the feel of things, sounds, the taste of food. And when they are older these sensations overwhelm them with longing and despair. In the barren room of Tremont Clay's filthy rags David was overcome by the smell of poorhouse turkeys, and he recalled how happy he had been in the poorhouse. The sound of a merry-go-round could bring back the image of dead Nora. The sight of green fields made his heart pound for Marcia Paxson, and the feel of books reminded him of Doc Chisholm. He was a prisoner of his sensory memories, and he would not have it otherwise, for through them he lived deeply, carrying with him to each new experience the full burden of his life up to that moment. He had never realized before how dependent his brain was upon its senses, and he loved the tangible world in which he had lived. He thought: "I'd like to see Paradise again on a rainy night. I'd like to smell the poorhouse once more. I'd like to see that old couple dashing at one another in the morning light." The world was upon him and in him, for he was one of the fortunate ones who carry their worlds with them. He was the man who as a boy had seen and listened and touched and smelled and tasted with love, and the treasure trove was with him forever.

"That's what sage smells like," Miss Adams whined.

"That's some smell," David replied, and for the rest of the day he was ashamed of himself for working in that office. But at the close of the day Tremont Clay took him aside and pointed with a manicured finger at a line in *Passionate Love*. "Did you write this?" he asked nervously.

David licked his lips and looked at the offending passage. A woman was trying to describe sexual intercourse. Her words had been too plain and David had substituted, *"You can guess what happened next."*

"Yes, sir," David admitted guiltily. "I did it."

"It's wonderful!" Clay exploded. "It's as good as Morris Binder! Hold on to that line! Use it two or three times an issue. It says everything, but they can't pin anything on you."

And David did use it. It had a fine insinuating leer. It was especially titillating to young readers, since it flattered their experience, and if they didn't know what happened next, Tremont Clay jolly well intended that they should find out.

When David saw himself among the little Italians of Third Street he suspected that he had become a man; but when he now considered himself he was sure that he must be. For always before he had lived with one simple, comprehensible group of people. Now he was plunged deeply into several worlds, and the complexity of his life assured him that he had assumed manhood's full responsibilities.

He was involved with the shadowy outlines of a novel. He was part of Mom's and Claude's hilarious life. At Tremont Clay's he was becoming daily more attached to Morris Binder and Miss Adams. He was editor of three cheap magazines. And he was in love with Alison Webster.

In spite of her having walked out on him during their meal, he still wanted to be with her. Sometimes at night it became unbearable for him to realize that Alison lay sleeping only a few floorboards away. When she grudgingly allowed him to take her to the movies he could not keep his hands off her. "Don't paw me!" she commanded.

On the way home he said, "I don't mean to offend you. But you're so darned lovely!"

She laughed and said, "I don't believe in trying to reform men. Not after what my mother went through. But if you want to date me, Dave, why don't you write something real instead of those flimsy sketches? Miss Clint says she'll take that story on Arizona."

"She will!" Dave cried. When he got back to the house he took Alison to her room and then dashed to tell Mom the news. "I'm going to write a story about Arizona!" he announced.

"Was you ever there?" Mom asked, leaning her elbows on a table.

"Sure. When I bummed across country."

"Well, if you was there, why'n hell do you want to tell anybody else about that lousy pile of sand?"

"I stayed three nights in a hobo camp near Phoenix. I'll never forget it."

"Don't bother anybody else about it," Mom advised. "I know all of Arizona, and there ain't a story worth tellin'."

"Where is there one, in your opinion? MacDougal Street?"

"Writin' is the bunk!" Mom insisted.

"Then why were you so excited when Alison published a story?" David argued.

"Because I like to see people do what they want to do. You should of seen the party we threw when the little Jewish girl across the street married the Italian boy. They were doin' what they wanted to do."

On the first night that he was supposed to write, he talked with Mom till two. They kicked around theories of life, why people get drunk, should two people of like interests get married, and the prospects of repeal. It was much the best talk David had participated in for months. Claude joined them at midnight and swung the topics around to immortality and birth control. In the morning Alison asked, "How'd the story go?" and David blinked.

"I . . . I was planning it," he said.

He planned it the next night, too, with more help from Mom and Claude. They drank beer till one and Mom spoke of the early days in Arizona. She said that the only person in God's earth she knew who was lower than the MacDougal Street fire inspector was an Indian garage mechanic in Tucson. "He had three monkey wrenches. He used the big one to wreck big cars, the little one to wreck little cars, and the middle-sized one to ruin radiators. And he'd look at you with big black eyes. I hauled off and knocked him out one day," she said. "Cost my old man two thousand dollars. That damn fool Indian had sense enough to claim I had ruined his sacroiliac!"

Finally, on the fifth night, David actually started to write. To a hobo camp in Arizona came three men on their way to California. Beyond the vast flats rose a vision . . .

He tore the paper up and started again. To a hobo camp in Arizona came four men on their way to California. They could see the purple hills, and one of them—David could see him now, terrible and haunting with a scar along his cheek— droned on about the bitter winters in Dakota . . .

In the morning Alison took one look at the yarn and said

in a gentle voice, "Dave! You don't have to write every story as if you were Maxim Gorky." She told him what a magazine like *Fashion* expected: a challenging lead, well-developed characters, plot and a zippy close.

Sweating in his room—"I can do this!" he told himself—he slaved out the story. Ruthlessly he cut away those parts which were close to him and substituted bits of local color so that the hobo camp became a delightful place filled with splendid characters who mouthed the world's wisdom. Toward morning he leaned back and studied what he had written. "Sounds like an eleven-year-old boy describing a poorhouse," he grunted.

But *Fashion* bought it! Then David acted like every other young writer with his first success. Upon news of acceptance he borrowed thirty dollars from Morris Binder and took Alison on a terrific outing. When the *Fashion* check arrived he took Alison and Mom and Claude to the theatre. Then, when the story actually appeared, he celebrated for a third time and wound up in debt. But he felt wonderful! Like an author!

On his way to work he maneuvered himself past as many newsstands as possible and eyed the trim piles of *Fashion*. "Boy!" he thought. "There she lies!" When he saw a woman on the subway with the magazine he snooped to see what she was reading. It was not his page and he felt strangely offended. Toward the end of the month he had the dismal experience of seeing *Fashion* lying in a muddy gutter, and there was a pang of tragedy in that moment. Even more disturbing was the day when the next issue of the magazine appeared. It was indecently prompt, David thought.

He was then inspired to read his story carefully, but he could form no clear opinion of it. At times his writing seemed better than he remembered it, but after he put the magazine aside he realized with astonishment that what he remembered was not his story but the ads that had run beside it. He saw with disillusioned clarity that his words had been used to lure readers back to the advertisements. "Well," he said, "the words were good enough for that."

Alison deemed him a success. She allowed him to take her out several times on the express condition that he would not spend more than eighty cents on her dinner. He found her an increasing enigma. Her petty calculations about people disturbed him, and her mathematics was astonishing. She said, "Mom oughtn't to wear twenty-dollar dresses. Not with the money she has."

"What difference does it make?"

"Well," she explained, "if I bought two cheap twenty-dollar dresses, what would I have? Two undistinguished sacks. But if I paid sixty dollars, as I did for this one . . ."

"That's twenty dollars more than you were talking about," David pointed out.

"Yes, but I just sold another story, so I have the extra twenty."

David blinked and asked, "Does that make sense to you?"

"Well," she detoured, "I swore I'd never be like Mom and Pop. Cheap."

"I thought your home was fine," David said reflectively.

"It was. On my money. Why do you suppose I wrote trash for Tremont Clay? To support my family. Why do you suppose I write so hard now? To support my father."

"Do you send him money?" David asked.

"Only momentarily. He holds it briefly and then passes it on to a Baltimore bootlegger."

"You mean he's a drunk?"

"He's worse. For years he's been trying to drink it faster than the bootlegger can haul it in. He might have won, too, but with my money the bootlegger bought himself a motor boat."

Once, coming home from a play, she sat with her knees crossed so that a man opposite her stared all the way from Times Square to Christopher Street. On the stairs David said, "Weren't you sitting pretty high?" and she explained: "Good-looking girls ought to do that once in a while. Helps other girls."

"What do you mean, Alison!"

"Oh, it's not easy for an ugly girl to get married. When I was fat I never had a date. That galoot who was staring at me will go home now and make passes at the ugly girl next door. That's how life keeps moving."

But she herself would never permit David to kiss her. "I can't get mixed up with you," she warned him. "Not you nor anyone. I've got work to do." Then one day she disappeared. She was gone for a week, and when she returned she was slimmer and more desirable than ever. She was subdued, too, and seemed glad when David asked her for a date. On the way home she even assented when he suggested that they sit on a bench in Washington Square. It was a beautiful, city night, with stars barely peeking through the metropolitan glare. There was a barking of dogs and the muffled whispers of lovers. Suddenly she swept herself into David's arms and allowed him to kiss her. She ran her hungry fingers along his neck and with a gasp he expressed his astonishment when she began kissing him as if she had longed for this moment.

Awkwardly he mumbled, "What's the matter, Alison?"

"My father died," she blurted out, and immediately she was engulfed in passionate tears. She kissed David many more times and then tore herself from him and sat staring at the sky. Slowly, as if from a great distance, she began talking, more to herself than to David. "Do you remember when you were sick at my home? The big tray on which I brought you breakfast? That was Pop's tray. It was my job to feed him, when he could eat.

"Three or four times a month he'd get blind, roaring, three-day drunk. Never kept a job." She stopped speaking and David sensed that she was crying. At last great bitterness, "Well . . . every . . . goddamned . . . time . . . I . . . handled . . . that . . . tray . . ." She stopped for a moment and said quickly, "You'll read about it in a book some day. And it'll be a wonderful book, too! Because whenever I took Pop that tray I made myself study him. I took notes on each . . . rotten . . . terrible . . . step . . . he . . . took . . . going . . . down." The fight went out of her and she said between sobs, "We buried him yesterday, and at the funeral people made believe he was just an ordinary husband instead of a piece of soaked-up human blotting paper."

Compassionately David tried to put his arm about her to console her, but she drew away from him. "Don't ever touch me again!" she said in harsh, bitter tones. She rose rapidly and hurried across the Square to Mom Beckett's. In the morning she waited for Mom in the restaurant and said, "I'll be leaving at the end of the week. I'm taking an apartment on Washington Square."

"Why?" Mom asked.

"You know why," the slim, brittle girl replied. "I need a good address. In a couple of months I'll be a full-time editor. In my business if a girl says she lives on MacDougal Street everybody asks, 'Wonder who she's sleeping with?' But when I say, 'Washington Square,' the same people whistle and say, 'Mmmm! She's got dough!' "

Mom grinned a big toothy grin and said, "You'll get ahead."

Alison knew that this was not intended as a compliment, but she stared right back at the big woman and said, "They're beginning to lay people off. You watch. David Harper is going to be fired. A lot of people in my office are going out. Well, this is the time they separate the men from the boys. I'm not going to be fired, Mom."

"I'm sure you won't be," the big, friendly woman agreed.

At dinner Mom reported the news to David. He was disturbed that Alison should think him about to be fired and he was disappointed that she should be leaving Mom's. He dashed upstairs and banged on Alison's door. "Go away!" she commanded. When he banged again she opened the door slightly and said in a harsh whisper, "Go away, Dave! Just because I was silly on that bench . . . I'll never see you again."

"What's the matter with me?" he blurted out in bewilderment.

"Nothing," Alison said through the door. "It's us. The world. It takes a tough person to live through the next years. Together we'd be soft." In proof of her own hardness, she slammed the door against his face.

She never talked with him again that year. In slim perfection she left Mom Beckett's and took an apartment on the Square. Sometimes at night David would see sports roadsters parked by the door, and he would sneak up to see where the cars were from. They were expensive and from Yale or Princeton. He studied the masthead of *Fashion* and saw that she had been promoted to head of the fiction department. Sometimes he would see her crossing the Square. Now she usually walked with important-looking people. They would huddle together, listening to someone's chatter, and then explode apart with merry laughter. David hated them.

The days of hunger were upon him, and he knew no vanity. He would call her at the office or at her home. She would tell him wearily to stop bothering her. Once she taunted him. "How's the great American novel?" she inquired. When he did not reply, she said, "Mine's almost done. Stop calling me!"

He stooped to silly tricks, deluding himself with daydreams. He said to Miss Adams, "I've heard it gossiped that I was going to be fired. I can't be! I'm going to be married."

The little woman's face grew very cold. "Don't do anything hasty, David! Please!" Then she peered carefully toward Clay's office and whispered, "There's going to be some layoffs pretty soon. Business is terrible."

"Will I . . ."

The hard gray woman looked at him compassionately. "You were the last editor taken on, weren't you?"

"They certainly wouldn't fire Morris Binder, would they?" he asked.

Miss Adams flushed deeply and snapped, "He can always work here. Where else could he work?"

David saw that his question about Binder had somehow wounded the little woman, and he felt sorry for her. He said, "So you'd advise me not to get married?"

"Don't do it. Bad times are ahead."

He also took his aching troubles to Mom. She prescribed her sovereign specific for all worries: gin. They got quietly drunk together while Claude cooked a stew. The big, compassionate woman listened for hours as David explained, in ever thicker syllables, what a hard life Alison had experienced. "You mustn't blame her, Mom. It's not her fault."

"I know!" Mom commiserated. "She's a tender, beautiful, gentle girl."

Then David would walk the streets of the Village, the old streets where so many young men had tramped for this best of all reasons. As his brain cleared he saw with fierce clarity that nothing had helped him forget Alison, not lying to Miss Adams, nor getting drunk, nor sharing his troubles with Mom. The hunger of life was upon him, the full wild hunger of manhood. "Oh, Alison!" he would mutter to the night.

He thought that no boy could ever become a man who had not felt this fire. He thought that no man could know himself until he knew exactly how important women were to him. He recalled the perfect beauty of his affection for little Nora amid the damp smells of Venice. He thought of Mona and the long days waiting for news from Hollywood. He recalled with passionate clarity the cool beauty of the girl he had lost, Marcia Paxson. Then his hungry mind would wander across the Square to Alison's house. And there it seemed to crash into an immovable obstacle. Alison, the calculating, determined, ambitious woman, would never, he realized, take off the armor in which she had sheathed herself. What was behind that steel? In spite of all he had learned, David had stubbornly made assault after assault against her hardness, hoping to reveal a human being. The quest, he now acknowledged, could never end successfully.

And yet from Alison he had learned how important women were to him. They were more important than writing

a book, or holding a job, or protecting his vanity. He knew!
To him that year they were more important than bread.

Then, with shocking force, David was wrenched away from
a consideration of his own troubles. It was late in 1931 and
David was editing a love story for *Passionate Love*. He had
already used *"You can guess what happened next,"* and was
searching his mind for something as good to describe the third
passage at arms.

The day was unseasonably warm and Morris Binder had
been agitated by a sex murder which had occurred the night
before in Yonkers. There were no clues, and even though
there were excellent pictures of the girl's parents weeping
and looking down a cellar door, Binder was dissatisfied. He
abhorred an unsolved crime. So he stayed close to the ticker,
hoping for a clue. David spoke to him several times and
noticed that the big man's face was florid. "Is it hot in here?"
David asked. When the huge editor said he felt all right,
David returned to his tale of seduction.

Suddenly behind him a terrible, penetrating, strangling
shriek filled the room, and he heard a chair crash. He leaped
from his desk in awful fright and shouted for Morris Binder.
But the immense man lay stretched on the floor, his face a
dark purple, his hands clenching and unclenching. He was
dying from strangulation, but David could not know this.

Then the door burst open and little Miss Adams dashed
toward the heaving body. Swiftly she pried open the massive
jaws and thrust a rubber eraser between them. Then, twisting
her finger like a hook, she pulled out the swollen, gashed
tongue. As the air eased its way to the stricken man's tortured lungs Miss Adams sat beside him on the floor, holding
the wounded tongue.

Mr. Clay came in. He was dressed in a precise gray suit,
but his hands were sweating, and he rubbed them nervously.
Awkwardly he nudged Miss Adams on the shoulder and
asked, "He all right?"

"Yes," she said. "Get the people out of here."

In the hall Mr. Clay said, "It's a frightful business. Some-
times he gets these seizures three or four times a month.
That's why he works here. I don't really mind it so long as
Miss Adams is around to care for him."

"Can't he be cured?" David asked.

"No," the nervous little man said. "And a word of caution.
Whenever this happens call for Miss Adams. You see, she

lives above him over by the river. He has a bell . . . But if she shouldn't be around . . ." He shivered with disgust. "Pull his tongue out and hold it. I've had to do it twice . . ." His face became ashen and he hurried into the men's room, where David could hear him retching.

Three days later Morris Binder collapsed again. He uttered his frightful, animal cry, stumbled about the room like a stricken bull, and crashed into his own filing cabinets. David forgot his instructions and went to the prostrate man's assistance. He was prying open the massive jaws when Miss Adams burst into the room. She fairly dived at David and smashed him against the desk. "Get away!" she screamed, and she began to mother the gasping body.

David sat hunched against the desk, watching the gruesome ritual by which life was coaxed back into its immense citadel. Mr. Clay came in, sweating worse than before. Seeing David on the floor, he could guess what had happened. "Come here!" he commanded.

In the hall he issued a stiff reprimand. "I warned you to call Miss Adams. It's her job. In a sense, it's her privilege." With acute agitation he wiped his hot face. "She's always loved Morris Binder. I think she sits down below day after day, waiting for the scream."

From then on David waited, too. There seemed to be no clue as to when the attacks would strike, only the animal screams and feet hurrying up the stairs. The effect on David was strange and powerful. He was reminded that men may be angels, but they are animals, too. They are driven by uncontrollable forces and only the love of other people makes it possible for them to survive. Men are lonely and are stricken in the night. They lock their jaws against themselves. They scream like animals, and even though they ridicule love and the forces of destruction, they are themselves theatres for the operation of such forces. Men are gross and they fall upon the floor. Tragedy is near them; and in the distance women wait, no more secure than they.

But Morris Binder taught David more than this. This gross and tragic man introduced his young assistant to the final quartets of Beethoven, and as David listened to the great, deaf German's music, considering how Beethoven had written it—lonely, silent, racked with disease—he knew that even though man is an animal, he is the divine animal.

There was practically no form of social intercourse in which

Morris Binder could indulge. He could not dine out, for at any moment a seizure might possess him and send him howling to the floor. The opera, which he much loved, was forbidden him as were the stage and the ball park. Occasionally the police took him to an ice hockey game. They sat in a box near the men's room, and if he suffered an attack, they held him on the floor and then dragged his inanimate body to the washroom, where they bathed his face.

He lived in three rooms on East Ninth Street, not far from the East River, a lonely giant of a man. Above him lived Miss Adams, waiting for the cry in the night, and she walked him back and forth to work as if he were a schoolboy.

He had one passion which he exercised to the full. Even more than murder he loved recorded music, and the largest of his three rooms was a miracle. He took David there one Friday afternoon. "We'll hear some music," he proposed. It was snowing, and Miss Adams walked between them. At the apartment house she said, "I don't like music. Have a good time." She said good night and climbed her extra flight of stairs. Morris Binder turned the key in his lock and cried, like a child with a toy, "You're going to see something!"

By the window a street lamp burned, and from its muted rays David could see a gothic room lined with record cabinets and albums of all colors. Above him, from seven different angles, hung horns and loud-speakers. By a closet door stood four boxes atop one another, housing the mechanical gear.

"It's a hobby of mine!" the editor said eagerly. "Stand anywhere you wish!" Like an eager boy he went to the machinery and started to click switches. On WJZ an orchestra played dinner music. Suddenly, from all directions the room exploded into sound! The seven speakers were so attuned as to produce an organ effect that completely filled the mind. "Good, eh?" the huge man beamed.

Then he began to switch certain speakers off and augmented others. The glorious sound rose and fell in cascading brilliance. Then the fat man turned off the radio and started the record player. He said, apologetically, "Sometimes the record changer doesn't work, but listen!" He now turned on all the speakers, and from the horns came a whisper of sound, a haunting sound of strings. Morris Binder stood with his head bowed and seemed to drink in the climbing music. David felt himself caught up in the glorious tentacles of the music and lifted about the room. The strings raced and danced and snarled and pleaded. "What is this?" David finally asked.

"One of the Rasoumowsky quartets," the fat man replied. "Opus 59 in C Minor."

"Did Beethoven write it?"

"Of course!" the huge man grunted, and David saw that his eyes were closed. For a moment David listened to the shimmering harmonies and for the first time in his life understood the poet's phrase "breathless in adoration."

"It's wonderful!" he finally cried. Morris Binder opened his eyes.

"This?" he asked incredulously. "This is really rather poor Beethoven. Would you like to hear the last quartet?"

"If it's better than this, sure!" David cried.

Morris Binder turned off the record changer and plodded out to the kitchen. Soon he reappeared with a tray containing beer, Roquefort cheese, rye bread, and rollmop herrings. As the pièce de résistance he produced a jar of anchovies. "If you don't like this kind of food, please don't tell me." He whisked out a napkin and tied it around David's neck. "This is the kind of meal Beethoven would have loved!" he said.

Then he went to his albums and returned with an English set. "This is the superb quartet," he said. "Opus 135 in F. It's not so long nor so moody as 130 and 132. But no man can write better music than this." He put the imported records on the changer and then slumped into a big chair, grabbing a chunk of bread and cheese as he sat down.

The music was unlike any David had ever heard before. It was patient music, building up slowly from the sounds of sixteen strings, but at times it seemed like more than a full orchestra, for the strings played upon every memory a young man could have. Gradually, as if there were no meaning to time, the wonderful quartet continued. Morris Binder made himself a huge sandwich of anchovies. He took a deep draught of bootleg beer and sighed, "God! This is wonderful!"

But then the inevitable Beethoven took over. In the last movement of the last quartet, as if he were a dying man, his strings began breathlessly to gallop. There were unpredictable and agonizing silences. There was a hurry of plucked notes as if death were at hand. The fleetingness and tragedy of living filled the room and drowned the taste of anchovies and beer and rollmops alike. Morris Binder stopped eating and listened transfixed as the music galloped to its close. The needle struck raspingly into the groove and the changer clicked. There was a moment of dreadful silence, as if Beethoven had actually died in that grotesque room. Then Binder said, "Let's hear that again."

Later, David found that whatever the huge man played induced a strange longing, so that when the last record of a set ended the editor invariably cried, like a child, "That was glorious! Let's hear that again!" And he would set the needle on the last record and play it once more, as if its harmonies had lingered in the air unfinished, as if he might never again hear that particular fall of notes, as if . . .

Harshly, one night, when Morris Binder played the last record of Brahms' Third many times, David realized why the mammoth man acted so. "He knows," David said, "that he may die. At any time. He may never hear this record again. How can he leave it?"

So whenever Morris Binder said, his eyes glowing, "Would you mind if I play that one side again?" David always said, "I'd like it." And he began to notice people and music and the look of the sky as if that were the last day he himself would ever live. When he did this, he saw that people were inexpressibly superb. He had never before actually seen a face: the way light falls across thin bones or bumps of fat to make a character, or the way some men walk sideways as if afraid to meet life head on. He had not seen Washington Square, not truly, until he looked at it one night coming home from Morris Binder's. Then he saw it fully, as if that were the last time on this earth he would ever see it, and there was a beauty about that Square he had never before even dimly perceived.

He went often to Morris Binder's and acquired a taste for anchovies and beer. In the gothic room with its absurd horns, he learned to know music that would sing in his memory forever: Dvorak's American quartet, Borodin's nocturne, the songs of Mahler. He became like Binder and wished to hear a single record a half dozen times, knowing that one good thing is better than a dozen poor. He recalled the lilting words of Shakespeare:

> That strain again! it had a dying fall:
> O! it came o'er my ear like the sweet sound
> That breathes upon a bank of violets,
> Stealing and giving odor . . .

But there was another music at Morris Binder's, and that was what made Beethoven and Dvorak so breathtaking. For David could never know when the huge man would thrust volcanically from his chair and fall upon the floor in writhing agony. Then Miss Adams, who hated music but who listened, would dash downstairs and minister to the fallen angel. "Why don't you get out of here?" she screamed at David one night. "You're bad for him! All this noise and excitement." She looked at David with such hatred that he fled the apartment even before Binder had recovered.

Next morning at Tremont Clay's he avoided her, but she surprised him by seeking him out. "Forgive me," she said quietly. "Especially since I have such bad news. You're to be fired."

"Me!" David gasped.

"Yes," she said gently. "Mr. Clay wants to see you. But listen, I have lots of odd jobs about this place. You keep coming back. I'll see you get them. You're a fine young man."

Mr. Clay spoke in crisp, nasal tones. "We've got to kill your magazines," he whined. "No reflection on you. As soon as things get better, you've got a good job here."

"When do you think that'll be?" David asked.

Mr. Clay sat down and fidgeted with a color drawing for one of his covers. "My guess is three years," he said. He saw David's face whiten and impulsively he jumped from his desk and grabbed the young editor. "You're a good man, Harper," he said with unaccustomed warmth. "These are the days when you have to prove it. Dig yourself in somewhere. You be the fellow that pulls through!" Then, ashamed of his outburst, he shoved David toward the door.

But Miss Adams whispered, as David went dejectedly past her desk, "I'll always have a little something for you to do."

And he was out in Lafayette Street, opposite the immigrant station, with no work and less than a hundred dollars. He looked at the red building where so many immigrants had brought their hopes and he said: "Hell, if all that gang could make the grade . . . Why, they didn't even know the language!"

But things were tougher in 1932 than they had been when immigrants were flooding our unsatiated labor markets. Now there were no jobs. Mom had said, "Whatever you do, don't go back to college. Worst bums I ever knew kept goin' back to university. Get a job takin' money on the subway. That leaves your mind free for writin'."

There were no jobs on the subway. There were no jobs at Macy's, at Bloomingdale's, nor with construction companies. There were no jobs sweeping streets nor with trucking firms. No men were wanted. Not anywhere. Yet the newspapers were filled with ads saying: "Energetic Man Wanted. Must have own car." David applied for one of these, and even though he had no car, was immediately hired.

"The job's easier with a car," a fast-talking man explained. "But if you don't mind work you can do almost as well without. This here electric sweeper weighs forty-three pounds. That's a big feature. Housewives love its free and easy motion."

The brisk talker gave David and thirty other young men a rapid one-day course on salesmanship and the operation of the cleaner. At the end of the day the man coughed and said, "Of course, there's no salary on this job. That's good, because it means there's no ceiling on what you can make." He gave a nervous laugh. "Fifty, hundred, three hundred a week! You set the limit. Ha ha!"

But his figures proved merely to be the number of families who said "No." By the fifth day David was glad when women simply slammed the door in his face. That was much better than listening to tragic stories of "My man's a good man. He's a hard worker, but he can't find a thing." There were so many tears each day, stories so desperate that David found himself helping to buy lunch for children who obviously had not eaten for days.

A deadly pall hung over New York that March of 1932. The full tide of unemployment reached the meaner streets and crept slowly toward the healthier thoroughfares. The women said: "I don't see how we can live unless something happens," and by the end of his second week David had to quit. He had not sold a cleaner.

The brisk-talking salesman slowed down now and said, as David turned in his papers. "We've got a wonderful cleaner here. But people can't afford to buy it. What's gonna happen in this country? Tell me that!" And when David left, he saw eighteen young men waiting to be hired as salesmen.

He now had fifty-three dollars left in bank, and if it had not been for Mom, he would have been helpless. As she had done before with almost a hundred young men, she allowed him to stay in his room without rent. She affected not to know that Claude was slipping David plates of food, and she even paid him a small salary to sweep up the place. He was now a janitor, and he plunged into his work with great energy. He made the restaurant spotless, something it had never been before. He even prevailed upon Mom to let him repaint the front of the house, and from his vantage point aloft a teetering ladder he watched the wonderful ebb and flow of life along MacDougal Street.

He came to know Mom better and discovered that she was one of the few people in life who had made peace with herself and with the world. She made no money from her restaurant, partially cleared taxes by renting rooms, and occasionally did well with a shipment of bootleg. Since she had three annuities ready for her old age—the gifts of admiring elderly men—she exercised no caution in spending her bootleg money, and it was well known that she quietly helped many young people to obtain a precarious footing in the jungles of New York.

Sometimes she would become maudlin drunk and pat David on the arm in a way that reminded him of the Gonoph. "You mark my words!" she would sniffle. "Some day I'll be studied at Columbia University. Why? Because I was the only friend Claude ever had." She stumbled about her very neat room and found one of the poet's books, printed at her expense. "You ever seen snow in Greenwich Village, after it's been on the streets a couple of days?" She became belligerent. "How would you describe it? You're no poet! But listen to that bearded goat." She fumbled with the pages and then read: "I shuffle through the worn-out snow." She put the book down and stared antagonistically at David. "I read that crap you wrote for *Fashion*. Boy, did that stink! Here, you can borrow this for a while. Knock off work and study it."

She sent David to his room with the slender volume. These days he was not even trying to find a job, content with his make-believe janitor's position. He stayed in his room for days analyzing Claude's peculiar verse. He found Claude's work amazingly compact. Words were used as scalpels to cut into the meaning of life. He had never thought of using words in that precise and restricted manner. He lay on his bed, nothing to do, no work, no prospect of any, and thought about writing.

Words seemed to him the sacred instruments through which the spirit's finest messages were conveyed. It was well and proper for the Metropolitan to boast of having acquired a picture worth $200,000. David was sure the glowing canvas was more valuable than that, for it was rare and spoke of the world's vast beauty; but what, he mused, would a nation pay for the only copy of *Don Quixote?* Let's suppose there were no printing presses or monks to copy manuscripts. How would the bidding go for a book like *The Way of All Flesh?* Or *Hamlet?* Who could price such works? Or a solitary copy of *The Eve of St. Agnes?* Or the King James Version?

Unemployed, he lay on his bed and tried to think of nothing. The hunger for Alison was still with him, but he put her out of his mind. He forced himself to ignore stricken Morris Binder, and he thought no more of jobs. His head became a whirl of nothingness, and after a while he found himself staring out of his window at the solid brick wall. He realized to his astonishment that he had never before seen that wall. It filled his window. Nothing else was there, but he had not seen the wall.

Each brick was of a subtly different color. Between the bricks the mortar was also as varied as life. During each hour of the day the wall changed its appearance. Each change of the sun's position illuminated the fine texture of brick in new ways. Here a fragment of plaster clung to one brick and shot a long shadow across three other bricks, so that their desert-brown shapes turned to purple. There a jagged crack lay blood red to the sun. As the day faded there was vivid motion of light along the face of the wall. Flecks of gold danced upon each irregular shape, and sandy colors, mingled with red and purple and gold and yellow, shone evanescent in the late afternoon.

Night fell, and the heavenly pantomime ended. Purple shadows, like spent blood, swept across the bricks, and David lay palpitating with emotion. In his life the moment had come, the breathless moment that has no name. It was the instant of dedication, when the illimitable and yet finite future lay ahead as brilliantly clear as the bricks had been. He said: "Writing is like that. Seeing what no one has ever seen before and writing it down so simply that everyone will say, 'Of course! I knew that all along.' If I can see, I can write. If I took a book and wrote down just one thing each day that I had actually seen . . ." The words stopped, for there were no words to describe the difference between looking and actually seeing. He fumbled with his ideas for a moment and said: "If I could see into the core of some one thing each day, say a horse eating oats, or a ferryboat, or the way a chair stands on the floor, I'd soon be so terribly filled with material that they couldn't stop me from writing. Not even with machine guns." In his dark room he saw with utmost clarity that art is merely the organization of things understood, and seeing is the heart of understanding. He said: "There's no reason why I couldn't write as well as Balzac . . ." Then he became ashamed of having made such a comparison, but it returned. "No! Damn it all!" he cried. "There is no reason why I couldn't!"

The darkness was about him, and the illuminating wall was gone, but within his own mind a light showed that would never go out. This was the moment without a name, when a young man stood alone and soberly acknowledged what he might accomplish. He could not guess it then, but he was sharing the fragile and explosive instant that comes with shocking and disrupting force to fumbling young men: "Why, I could be President!" "If he wrote an opera, why couldn't I?" "Why shouldn't I be the best architect?" "Somebody's going to marry her, why not me?"

Violently, he snapped on his light and attacked his typewriter as if it were his enemy. He would describe those bricks exactly as he had seen them, but as he wrote he was interrupted by Mom's strident voice: "Hey! Dave!"

"What's up?" he shouted.

"Someone to see you!" Then, in a lower voice, Mom said, "Go on up."

From the stairs below David could hear the approach of soft steps. Now his visitor was rounding the first landing, now approaching the last dark flight. David peered into the shadows and slowly perceived the emerging form of a woman. It was Mona Meigs.

"Hello, Dave," she said prosaically.

"Mona!" he cried in confused emotion. It was unbelievable, seeing her in his hallway. She wore a beret and a soiled blouse. She had on well-tailored slacks and a man's belt. She wore saddle shoes and rolled-down brown socks. She had no make-up on and seemed pallid. She was thinner than before and somewhat unkempt.

"I got to have a place to stay," she said directly. "I'm broke."

"Where's Cyril?" David asked.

She shrugged her shoulders. "We washed up months ago," she said. "Company folded."

"Well, come in."

Mona paused in the doorway and surveyed his room. "Not much of a dump," she said.

"I'm out of work," he explained.

A look of anguish came into Mona's face. "Oh, hell!" she cried. "Don't anybody have a job?"

"I'll put you up, somehow," he said.

"You've got to stake me!" she pleaded.

"I'll find some place to sleep . . ." he began. But when he said this a look of horror came into Mona's face. She had intended coming as a queen to dispense her favors, but she saw that David could not consider such an arrangement. Her shoulders sagged and she went to his mirror. There she saw her stringy hair, the greasy beret and the unwashed blouse. Her face was a mask, still beautiful, but her eyes were sunken. Not even her perfect breasts showed to advantage, and she saw how wretched she had become.

"I have a hot lead on a picture," she said. Then she pointed at herself in the mirror. "I got to find a place to repair that," she said with a tone of disgust.

"You can stay here," David said. He went downstairs to Mom's sitting room. "I feel like a damned fool," he began, apologetically.

Mom interrupted him. "I always figure a man has an inalienable right to make a horse's ass of himself once a year. I figure that's the actress you told me about."

"That's Mona Meigs," David said.

"And she wants a room. And she has no money. I'm the last person in the world's got a right to give anybody advice, considerin' the clown I've been. But if I was you, Dave, I'd tell her to haul tail out."

"How could I do that?" David asked.

"OK. You'd share your last dime with her. So we'll do it this way. You can have that room. She can have it. Or you and she can have it together."

"Can I sleep in the restaurant?"

"The fire inspector says no! No more bums sleepin' down there."

"I'll take her junk upstairs," David said. "I'll find a place to stay somewhere."

"Dave," Mom said quietly, "you're usin' up this year's quota. You're bein' a prime, A-1 Kansas City horse's ass."

"I said that first," David replied. He climbed back to his room and reported, "Mom says you can stay here for a while."

"What about you?" Mona asked.

"I'll find a place somewhere."

Mona pulled off her beret and tossed it onto the bed. She ruffed out her hair and combed it with her fingers. "I suppose the john's out in the hall?" she queried distastefully.

"That's right," David answered and went downstairs.

He left the restaurant and went to a bench in Washington Square. On the opposite side he could see Alison's house, a handsome red-brick structure with clean white trim. It looked like its inhabitant, and David thought how different Alison was from Mona in her present condition. He recalled how Mona had been offended when he had said that he would not stay with her, and her brash assumption that he would still want to love her infuriated him. Mona was cheap and tough and he wanted nothing to do with her. Inwardly, he admitted that he was glad she looked so drab, because that fortified his resolution.

But the more he thought of her, lying on his bed, the more excited he became. "I better go see Alison," he finally decided. Against his own judgment he crossed the Square to her cold, white building and rang her bell. When the door clicked he hurried up the carpeted stairs.

Alison waited at the top, but when she saw who it was she cried, "Oh, it's Dave. I don't want to see you." She retreated into her room and slammed the door. In the quiet and thickly carpeted hallway David banged on the door and cried, "Alison! I've got to talk with you. Mona Meigs came back."

"How dandy!" came the bright young voice from behind the door.

"Could she stay with you? For a while?"

"What's the matter with her fancy actor?"

"I don't know. They broke up." There was a long silence and finally the door opened slightly. Alison peered through the chink and David said with appalling frankness. "I don't want to fool around with Mona. Seeing her made me know how much I need you."

The intensity of this statement made Alison catch her breath, and she admitted David into her room, but when he tried to kiss her, she pushed him away. "Now we start all that again," she groaned.

She sat David on her expensive davenport and he tried not to study the room like a peasant, but it impressed him. He looked away from the rich furnishings to where Alison sat primly in a Chippendale chair. "I can't throw Mona out," he pleaded.

"I know you can't," Alison agreed. "In a way, I admire you." Then, suddenly, words bubbled forth and she said, "The crowd I have to go with make me sick, Dave. They're so phony! The people they make jokes about are twice as good as they are."

"Then why do you bother with them?" David asked.

"Because . . . Well, it's my job." The barrenness of this reply shocked David and he betrayed his disappointment.

"I didn't think you were the one who compromised," he said. "I do, but . . ."

"I don't compromise!" she said defiantly. "I study them like guinea pigs. You'll see them in my book. It's almost done." Then her tone became icy again and she inquired, "What have you accomplished?"

"Not much," he admitted. "I got fired as you predicted. I've done some sketches."

"Sketches!" the slim girl exploded, jumping to her feet. "You're starving in an attic and all you do is sketches! Dave," she pleaded, bending down and placing her hands in his, "believe me! I'll upset heaven and hell at *Fashion* to make them take articles from you. Do us something flashy or woman stuff . . ." Then she saw that she was using the wrong words. Angrily she turned from him and walked toward the window, but she stopped and stood with her hands upon her finely tailored hips.

"You may not believe it from things I've done to you, Dave, but you're terribly important to me. You were the first intelligent person to tell me I could be a writer. I wish . . . I wish to God we had been meant for each other. Because for all your dreaming nonsense, I can respect you. But I'm going to be a writer. You watch! I'll never let anything interrupt, and when we're old people, we'll meet and talk about it while we sit in the sun."

She held out her beautiful hands, but David kept his in his lap. He sensed that this was the last time he would ever talk with Alison. He said, "I've walked the streets with my heart pounding for you, Alison. I know you're not tough. I know it's a pose, because I know how scared you are down inside that you won't be first rate. And how do I know? Because I feel the same doubts." His voice grew intense, and he said, "I shall write good books, too. They're bursting within me. I can see whole sections written out in my mind . . ."

The fury of words was on him and he paced nervously. "I'll write as I never dreamed of writing before. I'm going to drag experience right into . . ."

"Have you actually written any of it yet?" Alison asked quietly.

"As I said, some sketches."

"And from that you can be sure?"

"Yes," David said.

"Well, I'll pray for you," Alison concluded. She allowed him to kiss her good-bye, the last kiss they would ever know, and for a moment he thought: "She's a warm, human person, after all." Thus encouraged, he asked impulsively, "Could you possibly lend Mona a hundred dollars?"

But as he looked into her bright face, her eyes grew remorselessly hard. "No," she said, and she closed the door forever.

He returned to Mom Beckett's, where he slipped into the restaurant and propositioned Claude. "How about letting me sleep on chairs for a couple of nights?" he begged.

The poet bit his lip for a moment and said, "You know Mom's been having trouble with the inspectors." But that night he arranged a rickety bed upon which David slept for five successive nights. In the daytime he worked feverishly at Claude's typewriter, banging out a *Fashion* story about the Taos Indians. He built a hard and glossy patina into the words, and at last his pages had the tight and stylized *Fashion* quality. When it was done he took it uptown himself and asked the girl at the desk to deliver it to Miss Webster.

But he was so tired that next morning he overslept and Mom found him sprawled on the chairs, his mouth dirty with the smell of stale tobacco smoke. "Ain't he one hell of a sight?" Mom asked the poet as she surveyed the sleeping form. She kicked one of the chairs and bellowed, "Hey! You! I gave strict orders for bums to sleep outside." Then, when David rubbed his eyes, she threw up her hands in mock horror and screamed, "My God! It's Harper!"

The comedy ended when the door opened and a little man in uniform cried with great satisfaction, "Ah-ha! Just as I thought! Sleeping customers in the restaurant."

"You pismire!" Mom shouted. "You get the hell out of this restaurant!" She started to throw a coffee cup at the little fellow when Claude interrupted her.

The inspector grinned triumphantly and announced, "This

time it's going to be a fine!" Mom broke loose from Claude's restraint and leaped at the little man, who ducked out, chuckling to himself.

"Now see what you done!" Mom exploded at David. She would have berated him further but a stentorian voice outside was shouting, "Is this Mom Beckett's?" She left David and thrust her head out the door. "Who'n hell you think it is?" The loud voice cried back, "But they told me Mom Beckett was an ugly old bag! You're beautiful!"

"It's Jensen!" Dave cried, and he brushed past Mom and into the broad arms of the Wild Man. The big football player clapped David on the back and barged into the restaurant. "Some joint!" he said approvingly. He lifted Mom in the air and gave her a kiss. "You're even prettier than Dave said," he joked.

"A big boy like you better have a drink!" Mom proposed.

"And I could use one. Even this early." The Wild Man tossed off a beer and a gin and then took David out into Washington Square.

"What's up?" David asked.

"Cyril Hargreaves. He's very sick."

"In New York?"

"Yes. You see, I wanted to help him, but . . ."

"I don't have a job either," David said.

"Times are sure tough," Jensen said. "What Cyril needs most is somebody to sit with him." The wonderful color in Jensen's face was gone and he seemed worn with the troubles of his times. "You see, Dave, the old boy is dyin'. Alone."

He led David to a dingy house on West Forty-eighth Street and then climbed four flights of narrow stairs. In a room with no curtains and a single forty-watt bulb they found the old actor. Cyril was thin, very gray, and he was visibly dying. When David entered Cyril nodded and allowed his leonine head to fall upon the pillow. His mouth hung open. He had not been shaved for two days, and saliva dripped from his beard.

"Let him sleep," the Wild Man said. "He may recognize you later."

"What's he got?" David asked in a whisper.

"Pneumonia and old age."

"Has he had a doctor?"

"Equity sent one. I had no dough." The Wild Man explained the medicines and added, "You take over. I been here two days."

"Where you living?" David asked.

"Here and there," the Wild Man replied. The two friends looked at each other and said no more. While Jensen checked the medicine David looked at the sick man. Tears came into his eyes and he wanted to wipe them away, but he was ashamed to do so while Jensen remained. Cyril Hargreaves, the proud man! Lying in a grimy white bed. The blankets were thin and had been soiled for years. In lusher days lovers had come to this room and had wrapped themselves in those blankets. About the old actor's face the edges of the blankets were frayed, and they formed a gruesome shroud for the greatness that had once moved that wasted body.

"This is awful!" David muttered.

"Oh, he had a pretty good life," the Wild Man mused. "I'm going now. I can hardly keep my eyes open. But I'd give my last buck to get my hands on that bitch Mona Meigs."

David controlled his face. "She missing?" he inquired.

"Yep. They hit hard times, and as soon as the dough was gone, she high-tailed it out. I saw her the other day. She wouldn't come up to see him. She looked like hell. Ran away from me."

"You get some sleep," David said.

"You were in love with her, weren't you?" Jensen asked at the door.

"Who?"

"Mona. She sure looks like hell now." The Wild Man shook his head and left.

At dusk Cyril awoke. The newspaper shielding the light had slipped away, and a yellow glare filled his gaunt face. He did not recognize David but called him a stumbling "Mr. J'ns'n." He hawked and huffed, as in the old days, and said graciously, "I believe I have some med'sin due me. And I'm afraid the lamp needs some adjustment." He took the medicine and made a wry face. "The theatre has had a very bad season, Mr. J'ns'n. Things . . . have . . . been . . . very . . . slow . . . indeed."

He lapsed into a coma and for one frantic moment David thought he had died. But when the breathing seemed to have stopped completely, the old voice said, "I'll take a little nap." David pulled the worn blankets about the foam-flecked beard.

This was the end of the artist! This was how artists and poets and actors and novelists died! In a lonely room, with rented furniture and a shaky bed. This was the echo of applause, the true face when the masking was ended. Bitterly, and without comprehension, David recalled the endless towns Cyril Hargreaves must have played in his long career. Now they were shadows, and the laughter had ceased. He was dying in a dirty room on West Forty-eighth Street.

For a moment David's consuming preoccupation with experience came back and he remembered the night he had lain in the truck while Vito and the Wild Man had gone inside for hot dogs. That same feeling of infinite remoteness now attacked him, and he knew that whether he willed it or not, his avaricious mind was noting each shred of the raveled blanket exactly as it had recorded sounds on that distant night, or as it had studied the light falling across barren bricks outside his window.

Hargreaves moved, but David's mind continued to note the peculiar shape the blankets took as they rested upon the dying man. And the four bottles, they could be described like this: "Near the curve of the scarred bedstead rose four bottles like the pediment of a Greek temple." David blinked his eyes. "For God's sake!" he cried at his mind. "Stop! Stop!"

The night wore on, and the room became familiar. David studied the way in which the wallpaper was soiled. Some man with much pomade had often sat in that chair with his feet upon the bed, resting his greasy hair upon the wall. Over there a man—perhaps the same one—had blown his nose with his finger, and again the wall was stained. He was not frightened by these things. He did not fear that he himself might one day die in such a room, for he knew that he was as deeply committed to the world of art as Cyril Hargreaves had been. This barren room with its obscene stains might be the end of the artist, but it would never be the end of art. He remembered consolingly a long-forgotten name he had seen scrawled upon a rafter, God alone knew where: "Robert Mantell. Hamlet. February 3, 1907."

At four o'clock the dying man awoke and immediately recognized David. "Mr. Harper!" he called feebly. "It's so very good of you to visit with me!" He extended a thin, worn hand in exactly the gracious manner he would have used had David been visiting him in an expensive suite. Yet his quick mind saw that David was shocked by the quality of the hand, and he laughed, "So much can happen in two years." He lay back and smiled at his visitor. "I've seen several of my old friends," he said, mentioning names David did not know.

"But one person has been much in my mind. What happened to Miss Emma Clews?"

"I don't know," David said.

"I've been chuckling over her superb performance . . . What were we playing, Mr. Harper?"

They recalled events from that last Chautauqua. "We were fortunate to share that final tour," the old actor said. "I would not have missed it. Is it day or night?"

"It's day," David replied. "It's dawn."

"Could I prevail upon you . . ." He fell back. A very thin finger rubbed his chin and he said, " . . . Yesterday I could not shave. I have a feeling that Miss Meigs may call today. Could I prevail upon you to help me?"

The process was almost unbearable. David held the old man up, a bundle of tired bones held tenuously together by will and undead tissues. He felt as if he were being dragged against his will into the stratagems of death. For a moment he thought that he would be sick, like the old women in the poorhouse, but Lord Cyril rubbed the fresh cheeks and said, "It's a superb feeling, to be fresh shaven. I have a decided presentiment that Miss Meigs will call today."

At eight Jensen banged noisily into the room and cried, "If it was summer, Cyril, we'd go out to a ball game." Then he whispered to David, "Get some sleep and come on back about six. He'll die for sure tonight."

Tired, and with sand in his eyes, David rushed to his room, where Mona still lay in bed. She had cold cream on her face and her hair was in curlers. She had been sleeping in her underwear. "What brings you here?" she asked.

"Get some clothes on!" David commanded with sudden fury.

"What goes on?"

"I just left Cyril Hargreaves."

Mona thew her hands over her face. "Don't! Don't!" she wailed.

"Get up, damn you!" David shouted. He ripped the bed-clothes from her, and she stood defiantly by the bed.

"I can't go up there!" she protested. "I saw him once in that awful room. He understands, Dave."

Mona!" David shouted. "He won't live through the night. Get your clothes on."

"No!" she screamed, and when he grabbed her, she became hysterical. Mom and Claude hurried upstairs.

"What goes on here?" Mom demanded. Mona continued to scream.

"Tell her to get dressed!" David commanded.

"No! No!" Mona cried. She fled to Mom's strong arms, and the big woman protected her from David.

"What is it, Dave?" Mom asked.

"An old man is dying. She lived with him until his money was gone."

"You better leave her alone," Mom said quietly.

"By God, I won't!" David swore. "I held that old man in my arms while he shaved, hoping that she'd come see him today . . ." His voice broke and in despair he lunged at Mona, but with a big, firm hand Mom pushed him away.

"Beat it, Dave," she counseled. Stubbornly he tried to reach Mona, but the landlady would not permit him to do so. "Some things," she said firmly, "you can't make a person do."

"But that lousy tramp . . ."

"Dave!" Mom pleaded. "Doin' some things ain't of much significance. I guess I've seen more'n three hundred people die, more or less, and it never made a bit of difference who was there or what fine things anybody said, because when a person dies . . . Wheeeewt!" She made a horrible, low, whistling sound, as if a stubborn lamp had been extinguished.

That night the doctor said, "The old fellow's very weak."

"Any change in the medicine?" Jensen asked.

"No. I'll drop by tomorrow," the doctor replied. He paused as if about to say something more. Then he left.

Cyril was fully rational and seemed glad that David and Jensen both were to stay with him. "And in the seventh hour," he said, "men of the village came to sit with him." He laughed weakly at David and cackled, "Don't ask me who said it. I said it."

David inquired which of his many roles he had most enjoyed. He thought for a minute, accentuating his fallen cheeks by sucking in their remnants. "It would have to be Polonius," he admitted. "An actor can do a great deal with Polonius."

"You played him in John Barrymore's company, didn't you?" David asked.

And Jensen sighed loudly and said, "John Barrymore! There was a man who could act!"

The worn old trouper turned onto his right elbow and with difficulty stared at Jensen. "Did you say John . . . Barrymore? Really, Mr. Jensen! I should have thought a summer in stock would have taught you some discrimination." He fell back on his pillow and stared sadly at the greasy wallpaper. "But I suppose," he mused, "that the movies have corrupted you." Then he snorted. "Simply because a man has a profile! Let me tell you, Mr. Jensen . . ."

He fell asleep, and the watchers kept each other awake by various means, so that his medicine would not be missed. At midnight they awakened him. He was extremely weak, and Jensen supported him so that he could swallow. The Wild Man was exquisitely tender and kidded Cyril along as if he were a child, "Now Goddamnit, Sir Cyril, open your mouth and let this good li'l ol' stuff trickle down!" He laid the frail old man back on the pillow and adjusted the blankets so that the frayed ends would not tickle.

"I hoped that you might find Miss Meigs," Cyril said. "If you ever do, see that she has a place to stay until she gets a part. She's a superb actress. We'll all be proud of her one day." He looked about the room as if he might find her where the others had failed. Seeing only shadows, he drifted back to sleep.

The watchers slumped forward in their chairs. They were now in the lonely hours when the darkest night gasped bitterly to hold back the dawn. The noises of the wakening city had not yet begun, and there were no birds.

In spite of their intentions, the two young men fell asleep, and toward four Cyril awoke in delirium and started to whisper hoarsely, "Watch that broken pole! Mr. Harper! I beg you! Watch that pole!" He mumbled for some minutes and failed to waken either of his friends. Then his mind slowly cleared. He saw them slumped forward in their chairs. His old mouth moved in uncontrolled starts. "Let them sleep," he said, and died.

David would surely have brooded upon Cyril's death had not the great MacDougal brawl intervened. Fights were common in the cosmopolitan Village, where fiery Italians assaulted one another and white men beat up Negro men for dating white women. Gay blades from uptown often took a few drinks and discovered themselves to be witty, irresistible Lotharios, whereupon someone bashed them in the face and taught them otherwise.

But a brawl on MacDougal Street had a special quality. It was louder and rougher than the others because Mom Beckett was usually involved. And across from Mom's lived an immense fat lady with a voice like a klaxon. Since she was too heavy to move about, she sat on a soap box in a second-story window and spied upon the restaurant. Whenever a good fight seemed imminent she whipped open her window and shouted in piercing screams. "Fight! Fight! Fight!" Then all of Mac-Dougal Street poured out to watch the ruckus.

On a warm day in December the fat lady was watching the empty street when she saw Mom Beckett throw the little fire inspector out of the restaurant. Then Mom shouted, "So you'll report me, will you? I'll break your goddamned neck!" The inspector made some brave reply, and Mom grabbed him by the coat lapels.

"Fight! Fight!" screamed the fat woman. From every door along the street men and women and children catapulted onto the sidewalks, and among them David appeared to see what Mom was doing. As he arrived, the neat, marcelled woman pushed the little inspector in the face.

"You little stinker!" she cried. David tried to rescue the inspector, for he knew that if Mom actually struck him she would be arrested; but when the big Arizona woman saw David attempting to break up the brawl she said, "Dave! You stand clear."

"He's the law!" David protested.

"He's a pismire!" Mom replied, and in the excitement she hauled her right arm back and socked the frightened little man. On her fifth wallop a flash bulb went off, and it was this picture that made the fight famous. It was printed in all the papers under the heading "Arizona Amazon," and it showed a meticulously dressed woman, her hair unruffled, swinging a terrific haymaker at a quaking little man. What made the picture truly hilarious was that Mom was biting her lower lip as if eager to muster all her power into the blow.

The case of the Arizona Amazon was a six-day wonder. One New York paper dubbed her the "MacDougal Mauler" and said, "She makes Gene Tunney look like a bum." The judge, of course, took a more serious view. He said that the appointed servants of the people could not be put in danger of their lives—here the courtroom began to heave with chuckles—simply because someone did not like the decisions of the appointed servants of the people. Mom Beckett had been clearly heard to say in the presence of witnesses that "she would break that little bastard's neck," and judging from the photograph entered as evidence—here the judge coughed —she had come pretty close to doing so. "Thirty days!"

So they carted Mom off to jail, and then an unforeseen thing took place. Claude became ill. He actually became sick because of his worry over Mom. For years people had seen him hanging around the restaurant and had taken for granted that he was Mom's whilom lover, but now the full quality of his passion for the big woman from Arizona manifested itself. He lay in bed and cried. He experienced deep pain at the degradation Mom had suffered, and he could not eat.

David ran the restaurant, which did a tremendous business, and between times went up to see Claude. The bearded poet lay wanly on his bed and said, "It was a frightful thing. Those damned fools just wanted her to make a spectacle of herself." Then tears came into his eyes. Later he said, "That violent voice shouting 'Fight! Fight!' She's the woman who should have been arrested. It's like the line from *Othello*: 'Silence that dreadful bell!' "

For two weeks Claude would not get up. Friends who had visited Mom in prison reported on her good health. They said she and the police got along fine, since they had so many common acquaintances. Finally one consistent old drunk said, "Mom'd like to see you, Claude."

This intelligence put the poet into a nervous state and a conclave was held. A collection was taken and David purchased a large bunch of flowers. The men combed and dressed Claude, but it was apparent that he could not negotiate the trip by subway, so they plopped him and David into a cab and sent them off to jail.

The police were very considerate. They took Claude right in and produced Mom. She looked better than ever and seemed to have been dining well. When she saw the flowers she winced and said, "I'm a prisoner, not a corpse." Then Claude began to weep, and he looked across the barren table at her as if his heart had been stricken. She comforted him as best she could and said the flowers were wonderful. Just what she needed. But when Claude left, sniffling and weak-kneed, she held onto David's sleeve.

"He must be nuts!" she whispered. "I need flowers like an ox needs a tail full of cement. Psst! Kid! How about sneakin' me in a pint of gin? That's what I really need."

So David sent Claude home in a taxi and then scrounged about the Village till he found a pint of gin. To his surprise the jailer laughed and said, "For Mom Beckett it's OK, but don't let the blue-noses hear about this." He let David go right back to Mom's cell, where the big handsome woman knocked the top off the bottle and took a lusty swig.

"Jesus!" she cried. "That's even worse than I used to sell. But it's good!"

Then David felt that he must explain. "I'm running the restaurant, Mom. And if you don't mind, I'm sleeping in your room."

Mom put down the bottle. "You mean that the scrawny actress is upstairs? And you're down?"

"Yes. After the old man's death I never want to see her again."

Mom took a deep swig of gin and shook her head. "Honest to God, Dave, you must have mush in your brains." She was going to add further comments but decided against it. "Look after Claude, will you?" she asked. "Tell him not to worry. All this jail means to me is a chance to get some regular sleep." When David left, she was sitting on her hard bed, with the gin bottle in one hand and a comb in the other.

"She's the best woman we ever had in this dump," the jailer said proudly. "Big-hearted sorta, like my wife."

The snow began about eight in the morning. Dreamily it fell upon the great city, and by mid-afternoon Washington Square was a place of formless beauty. The statue of Garibaldi, that chaotic adventurer, stood draped in a Roman toga, while upon the triumphal arch of Washington, a better organized adventurer, ruffles of white clung handsomely.

The sky was somber gray, and still the moist flakes fell. To the east the tall and ugly university buildings at last looked passably decent, as if their architect in shame had thrown a gossamer shroud about their hideousness. To the south slept the unimportant buildings that had housed the poets and the novelists and the painters. On these houses, where the creators had lived in their productive years, the snow fell with a kind of benison, as if it, senseless, knew that some painter, later than the rest, was watching it so that he might recall it for later use in some evocative canvas.

Actually, there was no watching painter, but in the middle of the Square, confused and reveling in the silent thunder of the snowstorm, stood David Harper in wet shoes, watching the whiteness fall upon the varied architecture he had grown to love. He turned around many times to see first the shrouded university buildings, then the painters' homes, and then the handsome Georgian doors along the north. The stark and

barren trees clutched for a moment at accumulating burdens
and then sent them tumbling to earth in a flurry of flakes.
The fountain was lost beneath a solemn mound such as might
have marked the grave of the ancient Indians who had owned
the Square. This was the old potter's field of New York, and
David thought, "My people are in potter's field, too." Mysteriously, the twisting curtain of snow segregated the Square
and the Village from the rest of the city, so that David could
feel that he was, for once, standing absolutely alone in the
heart of New York.

But he was not quite alone, for on a bench near Washington's arch, a venturesome couple, wrapped high in coats,
huddled together in kisses. It was unbelievable! Even in the
midst of this increasing storm, there were lovers in Washington Square, and David thought, "I've seen it in all kinds of
weather, and there's always been at least one couple kissing.
Maybe that's why it's such a wonderful place." He stamped
his wet feet and from a distance saluted the kissing pair.
"Hiya, champs!" he called into the storm. Then he became
aware of his feet and muttered, "I'm getting cold!"

Yet, like winter wheat, David thrived in the snow. Its great
beauty, in the heart of his city, reminded him of strange and
towering things. He watched the buses struggling to breast
the drifts. Taxis no longer scurried back and forth, and students leaving the university bowed their heads low to forge
a path through the indifferent flakes.

Tumultuous ideas possessed him as he stamped back and
forth across the drifted Square. He felt, strangely, as if God
had touched him that day, and his mind was in a ferment
of hugh cloudy symbols. Names and scenes flashed across
his memory, summoned by nothing but the storm. Words of
towering evocation sprang to his mind: *field, clouds, and
Hector lay face down upon the dust of Troy, this island of
my soul, hunger, petticoat* . . .

Up from the Hudson River, along the canyons, winds
whistled into the Square and made a momentary blizzard,
but then the echoing quietness of a city storm fell once more
upon the burdened buildings, and David muttered, "Boy! My
feet really are cold!"

Reluctantly, he plunged homeward to MacDougal Street.
He was still determined not to go near Mona, but his sight
of the lovers kissing in the snow had reminded him that the
slim actress was at that very moment in his bed, alone. He
recalled how entrancing Mona had seemed that morning when

she came downstairs for some of Mom's free food. Even
the circles under her eyes had disappeared. Twice David had
asked, "When are you leaving?" and she had replied, "You
know I got nowhere to go." She was there now, in his room.

He paused for one last look at the swirling snow and then
went down the flight of steps into the steamy restaurant. As
soon as he appeared, the loafers ran up to him in deputation
and handed him a long envelope. It was from *Fashion*, and
with cold fingers he ripped it open. Inside was a $300 check
for his story, and miserable Claude, who had not received
$300 for his whole output of poetry, became so excited that
he served free drinks to the entire crowd.

There was much talk as to who could cash the check, but
finally a man guzzling from a full bottle of rye said, "Lemme
see that check." He studied it for a moment and said, "That's
a real check. You sign it here and I'll cash it." He pulled
from his hip a roll of bills so large that he had to tug upon it
to tear it loose from his pocket. Peeling aside the thousand-
and five-hundred-dollar bills, he came at last to the mere
hundreds. "Here," he grunted, handing David three of them.
And that trivial incident was what launched the strange
events of that day.

The man was a notorious, cheap gangster. When he handed
David the three bills he was standing beside Claude, so that
with one glance David could see both men, and the discrep-
ancy between them was shocking. There stood the bearded
poet, and he had no money. Across from him stood the petty
thief, the gambler, the bootlegger, the dabbler in all the
rackets of the night, and this man had to peel away the big
bills before he could reach the hundreds.

There are certain acts in a man's life which spring from
no sensible cause. A young man may stand in a snowstorm
and immediately afterwards see a poet and a gangster, and
without cause he is constrained to act in a given way. He has
been stirred by the deep sources that agitate his race, and
the acts which follow may be called acts of faith, for by them
he reaffirms the hidden purposes of his life.

With his $300 David ran out of the restaurant and dashed
through the swirling streets so that he left behind him a
miniature blizzard. He ran to the jail, where the jovial keeper
said, "Even Mom Beckett ain't allowed to have $200 in this
jail."

"Could I see her anyway?" David asked.

"What for?"

"Let me give her the dough, and then you can keep it for her."

"Look, buddy! Awready we got a hundred special rules for that dame. Now you want me to open a bank!" But nevertheless the jailer led David to the small visiting room into which Mom finally entered. She was trim, well rested, well corseted. Her big face grinned happily at David and she said, "I suppose you're right well adjusted to my room by now. Well, haul ass outa there by Saturday night. They're springin' me!"

"Mom," David said, "I got a break today, and I want to pay you back some of the dough I owe you." Before she could protest he plopped $200 into her hand.

"Look, kid!" She laughed. "I never expect to get dough back. Especially not from writers. You need it. Look at your shoes!"

David pulled his hand away. "It's yours."

"But I don't need it!"

David stared at her and asked, "Didn't you ever get money that you didn't want?"

The big Arizona woman laughed at her star boarder and said, "Not very often, but once or twice I did pick up a buck or two I was ashamed to own." She yelled for the jailer and gave him the two hundred to be put with her things. Then she placed both hands on the table, palms down, and asked, "Since you gotta leave my room by Saturday, why don't you and Miss Mona make up?"

"I've been thinking about that all day," David admitted.

"Walkin' around in the blizzard, eh? Look, kid, let me give you one piece of advice. Knock yourself out for principle. Give away your dough. Knock yourself out for revenge, or power, or ambition. But never knock yourself out for love."

"What do you mean?" David asked.

"Just this. Power and ambition and writin' and all that crap is sort of extra. I guess good men bother themselves quite a bit about such stuff. But don't ever bother about love. Don't crucify yourself on that cross, because lovin' is so easy and natural there should never be no pain to it. If you still got that itchy feelin' for Mona, why hop to it. Save your ponderin' for somethin' tough and big. Love is too simple to make a fuss over."

The warden said that David would have to go, and as he left Mom shouted across the corridor, "Remember! Outa my bed by Saturday!"

Giving Mom $200 was a simple act of decency. What David did next was the act of faith. He wandered home through the silent streets, and at Mom's he slipped in by the main door so as to avoid the restaurant. He climbed the steps, not to Mom's room, but on up to his own. Mona was sitting hunched by the radio, and he said, "Turn it off, Mona," and when she had done so, he grinned at her and said, "I gave you the first hundred-dollar bill I ever had, because when you took that screen test it was my test, too." He thrust his last bill into her hands and said, "Right now I'm dead sure you'll be a great actress. You're part of me, and you just can't fail."

In their old clothes and poverty they looked at each other: at the faded dress and the worn coat, at the thin shoes and the thin faces. It would have been difficult to say which of the two had enough spiritual reserve left over to comfort the other, and yet when they went to bed their love-making was even more violent than it had been in the old days, except that now David sought release even more desperately than Mona. Outside their window the still-falling snow drifted down between the buildings like a veil drawn across the dirty panes.

Toward nine that night they rose and put on their old clothes. In David's mind unappeased longings lunged recklessly about. He said, "This may sound silly, Mona, but I'd like to take a walk in the snow."

"Why not?" she asked.

They slipped past the restaurant, and David saw the gangster still lounging at the bar. Claude remained on his stool, lost and lonely without Mom. In the muffled streets snow still fell, and standing at the head of one of them David felt that all the poets who had sung of snow upon rolling hillsides should see it just once as he saw it then. In the country snow is merely an additional adornment, but in a sprawling city it is—for brief moments until traffic and soot engulf it— the most beautiful dress that nature ever wears. It clothes the drabness and it hushes the strident noise. It erases the architect's willful blunders, and it hides away the garbage. It brings an absolute beauty to the shapes of tall buildings and makes serene the drunken lurchings of mean old houses that should have been torn down long since. And when, in addition to all this, a thousand electric stars play upon it, throwing ghostly banners across its placid surface, new-fallen city snow is a thing of cold and perfect beauty.

Mona and David plowed westward, and at last they came upon the Hudson. For some minutes they watched a lonely ferry boat battling its way to Jersey, and then David understood in one flashing moment what this day had been about. For in the crying distance the ferry boat sounded its mournful fog horn, and it was like a barge along the Delaware canal, petulantly crying for the lock keeper. In that single moment David saw the entire novel he had been wanting to write. As if all the tiny lights that played upon the snow had been collected into one penetrating beam, a light from somewhere illuminated the chaotic ideas that had been festering in his mind and reduced them to order.

"I've got it!" he cried across the snowstorm. "Mona! I'm going to write a novel about the canal where I grew up. I knew an old man . . . We called him Old Daniel . . . He lives on a canal barge, and you're his daughter!"

"If I'm in the book," Mona observed, "it'll be a wow!"

"You *are* the book!" David said, and then as if voices were speaking to him he heard the opening lines of his novel: *"Whenever the distant horns sounded, I ran to the top of the hill to watch my beloved barges drift down the canal."* He stopped in great happiness, as if at last the oboe in a chattering orchestra had sounded the note about which the musicians could organize their music.

"You're shivering," Mona said. "Let's go home."

With her hundred dollars Mona bought herself a new wardrobe. Helping her do so was a fascinating experience for David. To buy one dress, for example, she went to at least ten stores. She made out a list of contingencies. "If I buy a blue dress," she reasoned, "I'll have to have blue shoes and a new hat. But if I buy one of those snappy grays, I'll need a new hat and a new sweater, but I can use my old shoes." With these combinations in mind she plodded from store to store. "Do you think it sticks out a little too far in back?" she would ask David. "After all, I do have just a wee bit of an unnnh! back there." She tossed her hips like a burlesque queen.

Each dress looked perfect to David's enthusiastic eye, but Mona found something wrong with them all. Once David said, "Why don't you grab one and have done with it?" She stared at him with scorn. "That's all right for you," she said. "Most of the time you look as if your mom baked the bread and then made your suit out of the sack. But all I've got to go on is my looks."

When the ordeal was completed, it seemed as if Mona had spent not one hundred dollars but five or six hundred. And much of it had gone for odds and ends of things, so that she bewildered David by appearing always different, as if she had an endless supply of dresses. She fascinated him in other ways, too. He came to know the solid joy of living with another person. He loved the play of her personality as he saw it intimately. He liked to come back to his room—after doing nothing, for there were no jobs—and to find her there listening to the radio. It was warm and meaningful to be associated with another human being.

The radio was a source of pain to Mona. She kept it going as much as eighteen hours a day, her head swaying in time to popular airs. If a woman's voice began to sing "Dancing in the dark . . ." she would leap to her feet, and it was apparent that she was comparing the singer's voice to her own. Finally the moment would come when she could no longer bear to hear the song, for either the singer was better than she, and therefore intolerable, or the singer was much worse, and it was agony to hear a fine song tortured by ineptitude. She would snap the radio off and walk angrily up and down the room, beating one fist into the other palm. Sometimes tears would come to her eyes and she would cry, "Damn it! Damn it! Listen to that bag murder that song! And she's got a job!"

Each passing day frightened her, and she often stared at David. "Tell me, kid. Do the lines show in my face? Christ, it's terrible to be living now. No work and getting older."

When she smoked she used a long cigarette holder, carefully placing its tip far back in her mouth. "What's the trick?" David asked. She removed the holder and tapped her beautiful teeth. "Keeps the china closet clean," she explained. "Some day those teeth'll be my fortune." Nor would she drink red wine. "Stains the china," she said. With great care she watched her diet, often refusing to eat, even though Mom's food cost nothing. When Mom gave David enough money for two movie tickets, he took Mona, but the movies were no relaxation. Tensely she followed each scene until envy destroyed her. She would whisper, "Look at that bitch! She's got legs like a piano mover's. That lousy tramp!" Often she darted out of the theatre, and David would find her hunched up before the radio torturing herself there rather than in the movies.

Once on the radio she heard Vito's voice and she went practically mad with excitement. "He could get me a job!" she cried, hammering David on the chest.

They went to NBC where Vito introduced her to a half dozen people. Some men listened to her sing. "She's got talent," they agreed.

"They always say that," Vito whispered to David. "Everybody up here crawls with talent."

"Do you have any speaking parts?" Mona begged the men.

"We'll take your name," they said gravely. "If anything turns up, we'll call you."

Then Mona tortured herself about the telephone. She insisted upon keeping the door open, in case the phone might ring. This annoyed the man next door, because the incessant radio kept him awake. He protested and Mona stormed out into the hall. "You goddamned old sonofabitch!" she began, heaping upon him the black bilgewaters of her frustration. He protested to Mom, who told him to go to hell.

Finally, one day the phone rang, and Mona practically fell down the stairs in her dash to answer it. But it was only Vito. He wanted them to come up to his place for supper. She agreed, but when she got back to the room she began to tremble. "Dwarfs!" she said. "Dave, if I get too nervous, take me home. Promise me that."

The dwarfs had a tiny apartment, befitting their size, and Betty was pregnant. David kissed her warmly and cried, "I hope it's a big, bouncing boy!" But the sudden stillness that greeted this phrase was so awkward that David knew these little people had been thinking constantly of that ugly problem: "Will our child be normal?"

Hitherto such a silence would have embarrassed David. He would have blushed and been ashamed of himself, but his association with Mom had cured him of such nonsense. He saw that if there is anything people deeply need and want it is the frank discussion of submerged and mouldering problems.

"Yes," he said boldly, "I hope it's a boy and I hope it's a big fellow. Think how much a big boy would love a mother like you, Betty."

As if a dam had broken, little Vito began to talk fast. "Even if he was small, do you think we'd be an embarrassment to him? Of course, we'd bring him up with the knowledge that he was going to be small. Betty tells me that as soon as she could understand, her parents taught her she would be small. Mine tried to hide it from me. Of course, my people hadn't read any books when they got to America."

"How is your father?" Mona asked Betty in cold, controlled accents.

"My father lost his memory in the crash," Betty said quietly. "He shot himself."

Mona rose nervously and asked, "Mind if I turn on the radio!" She got some music and turned it very loud. "Listen to this!" Then, as suddenly, she turned it off and looked at Vito. "How soon could you tell if a child . . . If he's going to be big?"

The little man said, "About six months, I think."

Betty interrupted. "My parents said they knew about me in eight months, but with a boy I guess you could tell sooner."

Impulsively Mona sat beside the little woman and said, "I'll make a small bet. One copper penny that your kid's going to be a big one. But take my advice, Betty. Don't let Vito near him, because big or small, Vito'll string him up for a puppet."

"Speaking of Chautauqua," Vito cried happily, "what happened to the Gonoph?"

"I don't know," David replied.

"Wasn't she the world's worst?" Vito asked. "I have a small part in *Mother Turner's Triumph*. I'm a dopey old woman, and all I do is say to myself, 'How would the Gonoph say this line?' I'm a sensation."

"Does radio pay pretty well?" Mona inquired.

"Not the kind I get," Vito said.

"He's a monument to the fleeting voice!" Betty laughed. "He used to tell me, 'Listen at 2:15.' But if a car shifted gears I missed him. I don't bother any more."

The little people were effusive in their good-byes. "You must both come again," they insisted. "We haven't had so much fun in years." Little Betty took Mona's hand and said, "Really, come back."

On the street Mona said, "You were good for them, Dave. They wanted to talk about the baby."

"I was afraid you'd wreck things," David admitted. "You were swell."

"You can trust me," she assured him. "I don't like death, that's all. I don't like growing old or people who aren't getting along." She shivered and said, "It's terrible to be without work."

"I'm glad I saw you in action tonight," David said. "Because I know a wonderful guy who has fits. I've been afraid to take you there."

Mona and Morris Binder got along fine. They understood each other at once. All during the summer they played music together, and drank beer, and ate the weird foods that Binder liked so much. Twice Mona was present when Morris fell into cataleptic trances. She held his head until Miss Adams could arrive.

The big man told David that Mona was a great girl. "You planning to get married?" he asked.

"We might," David said, but even as he spoke he knew that Mona would marry no one until she attained success. When the next winter came he died many deaths for her. He would see her scanning the theatrical news. With her last pennies she would buy *Variety* and devour the argot of her trade. For those few hours she was herself, lost, lost in the world of make-believe. But reading of show people made her as tense as a caged thought, and she would burst from her small room and haunt the casting offices. She taught Claude to trim her hair, and the poet would work on it three or four hours a week, snipping single strands here and there to accentuate the curl.

But when snow fell and the season actually began, Mona became inconsolable. Neither she nor David had any money —a loan from Mom now and then—and there was no way for Mona to hide the fact that she was an actress, broke and out of work. David was not surprised, therefore, when he found the note. It was stuck between the bristles of his brush: *"Don't try to find me. Good luck, trouper."*

For two days David lived in his empty room, and each hour brought some new pang of regret that Mona was gone. Finally he took her message to Morris Binder, who said, "I'm sorry to see that note. She was a good girl." The ponderous man did not try to console David. "Things like this happen all the time," he said. "Each man gets his share. I think you accept them better on herring and beer than on almost any other philosophical underpinning."

Then, one night David found where Mona had gone. Mom gave him a quarter and he went to a cheap movie. When it came time to go home, he could not face the prospect of his dreary room. Before Mona had shared it with him it had been a good room. Now he felt that no room from which a woman was missing could be very satisfactory. So in his loneliness he went into an all-night restaurant on Eighth Street and ordered coffee and doughnuts. He liked the steamy friendliness of the place, and with a show of bravado, plunked his last dime on the counter, slipping his thumb into his belt as if he were an important man with a few idle moments to kill.

A night wanderer entered and sought attention. "Say!" he cried. "Did you see the pictures in tonight's paper?" The customers ignored him and he ordered some coffee. Then he tried again. "You ever see such awful pictures of an axe murder?" Again he was rebuffed, and finally he thrust the paper under David's nose. "They sure chopped him up, di'n' they?" he demanded. But David's eye was attracted to the lower right-hand corner where Mona Meigs and Max Volo were shown in an expensive night club under the heading: "Philadelphia Promoter and His Lovely."

This was the dark winter of 1933. It was a cold and frightening time. A political interregnum ruled the nation, and there were ugly rumors. Plants closed, and men like Betty Fletcher's father committed suicide.

David had now started to organize thought-chapters for his novel. He would wander about the fine old streets of the Village composing whole chapters in his mind. Some days he would repeat a single phrase more than a hundred times, constructing around it an ever-towering edifice of ideas. Even on the most snowy days he could visualize canal barges drifting down a summery canal. When he had perfected a chapter in his mind, he would feel good, almost as good as if it had been committed to paper. The characters of his book—still nameless—came to have greater reality to him than people he met on the Village streets.

Of course, he had no money. In anticipation of Repeal, Mom permitted him to rebuild the bar, and for this she gave him such odds and ends of change as he had to have. He also reported daily to Miss Adams, but usually she said, "Nothing today, David."

But occasionally she gave him a half dozen galleys to proofread. Sometimes he saw Mr. Clay, who was much older now. The trim gray man edited five magazines and Morris Binder took care of the rest. The other editors had all been fired.

On press days Miss Adams often said, "Here's a bunch of

art work for the engravers. And they have some packages for us." She gave him thirty cents, a nickel up, a nickel back, and twenty cents for himself. He took the parcels to an engraver's on East Thirty-ninth Street. Then he would run as fast as he could, all the way back to Lafayette Street, and thus save a nickel, so that he earned twenty-five cents a day.

But the nickel saved was never a nickel earned; for on his way home he would stop by Shriftgeisser's Bakery, where an old German woman sold him two stale chocolate eclairs for his hard-earned nickel. So he wound up with only twenty cents after all. But he loved the eclairs! His mouth would water when he saw them, stale though they were. He enjoyed his first bite through the soft chocolate, through the flaky egg crust, and into the cool whipped-cream filling. He ate his eclairs in six big bites, walking down Fourth Street. He usually finished the second one by the time he reached Washington Square, so that no matter what the weather or his disappointments, when he saw that friendly Square he felt good.

For most novelists, the next process after thought-writing is the actual preparation of a first draft, but for David this step was long postponed. His insecurity kept him from doing any sequential work; his agitated emotions imprisoned him in perpetual suspense, and the best he could do was to wander about the Village, erecting cloudy mental images of Bucks County. He lived on the hope that once he sat down to write, perfect scenes and passages would burst magically upon his paper. The novel was as good as written. So he loafed in Washington Square.

Once he spent a whole day trying to evolve a name for Mona Meigs. He strolled from MacDougal Street to Gay and on to Bank and Little West Twelfth, repeating to his inward ear the litany of names he had contrived: Marcia Derry? Alice Bates? Lucretia Berry? Rosa Kullman? He conceived the idea that if he could only find the right name, his book would be half written.

In his loneliness he took a new interest in Claude and talked with him for long afternoons about the use of words. Or he would take Claude's place in the restaurant. He became meticulous about making change correctly, so that if a Village bum forgot a nickel, David would run after him and remind him of the coin.

But in spite of the dedication he felt within, he acknowledged that these were the dark days. He discovered this when

he walked through the Village streets and found that for the most part he kept his eyes averted. He did not want people to see how lonely and useless he had become. There was a thin, beautiful Jewish girl who went to night school at NYU. She smiled at him night after night, and he borrowed thirty cents from Mom so that he could feel free to speak with her.
"Would you like a drink?" he asked.

"I don't drink," she said.

He blushed and ran down Third Street. She cried after him, "I meant I didn't drink, like that!" But he hurried away, ashamed.

On such nights he did not think: "Some day I'll remember this and put it in a book." This was not book stuff. It was a tired and rasping depression, and he could not look in other faces, for they were tired and hungry, too.

And then, strangely, he started to write, violently and eruptingly. It happened in this way. One morning he shuffled into the restaurant and Mom Beckett said, "Dave, pull yourself together. I've got bad news for you."

"What?" he asked stolidly.

"Let's sit over here." The big woman was visibly nervous, and she put her hand on David's. "Bad news comes to everybody," she said.

"What is it?" David demanded.

"A telegram came. I opened it. Your Aunt Reba's dead." She sniffed.

David looked at her big, handsome face and grinned. "Save the act," he laughed. "She was a mean old sonofabitch."

A big, happy smile broke over Mom's face. She said, "Claude! Draw us a couple of beers! So she was a stinker, eh?"

"Mom," David laughed, "she was the queen of stinkers. How about lending me some dough for a movie?"

"It ain't as simple as that, kid," Mom replied. She unfolded the telegram and said, "They ask you to come down and supervise the funeral."

"Should I go?"

"Yes. Claude'll lend you his black suit." So in a borrowed suit David Harper returned to Bucks County.

He had not envisaged such a setting for his return to Doylestown: a steaming day in August, less than a dollar in his pockets, a borrowed suit, and a funeral. He had rather imagined himself coming back with a briefcase in hand and a well-tied tie, bespeaking modest but substantial success.

Yet here he was. He knew no one at the poorhouse. Now even Luther Detwiler was dead, wildly crazy at the end and chained to the wall. Reba Stücke was grim and bitter in her cheap coffin. Against his will David looked at her as she lay in the poorhouse chapel, her lips tight-sealed and her eyes staring meanly ahead, even beneath closed lids. She had been an evil, bitter person, and he could feel no sorrow. A woman who had graced neither her own life nor humanity was dead. She must be buried.

But the burial presented a problem. While David gazed at his aunt's remains he was aware that two men were watching him from the shadows. After a decent interval one of them tapped him on the shoulder. It was the overseer, who whispered hoarsely, "You got the money to bury her?"

"I didn't know anything about money!" David protested.

The second man came up. "I'm the undertaker," he said mournfully. "This must have been a terrible shock to you."

"I don't have any money," David explained.

"She was your aunt!" the overseer insisted.

"But she saved money for her funeral!" David pressed, ashamed of himself yet seeing no other alternative.

"Of course!" the overseer agreed. "But her money's tied up. No one can get at it legally, not even for a funeral."

"We could bury her in potter's field," the undertaker suggested slowly.

"She's the boy's own flesh and blood!" the overseer said in disgust.

"How much?" David demanded bitterly.

"Fifty dollars," the undertaker said promptly. "And that's special. Poorhouse rates."

David left the chapel and walked about the poorhouse grounds. Where could he get fifty dollars? He couldn't tap Mom again. Mona would let him have it, but where was she? He couldn't ask Alison. Then he thought of Morris Binder. The overseer gave him the poorhouse truck and he drove into the railway station to send a telegram. But when the attendant read David's telegram he snorted and said, "We can't send a message like that. Ain't you got any respect?"

"Well," David insisted, "she was a mean old devil."

"You ought to be ashamed of yourself!" the operator moralized. "Your own flesh and blood!"

David grew furious. He stamped from the station and called Miss Adams on the phone, reversing charges. "A mean ugly old woman died," he said sharply. "They tell me I've got to bury her. Can you send me fifty dollars by wire?" There was no argument. The crisp woman said promptly, "Of course. Wait at the telegraph office." So during the hot hours David sat in the office while the operator glared at him. He heard the man whisper to a friend: "And she was his own flesh and blood!"

The phrase infuriated David. Reba Stücke was no flesh and blood of his. She was not related to him by bonds of sympathy, interest, ambition, hope or love. An unknown Chinese coolie struggling in the Shantung sun, he was David's brother! A Polish peasant battling the seasons was David's flesh and blood. The poet Claude was more his understanding aunt than Reba Stücke had ever been. He had hated her in life; in death he despised everything she had stood for. She was not his flesh and blood.

Finally the telegram came: "FIFTY DOLLARS. BURY THE OLD BAG. MORRIS." Now the operator was doubly incensed and handed David the money with great reluctance. Holding back the last bill, he pushed his eyeshade up and said, "You mind if I give you some good advice? You ought to learn humility." David waited until the man had surrended the bills and then said, "Now you'll get some advice, whether you mind or not. Why don't you . . ." But he was immediately ashamed of himself and blustered out of the station.

The funeral was arranged, and a solitary hearse drove Reba Stücke to Sellersville. David rode with the silent driver and helped the graveyard attendants lower the weightless coffin into the earth. Try as he might, he could generate no decent emotion for this woman's last moment among men. Again the minister said, "His flesh and blood," and again David's anger rose. She was not of his flesh! He loved all people and would spend himself in their behalf. He was sensitive to the slightest quivering of humanity. He loved the earth, even this cold brownish earth of Sellersville, where his own mother lay in a pauper's grave, and he thrilled to the smallest bird or the palest violet. He was not of Reba Stücke's blood.

The German minister who had known Reba unfavorably in life said a few consoling words, and heavy earth fell upon the echoing coffin. The grisly funeral was over.

But death cannot be so impersonal, and when David was driving homeward in the hearse he saw a sign which said, *New Hope 19 Miles.* "Would you let me out here?" he asked. The silent driver assented, and David walked along the magnificent roads of Bucks County. In time he came to land he knew. Hot sweat filled his eyes, and he was dusty, but this earth looked good to him. There was solid richness in it, and its barns were rugged against the hillsides. From the distant Delaware birds rose and winged their way inland; and it was while watching one of these birds that death flooded David's throat and he cried, "Aunt Reba! God have mercy on you!" He stood frozen like Paul in the dusty sunlight and bowed his head. Aunt Reba had been the last remaining person on earth connected to him by blood ties. Now he stood alone on the whirling world. "Have mercy on her, God," he prayed.

While he stood so, a Ford came up behind him. "Fine place to daydream!" a nasal country voice cried. "Kin I carry yew into New Hope?" The car was jerky, for the man had only recently learned to drive. "Just bought 'er," he explained. "D'yew think she was a bargain fer a hunnerd and fifty dollars?"

"Everything's a bargain these days," David agreed. The man must have been over seventy and took great pleasure in the car.

"Yew from these parts?" the man asked as the Ford rattled through Solebury.

"From Doylestown way," David said.

"Then why you walkin' over thisaway?"

"I've been to a funeral," David explained.

"Who ya buried?" the man inquired.

"My aunt. She used to work at the poorhouse."

The man slammed on the brakes and turned to look at David. "Why, yew little shaver!" he said. "Don't yew remember me?"

David studied his face, old and sun-beaten, but he could not recognize him. The man chuckled and said, "I saw yew the mornin' Mr. Paxson come fer me and my wife. Yew was watchin' us!"

"No!" David said slowly. "You're the man who wouldn't stay in the poorhouse! I didn't even think you saw me!"

"I see lots," the old man said.

Impulsively, David reached out and grabbed the old man's hand. "I was proud of you," he blurted. "I've never forgotten you. How's your wife?"

"She's fine!" the farmer cried. "Says I's a damn fool to buy this here Ford at my age but I said, 'What the hell?'"

"How's . . . How's Mr. Paxson?"

"Like ever' one else, he's been havin' his troubles."

"What?" David asked in alarm.

"His girl," the man said cryptically. He started the Ford and drove for a few minutes in silence. Then he said, "I owe all I got to Paxson, so I don't rumor none about him."

"But his girl? What about her."

"There's been talk," was all the old man would say.

At New Hope David dropped into a soda fountain and casually asked, "How're the Paxsons doing?" and the clerk said, "Fine."

David finished his drink and started to walk across the bridge into New Jersey, but he went back to the soda fountain and asked for some nickels. Nervously he called the Paxson farm. "Is Marcia there?" he asked. "No," replied a woman's voice he did not recognize. "When will she be back?" David pursued. "I don't know," the irritated voice replied and there was a bang as the receiver slammed onto its hook.

At the fountain David ordered another drink and drawled, "See much of the young Paxson girl these days?"

"No," the tall clerk said. "She ain't here no more."

"Where is she?" David asked nonchalantly.

"Folks say she's out west gettin' a divorce."

David held his glass very tightly and took a long drink. "Little trouble?" he finally drawled.

The tall clerk stared at David. "What you askin' these questions for? You from these parts?"

"Lambertville," David lied. "Know the Paxsons well."

"Well!" the clerk confided, leaning toward David, "they say she got mixed up with another man. What makes me laugh is that I heard this high and mighty Paxson dame chose for herself a handyman in a circus! How'd you like them potatoes?"

"Ha ha!" David laughed. The gossip was encouraged.

"So we all think her husband, that's Harry Moomaugh, the great athalete, gave her the gate. And I don't know a finer fellow than Harry Moomaugh."

Like one of Mona's habitués, David leaned on the counter and asked, "What'ya make of it? These rumors, I mean?"

"My personal opinion," the clerk whispered, "is that it's a judgment. I ain't a religious man, exactly, but I think it's God's judgment. Yessir, them Paxsons was always high and mighty." He learned back with a self-satisfied air, his elbows resting on syrup jars. "You can quote me as sayin' that this here business has really slowed them Paxsons down to a walk."

David tossed the man a nickel. "What's Moomaugh doing?" he asked.

"He's courtin' a decent girl."

Something in the way the tall man grinned infuriated David. With great asperity he asked, "You went to school with the Paxson girl, didn't you?"

"Why yes," the clerk admitted.

"And you were always in love with her, weren't you?"

"Well . . ."

"And she never gave you a tumble, did she?"

"Well . . ."

Quickly David reached across the counter and grabbed the clerk by the neck. "I oughta paste you!"

The store manager hurried up. "What's wrong?" he cried.

David shoved the clerk away and said, "You oughta wash his mouth out with soap. He's been a bad boy."

The clerk quickly recovered his footing and smiled. "I'll tell the people you were in," he said. "You'd be the circus handyman, wouldn't you?" The store manager began to laugh, and David stumbled out of the store and across the bridge.

He bummed his way back to New York. For most of the trip he was in a kind of daze, but when he passed through the Holland Tunnel and reached the ugly and familiar streets of New York, a great energy possessed him, and he rushed immediately to Morris Binder's and begged the big man to let him use the typewriter. "I hocked mine," he said.

Without stopping he hammered out fifteen pages of his novel, and on every page the golden glory of Bucks County and the canal transfused the words. At last he was started! The opening words of his book rushed forth exactly as he had planned them months before:

*Whenever the distant horns sounded, I ran to the top of the hill to watch my beloved barges drift down the canal. Although I was twelve and had many chores, it was my chief pleasure to see the snout-nosed boats come up to the locks and mysteriously rise and fall. But on this day the barge was different, and it changed my life forever. It was red-nosed, as if it had come from a bleeding fight, and on its prow stood a man with one leg, watching the mules. Behind him was a deckhouse, and at the door stood a young girl of eleven. I remember that she wore her hair in pigtails, and that was my first sight of Lucia Berry.*

Four times David wrote to Marcia and each time the

letter was unanswered. He had the uncharitable suspicion that perhaps the Paxsons had sequestered his letters, so he borrowed money from Mom and called Solebury. The operator said, "The Paxsons are out of town. I don't know when they'll be back."

In anger and confusion he returned to his writing, working at Morris Binder's long hours each day. Twice he was banging at the typewriter when the huge editor rose for breakfast. "What is it, David?" the fat man inquired.

"It's a book," David said. Like a pregnant woman, he felt embarrassed to talk about the ideas he was carrying. He felt that too much talk might bring his offspring bad luck.

One night Morris Binder said, "Your young friend seems to be doing all right with her gangster!" And he showed David a clipping from one of the more lurid newspapers. It showed Mona Meigs looking back over her shoulder at a photographer. Max Volo was speaking to a tall, thin man. The caption asked whether it was true that Philadelphia's Max Volo was going to muscle in on the slot-machine racket in New York?

David did not comment on the picture. He felt that Mona Meigs was gone permanently from his life. He still trusted in her ultimate success; in fact her success would be sweet to him, just as Alison's success in writing would be pleasing, for he felt a proprietary interest in his friends. But he hoped that the lonely days when he sought refuge with Mona were past.

He worked hard that beautiful September evening. Morris Binder played Beethoven, softly but with all seven horns, and the night grew splendid with tired eyes and ears heavy with sound. The delight was shattered, however, by a scream more frightful than any David had yet heard. For a moment he sat frozen at the typewriter, and then Miss Adams burst into the room and caught up the head of the stricken man.

It was a long time before she could bring him under control, and there was copious blood upon her hands when she did. This she ignored, rocking back and forth with the huge head in her arms, murmuring, "Poor man! He's getting worse."

"Is there anything I can do?" David inquired.

"You can get out!" the gray, combed woman cried.

So David left, and when he entered the moonlit Square where lovers grasped for autumn as if it were spring, he thought with dismay of the novel he had left unboxed on

Morris Binder's bed. He was constrained to run back for it, but decided that doing so would only agitate Miss Adams more. He would get it in the morning, but even before he woke there was a rude banging on his door. At first he could not recall where he was, and then a small boy from Tremont Clay's popped his head in the door and cried, "They want you at the office right away!"

David shaved in a hurry, while the little boy stood first on one foot and then the other. "Let's go!" he kept repeating. On Third Street David tried to ascertain what had happened, but the boy knew nothing. "They want you, that's all," he said. There was a cold chill about David's heart as he approached the building on Lafayette Street, for he thought that perhaps Morris Binder had finally . . . He expelled the thought from his mind.

As soon as he entered the office, Miss Adams caught him by the arm and pulled him over to her desk. She had his novel before her. "Did you write this?" she asked.

"Yes," David said defensively.

The tight little woman told him to sit down. "This is very good," she said. Primly she lifted single pages from the unfinished chapters and read odd lines. "You'll be able to have this published," she said, and then she added other phrases, short, crisp comments about style and characterization. "You'll be a fine writer some day," she said.

David was too agitated to speak. Here was the first person in the world to have seen a story upon which he had truly worked, and she was saying that it was good. She used four or five words that he had dreamed might one day be spoken of his writing: *movement, a swinging style, good words, people*. There could never again be a moment like this, and he could not speak.

"But you've a great deal to learn!" Miss Adams said, as if she were beginning a lesson that would last for years. "Have you ever given yourself a course in writing? No? would you mind terribly if I used a pencil?" She took an editorial pencil—Hardness #1—and started to draw lines through words and to insert provisional substitutes. Then she showed David his opening paragraph: *Whenever the distant horns sounded, I ran to the top of the hill to watch my beloved the barges drift down the canal. Although I was twelve and had many chores it was my chief pleasure to see the snout-nosed boats barges come up to go into the locks and mysteriously rise and or fall. But on this day the barge*

*was different, and it changed my life forever. It was red-nosed,
as if it had come from a bleeding fight, and on its prow stood
a man with one leg, watching the mules. Behind him was a
deckhouse, and at the door stood a young girl of eleven. I
remember that she wore her hair in pigtails, and that was
my first sight of Lucia Berry.*

"See how the style is tightened up by knocking out words!"
Miss Adams said with deep pleasure. "You use too many
adjectives and adverbs. I despise words like *forever, never,
whenever*. They're mock poetic. Avoid them. And don't use
*but* or *and* to begin sentences. They're cheap and mock-
philosophical connectives."

"You just used *and* yourself," David argued.

"I'm talking," Miss Adams snapped. "I'm not trying to
write a good book. And David, please don't use words like
*beloved*. If your little boy loves the barges, let him show it.
Don't use soft words. Same way with your descriptive adjectives. *Bleeding* fight? That doesn't make sense. A *young* girl
of eleven? Redundant. A girl of eleven *is* young. And why
would a barge drifting downstream need mules? Or how can
a barge in a lock rise *and* fall at the same time?"

"I like the sound of some words," David insisted.

"Even so, they have to make sense! Now the phrase I
dislike most . . . I guess it's the worst phrase in writing. *And
it changed my life forever*. That's really a cheap trick. It went
out of style years ago. If that barge changed the boy's life
forever, show it. Don't say it." She raised her pencil to rub
out the offending line completely, but David put his hand
over it.

"It's for that I'm writing," he said simply.

"What do you mean?" she asked. Two men came in with
bills. Impatiently she motioned them on back to Tremont
Clay. Then she returned to David, her eyes blazing with
excitement. "What do you mean?" she repeated.

"I used to live with a lot of old men," David began.

"Where?"

"In a certain place," he answered. "Strange and sometimes
wonderful things had happened to those men, but they weren't
aware of it. They never knew. When I write I want everything that happens to be absolutely clear. If I think the
reader won't catch it, I'm going to say it right out."

"It's still an outmoded trick."

"I don't care," David insisted. "If my boy begins to like

jelly beans on a certain day, and if that's important, I'm
going to say so."

Miss Adams started to re-argue the point, but her eye hit
the opening lines again. With a firm stroke she crossed out
*boats* and wrote in *barges*. "It's got to be either a barge or a
boat. Make up your mind."

"I was avoiding repetition," David explained.

"Nothing wrong with good repetition." Then she crossed
out *distant* again. "A horn can't be *distant* and still be heard,"
she said.

This was too much for David and he looked angrily at the
prim woman. "Do you like it better now?" he asked.

"Yes," she said. "The dead wood's cleared away."

"And so is the music," David argued.

"You're writing a novel, not a poem," she said.

"I don't see any difference," David challenged.

"Between a novel and a poem?" she asked, her voice rising.

"No!" David snapped. The two men returned for her signature. "Later," she cried peremptorily and shooed them out
the door. Then David leaned forward across her desk and a
torrent of words, long imprisoned in his mind, burst forth.
"I'd like to write as if every page were a poem. I'd like to
pour words out whether they mean anything or not. If I were
describing a brick wall I'd like to flood the pages with feelings and touches and even smells, and I wouldn't care whether
anyone read what I wrote or not. The words you've crossed
out, Miss Adams, are the ones I want."

Miss Adams coughed and leaned forward to meet this
challenge. "Art is mostly discipline," she said.

"I don't want discipline!" David cried. "No, I don't! I've
been all over this country and it isn't mean and tight the way
you say. There are mountains so big you could never describe
them. And little streams that would take a million words to
tell how they cross from one field to another. I know a poet
who says that a novel is like a golden kettle. You throw all
the world into it."

Miss Adams cleared her throat primly and said, "Up in
Vermont my mother has a kettle like that. She keeps it on
the back of the stove and tosses odds and ends into it. Do
you know what comes out?"

"What?" David asked.

"Mush."

There was a pregnant pause as Miss Adams stared at the
young man. He was the one who dropped his eyes. Slowly,

he said, "Miss Adams, you can help me. I've had a vision. I've seen a wonderful land, and the people were even better than the land. When I think about them I want to sing. You say it's mush."

"Art is a cruel discipline," she insisted. "Go look at the great painters. Or the best architects. The central problem is to find a clean, hard line. Clean, sharp, pure."

"It sounds too icy and forbidding," David said.

"The finest art is," she assured him. "It's a lonely paring away of everything that isn't needed. If you can apply such standards to your vision . . ." She paused and then said, "I used to have that vision. Morris Binder had it, too. I was to be the great editor. Young novelists would work with me. He would be the lawyer that went to the Supreme Court. Now . . ."

The vision faded and she leaned back and studied David. He was twenty-six. At that age her brother had owned a hardware store. At twenty-seven her father had had four children. Morris Binder, forced on by Jewish parents who knew the toll of sloth, had graduated from law school at twenty-three; but David seemed scarcely a man. Could it be, she wondered, that this clean face with no scars of defeat could have had a vision? Nervously she shuffled his manuscript together.

"So you want to write a great book?" she sighed.

"Yes," he said.

"Then don't let anything interrupt you. If you need money, see me . . . or Morris Binder. We stayed up most of last night and I read this to him. He thinks it's wonderful, David, but he's a loose thinker, as you know. He's prone to excesses, and he's never disciplined himself. But please don't talk to him about it. He's sick . . . He's very sick." She did not cry. She never cried, but she slumped in dejection, as if the burden of waiting for those frightful screams was greater than she could carry. "I'd be deeply pleased," she said, "if you'd let me study the chapters after you finish them. And remember. Don't let anything interrupt."

But a violent emotional experience did interrupt, and for more than a month David wrote nothing. It started with a phone call from Mrs. Paxson. She said that David's letters had been waiting when they got back. They didn't know where Marcia was. She had been divorced in Nevada and no one had heard of her since.

David borrowed some money from Mom and hurried down to Solebury. The Paxsons met him with Quaker austerity but not unfriendliness. He had been the cause of their daughter's dismay, but he was also one of the billions who shared the earth with them and that sovereign fact entitled him to their full sympathy. "Marcia felt a great burden of sin," Mrs. Paxson said quietly. "She knows she wronged Harry Moomaugh cruelly. If we had leper colonies around here, I'm sure thee'd find her there, expiating her guilt."

"We may not hear from her for a long time," Mr. Paxson said. "She may even seek thee out first."

"I'll want to marry her that day," David said.

The Paxsons would not commit themselves. "Integrity in children is hard to bear," Mrs. Paxson said. "Marcia may refuse thee, as thee refused her." David was embarrassed to know that Marcia had told her parents of his behavior.

The Paxsons offered him money, since his clothes were obviously inadequate, but he refused and hitch-hiked his way back to Washington Square. Since he must talk with someone, he elected Mom Beckett. She was unusually sympathetic. She sat in the restaurant and poked at her coiffured hair. "I'm always amazed," she said, "at the capacity good people have for kicking themselves in the stomach. That alley cat Mona! Hell! She could absorb anything and come out all right. But a girl like this one you're telling me about . . . Oh, heavenly days, the punishment they give themselves. But there's this about it, Dave. If such girls ever get settled, God, what lovely wives they make!"

Mom had fifteen different ideas as to how Marcia could be tracked down. "We could hire a private dick," she proposed eagerly.

"The Paxsons made me promise not to," David objected.

"Well, I could lend you three hundred dollars and you could slip out to Nevada and pick up her trail. That way you'd be the eye." Her fertile mind suggested other ways, but David, who knew that Marcia must ultimately solve the problem for herself, rejected them all.

He lay about his room, stared at the brick wall, and said, "Now tomorrow, damn it, I'll go over to Morris Binder's." But after he had stayed away for eight days Miss Adams came boldly to his room.

"What's the matter?" she asked. "You can't take criticism?"

"I can't get started again," he said.

"David!" the little woman cried, laying down her handbag. "This is your life! This is your immortal life, David!" She looked at him in despair and said, "If it's money, if it's a place to stay . . ." When she saw the depth of his stupor, she went away, but that afternoon he got a special-delivery letter from her. "Only a few people can write, and of them only a few ever get started. Don't waste yourself, David." She enclosed ten dollars to be spent as he wished. She said, "Maybe a trip into the country would help. Bus fares are very low."

Her letter shocked David into action. He was appalled that a woman as cold as Miss Adams should care what he did or why. "I'll get hold of myself," he swore, and he went to the public library and said to the librarian, "I'm out of work and I'd like a good, tough book to sort of hold myself together." She smiled warmly at him and said. "Have you ever read *Washington Square*, by Henry James?"

"I never heard of it!" David said. He took the small and often rebound book out into the Square itself and started to read. The old passion for identification swept over him. He imagined—as was indeed the case—that James had chosen for his sedate scene the very house in which Alison now lived. He pictured Alison as the banker's daughter and it was late at night, over a cup of coffee at Mom's, when he finished the book. Then he understood what Miss Adams had meant by control and line and purity in art. The novel had impressed him deeply, but at the same time he clung to an old idea of his: "If a man could write just as he wished, he'd write like Balzac." He went to bed tired and happy, resolved that in the morning he would try—to the limit of his capacity—to write like Balzac.

But in the morning there came a tender knocking at his door. He rose, irritated with himself at having been so long in bed, and looked into the hall. There stood Mona.

She wore an expensive mink coat, a saucy hat, very high-heeled shoes, and a severely plain dress that must have cost a hundred dollars. There were no lines under her eyes, and she was so beautiful that David's heart sank.

"What do you want?" he demanded.

Quickly, and in real fright, she ducked into his room, quietly closed the door, and slumped back against it in a gesture of despair. "You've got to help me!" she insisted.

David drew away from her and studied her coldly. "What's happened now?" he asked.

She put her beautiful hands over her face and shook her head as if in unbelief. "I'm scared silly," she said. "You've got to hide me for a while." She dropped her hands and looked at David as if she were a little girl detected in the act of stealing jam.

"Cut it out!" David growled. "That pleading look is pretty silly in a mink coat."

In one motion she hurried across the room and took David's hands. "This is no joke!" she cried with deep emotion. "Max Volo is at the bottom of the East River. In a barrel of concrete. If they find me, they'll shoot me. They think I know who did it." She licked her lips and stared up at David, holding onto his strong arms. "And I do know! I saw them kill Max. I was in a closet, hiding."

Reluctantly, David led the nervous and alluring girl to a chair. "I'll see if Mom has a drink," he fumbled.

"I don't need a drink," Mona objected. "All I need is time to think this out."

David studied her with distaste. "Think what out?" he asked.

"Don't look at me like that!" she snapped. "You look at me as if I did it! David, they have men out right now looking for me!" She sprang from her chair and grabbed David by the shoulders. "Don't you understand? I'm scared to death!"

"Mona! Don't talk silliness. You were never afraid of anything. You're just stalling for time till you figure out some way to use this to your advantage. All right, you can use my room." In real disgust he went to his bureau.

"You aren't going to leave?" she whined petulantly.

He reached for his clothes and awkwardly slipped into them. Grabbing a few shaving items he jammed them into his pockets and opened the door. "I won't say anything," he promised.

Mona began to cry. "Dave!" she mumbled. "When I went off with Max Volo, it was only to save you trouble. You had no money . . ."

"And Max did!"

"I did it to help you, Dave. A hundred times I said. 'I'll send Dave that hundred bucks.' Here!" She clawed open her purse and handed David a handful of bills. "Thanks, kid," she said. "You were a godsend that time."

"Put them away!" David said, stepping into the hall.

"I feel like a devil, shoving you out of your room." Mona sniffled. "You don't have to go, do you?"

"Yes," he said. He closed the door softly and went downstairs to Mom's room. The big, handsome woman was dusting her incongruous collection of small marble statues. Demure milkmaids and angels predominated, but there was one utterly indecent group of Pan and two wood nymphs.

"That's from Messina! Italy!" she said proudly. "Ain't it a pistol?"

"You ought to have a curtain around that one!" David gasped.

"A little guy with a squinted-up face carved that one special for a fellow I was touring Europe with." She stood back to survey the scabrous statue and laughed. "He was quite a fancy boy, that one."

"Who? The carver?"

"No!" Mom chuckled. "The fellow I was with." She leaned back and began: "He was the son of an Oklahoma oil millionarie, and he wore a wristwatch . . ."

"Mom," David interrupted. "Did you see Mona Meigs come in this morning?" The big woman put her cup down.

"Is she in this house?" she demanded. When David nodded she went to the door and bellowed for Claude. The bearded poet appeared and she stormed at him, "I thought I told you no whores was allowed in this house?"

Claude smiled at her patiently and said, "So I understood."

"Then how in hell did she get up to David's room?"

"She must have sneaked in the front door when someone was leaving." The bearded man looked so sincere in his explanation that Mom accepted it.

"Very good!" she said. "If she sneaked in, throw her out on her ass!" She went to the foot of the stairs and began to shout, "Hey! You two-bit tramp! Get the hell down here!"

"Mom!" David pleaded, pulling her back into the room, "I think it's serious this time. Her friend . . ." He mumbled. "The man she was living with was murdered. She says it's a gang killing."

"And she wants to hide out here?" Mom snorted. "With all the cheap torpedoes that lounge in my bar, she wants to hide upstairs so we all get shot. Get her to hell out!"

"Let her stay a couple of days. I'll find a bed somewhere."

"No!" Mom insisted. "Dave," she said, "men never understand women like that tramp. Out she goes."

"I'm through with her, Mom. I'm cured, but supposing she's telling the truth?"

"All right! Claude! You go get the papers." She dispatched him as if he were a child, and he nodded as if he were a servant. He tossed one of her shawls about his thin shoulders and ran into the street. In a few minutes he returned with proof of Mona's story. Max Volo in his barrel of concrete had been dredged up from the East River. It was a gang killing, and the police feared for the life of a beautiful young woman who was supposed to have the clues. Mom read the stories slowly, like one who had never bothered much with books, and said, "Claude! You take her up some chow. She can stay here three days."

David would not go back to his room. He was through with Mona forever; yet as he wandered about the streets of his Village—Gay, Jones, Bedford, Grove—he became terribly confused, for although he now despised the bright and cruel singer, his entire novel was founded upon her, and she was tied about the ventricles of his heart so that her slightest movement had the power to suffocate him. She was in him and of him and she possessed his imagination. She was the superb and challenging woman that all men meet; she was Lilith breathing fire into the nostrils of dead Adam. And yet the more David thought of her in those days, the more certain he was that he must never go near her again.

Then, on the third day, David heard newsboys hawking their headlines: "Blonde Tells All!" When he bought a paper, Mona smiled up at him. Her legs were generously displayed, and she was surrounded by eight self-conscious and admiring policemen.

Now it was Mona's lurid escapade that became David's reason for not writing. Inadvertently he was dragged into the whirlwind of her experience. She became known as "The Bravest Girl in America!" Instead of being censured for having lived with a cheap crook like Max Volo, she was enshrined for having had the courage to identify the killers. She played for a week in a New York vaudeville theatre and then went on tour. She sang and danced and gave a monologue telling about how she had sat for two days in a "mean, filthy tenement room, getting up courage to tell the police."

When the *New York Times* carried an editorial about her,

Tremont Clay himself came to see David. "Morris Binder tells me you know this girl!" he snapped.

"That's right," David agreed. So Clay handed David two hundred and fifty dollars for a series of lurid and provocative articles about Mona and her gallantry. Thanks to Clay's superb editing, the result was a girl who was a cross between a wanton sex maniac and Joan of Arc. The stories were so enticing that a feature syndicate bought them, and from Washington Mona wired: "You've made me famous! Hollywood is nibbling for the story of my life. Me to star!"

She returned to New York in triumph and did a stand in a Village night club, where an immense bar had been opened to celebrate the death of prohibition. Life-sized posters were made of her wearing practically nothing, and one day she returned to Mom's. "Tell David to come to see me," she ordered Claude. "Give him this."

When David saw her address—upper Fifth Avenue—he threw away the card, but she came back and found him sitting at a table with Mom. They were talking about Marcia Paxson and about how a person could remember scenes of childhood more vividly than things experienced a week ago. "Dave," Mona said. "I got to ask one more favor of you."

"You cheap sonofabitch!" Mom snorted. "Why don't you get to hell out of here?"

Mona did not flinch. Her fine, hard face looked as clean and young as when David had first seen her. Her breasts still seemed firm and small. Her neck was thin and lithe, and she leaned forward in a kind of halted excitement. "I need your help for two days," she said.

"For Christ's sake!" Mom exploded. "Can't you see this kid has had a bellyful of you? Claude! Throw this lousy tramp out on her ass!"

"The big chance has come." Mona said quietly.

That awful phrase of youth—the big chance—struck David very hard. It was this that he once prayed for: Mona's big chance. He had given her money when he needed it, and he had always felt that his planet was strangely intermingled with the force of her sun, so that no matter if he were thrust, like Jupiter, millions of miles from that glowing sun, he would still mysteriously wander through the dark places of the universe, held somehow by that bright creature. "OK, Mona. What do you want?"

"I want you to be my chauffeur for two days. I got to impress those bastards."

"My driver's license is no good," David explained.

"I don't mean to drive!" she protested quickly. "Just to bring me messages. In a snappy uniform."

"My God a'mighty!" Mom cried, staring at David in disbelief.

At first David was tempted to reply: "Mona, how dare you propose such a thing?" But he perceived that she would see nothing indecent in her request. Sick in his stomach, he asked quietly, "You want me to get dressed up? Like a chauffeur?"

Her carefully painted face brightened. "Would you?" she asked eagerly.

"All right," he said, and he left the restaurant with her.

For a moment Mom sat silent. Then she slammed the table with her fist. "You!" she shouted at Claude. "Get the hell out of this restaurant!"

"Why?" Claude asked, imperturbably.

"Because you're a stupid fool, like all men!" She shoved him out the door and then heard a noise in the kitchen. She kicked the door open and glared at the unoffending Chinese cook. "What the hell are you doin'?" she shouted. The cook looked at her with mournful eyes and said nothing. For a moment she considered firing him, but he was chopping meat with a large cleaver, so she banged the door shut and sat down at a lonely table. She slumped forward and studied the pattern on the oilcloth. Finally she groaned inwardly and walked wearily to the door. "OK, Claude. Come on back," she yelled. As the amused poet shuffled back to his place behind the counter she sighed and said, "Now, by God, I *have* seen everything. A chauffeur! For that lousy tramp!"

Mona took David to a costumer's who fitted him out resplendently. For two days he carried messages from one expensive suite to another, and finally he brought to Mona the news she had hoped for through all the years. She read the brief contract and saluted the mass of flowers that attended it. Then quietly she relaxed into a big chair and with an almost fragile beauty smiled up at Dave. "Thanks, kid," she said.

The moment was so much the culmination of a life that David found rich thoughts welling into his heart. From among them all he selected one and said, "I remember the first night I saw you. At John Philip Sousa's party. You were with

Klim." The old words were pregnant with power, and Mona's tense, hard beauty resolved in a placid mask of loveliness.

"They were good days we had!" she said.

She seemed so cherishable at that moment that David nervously fingered his chauffeur's costume and said, "How could you have lived with Max Volo?"

The singer closed her eyes and clenched the contract, as if for reassurance. "Sometimes you have to take what you can get," she said. "I didn't actually down deep like it any more than you did when his money got you started."

"Wait a minute!" David cried. "I gave Nora every cent Max Volo helped me to steal. I don't owe him a dime."

"I didn't mean about Paradise!" Mona said quickly, reaching out for his hand. "What a kid does when he's young, that's his business. I meant about Max sending you to college."

It was as if the room had suddenly exploded. Mona felt David's hand tighten, and with her sure instinct she guessed that he had not known of Volo's surreptitious gift to Dedham. "Didn't you ever know?" she asked intrusively.

"No," David said breathlessly. "I . . . I thought it was Uncle Klim. I almost went crazy when Klim killed himself because of you and me." He sat heavily on the edge of the chair and Mona felt his hand grow limp.

"Klim was a good guy. So was Max. Really he was! He used to do good things for lots of people. But he liked you best. The way you ran into the fire. Tell me the truth, Dave. There were some girls in that fire, weren't there?"

The vast ugliness of life encompassed David. Men steal and run whore houses and are buried in a barrel of cement in the East River. Desperate young girls become prostitutes and are burned to death. Girls of great promise sing for Sousa and then scratch their way up the ladder, claw by claw, and from their scratching old actors die and are buried in potter's field. Musicians of great promise wind up as something short of genius and are betrayed by their mistresses and friends, and shoot themselves. On the mad row crazy Dutchmen who own cigar factories—in their crazy minds—die chained to walls, and outside the snow falls, the snow of indifference and forgetfulness, to obliterate the shame and misery.

"It's snowing," David finally said. "I'd better go."

He rose and stood by the chair. Often, recently, he had experienced the sensation that never again would he see a particular scene or person. He had felt so on the final night of Chautauqua, when he saw for the last time the good brown tent come down, that night when the Gonoph had asked, blushing, "Why don't we kiss good-bye? We may never see each other again." He had kissed her, and it had been horrible, and he had never seen her again.

Once the poet Claude had said, "Poets are simply people who see things two ways. Like children, as if they had never seen them before. Like old men, as if they would never see them again." There was much to what Claude had said, for now David felt that oppressive and yet explosive sense of wonder: This is the last time I shall see her, and I would have walked a thousand miles on coals to see her now.

"Mona . . ." he began, but there was too much to say. Then he stumbled on. "I don't care about Max Volo. I guess you and I are an awful lot alike." Impulsively he threw himself upon the chair and buried his face against hers. In sweet relaxation she lay there and did not even place her arms about him. He kissed her for a moment and then hastened to the door.

"You can keep the chauffeur's suit," she said. "It's paid for."

Now David began to experience one of the most unbelievable phenomena of art. He had a novel completely written in his mind. His characters were vivid and more alive than people he met upon the street. The canal and its barges actually followed him about the Village, and he was living at a pitch of emotional perception such as he had never known before. Yet he could not write!

How can it be that a man can even see the finished printed page in his eye, can taste the plaudits of a job well done, and yet be unable to push a pen across a paper or strike one reluctant key? David could not guess.

He fell into a kind of endless stupor and tramped about the streets of New York in the snow. He had never previously bothered about drinking, but now when he could borrow money from Mom he wandered into one recently opened bar after another, explaining to anyone who would listen the details of his book. Even when bartenders, those compulsive listeners, turned away in boredom, David gabbled on.

Once, when he was ashamed to beg from Mom, he stumbled into Tremont Clay's office and braved the wrath of Miss Adams. She took one look at him and gave him two dollars' worth of galleys to correct, ignoring completely the unwritten novel. When he took them in to Mr. Clay the tired thin man looked up with eyes haggard from much night work and said, "You look awful."

David was still partially drunk and replied, "You don't look so hot yourself."

"I feel terrible," Clay admitted. "I'm probably killing myself, but it really gives me a good chuckle! Everyone around here used to think of me as the pampered rich man's son. Now they can see why I'm president." He rubbed his eyes and then cackled maliciously, "I suppose you saw where Forward Press folded up. I understand that Ace Publications is on the rocks, too. But not this place!"

The nervous little man fixed his hair, using his fingers as a comb and then said sharply, "Get hold of yourself, Harper. Can you keep a secret? I'm going to need you any day now. Good salary and a good job."

"Things picking up?" David asked, shaking his head to clear his mind.

"Not yet. What I have in mind," and the tight little man looked about him, "is that Morris Binder's spells are getting worse. He may die any minute."

"Jesus!" David gulped.

"I'm not cruel or merciless," the editor insisted. "Binder can work here as long as he lives. I'll give him a pension if he becomes incapacitated. But I think he's going to die. I've got to figure out what to do if he does. How much did Miss Adams give you for this job?"

"Two dollars."

"That's fair, but here's three more. An even five. Go out and get a shave. Buy yourself a clean shirt. And keep hold of yourself, Harper."

But David took the five dollars into a bar where some men had once stood him drinks. He invited everyone to join him in a drink, and at midnight he was still there, confiding in lisping whispers that it was terrible to be waiting around to fill a dead man's shoes. He drank himself into a stupor of forgetfulness, and in the frozen morning a MacDougal Street pants presser found him huddled in a doorway, purple with cold. He guided David to Mom Beckett's, and she threw some water in his face. "So the Bowery bum finally came home! You look just fine! There's a package for you upstairs."

He stumbled up to his room where he found a book waiting

for him. It was bound in shiny black cloth and was called *The Black Prince,* by Alison Webster. It contained a short inscription from Alison: "I told you I'd get it all down on paper." With great excitement he fumbled his way into bed and started to read the novel. Shamelessly, Alison had drawn a bitter picture of her father, the Black Prince. With cold, sure words she had delineated the man's self-destruction and the gradual erosion of his family. It was all there, the house, the tray, the heroine who fought against it, and the moral dissolution of a man.

Strangely, it was not hard and glossy like Alison herself. It was a strong novel that tried to be even better than it was, and it bespoke a brilliant future. David's eyes were bloodshot when he finished reading, and his head was hot with excitement. He dashed off a note to Alison: "Only you can guess how happy I am about this. It's terrific, and you're going to be a wonderful writer. Hooray! Hooray!"

He stumbled downstairs with his note and Mom cried, "You prime damn fool! You're not going out still half drunk?"

"I want to mail a letter!" David explained.

"Come in and have some hot food!" she insisted, but David was already gone. He felt a wild exhilaration over Alison's novel. He felt that it was good to know people who could do what they said they were going to, even if they hurt you bitterly in doing so. When he mailed the note he felt so expansive that he stumbled along the cold streets of the Village and sang a kind of chant to himself. Excited, like an addict of strange drugs, he concluded, "Boy! Tomorrow I'm going to get to work myself! If she can do it, I can do it!"

Then he came to Mrs. Shriftgeisser's bakery, and the fresh eclairs looked so enticing that he bought two stale ones and munched them on the way back to Washington Square. Half an hour later he was in agony from a terrible pain. He was literally knocked double and was unable to run the two blocks to Mom Beckett's. He fell in the snow and began to vomit. He fouled his pants, as well, and when a policeman saw his green and ashen face an ambulance was called.

Only the prompt application of a stomach pump saved his life. When he finally realized where he was, he lay back upon the hospital pillows and felt his world come gradually to a soft but irrevocable stop. He was weak and thin and unshaved. He weighed twenty-four pounds less than he had in college, and his eyes were badly strained. His breath came in short gasps, and he was close to nervous collapse.

The doctors asked, "What did you eat?"

"Nothing," David said.

"Look!" they snapped. "You're lucky you aren't dead. What was it?"

David knew that if he told, Mrs. Shriftgeisser would be arrested, and she had too often befriended him for him to betray her now. "It wasn't anything," he insisted.

"It was some kind of cream puff, wasn't it?" the health inspector probed.

"I didn't eat anything," David answered stubbornly.

"You damned fool!" a doctor cried. "We pumped it out of you. You think we're stupid?"

Later on, when Mom came to see him, he told her to warn Mrs. Shriftgeisser. Mom was proud of him for having defied the law. "It's always a horse's ass," she observed. "Seems a man can stand up under anything but a uniform. Makes damn fools of 'em all." She talked a lot to hide her astonishment at the physical report. "If you want anything," she insisted, "let me know."

When she left, David was alone, even though the ward was crowded with derelicts like himself. He was alone with the perilous thought that perhaps it would have been better had he stayed in the Square with the frightful pain in his stomach, oblivious at last to the cross-currents in which he was caught up. His novel had been dissipated by his own puling indecision. His various determinations had been derailed by any slight external disruption. Alison and Marcia were vague and lost memories, and he recognized himself to be one hell of a mess.

And there was still Mona. Even though he sensed that he would never see her again, she was deep in his blood stream. She was the virus against which he had been powerless to fight. Let the doctors diagnose his illness however they would, Mona was its name. Of her he had to be cured first. She was the fruit of the tree of his young life; he had eaten it and now he was sick with first knowledge.

He had entered the valley of despair, that somber valley which no man who grows to white hairs can escape. For some the valley is synonymous with war, or the great depressions that grip a land and its people, or the ages of discontent and failing hope. They are the terrible valleys in which the spirit founders. Other men seek out their despair in broken loves or lost illusions or decaying dreams or the petty failure of everyday excursions. Some unfortunates stumble from one valley to another: war, depression, an age of disillusion, a lost love, failure, and then the night. But no man escapes the valleys altogether, and those who claim they do are either cowards or fools.

David, in his despair, could not know that he was sharing the experience of all men. During his first long hospital night he saw visions, tremendous spirals that twisted upward and inward, and he was lost among them. Phantasms of color whirled through space, dragging him along, so that at midnight the nurse said he had five degrees of fever.

But toward the morning hours, those during which Cyril Hargreaves had died, David's fevered mind recalled a familiar scene that he had never once previously remembered. He was far above the world, and below him people like flies drifted here and there. A malignant spirit reached out and clutched at the flies, pulling off their wings, leaving them to stumble about in confusion. Then the harpy drew about the world a circle of red spit, and as long as the flies stayed within that prison, they could move—wingless—where they willed. They could breed or build or quarrel or leave specks in patterns, but they were free; yet once they trespassed the red circle a ponderous, impartial thumb exterminated them.

The vision was frightful, and David woke from it crying. There were others that night screaming worse than he, so that his protest went unnoticed, and for this he was glad, because when his first hysteria ended, he was able to survey his vision.

The flies were free. Only when they approached the line were they in danger, and from this simple truth David derived great consolation. There are two degrees of freedom. A few flies can soar at will, with their wings intact. Most surrender their wings, yet still retain a measure of freedom.

"A man's crazy not to see that pretty soon he gives up his wings," David mused. "Some of us even seem to rip them off ourselves, as if we couldn't bear freedom. But even in prison we have certain freedoms."

Toward daylight he regained full sanity and lay weak upon his pillow. "There goes my dream of a great novel," he muttered. "Well, there'll be work to do some place else. Maybe I don't have wings . . ." He relaxed, content with his prison.

And in that critical moment he joined the millions of the world who have seen a great vision—love, universal peace, decency, brotherhood—but who surrender the vast hope and immure themselves jealously within the walls of their petty prisons.

When morning dawned, David still had a high fever, and for a moment he thought crazily that he was burning. Then he laughed at himself and with his eyes closed recalled two memorable fires that he had seen. The first had destroyed a forest in Colorado, and it had been terrible to witness, for on a neighboring mountain stood a field of jagged stumps, charred and forever barren; and David had known that the forest he was watching die in smoke could not rise again. Its lonely stumps would always remind men of that day's conflagration.

But there had been another fire that had danced in his memory for a long time. In Iowa a farmer had burned off his fields so as to enrich the soil for spring planting; and this fire had been life-bringing, for it cleansed away old encrustations and laid the true soil bare for tilling.

A calmness came over David, and he actually felt his fever subsiding. He prayed briefly that the fires of his life had been like those set consciously by the Iowa farmer. He hoped that the encrustations and trivia of youth had been burned away and that his fields were now ready for adult harvests. He thought: "I'll bet there are men who've never had a day's worry growing up. There must be a million fellows who'd never have given Mona Meigs a second look." Then, sleepily, he concluded that such men would have to be like those who wilfully avoided the great valleys of experience. "They'd either be cowards or fools," he chuckled, and he went to sleep.

Some time after the lunch hour—he was too weak to eat— he heard through the ward the soft voice of an Italian housewife. She was reading to the sick men from an essay to which she had become much attached, for it spoke of her own longings: "Men are not born citizens of the countries they inhabit. They are like wanderers on whom fall the ashes of many places, and some men live forever in countries they never even dimly understand. No! Men grow to citizenship. They earn it. How do they earn it? By love, work, a passion for things better than they are, or by flashes at night when all the vast land from New York to California stands illuminated. That is how men gradually come to know where they live and why."

The words were so astonishing in a charity ward that David called feebly to a passing nurse. "Whatcha want?" she demanded.

"That woman reading? Who?"

"One of the WPAers."

"Ask her if she'd stop here," David requested quietly.

"She a'ready stopped, but you were asleep."

Nevertheless, the nurse spoke to the Italian woman. The sick man to whom she was reading had long ago fallen asleep. That was her daily experience, but in her quiet way she had determined that even if the entire hospital fell asleep, she would nevertheless continue to read the things she thought worthwhile.

"Hello," she said softly to David. "I'm Mrs. Allegri." She was a big woman, in her forties, and her hips were immense.

"That selection you were reading? What is it?"

"It's from an essay," she explained, beaming with satisfaction.

"It was very good. Who wrote it?"

"My boss!" she said proudly. "That is, the regional boss for the Eastern states. I'm on WPA, you know."

"Your boss writes well. Who is he?"

"Mr. Joseph Vaux," she said with great pride.

David grinned and thought of the steel-hard fellow he had known in college, the radical, the know-it-all, the intransigeant fighter. Jesus! It was good to hear about your friends. "Would you read me that again?" he asked.

Mrs. Allegri sat down and patiently shuffled her papers. "Men are not born citizens of the country they inhabit," she began. When she finished the flowing essay David repeated his former verdict. "That's wonderful!" he said. Mrs. Allegri beamed at him, but from long experience with her own children she recognized David's constricted breathing and told him to go to sleep again. "I'll come back tomorrow," she said.

He watched her go, a large, soft woman who walked with grace and who saw each wornout defeated man as her special charge. She nodded gently to each inmate as she left, and when her large body turned the last corner, it was as if goodness itself had departed from that hall.

That night David had no nightmares. Visions prompted by Mrs. Allegri's reading filled his mind. This was the vast land! This America thrown between oceans, perfect in prospect and reassuring in achievement. He thought slowly and with heavy breathing of the states he had bummed through after Chautauqua folded: Kansas and Colorado and Oregon! They were names of beauty; even as words they were cherishable. The Dakotas and Texas, Missouri and Wisconsin, and strange Alabama where he had not felt at home.

He could not believe that his vast country had run down. He refused to acknowledge that it had come to a halt or that its spirit was dead. The depression was terrible—he knew how terrible—and his nightmare of the wingless flies was worse, but one Mrs. Allegri slowly refusing to surrender gave David courage.

The next afternoon he found himself eagerly awaiting her arrival, and about two she appeared with several other women. She walked with stately mien down the long aisle to David's bed and said, "I've brought an assistant who likes to read."

But the helper took one look at David, threw her hand to her mouth and dashed from the ward. David tried to leap from his bed but stumbled weakly and was caught by Mrs. Allegri. "Marcia!" he cried. "Come back!"

She wouldn't. She rushed down the long aisle and slammed open the door. Then she turned and disappeared. Mrs. Allegri and the nurse put David back in bed.

"How do you know her?" David gasped.

"She lives with me. She's on WPA, too." Mrs. Allegri dismissed the nurse and sat with David. "She told me about you. She's been looking for you, and she's been afraid she'd find you."

"Is she divorced?" David asked.

"Yes," Mrs. Allegri said. "She never talks much, but one night she saw me washing Achilles . . ."

David asked more than a hundred questions before the visiting period was over, and Mrs. Allegri answered each one as if he were one of her children asking: "What makes the wind?" Then she rose gracefully and walked slowly down the aisle, smiling at the sick men.

When Marcia and Mrs. Allegri appeared the next afternoon, the experience was different from anything David had previously known. Marcia was older. Unlike Mona Meigs, she had been unable to slough off the consequences of her actions. They showed clearly in her face. She was thinner, too, and less neat than David had remembered her. But she was still straight and she still looked at David directly. Her clothes showed numerous signs of having been mended. She wore no makeup and was noticeably pallid, but she was the same girl he had always known, defiant, eager for contest, alive and hopeful. She blushed deeply and said hello.

"I'll read farther down," Mrs. Allegri said. She had with her the Beards' *The Rise of American Civilization* and she was prepared to read it whether anyone on the aisle could understand it or not, because she understood it, now, after years in this country.

David stared at Marcia and said, "Won't you sit down?" She was embarrassed. She opened an oilcloth bag and produced a novel.

"This is *The Good Earth*," she said.

"Your parents are wondering where you are," he interrupted.

"We've lots of time to talk later," she said, but as she read the Chinese novel, her hand shook, and she was visibly relieved when Mrs. Allegri came to take her home.

"We'll be back!" the soft Italian woman said, and when the day came for David to be discharged she insisted that he come to live with her for a week. "You need nursing," she said, and she took him to her home.

At Mrs. Allegri's David was surrounded by a degree of love he had never known before. It was his first experience in living with an actual family whose members loved one another, and the impact upon him was very great. Mr. Allegri was a fiery man, older than his wife and weighing about half as much. He had been unemployed for three years, a catastrophe that he laid loudly and personally upon the doorstep of one Herbert Hoover, whose infamy he could discuss for hours. He had six children. The oldest was a girl studying law at NYU. Two sons were in the CCC and wrote long letters about Wyoming which Mr. Allegri read to anyone who would listen. Two children were in school and baby Achilles was three years old.

Where the money came from to sustain this sprawling household David never knew. Allegri worked at odd jobs. Mrs. Allegri was on WPA. Marcia paid some rent and the CCC boys sent home a few dollars. It was not money, it was Mrs. Allegri that held the home together. She did immense washes, scrubbed the place once a week, and took care of her children. She babied her hot-tempered husband and laughed with the neighbors at night as they all sat on fruit crates in Bleecker Street. She felt ashamed to take her dole from WPA, for all she had to do was to sit and read books that she had always yearned to study. She had a rich, wonderful life, and her happiness in it glowed from her big round face.

David was given a bed on the ground floor. He tried to walk about but found himself far too weak. He still breathed heavily and was unable even to argue with Mr. Allegri for long. Once he asked the little fighting cock what happened to men who got sick and had no place like this to come to. Allegri stuck his jaw way out and said, "They croak, that's what!"

David's appreciation of his refuge made him consider the even greater kindness that had been extended him by Mom Beckett. He was ashamed of not having gone back to her hilarious restaurant and he explained the situation to Marcia, begging her to visit Mom and to extend his apologies. Marcia agreed that someone must do so, and when she reached Mom's flowing bar she was glad that she had come.

"He'll be coming back in about a week," she explained.

"Keep him till he gets well!" Mom insisted. "Eatin' this grub would kill a healthy guy."

"You've been very kind to David," Marcia said. "Even if he's never told you, he appreciates what you've done."

"The important thing," Mom interrupted, "is gettin' you and him married. When's it gonna be?"

"I don't know," Marcia said. "David's changed. He seems to have lost his courage."

"Hell!" Mom exploded. "He ain't had a job for three years."

"But I can't marry a weakling, Mrs. Beckett."

"It's Miss Beckett!" Mom corrected. "But hell, sister! All men are weaklings. Women marry 'em and make 'em strong." Impatiently she went to the kitchen door and kicked it open. Marcia could see the tall, thin, bearded figure of a man who wore a chef's funny white cap and a dirty apron. He was bending over the stove, tasting a stew with his thumb. Grandiloquently, Mom pointed at him.

"There he is!" Mom said. "Ain't he a godforsaken, pitiful wreck of a man?" She closed the door and said powerfully to Marcia, "They tell me he's America's greatest poet, but he's so goddamned dumb that if I didn't look after him he'd starve to death. In one way or another, all men are like that. You marry Dave and make a man of him."

But Marcia was not so sure of David's future. She saw defeat written in his face and she guessed clearly that he had surrendered. What he had relinquished she did not know: hope, a play, the dream of the future, perhaps a book of poems. She took Mr. Allegri aside and said, "Get him out into the fresh air, even if it is winter." The little man led David through the Italian quarter to a group of narrow clay courts on which a score of men were playing bocce. Then he bundled David up and sat him on a cold bench, adding, "Now if you could lend me even so much as ten cents, you and I could make a lot of money. But for the love of the Virgin, don't tell my wife I played bocce!"

The players cheered in Italian when he stepped onto the courts. He was like a fighting cock, and bocce—the Italian game of bowls—was a wild experience when he played. He cursed the balls, wept at a bad shot, used exaggerated body English, refused to accede a single point, and went crazy with joy when he won.

After each game he rushed up to David and handed him some money. "Keep it for me! Now don't get cold. Only one more game!" David shivered, but the fresh air did him good, and the wild pleasure of the Italian men—all unemployed—delighted him.

"Do you play here every day?" he asked the men about him.

"Oh, yes!" a watcher replied. "I can remember when Allegri would win as much as ninety dollars. Now they play for pennies, but they get as much fun." He paused to laugh at little Allegri screaming passionately over a foul. "It's better when he's here. But his wife won't let him play much any more. No money. You must have lent him some?"

Mr. Allegri won eighty cents. Hoarse and trembling with excitement, he cried, "We'll have a beer! For you, orange juice." He led the way to an espresso shop where the players reconstructed the games. Once Allegri became so excited that it seemed to David as if murder by knife could be the only solution when suddenly everybody burst into wild laughter, slapped Allegri on the back, and sent him home to his wife.

The streets were cold and dark, and Mr. Allegri became afraid. "She'll know for sure what I was doing!" he wailed. Then he said accusingly to David, "You should have made me come right home." He grasped David by the arm and said, bravely, "It'll be all right. Let me do the talking! If she asks you, deny everything."

There was no necessity to lie. Mrs. Allegri looked at her guilty little husband and said, "You took David for a walk?

Good!" She cooked a big meal and said, "With the money you won at bocce, David, you should take Marcia to a movie!"

They didn't go to a movie. They walked about the streets and finally sat in a drug store, talking. "I've never known so much love before," David said quietly.

"That's why I live there," Marcia said.

"We could be like that," David said haltingly.

"We could be," Marcia said. "I've always wanted a home like theirs. A home where there was so much love it could spill over onto people. That would be a good home."

"We should get married," David said.

"It's what I long for most," Marcia replied.

"When can we?" David asked.

He was shocked by her answer. "How can I be sure you're ready?" she asked. "Have you changed yourself in humility, as I've had to?"

"Can't you see that I have?" he said.

"No. You look merely frightened to me."

"Watch me for a while," he said humbly. "If you think I've learned, will you marry me?"

"Of course!" she replied. "Why else have these things happened?"

They walked home slowly and David told the Allegris that in the morning he would go back to MacDougal Street and find a job. They were unhappy to have him go, and late that night Mr. Allegri crept to his bedside and whispered, "Any time you need a home, you got one. Right here." There was a long pause while they shook hands in the dark room. Then Allegri said very slowly. "If you happen to have any change left, I could do a nice piece of business tomorrow at the bocce courts. Why, with a proper stake I could make a living off them damned fools. They can't play. Did you notice that?"

David pounded pavements for eleven days and finally uncovered a rumor of a job. At Wanamaker's freight shed the foreman admitted, "Things are better. Some time later this month we may have a job unloadin' trucks. Pays $18 a week. Keep comin' back."

David was so pleased that he galloped directly to Marcia, who was as proud of him as if he had really started work. In search of celebration, he snapped his fingers and said, "There's a wonderful man I'd like you to meet. But he has fits."

"Why would that make a difference?" Marcia asked. When they arrived, the immense editor was playing Brahms, and as the rich clean chords sounded he voiced his approval of Marcia. "A lovely girl, much better than the last. Whew! You should have seen her, Miss Paxson. An actress, but she got her man soaked up in concrete."

"Was it Miss Meigs?" Marcia asked suspiciously.

"Yes," Binder laughed merrily. "And he put her in his novel, too. She was the heroine."

"David!" Marcia cried. "I didn't know you were writing a book."

"I'm not," he said abruptly. "Not any more." Then Marcia understood what surrender David had made. She could see the glory missing from his face, and she became sad, even though he had a job unloading trucks.

But Morris Binder, himself a man who had surrendered, thought David's new job something to celebrate. He suggested, with great trepidation, "Why couldn't we go to the symphony tonight? Stokowski is conducting." He pointed to a clipping from the *Times* which he had tacked above his record player. It gave the program, and David knew that the huge man had intended playing the records that night, imagining himself at the symphony. The editor bowed to Marcia and said, "Miss Paxson, would you risk it?" His big hands were nervously twitching as he stumbled to explain, "We could sit in the back and I'd pay the ushers to watch me. Recently I've been able to anticipate . . . I could hold your hand, David to let you know." He unfolded a campaign that had obviously been in his mind for a long time. "And Marcia can carry this little pillow to stuff against my face in case . . ."

He called a cab and they went to Carnegie Hall. He bought three seats in the row near the door and gave two ushers a dollar each to be ready. Then he ponderously let himself down into his seat between David and Marcia and said, "The acoustics of this hall are superb. I came here often as a boy."

The first part of Stokowski's program consisted of two numbers David had often heard him play in Philadelphia, the Classical and Mozart's 39th. He had long appreciated the latter with its quiet rustle of immortality, but until this night he had never fully understood the music. Now, sitting with Morris Binder's fat hand in his, he could actually feel the impact of music upon the big man's spirit. Binder's pulses quickened, and David's own perceptions were trebled by contact with the trembling man.

During intermission Binder sat very still and would not talk, as if he were saving his energies for the inward battle. But when the musicians returned to the stage and the bassoon practiced the important notes it would soon play, he opened his lips with almost childish delight and said, "It's the first live music I've heard in nineteen years."

Tears filled his eyes when Stokowski began to conduct Beethoven's Pastoral. David did not like this symphony. He felt that the deaf master had allowed his mind to dwell upon trivial items, so that the second movement especially seemed repetitious. He had often thought that the long-windedness of the first two movements was the only evidence Beethoven ever gave of his increasing deafness. But tonight, sitting beside an immense hulk whose mind was somehow crippled, listening to music by a man whose ears were stopped, David experienced the terrible meaning of mortality. Men are actually living chunks of matter that some day die. He forgot the music and remembered his first acknowledgment of this fact. It had occurred three days after Cyril Hargreaves had engineered it so that Max Volo's men assaulted him. He had hated Cyril desperately and had plotted rich revenge. But he happened to open a door and saw Cyril sitting on the toilet. The pompous actor, the vain man, the strutter, and the false accent all disappeared in that brief moment. From then on Cyril Hargreaves was only a man. He ate and slept and went to the toilet, and all the men in the world were like him.

A tremor passed along Morris Binder's hand and surged upon David's, so that the presence of mankind was strong upon David. He thought of Beethoven in the streets of Bonn. The ugly deaf man had loved and hated and been despised. He had boils and indigestion and he liked beer and he went to the toilet, sick with fear. Yet his music transcended all this, but if one listened closely one could hear the tread of a real man, on this whirling earth, tormented as only men on this earth can be.

Now the lusty bassoon uttered its peasant dance, and Morris Binder grinned with pleasure. The storm came, and with it the storm of fear across Binder's face. David could feel his muscles tighten, and for a moment the huge man looked panic-stricken. His hand began to shake, and the ushers moved into position.

But David put his arm about Binder's huge neck and pressed close to him. "No!" he whispered. "You can stick it out." The big man relaxed, and closed his eyes as the storm ended. Almost at the same instant Beethoven's storm passed, too, and from the orchestra came the wonderful and stately rhythm of thanksgiving. There was a flood of noble sound, as if the angry deaf man had cried, "I'll make the world sway!" The closing movement became so wooded and entrancing that it reminded Morris Binder of the days when his parents had taken him to the Catskills. David saw the valleys of the Delaware, and Marcia thought of her father's fields, where she had tended cattle. Like Beethoven, they were people of the earth.

Slowly, magnificently, the symphony came to a close. The hall and all the people were transfused with sunlight from the splendid chords, but when the last note sounded, Morris Binder and David slumped forward in their seats. The ushers came up and whispered, "We'll carry him out," but the giant editor grunted and said, "Thank you. I'm all right." He rose slowly and walked with great precision to the street. In a taxi he sat upright, as if he were a girl going to her wedding in a stiff gown, and even when he climbed his stairs, he moved like an automaton.

But once at home, he collapsed into his chair. His eyes became glassy and he stared ahead, his huge mouth agape. Marcia went to find a damp cloth and David, preparing to help the editor to bed, took off his coat. Then Binder saw the gray arcs of nervous sweat under David's arms. "Was it as bad as that?" he asked.

"I never heard music before," David replied.

"I felt the same way! I wish we could . . ." But the worst attack of all began. He reared from his chair in one violent lunge toward the ceiling and uttered a shattering scream. He crashed to the floor, and even though David and Marcia had been waiting for this great attack, they held back aghast.

The space was clear, therefore, when Miss Adams burst into the room, "You took him to the theatre!" she screamed at David hysterically. "You're killing him! Get out, you good-for-nothing. Get out!"

The next morning at ten-thirty a taxi rushed up to Mom Beckett's, accompanied by two policemen. A white, trembling Tremont Clay jumped out and began to cry, "Where's Mr. Harper?"

From her door Mom, her hair plastered down with pomade, peered inquisitively. "Hey, you!" she cried. "What's all the noise?"

"I've got to see Mr. Harper!" the excited publisher answered.

"Well, he's sleepin'!" Mom replied. "He may get a job next week and he's restin'."

"Please call him!" Clay pleaded. One of the policemen appeared.

"Dave!" Mom bellowed. "Haul ass down here! The law!"

David appeared, unshaved and blinking. "Mr. Clay!" he mumbled. The publisher gripped him by the forearm and hustled him into the street. A crowd had gathered and suddenly the fat woman's window shot up. "Fight! Fight!" she screamed. From a dozen doors people catapulted into Mac-Dougal Street.

"Stand back!" the two policemen ordered, but from above them came the deafening exhortation, "Fight! Fight!" A crowd of loungers stared in the cab window at David and started to cry. "He did it! He's the one!" Slowly the cab pulled away, and in the rear seat David stared at Mr. Clay. The little publisher licked his lips.

"Miss Adams just killed Morris Binder," he said hoarsely.

"My God!" David gasped.

"He had a tremendous fit. She seemed to lose her head." He covered his thin face with his hands. "It was horrible. She stabbed him at least a dozen times."

"Why?" David demanded.

"Why!" the specialist in crime echoed. "Why does anybody . . ." He lowered his voice and said, "She saw that he was going slowly crazy. She . . ." He hammered his forehead and shouted accusingly, "Don't ask me why! Figure it out for yourself!"

"What will they do to her?" David asked in a whisper.

"Miss Adams?" The tense little man looked angrily at David and said, "Nothing. They won't do a damned thing, because she killed herself, too."

"Ugh," David grunted, as if he had been struck. "Oh, God!" His face grew dark and he cried, "Mr. Clay, I . . ."

"Son!" Mr. Clay interrupted, grabbing David by the shoulder exactly as David had grabbed Morris Binder the night before. "Pull yourself together. I don't want to hear anything. You've got a tremendous job to do. Five magazines. I'm giving you forty a week, right now! Better times are coming, kid. This is your big chance."

David pulled away in disgust as the taxi entered Lafayette Street. "But why would she . . ."

Clay gripped him furiously. "I'll get you a helper, too. You can have practically anything you want, Harper. But you and I have got to pull these magazines through." The little editor took a deep breath. "Here we are," he said. "Now play the man! You'll see a rough scene, but keep your wits." He banged open the taxi door and muscled his way through the mob. David followed him and heard men whispering, "That's Clay himself. He found the bodies."

Photographers were busy in the editorial office. There was a noisy confusion of policemen and intruders, and for a moment David could see nothing, and then slowly the noise ceased and a pathway was made for Tremont Clay. Down it David saw the tragedy. His finest friend lay shambled across the floor. Blood dripped indecently from unnecessary wounds, and the huge, expressive face was distorted in its final passion. The tongue from which David had learned so much wisdom —the very tongue David had sometimes held—was protruded and purple. Death, in triumphant confusion, possessed Morris Binder in all possible ways. Tears gushed to David's eyes, but a firm hand gripped him. "Take it easy," Mr. Clay commanded.

Then more flash bulbs exploded, and with an impulsive gasp the late comers saw the long steel paper knife protruding from Miss Adams' body. Her trim gray suit was smeared with blood. There was a sickening moment as the flash bulbs defined her hard features, and then a young policeman whispered, "I guess she was the other woman."

David started to protest, but to his horror he saw Mr. Clay directing the photographers how to take additional pictures which would show both bodies. And then David saw what was in the little man's mind. This story could run in the Clay magazines for years. It had everything! A brilliant criminologist, a sex-starved clerk, mania, passion, a long steel knife, and superb pictures. Why, this story could go on forever!

"Take a couple more from here," Mr. Clay stage-directed, and inadvertently David looked down at the bleeding hulk of the betrayed giant, the proscribed lawyer, the great detective who functioned from a grubby desk, the opera savant who heard no operas, the man who loved all people and who lived alone. Now he had found his Valhalla, immortalized in Tremont Clay's murder magazines. In death Morris Binder would become like a prehistoric monster, imprisoned forever in the glacial moraine of a filth he had helped to create.

When the last photographs were taken, when the limp bodies were dragged away, a charwoman came in to wash the defiled floor. When she was done, Mr. Clay said, "Now the place is yours!"

David was inspired to rush out of the door and never return, but at that moment a messenger boy arrived with the latest batch of manuscripts. "Where shall I put them?" he asked.

"Why, on Mr. Harper's desk!" Mr. Clay cried, banging the old, scarred desk. "He's head man up here now!" Gently he pushed David into Morris Binder's huge chair. "Boy!" he cried. "Fetch a pillow!" Then he half-laughed and patted David on the shoulder. "Don't mind," he said. "No one could fill that chair, but you'll come as close as anyone." He stepped in front of David and said with great force, "A lot of my life rides with you, son. These are the days when a man shows what he's got."

Then David was alone in the dark room. The knife-scarred desk with its load of filth was his. As he envisaged the endless, indecent pages he would have to write, he grew ashamed and muttered, "I can't work here! I'll unload trucks." But the call of a job was too great. For three long years he had been unemployed, and now he had a job again. Maybe people would laugh at a grown-up man who was a pulp editor, but had they, by God, walked the streets alone and hungry and ashamed and cold and useless and broke, watching themselves each day becoming more and more inevitably bums? Had they known the stark, gnawing rottenness of being out of work day after day in the full power of youth? Had they stood in some midnight square with not a cent to their names and thought of taking pretty girls to dinner or to the theatre or even to a goddamned lousy ten-cent movie? Had they known the longings of youth forestalled and aborted by an economic accident called depression? If they had not, David cried, let them keep their mouths shut.

But when he read the first sentences of his first manuscript—"This murder took place in my own town and if you don't believe me you can read about it in the pittsburg papers which also have good photographs in case you want some" —he felt a moment of revulsion. His mind mumbled a kind of death chant: "Men don't want to be free. They don't want the feel of meadows under their feet nor the cry of wood-birds leading them on. They fear the desert and the sun that sinks behind the endless ocean. The sky must be broken by clouds and stars or it would be intolerable. And the inward clutches of the heart, disappearing in the very womb of time itself, are even more forsaken and forlorn."

The parable of the wingless flies had come home. David's spirit shuddered at the prospect of freedom. Like a horse caught in a fire, he whinnied shamelessly to be kept in his stall; and the name of surrender that echoed through all the fly-specked offices of the world echoed through his dark office and darker mind: Work.

But even though David was successful in convincing himself that being an editor for Tremont Clay was decent because it was work, he had a nervous moment when he reported that evening to Bleecker Street and informed Marcia of his good luck. She said, coldly, "You mean grown-up men work on such magazines?"

"You liked Morris Binder," he argued.

"But he wasn't a grown-up man!" she protested. She would say no more than this, and it was apparent that she was completely disgusted with David. He began to feel this disgust himself when he discovered that both Morris Binder and Miss Adams had left him all their money. Each had less than four hundred dollars, and David was bewildered as to why these lonely people had left their money to him and not to one another. Marcia explained the reason very simply.

"They were cowards," she said. "Fear corroded their lives. I don't know why Morris Binder was ashamed to marry her. Perhaps he felt his sickness . . . Maybe it was she who was afraid. They were cowards, and they killed themselves long ago. Didn't you see that?"

He hadn't seen the cowardice that had killed these people. In fact, he did not even yet comprehend that had they married and lived together little would have been changed except the most fundamental thing in both their lives: they could have shared their accomplishments and defeats, and bitter Miss Adams would have had no necessity to kill either the hulking editor or herself, because fear would thus have been expelled.

David understood this when he took Marcia to Morris Binder's apartment one Saturday morning. Workmen were ripping down the fabulous horns. They were joking about the intricate system as they destroyed it, and David realized that it could never be replaced. The grandeur of that room was gone. "It gives you a sick feeing," David said. "Like watching a cathedral being torn down."

"David!" Marcia cried. "Morris Binder never built a cathedral! Cowards build refuges, perhaps, or maybe stuck-away chapels. But not open-air cathedrals! Not with spires and organ music!"

"What's troubling you, Marcia?" David asked in real confusion.

"There's danger in the world," Marcia replied. "Brave people are needed. Every day you work for Tremont Clay proves to me I could never marry you."

"Men have to work at lots of different things," David protested.

"But men also have to build a life, David!" Marcia pleaded. She pointed angrily at the barren rooms in which Morris Binder had spent his long travail. "Was this a life?" she asked.

"He was a sick man! Almost a cripple!"

"No man needs to be sick in the heart," Marcia said furiously. "That's the test of whether you're living or not." David tried to reply, but she overrode him. "You're a stranger to me!" she cried. "You've become a coward. I could never marry you."

David started to refute this statement, but a workman on a stepladder ripped away a wire and began to shout, "Hey! Whaddaya know? This wire led upstairs to the dame's room! Pretty tidy, eh?"

"Whaddaya mean?" another workman shouted.

"Curb service!" the man on the ladder explained. He jerked the wire and yelled. "Yoo-hoo! Bessie! Come on down!" The men burst into loud laughter.

David was infuriated by Marcia's reaction to his job. "Damn it all," he growled, as he walked to work, "for three years I had no job. Now I get hell for finding one. It just don't make sense." Yet at strange intervals during his editorial work, Marcia's image would whir across his desk, mocking him for being an intellectual garbage man.

He finally went to see Mom and explained the whole situation to her, ending, "So I've been out of work for three years, and I finally get a job. Maybe it isn't the best job in the world, but which would you rather have, an unemployed bum or a guy trying to make his way?"

"Well," Mom reflected, "seems to me you came to see me in jail with two hundred bucks you were ashamed to hold on to. I told you I understood perfectly, and I did. But what I don't understand is how them bills could have been stained any darker than the ones you get on your present job." She leaned back from the table and studied the effect of her words. David scratched his ear.

"You mean you'd rather have me lounging around here than working?" David asked.

"Look at Claude!" she said, pointing at the poet with her manicured hand. "Every seven or eight years he turns out a book of poems. Folks say they're the best in America. Rest of the time he sponges offa me. I got to admit that he does help out on the cookin', God fabbid. But that seems to me an honorable way to live."

"How about you . . ." David exploded.

"Wait a minute!" the big woman interrupted, placing her hand on David's wrist. "Slow down, sonny! You started this conversation, not me. I wouldn't never have said nothin'. But you ast me, and I'm tellin' you."

"All right! Let me say it slower. You've been a bootlegger, pretty much of a bum at times. How does this apply to you?"

"Very easy!" Mom said with great force. "It's like this. How a woman makes her livin' is unimportant. On the street, bootleggin', griftin'. It's part of a woman's nature, because the best she can hope for is to grub her dough off'n some man. But for a man it makes all the difference in the world. A man has got to hold his head up, or he's plumb lost. I'm a bootlegger, OK. Claude ain't. He won't touch the stuff, says it's a filthy business."

"Yet he lives off your dough."

"Not exactly," Mom said. At this moment the poet rang up a small sale. "You see, we've agreed to call that his work. That's his job. In a way, he owns the restaurant. He reinvests his wages, you might say. He takes only dimes and quarters as he needs them and now and then a pair of shoes. That ways things are honest. No real man would be satisfied with less."

"You're saying I should quit my job?"

"If you're askin' me, yes."

"But what in God's name can I live on? I want to get married."

"You can write," Mom said.

The two friends looked at each other. Mom's face was a

heavy mask, well made up and placid. She was in no sense accusing David, but spiritually she was assuming the role formerly held by Miss Adams. "You can write," she said, adding silently, "and a guy who can do that is silly to . . ."

"What do you think I should do, Mom?"

"I think maybe you should help Claude. You could be assistant cook."

David bit his lip and asked, "You've met Marcia Paxson. Would she marry me if I was assistant cook?"

"I can tell you, she won't marry you unless you are. Or the equivalent."

For three days David considered his problem. During these days he thought a great deal about Morris Binder. He reviewed the man's bleak life, and his terrible indecency in having Miss Adams listening from an equally bleak room above him. He thought of the trivial impact these people had made upon their city. They had been cliff dwellers and they had accomplished nothing: no children, no love, not even a home; no singing accomplishments, nothing but a series of filthy magazines stretching from the sewage pits of society to the minds of morons.

"Forty years from now I could be like that!" he shuddered. He began to see his life as a limited journey. There were only a few places he could visit, a few objectives to be attained, and when his brief efforts were over, the journey and its memories would be forgotten. During these days of review he came to hate New York City, both in the morning when he walked down Third Street and late at night when he came home along Fourth. He recalled how blessed by nature had been his poorhouse life; but here in the city it sometimes seemed as if there were no life. There were no birds nor turning furrows in the spring. Nights were often wintry but never frosty, and some seasons slipped past without his even knowing they had come; for there were no dogtooth violets, no mosses by the creek nor cattails fluffing in the autumn breeze.

By the fourth day his mind was made up. He stopped at a corner shop and bought a big bouquet of flowers. Then he went up to his room and grabbed the folder in which his forgotten and unfinished novel lay gathering dust. He tucked it under his arm and stepped out in MacDougal Street. Immediately, from the fat woman's window across the way came the strident cry, "Lover! Lover! Lover!"

A group of little boys surrounded him and teased him as

he walked toward Bleecker Street. Even after he had turned the corner he could hear the fat woman crying, "Lover! Lover!" At Sixth Avenue the boys left him, and he trudged across to Seventh. There a new group of idle urchins began to joke with him, and among them was Mrs. Allegri's boy. Like a bolt he left the crowd and went screaming down the street: "Here comes Harper with the biggest goddamn bunch of flowers . . ." Mrs. Allegri met her son at the stoop and slapped his face soundly. "Have some manners!" she commanded. Little Mr. Allegri got up from his peach basket and shouted, "Marcia! Here he is!" The excited man led David through the dark hall and into Marcia's room. "Behold the lover!" he cried approvingly. "I'll fetch a vase."

When David was alone with Marcia he said abruptly, "Now I know what you were talking about. I quit my job . . ."

Like a woman, Marcia popped her knuckles to her teeth and cried, "What will you do for a living?" David grinned.

"Mom has offered me a job as assistant cook. What she means is that she'll stake me until I finish writing . . . Well, I've been working on a novel."

"Yes," Marcia said. "I imagined that was your surrender."

"What do you mean?"

They sat on the edge of the bed and Marcia held his hands. "From the time I first met you in the poorhouse, I knew we'd get married, Dave. When Daddy read your poem aloud, I wanted to know a boy like you. At basketball games I used to watch every jump you made, and the bright wonder in your eyes came to be in mine, too. But when I saw you in the hospital I knew that you had surrendered. What it was I didn't know, but it was something big. It was a novel, eh?"

"This sounds foolish," David said in embarrassment. "But I guess I was going through a period of pretty wild self-intoxication. I thought I was going to be a second Balzac." The old fire came upon him and he simply had to rise and move about. "God! What novels I was going to write! I guess I did it mostly to keep my spirits . . ." He stopped abruptly and handed Marcia the folder. "Will you read this? And if it's any good, will you marry me?"

"Dave!" the glowing girl replied, "I'm going to marry you whether it's any good or not. You don't have to be a success. Just so long as you haven't quit where the big dreams are concerned."

"When can we get married?" David asked.

"Right away! We'll live at Mom's, and then later on I'll have courage enough to go back to Bucks County. I want to live near the canal and to go shopping in Doylestown as Mrs. David Harper. I want you so very much, and if I'm ever tough or cold or haughty, I want you to slap my ears down." She held out her arms to David, and they fell backwards onto the bed. After they had been ominously silent for some minutes Mr. Allegri coughed very noisily in the hall and banged on the door.

"I brought you some wine!" he announced. "And some cookies!" He placed a tray upon a chair, and all the Allegris and some of their friends piled into the room.

"An engagement!" Mrs. Allegri beamed.

And David thought: "It's like coming home to yourself at last."

For this is the journey that men make: to find themselves. If they fail in this, it doesn't matter much what else they find. Money, position, fame, many loves, revenge are all of little consequence, and when the tickets are collected at the end of the ride they are tossed into the bin marked FAILURE.

But if a man happens to find himself—if he knows what he can be depended upon to do, the limits of his courage, the positions from which he will no longer retreat, the degree to which he can surrender his inner life to some woman, the secret reservoirs of his determination, the extent of his dedication, the depth of his feeling for beauty, his honest and unpostured goals—then he has found a mansion which he can inhabit with dignity all the days of his life.

Among the many people he had known, David could recall only one real enemy, his aunt Reba Stücke, and he finally got even with her in a manner so bizarre that for the rest of his life he had to laugh with joyous pleasure whenever he remembered that evil woman. By the same stratagem he gained his freedom from the sentimental bondage in which he had been held by Mona Meigs. It happened this way.

When Marcia brought him the incomplete novel she said, "It's wonderful, Dave! You be second cook till it's finished. I'll be proud to be chambermaid." Then she frowned ever so slightly and said, "I can see from the book that you really loved Miss Meigs."

David blushed and asked, "Is it as clear as that?"

"It's very clear," Marcia said seriously. "Are you still in love with her?"

David had sense enough to reply, "Not the way I am with you," and the frown disappeared. Then he added, "It's just that no man could ever forget Mona completely. I saw a man die one night, and his last question was about her." Marcia frowned again, a woman's flickering frown that seemed to cut deep because it stayed so very briefly.

Then the will was probated.

Actually, there was no will. Reba Stücke had been so grasping that she was emotionally unable to write a will. She simply could not imagine giving up her hoarded money to anyone, so the court said that by default it must go to David. They sent him eight hundred and sixty dollars and many papers to sign. He said to Marcia, "We don't want to start our married life with money from that old witch."

"You bet we don't!" Marcia agreed, and they decided to give it to the Friends' Service Committee, but they were prevented from such an obvious gesture by Mona's letter:

Dear Dave

I suppose your all fixed up now with a good job I wouldent for the world bother you again but Ive had some trouble and I feel dead certin that its all over and that my big chance is just arround the corner Theres a new company starting with some MGM characters and Im dead certin to land big with them I had a bit part in the last John Barrimore turkey but you probably dident see me as I was like Vito on the radio Dave theres this very good friend of mine Richard Hansen and he writes these wonderful songs any day I expect him to click but big Could you let me have a couple of hundred bucks its a good risk because as you know I pay back loans and Dick says I can have the first money he gets from Paramount on his songs If you could hear them youd know he was dead certin to be a big success . . .

David handed the scrawl to Marcia, who read it slowly and shook her head. "What are you going to do?" she asked. Then she noticed that he was laughing.

"Do?" he chuckled. "This solves everything!" He laughed all the way to the bank, where he made out a cashier's check, and on to the postoffice, where he mailed a registered letter, and all during the rest of the day, so that forever afterwards when he thought of Aunt Reba a warm glow suffused him, and he felt wonderful. He might be in a restaurant, and he would begin to chuckle for no apparent reason, and then Marcia would know that he was thinking of Aunt Reba's poorhouse money out in Hollywood, spent in niggardly amounts to support an actress and a song writer who lived together in open sin.

So whenever David laughed, Marcia laughed too, for she knew that at long last the poorhouse, and Aunt Reba, and perhaps even Mona had been exorcized by the subtle warmth of comedy. "At last he's ready to get married," she whispered to herself.

The wedding was held in a small white room on East Seventeenth Street. The guests arrived by mid-afternoon. From Bucks County only the Paxsons appeared, and they sat apart in one corner of the room, ashamed and confused at their daughter's headstrong history yet pleased that she was at last marrying David Harper.

David's friends attended the Quaker wedding self-consciously. Tremont Clay wore formal dress and felt ill at ease. He thought that this young man had let him down. Mom Beckett and Claude sat together, holding hands, and as always at a wedding Mom had tears in her eyes. Her mascara smeared, and she was not a lovely sight. Vito was in the front row where he could see, while little Betty, pregnant again, was to accompany Marcia to the wedding chairs. Wild Man Jensen was to walk with David. In the rear Mrs. Allegri wiped her nose even before the procession started, but Mr. Allegri commanded her sharply to stop. He pointed out that it couldn't be much of a wedding with no priest or flowers.

Four elderly Quakers entered from a side door and sat facing the small Meeting. Three were men, and they looked like Solebury farmers, transplanted into the city. The woman was small and nervous. With sharp eyes she indicated where everyone was to sit, jumped up to adjust the curtains, and marked the minutes by a tapping foot. These four were that day the repositories of God's will, and through them David and Marcia would be married.

At four-thirty Marcia and the dwarf Betty Bellotti walked into the room, followed by David and Wild Man Jensen. The bridal pair sat on two plain chairs that faced the audience. There was silence, and the peace of God descended upon that room, and behind him David could hear the three men breathing heavily. He could hear the woman tapping.

He looked among the strange faces and felt that he could never find courage to rise and begin the ceremony. Slowly, as if testing his strength, he gritted his teeth, but strength fled from him, for he heard Marcia gasp and followed her eyes across the room. Then he gasped too, for sitting in the corner was Mrs. Trueblood.

She was an elderly woman, thin and tall. She had a slightly peaked nose and eyes that burned like embers in a dying grate. She was always dressed in black and spoke at Yearly Meetings. Marcia had not invited her, nor had David. She had no doubt come as the representative of Solebury Meeting in this official marriage of a daughter of Solebury. She sat primly, unwanted, unlovely, bitter; and the wedding couple was shaken by this Coleridgean wedding guest.

Twenty minutes of silence elapsed, and David thought of Mrs. Trueblood and Harry Moomaugh and Alison Webster and Mona Meigs and of each item of sin that rested on him that day. In the audience, members began to wonder if he had forgotten his words, but Mr. Paxson stared at him and almost imperceptibly nodded his head. David took a deep breath and rose to face the members of the Meeting.

"In the presence of God and these our friends assembled," he said softly, "I take thee, Marcia, to be my wife . . ." He continued the simple ritual, placed the ring upon Marcia's finger, and kissed her. Marcia acknowledged to the Meeting —and through it to the world—that she was taking David to be her lawful husband. With these simple words the marriage was consecrated.

They sat down, and there came a greater silence. As in the old poorhouse Meeting, a fly droned endlessly about David's head and inadvertently he looked beside him, half expecting to see mad Luther Detwiler sitting with his hat on; but instead he saw his wife, and he remembered how he had first seen her, in just such a quiet Meeting, and he thought: "It seems so right."

But the essential wrongness of this marriage could not go unchallenged. Mrs. Trueblood rose and pointed her long beak at the couple. "Marcia Paxson Moomaugh Harper," she said in godlike tones, "thee has been a wilful child. Thee has been headstrong, has loved thine own ways and has shown no aptitude for true marriage. What token is there that thee has changed?"

In their corner Mr. and Mrs. Paxson stared at the floor. David looked away in shame, but Marcia stared back at Mrs. Trueblood. The woman constructed a long and thoughtful analysis of marriage as a sacrament. The very presence of God Himself was dragged into the small room, and flies buzzed while she excoriated divorce and broken vows. She spoke as a prophet from the Old Testament, and her voice had a monitory ring that frightened David and left him quivering when she finally sat down, clothed in lonely dignity, trembling from the force of what the Lord had made her say.

Again the room was silent and David could hear labored breathing. It was the moment of consecration, when two people, strangers up to now, were being fused into one. David thought of the fiery charges Mrs. Trueblood had made. She seemed to be like Morris Binder: "There are good men and bad men. Good girls and bad girls. Never leave the reader in doubt. Good girls wear simple colors like honest yellow or blue."

But human beings, David among them, could not be so labeled. There was sin upon him, yes. In the drowsy, quiet room he thought of this sin. He concluded that sin was any folly which hurt or even ruined the man who persisted in it. Sin was the erosion of spirit that finally left fields of the soul gullied, their substance washed away, their stalks of grain bent and fruitless. Each human being was subject to sin and each bore his penalties in peculiar and often terrible ways.

But sin was not evil. No, evil must be in a lower category. Evil was wrong-doing directed not at one's self but at another. Evil was sin persisted in, arrogantly and to no known purpose. And it was this confusion between sin and evil that so blinded the world. Tremont Clay was an evil man, and in the quiet room David looked at the dapper man and thought: "I'll never stoop so low again." For Clay had set out consciously to debauch the world, and he had established good rules for accomplishing his purpose. He did not even sin against himself in doing so, for the magazines did not corrode him; but they were evil, and David would always despise himself for having helped that work along.

Then he saw the mascaraed face of Mom Beckett. She stared impassively ahead, her hand clutching Claude's. He watched her for a moment and realized that he had no words of description for her. Neither sin nor evil seemed to apply to that strange and provocative woman.

As he studied his friends and thought of their problems—Jensen was still unemployed; Vito's first child had been a dwarf, but they had hopes that the second might not be—he became angry with Mrs. Trueblood. "There's no reason why she should have spoken so!" he muttered to himself, staring at the uncompromising Quaker saint. He could not believe that his marriage with Marcia was perpetually condemned because it happened to have been conceived in sin. That was beside the point. There was a phrase from Marcia's favorite poem: "And peace proclaims olives of endless age." There was no reason why that should not describe their dedicated marriage. They would live as if their lives were an atonement for the errors they had made.

He thought of his own country. It had started its noble life with the greatest crime of all: matricide. Its finest patriots were stained with the intolerable crime: treason. Its corporate life was still stained with minor forms of slavery. And yet from these lewd beginnings a nation of free and reasonably good men had risen and prospered and shown a light to all the world. David thought of the little Italians fighting over their bocce far from home, and they were better here. He recalled the shivering Jews in Lafayette Street, and here they were free. Either a nation or a man—or a marriage, for that matter—can start in sin and accomplish the perfection to which it aspires. Only the wilfully evil are proscribed and nugatory. David looked humbly at his feet as if he were unworthy of this cleansing truth.

Then from a side bench a man in gray rose and began to speak. Neither David nor Marcia knew this Quaker, nor would they ever know his name, but his words fell over the ugly architecture of their past like snow upon the buildings of Washington Square. He said, "The most misleading concept in religion is that of the recording angel. I cannot believe that God remembers or cares to remember a single incident of our lives. I am the recording angel. My spirit and my body are the record. My good deeds show in me, and my wrong deeds can never be hidden. My spirit either grows to fullness or declines to nothing. God has no need of recording devices. We must not think of Him as a vengeful or shopkeeping dictograph. He has created a better instrument than a strip of all-recording film. He has made me. He needs only look at me, and all is recorded.

"Therefore we must conclude that we retain the privilege of erasing past mistakes. Sometimes I think we Quakers do not attend carefully enough to the teachings of the Catholic Church. I refer especially to their doctrine of final salvation. I know it is repugnant for some Friends to contemplate a totally evil man's being saved in the last gasp of life, but if what I have just said about God's establishing us as his immortal recording devices is true, I for one believe this to be possible."

He spoke briefly of marriage as the beginning of a new memory. Then he sat down. The flies buzzed on, and the sun, falling low in the west, slipped in beneath the curtains as it had each Sunday in the poorhouse church.

The words of the man in gray had a powerful effect upon Marcia, and she felt that this day was indeed the beginning of a new life. The phrase was trite, but it had been good enough for Dante centuries ago and it was still the best single description of a Christian marriage. She thought with a great tenderness of the brown-haired fellow beside her. She knew his every fault: his pusillanimous nature, his fuzzy idealism, his pantheism, his uncritical belief in people, and his financial irresponsibility. But she remembered what Mom Beckett had said: "Hell, there ain't no good single men. A girl picks out the best she can lay her hands on and then tries to make somethin' of him." She kept her eyes on the floor and knew without question that her man would live with dignity. His book would be good, too, perhaps not the perfect thing he had imagined, but good.

Slowly she became aware that David had turned toward her. She looked up and saw him bidding her to stand. He shook hands with her. Behind her the spiritual seers of the Meeting also shook hands. In the audience friends and strangers grasped one another's hands, and the wedding was over.

David and Marcia Harper left the Meeting House. Of their free will and with their own words they had married, and ahead of them reached a prospect of endless worth. But when they reached Third Avenue, a newsboy was screaming his evening papers: "Hitler withdraws from the League of Nations!" David looked at the headlines casually and wondered what new wretchedness was afoot; but Marcia, who pondered these things, clutched David closely, and though the day was warm she drew herself beside him as if a cold wind had suddenly swept across the world.